# THE WALLACE

BLIND HARRY was an acclaimed poet of fifteenth-century Scotland about whom very little is known.

DR ANNE McKIM was born in Glasgow and educated at the Universities of Dundee, Manitoba and Edinburgh. She is a Senior Lecturer at the University of Waikato in New Zealand.

# The Wallace

## Blind Harry

*Edited and introduced by*
Anne McKim

CANONGATE
CLASSICS
112

First published as a Canongate Classic simultaneously in
Great Britain and the United States of America in 2003
by Canongate Books Ltd, 14 High Street, Edinburgh EHI
ITE.

Maps courtesy of Max Oulton

10 9 8 7 6 5 4 3 2 1

The publishers gratefully acknowledge general subsidy
from the Scottish Arts Council towards the Canongate
Classics series and a specific grant towards the publica-
tion of this title.

Set in 10pt Plantin by Hewer Text Ltd, Edinburgh.
Printed and bound by Nørhaven Paperback A/S, Denmark

*British Library Cataloguing-in-Publication Data*
A catalogue record for this volume is available on
request from the British Library

ISBN I 84195 413 6

www.canongate.net

# Acknowledgements

I first read 'The Wallace' in the Scottish Text Society edition by the late Dr Matthew McDiarmid when I was a graduate student in Canada over twenty-five years ago, and my longstanding and considerable debt to his work will be apparent in this new edition. To Professor John MacQueen, formerly Director of the School of Scottish Studies at Edinburgh University, I remain deeply grateful for guiding my doctoral studies in early Scottish heroic literature.

I benefited from Professor Russell Peck's valuable comments on selections from the poem I prepared for a student edition (forthcoming from Medieval Institute Publications), and from that indispensable resource, the *Dictionary of the Older Scottish Tongue*.

I would like to thank the Faculty of Arts and Social Sciences at the University of Waikato for a research grant which enabled me to travel to Edinburgh to work with the manuscript. My thanks are also due to the Trustees of the National Library of Scotland, to Max Oulton for producing the maps, Michelle Keown and Catherine Silverstone for research assistance, and Lisa McLean and Joanna Janssen, as well as the staff of University Secretarial Services, for typing various drafts of the text.

I am forever indebted to Bert and Ruby McKim for their warm hospitality when I stay in Edinburgh, and to John and Mary Miller in London. I can never thank enough my husband and children for their loving support over the long period I worked on this project.

# Introduction

The historical verdict may be that William Wallace was a failure, but in the popular imagination he has long been venerated as a Scottish national hero and freedom fighter.[1] There can be no doubt that Hary's *The Wallace*, written more than a century and a half after the subject's death, played – and continues to play, though less directly – a major role in promoting Wallace as an icon of Scotland's first struggle for independence.[2] When the hugely successful film *Braveheart* was first shown at my local cinema in Hamilton, New Zealand, I received telephone calls from people exercised by what they saw as a Hollywood version of history. Wallace's supposed relationship with the daughter-in-law of Edward I, and the future Queen of England, was singled out as a particularly blatant example of falsification. The point is, it is a very old, and certainly not a new, falsification, since Blind Harry invented the original story of a meeting between Wallace and Edward's queen and toyed with the suggestion that the latter may have been a little in love with the Scottish champion.

AUTHOR

We know very little about the author of *The Wallace*; even his name remains something of a mystery. The Scottish historian John Major, writing in the early sixteenth century, is the first to confirm that 'the whole book of William Wallace' was written by a certain Henry or Hary, though whether this was his first or last name is not clear.[3] McDiarmid notes that the surname Hare or Henry (as well as variants such as Henrison) was quite common in the Linlithgow area in the second half of the fifteenth century. He ventures the opinion that the writer was born there or thereabouts around 1440, citing in support what he considers to be evidence in *The Wallace* of the author's detailed regional knowledge of Stirlingshire and Perthshire.[4] Others believe that the name Hary, or Blind Harry as he is often called, was an alias or nickname of some poet whose identity may or may not have been known to his contemporaries but who remains otherwise unidentified.[5] The poet William Dunbar simultaneously attested and perpetuated the currency of the name *Blind*

*Hary* when he registered his death as a recent event in the poem best known as 'The Lament for the Makars' (c. 1505).

Harry's blindness is confirmed both by the royal records and by John Major, although the latter's claim that the poet was blind from birth has been challenged, particularly by readers who are convinced that only a sighted person could have written the graphic descriptions and detailed topographical accounts that distinguish *The Wallace*.[6] The richly allusive and highly literary quality of Blind Harry's writing indicates an educated and widely read man, while a strong respect for reading is also conveyed right from the start of the poem in his references to what readers can learn from books and in his injunctions to his readers to go and read certain books (Book 1, 1, 17, 34, 37; see also Book 7, 613, 1293).

He appears to have been a well-travelled man. The poem provides ample illustration of his detailed geographical knowledge of Scotland, Northern England and parts of France. The detailed accounts of the various routes Wallace follows allow these to be mapped. His excellent military knowledge, especially of battle sites and strategies, and his acute awareness of the need to supply armies with provisions of various kinds led the last editor of his poem to conclude that he must have served as a soldier at some stage.

John Major informs us that Blind Harry recited his poem in the presence of princes. Whether he ever entertained the king in this way we do not now know, although the royal treasury records reveal that between 1490 and 1492 he received gifts of money from the young King James IV on five separate occasions at Linlithgow Palace, indicating that he had connections with the royal court, though in what capacity is not specified.[7] Two of the payments were made at Yuletide, when the king rewarded various court entertainers. He probably died between 1492 and 1494, since there are no further royal payments recorded after 1492 and William Dunbar links his death with that of another poet, Patrick Johnstone, who is known to have died in 1494.

TIME OF WRITING

We can be certain that Blind Harry had completed his poem before 1488, the last year of James III's reign, because it was copied that year by a scribe called John Ramsay, probably as a commission. Towards the end of his poem Blind Harry acknowledges that he consulted and was influenced in at least one editorial decision by two of his contemporaries, Sir William Wallace of Craigie and Sir James Liddale of Halkerston (12, 1444–46), which pushes the time of composition back into the 1470s, since both were knighted in 1471 and Sir William died in 1479. This was the decade in which James III's policy of matrimonial alliances with England might explain Blind Harry's criticism in the poem's opening lines (1, 5–10) of those who 'honour ennymyis'. James's active peace-mongering, including his pursuit of a marriage alliance between his son and Edward IV's daughter in 1474, was not popular in some quarters and considered too pro-English, especially among the great magnates in the Scottish borders. While there had been sufficient goodwill in 1462 to agree a truce of fifteen years, by the late 1470s relations between the two countries had deteriorated to such an extent that the threat of another outbreak of war was imminent, as armies attacked each other's borderland in the summer and autumn of 1480.[8]

It has been suggested that Blind Harry's supposed sympathies with Alexander, Duke of Albany, the king's estranged brother, would account for what has been taken as his criticism of James in the poem's opening lines. In this connection, McDiarmid notes that one of Blind Harry's consultants, Sir James Liddale, was Albany's steward and might be expected to share with his superior and other southern magnates a deep opposition to James's 'pro-English' foreign policy. The roles given to Crawford, ancestor of the out-of-favour magnate, the earl of Crawford, and to Sir Archibald Douglas, forebear of the once mighty fifteenth-century lords of Douglasdale, might also be thus explained.

Blind Harry seems to be particularly knowledgeable about the names of Cumberland, Northumberland and, indeed, Westmoreland, knights who campaigned in Scotland during the Wars of Independence, many of whom bear the names of families known to have been engaged in cross-border warfare throughout the wars. This may indicate a particular familiarity with the border area and local traditions, of the kind a native of the region might have. Hary's obvious respect for Sir Henry Percy, the Northumberland knight appointed as warden of Ayr and Galloway by Edward I when he established his occupation regime in 1296, contrasts with the characteristically partisan and generally xenophobic attitudes invariably shown to the English in the poem, and may be evidence of the kind of 'common heroic inheritance' one quite recent study of fifteenth-century border society has discovered in late medieval border ballads and songs.[9]

Blind Harry's virulent anti-English sentiments and frequent use of vituperation, evident in such terms as 'curssit Saxonis blud', have been singled out for attention by previous readers but xenophobia was common on both sides, fostered by nearly two centuries of intermittent war between the neighbouring countries, and almost constant cross-border raids. Medieval chronicles, as well as political songs, provide ample testimony to this. In the late 1470s similar bones of contention as when Edward I invaded in 1296 were present, notably a Scottish king's refusal to pay homage to an English overlord and the restoration of the 'auld alliance' between Scotland and France, negotiated in 1474, which England regarded as provocative.

GENRE

Blind Harry's composition is best described as a romantic biography. He himself refers to his work as an account 'of Wallace lyff' (12, 1410), and within Blind Harry's lifetime the copyist Ramsay called the work a *vita*, that is, a life or biography, of the noble knight and champion of the Scots, William Wallace (*vita nobilissimi defensoris Scotie Wilelmi Wallace militis*).[10] All but one of the surviving printed editions until 1705, and the majority of those printed after that, have a title beginning 'The Life and Acts'.[11]

Life writing and encomium, or eulogy, were inextricably intertwined in the Middle Ages.[12] Since the object was to praise the subject, not to present an objective, let alone a 'warts and all' biography, the emphasis was on great and exemplary deeds, and incidents were included, and often embellished, in order to make an ethical impression on the reader.[13] When Blind Harry finally gets round to providing a full physical description of Wallace, towards the end of his narrative (10, 1221–40), it is not a realistic portrait but a highly stylised one modelled on the description of Charlemagne in the very popular History of Charles the Great (*Historia Karoli Magni*), as previous readers have noted.[14] On the other hand, accuracy seems to have been an important consideration when Blind Harry followed convention by including his subject's genealogy at the outset of his 'lyff' (I, 21–34). The narrative then follows an essentially linear trajectory, from Wallace's birth (the second son of Malcolm Wallace) to his death by execution at the hands of Edward I. After fleeing with his mother to Gowry, he passes his schooldays in occupied Scotland until, as an eighteen-year-old youth, he kills the son of the captain of Dundee, after some provocation, and is forced to become an outlaw. Thereafter his heroic career begins and is only brought to a close, according to Hary, by the treachery of a trusted associate, not the superior force of his foes. Towards the end of his narrative Blind Harry states that Wallace was forty-five years of age when he was betrayed, having spent the previous twenty-nine years, from the age of sixteen, as a freedom fighter (12, 1426–28). The trouble is that the historical events Blind Harry refers to as

preceding his hero's rebellion, such as the sack of Berwick, which
took place in March, 1296, and the trial and execution in London,
which ended it in August, 1305, make the statement about the length
of his active career patently false. Within the narrative itself invented battles and incidents are included as well as verifiable ones.
As the eighteenth-century judge and historian Lord Hailes so
memorably put it, Blind Harry 'celebrated the actions which Wallace did not perform, as well as those which he did'.[15] Embellishment hardly seems adequate as a term to cover the liberties Blind
Harry takes with history!

Yet the modern historian's tendency to consider the memorialist
less reliable than the chronicler and only slightly more reliable than
the chivalric historian does not take sufficiently into account medieval
understandings of the conventions suitable to a biographical treatment of a subject.[16] Literary embellishment of content as well as style
were accepted and even expected. Blind Harry's apology for his
rhetorical inadequacies at the close of his narrative is itself a rhetorical
ploy, which only serves to underline his literary aspirations.

SOURCES

The Wallace story had become the stuff of legend long before Blind
Harry memorialised his hero. Although he claims as his authority an
eye-witness account written in Latin by Wallace's chaplain and
former schoolmate, John Blair (5, 537–41; 12, 1410–15), no such text
survives nor is its existence attested by any other records. The earliest
Scottish account of William Wallace is preserved in brief annals by
John of Fordun (*Gesta Annalia* caps. 98–103), later included in his
*Chronica Gentis Scotorum* (c. 1380), which was a primary source for
the fifteenth-century chroniclers, Andrew of Wyntoun (c. 1420) and
Walter Bower (c. 1440), whose fuller accounts of Wallace, one written
in the vernacular, the other in Latin, Blind Harry almost certainly
knew. Like his predecessors, Blind Harry also drew on traditional
tales of Wallace's exploits, including perhaps some of the 'gret gestis'
Wyntoun mentions as circulating in the early fifteenth century
(*Orygynale Cronykil of Scotland*, Book VIII, 2300).

The single most important model and, ironically, 'source' for
Blind Harry's composition is a fourteenth-century vernacular verse
biography of the other most renowned Scottish national hero,
Robert the Bruce. Blind Harry refers to *The Bruce* (c. 1375) and
its author, John Barbour, a long-serving Archdeacon of Aberdeen, a
number of times in *The Wallace* and in ways that convey his respect
for Barbour's biography of the king. If imitation is indeed the
sincerest form of flattery, Blind Harry pays Barbour a considerable

compliment by going so far as to 'borrow' several episodes from the
archdeacon's account of Bruce's military career – in which Wallace
is not once mentioned – and assigning them to Wallace! Early in his
poem, Blind Harry reveals his belief that Wallace merits comparison
with Bruce and, while he qualifies this with the acknowledgement
that Bruce was the legitimate 'heir' of the kingdom, his preference
for Wallace is evident in his claim that the latter was the greater hero
because he was braver and more patriotic, as witnessed, he says, by
the number of times he rescued Scotland from the English, and even
challenged the enemy on their own ground:

> All worthi men that has gud witt to waille,       at command
> Be war that yhe with mys deyme nocht my.      Beware; do not find fault
>      taille
> Perchance yhe say that Bruce he was none sik.    such
> He was als gud quhat deid was to assaill        as; action; attempt
> As of his handis and bauldar in battaill,       bolder
> Bot Bruce was knawin weyll ayr of this kynrik;  heir; kingdom
> For he had rycht we call no man him lik.
> Bot Wallace thris this kynrik conquest haile,    conquered
> In Ingland fer socht battaill on that rik.       far; realm
>      (2, 351–59)

Appropriately enough, the only surviving manuscript of *The Wallace*, written in 1488, is preserved and bound along with one of only
two extant manuscripts of *The Bruce*, written in 1489, in the
National Library of Scotland (Advocates 19.2.2). The handwriting
and separate colophons at the end of each poem proclaim them to be
the work of the same scribe, John Ramsay, whom Neilson identifies
as a cleric and notary of St Andrews diocese.[17] Whether they were
commissioned by the same patron, which might suggest early
recognition of the affinity between the two works, cannot be
established. We do know from one of the colophons that the copy
of *The Bruce* was made at the request of Sir Symon Lochmalony,
vicar of Auchtermoonzie in Fife.

## PURPOSE, THEME AND STRUCTURE

Like Barbour, Blind Harry's purpose was commemorative and
eulogistic. As well as encouraging his readers to honour worthy
ancestors, he begins his account of the already renowned Wallace (1,
17) with a brief genealogical sketch (1, 21–38), in which Wallace's
ancestry is traced back through the Crawford line on his mother's
side, and on his father's side to the first 'gud Wallace', whom Blind

Harry, following Barbour's lost Genealogy of the Royal House of
Stewart (referred to as 'The Stewartis Orygenalle' by Wyntoun),
identifies as the companion of Walter, the first Scottish Stewart.
Introducing his hero in this way is entirely conventional, but Blind
Harry also aims to establish beyond doubt Wallace's noble Scottish
lineage. In doing so, he repudiated received depictions of Wallace as
a common thief, rebel and traitor found in the English records and,
at the same time, he challenged any lingering perception in Scotland
that, because of his inferior rank, Wallace had never commanded the
full support of the Scottish nobles.

It is above all for his 'nobille worthi deid' (1, 2) in defence of his
country that Blind Harry celebrates Wallace. He portrays him as a
great national liberator, 'the rescew of Scotland' (1, 38), a hero on a
mission that is divinely sanctioned – 'he fred it weyle throu grace' (1,
40), – and ultimately a martyr for the cause. Early in the narrative the
famous seer Thomas the Rhymer prophesies that Wallace will liberate
Scotland from English domination and restore peace three times (2,
346–50). Later Wallace himself is granted a vision in which St
Andrew, Scotland's patron saint, and the Virgin Mary present him
with an avenging sword, a parti-coloured wand and a precious book,
interpreted by his chaplain John Blair as confirmation of his divinely
ordained mission (7, 65–152). As Brown and McDiarmid have noted,
the suggestion for the prophetic dream probably came from the
alliterative *Morte Arthure* in which King Arthur is visited by Lady
Fortune in a dream, but the religious interpretation does not.[18]
Indeed, there are a number of explicit allusions to Arthur in Blind
Harry's poem, including the claim that 'Wallace of hand sen Arthour
had na mak' (8, 845) which, along with allusions to Hector, Alexander
the Great, Julius Caesar, Roland and Godfrey of Boulogne, strongly
suggest that Blind Harry wished Wallace to be added as a kind of
tenth 'noble' or 'worthy' to the illustrious 'Nine Worthies' celebrated
in literature, art and architecture in the Middle Ages.[19]

Blind Harry presents himself as a disinterested as well as a
patriotic writer. Although he appeals to fellow patriots – at one
point calling on 'Yhe nobill men that ar of Scottis kind' (7, 235) to
avenge atrocities that he alleges the English have committed – he
claims that he was not commissioned by 'king nor other lord' to
write the book, and that he was not prompted by the prospect of any
reward (12, 1433–5). Like many other medieval poets, Blind Harry
expresses feigned anxiety about the reception of his 'nobill buk' (12,
1451–54), which some may dismiss as the 'rurall dyt' (12, 1431) of a
self-confessed rustic or 'burel man' (12, 1461). In the event, *The
Wallace* was an immediate and lasting success. By 1488 it had been

copied, probably as a commission, by John Ramsay, as we have noted, and after the first Scottish printing press was set up in Edinburgh in 1507–8, it was one of the first books printed, almost certainly by Chepman and Myllar, the bibliographer John Miller noting that at least twenty-two other editions were printed before 1707. Adaptations of Blind Harry's work, from the selective revisions of the Protestant printer Lekpreuik (1570) to cater to the tastes of a post-Reformation readership to the complete 'modernisation' of William Hamilton of Gilbertfield (1722), ensured that *The Wallace* always found an audience. Some readers were more critical than others. Early sixteenth-century Scottish historians tended to be sceptical about Blind Harry's reliability, even as they drew heavily on his account as a source for Wallace's career. Major was particularly influential in developing the tradition of the blind minstrel dependent for his livelihood on pleasing wealthy patrons by regaling them with stories drawn from popular sources.

Blind Harry himself locates his work within a learned literary tradition when he purports to translate from a Latin life of Wallace; when he cites and recommends particular books to his readers; and again when he alludes to chronicle sources. His primary model as we have seen is Barbour's *Bruce,* which was evidently respected by fifteenth-century chroniclers, and which provided Blind Harry with a suitable structure to emulate – a sequence of linked episodes describing the heroic actions and incidents in the life of a national hero. While the formal ordering of the narrative into twelve books can be clearly detected from Ramsay's transcription (even though he overlooked the start and end of Book 9 with the result that his manuscript has only eleven books), *The Wallace* is essentially structured according to the protagonist's threefold 'rescues' of Scotland from English domination, a narrative strategy which is complemented by a range of rhetorical strategies including repetition with variation of motifs, many of them also deployed by Barbour. Recent scholarship has highlighted the use of traditional material, including folklore, by even respectable medieval historians like Andrew Wyntoun and Walter Bower, so it is not at all surprising to find that Hary too drew on folklore, most strikingly in the Fawdoun episode in which Wallace encounters the ghost of a man he has beheaded.

INFLUENCES

It is the 'conscious blending of folk-myth and Chaucerian literary conventions' which perhaps makes *The Wallace* such an interesting work.[20] Although Blind Harry's knowledge of Chaucer's poetry – which was quite widely available in fifteenth-century Scotland – has long been noted, with specific echoes of *The General Prologue* to *The Canterbury Tales*, *The Knight's Tale* and *The Franklin's Tale*, *Troilus and Criseyde*, and *The Legend of Good Women* noticed in the Notes section of this edition, critical appreciation of the literary merits of *The Wallace* has come only quite recently.

Familiarity with the great medieval romance cycles of Arthur and Alexander, Scottish translations and derivatives of which were composed and circulated in the fifteenth century, is evident in Blind Harry's poem, particularly in his depiction of Wallace as an exemplary warrior and 'chyftayne in wer' (5, 842). As well as being handsome, strong, brave and wise (1, 184), as a military leader he inspires loyalty and admiration by his personal prowess, his prudence (e.g. in avoiding open battle when seriously outnumbered), his sound military strategy and tactics, and his generosity to his followers (6, 784–86). Wallace, 'the flour of armys' (6, 56), is almost invariably chivalrous in his treatment of noncombatants and we are repeatedly told that he refused to harm women, children and priests. Off the battlefield, he is 'curtas and benyng' (1, 202), but because *The Wallace* is so centrally concerned with war, these particular attributes are more stated than demonstrated. Nevertheless, Blind Harry conveys his appreciation of the value that attaches to courtly and courteous conduct when he takes the trouble to praise the son of John Ramsay, one of Wallace's allies, as the 'flour of courtlyness' (7, 900) and when he stages a completely unhistorical meeting and conversation between the English queen and his hero, in which courtly decorum is displayed (8, 1215–1466).

The conflicting claims of war and love exercise the young Wallace (5, 611–48) when he is smitten by a young woman in Lanark. Apparently aware of the philosophy that love can spur a warrior on to great feats of prowess, Wallace declares to his friend Kerle that the case is rather different when the liberation of his country is at stake. As a champion of such a cause, he believes love will only distract him from his mission:

| | |
|---|---|
| He that thinkis on his luff to speid, | help prosper |
| He may do weill, haiff he fortoun and grace. | if he has |
| Bot this standis all in ane other cas: | things stand differently in this case |
| A gret kynryk with feill fayis ourset. | kingdom [is] with many enemies overrun |

Rycht hard it is amendis for to get     *to obtain amendis from them*
At anys of thaim and wyrk the observance     *and at the same time perform the duties*
Quhilk langis luff and all his frevill chance.     *belong to; fickle*
    (5, 640–46)

He also knows from experience how dangerous a distraction love can be since an earlier liaison with a paramour in Perth had very nearly cost him his life and endangered his men. But despite his asseveration that love is 'nothing bot folychnes' (631), like Troilus, he finds the power of love irresistible once it has made its 'prent' (606) on his heart. Unlike Troilus, he marries his beloved, and comes to regret this only because it costs her her life.

Wallace's personal bereavement serves to deepen his resolve against his enemies, as righteous anger and desire for vengeance unite his personal and political motives:

The saklace slauchter of hir blith and brycht,
That I avow to the Makar of mycht,     *almighty God*
That of that nacioune I sall never forber     *spare*
Yhong nor ald that abill is to wer.     *old; fit to fight*
    (6, 215–18)

He proceeds to kill the sheriff and English inhabitants of Lanark, and his personally motivated reprisal marks the beginning of Scotland's recovery as Scots who flock to his lead recognise:

Quhen Scottis hard thir fyne tithingis of new     *heard this excellent news*
Out of all part to Wallace fast thai drew,     *From all over*
Plenyst the toun quhilk was thar heretage.     *Settled*
Thus Wallace straiff agayne that gret barnage.     *strove against; barons*
Sa he begane with strenth and stalwart hand     *So*
To chewys agayne sum rowmys of Scotland.     *recover; parts*
The worthi Scottis that semblit till him thar     *flocked to*
Chesit him for cheyff, thar chyftayne and ledar.     *Chose*
    (6, 265–72)

Blind Harry never lets his readers forget that his hero is a man moved by 'pitte' for his country and 'ire of wrang' (6, 624) that is, the righteous anger caused by wrongs that must be redressed. Provocation ranges from the scorn and insults the young Wallace regularly encounters as he attempts to go about his everyday business in occupied Scotland to the killing of his kin which in the course of the narrative, includes his father, elder brother and uncle, as well as his wife. Wallace reacts to these provocations by cutting throats, dashing out brains, shattering bones, striking out eyes and tongues and beheading others in an orgy of violence described with a relish some readers have found distasteful. Blind Harry's frequently emotive language seems designed not only to express Wallace's rage and Blind Harry's antipathy but also to incite hatred of the English in his readers.

*The Wallace* catalogues the sheer brutality of war. We are regaled with such detailed accounts of the sacking of towns and the burning-down of buildings full of screaming inhabitants that the smells and sounds, as well as the terrible sights of war, are graphically conveyed. The hero may spare women but he gives the severed head of Fitzhugh, here said to be Edward I's nephew, to his wife and sends her with it to the English king.

If Blind Harry dwells on the bloodshed in a way that leaves him open to the charge of glorifying slaughter, there is nevertheless a surprising amount of humour in the poem. Much of it, of course, is at the expense of the English. For example, when Edward's drunk and insensible soldiers are burned to death as they sleep in barns outside Ayr, Blind Harry offers an early example of typically Scottish understatement: 'Till slepand men thar walkand [waking] was nocht soft' (7, 440). On other occasions the humour derives from the improbability of the seven-foot-tall hero successfully passing himself off as a woman to elude capture. Pursued after he kills the constable of Dundee early in his career, Wallace quickly dons a woman's gown, headscarf and hat, and swaps his bloody knife for a spinning 'rok', prompting the poet to comment:

> thai socht him beselye
> Bot he sat still and span full conandly,          skilfully
> As of his tym, for he nocht leryt lang.          considering he had not
>                                                   learned long

(1, 247–9)

Blind Harry also gives Wallace a sense of humour, as well as a keen sense of injustice. When the captain of Lochmabon scornfully has the tails of Scottish horses docked, Wallace proffers a 'reward', introducing himself as 'a barbour of the best' who has come from the west 'to cutt and schaiff' and 'lat blud' (5, 758–60), before he dispatches the captain and a companion with his sword. Indeed much of the humour of *The Wallace* is found in the many verbal exchanges that frequently precede physical encounters between the hero and his English enemies, where the jokes are shared with the reader, as when, for example, challenged by the gatekeeper at Perth, Wallace gives his name as 'Will Malcomsone' (4, 368), which, of course, he is (Will, son of Malcolm). On another occasion, irreverent humour and witty wordplay are enjoyed by Wallace and his uncle Auchinleck as they prepare to mount a front- and rearguard attack on an army led by Bishop Bek near Glasgow:

'Uncle,' he said, 'be besy in to wer.                    prepare for battle
Quhether will yhe the byschoppys taill upber,            Whether; carry
Or pas befor and tak his benysone?'                      in front; blessing
He answerd hym with rycht schort provision,             little hesitation
'Unbyschoppyt yeit forsuth I trow ye be.                 unblessed by a bishop
Your selff sall fyrst his blyssyng tak for me,
For sekyrly ye servit it best the nycht.                 surely; deserved; tonight
To ber his taill we sall in all our mycht.'              carry; with
        ( 7, 545–52)

Wallace may show little respect for an English bishop, but his devoutness is nevertheless illustrated a number of times in the poem when he attends mass, offers up prayers, and finally endures torture by steadfastly reading the psalter he has, we are told, kept on his person since childhood. (Blind Harry adds an ironic touch when he makes the Bishop of Canterbury defy Edward I by hearing the last confession of this 'rebell'.) His execution, following betrayal by a trusted associate, and the father of his godchildren, is presented as a martyrdom (12, 1305–8) – as it was by Andrew Wyntoun – and divine approbation is conferred through the spirit of an elderly monk who appears in a vision to confirm that Wallace, 'a gret slaar of men' and 'defendour of Scotland' (12, 1278, 1285), will be honoured in heaven.

VERSE AND LANGUAGE

*The Wallace* has the distinction of being the first extant Middle Scots poem to use the decasyllabic couplet.[21] Blind Harry also employs a nine-line decasyllabic stanza rhyming aabaabbab (2, 171–359), first used by Chaucer in *Anelida and Arcite* and later by all the major Middle Scots poets, Robert Henryson (*The Testament of Cresseid* 407–69), William Dunbar (*The Goldyn Targe*) and Gavin Douglas (*The Palice of Honour*, Prologue and Parts One and Two); and a decasyllabic eight-line stanza rhyming ababbcbc (6, 1–104), employed by Chaucer in *The Monk's Tale* and by Dunbar in a number of poems.

Like Matthew P. McDiarmid's scholarly edition for the Scottish
Text Society (1968–69), this edition is based on the sole surviving
manuscript, Advocates 19.2.2., and the division into twelve books
found in Lekpreuik's 1570 edition is also adopted here. Occasionally
missing lines and improved readings are supplied from the remain-
ing fragments of the first printed edition (1507–8) preserved in the
National Library of Scotland and its derivative printed by Lekpreuik in 1570. Spellings have been normalised to the extent that
scribal yogh is transcribed as *y*, *i* as *j*, *u* and *w* as *v*, and *w* as *u* in line
with modern expectations. *Of* has been distinguished from *off*, *thee*
from *the*, and roman numerals translated into letters within the
poem. Contractions in the manuscript have been silently expanded,
and capitalisation and punctuation follow modern practice.

Anne McKim

NOTES

1 G.W.S. Barrow, *Robert Bruce and the Community of the Realm of Scotland*
3rd edition (Edinburgh: Edinburgh University Press, 1988), 137–38; Andrew
Fisher, *William Wallace* (Edinburgh: John Donald, 1996), 134.

2 While his death on 23 August, 1305 is a matter of public record, the date
and place of his birth remain the subject of considerable debate. A recent
biographer argues for 1272 or 1273 in Ellerslie, Ayrshire, although a number
of traditions associate him with Elderslie, Renfrewshire. James Mackay,
*William Wallace: Brave Heart* (Edinburgh: Mainstream, 1995).

3 *Historia Majoris Britanniae* (Paris, 1521), Book IV, ch. 15.

4 *Hary's Wallace*, Scottish Text Society (Edinburgh & London, 1968–9), 2
vols. Introduction, xxvii–xxviii.

5 W.H. Schofield, *Mythical Bards and the Life of William Wallace* (Cambridge, Mass. and London, 1920), p. 12; John Balaban, 'Blind Harry and *The
Wallace*.' *The Chaucer Review* 8 (1974): 241–51, p. 247.

6 George Neilson, 'On Blind Harry's *Wallace*.' *Essays and Studies* I (1910):
85–112, p. 85; McDiarmid, Introduction xxxiv–xxxvii.

7 There may have been more payments but the exchequer records for the
1470s and for 1488 are missing.

8 Cynthia J. Neville, 'Local Sentiment and the "National" Enemy in
Northern England in the Later Middle Ages', *Journal of British Studies*
vol. 35, no. 4 (Oct., 1996): 419–37, p. 430.

9 Anthony Goodman, 'The Anglo-Scottish Marches in the Fifteenth Century: A Frontier Society?' in *Scotland and England 1286–1815*, ed. R.A.
Mason (Edinburgh: J. Donald 1987), 18–33, p. 29.

10 National Library of Scotland MS Advocates 19.2.2, folio 194[a]

11 The 1630 quarto edition has the title 'The Acts and Deeds of Sir William
Wallace'.

12 Ruth Morse, *Truth and Convention in the Middle Ages: Rhetoric, Re-
presentation, and Reality* (Cambridge: Cambridge University Press, 1991), p.
257.

13 Morse, p. 261.

14 McDiarmid notes that a copy of the *Historia* was available at Coupar Angus Abbey in the late fifteenth century, so it was possible that Hary consulted it. *Hary's Wallace, vol. II, p.* 230.

15 *Ancient Scottish Poems, published from the MS of George Bannatyne 1568* ed. David Dalrymple, Lord Hailes (Edinburgh, 1770).

16 Morse, p. 265.

17 'On Blind Harry's *Wallace*', p. 86.

18 J.T.T. Brown, *The Wallace and The Bruce Restudied* (Bonn, 1900), p. 38; McDiarmid vol. II, p. 200.

19 Robert Bruce is added as a tenth worthy in a *ballat* preserved in a sixteenth-century manuscript of Fordun's *Chronica* held by Edinburgh University Library.

20 Balaban, 250.

21 Walter Scheps, 'Middle English Poetic Usage and Blind Harry's *Wallace*. *The Chaucer Review* 4 (1970), 291–302.

# BOOK ONE

Our antecessowris that we suld of reide   *ancestors; should; read*
And hald in mynde thar nobille worthi   *hold*
  deid,
We lat ourslide throu verray sleuthfulnes,   *bypass through very sloth*
  And castis us ever till uther besynes.   *turn ourselves to*
5  Till honour ennymyis is our haile entent:   *To; whole intention*
It has beyne seyne in thir tymys bywent.   *been seen; past*
Our ald ennemys cummyn of Saxonys   *old*
  blud,
That nevyr yeit to Scotland wald do gud
Bot ever on fors and contrar haile thar will,   *of necessity*
10  Quhow gret kyndnes thar has beyne kyth   *How; shown to them*
  thaim till.
It is weyle knawyne on mony divers syde
How thai haff wrocht in to thar mychty   *acted*
  pryde
To hald Scotlande at undyr evermar,   *perpetually in subjection*
Bot God abuff has maid thar mycht to par.   *diminish*
15  Yhit we suld thynk one our bearis befor;   *Yet; on; forebears*
Of thar parablys as now I say no mor.   *teachings*
We reide of ane rycht famous of renowne,   *one [person]*
Of worthi blude that ryngis in this   *rules [reigns]*
  regioune,
And hensfurth I will my proces hald   *narrative*
20  Of Wilyham Wallas yhe haf hard beyne   *have heard*
  tald.
His forbearis, quha likis till understand,
Of hale lynage and trew lyne of Scotland,   *good lineage*
Schir Ranald Crawfurd, rycht schirreff of   *Sir; rightful sheriff*
  Ayr,
So in hys tyme he had a dochter fayr,   *daughter*
25  And yonge Schir Ranald, schirreff of that
  toune;
His systir fair of gud fame and ranoune,
Malcom Wallas hir gat in mariage,
That Elrisle than had in heretage,
Auchinbothe and othir syndry place;
30  The secund o he was of gud Wallace,   *grandson*
The quhilk Wallas full worthely at wrocht   *acted*
Quhen Waltyr hyr of Waillis fra Warayn   *When; heir*
  socht.

Quha likis till haif mar knawlage in that part     *Who; to have more*

Go reid the rycht lyne of the fyrst Stewart.     *authentic lineage*

35 Bot Malcom gat upon this lady brycht

Schir Malcom Wallas, a full gentill knycht,

And Wilyame als, as cornyklis beris on hand,     *chronicles tell*

Quhilk effter was the reskew of Scotland.     *Who*

Quhen it was lost with tresoune and falsnas,     *by*

40 Ourset be fais, he fred it weyle throu grace.     *foes; freed*

Quhen Alexander our worthi king had lorn     *lost*

Be aventur his liff besid Kyngorn.     *By chance; Kinghorn*

Thre yer in pes the realm stude desolate.

Quharfor thair rais a full grevous debate.

45 Our prynce Davy, the Erle of Huntyntoun,

Thre dochtrys had that war of gret ranoun,     *daughters*

Of quhilk thre com Bruce, Balyoune, and Hastyng.     *Balliol*

Twa of the thre desyryt to be kyng.

Balyoune clamyt of fyrst gre lynialy,     *as lineal heir by first degree*

50 And Bruce fyrst male of the secund gre by.     *by the second degree*

To Paryse than and in Ingland thai send

Of this gret striff how thai suld haif ane end.

Foly it was forsuth it happynnyt sa,

Succour to sek of thar alde mortale fa.     *seek; foe*

55 Edwarde Langschankis had new begune his wer     *war*

Apon Gaskone fell awfull in effer.     *Gascony very fearful in array*

Thai landis thane he clamde as heretage

Fra tyme that he had semblit his barnage     *assembled; baronage*

And herd tell weyle Scotland stude in sic cace.     *such a state*

60 He thocht till hym to mak it playn conquace.     *conquest*

Till Noram kirk he come withoutyn mar;     *To; without delay*

The consell than of Scotland mett hym thar.     *representatives*

Full sutailly he chargit thaim in bandoune     *commanded; subjection*

As thar ourlord till hald of hym the croun.     *overlord*

65 Byschope Robert in his tyme full worthi

Of Glaskow lord, he said that 'we deny

Ony ourlord bot the gret God abuff.'

The king was wrath and maid hym to
    ramuff.                                                          *depart*
Covatus Balyoune folowid on hym fast.
70 Till hald of hym he granttyt at the last.                    *hold the land [as an inferior]*
In contrar rycht a king he maid hym thar               *Against just practice*
Quhar throuch Scotland rapentyt syne full             *repented afterwards sorely*
    sar.
To Balyoune yhit our lordis wald nocht                 *yet; would*
    consent.
Edward past south and gert sett his                    *arranged*
    parliment.
75 He callyt Balyoune till answer forScotland.            *summoned; be accountable*
The wys lordis gert hym sone brek that                 *caused; bond*
    band.
Ane abbot past and gaif our this legiance.             *handed over; allegiance*
King Edward than it tuk in gret grevance.              *displeasure*
His ost he rasd and come to Werk on                    *host [army]; raised*
    Twede
80 Bot for to fecht as than he had gret drede.            *fight*
To Corspatryk of Dunbar sone he send,
His consell ast for he the contre kend                 *counsel asked; countryside*
                      *knew*

And he was brocht in presence to the king.
Be sutalle band thai cordyt of this thing.            *By secret agreement;*
                      *accorded*

85 Erle Patrik than till Berweik couth persew;            *went*
Ressavide he was and trastyt verray trew.             *Received; believed [to be]*
                      *very loyal*

The king folowid with his host of ranoun;             *army*
Effter mydnycht at rest wes all the toun.
Corspatrik rais, the keyis weile he knew,             *arose*
90 Leit breggis doun and portcules thai drew,            *bridges; portcullis; drew [up]*
Sett up yettis, syne couth his baner schaw;           *opened gates; then displayed*
                      *his banner*

The ost was warand towart hym thai draw.             *aware*
Edward entrit and gert sla hastely
Of man and wiff seven thousand and fyfty,
95 And barnys als, be this fals aventur                  *children also*
Of trew Scottis chapyt na creatur.                    *escaped*
A captayne thair this fals Edward maid.               *appointed*
Towart Dunbar without restyng thai raid              *rode*
Quhar gaderyt was gret power of Scotland,            *gathered; forces*
100 Agayne Edward in bataill thocht to stand.

Thir four erllis was entrit in that place — These
Of Mar, Menteith, Adell, Ros upon cace. — by chance
In that castell the erle gert hald thaim in, — prepared for siege
At to thar men without thai mycht nocht
wyn, — So that to their; outside; get to
105 Na thai to thaim suppleying for to ma. — Nor; to bring relief
The battaillis than togiddyr fast thai ga. — battalions then; go
Full gret slauchtyr at pitte was to se — slaughter
Of trew Scottis oursett with sutelte. — cunning
Erle Patrik than quhen fechtyng was fellast — fiercest
110 Till our fa turnd and harmyng did us mast: — did us most harm
Is nayne in warld at scaithis ma do mar — none; injuries
Than weile trastyt in borne familiar. — well trusted [associates] in a familiar place

Our men was slayne withoutyn
redempcioune; — ransoming
Throuch thar dedis all tynt was this
regioune. — lost
115 King Edward past and Corspatrik to Scune — Scone
And thar he gat homage of Scotland sune, — soon
For nane was left the realme for to defend.
For Jhon the Balyoune to Munros than he
send
And putt hym doune for ever of this
kynrik. — kingdom
120 Than Edwarde self was callit a roy full ryk. — king; mighty
The croune he tuk apon that sammyne
stane — same stone [of destiny]
At Gadalos send with his sone fra Spane, — from
Quhen Iber Scot fyrst in till Irland come;
At Canmor syne King Fergus has it nome, — That; after; taken
125 Brocht it till Scune and stapill maid it thar, — established
Quhar kingis was cround eight hundyr yer
and mar
Befor the tyme at King Edward it fand. — found
This jowell he gert turs in till Ingland, — treasure; had [it] packed off to

In Lund it sett till witnes of this thing,
130 Be conquest than of Scotland cald hym
king. — himself
Quhar that stayne is Scottis suld master be. — should
God ches the tyme Margretis ayr till see!

Seven scor thai led of the gretast that thai
 fand
Of ayris with thaim, and Bruce, out of  *heirs*
 Scotland.
135 Edward gayf hym his fadris heretage
Bot he thocht ay till hald hym in thrillage.  *subjection*
Baith Blacok mur was his and Huntyntoun.
Till Erle Patrik thai gaif full gret gardoun.  *reward*
For the frendschipe King Edward wyth
 hym fand,
140 Protector haile he maid hym of Scotland.
That office than he brukyt bot schort tyme.  *enjoyed but*
I may nocht now putt all thar deid in ryme.
Of cornikle quhat suld I tary lang?  *Why should I tarry long over general history?*

To Wallace agayne now breiffly will I  *go*
 gange.
145 Scotland was lost quhen he was bot a child
And ourset throuch with our ennemys  *overthrown through*
 wilde.
His fadyr Malcom in the Lennox fled;
His eldest sone theder he with hym led.
His modyr fled wyth hym fra Elrisle,
150 Till Gowry past and dwelt in Kilspynde.
The knycht hir fader thedyr he thaim sent
Till his uncle that with full gud entent  *good intentions*
In Gowry dwelt and had gud levyng thar,  *good livelihood*
Ane agyt man the quhilk resavyt thaim far.  *aged*
155 In till Dunde Wallace to scule thai send
Quhill he of witt full worthely was kend.  *learning; known*
Thus he conteynde in till his tendyr age,  *continued*
In armys syne did mony hie vaslage  *many feats of prowess*
Quhen Saxons blud in to this realm
 cummyng
160 Wyrkand the will of Edward, that fals king.
Mony gret wrang thai wrocht in this
 regioune:
Distroyed our lordys and brak thar  *buildings*
 byggynys doun;
Both wiffis, wedowis thai tuk all at thar will,
Nonnys, madyns, quham thai likit to spill.  *spoil*
165 King Herodis part thai playit in to Scotland
Of yong childer that thai befor thaim fand.

The byschoprykis that war of gretast vaile     bishoprics; importance
Thai tuk in hand of thar archybyschops     took over completely from
    haile.
No for the pape thai wald no kyrkis forber     Nor; would they spare
                                          churches

170   Bot gryppyt all be violence of wer.     seized; by violence
Glaskow thai gaif, as it our weile was kend,     very well was known
To dyocye in Duram to commend.     in commendation
Small benifice that wald thai nocht persew.
And for the richt full worthy clerkis thai
    slew,
175   Hangitt barrounnys and wrocht full mekill     caused great suffering
    cayr.
It was weylle knawyn in the bernys of Ayr,     barns
Eighteen score putt to that dispitfull dede.     cruel death
Bot God abowyn has send us sum ramede:     above; remedy
The remenbrance is forthir in the taile.     story [i.e. in Book Seven]
180   I will folow apon my proces haile.     go on with; narrative
Willyham Wallace or he was man of armys     before
Gret pitte thocht that Scotland tuk sic     such
    harmys.
Mekill dolour it did hym in hys mynd,     Much distress; caused
For he was wys, rycht worthy, wicht and     bold
    kynd.
185   In Gowry dwelt still with this worthy man.
As he encressyt and witt haboundyt than     knowledge abounded
In till his hart he had full mekill cayr.
He saw the Sothroun multipliand mayr,     English
And to hymself offt wald he mak his
    mayne.     lament
190   Of his gud kyne thai had slane mony ane.     kinsmen; many a one
Yhit he was than semly, stark and bauld,     seemly; strong; bold
And he of age was bot eighteen yer auld.
Wapynnys he bur, outhir gud swerd or     bore; either
    knyff,
For he with thaim hapnyt rycht offt in     often
    stryff.
195   Quhar he fand ane withoutyn othir     one alone
    presance
Efter to Scottis that did no mor grevance.     that [one]; injury
To cutt his thrott or steik hym sodanlye     stab
He wayndyt nocht, fand he thaim savely.     hesitated; [if] he found [he
                                        could do it] safely

Syndry wayntyt, bot nane wyst be quhat way, — Many were missing
200 For all to him thar couth na man thaim say. — attribute
Sad of contenance he was bathe auld and — Serious
    ying, — young
Litill of spech, wys, curtas and benyng. — [A man] of few words; kind
Upon a day to Dunde he was send;
Of cruelnes full litill thai him kend. — Of his warlike nature; knew
205 The constable, a felloun man of wer, — fierce
That to the Scottis he did full mekill der, — harm
Selbye he hecht, dispitfull and outrage. — was called; cruel; violent
A sone he had ner twenty yer of age,
Into the toun he usyt everilk day. — was wont to go
210 Thre men or four thar went with him to
    play, — amuse themselves
A hely schrew, wanton in his entent. — complete wretch;
    — unrestrained

Wallace he saw and towart him he went.
Likle he was, rycht byge and weyle beseyne — Well-made; well-dressed
In till a gyde of gudly ganand greyne. — garment; fine green
215 He callyt on hym and said, 'Thou Scot,
    abyde.
Quha devill thee grathis in so gay a gyde? — dresses
Ane Ersche mantill it war thi kynd to wer, — Irish cloak; nature
A Scottis thewtill undyr thi belt to ber, — knife
Rouch rewlyngis apon thi harlot fete. — rough brogues; worthless feet
220 Gyff me thi knyff. Quhat dois thi ger so — Why do you dress so
    mete?' — smartly?
Till him he yeid his knyff to tak him fra. — went; from
Fast by the collar Wallace couth him ta. — seize
Undyr his hand the knyff he bradit out, — drew
For all his men that semblyt him about, — gathered
225 Bot help him selff he wyst of no remede. — Unless he helped; knew
Without reskew he stekyt him to dede. — stabbed him to death
The squier fell, of him thar was na mar.
His men folowid on Wallace wonder sar. — pursued; intently
The pres was thik and cummerit thaim full — hand to hand fighting; thick;
    fast. — hindered
230 Wallace was spedy and gretlye als agast, — quick and also very terrified
The bludy knyff bar drawin in his hand;
He sparyt nane that he befor him fand.
He knew the hous his eyme had lugit in; — uncle; lodged
Theder he fled for out he mycht nocht
    wyn. — get

235 The gude wyff than within the clos saw he — *mistress of the house; courtyard*

And 'help!' he cryit, 'for him that deit on tre. — *[Jesus]; died; cross*

The yong captane has fallyn with me at stryff.' — *got into a fight with me*

In at the dure he went with this gud wiff. — *door*

A roussat gown of hir awn scho him gaif — *russet; she gave him*

240 Apon his weyd at coveryt all the layff, — *[Put on] over his clothes; rest*

A soudly courche our hed and nek leit fall; — *dirty headdress [kerchief]*

A wovyn quhyt hatt scho brassit on withall, — *woven white hat; clasped*

For thai suld nocht lang tary at that in; — *house*

Gaiff him a rok, syn set him doun to spyn. — *spinning wheel*

245 The Sothroun socht quhar Wallace was in drede. — *Englishmen; danger*

Thai wyst nocht weylle at quhat yett he in yeide. — *knew; gate; went in*

In that same hous thai socht him beselye — *skilfully*

Bot he sat still and span full conandly,

As of his tym, for he nocht leryt lang. — *Considering his [short learning] time; learned*

250 Thai left him swa and furth thar gait can gang — *so; thus went their way*

With hevy cheyr and sorowfull in thocht. — *sad cheer, melancholy*

Mar witt of him as than get couth thai nocht. — *More knowledge*

The Inglis men all thus in barrat boune — *prepared for a hostile encounter*

Bade byrn all Scottis that war into that toun. — *Ordered [that they] burn*

255 Yhit this gud wiff held Wallace till the nycht, — *kept*

Maid him gud cher, syne put hym out with slycht. — *Made him welcome then; stealth*

Throu a dyrk garth scho gydyt him furth fast; — *dark garden; led; out*

In covart went and up the watter past, — *[He] went into hiding; river*

Forbure the gate for wachis that war thar. — *Avoided; sentries*

260 His modyr bade in till a gret dispar. — *waited*

Quhen scho him saw scho thankit hevynnis queyn — *heaven's queen [Mary]*

And said, 'Der sone, this lang quhar has thou beyne?' — *long while where*

He tald his modyr of his sodane cas. — *misfortune*
Than wepyt scho and said full oft, 'Allas!
265 Or that thou cess thou will be slayne — *Unless*
    withall.'
'Modyr,' he said, 'God reuller is of all.
Unsoverable ar thir pepille of Ingland. — *Insufferable; these*
Part of thar ire me think we suld
    gaynstand.' — *oppose*
His eme wist weyle that he the squier slew; — *uncle knew*
270 For dreid tharof in gret languor he grew. — *distress*
This passit our quhill divers dayis war — *continued until;*
    gane. — *went*
That gud man dred or Wallace suld be — *lest*
    tane, — *taken*
For Suthroun ar full sutaille everilk man. — *Englishmen; cunning*
A gret dyttay for Scottis thai ordand than. — *indictment*
275 Be the lawdayis in Dunde set ane ayr. — *days for holding trials; justice-ayre*

Than Wallace wald na langar sojorne thar.
His modyr graithit hir in pilgrame weid; — *dressed garb*
Hym disgysyt, syne glaidlye with hir yeid, — *then; went*
A schort swerd undyr his weid prevale. — *clothing secretly*
280 In all that land full mony fays had he. — *foes*
Baith on thar fute, with thaim may tuk thai — *Both on foot; [they] took no*
    nocht. — *more*
Quha sperd, scho said to Sanct Margret — *Whoever asked;*
    thai socht: — *went*
Quha servit hir, full gret frendschipe thai — *Whoever worshipped*
    fand
With Sothroun folk, for scho was of — *English*
    Ingland.
285 Besyd Landoris the ferrye our thai past, — *by ferry they crossed*
Syn throu the Ochtell sped thaim wonder — *Ochil hills*
    fast.
In Dunfermlyn thai lugyt all that nycht. — *lodged*
Apon the morn quhen that the day was
    brycht,
With gentill wemen hapnyt thaim to pas, — *go*
290 Of Ingland born, in Lithquhow wounnand — *[who were] dwelling in*
    was. — *Linlithgow*
The captans wiff, in pilgramage had beyne,
Fra scho thaim mett and had yong Wallace
    sene,

Gud cher thaim maid, for he was wondyr
fayr,

Nocht large of tong, weille taucht and     *too free of speech*
debonayr.     *courteous*

295   Furth tawkand thus of materis that was     *things that had been done*
wrocht

Quhill south our Forth with hyr son scho
thaim brocht,[1]

In to Lithkow. Thai wald nocht tary lang.

Thar leyff thai tuk, to Dunypace couth     *leave; went*
gang;

Thar dwelt his eyme, a man of gret riches.

300   This mychty persone, hecht to name     *parson, was named*
Wallas,

Maid thaim gud cher and was a full kynd
man,

Welcummyt thaim fair and to thaim tald he
than,

Dide him to witt, the land was all on ster;     *Made him [Wallace]*
    *understand; in turmoil*

Trettyt thaim weyle, and said, 'My sone so
der,

305   Thi moder and thou rycht heir with me sall     *here; shall stay*
bide

Quhill better be, for chance at may betyde.'     *Until things improve*

Wallace answerd, said, 'Westermar we will.     *Further west we will [go]*

Our kyne ar slayne and that me likis ill,     *kinsfolk*

And othir worthi mony in that art.     *many other worthy people in*
    *that area*

310   Will God I leiffe, we sall us wreke on part.'     *live; avenge in part*

The persone sicht and said, 'My sone so     *parson sighed*
fre,     *noble*

I can nocht witt how that radres may be.'     *revenge*

Quhat suld I spek of fruster? As this tid     *needlessly; At this time*

For gyft of gud with him he wald nocht     *giving of good*
bide.

315   His modyr and he till Elrisle thai went.

Upon the morn scho for hir brother sent,

In Corsby dwelt and schirreff was of Ayr.     *sheriff*

Hyr fadyr was dede, a lang tyme leyffyt had     *had lived*
thar.

1 Until south across the [river] Forth she brought them with her

Hyr husband als at Lowdon hill was slayn.

320 Hyr eldest son that mekill was of mayn,     *very strong*
Schir Malcom Wallas was his nayme but     *truly*
less,
His houch senons thai cuttyt in that press.     *tough sinews [i.e. behind the knee]*

On kneis he faucht, felle Inglismen he slew.     *many*
Till hym thar socht may fechtaris than     *more than enough fighters*
anew,

325 On athyr side with speris bar him doun.     *either; bore*
Thar stekit thai that gud knycht of renoun.     *stabbed*
On to my taile I left. At Elrisle     *story*
Schir Ranald come son till his sister fre,     *noble*
Welcummyt thaim hayme and sperd of hir     *asked*
entent.

330 Scho prayde he wald to the lord Persye     *She;*
went,     *go*
So yrk of wer scho couth no forthir fle     *weary of war*
To purches pes in rest at scho mycht be.[1]
Schyr Ranald had the Perseys proteccioune,
As for all part to tak the remissioune.     *pardon*

335 He gert wrytt ane till his syster that tyde.     *had one written for his sister*
In that respyt Wallas wald nocht abyde;     *reprieve*
Hys modyr kyst; scho wepyt with hart sar;     *kissed*
His leyff he tuk, syne with his eyme couth     *then; uncle made his way*
far.

Yonge he was and to Sothroun rycht     *English*
savage.     *fierce*

340 Gret rowme thai had, dispitfull and     *power; cruel and violent*
outrage.
Schir Ranald weylle durst nocht hald     *keep*
Wallas thar
For gret perell he wyst apperand war.     *was*
For thai had haile the strenthis of Scotland;     *completely occupied; strongholds*

Quhat thai wald do durst few agayne thaim     *Whatever*
stand.

345 Schyrreff he was and usyt thaim amang.     *used to go*
Full sar he dred or Wallas suld tak wrang,     *Greatly he dreaded lest; suffer harm*

For he and thai couth never weyle accord.

1 To obtain a pardon so that she might be at peace

He gat a blaw, thocht he war lad or lord,            servant
That profferyt him ony lychtlynes.                   offered; insult
350  Bot thai raparyt our mekill to that place.      frequented too much
     Als Inglis clerkis in prophecys thai fand       found in prophecies
     How a Wallace suld putt thaim of Scotland.      out of
     Schir Ranald knew weill a mar quiet sted        more quiet place
     Quhar Wilyham mycht be better fra thar
        fede                                          hostility
355  With his uncle Wallas of Ricardtoun.
     Schir Richart hecht that gud knycht of          was called
        renoun;
     Thai landis hayle than was his heretage.        All these lands
     Bot blynd he was—so hapnyt throu curage,
     Be Inglis men that dois us mekill der;          much injury
360  In his rysyng he worthi was in wer—             early career; war
     Throuch hurt of waynys and mystymit of
        blude;[1]
     Yeit he was wis and of his conseill gud.
     In Feveryer Wallas was to him send;             February
     In Aperill fra him he bound to wend.            prepared to go
365  Bot gud service he dide him with plesance       gladly
     As in that place was worthi to avance.          praise
     So on a tym he desyrit to play.
     In Aperill the twenty third day
     Till Erevyn watter fysche to tak he went;       Irvine river
370  Sic fantasye fell in his entent.                Such a notion [whim] came
                                                         into his mind

     To leide his net a child furth with him         youth; went
        yeid,
     Bot he or nowne was in a felloune dreid.        before noon; terrible danger
     His swerd he left, so did he never agayne;      he did so
     It dide him gud suppos he sufferyt payne.
375  Of that labour as than he was nocht sle;        then; skilled
     Happy he was, tuk fysche haboundanle.           in plenty
     Or of the day ten houris our couth pas,         Before ten o'clock
     Ridand thar com ner by quhar Wallace was
     The lorde Persye, was captane than of Ayr.
380  Fra thine he turnde and couth to Glaskow        thence
        fair.                                         go
     Part of the court had Wallace labour seyne,     retinue
     Till him raid five cled into ganand greyne,     rode; clad in suitable green

1 Pierced through the veins and unlucky [in loss] of blood

And said sone, 'Scot, Martyns fysche we
   wald have.'
Wallace meklye agayne answer him gave:     mildly
385 'It war resone me think yhe suld haif part.     right
Waith suld be delt in all place with fre     Fishing spoils; divided,
   hart.'     generous
He bade his child, 'Gyff thaim of our     ordered
   waithyng.'     spoils
The Sothroun said, 'As now of thi delyng     dealing
We will nocht tak; thou wald giff us our     would give us too little
   small.'
390 He lychtyt doun and fra the child tuk all.     alighted
Wallas said than, 'Gentill men gif ye be,     if
Leiff us sum part, we pray, for cheryte.
Ane agyt knycht servis our lady today.
Gud frend, leiff part and tak nocht all
   away.'
395 'Thou sall haiff leiff to fysche and tak thee
   ma;     more
All this forsuth sall in our flytting ga.     we shall remove
We serff a lord. Thir fysche sall till him     These
   gang.'     go
✳ Wallace answerd, said, 'Thou art in the
   wrang.'
'Quham dowis thou Scot? In faith thou     you deserve
   servis a blaw.'
400 Till him he ran and out a swerd can draw.
Willyham was wa he had na wapynnis thar     grieved
Bot the poutstaff, the quhilk in hand he     fishing pole; which
   bar.
Wallas with it fast on the cheik him tuk     struck
Wyth so gud will quhill of his feit he     until; feet; shook
   schuk.
405 The swerd flaw fra him a fur breid on the     flew; furrow breadth
   land.
Wallas was glaid and hynt it sone in hand,     caught
And with the swerd ane awkwart straik him     crosswise stroke
   gave,
Undyr the hat his crage in sonder drave.     neck asunder struck
Be that the layff lychtyt about Wallas.     By that time; rest;
    dismounted

410 He had no helpe, only bot Goddis grace.     except
On athir side full fast on him thai dange;     struck blows

Gret perell was giff thai had lestyt lang.   *if*
Apone the hede in gret ire he strak ane;
The scherand swerd glaid to the colar bane.   *cutting; glided; bone*
415 Ane other on the arme he hitt so hardely   *vigorously*
Quhill hand and swerd bathe on the feld   *Until*
    can ly.   *lay*
The tothir twa fled to thar hors agayne.
He stekit him was last apon the playne.   *stabbed*
Thre slew he thar, twa fled with all thar
    mycht
420 Efter thar lord, bot he was out of sicht
Takand the mure or he and thai couth   *Reaching; moor before*
    twyne.   *part*
Till him thai raid onon or thai wald blyne   *at once before; stop*
And cryit, 'Lord abide, your men ar
    marterit doun
Rycht cruelly her in this fals regioun.
425 Five of our court her at the watter baid   *retinue; waited*
Fysche for to bryng, thocht it na profyt
    maid.
We ar chapyt, bot in feyld slayne ar thre.'   *have escaped*
The lord speryt, 'How mony mycht thai   *asked*
    be?'
'We saw bot ane that has discumfyst us all.'   *discomfited [overcome]*
430 Than lewch he lowde and said, 'Foule mot
    you fall,[1]
Sen ane you all has putt to confusioun.   *Since one person*
Quha menys it maist the devyll of hell him   *Who laments*
    droun!
This day for me in faith he beis nocht
    socht.'
Quhen Wallace thus this worthi werk had
    wrocht,
435 Thar hors he tuk and ger that levyt was   *weapons [gear]; left*
    thar,
Gaif our that crafft, he yeid to fysche no   *Gave up; occupation*
    mar;
Went till his eyme and tauld him of this
    drede,   *fearful situation*
And he for wo weyle ner worthit to weide;   *nearly went mad*
And said, 'Sone, thir tithingis syttis me sor,   *Son; grieve me*

[1] Then laughed he loudly and said, 'May ill befall you'

440   And be it knawin thou may tak scaith       harm
       tharfor.'
    'Uncle,' he said, 'I will no langar bide.
    Thir southland hors latt se gif I can ride.'     if
    Than bot a child him service for to mak,      with only
    Hys emys sonnys he wald nocht with him    uncle's
       tak.
445   This gud knycht said, 'Deyr cusyng, pray I   Dear cousin
       thee,
    Quhen thou wanttis gud cum fech ynewch    good men; enough
       fra me.'
    Sylver and gold he gert on to him geyff,     had given to him
    Wallace inclynys and gudely tuk his leyff.    bowed; graciously

## BOOK TWO

Yong Wallace, fulfillit of hie curage,  *full of noble courage*
In prys of armys desyrous and savage,  *Eager for renown in arms and fierce*

Thi vaslage may never be forlorn,  *courage; destroyed*
Thi deidis ar knawin thocht that the warld had sworn;  *though; sworn [to the contrary]*
5 For thi haile mynde, labour and besynes,
Was set in wer and verray rychtwisnes,  *war; true*
And felloune los of thi deyr worthi kyn.  *grievous loss*
The rancour more remaynde his mynd within.
It was his lyff and maist part of his fude,  *sustenance*
10 To se thaim sched the byrnand Sothroun blude.  *burning English blood*
Till Auchincruff withoutyn mar he raid,  *without more delay*
And bot schort tyme in pes at he thar baid.  *only; stayed*
Thar dwelt a Wallas welcummyt him full weill,
Thocht Inglismen thar of had litill feille.  *knowledge*
15 Bathe meite and drynk at his will he had thar,  *as he wished*
In Laglyne wode quhen that he maid repayr.  *Laglyn wood; went*
This gentill man was full oft his resett,  *very often; refuge*
With stuff of houshald strestely he thaim bett.[1]
So he desirit the toune of Air to se.
20 His child with him as than na ma had he.  *more*
Ay next the wode Wallace gert leiff his hors,  *Always; wood; did leave*
Syne on his feit yeid to the merkat cors.  *Since on foot [he] went; market cross*

The Persye was in the castell of Ayr  *Percy*
With Inglismen, gret nowmer and repayr.  *number and concourse of people*

25 Our all the toune rewlyng on thar awne wis  *Over; ruling; own way*
Till mony Scot thai did full gret suppris.  *To many; injury*
Aboundandely Wallace amang thaim yeid.  *Boldly; went*
The rage of youth maid him to haif no dreid.

---

1 With household provisions he diligently supplied them

A churll thai had that felloune byrdyngis bar.   *heavy burdens*
30  Excedandlye he wald lyft mekill mar   *Surpassingly; lift much more*
Than ony twa that thai amang thaim fand,   *any two*
And als be us a sport he tuk on hand.   *by custom*
He bar a sasteing in a boustous poille;   *bucket on strong pole*
On his braid bak of ony wald he thoille   *broad back; endure*
35  Bot for a grot, als fast as he mycht draw.   *groat; strike*
Quhen Wallas herd spek of that mery saw,   *claim*
He likit weill at that mercat to be   *market*
And for a strak he bad him grottis thre.   *blow; offered*
The churll grantyt, of that proffer was fayn.   *offer; glad*
40  To pay the silver Wallas was full bayne.   *ready*
Wallas that steing tuk up in till his hand.   *pole*
Full sturdely he coud befor him stand.
Wallace with that apon the bak him gaif   *struck*
Till his ryg bayne he all in sondyr draif.   *Until; back bone*
45  The carll wes dede. Of him I spek no mar.   *fellow*
The Inglismen semblit on Wallace thair,   *gathered around*
Feill on the feld of frekis fechtand fast,   *Many; men fighting hard*
He unabasyt and nocht gretlie agast.   *undaunted; frightened*
Upon the hed ane with the steing hitt he,   *pole*
50  Till bayn and brayn he gert in pecis fle.   *Until bone; shattered*
Ane othir he straik on a basnat of steille   *helmet; steel*
The tre to raiff and fruschit everedeille.   *wood snapped; broke completely*

His steyng was tynt, the Inglis man was dede,   *pole; ruined*

For his crag bayne was brokyn in that stede.   *neck bone; instantaneously*

55  He drew a swerd at helpit him at neide.   *sword that*
Throuch oute the thikest of the pres he yeid   *press*

And at his hors full fayne he wald haif beyne.   *glad*

Twa sarde him maist that cruell war and keyne.   *Two vexed; most; fierce were; warlike*

Wallace returned as man of mekyll mayne   *strength*
60  And at a straik the formast has he slayne.   *one blow; foremost*
The tother fled and durst him nocht abide.
Bot a rycht straik Wallas him gat that tyd.   *well-aimed stroke; dealt; moment*

In at the guschet brymly he him bar;   *armhole gusset fiercely; struck*

The grounden swerd throuch out his cost it    sharp, rib it sliced
    schar.
65  Five slew he thar or that he left the toune.    before
He gat his hors, to Laglyne maid him
    boune,    bound
Kepyt his child and leyt him nocht abide.    Defended
Feille folowit him on hors and eik on futte    Many; also
70  To tak Wallace, bot than it was no butte.    to no avail
Covert of treis savit him full weille,    Hiding in woods protected
Bot thar to bid than coude he nocht adeille.    stay; at all
Gud ordinance that serd for his estate    provisions; were fitting;
        position
His cusyng maid at all tyme ayr and late.    kinsman; whatever the time
        of day

75  The squier Wallace in Auchincruff that was
Baith bed and meite he maid for thaim to pas
As for that tyme that he remanyt thar.
Bot sar he langit to se the toune of Ayr.    sorely; longed
Thedyr he past apon the mercate day.    market
80  Gret God gif he as than had beyne away!    if [only]; at this time
His emys servand to by him fysche was    uncle's servant; buy
    send,
Schir Ranald Crawfurd, schirreff than was
    kend.    known
Quhen he had tane of sic gud as he bocht,    taken; such goods
The Perseys stwart sadly till him socht    steward sternly went up to
        him

85  And said, 'Thou Scot, to quhom takis thou
    this thing?'
'To the schirreff,' he said. 'Be hevynnys
    king,
My lord sall haiff it and syne go seke thee    then you go seek more
    mar.'
Wallace on gaite ner by was walkand thar.    on a nearby street
Till him he yeid and said, 'Gud freynd,    went
    pray I thee,
90  The schireffis servand thou wald let him
    be.'
A hetfull man the stwart was of blude    hot-tempered
And thocht Wallace chargyt him in termys    challenged
    rude.
'Go hens, thou Scot, the mekill devill thee    mighty devil speed you
    speid.

|  | | |
|---|---|---|
| | At thi schrewed us thou wenys me to leid.' | wicked will; think |
| 95 | A huntyn staff in till his hand he bar; | in his hand he carried |
| | Thar with he smat on Willyam Wallace thair. | struck |
| | Bot for his tre litill sonyhe he maid, | because of; wooden staff; hesitation |
| | Bot be the coler claucht him withoutyn baid | caught / delay |
| | A felloun knyff fast till his hart straik he, | fatal |
| 100 | Syn fra him dede schot him doun sodanle. | he fell down suddenly |
| | Catour sen syne he was but weyr no mar.[1] | |
| | Men of armes on Wallace semblit thar; | surrounded Wallace |
| | Four scor was sett in armys buskyt boun | ready-prepared |
| | On the merket day for Scottis to kepe the toun, | from; defend |
| 105 | Bot Wallace bauldlye drew a swerd of wer. | |
| | In to the byrneis the formast can he ber, | breast-plate; did he strike |
| | Throuch out the body stekit him to dede | stabbed; death |
| | And syndry ma or he past of that stede. | many more before; place |
| | Ane other awkwart a sarye straik tuk thar, | cross-wise; sorry blow |
| 110 | Aboun the kne the bayne in sonder schar. | Above; shattered |
| | The thrid he straik throuch his pissand of maile | gorget |
| | The crag in twa, no weidis mycht him vaill. | armour; avail |
| | Thus Wallace ferd als fers as a lyoun. | acted as fierce |
| | Than Inglismen that war in bargane boun | battle ready |
| 115 | To kepe the gait with speris rud and lang, | strong |
| | For dynt of swerd thai durst nocht till hym gang. | sword blows; proceed against him |
| | Wallace was harnest in his body weyle; | armed |
| | Till him thai socht with hedis scharp of steyle | sharp steel [spear] heads |
| | And fra his strenth enveronde him about. | on his strong ground encircled |
| 120 | Bot throu the pres on a side he went out | throng |
| | In till a wall that stude by the se syde; | Up to; sea |
| | For weyle or wo thar most he nedis abide, | await them |
| | And of thar speris in pecis part he schar. | cut |
| | Than fra the castell othir help come mar. | |
| 125 | Atour the dike thai yeid on athir side, | Over; dyke [wall]; went |
| | Schott doun the wall; no socour was that tyde. | |

1 His days as a caterer were certainly over after that.

Than wist he nocht of no help bot to de.  *knew; die*

To venge his ded amang thaim lous yeid he,  *death; freely went*

On athyr part in gret ire hewand fast.  *either side; anger hacking*

130 Hys byrnyst brand tobyrstyt at the last,  *burnished sword shattered*

Brak in the heltis, away the blaid it flaw.  *Broke; hilts; blade; flew*

He wyst na vayne bot out his knyff can draw.  *knew no hope*

The fyrst he slew that him in hand has hynt  *laid hold of*

And other twa he stekit with his dynt.  *stabbed; blow*

135 The ramanand with speris to him socht,  *remainder; fell on him*

Bar him to ground, than forthir mycht he nocht.

The lordis bad that thai suld nocht him sla.  *ordered; kill*

To pyne him mar thai chargyt him to ga.  *torment; commanded; proceed*

Thus in thar armys suppos that he had sworn,  *sworn [to the contrary]*

140 Out of the garth be fors thai haff him born.  *enclosure by force; borne*

Thus gud Wallace with Inglismen was tane  *taken*

In falt of helpe for he was him allayne.  *For want; alone*

He coud nocht cheys, sic curage so hym bar.  *had no choice; such*

Frevill Fortoun thus brocht him in the swar,  *Fickle / snare*

145 And fals Invye ay contrar rychtwisnes,  *malice [envy]; always*

That violent god full of doubilnes,  *deceit*

Thai fenyeit goddis Wallace never knew.  *Those false*

Gret rychtwisnes him ay to mercy drew.  *virtue; always*

His kyn mycht nocht him get for na kyn thing,  *kinsfolk; get back; no kind of*

150 Mycht thai have payit the ransoune of a king.

The more thai bad, the more it was in vayne.  *offered [bid] / vain*

Of thar best men that day seven has he slayne.

Thai gert set him in till a presoune fell,  *had him placed; cruel prison*

Of his turment gret payne it war to tell.  *torture*

155 Ill meyt and drynk thai gert on till him giff.  *Bad food*

Gret mervaille was lang tyme gif he mycht    live
  leyff;
And ek tharto he was in presoune law    also; dungeon deep
Quhill thai thocht tyme on him to hald the    Until; carry out the law
  law.
Leyff I him thar into that paynfull sted.    Leave; place
160  Gret God above till him send sum ramede!    help
The playne compleynt, the pittous    loud lamenting; wretched
  wementyng,      mourning
The wofull wepyng that was for his takyng,    arrest
The tormentyng of every creatur!
'Alas,' thai said, 'how suld our lyff endur?
165  The flour of youth in till his tender age    flower
Be fortoun armes has left him in thrillage,    thraldom
Lefand as now a chifftane had we nane    Living at this time
Durst tak on hand bot young Wallace alane.    undertake except
This land is lost, he caucht is in the swar.    snare
170  Prophesye out, Scotland is lost in cayr.'    Declare everywhere; despair

    Barrell heryng and watter thai him gave    Salt herring; gave
    Quhar he was set into that ugly cave.    placed; cave
Sic fude for him was febill to comend.    Such; poor [insufficient]
Than said he thus, 'All weildand God    powerful
  resave    receive
175  My petous spreit and sawle amange the lav.    wretched spirit; soul; humble
My carneill lyff I may nocht thus defend.    carnal
Our few Sothroune on to the dede I drave.    Too; death
Quhen so thou will out of this warld I
  wend,
Giff I suld now in presoune mak ane end.    If

180  Eternaile God, quhy suld I thus wayis
  de,    die
  Syne my beleiff all haile remanys in
  Thee,
At Thin awn will full worthely was wrocht?    That
Bot Thou rademe, na liff thai ordand me.    redeem; decreed for
Gastlye fadyr that deit apon the tre,    Spiritual; died; cross
185  Fra hellis presoune with thi blud us bocht,    redeemed
Quhi will thou giff thi handewerk for
  nocht,
And mony worthy in to gret payne we se,
For of my lyff ellys nothing I roucht?    life otherwise; cared
  O wareide swerd, of tempyr never trew!    accursed

190   Thi fruschand blaid in presoune sone me    breaking
      threw
      And Inglismen our litill harme has tane.    too little; suffered
      Of us thai haiff undoyne may than ynew!    more than enough
      My faithfull fadyr dispitfully thai slew,    mercilessly
      My brother als and gud men mony ane.    also; many a one
195   Is this thi dait? Sall thai ourcum ilkane?    appointed time; everyone
      On our kynrent, deyr God, quhen will thou    kinsfolk; have pity
      rew,
      Sen my power thus sodandlye is gane?

      All worthi Scottis, all michty God you
      leid,
      Sen I no mor in vyage may you speid.    expedition; help
200   In presoune heir me worthis to myscheyff.    here; I must die
      Sely Scotland that of help has gret neide,    Defenceless
      Thy nacioune all standis in a felloun    an extreme danger
      dreid.
      Of warldlynes all thus I tak my leiff.    From worldly things; leave
      Of thir paynys God lat you never preiff,    experience
205   Thocht for wo all out of witt suld weid.    Though; should be driven
                                                    mad

      Now othir gyft I may none to you gyff.'

      O der Wallace, umquhill was stark and    [who] once was strong;
      stur,                                         vigorous
      Thou most o neide in presoune till    to
      endur.
      Thi worthi kyn may nocht thee saiff for    save with money
      sold.
210   Ladys wepyt that was bathe myld and mur,    gentle
      In fureous payne the modyr that thee bur,    bore
      For thou till hir was fer derer than gold.
      Hyr most desyr was to be undyr mold.    under ground, i.e., buried
      In warldlynes quhi suld ony ensur,    should anyone trust
215   For thou was formyt forsye on the fold!    strong in life

      Compleyn, sanctis, thus as your sedull    beloved ladies petition
      tellis;
      Compleyn to hevyn with wordis that
      nocht fell is;    cruel
      Compleyne your voice unto the God abuffe;    above
      Compleyne for him into that sitfull sellis;    [who is] in that sorrowful cell

220    Compleyne his payne in dolour thus that    *suffering*
            dwellis,
       In langour lyis for losyng of thar luff.    *distress*
       His fureous payne was felloune for to pruff.    *fierce suffering; cruel; endure*

       Compleyne also yhe birdis blyth as bellis;    *you maidens cheerful*
       Sum happy chance may fall for your    *benefit*
            behuff.

225    Compleyne lordys, compleyne yhe ladyis    *lovely*
            brycht,
       Compleyne for him that worthi was and
            wycht,    *bold*
       Of Saxons sonnys sufferyt full mekill der;    *At the hands of the English; great harm*

       Compleyne for him was thus in presone    *condemned*
            dicht
       And for na caus, bot Scotland for thi richt.    *rights*
230    Compleyne also yhe worthi men of wer;    *war*
       Compleyn for hym that was your aspersper    *champion [lit. sharp spear]*
       And to the dede fell Sothron yeit he dicht;    *death many Englishmen yet; sent*

       Compleyne for him your triumphe had to    *victory*
            ber.

       Celinus was maist his geyeler now.    *Mercury; jailer*
235        In Inglismen, allace, quhi suld we trow,    *trust*
       Our worthy kyn has payned on this wys?    *injured*
       Sic reulle be rycht is litill till allow.    *Such rule by; can't be allowed*

       Me think we suld in barrat mak thaim bow    *strife*
       At our power, and so we do feill sys.[1]
240    Of thar danger God mak us for to rys,
       That weilll has wrocht befor thir termys    *these times*
            and now,
       For thai wyrk ay to wayt us with supprys.    *always to lie in wait to surprise us*

       Quhat suld I mor of Wallace turment
            tell?
       The flux he tuk in to thar presoune fell.    *dysentery; in their terrible prison*

---

1 We should make them feel our strength, i.e. subdue them, in combat

245 Ner to the dede he was likly to drawe.
Thai chargyt the geyler nocht on him to          jailer; lose time
     dwell,
Bot bryng him up out of that ugly sell          loathsome cell
To jugisment, quhar he suld thoill the law.          trial; endure
This man went doun and sodanlye he saw,
250 As to his sycht, dede had him swappyt
     snell,[1]
Syn said to thaim, 'He has payit at he aw.'[2]

Quhen thai presumyt he suld be verray          dead for certain
     ded,
Thai gart servandys withoutyn langer
     pleid,          argument
Wyth schort avis on to the wall him bar.          Without delay
255 Thai kest him our out of that bailfull steid-          threw him over; woeful place
Of him thai trowit suld be no mor ramede-          For; believed; remedy
In a draff myddyn quhar he remaynt thar.          refuse heap
His fyrst norys, of the Newtoun of Ayr,          nurse
Till him scho come, quhilk was full will of          troubled
     reid,
260 And thyggyt leiff away with him to fayr.          begged leave; go [take him
                                                            away]

In to gret ire thai grantyt hir to go.
Scho tuk him up withoutin wordis mo
And on a caar unlikly thai him cast;          a rough cart
Atour the watter led him with gret woo          Over; river
265 Till hyr awn hous withoutyn ony hoo.          delay
Scho warmyt watter, and hir servandis fast          quickly
His body wousche quhill filth was of hym          washed until the filth was
     past.                                              removed
His hart was wicht and flykeryt to and fro,          strong; flickered
                                                        spasmodically
Also his twa eyne he kest up at the last.          opened

270 His foster modyr loved him our the laiff,          above the rest
Did mylk to warme, his liff giff scho          Had milk warmed; if
     mycht saiff,
And with a spoyn gret kyndnes to him          spoon
     kyth.                                              showed

1 So it appeared to him, death had seized him quickly
2 Then said to them, 'He has paid what he owed [to Nature],' i.e., he has
died

Hyr dochter had of twelve wokkis ald a knayff:   *daughter had a twelve-week-old boy*

Hir childis pape in Wallace mouth scho gaiff.[1]

275  The womannys mylk recomford him full swyth.   *revived quickly*

Syn in a bed thai brocht him fair and lyth,   *Then; kindly and gently*

Rycht covertly thai kepe him in that caiff,   *secretly; hiding place*

Him for to save so secretlye thai mycht.

In thar chawmyr thai kepyt him that tide.   *for a time*

280  Scho gert graith up a burd be the hous side   *had a board set up*

Wyth carpettis cled and honouryt with gret lycht;   *Covered with woollen cloth*

And for the voice in every place suld bide   *word; spread*

At he was ded, out throu the land so wide,   *That; throughout*

On presence ay scho wepyt undyr slycht.   *company she always pretended to weep*

285  Bot gudely meytis scho graithit him at hir mycht.   *food; prepared; the best she could*

And so befell in to that sammyn tid   *in the meanwhile*

Quhill forthirmar at Wallas worthit wycht.   *Until later on; grew strong*

Thomas Rimour into the Faile was than   *Fail [monastery]*

With the mynyster, quhilk was a worthi man.   *head of monastery, who*

290  He usyt offt to that religious place.   *often frequented*

The peple demyt of witt mekill he can;   *believed that he knew a great many things*

And so he told, thocht at thai blis or ban,   *whether they blessed or cursed [him]*

Quhilk hapnyt suth in mony divers cace,   *Which turned out to be true*

I can nocht say be wrang or rychtwisnas,   *through wrong or right*

295  In rewlle of wer quhether thai tynt or wan.   *lost or won*

It may be demyt be divisioun of grace.   *deemed by gift*

Thar man that day had in the merket bene;   *Their*

On Wallace knew this cairfull cas so kene.   *painful grievous*

His master speryt quhat tithingis at he saw.   *asked what tidings*

1  She offered her milk-filled breast to Wallace

300 This man answerd, 'Of litill hard I meyn.'    *heard I say*
The mynister said, 'It has bene seildyn seyn    *seldom seen*
Quhar Scottis and Inglis semblit bene on raw    *have been gathered together*
Was never yit als fer as we coud knaw,    *as far as we know*
Bot other a Scot wald do a Sothroun teyn    *either; harm*
305 Or he till him, for aventur mycht faw.'    *[whatever] chance might befall*

'Wallas,' he said, 'ye wist tayne in that steid,    *You know [was] taken; place*
Out our the wall I saw thaim cast him deide,    *over*
In presoune famyst for fawt of fude.'    *starved for want*
The mynister said with hart hevy as leid,    *lead*
310 'Sic deid to thaim me think suld foster feid,    *Such [a] deed; feud*
For he was wicht and cummyn of gentill blud.'    *noble*
Thomas answerd, 'Thir tithingis ar noucht gud.
And that be suth my self sall never eit breid,    *If that be true*
For all my witt her schortlye I conclud.'    *here*

315 'A woman syne of the Newtoun of Ayr    *then*
Till him scho went fra he was fallyn thar
And on hir kneis rycht lawly thaim besocht    *lowly*
To purches leiff scho mycht thin with him fayr.    *obtain leave [so]; thence go*
In lychtlynes tyll hyr thai grant to fayr.    *scorn; proceed onward*
320 Our the watter on till hir hous him brocht    *unto; her*
To berys him als gudlye as scho mocht.'    *bury; might*
Yhit Thomas said, 'Than sall I leiff na mar    *shall; live*
Gyff that be trew, be God that all has wrocht!'    *If*

The mynister herd quhat Thomas said in playne.    *plainly*
325 He chargyt him, 'Than go speid thee fast agayn    *ordered him [the servant]*
To that sammyn hous and verraly aspye.'    *same; see for certain*
The man went furth at byddyng was full bayn.    *ready*

To the Newtoun to pas he did his payn     *exerted himself*
To that ilk hous and went in sodanlye.     *same*
330 About he blent on to the burd him bye.     *glanced*
This woman rais. In hart scho was nocht     *glad*
    fayn.
'Quha aw this lik?' he bad hir nocht deny.     *Whose body is this?*

'Wallace,' scho said, 'That full worthy
    has beyne.'
Than wepyt scho that pete was to seyne.
335 The man thar till gret credens gaif he     *there to*
    nocht.
Towart the burd he bouned as he war     *went quickly as [if]*
    teyne.     *angry*
On kneis scho felle and cryit, 'For Marye
    scheyne     *glorious*
Lat sklandyr be and flemyt out of your     *blame; banished*
    thocht,
This man hir swour, 'Be Hym that all has     *swore*
    wrocht,
340 Mycht I on lyff him anys se with myn eyn     *once*
He suld be saiff thocht Ingland had him
    socht!'

Scho had him up to Wallace be the des.     *brought; by the dais*
He spak with him, syne fast agayne can     *hurried back again*
    pres
With glaid bodword thar myrthis till     *message; spirits to improve*
    amend.
345 He told to thaim the fyrst tithingis was les.     *lies*
Than Thomas said, 'Forsuth, or he deces     *before he dies*
Mony thousand in feild sall mak thar end.
Of this regioune he sall the Sothroun send     *[Out] of*
And Scotlande thris he sall bryng to the     *thrice*
    pes;     *peace*
350 So gud of hand agayne sall never be kend.'     *known*

All worthi men that has gud witt to     *at*
    vaille,     *command*
Be war that yhe with mys deyme nocht     *Beware; do not find fault*
    my taille.
Perchance yhe say that Bruce he was none
    sik.     *such*

He was als gud quhat deid was to assaill    *as; action; attempt*

355   As of his handis and bauldar in battaill,    *bolder*
Bot Bruce was knawin weyll ayr of this    *heir*
    kynrik;    *kingdom*
For he had rycht we call no man him lik.
Bot Wallace thris this kynrik conquest    *conquered*
    haile,
In Ingland fer socht battaill on that rik.    *far; realm*

360   I will ratorn to my mater agayne.    *return; subject*
Quhen Wallace was ralesched of his payn,    *released from*
The contre demyd haile at he was dede;    *completely believed that*
His derrest kyn nocht wist of his ramede    *knew; recovery*
Bot haile he was likly to gang and ryd.
365   Into that place he wald no langar byde.
His trew kepar he send to Elrisle.    *loyal keeper [i.e., the nurse]*
Efter him thar he durst nocht lat thaim be.    *Behind*
Hir dochter als, thar servand and hir
    child,
He gart thaim pas on to his modyr myld.
370   Quhen thai war gayne na wapynnys thar he    *gone*
    saw
To helpe him with quhat aventur mycht
    befaw.    *befall*
A rousty swerd in a noik he saw stand    *corner*
Withoutyn belt, but bos, bukler or band.    *without boss, shield*
Lang tyme befor it had beyne in that steid;
375   Ane agyt man it left quhen he was dede.
He drew the blaid: he fand it wald bitt    *cut*
    weill;
Thocht it was foule, nobill it was of steyll.    *in bad condition; steel*
'God helpis his man, for thou sall go with
    me
Quhill better cum, will God, full sone may    *Until a better [sword]*
    be!'
380   To Schir Ranald as than he wald nocht fair.    *go*
In that passage offt Sothroun maid repar.    *route; frequented*
At Rycardtoun full fayn he wald have
    beyne
To get him hors and part of armour
    scheyne.    *shining*
On thederwart as he bounyt to fair    *In that direction; prepared to*
    *go*

385 Thre Inglismen he met, ridand till Ayr,
    In thair viage at Glaskow furth had beyne.    *travelling*
    Ane Longcastell, that cruell was and keyne,    *fierce*
    A bauld squier, with him gud yemen twa.    *bold; retainers two*
    Wallace drew by and wald haiff lattyn    *drew to the side; let*
       thaim ga.
390 Till him he raid and said dispitfully,    *To*
    'Thou Scot abide. I trow thou be sum spy,
    Or ellis a theyff, fra presens wald thee hid.'    *presence [of others]*
    Than Wallace said with sobyr wordis that
       tid,    *time*
    'Schir, I am seik. For Goddis luff latt me ga!'
395 Longcastell said, 'Forsuth it beis nocht sa.
    A felloune freik thou semys in thi fair.    *fighting man; bearing*
    Quhill men thee knaw thou sall with me till
       Ayr.'[1]
    Hynt out his swerd that was of nobill hew.    *[He] pulled*
    Wallace with that at his lychtyn him drew,    *dismounting*
400 Apon the crag with his swerd has him tayne,    *neck; struck*
    Throu brayne and seyne in sonder straik    *brawn; sinew; bone*
       the bayne.
    Be he was fallyn, the twa than lichtyt doun,    *Once; alighted*
    To veng his dede to Wallace maid thaim    *avenge; death*
       boun.
    The tayne of thaim apon the hed he gaiff,    *The one; hit*
405 The rousty blaid to the schulderis him claiff.    *shoulders; cleaved*
    The tother fled and durst no langer bide;
    With a rud step Wallace coud efter glide.    *powerful stride; go easily*
    Our thourch his rybbis a seker straik drewe    *Up through; sure stroke he*
       he,    *delivered*
    Quhill lever and lounggis men mycht all    *So that liver; lungs*
       redy se.
410 Thar hors he tuk, bathe wapynnys and
       armour,
    Syne thankit God with gud hart in that    *Then*
       stour.    *fight*
    Sylver thai had, all with him has he tayne
    Him to support, for spendyng had he nayne.    *spending money*
    In to gret haist he raid to Ricardtoun.
415 A blyth semblay was at his lychtin doun    *A happy reunion;*
                             *dismounting*

1 Until we know who you are you shall [come] with me to Ayr

Quhen Wallace mett with Schir Richart the knicht,

For him had murnit quhill feblit was his mycht.    [Who] had grieved for him; enfeebled

His thre sonnys of Wallace was full fayne;    Wallace's return; glad

Thai held him lost, yit God him sawth agayne.    saved

420  His eyme, Schir Ranald, to Rycardtoun come fast;    uncle

The wemen told by Corsby as thai past    women

Of Wallace eschaipe, syne thar viage yeid.[1]

Schyr Ranald yit was in a felloune dreid:    terrible fear

Quhill he him saw in hart he thocht full lang;    Until; was downcast

425  Than sodanlye in armys he coud him thrang.    embrace

He mycht nocht spek, bot kyst him tenderlye;

The knychtis spreit was in ane extasye.    spirit

The blyth teris tho bryst fro his eyne two    happy; then burst

Or that he spak, a lang tyme held him so,    Before

430  And at the last rycht freindfully said he,    kindly

'Welcum nevo, welcum, deir sone to me.    nephew

Thankit be He that all this warld has wrocht,

Thus fairlye thee has out of presoune brocht!'    wonderfully

His modyr come and other freyndis enew    enough

435  With full glaid will to feill thai tithingis trew.    learn

Gud Robert Boyd, that worthi was and wicht,    strong

Wald nocht thaim trow quhill he him saw with sicht.    believe until; with his own eyes

Fra syndry part thai socht to Ricardtoun,    From diverse places; went

Feille worthi folk that war of gret renoun.    Many

440  Thus leiff I thaim in mirth, blys and plesance,    leave

Thankand gret God of his fre happy chance.    for; great good fortune

1 Of Wallace's escape, then continued on their way

# BOOK THREE

|     | | |
|-----|-------------------------------------------------|-----------------------------|
|     | In joyous Julii, quhen the flouris swete        | joyful July |
|     | Degesteable, engenered throu the heet,          | Were made to bloom, engendered by |
|     | Baith erbe and froyte, busk and bewis, braid    | herb; fruit, bush and boughs grew |
|     | Haboundandlye in every slonk and slaid;         | Abundantly; hollow and valley |
| 5   | Als bestiall, thar rycht cours till endur,      | Also beasts; proper; maintain |
|     | Weyle helpyt ar be wyrkyn of natur,             | working |
|     | On fute and weynge ascendand to the hycht,      | wing; coming to full growth |
|     | Conserved weill be the Makar of mycht;          | Preserved [tended]; by |
|     | Fyscheis in flude refeckit rialye               | river revived royally |
| 10  | Till mannys fude the warld suld occupye;        | busy itself |
|     | Bot Scotland sa was waistit mony day,           | laid waste |
|     | Throu wer sic skaith at labour was away.        | war such harm that; useless |
|     | Wictaill worth scant or August coud apper,      | Provisions became; before; arrived |
|     | Throu all the land that fude was hapnyt der.    | became dear |
| 15  | Bot Inglismen, that riches wantyt nayne,        | lacked none |
|     | Be caryage brocht thar wictaill full gud wayne; | By baggage; food in good quantity |
|     | Stuffit housis with wyn and gud wernage         | Supplied castles |
|     | Demaynde this land as thar awne heretage;       | Governed |
|     | The kynryk haile thai reullyt at thar will.     | ruled |
| 20  | Messyngeris than sic tithingis brocht thaim till, | |
|     | And tald Persye that Wallace leffand war,       | was [still] alive |
|     | Of his eschaip fra thar presoune in Ayr.        | escape; prison |
|     | Thai trowit rycht weill he passit was that steid | place |
|     | For Longcastell and his twa men was deid.       | were dead |
| 25  | He trowit the chance that Wallace so was past.  | cursed the [lost] opportunity |
|     | In ilka part thai war gretlye agast             | On every side |
|     | Throu prophesye that thai had herd befor.       | |
|     | Lord Persye said, 'Quhat nedis wordis mor?      | |
|     | Bot he be cest he sall do gret mervaill.        | Unless; stopped; wonders |
| 30  | It war the best for King Edwardis availl        | advantage |
|     | Mycht he him get to be his steidfast man,       | |

For gold or land his conquest mycht lest          last
  than.
Me think beforce he may nocht gottyn be.          by force
Wysmen the suth be his eschaip may se.'           by
35  Thus deyme thai him in mony divers cas;          they consider; diverse points
                                                     of view

We leiff thaim her and spek furth of
  Wallas.
In Rycardtoun he wald no langer byde,
For freindis consaill nor thing that mycht
  betide;
And quhen thai saw that it availlit nocht,
40  His purpos was to venge him at he mocht
On Sothron blud quhilk has his eldris          forebears
  slayne,
Thai latt him wyrk his awn will in to          openly
  playne.
Schir Richart had thre sonnys as I you tald,
Adam, Rychart and Symont that was bald.          bold
45  Adam eldest was growand in curage,
Forthward, rycht fayr, eighteen yer of age,      Promising
Large of persone, bathe wis, worthi and
  wicht.                                           bold
Gude King Robert in his tyme maid him
  ' knycht.
Lang tyme eft in Brucis weris he baid,          after; fought
50  On Inglismen mone gud jorne maid.            many; combats
This gud squier with Wallace bound to ryd      prepared
And Robert Boid quhilk wald no langar
  bide                                            remain
Under thrillage of segis of Ingland.            thraldom; Englishmen [lit.
                                                   men of England]
To that fals king he had never maid band.      [an] oath of fealty
55  Kneland was thar, ner cusyng to Wallace,      cousin
Syne baid with him in mony peralous place,      Afterwards remained
And Edward Litill, his sister sone so der.
Full weill graithit in till thar armour cler    equipped; bright
Wyth thar servandis fra Ricardtoun thai
  raid
60  To Mawchtlyne mur and schort tyme thar
  abaid,                                          waited
For freindis thaim tauld, was bound under       tribute
  trewage,

That Fenweik was for Perseys caryage:    was [away]; baggage
Within schort tyme he will bryng it till
    Ayr
Out of Carleile; he had resavyt it thair.
65 That plesyt Wallace in his hart gretumlye.    greatly
Wytt yhe thai war a full glaid cumpanye.    For sure
Towart Lowdoun thai bounyt thaim to ride    prepared
And in a schaw a litill thar besyde    wood
Thai lugyt thaim, for it was nere the nycht,    camped
70 To wache the way als besyly as thai mycht.    vigilantly
A trew Scot quhilk hosteler hous thair held    who [an] innkeeper's house
                                        occupied there
Under Lowdoun, as myn autor me teld,    Below
He saw thar com, syne went to thaim in    coming, then; quickly
    hye.
Baithe meite and drynk he brocht full
    prevalye    secretly
75 And to thaim tald the cariage in to playn.    told them about; plainly
Thair for-rydar was past till Ayr agayne,    advance rider
Left thaim to cum with power of gret    company of great advantage
    vaille.
Thai trowit be than thai war in    believed
    Avendaille.
Wallace than said, 'We will nocht sojorne
    her,
80 Nor change no weid bot our ilk dayis ger.    clothes; everyday garments
At Corssencon the gait was spilt that tide,    road; destroyed; time
Forthi that way behovid thaim for to ride.    Therefore
Ay fra the tyme that he of presoune four    Ever since; out of prison
                                        went
Gude souer weide dayly on him he wour:    trusty armour
85 Gude lycht harnes fra that tyme usyt he    armour
    ever,
For sodeyn stryff fra it he wald nocht    In case of surprise attack;
    sever.    never without it
A habergione under his gowne he war,    breastplate
A steylle capleyne in his bonet but mar,    cap; hat; more
And glovis of plait in claith war coverit
    weill,[1]
90 In his doublet a clos coler of steyle.    jerkin; fitted collar
His face he kepit for it was ever bar,    guarded; bare

---

1 And gloves of plate-armour were covered well with cloth

With his twa handis the quhilk full worthi
war.
In to his weid and he come in a thrang        In his armour; if; battle
Was na man than on fute mycht with him
gang.        compete
95   So growane in pith, of power stark and        grown in strength; strong;
stur,        sturdy
His terryble dyntis war awfull till endur.        blows; daunting
Thai trastyt mar in Wallace him allane
Than in a hundreth mycht be of Ingland
tane.        taken
The worthi Scottis maid thar no sojornyng,
100   To Lowdoun hill past in the gray dawyng,        dawning
Devysyt the place and putt thair hors thaim        Surveyed
fra
And thocht to wyn or never thin to ga:        go from there
Send twa skowrrouris to wesy weyll the        They sent two scouts;
playne,        reconnoitre
Bot thai rycht sone raturnde in agayne,        quickly
105   To Wallace tald that thai war cummand
fast.
Than thai to grounde all kneland at the last        Then
With humyll hartis prayit with all thar
mycht
To God aboune to help thaim in thar rycht.        above
Than graithit thai thaim till harnes hastely.        equipped themselves with
armour
110   Thar sonyeit nane of that gud chevalrye.        none hesitated
Than Wallace said, 'Her was my fader
slayne,
My brother als, quhilk dois me mekill
payne;
So sall my selff, or vengit be but dreid.        avenged be without doubt
The traytour is her, caus was of that deid.'
115   Than hecht thai all to bide with hartlye        vowed; heartfelt
will.
Be that the power was takand Lowdoun
hill.[1]
The knycht Fenweik convoide the caryage;        escorted
He had on Scottis maid mony schrewide        against; accursed raids
viage.

1 By that time the English force was making their way to Loudoun hill

The sone was rysyne our landis schenand    sun; over; shining
  brycht.
120 The Inglismen so thai come to the hycht;    hill
Ner thaim he raid and sone the Scottis saw.    rode; soon
He tald his men and said to thaim on raw,    together
'Yhonne is Wallace that chapit our    escaped from our prison
  presoune.
He sall agayne and be drawyn throu the
  toune.¹
125 His hede mycht mar, I wait, weill ples the    more, I think, well
  king
Than gold or land or ony warldly thing.'    [More] than
He gart servandis bide with the cariage    caused; stay
  still.
Thai thocht to dauntyt the Scottis at thar    subdue
  will.
Nyne scor he led in harnes burnyst brycht,    armour
130 And fyfty was with Wallace in the rycht.
Unraboytyt the Sothroun was in wer    Undaunted
And fast thai come, fell awfull in affer.    very; appearance
A maner dyk of stanys thai had maid,    A sort of stone wall they [the
                            Scots]
Narrowyt the way quhar throuch thai thikar    through which they crowded
  raid.
135 The Scottis on fute tuk the feld thaim
  befor;
The Sothroun saw: thar curage was the mor.
In prydefull ire thai thoucht our thaim to
  ryde,
Bot other wys it hapnyt in that tide.
On athir side togidder fast thai glaid;    went easily
140 The Scottis on fute gret rowme about
  thaim maide,
With ponyeand speris throuch platis prest    piercing
  of steylle.
The Inglismen that thocht to veng thaim
  weylle,
The harnest hors about thaim rudely raide,    harnessed; roughly
That with unes upone thar feit thai baid.    difficulty upon; stayed
145 Wallace the formast in the byrney bar;    breastplate struck
The grounden sper throuch his body schar.    sharp; cut

¹ And he shall again be dragged through the town

The schafft to-schonkit offe the fruschand tre;  *shaft broke off; splintering wood*

Devoydyde sone sen na better mycht be,  *Split; since*

Drew swerdis syne, bathe hevy, scharp and lang.  *then*

150 On athyr syd full cruelly thai dang,  *struck*

Fechtand at anys in to that felloune dout.  *cruel danger*

Than Inglismen enveround thaim about,  *encircled*

Beforce etlyt throuch out thaim for to ryde.  *By force aimed*

The Scottis on fute that baldly couth abyde

155 With swerdis schar throuch habergeons full gude,  *pierced; breastplates*

Upon the flouris schot the schonkan blude  *flowers; spouting blood*

Fra hors and men throu harnes burnyst beyne.  *polished armour spurting*

A sayr sailye forsuth thar mycht be seyne.  *pitiful assault*

Thai traistyt na liff bot the letter end.  *expected; latter end [i.e., death]*

160 Of sa few folk gret nobilnes was kend,  *For; shown*

Togydder baid defendand thaim full fast;  *stood defending themselves*

Durst nane sever quhill the maist pres was past.[1]

The Inglismen that besye was in wer  *who trained were in warfare*

Befors ordand in sonder thaim to ber.[2]

165 Thair cheyff chyftan feryt als fers as fyr,  *charged as fiercely*

Throu matelent and verray propyr ire,  *rage; pure anger*

On a gret hors in till his glitterand ger  *equipped in glittering armour*

In fewter kest a fellone aspre sper.  *fewter [socket] placed; cruel sharp spear*

The knycht Fenweik that cruell was and keyne,  *fierce; merciless*

170 He had at dede of Wallace fader beyne,  *at the death of*

And his brodyr, that douchty was and der.  *who courageous; dearly loved*

Quhen Wallace saw that fals knycht was so ner

His corage grew in ire as a lyoune;

Till him he ran and fell frekis bar he doune.  *many men he struck down*

175 As he glaid by awkwart he couth him ta,  *agilely passed crosswise; take*

The and arsone in sonder gart he ga.  *Thigh; saddlebow; he sliced through*

1 None dared separate until the press to battle was past
2 Planned by force asunder to drive them

Fra the coursour he fell on the fer syd.    *steed*

With a staff swerd Boyd stekit him that tyde.    *strong sword; stabbed*

Or he was dede the gret pres come so fast    *Before*

180 Our him to grounde thai bur Boyde at the last.    *bore*

Wallace was ner and ratornde agayne

Him to reskew, till that he rais of payne,    *rose with difficulty*

Wichtly him wor quhill he a swerd had tayne.    *Bravely; defended him until*

Throu out the stour thir twa in feyr ar gayne.    *fighting these two together*

185 The ramanand apon thaim folowit fast;    *remainder*

In thar passage fell Sothron maid agast.    *many Englishmen were terrified*

Adam Wallace, the ayr of Ricardtoun,    *heir*

Straik ane Bewmound, a squier of renoun,    *one*

On the pyssan with his brand burnyst bar.    *gorget; sword*

190 The thrusande blaid his hals in sonder schayr.    *cutting; neck; sheared asunder*

The Inglismen, thocht thar chyftayn was slayne,    *although*

Bauldly thai baid as men mekill of mayn.    *Boldly stood their ground; stalwart*

Reth hors repende rouschede frekis under feit;[1]

The Scottis on fute gert mony lois the swete.    *made many lose their lives*

195 Wicht men lichtyt thaim selff for to defend;    *Bold; dismounted*

Quhar Wallace come thar deide was litill kend.    *deeds amounted to little*

The Sothroune part so frusched was that tide    *The English side; crushed; time*

That in the stour thai mycht no langar bide.    *battle*

Wallace in deide he wrocht so worthely,

200 The squier Boid and all thar chevalry,

Litill, Kneland, gert of thar ennymys de.

The Inglismen tuk playnly part to fle.    *openly*

On hors sumpart to strenthis can thame found    *castles; went*

1 Fierce kicking horses trampled men underfoot

To socour thaim, with mony werkand          save themselves; painful
   wound.
205  A hundreth dede in feild was levyt thar,   were left there
And three yemen that Wallace menyde fer      mourned
   mar;
Twa was of Kyle, and ane of Conyngayme
With Robert Boide to Wallace com fra         had come from home
   hayme.
Four scor fled that chapyt on the south      escaped
   syde.
210  The Scottis in place that bauldly couth
   abyde
Spoilyeid the feld, gat gold and othir ger,  Plundered; gear
Harnes and hors, quhilk thai mysteryt in     Armour; needed in warfare
   wer.
The Inglis knawis thai gart thar caryage leid[1]
To Clidis forest; quhen thai war out of
   dreid                                    danger
215  Thai band thaim fast with wedeis sad and   withes [twisted bark] tight;
   sar,                                         painful
On bowand treis hangyt thaim rycht thar.     bending; hanged
He sparyt nane that abill was to wer,        spared; able to fight
Bot wemen and preystis he gart thaim ay      priests; always spared them
   forber.
Quhen this was doyne to thar dyner thai
   went
220  Of stuff and wyne that God had to thaim    food
   sent.
Ten scor thai wan of hors that cariage bure, baggage; carried
With flour and wyne als mekill as thai
   mycht fur                                carry
And other stuff that thai of Carleile led.   from
The Sothron part out of the feild at fled    that
225  With sorow socht to the castell of Ayr
Befor the lord and tauld him of thar cair:   distress
Quhat gud thai lost and quha in feild was    goods
   slayne
Throu wicht Wallace that was mekill of
   mayne,
And how he had gart all thar servandis
   hang.

1 They made English serving men [knaves] transport their baggage

230 The Persye said, 'And that squier lest lang     *if*
    He sall us exille out of this contre cleyne.
    Sa dispitfull in wer was never seyne.     *cruel*
    In our presoune her last quhen that he was     *when he was last here*
    Our sleuthfully our keparis lett him pas.     *Too carelessly; wardens*
235 Thus stuff our land I fynde may nocht     *provisioned*
       weill be;
    We mon ger bryng our victaill be the se.¹
    Bot los our men it helpis us rycht nocht.     *[to] lose*
    Thar kyne may ban that ever we hydder     *kindred; curse that we ever*
       socht.'
    Lat I thaim thus blamand thar sory chance,     *I leave; unfortunate*
240 And mar to sper of Scottis mennys     *more [I will] enquire;*
       governance.
    Quhen Wallace had weyle venquist into     *completely vanquished*
       playne
    The fals terand that had his fadyr slayne,     *tyrant*
    Hys brother als quhilk was a gentill knycht,     *noble*
    Othir gud men befor to dede thai dycht,     *put to death before*
245 He gert devys and provide thar victaille,     *made arrangements*
    Baith stuff and hors that was of gret availle.     *provisions*
    To freyndis about richt prevalye thai send.
    The ramanand full glaidlye thar thai spend.     *passed time*
    In Clydis wode thai sojornyt twenty dayis;     *dwelled*
250 Na Sothren that tyme was persavyt in thai     *those areas*
       wais
    Bott he tholyt dede that come in thar danger.     *suffered death*
    The worde of him walkit baith fer and ner.     *spread*
    Wallace was knawin on lyff leyffand in     *[to be] alive living openly*
       playne,
    Thocht Inglismen tharof had gret payn.
255 The Erle Persye to Glaskow couth he fair     *made his way*
    With wys lordis and held a consell thair.     *council*
    Quhen thai war mett weylle, ma na ten     *more than*
       thousand,
    Na chyftane was that tyme durst tak on     *dared*
       hand
    To leide the range on Wallace to assaill.     *pursuit*
260 He speryt about quhat was the best consaill.     *asked; counsel*
    Schir Amar Wallange, a fals traytour     *strong*
       strange,

¹ We must have our provisions brought in by sea

In Bothwell dwelt and thar was thaim
    amange,                                                    *was among them there*
He said, 'My lorde, my consaill will I giff.
Bot ye do it fra scaith ye may nocht
    scheyff.                                                    *Unless; harm; escape*
265  Yhe mon tak pes without mar tarying,            *more delay*
As for a tyme we may send to the king.'            *until such a time [as]*
The Persye said, 'Of our trewis he will nane.     *truce; have nothing (to do)*
Ane awfull chyftane trewly he is ane;             *A fearsome*
He will do mair in faith or that he blyne.        *before; ceases*
270  Sothroun to sla he thinkis it na syne.'        *no sin*
Schir Amar said, 'Trewis it wordis tak            *behoves us*
Quhill eft for him provisioune we may mak.        *after; plans*
I knaw he will do mekill for his kyne.            *kin*
Gentrys ande trewtht ay restis him within.        *Nobility; loyalty always*
275  His uncle may, Schir Ranald, mak this
    band.                                                     *agreement*
Gyff he will nocht, racunnys all his land          *confiscate*
On to the tyme that he this werk haiff            *Until such time as*
    wrocht.'                                                  *done*
Schir Ranald was sone to that consell
    brocht.
Thai chargyt him to mak Wallace at pes
280  Or he suld pas to Londone withoutyn les.       *doubt*
Schir Ranald said, 'Lordis, yhe knaw this
    weill,
At my commande he will nocht do a deill.           *at all*
His worthi kyn dispitously ye slew,                *mercilessly*
In presone syne ner to the dede him threw.
285  He is at large and will nocht do for me
Thocht ye tharfor rycht now suld ger me de.'
Schir Amar said, 'Thir lordis sone sall send       *These*
On to the king and mak a finall end.
Of his conquest forsuth he will it haiff;
290  Wallace na thou ma nocht this kynrik
    saiff.[1]
Mycht Edward king get him for gold or
    land
To be his man than suld he bruk Scotland.'         *enjoy possession of*
The lordis bade ces. 'Thou excedis to that         *go too far with*
    knycht

---

1 Neither Wallace nor you may save this kingdom

Fer mayr be treuth than it is ony rycht.
295 The wrang conquest our king desiris ay        wrongful
On hym or us it sall be seyne some day.
Wallace has rycht, bathe force and fair
    fortoun.
Ye hard how he eschapyt our presoune.'
Thus said that lord, syne prayit Schir
    Ranald fair
300 To mak this pes: 'Thou schirreff art of
    Ayr.
As for a tyme we may avisit be,               advised
Undyr my seylle I sall be bound to thee
For Inglismen that thai sall do him nocht,    do no [harm to] him
Nor to no Scottis, les it be on thaim socht.' unless
305 Schir Ranald wist he mycht thaim nocht
    ganestand.                                 gainsay
Of Lord Persye he has resavit this band.      From; bond
Perseys war trew and ay of full gret vaill,   service
Sobyr in pes and cruell in battaill.          fierce
Schir Ranald bounyde upon the morn but        prepared; without
    baid                                          delay
310 Wallace to seke in Clydis forest braid.    broad
So he him fand bounand to his dyner,          getting ready for
Quhen thai had seyne this gud knycht was
    so ner,
Weyle he him knew and tauld thaim quhat       He knew him well
    he was.
Mervaille he had quhat gart him hidder        made
    pas,
315 Maide him gud cheyr of meyttis fresche     foods
    and fyne.
King Edwardis self coud nocht get better
    wyn
Than thai had thar, warnage and              malmsey wine; venison
    venysoune,
Of bestiall into full gret fusioun.           meat; plenty
Syn efter mett he schew thaim of his deide    dinner; told
320 How he had beyne into so mekill dreid.     great danger
'Nevo', he said, 'wyrk part of my consaill.
Tak pes a quhill as for the mair availl;      to gain the greater advantage
Bot thou do so forsuth thou dois gret syne,   unless
For thai ar set till undo all thi kyn.'       ruin
325 Than Wallace said till gud men him about,

'I will no pes for all this felloune dout　　*will [accept]; truce; terrible danger*

Bot gif it ples better to you than me.'　　*Unless*
The squier Boide him answerd sobyrle,
'I gif consell or this gud knycht be slayne,　　*before*
330　Tak pes a quhill suppos it do us payne.'　　*even though it grieves us*
So said Adam, the ayr of Rycardtoune,
And Kneland als grantyt to thar opynyoun.　　*agreed with*
With thair consent Wallace this pes has tayn,
As his eyme wrocht, till ten moneth war gayn.　　*uncle arranged; gone by*
335　Thar leyff thai tuk with comforde into playn,　　*comfortably; truly*
Sanct Jhone to borch thai suld meyt haille agayn.　　*with St John's protection; meet safely*
Boyde and Kneland past to thar placis hayme,　　*houses*
Adam Wallace to Ricardtoun be nayme,
And Wilyham furth till Schir Ranald can ride
340　And his houshald in Corsby for to bide.[1]
This pees was cryede in August moneth myld.　　*proclaimed*
Yhet goddis of battaill furius and wild,
Mars and Juno, ay dois thar besynes,
Causer of wer, wyrkar of wykitnes,
345　And Venus als the goddes of luff
Wytht ald Saturn his coursis till appruff –　　*With; approve*
Thir four scansyte of divers complexioun,　　*displayed*
Bataill, debaite, invy and destruccioun –　　*strife; envy*
I can nocht deyme for thar malancoly.　　*pronounce judgement on; malice*

350　Bot Wallace weille coude nocht in Corsby ly.　　*lie*
Hym had lever in travaill for to be,　　*preferred; active*
Rycht sar he langyt the toune of Ayr to se.　　*sorely; longed*
Schir Ranald past fra hame apon a day,
Fyfteyne he tuk and to the toune went thai,　　*he [Wallace]*
355　Coverit his face that no man mycht him knaw;　　*covered*
Nothing him roucht how few ennymyis him saw:　　*cared*

1 To dwell in his household in Corsby

In souer weide disgysyt weill war thai.                      trusty clothes
Ane Inglisman on the gait saw he play[1]
At the scrymmage, a bukler on his hand.                      At scrimmage; shield
360 Wallace ner by in falouschipe couth stand                  stood
Lychtly he sperde, 'Quhi, Scot, dar thou                     Scornfully; asked;
   nocht preiff?'                                                try
Wallace said, 'Ya, sa thou wald gif me
   leiff.'
'Smyt on,' he said, 'I defy thine accioune.'                 Strike
Wallace tharwith has tane him on the                         hit; crown [of the head]
   croune,
365 Throuch bukler, hand and the harnpan also,                skull
To the schulderis the scharp swerd gert he
   go.
Lychtly raturnd till his awne men agayne.                    Nimbly
The wemen cryede, 'Our bukler player is
   slane!'
The man was dede. Quhat nedis wordis
   mair?
370 Feille men of armys about him semblit                     Many; gathered
   thair:
Sevyn scor at anys agayne sixteen war sett;                  Seven score [140]; against
Bot Wallace sone weille with the formest
   mett,
With ire and will on the hede has him
   tayne,                                                    struck
Throuch the brycht helm in sonder bryst                      helmet; shattered; bone
   the bane.
375 Ane other braithly in the breyst he bar;                  violently; breast; wounded
His burnyst blaid throuch out the body
   schar,                                                   sliced
Gret rowme he maid; his men war fechtand                     headway
   fast
And mony a growme thai maid full sair                        man [lit. groom]
   agast –
For thai war wicht and weill usyt in wer –                   very experienced; war
380 Of Inglismen rycht bauldly doun thai ber.
On thar enemys gret martirdome thai maik.
Thar hardy chiftane so weill couth
   undyrtak:
Quhat Inglisman that baid in till his gait                   got in his path

---

1 On the street he saw an Englishman playing

Contrar Scotland maid never mar debait. — never more fought
385 Felle frekis on fold war fellyt undir feit;[1]
Of Sothroune blude lay stekit in the streit. — stabbed
New power come fra the castell that tyde. — Reinforcements; time
Than Wallace drede and drew towart a side; — was filled with dread
With gude will he wald eschew a supris — avoid an attack
390 For he in wer was besy, wicht and wis. — diligent; prudent
Harnes and hedis he hew in sonderys fast; — Armour; cut to pieces
Be force out of the thikest preys thai past. — press [of battle]
Wallace raturnyde behynde his men agayne;
At the reskew feile enemys has he slayne. — many
395 His men all samyn he out of perill brocht — together
Fra his enemys, for all the power thai mocht. — power; might [have]
To thar horsis thai wan but mair abaide; — got without
For danger syne to Laglyne wode thai raid. — Because of; then; rode
Twenty and nine thai left into that steide — place
400 Of Sothroun men that bertynit war to dede. — were left for dead
The ramaynand agayne turnyt that tide, — time
For in the woode thai durst nocht him abyde.
Towart the toune thai drew with all thar mayn, — forces
Cursand the pes thai tuk befor in playne. — openly
405 The lord Persye in hart was gretlye grevyt. — grieved
His men supprisyt agayne to him relevyt — defeated; rallied
And feille war dede into thar armour cler, — many; bright
Thre of his kyne that war till him full der. — [Including] three
Quhen he hard tell of thar gret grevance, — harm
410 Thar selff was caus of this myschefull chance. — evil
Murnyng he maid, thoucht few Scottis it kend. — Mourning; knew
A herald than to Schir Ranald he send
And tald till him of all thar sodeyne cas, — unexpected case
And chargyt him tak souerte of Wallas: — stand surety
415 He suld him kepe fra merket toune or fair, — market
Quhar he mycht best be out of thar repair. — path
The Sothroun wist that it was wicht Wallace — knew
Had thaim ourset in to that sodand cas. — defeated

[1] Many valued men on the battlefield were felled under foot

Thair trewis for this thai wald nocht brek
adeill.                                                    at all
420 Quhen Wallace had this chance eschewit            danger; escaped
weill,
Upon the nycht fra Lagleyne hayme he
raid.
In chaumeris sone thair residence thai            chambers
maid.
Upon the morn quhen that the day was
lycht,
Witht Wallace furth went Schir Ranald the         With
knycht,
425 Schew him the wryt lord Persie had him            Showed; writ
sent.
'Deir sone,' he said, 'this war my haile           this is my greatest desire
entent,
That thou wald grant quhill thir trewis war        until
worn,                                                  lapsed
Na scaith to do till Inglisman that is born,       harm
Bot quhar I pas dayly thou bid with me.'           accompany
430 Wallace answerd, 'Gud schir, that may
nocht be.
Rycht laith I war, deyr uncle, you to greiff.      reluctant (i.e., loathe); vex
I sall do nocht till tyme I tak my leyff,
And warn you als or that I fra you pas.'           I [will] warn; before
His eyme and he thus weill accordyt was.
435 Wallace with him maid his continuance.           stayed with him
Ilk wicht was blyth to do till him plesance.       Each man; kindness
In Corsby thus he resyd thaim amang                resided
Thai sixteen dayis, suppos him thocht it           [too]
lang.                                                  long
Thocht thai mycht ples him as a prince or          serve
king,
440 In his mynde yit remanyt ane other thing:
He saw his enemys maisteris in this
regioune,
Mycht nocht him ples thocht he war king           please
with croune.
Thus leyff I him with his der freyndis still;
Of Inglismen of sumpart spek I will.              something

## BOOK FOUR

In September, the humyll moneth swette,   *humble*
Quhen passyt by the hycht was of the
hette,   *heat*
Victaill and froyte ar rypyt in   *ripened*
aboundance
As God ordans to mannys governance.   *ordains*

5  Sagittarius with his aspre bow,   *cruel*
Be the ilk syng veryte ye may know   *By the same sign*
The changing cours quhilk makis gret
deference;   *difference*
And levys had lost thair colouris of   *leaves*
plesence.
All warldly thing has nocht bot a sesoune,

10  Both erbe and froyte mon fra hevyn cum   *must from heaven*
doun.
In thys ilk tyme a gret consell was sett
In to Glaskow, quhar mony maisteris mett   *chiefs*
Of Inglis lordis to statute this cuntre.   *rule*
Than chargyt thai all schirreffis thar to be.   *sheriffs*

15  Schir Ranald Crawfurd behowide that tyme   *was obliged to be there at*
be thar   *that time*
For he throu rycht was born schirreff of
Ayr.
His der nevo that tyme with hym he tuk,   *nephew*
Willyham Wallace, as witnes beris the buk,
For he na tyme suld be fra his sicht;

20  He luffyt him with hart and all his mycht.
Thai graith thaim weill without langar   *readied*
abaid.   *delay*
Wallace sum part befor the court furth raid,   *in advance; retinue; rode*
With him twa men that douchtye war in   *bold*
deid,
Our tuk the child Schir Ranaldis sowme   *Overtook; young man;*
couth leid.   *baggage*

25  Softlye thai raid quhill thai the court suld   *Easily; until; retinue; see*
knaw.
So sodeynly that Hesilden he saw   *at Hazelden*
The Perseys sowme, in quhilk gret riches   *baggage*
was.
The hors was tyryt and mycht no forther   *tired*
pas.

Five men was chargit to keipe it weill all sid;

30 Twa was on fute, and thre on hors couth ride.

The maister man at thar servandis can sper,    *their [Sir Ranald's]; enquired*

'Quha aw this sowme? The suth thou to me ler.'    *owns; Tell me the truth*

The man answerd withoutyn wordis mar,

'My lordis,' he said, 'quhilk schirreff is of Ayr.'

35 'Sen it is his, this hors sall with us gang    *since; shall go with us*

To serve our lord, or ellis me think gret wrang.

Thocht a subjet in deid wald pas his lord,    *deeds; surpass*

It is nocht levyt be na rychtwis racord.'    *permitted; opinion*

Thai cut the brays and leyt the harnes faw.    *straps; gear; fall*

40 Wallace was ner. Quhen he sic revere saw,    *robbery*

He spak to thaim with manly contenance;

In fayr afforme he said but variance,    *manner; firmly*

'Ye do us wrang, and it in tyme of pes.    *truce*

Of sic rubry war suffisance to ces.'    *proper*

45 The Sothron schrew in ire answerd him to:    *scoundrel*

'It sall be wrocht as thou may se us do.

Thou gettis no mendis. Quhat wald thou wordis mar?'    *amends*

Sadly avisit, Wallace remembrith him thar    *Firmly resolved*

On the promys he maid his eyme befor.    *uncle*

50 Resoun him rewllyt; as than he did no mor.    *ruled for the time being*

The hors thai tuk for aventur mycht befall,    *whatever might happen*

Laid on thar sowme, syne furth the way couth call.    *baggage; then / drove*

Thar tyryt sowmer so left thai in to playne.    *tired pack horse; indeed*

Wallace raturnd towart the court agayne.    *returned; retinue*

55 On the mur syde sone with his eyme he mett    *moor*

And tauld how thai the way for his man sett:    *stopped*

'And war nocht I was bonde in my legiance,    *honour-bound*

We partyt noucht thus for all the gold in France.

The hors thai reft quhilk suld your harnes ber.'    *took; equipment*

60 Schir Ranald said, 'That is bot litill der.    *harm*

We may get hors and othir gud in playne;                 soon enough
And men be lost, we get never agayne.'                   But if
Wallace than said, 'Als wisly God me save,               save
Of this gret mys I sall amendis have                     wrong
65    And nother latt for pes na your plesance.           neither refrain; pleasure
With witnes her I gif up my legiance,[1]
For cowardly ye lik to tyne your rycht.                  lose
Your selff sone syne to dede thai think to               death; condemn
     dycht.'
In wraith tharwith away fra him he went.                 anger
70    Schyr Ranald was wis and kest in his               considered carefully
     entent,
And said, 'I will byde at the Mernys all                 Newton Mearns
     nycht
So Inglismen may deyme us no unrycht                     judge us [guilty of] no
                                                           offence

Gyff ony be deide befor us upon cas,                     If any happen to be dead
That we in law may bide the rychtwisnas.'                truth
75    His luging tuk, still at the Mernys baid.           lodging; waited
Full gret murnyng he for his nevo maid,                  grieving
Bot all for nocht; quhat mycht it him availl?
As in till wer he wrocht nocht his consaill.[2]
Wallace raid furth, with him twa yemen
     past;
80    The sowmer man he folowid wondyr fast.             baggage man
Be est Cathcart he ourhyede thaim agayne.                By; overtook
Than knew thai weille that it was he in
     playne,
Be hors and weide, that argownd thaim                    challenged
     befor.
The fyve to thaim retornde withoutyn mor.                turned back
85    Wallace to ground fra his courser can glide;       steed; descended
A burnyst brand he bradyt out that tyde.                 polished; drew
The maister man with sa gud will straik he,              such force
Bathe hatt and hede he gert in sonder fle;               helmet; caused
Ane other fast apon the face he gaiff,                   hard; hit
90    Till dede to ground but mercy he him               Until; dashed
     draiff;
The thrid he hyt with gret ire in that steid;
Fey on the fold he has him left for deid.                Doomed in life

1 In front of witnesses here I give up my allegiance
2 In matters of war he did not follow his counsel

Wallace slew three; be that his yemen wicht    *bold*
The tother twa derfly to dede thai dycht.    *violently killed*
95 Syne spoilyeid thai the harnais or thai wend    *plundered the gear before*
Of silver and gold aboundandlye to spend.
Jowellis thai tuk, the best was chosyn thar,    *Valuables*
Gud hors and geyr, syne on thar wayis can fayr.    *weapons; went*
Than Wallace said, 'At sum strenth wald I be.'    *stronghold*
100 Our Glid that tyme thar was a bryg of tre;[1]
Thidder thai past in all thar gudlye mycht.
The day was gayne and cummyn was the nycht.
Thai durst nocht weylle ner Glaskow still abide.
In the Lennox he tuk purpos to ryde,
105 And so he dyde, syne lugyt thaim that nycht    *lodged*
As thai best mowcht quhill that the day was brycht.    *until*
Till ane ostrye he went and sojorned thar    *inn*
With trew Scottis quhilk at his freindis war.    *who were his friends*
The consaill mett rycht glaidly on the morn,
110 Bot fell tithingis was brocht Persie beforn:    *bad news*
His men war slayne, his tresour als bereft
With fell Scottis and thaim na jowellis left.    *By cruel*
Thai demede about of that derff doutous cas.    *gave their opinion in turn; violent; uncertain*
The Sothren said, 'Forsuth it is Wallas:
115 The schirreffis court was cumand to the toun
And he as ane for Scot of most renoun.'    *He [came] as one of the Scots*
Thai gert go seik Schir Ranald in that rage    *sent for*
Bot he was than yeit still at herbryage.    *[his] lodgings*
Sum wis men said, 'Herof na thing he kend.    *He knew nothing of this*
120 The men war slayne rycht at the townis end.'
Schir Ranald come be ten houris of the day.    *by ten o'clock in the morning*

1 Over [the River] Clyde at that time there was a wooden bridge

Befor Persye than seir men brocht war thai.          *several*
Thai folowit him of felouny that was wrocht;          *charged*
The siys of this couth say to him rycht nocht.          *assize*
125  Thai demede about of that feill sodeyne cas.          *deliberated*
Befor the juge thar he denyit Wallas,[1]
And so he mycht, he wist nocht quhar he was.          *knew*
Fra this consaill my purpos is to pas,          *From [my account of]*
Of Wallace spek in wyldernes so wyde:          *[to] speak*
130  The eterne God his governour be and gyde!
Styll at the place four days he sojorned haill          *Quietly* / *safely*
Quhill tithingis come till hym fra thar consaill.          *Until*
Than statute thai in ilk steide of the west          *decreed; each place*
In thar boundis Wallace suld haiff no rest.          *Within*
135  His der uncle gret ayth thai gert him swer          *oath; made him swear*
That he but leiff suld no freindschipe him ber;          *without permission*
And mony othir was full woo that day.          *sad*
Robert the Boide stall of the toune his way,          *stole away from*
And Kneland als, befor with him had beyne.
140  Thai had lever haif seyne him with thar eyne          *would rather have* / *eyes*
Leyffand in lyff as thai knew him befor,          *Alive and well*
Than of cler gold a fyne mylyone and mor.
Boid wepyt sor, said, 'Our leidar is gayne.
Amang our fays he is set him allayne.'          *all alone*
145  Than Kneland said, 'Fals fortoun changis fast.
Gret God sen we had ever with him past.'          *grant [that]*
Edward Litill in Annadyrdaill is went          *Annandale*
And wait rycht nocht of this newe jugement.          *knew nothing about*
Adam Wallace baid still in Ricardtoun.          *stayed*
150  So fell it thus with Wallace of renoun,
He with power partyt mervalusly.          *company*
Be fortoun chance ourturnys doubilly.          *overturns*

1 Before the judge there he denied [knowledge of Wallace's whereabouts]

|   | | |
|---|---|---|
| | Thar petuous mone as than couth nocht be bett; | lament; helped |
| | Thai wyst no wyt quhar that thai suld him get. | had no idea |
| 155 | He left the place quhilk he in lugyng lay: | where |
| | Till Erle Malcome he went upon a day. | |
| | The Lennox haile he had still in his hand; | wholly |
| | Till king Edward he had nocht than maid band. | made / an oath of fealty |
| | That land is strait and maisterfull to wyn; | narrow; difficult; conquer |
| 160 | Gud men of armys that tyme was it within. | |
| | The lord was traist, the men sekyr and trew; | trustworthy; sure |
| | With waik power thai durst him nocht persew. | |
| | Rycht glaid he was of Wallace cumpany, | |
| | Welcummyt him fayr with worschipe reverandlye. | honour |
| 165 | At his awne will desyryt gyff he walde | |
| | To byde thair still, maistyr of his houshald, | |
| | Of all his men he suld haile chyftayne be. | complete |
| | Wallace answerd, 'That war yneuch for me. | |
| | I can nocht byde, my mynde is sett in playne | completely made up |
| 170 | Wrokyn to be or ellis de in the payne. | Revenged; attempt |
| | Our wast contre thar statute is so strang, | Over [the] west country |
| | Into the north my purpos is to gang.' | go |
| | Stevyn of Irland than in the Lennox was; | |
| | With wicht Wallace he ordynyt him to pas | he i.e., Malcolm; ordered him [Steven] |
| 175 | And other als that borne war of Argill. | |
| | Wallace still thair residence maid a quhill, | dwelling |
| | Quhill men it wist and semblit sone him till. | Until; knew; assembled |
| | He chargyt nayne bot at thar awne gud will. | commanded |
| | For thai war strang, yeitt he couth nocht thaim dreid | fear |
| 180 | Bot resavit all in weris thaim to leid. | |
| | Sum part of thaim was into Irland borne, | native Highlanders |
| | That Makfadyan had exilde furth beforne. | earlier |
| | King Edwardis man, he was sworn of Ingland, | had sworn fealty to |
| | Of rycht law byrth suppos he tuk on hand. | low |

185 To Wallace thar come ane that hecht    *was named*
     Fawdoun.
    Malancoly he was of complexioun,    *disposition*
    Hevy of statur, dour in his contenance,    *Heavily built; gloomy-featured*
    Sorowfull, sadde, ay dreidfull but plesance.    *grave; suspicious without kindness*

    Wallace resavit quhat man wald cum him till;
190 The bodelye ayth thai maid him with gud    *bodily oath*
     will
    Befor the erle, all with a gud accord,    *agreement*
    And him resavyt as captane and thar lord.
    His speciall men that come with him fra hame,
    The tayne hecht Gray, the tother Kerle be    *the one called*
     name,
195 In his service come fyrst with all thar
     mayne    *followers*
    To Lowdoun hill quhar that Fenweik was
     slayne.
    He thaim comandyt ay next him to persew    *follow*
    For he thaim kend rycht hardye, wis and    *knew them [to be]*
     trew.
    His leyff he tuk rycht on a fair maner.    *leave*
200 The gud erlle than he bad him gyftis ser.    *offered; several*
    Wallace wald nayne, bot gaiff of his fell sys    *many times*
    To pour and rych upon a gudlye wis.
    Humyll he was, hardy, wis and fre;    *generous*
    As of ryches he held na propyrte.    *personal property*
205 Of honour, worschipe, he was a merour[1]
     kend;
    Als he of gold had boundandlye to spend;    *plenty*
    Upon his fayis he wan it worthely.    *foes*
    Thus Wallace past and his gud chevalry,    *moved on; horsemen*
    Sexty he had of lykly men at wage;    *hired*
210 Throuch the Lennox he led thaim with
     curage.
    Aboun Lekke he lugyt thaim in a vaille;    *Above; valley*
    A strenth thar was quhilk thai thocht till    *stronghold*
     assaill.
    On Gargownno was byggyt a small peill    *stockade*
    That warnyst was with men and wictaill    *provisioned; food*
     weill,

---

1 Of honour and valour he was a known mirror

215 Within a dyk, bathe clos, chawmer and hall; *boundary-wall; courtyard*
    Capteyne tharof to nayme he hecht
        Thrilwall,
    Thai led Wallace quhar that this byggynge *building*
        was;
    He thocht to assaill it ferby or he wald pas. *farther before*
    Twa spyis he send to wesy all that land; *reconnoitre*
220 Rycht laith he was the thing to tak on hand *unwilling; undertake*
    The quhilk be force that suld gang hym *by; goes against him*
        agayne;
    Lever had he throu aventur be slayne. *He would rather; chance*
    Thir men went furth as it was large *These; fully midnight*
        mydnycht;
    About that hous thai spyit all at rycht. *fort; thoroughly*
225 The wachman was hevy fallen on sleipe;
    The bryg was doun at that entre suld keipe, *guard*
    The lauboreris latt rakleslye, went in. *workmen; carelessly left*
    Thir men retornede withoutyn noyes or
        dyn
    To thar maister, told him as thai had seyne.
230 Than grathit sone thir men of armys keyne, *got ready; strong*
    Sadlye on fute on to the hous thai socht *Resolutely*
    And entryt in, for lattyn fand thai nocht. *opposition*
    Wicht men assayede witht all thar besy cur *attacked; attention*
    A loklate bar was drawyn ourthourth the *locked; across*
        dur, *door*
235 Bot thai mycht nocht it brek out of the *wall*
        waw.
    Wallace was grevyt quhen he sic tary saw. *vexed; delay*
    Sumpart amovet, wraithly till it he went; *affected, angrily*
    Be fors of handis he raist out of the stent *wrenched; support*
    Thre yerde of breide als of the wall puld *breadth*
        out.
240 Than merveld all his men that war about
    How he dide mair than twenty of thaim
        mycht. *might*
    Syne with his fute the yett he straik up *Then; gate; struck*
        rycht
    Quhill brais and band to byrst all at anys. *brace; chain; once*
    Ferdely thai rais that war into thai wanys. *Full of fear; dwellings*
245 The wachman had a felloune staff of steill, *cruel sword*
    At Wallace strake bot he kepyt hym weill. *defended himself*
    Rudely fra him he reft it in that thrang, *Roughly; seized; throng*

Dang out his harnys, syne in the dik him flang.  *Knocked; brains; ditch*

The remaynand be that was on thar feit.

250 Thus Wallace sone can with the capteyn meite.

That staff he had, hevy and forgyt new;  *sword; heavy*

With it Wallace upon the hede him threw  *struck*

Quhill bayn and brayn all into sonder yeid.  *bone; brawn; flew into pieces*

His men entryt that worthy war in deid,

255 On handis hynt and stekit of the layff.  *laid hold; stabbed; rest*

Wallace commaundede thai suld na wermen saiff:  *warriors; spare*

Twenty and twa thai stekit in that steid.  *place*

Wemen and barnys quhen at the men war deide,  *children; dead*

He gert be tayn in clos hous kepyt weill  *had taken; locked*

260 So thai wythtout tharof mycht haiff no feill.  *outside; knowledge*

The dede bodyes thai put sone out of sycht,

Tuk up the bryg or that the day was lycht,  *bridge before*

In that place baid four dayis or he wald pas

Wist nane without how at this mater was.  *outside; matters stood*

265 Spoilyeide that steid and tuk thaim ganand ger;  *Plundered; fine property*

Jowellis and gold away with thaim thai ber.  *carried*

Quhen him thocht tyme thai ischede on the nycht,  *issued*

To the next woode thai went with all thar mycht.

The captenys wiff, wemen and childer thre

270 Pas quhar thai wald, for Wallas leit thaim be.

In that forest he likit nocht to bide;

Thai bounyt thaim atour Forth for to ride.  *prepared; around*

The mos was strang, to ryde thaim was no but;  *baggy moorland; hard-going; advantage*

Wallas was wicht and lychtyt on his fute.  *alighted on foot*

275 Few hors thai had, litill tharof thai roucht;  *cared little about that*

To save thar lyves feill strenthis oft thai socht.  *lives; many strongholds*

Stevyn of Irland he was thar gyd that nycht  *guide*

Towart Kyncardyn; syne restit thar at rycht  *right of way*

In a forest that was bathe lang and wide,

280 Rycht fra the mos grew to the watter syde.  *marsh*

Efter the sone Wallas walkit about — *sunset*
Upon Tetht side quhar he saw mony rout — *Teith; herds*
Of wyld bestis waverand in wode and — *wandering*
 playn.
Sone at a schot a gret hart has he slayn, — *with a shot*
285 Slew fyr on flynt and graithit thaim at — *Struck; got themselves ready*
 rycht.
Sodeynlye thar fresche venesoun thai dycht. — *prepared*
Wictaill thai had, bathe breid and wyne so — *bread*
 cler,
With other stuff yneuch at thar dyner. — *enough*
His staff of steill he gaiff Kerly to kepe, — *sword*
290 Syn passit our Tetht watter so depe.
In to Straithern thai entrit sodeynly, — *immediately*
In covert past or Sothren suld thaim spy. — *Secretly; before*
Quhen at thai fand of Scotlandis
 adversouris
Without respyt cummyn was thar fatell
 houris.
295 Quham ever thai mett was at the Inglis fay — *in the English allegiance*
Thai slew all doun with out langer delay.
Thai sparyt nane that was of Inglis blude;
To dede he yeid thocht he war never so
 gude.
Thai savyt nother knycht, squier nor knaiff;
300 This was the grace that Wallace to thaim
 gaiff;
Bot wastyt all be worthynes of wer — *valour*
Of that party that mycht weild bow or sper.
Sum part be slycht, sum throu force thai — *cunning*
 slew,
Bot Wallace thocht thai stroyit nocht half — *destroyed; enough*
 enew.
305 Silver thai tuk and als gold at thai fand,
Othir gud ger full lychtly yeid be hand:
Cuttyt throttis and in to cuvys thaim kest, — *caves; cast*
Put out of sycht for that him thocht was
 best.
At the Blakfurd as at thai suld pas our,
310 A squier come and with him bernys four — *barons*
Till Doun suld ryde, and wend at thai had — *thought*
 beyne
All Inglismen at he befor had seyne.

Tithingis to sper he hovid thaim amang.   *ask; hovered*

Wallace tharwith swyth with a swerd out   *swiftly*
swang,

315 Upon the hede he straik with so gret ire

Throu bayne and brayn in sonder schar the   *cut*
swyr.   *neck*

The tother four in handis sone war hynt,

Derfly to dede stekit or thai wald stynt.   *Violently stabbed to death*

Thar hors thai tuk and quhat thaim likit best,

320 Spoilyeid thaim bar, syne in the brook   *Stripped*
thaim kest.

Of this mater no mor tary thai maid,

Bot furth thar way passit withoutyn baid.

Thir werlik Scottis all with one assent   *These war-like*

Northt so our Ern throuch out the land thai   *North; across River Earn*
went,

325 In Meffan woode thar lugyng tuk that   *Methven*
nycht.

Upon the morn quhen it was dayis lycht

Wallace rais up, went to the forest side,

Quhar that he sawe full feill bestis abide,   *a great many*

Of wylde and tayme, walkand   *roaming freely [with*
haboundandlye.   *abandon]*

330 Than Wallace said, 'This contre likis me.   *region*

Wermen may do with fud at thai suld haiff,   *Warriors; perform*

Bot want thai meit thai rak nocht of the   *If they; care nothing about*
laiff.'   *the rest*

Of dyet fayr Wallace tuk never kepe   *fine food; heed*

Bot as it come welcum was meit and sleip.

335 Sum quhill he had gret sufficience within;   *sometimes*

Now want, now has, now los, now can wyn;   *lacks*

Now lycht, now sadd, now blisfull, now in   *glad; happy*
baill;   *sorrow*

In haist, now hurt; now sorowffull, now
haill;   *healthy*

Nowe weildand weyle, now calde wedder,   *enjoying good [fortune];*
now hett;   *weather; hot*

340 Nowe moist, now drowth, now waverand
wynd, now wett.

So ferd with him for Scotlandis rycht full   *fared; evenly*
evyn

In feyle debait six yeris and monethis   *great strife*
sevyn.

Quhen he wan pees and left Scotland in                    *openly*
    playne,
The Inglismen maid new conquest agayne.
345  In fruster termys I will nocht tary lang.                 *In pointless words*
Wallace agayne unto his men can gang                       *went*
And said, 'Her is a land of gret boundance.                *plenty*
Thankit be God of his hye purvyans!                        *provision*
Sevyn of you feris graith sone and ga with                 *companions prepare*
    me.
350  Rycht sor I long Sanct Jhonstoun for to se.             *Perth*
Stevyn of Irland, als God of hevyn thee
    saiff,
Maister leiddar I mak thee of the laiff.                   *Chief leader; rest*
Kepe weill my men; latt nane out of thi
    sycht                                                     *sight*
Quhill I agayn sall cum with all my mycht.                 *Until*
355  Byde me sevyn dayis in this forest strang.             *Wait [for]*
Yhe may get fude, suppos I dwell so lang.
Sumpart yhe haiff, and God will send us
    mair.'
Thus turnyt he and to the toun couth fair.                 *went*
The mar kepyt the port of that village;                    *officer in charge of the gate*
360  Wallace knew weill and send him his
    message.
The mar was brocht, saw him a gudlye
    man,
Rycht reverandlye he has resavyt thaim                     *respectfully*
    than.
At him he speryt all Scottis gyff thai be.                 *if*
Wallace said, 'Ya, and it is pees trow we.'                *peace time*
365  'I grant,' he said, 'that likis us wonder
    weill.
Trew men of pees may ay sum frendschipe
    feill.
Quhat is your nayme? I pray you tell me it.'
'Will Malcomsone,' he said, 'sen ye wald
    witt.                                                     *know*
In Atryk forest has my wonnyng beyne.                      *Ettrick; dwelling*
370  Thar I was born amang the schawis                       *fair woods*
    scheyne.
Now I desyr this north land for to se,
Quhar I mycht fynd better dwellyng for
    me.'

The mar said, 'Schir, I sper nocht for nane ille, — enquire

Bot feill tithingis oft syis is brocht us till — many tidings often

375 Of ane Wallace, was born in to the west.

Our kingis men he haldis at gret unrest, — distress

Marteris thaim doun, gret pete is to se. — Slaughters

Out of the trewis, forsuth, we trow he be.' — Breaking the truce

Wallace than said, 'I her spek of that man. — hear speak

380 Tithingis of him to you nane tell I can.'

For him he gert ane innys graithit be — dwelling–place prepared

Quhar nane suld cum bot his awne men and he.

Hys stwart Kerlye brocht thaim in fusioun — abundance

Gude thing eneuch quhat was in to the toun. — Enough good provisions

385 Als Inglismen to drynkyn wald him call — Also

And commounly he delt nocht thar withall. — had no dealings with them

In thar presence he spendyt resonably,

Yheit for him self he payit ay boundandlye. — abundantly

On Scottis men he spendyt mekill gud

390 Bot nocht his thankis upon the Sothren blud. — willingly

Son he consavyt in his witt prevalye — Soon; understood

In to that land quha was of maist party. — most power

Schir Jamys Butler, ane agit, cruell knycht, — fierce

Kepyt Kynclevyn, a castell wondyr wycht. — Kinclaven; very strong

395 His sone Schir Jhon than dwelt in to the toun,

Under capteyn to Schir Garraid Heroun.

The wemen als he uysyt at the last; — [Wallace] visited

And so on ane hys eyne he can to cast, — one

In the south gait, of fassoun fresche and fayr. — street; appearance

400 Wallace to hir maid prevalye repair. — secret visits

So fell it thus, of the toun or he past, — before

At ane accorde thai hapnyt at the last.

Wallace with hyr in secre maid him glaid; — secret

Sotheren wist nocht that he sic plesance haid. — Englishmen; pleasure

405 Offt on the nycht he wald say to him sell, — self

'This is fer war than ony payn of hell, — far worse, any

At thus with wrang thir devillis suld bruk our land, — possess

And we with force may nocht agayne thaim stand.

To tak this toun my power is to small;  *too*
410 Gret perell als on my self may fall.
Set we it in fyr it will undo my sell,  *[If] we set it on fire; self*
Or los my men; thar is no mor to tell.
Yhettis ar clos, the dykis depe withall;  *Gates; shut; ditches; deep*
Thocht I wald swyme, forsuth so can nocht all.
415 This mater now herfor I will ourslyde,  *put aside*
Bot in this toun I may no langar byde.'
Als men tald him quhen the captayne wald pas  *Also*
Hayme to Kynclevyn, quharof rycht glaid he was.  *Home*
His leiff he tuk at heris of the toun;  *leave; lords*
420 To Meffane wode rycht glaidly maid him boun.  *bound*
His horn he hynt and bauldly loud can blaw;  *seized; boldly*
His men him hard and tharto sone couth draw.  *heard, drew*
Rycht blyth he was for thai war all in feyr;  *in array*
Mony tithingis at him thai wald nocht speyr.  *find out*
425 He thaim commaunde to mak thaim redy fast;
In gud array out of the woode thai past.
Towart Kynclevyn thai bounyt thaim that tid,  *headed / time*
Syn in a vaill that ner was thar besid,  *Then; valley*
Fast on to Tay his buschement can he draw.  *River Tay; ambush*
430 In a dern woode thai stellit thaim full law,  *dark; crept stealthily; low*
Set skouriouris furth the contre to aspye  *scouts; spy*
Be ane our nowne thre for rydaris went bye.  *By one past noon; advance riders*
The wach turned in to witt quhat was his will.  *watch; returned; know*
He thaim commaund in covert to bide still.  *hiding; wait*
435 'And we call feyr the hous knawlage will haiff  *If we give warning [i.e., call 'fire']*
And that may sone be warnyng to the laiff.  *rest*
All fors in wer do nocht but governance.'  *warlike action; without discretion*

Wallace was few bot happy ordinance     *had few men; fortunate provision*

Maid him fell syis his adversouris to wyn.[1]

440 Be that the court of Inglismen com in,     *retinue*

Four scoyr and ten weill graithit in thar ger,     *equipped; armour*

Harnest on hors, all likly men of wer.     *Armed; promising*

Wallace saw weill his nowmer was na ma;     *more*

He thankit God and syne the feild couth ta.     *battlefield*

445 The Inglismen merveild quhat thai suld be,

Bot fra thai saw thai maid thaim for melle.     *from when; prepared to do battle*

In fewter thai kest scharpe speris at that tide;     *From their supports*

In ire thai thoucht atour the Scottis to ryd.     *around*

Wallace and his went cruelly thaim agayne;     *fiercely; against*

450 At the fyrst rusche feill Inglismen war slayne.     *attack; many*

Wallace straik ane with his gude sper of steill

Throu out the cost; the schafft to brak ilk deyll.[2]

A burnyst brand in haist he hyntis out;     *burnished sword; pulled*

Thrys apon fute he thrang throuch all the rout.     *pressed; throng*

455 Stern hors thai steik suld men of armys ber;     *Strong; stab should*

Sone undir feit fulyeid was men of wer.     *trampled*

Butler lychtyt him self for to defend     *alighted*

Witht men of armys quhilk war full worthi kend.     *reputed*

On athyr syde feill frekis was fechtand fast.     *many men; fighting*

460 The captayne baid thocht he war sor agast.     *withstood; was terrified*

Part of the Scottis be worthines thai slew;     *valour*

Wallace was wa, and towart him he drew.     *melancholy*

His men dred for the Butler bauld and keyn.     *dreaded; bold; fierce*

On him he socht in ire and propyr teyn;     *pure rage*

465 Upon the hed him straik in matelent,     *furiously*

The burnyst blaid throu out his basnett went.     *helmet*

1 Caused him many times to triumph over his adversaries
2 Right through the rib; the shaft broke completely

Bathe bayne and brayn he byrst throu all
the weid.                                            bone; flesh; burst
                                                     armour
Thus Wallace hand deliverit thaim of dreid.          Wallace's hand; from danger
Yeitt feill on fold was fechtand cruelly;            on earth [alive]
470   Stevyn of Irland and all the chevalry           horsemen
In to the stour did cruelly and weill;               battle; fiercely
And Kerle als with his gud staff of steill.          sword
The Inglismen, fra thar cheftayne was                once
slayne,
Thai left the feild and fled in all thar mayn.       force
475   Thre scoyr war slayne or thai wald leif that    before
steid.                                               place
The fleande folk, that wist of no rameid             fleeing; remedy
Bot to the hous, thai fled in all thar mycht;        castle
The Scottis folowit that worthi war and              were valiant and
wycht.                                               bold
Few men of fens was left that place to kepe.         defence; guard
480   Wemen and preistis upon Wallace can wepe,
For weill thai wend the flearis was thar             they knew well those fleeing;
lord;                                                  lords
To tak him in thai maid thaim redy ford,             prepared themselves
Leit doun the bryg, kest up the yettis wide.         bridge; cast open; gates
The frayit folk entrit and durst nocht byde;         frightened; dared; stay
485   Gud Wallace ever he folowit thaim so fast       always
Quhill in the hous he entryt at the last.            Until; castle
The yett he wor quhill cumin was all the             gate; defended; until
rout.                                                troops
Of Inglis and Scottis he held no man                 kept none out
tharout.
The Inglismen that won war in that steid,            were captured
490   Withoutyn grace thai bertnyt thaim to deid.     mercy; put to death
The capteynis wiff, wemen and preistis twa,          [Lady Butler]
And yong childer, forsuth thai savyt no ma,          truly; spared no more
Held thaim in clos efter this sodeyn cas             Shut them in
Or Sothron men suld sege him in that                 Before English; besiege him
place;                                                 [Wallace]
495   Tuk up the bryg and closyt yettis fast.         quickly
The dede bodyes out of sicht he gart cast,[1]
Baith in the hous and without at war dede;           Both [those] in and outside
                                                       the castle
Five of his awne to berynis he gart leid             own [men]; burial

1 He had the dead bodies cast out of sight

| | | |
|---|---|---|
| | In that castell thar seven dayis baide he, | stayed |
| 500 | On ilka nycht thai spoilyeid besyle, | each; plundered |
| | To Schortwode schaw leide victaill and wyn wicht,[1] | |
| | Houshald and ger, baithe gold and silver brycht. | Furnishings and equipment |
| | Women and thai that he had grantyt grace, | mercy |
| | Quhen him thoucht tyme thai put out of that place. | |
| 505 | Quhen thai had tayne quhat he likit to haiff, | |
| | Straik doun the yettis and set in fyr the laiff, | Demolished; rest [of the castle] |
| | Out of wyndowis stanssouris all thai drew, | stanchions [i.e., supports] |
| | Full gret irn wark in to the watter threw; | work; moat |
| | Burdyn duris and lokis in thair ire, | Doors made of boards; locks |
| 510 | All werk of tre, thai brynt up in a fyr; | wood |
| | Spylt at thai mycht, brak brig and bulwark doun. | Destroyed; what they could; broke |
| | To Schortwode Schawe in haist thai maid thaim boun, | bound |
| | Chesyt a strenth quhar thai thar lugyng maid; | stronghold |
| | In gud affer a quhill thar still he baid. | array |
| 515 | Yit in the toun no wit of this had thai. | knowledge |
| | The contre folk quhen it was lycht of day | |
| | Gret reik saw rys and to Kynclevyn thai socht, | smoke |
| | Bot wallis and stane mar gud thar fand thai nocht. | Except for; stone; more goods |
| | The captennis wiff to Sanct Jhonstoun scho yeid | |
| 520 | And to Schir Garrate scho tald this felloune deid, | terrible |
| | Als till hyr son quhat hapnyt was be cas. | chance |
| | Than demyt thai all that it was wicht Wallas, | thought |
| | Of for tyme thar he spyit had the toun. | Earlier |
| | Than chargyt thai all thai suld be redy boun, | |
| 525 | Harnest on hors in to thair armour cler. | |

1 To Shortwood forest removed food and strong wine

To seik Wallace thai went all furth in feyr, · in array
A thousand men weill garnest for the wer, · equipped
Towart the woode rycht awfull in affer, · appearance
To Schortwode schaw and set it all about · surrounded it
530 Wytht five staillis that stalwart was and stout. · parties of armed men
The sext thai maid a fellon range to leid · line
Quhar Wallace was full worthi ay in deid.
The strenth he tuk and bade thaim hald it still · stronghold
On ilka syde, assailye quha sa will. · every
535 Schir Jhon Butler in to the forrest went
With two hundreth, sor movit in his entent; · moved
His fadris dede to venge him gif he mocht. · avenge
To Wallace sone with men of armys socht.
A cleuch thar was, quharof a strenth thai maid · hollow
540 With thwortour treis, bauldly thar abaid. · Trees growing across
Fra the ta side thai mycht ische till a playne, · the one; issue
Syn throuch the wode to the strenth pas agayn.
Twenty he had that nobill archaris war
Agayne sevyn scoyr of Inglis bowmen sar. · stern
545 Four scoyr of speris ner hand thaim baid at rycht, · spearmen; properly
Giff Scottis ischit to help thaim at thair mycht,
On Wallace set a bykkyr bauld and keyn. · attack
A bow he bair was byg and weyll beseyn · fine-looking
And arrows als bath lang and scharpe withall;
550 No man was thar that Wallas bow mycht drall. · draw
Rycht stark he was and in to souer ger, · sure armour
Bauldly he schott amang thai men of wer.
Ane angell hede to the hukis he drew · barbed head of an arrow; hooks
And at a schoyt the formast sone he slew.
555 Ynglis archaris that hardy war and wicht
Amang the Scottis bykkerit with all thar mycht. · attacked
Thar awfull schoyt was felloun for to byd; · terrible; withstand

Of Wallace men thai woundyt sor that tid.
Few of thaim was sekyr of archary;                    skilled in
560   Bettyr thai war and thai gat evyn party           evenly matched
In feild to byde other with swerd or speyr.
Wallace persavit his men tuk mekill deyr:             harm
He gart thaim change and stand nocht in to            remain; in that place
    steid;
He kest all wayis to saiff thaim fra the
    dede.
565   Full gret travaill upon him self tuk he,          labour
Of Sothron men feill archaris he gert de.
Of Longcaschyr bowmen was in that place:              Lancashire
A sar archar ay waytit on Wallace                     dangerous
At ane opyn quhar he usyt to repair.                  opening
570   At him he drew a sekir schot and sar              sure
Under the chyn, throuch a coler of steill,            steel collar
On the left side and hurt his hals sumdeill.          neck
Astonaide he was, bot nocht gretlye agast.            Astounded
Out fra his men on him he folowit fast,
575   In the turnyng with gud will has him tayne
Upon the crag, in sondyr straik the bayne.            neck; struck; bone
Feill of thaim ma na freyndschip with him             many more of them
    fand;
Fyfteyn that day he schot to dede of his
    hand,
Be that his arrows waistyt war and gayne;             By then
580   The Inglis archaris forsuth thai wantyt           lacked
    nayne.
Without thai war thar power to ranew,
On ilka side to thaim thai couth persew.              each
Wylyham Loran com with a boustous staill              large army
Out of Gowry on Wallace to assaill.
585   Nevo he was, as it was knawin in playn,           Nephew; plainly known
To the Butler befor that thai had slayn.
To venge his eyme he come with all his                avenge; uncle
    mycht;
Thre hundreth he led of men in armys
    brycht.
To leide the range on fute he maid him                column
    ford;                                             ready
590   Wallace to God his conscience fyrst
    remord,                                           laid bare
Syne comfort thaim with manly contenance.

'Yhe se,' he said, 'gud schiris, thar
    ordinance.
Her is no chos bot owder do or de.     *either*
We haiff the rycht, the happyar may it be     *luckier*
595 That we sall chaipe with grace out of this     *escape*
    land.'
The Loran be that was redy at his hand.     *by that time*
Be that it was efter nown of the day,     *By then; noon*
Feill men of witt to consaill sone yeid thai.
The Sothron kest scharply at ilka side     *looked carefully all around*
600 And saw the wood was nother lang no
    wide.
Lychtly thai thocht he suld hald it so lang;     *Scornfully*
Fyve hundreth maid throu it on fute to     *go*
    gang,
Sad men of armes that war of eggyr will.     *Bold; eager*
Schir Garratis selff without the woode baid     *outside; remained*
    still.
605 Schir Jhon Butler the ta sid chesyt he,     *one*
The tother Loran with a fell menyhe.     *fierce contingent*
Than gud Wallace that of help had gret
    neid
Was fyfty men in all that felloun dreid.     *danger*
Ane awfull salt the Sothren son began,     *assault; soon*
610 About the Scottis socht mony likly man     *many a promising*
With bow and sper and swerdis stiff of
    steill;
On ather side no frendschip was to feill.
Wallace in ire a burly brand can draw     *strong sword*
Quhar feill Sothron war semblit upon raw,     *many; gathered in a row*
615 To fende his men with his deyr worthi     *defend*
    hand.
The folk was fey that he befor him fand.     *doomed [to die]; found*
Throu the thikkest of the gret preis he past,     *press [of people]*
Upon his enemys hewand wonder fast.     *slashing*
Agayne his dynt na weidis mycht availl:     *blow; armour; avail*
620 Quham so he hyt was dede withoutyn faill.     *Whomsoever*
Of the fersest full braithly bair he doun     *fiercest; violently; bore*
Befor the Scottis that war of gret renoun.
To hald the strenth thai preist with all thar     *pressed*
    mycht.
The Inglismen that worthi war and wicht
625 Schir Jhon Butler relevit in agayne,     *rallied*

Sundryt the Scottis and did thaim mekill payn,    Separated

The Loran als that cruell was and keyn.

A sar assay forsuth thar mycht be seyn.    bitter assault

Than at the strenth thai mycht no langer bide;    stronghold

630  The range so strang com upon ather side.    pursuit

In the thikkest woode thar maid thai felle defens    fierce

Agayn thar fayis so full of violens.

Yit felle Sothron left the lyff to wed,    left their lives as a pledge

Till a new strenth Wallace and his men fled.

635  On adversouris thai maid full gret debait;    adversaries; resistance

Bot help thaim self no socour ellis thai wait.    other help; knew

The Sothron als war sundryt than in twyn,    divided; two

Bot thai agayne togidder sone can wyn.    came together

Full sutellye thar ordinance thai maid,    marshalling

640  The rang agayne bounyt but mar abaid.    without further delay

The Scottis war hurt and part of thaim war slayn;

Than Wallace said, 'We laubour all in vane.

To slay commounis it helpis us richt nocht.

Bot thair chiftanis that hes thame hidder brocht,

645  Micht we wirk swa that ane of thame war slane,    so

So sair assay thai couth nocht mak agayn.'    [an] attack

Be this the host approchand was full ner;    By this time

Thus wrandly thai held thaim upon ster.    actively; busy

Quhen Wallace saw the Sothroune was at hand,

650  Him thocht no tym langar for to stand.

Rycht manfully he graithit has his ger,    got ready

Sadly he went agayne thai men of wer;    Resolutely

Throuout the stour full fast fechtand he socht    conflict

With Goddis grace to venge him gif he mocht.

655  Upon the Butler awfully straik he;

Saiffgarde he gat under a bowand tre.

The bowcht in twa he straik aboune his hede    bough; above

Als to the ground and feld him in that           felled; place
    stede.
The haill power upon him com so fast              host
660 At thai beforce reskewit him at the last.
Loran was wa and thidder fast can draw;          woeful
Wallas ratornd sa sodeynly him saw.
Out at a syde full fast till him he yeid;
He gat no gyrth for all his burnyst weid.        shelter
665 With ire him straik on his gorgeat of steill,  gorget [i.e., throat armour]
The trensand blaid to persyt everydeill,         trenchant; pierced completely
Throu plaitt and stuff mycht nocht agayn it      armour plate; cloth
    stand;
Derffly to dede he left him on the land.
Hym haif thai lost thocht Sotheren had it         sworn [the contrary]
    sworn,
670 For his crag bayne was all in sonder           neck-bone; pieces; cut
    schorn.
The worthy Scottis did nobilly that day
About Wallace till he was wonn away.              delivered
He tuk the strenth magre thar fayis will,         in spite of; foes'
Abandonly in bargan baid thar still.              Boldly fighting
675 The scry sone rais the bauld Loran was dede.   cry; rose; bold
Schir Garrat Heroun tranontit to that stede       moved camp
And all the host assemblit him about.             army
At the north side than Wallace ischet out,        sallied
With him his men, and bounyt him to ga,           prepared; go
680 Thankand gret God at thai war partyt sa.       that; parted; so
To Gargyll wood thai went that sammyn             same
    nycht.
Sevyn of his men that day to dede was             put to death
    dycht;
In feld was left of the Sothren sex scoyr,        field
And Loran als, thar murnyng was the mor.
685 The rang in haist thai rayit sone agayne,      arrayed; soon
Bot quhen thai saw thar travaill was in           labour; vain
    vayne
And he was past, full mekill mayne thai           a great deal of lamenting
    maid
To rype the wood, bath vala, slonk and            search; valley; slope; glen
    slaid,
For Butleris gold Wallace tuk of befor.
690 Bot thai fand nocht, wald thai seke
    evermor.

Hys hors thai gat and nocht ellis of thar
   ger. — *equipment*
With dulfull mayn retorned thir men of wer — *sorrowful moan; these*
To Sanct Jhonnston in sorow and gret cayr.
Of Wallace furth me likis to spek mair. — *henceforth*
695 The secunde nycht the Scottis couth thaim
   draw
Rycht prevaly agayne to Schortwod schaw; — *secretly; forest*
Tuk up thar gud quhilk was put out of
   sicht, — *Picked up; belongings*
Cleithing and stuff, bathe gold and silver
   brycht; — *Clothing; army provisions*
Upon thar fute, for horsis was thaim fra, — *On foot; because they had no horses*
700 Or the son rais to Meffen wood can ga. — *Before; sun rose; went*
Thai twa dayis our thar lugyng still thai
   maid.
On the thrid nycht thai movit but mar
   abaid, — *moved without further delay*
Till Elkok park full sodeynly thai went; — *quickly*
Thar in that strentht to bide was his entent. — *stronghold; wait; intention*
705 Than Wallas said he wald go to the toun,
Arayit him weill in till a preistlik gown. — *Dressed; priest-like*
In Sanct Johnstoun disgysyt can he fair — *disguised; went*
Till this woman the quhilk I spak of ayr. — *before*
Of his presence scho rycht rejosit was — *pleased*
710 And sor adred how he away suld pas. — *sorely afraid*
He sojornyt thair fra nowne was of the day — *noon*
Quhill ner the nycht or that he went away. — *Until almost night before*
He trystyt hyr quhen he wald cum agayne — *arranged with her; again*
On the thrid day; than was scho wondyr
   fayne. — *very happy*
715 Yeitt he was seyn with enemys as he yeid. — *by; left*
To Schir Garraid thai tald of all his deid,
And to Butler that wald haiff wrokyn
   beyne. — *have been avenged*
Than thai gart tak that woman brycht and
   scheyne — *caused to be taken; fair*
Accusyt hir sar of resset in that cas. — *angrily; sheltering an outlaw*
720 Feyll syis scho swour that scho knew nocht
   Wallas. — *Many times; swore*
Than Butler said, 'We wait weyle it was he — *know well*
And bot thou tell in bayle fyre sall thou de. — *unless; by burning; die*

Giff thou will help to bryng yon rebell doun,                    If

We sall thee mak a lady of renoun.'

725 Thai gaiff till hyr baith gold and silver brycht,

And said scho suld be weddyt with ane knycht,

Quham scho desirit, that was but mariage.                    Whomever; unmarried

Thus tempt thai hir throu consaill and gret wage,                    counsel; reward

That scho thaim tald quhat tyme he wald be thar.

730 Than war thai glaid, for thai desirit no mar

Of all Scotland bot Wallace at thar will.

Thus ordaynyt thai this poyntment to fullfill.                    arranged; appointment

Feyle men of armes thai graithit hastelye                    Many; got ready

To kepe the yettis, wicht Wallas till aspye.                    guard; gates; bold

735 At the set trist he entrit in the toun,                    meeting-time

Wittand nothing of all this fals tresoune.                    Knowing nothing

Till hir chawmer he went but mair abaid;                    To; chamber; delay

Scho welcunmyt him and full gret plesance maid.                    pleasure showed

Quhat at thai wrocht I can nocht graithly say,                    readily

740 Rycht unperfyt I am of Venus play;                    imperfect

Bot hastelye he graithit him to gang.                    prepared; go

Than scho him tuk and speryt giff he thocht lang.                    Then; took hold; asked if; wearied

Scho askit him that nycht with hir to bid.                    stay

Sone he said, 'Nay, for chance that may betide.                    Soon; for [fear of] any [evil] chance

745 My men ar left all at mysrewill for me.                    in disorder because of

I may nocht sleipe this nycht quhill I thaim se.'                    until

Than wepyt scho and said full oft, 'Allace!

That I was maide! Wa worthe the courssit cas!                    born; Alas the accursed case!

Now haiff I lost the best man leiffand is.                    living

750 O feble mynd to do so foull a mys!                    offence

O waryit witt, wykkyt and variance,                    cursed knowledge; fickle

That me has brocht in to this myschefull chance!                    evil

Allace!' scho said, 'in warld that I was wrocht! — *created*

Giff all this payne on my self mycht be brocht! — *If*

755  I haiff servit to be brynt in a gleid.' — *deserved; to an ember*

Quhen Wallace saw scho ner of witt couth weid, — *was nearly driven mad*

In his armes he caucht hir sobrely — *gently*

And said, 'Der hart, quha has mysdoyn ocht? I?' — *done something wrong? Me?*

'Nay, I,' quod scho, 'has falslye wrocht this trayn. — *deception*

760  I haiff you sald. Rycht now yhe will be slayn.' — *betrayed*

Scho tauld to him hir tresoun till ane end — *treachery from start to finish*

As I haiff said. Quhat nedis mair legend?[1]

At hir he speryt giff scho forthocht it sar. — *sorely repented it*

'Wa, ya,' scho said, 'and sall do evermar. — *Alas, yes*

765  My waryed werd in warld I mon fullfill; — *cursed fate; must*

To mend this mys I wald byrne on a hill.' — *amend; wrong; burn*

He confort hir and baide hir haiff no dreide. — *told her to have no fear*

'I will,' he said, 'haiff sumpart of thi weid.' — *clothing*

Hir gown he tuk on hym and courches als. — *head scarves*

770  'Will God I sall eschape this tresoune fals.

I thee forgyff.' Withoutyn wordis mair

He kissyt hir, syne tuk his leiff to fayr. — *go*

His burly brand that helpyt him offt in neid, — *large sword*

Rycht prevalye he hid it undir that weid. — *secretly*

775  To the south yett the gaynest way he drew, — *gate; nearest*

Quhar that he fand of armyt men enew. — *enough*

To thaim he tald, dissemblyt contenance, — *under this false appearance*

To the chawmer quhar he was upon chance. — *[To go] to the chamber*

'Speid fast,' he said, 'Wallace is lokit in.' — *locked*

780  Fra him thai socht withoutyn noyis or dyn, — *From; went*

To that sammyn hous about thai can thaim cast. — *look*

Out at the yett Wallas gat full fast,

Rycht glaid in hart; quhen that he was without, — *outside*

[1] What need is there to write more?

Rycht fast he yeide a stour pais and a stout.   went [at] a strong and sturdy
                                                  pace

785   Twa him beheld and said, 'We will go se.   see
      A stalwart queyne, forsuth, yon semys to   woman
        be.'
      Thai folowit him throue the South Inche    park area at south of town
        thai twa.
      Quhen Wallace saw with thaim thar come
        na ma,
      Agayne he turnede and has the formast      He turned back
        slayn.
790   The tother fled. Than Wallace with gret
        mayn                                      force
      Upon the hed with his swerd has him
        tayne;                                    struck
      Left thaim bathe dede, syne to the strenth  then; stronghold
        is gayne.                                 went
      His men he gat, rycht glaid quhen thai him  found
        saw.
      Till thair defence in haist he gart thaim   To their defence position
        draw;
795   Devoydyde him sone of the womannys         Divested himself
        weid.                                     clothes
      Thus chapyt he out of that felloun dreid.   he escaped; terrible danger

## BOOK FIVE

The dyrk regioun apperand wonder fast     *i.e., winter*
In Novenber quhen October was past,
The day faillit, throu the rycht cours     *course of the sun; became*
   worthit schort;
Till banyst men that is no gret comfort
5  With thar power in pethis worthis gang;[1]
Hevy thai think quhen at the nycht is lang.
Thus Wallas saw the nychtis messynger,
Phebus, had lost his fyry bemys cler.     *beams bright*
Out of the wood thai durst nocht turn that     *at that time*
   tyd
10  For adversouris that in thair way wald     *Because of foes*
   byde.
Wallace thaim tauld that new wer wes on     *war*
   hand,
The Inglismen was of the toun cummande.     *coming*
The dure thai brak quhar thai trowyt     *door; believed*
   Wallace was:
Quhen thai him myst thai bounyt thaim to     *failed to catch; readied*
   pas.
15  In this gret noyis the woman gat away,     *commotion*
Bot to quhat steide I can nocht graithlye     *readily*
   say.
The Sothroun socht rycht sadly fra that     *went*
   stede     *place*
Throu the South Inch and fand thir twa     *found these*
   men dede;
Thai knew be that Wallace was in the
   strenth.     *stronghold*
20  About the park thai set on breid and lenth     *They surrounded the park*
With six hundreth weill graithit in thar     *equipped*
   armes,
All likly men to wrek thaim of thar harmes;     *avenge*
A hundreth men chargit in armes strang     *commanded*
To kepe a hunde that thai had thaim     *hound*
   amang.
25  In Gyllis land thar was that brachell brede,     *hunting dog bred*
Sekyr of sent to folow thaim at flede.     *Sure; scent; that*
So was scho usyt on Esk and on Ledaill,     *accustomed*

---

1 [who] have to wander along paths with their troops, i.e., who are outlaws

Quhill scho gat blude no fleyng mycht            fleeing
  availl.
Than said thai all Wallace mycht nocht
  away,
30  He suld be tharis for ocht at he do may.
The ost thai delt in divers part that tyde:      army; divided
Schir Garrat Herroun in the staill can           main party
  abide;
Schir Jhon Butler the range he tuk him till      column of solidiers
With thre hunder quhilk war of hardy will;
35  In to the woode apon Wallace thai yeid.        approached
The worthi Scottis, that wer in mekill           great
  dreid,
Socht till a place for till haiff yschet out      issued
And saw the staill enverounyt thaim about.
Agayne thai went with hydwys strakis             strokes
  strang;
40  Gret noyis and dyne was rayssit thaim          din; raised
  amang.
Thar cruell deide rycht mervalus to ken
Quhen forty macht agayne thre hunder             [were] matched against
  men.
Wallace so weill apon him tuk that tide
Throu the gret preys he maid a way full
  wide,
45  Helpand the Scottis with his der worthi
  hand.
Fell faymen he left fey upon the land.           Many foes; dying
Yheit Wallas lost fifteen into that steid,
And forty men of Sothroun part war dede.
The Butleris folk so fruschit was in deid,       disarrayed
50  The hardy Scottis to the strenthis throu
  thaim yeide.
On to Tayside thai hastyt thaim full fast;
In will thai war the watter till haiff past.
Halff couth nocht swym that than with
  Wallas was,
And he wald nocht leiff ane and fra thaim
  pas.
55  Better him thocht in perell for to be
Upon the land, than willfully to se
His men to droun quhar reskew mycht he
  nane.

Agayne in ire to the feild ar thai gayne.

Butler be than had putt his men in ray;    *order*

60  On thaim he sett with ane awfull hard assay

On ather side with wapynys stiff of steill.    *weapons*

Wallace agayne no frendschipe lett thaim feill

Bot do or de, thai wist no mor socour.    *knew; no other help*

Thus fend thai lang in to that stalwart stour.    *defend; a long time; valiant fight*

65  The Scottis chyftayne was yong and in a rage,    *spirited*

Usyt in wer and fechtis with curage.    *Practised in war; fights*

He saw his men of Sothroun tak gret wrang.    *the English suffer*

Thaim to raveng all dreidles can he gang,    *avenge; fearless he proceeded*

For mony of thaim war bledand wonder sar.    *many; bleeding profusely*

70  He couth nocht se no help apperand thar

Bot thar chyftayne war putt out of thair gait,    *Unless*  *way*

The bryme Butler so bauldlye maid debait.    *fierce; [who] boldly resisted*

Throu the gret preys Wallace to him socht;    *press [of folk] sought him*

His awfull deid he eschewit as he mocht.    *deeds; avoided; might*

75  Under ane ayk wycht men about him set,    *oak*

Wallace mycht nocht a graith straik on him get.    *direct blow*

Yeit schede he thaim; a full royd slope was maide.    *he parted them; wide breach*

The Scottis went out, no langar thar abaid.    *no longer stayed there*

Stevyn of Irland quhilk hardy was and wicht,    *bold*

80  To helpe Wallace he did gret preys and mycht,    *feats; mighty*  *deeds*

With trew Kerle douchty in mony deid.    *valiant; action*

Upon the grounde feill Sothroun gert thai bleid.    *many English they caused to bleed*

Sexty war slayne of Inglismen in that place

And nine of Scottis thair tynt was throuch that cace.    *lost*

85  Butleris men so stroyit war that tide    *destroyed; time*

In to the stour he wald no langar bide.    *fighting; remain*

To get supple he socht on to the staill.    *reinforcements; main army*

Thus lost he thar a hundreth of gret vaill.　　　a hundred valiant men

As thai war best arayand Butleris rout　　　Butler's company was
　　　　　　　　　　　　　　　　　　　　　　　　　preparing

90　Betwex parteys than Wallace ischit out.[1]

Sixteen with him thai graithit thaim to ga;　　readied them to go

Of all his men he had levyt no ma.　　　　　　left

The Inglis men, has myssyt him, in hy　　　　missing him; haste

The hund thai tuk and folowit haistely.　　　　hound

95　At the Gask woode full fayne he wald haiff　gladly
　　beyne,

Bot this sloth brache, quhilk sekyr was and
　　keyne,[2]

On Wallace fute folowit so felloune fast,　　　track; extremely

Quhill in thar sicht that prochit at the last.　　Until; had him in sight;
　　　　　　　　　　　　　　　　　　　　　　　　　approached

Thar hors war wicht had sojorned weill and　strong; lasted
　　lang.

100　To the next woode twa myil thai had to
　　gang　　　　　　　　　　　　　　　　　　　　　go

Of upwith erde thai yeid with all thar　　　　Up rising ground; went
　　mycht.

Gud hope thai had for it was ner the nycht.

Fawdoun tyryt and said he mycht nocht　　　not go [further]
　　gang.

Wallace was wa to leyff him in that thrang.　loath; leave; danger

105　He bade him ga and said the strenth was　　move
　　ner,[3]

Bot he tharfor wald nocht faster him ster.　　move

Wallace in ire on the crag can him ta　　　　struck him on the neck

With his gud swerd and straik the hed him　cut
　　fra.

Dreidles to ground derfly he duschit dede.　Without a doubt; fell
　　　　　　　　　　　　　　　　　　　　　　　　　violently

110　Fra him he lap and left him in that stede.　　leapt back; place

Sum demys it to ill and other sum to gud,　consider

And I say her in to thir termys rude,　　　　here; unpolished words

Better it was he did, as thinkis me.

Fyrst to the hunde it mycht gret stoppyn　means of stopping
　　be;

1 Between the two parties [i.e. the English armies] Wallace sallied out
2 But this (female) sleuth hound, which was reliable and fierce
3 He ordered him to go on and said the stronghold [i.e., the Gask Hall] was
near

| | | |
|---|---|---|
| 115 | Als Fawdoun was haldyn at suspicioun | Also; held in |
| | For he was haldyn of brokill complexioun. | regarded as; fickle character |
| | Rycht stark he was and had bot litill gayne. | strong; travelled |
| | Thus Wallace wist had he beyne left allayne, | knew |
| | And he war fals to enemys he wald ga, | |
| 120 | Gyff he war trew the Sothroun wald him sla. | If; loyal; English |
| | Mycht he do ocht bot tyne him as it was?[1] | |
| | Fra this questioun now schortlye will I pas. | From |
| | Deyme as yhe lest, ye that best can and may, | Consider; please |
| | I bott rahers as my autour will say. | only recite |
| 125 | Sternys be than began for till apper. | Stars |
| | The Inglismen was cummand wondyr ner; | |
| | Five hundreth haill was in thar chevalry. | |
| | To the next strenth than Wallace couth him hy. | hurry |
| | Stevyn of Irland, unwitting of Wallas, | unbeknown to |
| 130 | And gud Kerle, baid still ner hand that place | |
| | At the mur syde, in till a scrogghy slaid | bushy glen |
| | Be est Dipplyne quhar thai this tary maid. | delay |
| | Fawdoun was left besid thaim on the land; | |
| | The power come and sodeynly him fand, | army |
| 135 | For thair sloith hund the graith gait till him yeid; | went directly to him |
| | Of other trade scho tuk as than no heid. | way |
| | The sloith stoppyt, at Fawdoun still scho stude: | |
| | No forthir scho wald fra tyme scho fand the blud. | |
| | Inglismen dempt, for ellis thai couth nocht tell, | thought |
| 140 | Bot at the Scottis had fochtyn amang thaim sell. | that / selves |
| | Rycht wa thai war that losyt was thar sent. | grieved; scent |
| | Wallace twa men amang the ost in went, | |
| | Dissemblit weylle that no man suld thaim ken, | Disguised / know |
| | Rycht in affer as thai war Inglismen. | appearance |
| 145 | Kerle beheld on to the bauld Heroun | regarded; bold |

1 Could he have done other than let him perish as he did?

Upon Fawdoun as he was lukand doun,
A suttell straik upwart him tuk that tide; *cunning thrust*
Under the chokkeis the grounden swerd *jaw; sharp*
  gart glid
By the gude mayle, bathe hals and his crag *mail armour; neck; neck-bone*
  bayne
150 In sonder straik. Thus endyt that *pieces dashed*
  cheftayne.
To grounde he fell, feile folk about him
  thrang.
'Tresoune!' thai criyt, traytouris was thaim
  amang.
Kerlye with that fled out sone at a side;
His falow Stevyn than thocht no tyme to
  bide. *stay*
155 The fray was gret and fast away thai yeid, *confusion*
Lawch towart Ern. Thus chapyt thai of *[Keeping] low*
  dreid. *danger*
Butler for woo of wepyng mycht nocht
  stynt.
Thus raklesly this gud knycht haiff thai *carelessly*
  tynt. *lost*
Thai demyt all that it was Wallace men, *believed*
160 Or ellis him self, thocht thai couth nocht
  him ken.
'He is rycht ner. We sall him haif but faill.
This febill woode may him litill availl.' *puny*
Forty thar past agayne to Sanct Jhonstoun
With this dede cors, to berysing maid it *body; burial*
  boun, *ready*
165 Partyt thar men, syne divers wayis raid. *Divided; then; diverse; rode*
A gret power at Dipplyn still thar baid. *army*
Till Dawryoch the Butler past but let; *without delay*
At syndry furdis the gait thai umbeset; *various fords; beset*
To kepe the wode quhill it was day thai *guard*
  thocht.
170 As Wallace thus in the thik forrest socht,
For his twa men in mynd he had gret
  payne;
He wist nocht weill giff thai war tayne or
  slayne,
Or chapyt haile be ony jeperte. *escaped completely; chance*
Thirteen war left with him, no ma had he; *more*

| | |
|---|---|
| 175 | In the Gask hall thair lugyng haif thai tayne. |
| | Fyr gat thai sone, bot meyt than had thai nayne. |
| | Twa scheipe thai tuk besid thaim of a fauld, |
| | Ordanyt to soupe in to that sembly hauld, |
| | Graithit in haist sum fude for thaim to dycht. |
| 180 | So hard thai blaw rude hornys upon hycht.[1] |
| | Twa sende he furth to luk quhat it mycht be. |
| | Thai baid rycht lang and no tithingis herd he, |
| | Bot boustous noyis so brymly blew and fast. |
| | So other twa in to the woode furth past; |
| 185 | Nane come agayne, bot boustously can blaw.[2] |
| | In to gret ire he send thaim furth on raw. |
| | Quhen that allayne Wallace was levyt thar |
| | The awfull blast aboundyt mekill mayr. |
| | Than trowit he weill thai had his lugyng seyne. |
| 190 | His swerd he drew of nobill mettall keyne, |
| | Syn furth he went quhar at he hard the horn. |
| | Without the dur Fawdoun was him beforn, |
| | As till his sycht his awne hed in his hand. |
| | A croys he maid quhen he saw him so stand. |
| 195 | At Wallace in the hed he swaket thar[3] |
| | And he in haist sone hynt it by the hair, |
| | Syne out agayne at him he couth it cast. |
| | In till his hart he was gretlye agast. |
| | Rycht weill he trowit that was no spreit of man; |
| 200 | It was sum devill at sic malice began. |
| | He wyst no vaill thar langer for to bide: |

Glosses (right column):

- lodging
- soon; food
- none
- sheep; from a fold
- Prepared to sup; fine stronghold
- Made ready
- cook
- were away a long time; news
- loud; fiercely
- two others
- Angry; out altogether
- alone; left
- increased much more
- believed
- sharp
- Then; heard
- Outside the door
- As it appeared; own head
- He crossed himself
- soon seized
- Then
- believed; spirit
- such
- knew no reason

1 Just then they heard rough horns sound loudly
2 None came back, but [the horn] continued to blow loudly
3 He flung the head in at Wallace there

Up throuch the hall thus wicht Wallace can   *went quickly*
  glid
Till a clos stair, the burdis raiff in twyne;[1]
Fifteen fute large he lap out of that in.   *feet high; leapt; dwelling*
205 Up the watter sodeynlye he couth fair;   *quickly he went*
Agayne he blent quhat perance he sawe   *looked; appearance*
  thar.
Him thocht he saw Faudoun that hugly syr,   *horrid man*
That haill hall he had set in a fyr:   *whole; set on fire*
A gret raftre he had in till his hand.   *rafter*
210 Wallace as than no langar walde he stand.
Of his gud men full gret mervaill had he   *wonder*
How thai war tynt throuch his feyle fantase.   *lost; terrible folly*
Traistis rycht weill all this was suth in   *Be assured; true indeed*
  deide,
Suppos that it no poynt be of the creide.[2]
215 Power thai had witht Lucifer that fell,
The tyme quhen he partyt fra hevyn to   *departed from heaven*
  hell.
Be sic myscheiff giff his men mycht be lost,   *By such evil if*
Drownyt or slayne amang the Inglis ost   *host*
Or quhat it was in liknes of Faudoun   *in the likeness of*
220 Quhilk brocht his men to suddand   *sudden*
  confusioun;   *destruction*
Or gif the man endyt in evill entent,   *if; evil disposition*
Sum wikkit spreit agayne for him present;   *spirit appearing again for him*
I can nocht spek of sic divinite,   *such theology*
To clerkis I will lat all sic materis be.   *leave*
225 Bot of Wallace furth I will you tell.   *further*
Quhen he was went of that perell fell   *out of that terrible danger*
Yeit glaid wes he that he had chapyt swa,   *escaped so*
Bot for his men gret murnyng can he ma,   *make*
Flayt by him self to the Makar of buffe   *Complained; above*
230 Quhy he sufferyt he suld sic paynys pruff.   *allowed [that]; endure*
He wyst nocht weill giff it wes Goddis will   *knew; if*
Rycht or wrang his fortoun to fullfill.
Hade he plesd God he trowit it mycht
  nocht be
He suld him thoill in sic perplexite;   *suffer*
235 Bot gret curage in his mynd ever draiff,   *desire; drove [him]*

---

1 To a stair leading to a close, the boards [he] smashed in two
2 Although it is not in the [Apostles'] creed

Of Inglismen thinkand amendis to haiff.                    have
As he was thus walkand be him allayne                      by himself
Apon Ern side makand a pytuous mayne,                      lament
Schyr Jhone Butler to wache the furdis
     rycht,
240  Out fra his men, of Wallace had a sicht.
The myst wes went to the montanys                          gone
     agayne.
Till him he raid quhar at he maid his                      rode; where that
     mayne.
On loude he sperd, 'Quhat art thou walkis                  Aloud; asked
     that gait?'
'A trew man schir, thocht my viage be layt,                journey
245  Erandis I pas fra Doun to my lord.
Schir Jhon Sewart, the rycht for to record,                truth to tell
In Doune is now, new cummyn fra the                        recently come
     king.'
Than Butler said, 'This is a selcouth thing.               strange
Thou leid all out, thou has beyne with                     lied outright
     Wallace.
250  I sall thee knaw or thou cum of this place.'           before; leave
Till him he stert the courser wonder wicht,                directed; very strong steed
Drew out a swerd, so maid hym for to
     lycht.                                                 alight
Aboune the kne gud Wallas has him tayne,                   struck
Throu the and brawn in sonder straik the                   thigh
     bayne;
255  Derffly to dede the knycht fell on the land.           Violently
Wallace the hors sone sesyt in his hand,
Ane awkwart straik syne tuk him in the                     gave
     sted.
His crag in twa, thus was the Butler dede.                 neck; [broken] in two
Ane Inglisman saw thar chiftayne wes
     slayn;
260  A sper in reyst he kest with all his mayne,[1]
On Wallace draiff fra the hors him to ber.                 drove; knock
Warly he wrocht as worthi man in wer;                      Warily; war
The sper he wan, withoutyn mor abaid                       captured
On hors he lap and throu a gret rout raid                  throng
265  Till Dawryoch; he knew the ford full weill.
Befor him come feyll stuffyt in fyne steill.              many furnished with

1 A spear he placed in position with all his might

He straik the fyrst but baid in the blasoune[1]

Quhill hors and man bathe flet the watter doune;  *Until; floated*

Ane othir sone doun fra his hors he bar,

270 Stampyt to grounde and drownyt withoutyn mar;  *Trampled; immediately*

The thrid he hyt in his harnes of steyll,  *armour*

Throuout the cost the sper to-brak sumdeyll.  *ribs; broke* / *in part*

The gret power than effter him can ryd:  *army*

He saw na vaill no langar thar to byd.  *advantage*

275 His burnyst brand braithly in hand he bar;  *shining sword; violently*

Quham he hyt rycht thai folowit him no mar.  *struck sure*

To stuff the chas feyll frekis folowit fast  *provide pursuit many*

Bot Wallace maid the ganast ay agast.  *nearest*

The mur he tuk and throu thar power yeid.  *boggy land*

280 The hors was gud, bot yeit he had gret dreid

For failyeing or he wan to a strenth.  *reached; stronghold*

The chas was gret, scalyt our breid and lenth;  *spread*

Throu strang danger thai had him ay in sycht.  *great range*

At the Blakfurd thar Wallace doune can lycht,  *alight*

285 His hors stuffyt, for the way was depe and lang;  *was winded*

A large gret myile wichtly on fute couth gang.  *vigorously*

Or he was horst ridaris about him kest;  *Before; gathered*

He saw full weyll lang swa he mycht nocht lest.

Sad men in deid upon him can renew;  *Resolute*

290 With retornyng that nycht twenty he slew.  *counter-attacking*

The forseast ay rudly rabutyt he,  *strongest; vigorously repulsed*

Kepyt his hors and rycht wysly can fle

Quhill that he come the myrkest mur amang.  *Until; darkest*

His hors gaiff our and wald no forthyr gang.  *gave up*

295 Wallace on fute tuk him with gude entent;

---

1 He struck the first one through his coat of arms without hesitation

The hors he straik or that he fra him went;     before
His houch sennounnis he cuttyt all at anys       hough sinews; at once
And left him thus besyde the standand
   stanys,
For Sotheren men no gud suld of him wyn.         obtain
300 In heich haddyr Wallace and thai can twyn.       heather; parted ways
Throuch that dounwith to Forth sadly he          downward; resolutely
   soucht,
Bot sodandly than come in till his thocht
Gret power wok at Stirlyng bryg of tre.          kept watch; wooden bridge
Seychand he said, 'No passage is for me.         Sighing
305 For want of fude, and I haiff fochtyn lang,
On wer men now me thynk no tyme to
   gang;
At Kamyskynnett I sall the watter till.          Cambuskenneth; [go] to
Lat God aboune do with me quhat he will.
Into this land langer I may nocht byd.'
310 Tary he maid sum part on Forthis syd,           Delay
Tuk off his weid and graithit him but mar.       clothes
Hys swerd he band, that wonder scharply          bound
   schar,                                        cut
Amang his ger be his schuldris on loft.          gear; above
Thus in he went, to gret God prayand oft
315 Of his hye grace the caus to tak on hand.
Our the wattyr he swame to the south land,
Arayede him sone; the sessone was rycht          Dressed; quickly
   cauld,
For Piscis was in tyll his dayis of auld.        customary
Ourthwort the Kers to the Torwode he             Across
   yeide;
320 A wedow thar dwelt that helpyt him in neid.
Thidder he come or day begouth to daw
Till a wyndow and prevaly couth caw.             call out
Thai sperd his nayme bot tell thaim wald         asked
   he nocht
Quhill scho hir selff ner till his langage       Until; came near to talk to
   socht.                                        hm
325 Fra tyme scho wist at it was wicht Wallace
Rejossyt scho wes and thankit God of his         Joyful
   grace.
Scho sperd sone quhy he was him allayne.         soon
Murnand he said, 'As now may haiff I             Grieving; many men
   nane.'

|   | | |
|---|---|---|
| | Scho askyt him quhar at his men suld be. | that |
| 330 | 'Fayr deyme,' he said, 'go get sum meit for me. | |
| | I haiff fastyt syne yhisterday at morn. | |
| | I dreid full sar that my men be forlorn. | are lost |
| | Gret part of thaim to the dede I saw dycht.' | killed |
| | Scho gat him meyt in all the haist scho mycht. | |
| 335 | A woman he cald and als with hyr a child; | youth |
| | Syne bade thaim pas agayne thai wayis wild | |
| | To the Gask hall, tithingis for to sper | |
| | Giff part war left of his men in to fer;[1] | |
| | And scho suld fynd a hors sone in hir gait. | on her way |
| 340 | He bad thaim se giff that place stud in stait: | good condition |
| | Tharof to her he had full gret desyr | hear |
| | Becaus he thocht that it was all in fyr. | |
| | Thai passyt furth withoutyn tary mar. | without more delay |
| | Him for to rest Wallace ramaynit thar. | |
| 345 | Refreschit he wes with meyte, drynk and with heit, | heat |
| | Quhilk causyt him throuch naturall cours to weit | enquire |
| | Quhar he suld sleipe, in sekyrnes to be. | safety |
| | The wedow had of hyr awne sonnys thre. | |
| | Fyrst twa of thaim scho send to kepe Wallace, | guard |
| 350 | And gert the thrid go sone to Dunypace | quickly |
| | And tald his eyme that he was hapnyt thar. | uncle; had come |
| | The persone yeid to se of his weyllfar. | parson went |
| | Wallace to sleipe was laid in the wood syde; | |
| | The twa yonge men without hym ner couth byd. | outside; stay |
| 355 | The persone come ner and thar maner saw; | |
| | Thai beknyt him to quhat stede he suld draw. | signalled |
| | The rone wes thik that Wallace slepyt in; | thicket |
| | About he yeid and maid bot litill dyn. | |
| | So at the last of him he had a sycht, | |
| 360 | Full prevalye how that his bed was dycht. | arranged |
| | He him beheld and said syne to him sell | then |

1 If any of his company were left

'Her is mervaill, quha likis it to tell.     *Here; a miracle*
This a persone be worthines of hand     *a [single] person*
Trowys to stop the power of Ingland.     *[Who] expects*
365 Now fals fortoune, the myswyrkar of all,     *undoer*
Be aventur has gyffyn him a fall,     *By ill chance*
At he is left without supple of ma;     *[So] that; aid; more*
A cruell wyff with wapynnys mycht him     *bold woman*
    sla.'
Wallace him herd quhen his slepe ourpast.     *came out of his sleep*
370 Fersly he rays and said till him als fast,     *rose*
'Thou leid, fals preyst. War thou a fa to me,     *lied; foe*
I wald nocht dreid sic other ten as thee.
I haiff had mar syne yhisterday at morn
Than syk sexty war semblyt me beforn.'     *such; assembled*
375 His eyme him tuk and went furth with
    Wallace.
He tald till hym of all his paynfull cace.
'This nycht,' he said, 'I was left me allayne,
In feyle debait with enemys mony ane.     *fierce conflict; many a one*
God at his will my liff did ay to kepe:[1]
380 Our Forth I swame that awfull is and depe.     *Across the River Forth*
Quhat I haiff had in wer befor this day,     *war*
Presoune and payne to this nycht was bot     *suffering*
    play,
So bett I am with strakis sad and sar.     *beaten; blows grave; sore*
The cheyle watter urned me mekill mar,     *chill; afflicted; much more*
385 Efter gret blud throu heit in cauld was     *[losing] blood; heat; cold*
    brocht,
That of my lyff almost nothing I roucht.     *cared*
I meyn fer mar the tynsell of my men     *lament far more; loss*
Na for my selff, mycht I suffer sic ten.'     *Than; harm*
The persone said, 'Der sone, thou may se     *parson*
    weyll
390 Langar to stryff it helpis nocht adeyll.     *contend; at all*
Thi men are lost and nayne will with thee     *none;*
    rys,     *rise up*
For Goddis saik wyrk as I sall devys.     *do; shall advise*
Tak a lordschipe quhar on at thou may liff;     *Accept; on which; live*
King Edward wald gret landis to thee giff.'
395 'Uncle,' he said, 'Of sic wordis no mar.     *more*
This is nothing bot eking of my car.     *an increasing of my care*

[1] It was God's will ever to preserve my life

I lik better to se the Sothren de                    see
Than gold or land that thai can giff to me.
Trastis rycht weyll, of wer I will nocht ces         Believe me; war; cease
400  Quhill tyme that I bryng Scotland in to          Until [the] time
        pes,                                          peace
Or de tharfor in playne to understand.'              die for [that cause] plainly
So come Kerle and gud Stevyn of Irland.              so then came
The wedowis sone to Wallace he thaim
        brocht.
Fra thai him saw of na sadnes thai roucht,           From [the time] cared
405  For perfyt joy thai wepe with all thar eyne.     wept
To ground thai fell and thankit hevynnys
        queyn.
Als he was glaid for reskew of thaim twa;            Also; about the rescue
Of thair feris leyffand was left no ma.[1]
Thai tald him that Schir Garrat wes dede;
410  How thai had weyll eschapyt of that stede.       fortunately; from that place
Throuch the Oychall thai had gayne all that
        nycht
Till Erth ferry or that the day was brycht;          before
How a trew Scot for kyndnes of Wallace              friendship for
Brocht thaim sone oure, syne kend thaim to           over; directed
        that place.
415  Als Kerle wyst gyff Wallace leyffand war         was living
Nere Dunypace that he suld fynd him thar.
The persone gart gud purviance for thaim            supplies
        dycht.                                        ready
In the Torwode thai lugyt all that nycht,           camped
Quhill the woman that Wallace north had
        send
420  Retornd agayne and tald him till ane end
Quhat Inglismen in the way scho fand                 found
        dede:
Feyll was fallyn, fey in mony syndry sted.           doomed to die; different
The hors scho saw that Wallace had bereft,           stolen
And the Gask hall standand as it was left,
425  Without harme, nocht sterd of it a stane;        moved
Bot of his men gud tithingis scho gat nane.
Tharof he grevyt gretlye in that tyd.                grieved; time
In the forrest he wald no langar bid.
The wedow him gaiff part of silver brycht,           some

1 of their companions no more were left alive

430 Twa of hyr sonnys that worthi war and
        wycht;
    The thrid scho held becaus he lakit age,
    In wer as than mycht nocht wyn vesselage.    honour
    The persone than gat thaim gud hors and
        ger,                                      equipment
    Bot wa he was his mynd wes all in wer.       sad; [set] on war
435 Thus tuk he leyff withoutyn langar abaid;
    In Dundaff mur that sammyn nycht he
        raid.
    Schir Jhone the Grayme quhilk lord wes of
        that land,
    Ane agyt knycht, had maid nane other band   no other allegiance
    Bot purchest pes in rest he mycht bide still, solicited a truce [so that]
440 Tribute payit full sor agayne his will.
    A sone he had, bathe wys, worthi and
        wicht;
    Alexander the fers at Berweik maid him       fierce
        knycht,
    Quhar schawyn wes of battaill till haif      shown
        beyne
    Betwex Scottis and the bauld Persie keyne.
445 This yong Schir Jhone rycht nobill wes in
        wer.
    On a braid scheyld his fader gert him swer
    He suld be trew till Wallace in all thing
    And he till him quhill lyff mycht in thaim    as long as they lived
        ryng.
    Thre nychtis thar Wallace baid out of
        dreid,                                    danger
450 Restyt him weill, swa had he mekill neid.
    On the ferd day he wald no langer bide;      fourth
    Schir Jhone the Grayme bounyt with him       prepared
        to ryd,
    And he said nay, as than it suld nocht be.
    'A playne part yeit I will nocht tak on me.   open
455 I haiff tynt men throu my our rakles deid:    reckless action
    A brynt child mayr sayr the fyr will dreid.   burned; more keenly
    Freyndis haiff I sumpart in Clyddysdaill;
    I will go se quhat may thai me availl.'
    Schir Jhone answerd, 'I will your consaill
        do.
460 Quhen yhe se tyme send prevale me to,        secretly

Than I sall cum with my power in haist.'

He him betuk on to the Haly Gaist,                    *entrusted*

Saynct Jhone to borch, thai suld meite haill          *To the protection of St John*
and sound.

Out of Dundaff he and thir four couth
found.

465 In Bothwell mur that nycht remaynyt he              *Bothwell, in Lanarkshire*

With ane Crawfurd that lugyt him prevale.             *one [of the] Crawfords*

Upon the morn to the Gilbank he went,

Rasavit was with mony glaid entent,                   *Welcomed*

For his der eyme yong Auchinlek dwelt                 *dear uncle*
thar;

470 Brothyr he was to the schireff of Ayr.

Quhen auld Schir Ranald till his dede wes             *killed*
dycht,

Than Auchinlek weddyt that lady brycht                *fair*

And childer gat, as storyes will record,              *children; histories*

Of Lesmahago, for he held of that lord.               *held land [as a vassal]*

475 Bot he wes slayne, gret pete wes the mar,

With Perseys men in to the toun of Ayr.

His sone dwelt still, than nineteen yeris of           *lived there*
age,

And brokit haille his fadris heretage.                *enjoyed possession of*

Tribute he payit for all his landis braid             *wide*

480 To lord Persie, as his broder had maid.

I leyff Wallace with his der uncle still;             *leave*

Of Inglismen yeit sum thing spek I will.

A messynger sone throu the contre yeid.

To lord Persie thai tald this fellone deid;           *cruel deed*

485 Kynclevyn was brynt, brokyn and castyn               *burned*
doun,

The captayn dede of it and Saynt
Jhonstoun;

The Loran als at Schortwod schawis
scheyn.

'In to that land gret sorow has beyne
seyn

Throuch wicht Wallace that all this deid              *bold*
has done.

490 The toune he spyit and that forthocht we             *regretted*
sone.                                                 *soon*

Butler is slayne with douchty men and                *[along] with brave*
deyr.'                                                *loved*

In aspre spech the Persye than can speyr:　　*sharp; asked*

'Quhat worth of him, I pray you graithlye tell.'　　*became of him; promptly*

'My lord,' he said, 'rycht thus the cas befell.

495　We knaw for treuth he was left him allayne,　　*know for a fact; alone*

And as he fled he slew full mony ayne.　　*many a one*

The hors we fand that him that gait couth ber,　　*way carried him*

Bot of hym self no other word we her.　　*hear*

At Stirlyng bryg we wait he passit nocht:　　*bridge; know*

500　To dede in Forth he may for us be brocht.'　　*River Forth*

Lorde Persye said, 'Now suthlye that war syne.　　*would be [a] sin*

So gud of hand is nayne this warld within.　　*i.e., valiant in combat; none*

Had he tayne pes and beyne our kingis man　　*accepted a truce*

The haill empyr he mycht haiff conquest than.　　*whole; have conquered*

505　Gret harme it is our knychtis that ar ded;　　*that [so many of] our knights*

We mon ger se for other in that sted.[1]

I trow nocht yeit at Wallace losyt be:　　*is dead*

Our clerkys sayis he sall ger mony de.'　　*cause many to die*

The messynger said, 'All that suth has beyne.　　*truly*　　*come to pass*

510　Mony hundreth that cruell war and keyne　　*hundreds; fierce; bold*

Sene he begane ar lost without ramede.'[2]

The Persye said, 'Forsuth he is nocht ded.

The crukis of Forth he knawis wondyr weylle.　　*the windings of the Forth*

He is on lyff that sall our nacioune feill.　　*alive; know*

515　Quhen he is strest than can he swym at will.　　*hard pressed then*

Gret strenth he has, bathe wyt and grace thartill.'　　*both skill*　　*thereto*

A messynger the lord chargyt to wend　　*ordered to go*

And this commaunde in wryt with him he send.　　*writing*

Schir Jhone Sewart gret schirreff than he maid　　*grand sheriff*

1 We must arrange for others to take their place
2 Since he began [his rebellion] are lost beyond help [i.e., fatally wounded]

| | |
|---|---|
| 520 | Of Sanct Jhonstoun and all thai landis braid. |
| | In till Kynclevyn thar dwelt nayne agayne: |
| | Thar was left nocht bot brokyn wallis in playne. |
| | Leiff I thaim thus reulland the landis thar |
| | And spek I will of Wallace glaid weillfar. |
| 525 | He send Kerle to Schir Ranald the knycht, |
| | Till Boyd and Blayr that worthi war and wicht |
| | And Adam als, his cusyng gud Wallace; |
| | To thaim declarde of all this paynfull cas, |
| | Of his eschaipe out of that cumpany, |
| 530 | Rycht wonder glaid was this gud chevalry; |
| | Fra tyme thai wyst that Wallace leiffand was, |
| | Gude expensis till him thai maid to pas. |
| | Maister Jhone Blayr was offt in that message, |
| | A worthy clerk bath wys and rycht savage. |
| 535 | Levyt he was befor in Parys toune |
| | Amang maisteris in science and renoune. |
| | Wallace and he at hayme in scule had beyne. |
| | Sone efterwart, as verite is seyne, |
| | He was the man that pryncipall undertuk, |
| 540 | That fyrst compild in dyt the Latyne buk |
| | Of Wallace lyff, rycht famous of renoun, |
| | And Thomas Gray, persone of Libertoune. |
| | With him thai war and put in storyall, |
| | Offt ane or bath mekill of his travaill, |
| 545 | And tharfor her I mak of thaim mencioune. |
| | Master Jhone Blayr to Wallace maid him boune; |
| | To se his heyle his comfort was the mor,[1] |
| | As thai full oft togyddyr war befor. |
| | Sylver and gold thai gaiff him for to spend; |
| 550 | Sa dyde he thaim frely quhen God it send. |
| | Of gud weylfayr as than he wantyt nane. |
| | Inglismen wyst he was left him allane. |
| | Quhar he suld be was nayne of thaim couth say, |

Glosses (right margin):
520 wide
In till Kynclevyn — none again
Thar was left — nothing
Leiff — Leave
weillfar — welfare
526 wicht — strong
cusyng — cousin
declarde — made known
eschaipe — escape
530 Rycht wonder glaid — Extremely glad; band of knights
leiffand — living
expensis — supplies of money
message — the messenger employed in that errand
savage — bold
535 Levyt he was — He had been left
hayme — home [Scotland]; scule — school
pryncipall — chiefly
540 dyt — writing
persone — parson
storyall — a history
travaill — Often one or both; struggle
545 her — here
boune — bound
As thai full oft — frequently
550 gaiff him — [to] them generously
wantyt nane — lacked none
Quhar he suld be — Where he could be; couth — could

1 To see his [good] health was all the more comforting

Drownyt or slayne, or eschapyt away,

555 Tharfor of him thai tuk bot litill heid.    *heed*

Thai knew him nocht, the les he was in dreid.    *did not recognise him*

All trew Scottis gret favour till him gaiff,

Quhat gude thai had he mysterit nocht to craiff.    *goods; he had no need to ask*

The pes lestyt that Schir Ranald had tayne.    *truce; lasted; accepted*

560 Thai four monethis it suld nocht be out gane.    *For those; trespassed against*

This Crystismes Wallace ramaynyt thar,    *Christmas season; remained*

In Laynrik oft till sport he maid repayr.    *Lanark*

Quhen that he went fra Gilbank to the toune,

And he fand men was of that fals nacioune,    *If; found*

565 To Scotland thai dyde never grevance mar.    *never more caused injury*

Sum stekyt thai, sum throttis in sonder schar.[1]

Feill war sone dede, bot nane wyst quha it was.    *Many; none knew who was responsible*

Quham he handlyt he leyt no forther pas.    *Whomever he dealt with; let*

Thar Hesylryg dwelt, that curssyt knycht to vaill;    *in respect of worth*

570 Schyrreff he was of all the landis haill,    *entirely*

Felloune, outrage, dispitfull in his deid;    *Fierce; violent, cruel; deeds*

Mony of him tharfor had mekill dreid.    *great fear*

Mervell he thocht quha durst his peple sla;    *He wondered who dared*

Without the toune he gert gret nowmer ga.    *Out of; a great company go*

575 Quhen Wallace saw that thai war ma than he,    *more*

Than did he nocht bot salust curtasle.    *nothing except gave greeting*

All his four men bar thaim quietlik,    *held; quietly*

Na Sotheron couth deme thaim mys, pur no rik.[2]

In Lanryk dwelt a gentill woman thar,    *noble*

580 A madyn myld as my buk will declar,    *gentle maiden*

Of eighteen yeris ald or litill mor of age:

Als born scho was till part of heretage.    *Also; a portion of an inheritance*

1 Some were stabbed, some had their throats cut apart
2 No Englishman could find fault with them, poor or rich

Hyr fadyr was of worschipe and renoune,
And Hew Braidfute he hecht of    *was called*
   Lammyngtoune,
585  As feylle other was in the contre cald;    *many others; region called*
Befor tyme thai gentill men war of ald.    *Formerly; old*
Bot this gud man and als his wiff wes ded.
The madyn than wyst of no other rede,    *knew; course [of action]*
Bot still scho dwelt on trewbute in the    *tribute*
   toune
590  And purchest had King Edwardis
   protectiounne.
Serwandys with hyr, of freyndis at hyr    *Servants; ready at hand*
   will,
Thus leyffyt scho without desyr of ill;    *lived; wishing ill [of anyone]*
A quiet hous as scho mycht hald in wer,[1]
For Hesylryg had done hyr mekill der,    *her great injury*
595  Slayne hyr brodyr, quhilk eldast wes and
   ayr.    *heir*
All sufferyt scho and rycht lawly hyr bar.    *meekly carried herself*
Amyabill, so benyng, war and wys,    *Agreeable; gracious; prudent*
Curtas and swete, fulfillyt of gentrys,    *accomplished in noble conduct*

Weyll rewllyt of tong, rycht haill of    *Discreet in speech; fresh*
   contenance,
600  Of vertuous scho was worthy till avance;    *In virtues; praiseworthy*
Hummylly hyr led and purchest a gud    *conducted; obtained*
   name,
Of ilkyn wicht scho kepyt hyr fra blame.[2]
Trew rychtwys folk a gret favour hir lent.    *virtuous; granted*
Apon a day to the kyrk as scho went,    *church*
605  Wallace hyr saw as he his eyne can cast.    *looked around*
The prent of luff him punyeit at the last    *pierced*
So asprely, throuch bewte of that brycht,    *sharply; fair lady*
With gret unes in presence bid he mycht.    *difficulty in her presence remain*

He knew full weyll hyr kynrent and hyr    *kinsfolk*
   blud    *lineage*
610  And how scho was in honest oys and gud.    *lived an honourable; good life*
Quhill wald he think to luff hyr our the    *Sometimes; resolve; above all*
   laiff,    *others*

1 She kept as quiet a house as she could in war
2 She took care to give no one cause for blame

|  |  |  |
|---|---|---|
| | And other quhill he thocht on his dissaiff, | times; betrayal |
| | How that hys men was brocht to confusioun | destruction |
| | Throu his last luff he had in Saynct Jhonstoun. | the last lady he loved |
| 615 | Than wald he think to leiff and lat our slyd, | resolved to forget [her] |
| | Bot that thocht lang in his mynd mycht nocht byd. | stay |
| | He tauld Kerle of his new lusty baille, | pleasant suffering |
| | Syne askit him of his trew best consaill. | loyal and best counsel |
| | 'Maister,' he said, 'als fer as I haiff feyll, | as far as I know [about love] |
| 620 | Of lyklynes it may be wonder weill. | In all likelihood; very well |
| | Sen ye sa luff, tak hir in mariage. | Since; love |
| | Gudlye scho is, and als has heretage. | She is handsome; [an] inheritance |

|  |  |  |
|---|---|---|
| | Suppos at yhe in luffyng feill amys,[1] | |
| | Gret God forbede it suld be so with this!' | |
| 625 | 'To mary thus I can nocht yeit attend: | expect |
| | I wald of wer fyrst se a finaill end. | war |
| | I will no mor allayne to my luff gang. | alone; go |
| | Tak tent to me or dreid we suffer wrang. | Heed me; fear |
| | To proffer luff thus sone I wald nocht preffe; | propose [marriage], soon try |
| 630 | Mycht I leyff off, in wer I lik to leyff. | leave; war; live |
| | Quhat is this luff? No thing bot folychnes. | love; foolishness |
| | It may reiff men bathe witt and stedfastnes.' | deprive men of |
| | Than said he thus: 'This will nocht graithly be, | readily |
| | Amors and wer at anys to ryng in me. | Love and war; once; rule |
| 635 | Rycht suth it is, stude I in blis of luffe, | |
| | Quhar dedis war I suld the better pruff.[2] | |
| | Bot weyle I wait quhar gret ernyst is in thocht | know; the mind is anxious |
| | It lattis wer in the wysest wys be wrocht, | prevents; war; fought |
| | Les gyf it be bot only till a deid; | Unless; one deed |
| 640 | Than he that thinkis on his luff to speid, | prosper |
| | He may do weill, haiff he fortoun and grace. | if he has |

1 Although you were wronged in love
2 I should the better succeed in feats of arms

Bot this standis all in ane other cas:
A gret kynryk with feill fayis ourset.[1]
Rycht hard it is amendis for to get     to obtain amends from them
645   At anys of thaim and wyrk the observance     and at the same time perform
                                 the duties

Quhilk langis luff and all his frevill     belong to; fickle fortune
    chance.
Sampill I haif; this me forthinkis sar;     Experience; I sorely regret
I trow to God it sall be so no mar.
The trewth I knaw of this and hyr lynage.
650   I knew nocht hyr tharfor I lost a gage.'     her [the maid in St
                                  Johnstone]; pledge

To Kerle he thus argownd in this kynd,     debated; manner
Bot gret desyr remaynyt in till his mynd
For to behald that frely of fassoun.     behold; lovely lady
A quhill he left and come nocht in the     desisted; came
    toun;
655   On other thing he maid his witt to walk,     he kept his thoughts
Prefand giff he mycht of that langour slalk.     Trying; distress; slake
Quhen Kerle saw he sufferit payne forthi,     on account of this
'Der schir,' he said, 'ye leiff in slogardy.     live; idleness
Go se youre luf, than sall yhe get comfort.'     beloved
660   At his consaill he walkit for to sport,     went out; play
On to the kyrke quhar scho maid
    residence.     lingered
Scho knew him weill, bot as of eloquence     speech
Scho durst nocht weill in presens till him     disclose her mind in his
    kyth.                                   presence
Full sor scho dred or Sotheron wald him     feared the English
    myth,                                   observe
665   For Hesilryg had a mater new begone     begun
And hyr desirde in mariage till his sone.     son
With hir madyn thus Wallace scho besocht     beseeched
To dyne with hyr and prevaly hym brocht     secretly
Throuch a garden scho had gart wyrk of     had had made recently
    new,
670   So Inglis men nocht of thar metyng knew.
Than kissit he this gudle with plesance,     comely lady; pleasure
Syne hyr besocht rycht hartly of quentance.     beseeched ardently;
                                       friendship

---

1 But things stand differently in this case: A great Kingdom [is] overrun
with many enemies

Scho answerd hym with humyll wordis wise: — humble

'War my quentance rycht worthi for till pryse — were; friendship / prize

675 Yhe sall it haiff, als God me saiff in saille; — as God save my soul

Bot Inglismen gerris our power faill — causes; [to] fail

Throuch violence of thaim and thar barnage, — baronage

At has weill ner destroyt our lynage.' — That; lineage

Quhen Wallace hard hyr plenye petously — lament pitifully

680 Agrevit he was in hart rycht gretunly. — Grief-stricken; greatly

Bathe ire and luff him set in till a rage, — Both; passion

Bot nocht forthi he soberyt his curage. — nevertheless; moderated; feelings

Of his mater he tald as I said ayr — concerns; earlier

To that gudlye, how luff him strenyeit sar. — love; constrained grievously

685 Scho answerd him rycht resonably agayne

And said: 'I sall to your service be bayne — I shall be ready to serve you

With all plesance in honest causis haill; — wholly

And I trast yhe wald nocht set till assaill, — trust; attempt to

For yhoure worschipe, to do me dyshonour, — Because of your honour

690 And I a maid and standis in mony stour — struggles

Fra Inglismen to saiff my womanheid, — preserve; womanly honour

And cost has maid to kepe me fra thar dreid. — incurred expense; danger

With my gud wyll I wyll no lenman be — paramour

To no man born, tharfor me think suld yhe

695 Desyr me nocht bot in till gudlynas. — honourably

Perchance ye think I war to law purchas[1]

For tyll attend to be your rychtwys wyff. — to expect; lawful

In your service I wald oys all my lyff. — work

Her I beseik for your worschipe in armys, — appeal to your

700 Yhe charge me nocht with no ungudly harmys, — do not subject me to / unseemly

Bot me defend for worschipe of your blude.' — 

Quhen Wallace weyll hyr trew tayll understud, — honest speech

As in a part hym thocht it was resoun — right

Of hyr desir, tharfor till conclusioun — [To accede to] her wish

705 He thankit hyr, and said, 'Gif it mycht be — If

Throuch Goddis will that our kynryk war fre, — kingdom was

[1] Perhaps you consider I would be too low a prize

I wald you wed with all hartlie plesance;                heartfelt joy
Bot as this tym I may nocht tak sic chance,
And for this caus, none other, now I crayff;
710 A man in wer may nocht all plesance haiff.'          at war
Of thar talk than I can tell you no mar                   more
To my purpos, quhat band that thai maid                  agreement
     thar.
Conclud thai thus and syne to dyner went.
The sayr grevans ramaynyt in his entent,[1]
715 Los of his men and lusty payne of luff.               [Caused by] loss; pleasant
His leiff he tuk at that tyme to ramuff,                   leave; depart
Syne to Gilbank he past or it was nycht.                   before
Apon the morn with his four men him                       prepared
     dycht;
To the Corhed without restyng he raid,                    Corehead [near Moffat]; rode
720 Quhar his nevo Thom Haliday him baid,                 awaited him
And Litill als, Edward his cusyng der,                     dear cousin
Quhilk was full blyth quhen he wyst him so                 knew
     ner,
Thankand gret God that send him saiff                     safe
     agayne,
For mony demyt he was in Strathern slayn.                  believed
725 Gud cher thai maid all out thai dayis thre.          They feasted
Than Wallace said that he desirde to se
Lowmaban toun and Ynglismen that was                      Lochmaban
     thar.
On the ferd day thai bounyt thaim to far;                  fourth; prepared to go
Sixteen he was of gudle chevalre;                          fine knights
730 In the Knokwood he levyt all bot thre.                left
Thom Halyday went with him to the toun;
Edward Litill and Kerle maid thaim boun.                   ready
Till ane ostrye Thom Halyday led thaim                     To an inn
     rycht,
And gaiff commaund thar dyner suld be
     dycht.                                                 prepared
735 Till her a mes in gud entent thai yeid;               hear; mass with; went
Of Inglis men thai trowit thar was no dreid.               believed; danger
Ane Clyffurd come, was emys sone to the                    uncle's son [nephew]
     lord,
And four with him, the trewth for to                       to tell the truth
     record.

1 He remained sorely distressed [by] grievance

Quha awcht thai hors in gret heithing he ast.    owned; derision; asked

740 He was full sle and ek had mony cast.    sly; also; tricked

The gud wyff said, till applessyt him best,    mistress of the house; please

'Four gentill men is cummyn out of the west.'    [who] come from

'Quha devill thaim maid so galy for to ryd?    Who the devil; handsomely

In faith with me a wed thar most abide.    pledge; must

745 Thir lewit Scottis has leryt litill gud:    These ignorant; have learned

Lo! all thar hors ar schent for faut of blud.'    ruined because of defective lineage

In to gret scorn withoutyn wordis mayr    more

The taillis all of thai four hors thai schayr.    sheared

The gud wyff cryede and petuously couth gret    wept

750 So Wallace come and couth the captayne mete.    met the captain

A woman tald how thai his hors had schent.    injured

For propyr ire he grew in matelent.    pure; rage

He folowid fast and said, 'Gud freynd abid,    wait

Service to tak for thi craft in this tyde.    Payment; occupation; time

755 Marschell thou art without commaund of me;    Farrier; instruction from

Reward agayne me think I suld pay thee.

Sen I of laitt now come out of the west    Since recently

In this contre, a barbour of the best    region; barber

To cutt and schaiff, and that a wonder gude,    shave; marvellously well

760 Now thou sall feyll how I oys to lat blud.'    am accustomed; let

With his gud swerd the captayn has he tayn,    sword; struck

Quhill hors agayne he marscheld never nayn;[1]

Another sone apon the hed strak he,    Another soon

Quhill chaftis and cheyk upon the gait can fle.    So that; street; flew

765 Be that his men the tother twa had slayne.    By that time; other two

Thar hors thai tuk and graithit thaim full bayne

Out of the toun; for dyner baid thai nayne.[2]

1 So that he never again marshalled horses
2 Their horses they took and promptly made themselves ready/ To leave the town; they did not stay for dinner

The wyff he payit that maid so petuous            woman; piteous
   mayne.                         lament
Than Inglismen fra that chyftayne wes           once; was
   dede                           dead
770  To Wallace socht fra mony syndry stede.   sought
Of the castell come cruell men and keyne.        From; bold; fierce
Quhen Wallace has thar sodand semle seyne        quick assembly seen
Towart sum strenth he bounyt him to ryd,         stronghold; prepared
For than him thocht it was no tyme to byd.       wait
775  Thar hors bled fast, that gert him dredyng   heavily; made him fearful
   haiff;
Of his gud men he wald haif had the laiff.       rest
To the Knokwoode withoutyn mor thai             without delay
   raid,
Bot in till it no sojornyng he maid;             tarrying
That wood as than was nother thik no lang.       neither dense nor
780  His men he gat, syn lychtyt for to gang   then dismounted; go
Towart a hicht and led thar hors a quhill.       hill; while
The Inglismen was than within a myill,
On fresche hors rydand full hastely;
Sevyn scor and ma was in thar chevalry.          company of horsemen
785  The Scottis lap on quhen thai thar power   leapt on [horseback]; army
   saw,
Frawart the south thaim thocht it best to        Away from
   draw.
Than Wallace said, 'It is no witt in wer         skill
With our power to byd thaim bargane her.[1]
Yon ar gud men, tharfor I rede that we           counsel
790  Evermar seik quhill God send sum supple.'   press on until; help
Halyday said, 'We sall do your consaille,
Bot sayr I dreid or thir hurt hors will fayll.'  sorely; fear; these
The Inglis men in burnyst armour cler           burnished; bright
Be than to thaim approchyt wonder ner.          By then; very near
795  Horssyt archaris schot fast and wald nocht   Mounted archers shot
   spar;                            quickly; spare
Of Wallace men thai woundyt twa full sar.        grieviously
In ir he grew quhen that he saw thaim            anger; [Wallace]
   bleid;
Him self retornde and on thaim sone he          turned back
   yeid,                            advanced
Sixteen with him that worthi was in wer.         war

1 with our [smaller] power to wait to [give] them a battle here

800 Of thai formast rycht freschly doun thai          vigorously
        ber.                                                      bore
    At that retorn fifteen in feild war slayne;       counter-attack
    The laiff fled fast to thar power agayne.         rest; army
    Wallace folowid with his gud chevalrye.
    Thom Halyday in wer was full besye,               fighting; very busy
805 A buschement saw that cruell was to ken,          An ambush; fierce; indeed
    Twa hundreth haill of weill gerit Inglismen.      well-armed
    'Uncle,' he said, 'our power is to smaw;
    Of this playne feild I consaill you to draw.[1]
    To few we ar agayne yon fellone staill.'          Too; fierce armed party
810 Wallace relevit full sone at his consaill.        rallied [his men]; quickly; on
    At the Corheid full fayne thai wald haif beyne,   gladly they would have been
    Bot Inglismen weyll has thar purpos seyne.
    In playne battaill thai folowid hardely;
    In danger thus thai held thaim awfully.           formidably
815 Hew of Morland on Wallace folowid fast;
    He had befor maid mony Scottis agast.             terrified
    Haldyn he was of wer the worthiast man
    In north Ingland, with thaim was leiffand         living
        than.                                             then
    In his armour weill forgyt of fyne steill
820 A nobill cursour bur him bath fast and            steed carried
        weill.
    Wallace retorned besyd a burly ayk                turned round; strong oak
    And on him set a fellone sekyr straik;            grievous, firm blow
    Baith cannell bayne and schulder blaid in         [cutting] both collarbone
        twa,
    Throuch the myd cost the gud swerd gert           rib; sword caused
        he ga.
825 His speyr he wan and als the coursour             spear; captured
        wicht,                                            strong
    Syne left his awn for he had lost his mycht;      Then; own; become feeble
    For lak of blud he mycht no forther gang.         go
    Wallace on hors the Sotheron men amang,           Englishmen
    His men relevit, that douchty was in deid,        relieved; valiant; deed
830 Him to reskew out of that felloune dreid.         terrible danger
    Cruell strakis forsuth thar mycht be seyne        Fierce strokes truly
    On ather side quhill blud ran on the              either; green [grass]
        greyne.
    Rycht peralous the semlay was to se:              encounter

    1 From this open battlefield I advise you to withdraw

Hardy and hat contenyt the fell melle,  *heated continued; fierce fighting*

835 Skew and reskew of Scottis and Inglis als.  *Rescue and rescue again*
Sum kervyt bran in sonder, sum the hals,  *flesh; neck*
Sum hurt, sum hynt, sum derffly dong to dede;  *wounded; captured; violently killed*
The hardy Scottis so steryt in that sted,  *bestirred themselves; place*
With Halyday on fute bauldly that baid,  *foot boldly; withstood*
840 Amang Sotheron a full gret rowme thai maid.  *breach*
Wallas on hors, in hand a nobill sper,  *spear*
Out throuch thaim raid as gud chyftayne in wer.  *war*
Thre slew he thar or that his sper was gayn,  *before*
Than his gud swerd in hand sone has tayne,  *sword; soon*
845 Hewyt on hard with dyntis sad and sar;  *Hacked vigorously; blows heavy, grievous*

Quhat ane he hyt grevyt the Scottis no mar.[1]
Fra Sotheron men be naturall resone knew  *Once Englishmen*
How with a straik a man ever he slew,  *blow; every [time]*
Than merveld thai he wes so mekill of mayne;  *marvelled; mightily strong*
850 For thar best man in that kynd he had slayne,  *manner*
That his gret strenth agayne him helpyt nocht
Nor nayne other in contrar Wallace socht.  *no other against*
Than said thai all, 'Lest he in strenth untayne  *If he continues / uncaptured*
This haill kynryk he wyll wyn him allayne.'  *whole kingdom; win back*
855 Thai left the feild syne to thar power fled  *then*
And tald thar lord how evill the formest sped,  *ill / succeeded*
Quhilk Graystok hecht, was new cummyn in the land,  *was called*
Tharfor he trowyt nane durst agayne him stand.  *believed*
Wonder him thocht quhen that he saw that sicht,

1 Whomever he struck annoyed the Scots no more

| | |
|---|---|
| 860 Quhy his gud men for sa few tuk the flycht. | on account of so; fled |
| At that retorn twenty in feild was tynt, | turning-back |
| And Morland als; tharfor he wald nocht stynt, | stop |
| Bot folowed fast with three hundred but dreid, | without doubt |
| And swour he suld be vengit on that deid. | |
| 865 The Scottis wan hors becaus thar awne couth faill, | obtained |
| In fleyng syne chesd thaim the maist availl. | fleeing; they chose; advantage |
| Out of that feild thus wicht Wallas is gayn; | |
| Of his gud men he had nocht losyt ayne; | one |
| Five woundyt wes, yeit blythly furth thai raid. | |
| 870 Wallace a space behynd thaim ay he baid, | |
| And Halyday prevyt weill in mony place. | proved himself |
| Sib sister sone he wes to gud Wallace. | By kinship [i.e., he is Wallace's nephew] |
| Warly thai raid and held thar hors in aynd, | warily; breath |
| For thai trowide weyll Sotheron wald afaynd | try |
| 875 With haill power at anys on thaim to sett. | once |
| Bot Wallace kest thar power for to let; | planned; army; stop |
| To brek thar ray he besyit hym full fast. | battle order |
| Than Inglismen so gretly wes agast | |
| That nane of thaim durst rusch out of the staill, | main body |
| 880 All in a ray held thaim togidder haill. | array |
| The Sotheron saw how that so bandounly | boldly |
| Wallace abaid ner hand thar chevalry. | near; knights |
| Be Morlandis hors thai knew him wonder weill, | By |
| Past to thar lord and tauld him everilkdeill. | every detail |
| 885 'Lo schir,' thai said, 'forsuth yon sammyn is he | he is the same one |
| That with his hand gerris so mony de. | causes |
| Haiff his hors grace apon his feyt to bid[1] | |
| He dredis nocht throu five thousand to ryd. | |
| We rede ye ces and folow him no mar, | cease |
| 890 For drede that we repent it syn full sar.' | |
| He blamyt thaim and said, 'Men weyll may se | rebuked |

---

1 So long as his horse can stand

Cowartis ye ar that for so few wald fle.'

For thar consaill yeit leiff thaim wald he
   nocht.

In gret ire he apon thaim sadly socht,         *resolutely*

895  Vailland a place quhar he mycht bargane    *Seeking; battle*
   mak.

Wallace was wa apon him for to tak,        *reluctant; take on [battle]*

And he so few, to bid thaim on a playne;   *[with] so few; in the open*

At Quenysbery he wald haiff beyne full    *gladly have been*
   fayne.

Apon him self he tuk full gret travaill

900  To fend his men gyff that mycht ocht     *defend; avail in any way*
   availl.

A swerd he drew rycht manlik him to wer,   *manfully; defend*

Ay wayttand fast gyff he mycht get a sper.  *Always watching out; spear*

Now her, now thar, befor thaim to and fra.

His hors gaiff our and mycht no forther
   ga.

905  Rycht at the skyrt of Quenysbery befell,   *edge; [it] happened*

Bot upon grace as my autour will tell,    *source*

Schir Jhone the Grayme that worthi wes
   and wicht,

To the Corhed come on the tother nycht,   *previous*

Thirty with him of nobill men at wage.    *in his pay*

910  The fyrst dochter he had in mariage

Of Halyday was nevo to Wallace.

Tithandis to sper Schir Jhone past of that  *To ask for news; left*
   place

With men to spek quhar thai a tryst had   *meeting*
   set,

Rycht ner the steid quhar Scottis and
   Ynglis mete.

915  Ane Kyrkpatryk, that cruell was and keyne,  *One; fierce*

In Esdaill wood that half yer he had beyne.  *Ewesdale*

With Inglismen he couth nocht weyll
   accord.

Of Torthorowald he barron wes and lord.

Of kyn he was and Wallace modyr ner,[1]

920  Of Crawfurd syd that mydward had to ster.

Twenty he had of worthi men and wicht.

Be than Wallace approchit to thar sicht.    *By then*

---

1 He was a relation, a near relative of Wallace's mother

Schir Jhon the Grayme quhen he the
  counter saw,                                    *encounter*
On thaim he raid and stud bot litill aw.          *had little fear*
His gud fader he knew rycht wonder weyll,   925    *father-in-law*
Kest doun his sper and sonyeit nocht              *Threw; hesitated not at all*
  adeyll.
Kyrkpatryk als with worthi men in wer
Fyfty in fronte at anys doun thai ber.            *once*
Throuch the thikkest of thre hundreth thai
  raid,
On Sotheron men full gret slauchter thai   930
  maid,
Thaim to reskew that was in fellone thrang.       *extreme danger*
Wallace on fute the gret power amang,
Gud rowme he gat throuch help of Goddis           *space*
  grace.
The Sotheren fled and left thaim in that
  place.
Horsis thai wan to stuff the chas gud spede,   935   *obtained; provide pursuit*
Wallace and his that douchty wes in dede.
Graystok tuk flycht on stern hors and stout,      *strong*
A hundreth held togydder in a rout.               *pack*
Wallace on thaim full sadly couth persew;         *determinedly*
The fleyng weyll of Inglis men he knew,[1]   940
At ay the best wald pas with thar                 *That always*
  chyftayne.
Befor him he fand gud Schir Jhone the
  Grayme
Ay strykand doun quham ever he mycht              *Ever; whomever*
  ourhy.                                          *overtake*
Than Wallace said, 'This is bot waist foly,       *vain folly*
Comons to slay quhar chyftayns gayis away.   945   *get*
Your hors is fresche, tharfor do as I say.
Gud men yhe haiff ar yeit in nobill stait.
To yon gret rout for Goddis luff hald your        *throng; hold your way*
  gait.
Soundyr thaim sone. We sall cum at your           *Break them up quickly*
  hand.'
Quhen Schir Jhon had his tayll weyll   950        *speech*
  understand,
Of nane other fra thine furth tuk he heid.        *thenceforth; heed*

1 He was very familiar with the flight of Englishmen

To the formast he folowid weill gud speid.  foremost; very speedily
Kyrkpatryk als consideryt thar consaill,  advice
Than chargyt thar men all folow on the stayll.  commanded; [retreating] party

955 At hys command full sone with hym thay met,
Sad straikys and sayr apone thaym sadly set.  Firm; resolutely
Schyr Jhone the Grayme to Graystok fast he socht;
Hys prys pissan than helpyt him rycht nocht.  fine gorget
Upon the crage a graith straik gat him rycht.  neck; direct blow

960 The burly blaide was braid and burnyst brycht,  strong; broad; burnished
In sonder kervyt the mailyeis of fyne steyll.  cleft; mail
Throuch bayne and brawne it prochyt everilkdeill;  pierced
Dede with that dynt to the erd doun him draiff.  blow [was] driven
Be that Wallace was semland with the laiff.  By that time; meeting; rest

965 Derfly to dede feyle frekys thar he dycht;  many men; consigned
Rays never agayne quhat ane at he hyt rycht.  whatever one
Kyrkpatrik than, Thom Halyday and thar men,
Thar douchty deid was nobill for to ken.  acknowledge
At the Knokheid the bauld Graystok was slayne

970 And mony man quhilk wes of mekill mayne.  great valour
To saiff thar lyff part in the wood is past;
The Scottis men than relevit togidder fast.  rallied
Quhen that Wallace with Schir Jhone Grayme wes met
Rycht gudlye he with humylnes him gret.  greeted

975 Pardoun he ast of the repreiff befor  asked; reproof
In to the chas and said he suld no mor  chase
Formacioune mak of him that was so gud.  Give direction to
Quhen that Schir Jhon Wallace weyll undirstud

'Do way,' he said, 'tharof as now no mar.                'Away with you'
980  Yhe dyd full rycht; it was for our weylfar.
Wysar in weyr ye ar all out than I.                      warfare
Fader in armes ye ar to me forthi.'
Kyrkpatryk syne that wes his cusyng der,                 relative
He thankit hym rycht on a gud maner.
985  Nocht ane was lost of all thar chevalry.            horsemen
Schir Jhone the Grayme to thaim come
        happely.                                         luckily
The day was downe and prochand wes the                   past; approaching
        nycht;
At Wallace thai askit his consaill rycht.                Of
He answerd thus, 'I spek bot with your
        leiff.                                           permission
990  Rycht laith I war ony gud man to greyff,            reluctant; anger
Bot thus I say in termes schort for me:
I wald sailye, gyff ye think it may be,                  attack, if
Lowmaban hous quhilk now is left allayne,                castle; abandoned
For weyll I wait power in it is levyt nayne.             forces; left none
995  Carlaverok als yeit Maxwell has in hand;            under control
And we had this thai mycht be bath a wand                both be a weapon
Agayne Sotheroune that now has our
        cuntre.
Say quhat ye will, this is the best think
        me.'
Schir Jhone the Grayme gaiff fyrst his gud
        consent,
1000 Syne all the layff rycht with a haill entent.       Then; rest; wholeheartedly
To Lowmaban rycht haistely thai ryd.
Quhen thai come ner nocht half a myill
        besid,
The nycht was myrk, to consaill ar thai                  dark; council
        gayne.                                           gone
Of mune not stern gret perans was thar                   moon; stars; there was little
        nayne.                                              sight
1005 Than Wallace said, 'Me think the land at
        rest.
Thom Haliday, thou knawis this cuntre
        best.
I her no noyis of feyll folk her about,                  many; here
Tharfor I trow we ar the les in dout.'                   less in danger
Haliday said, 'I will tak ane with me
1010 And ryde befor the maner for to se.'                ahead; to see how things are

Watsone he callit, 'With me thou mak thee    *make yourself ready*
  boun.
With thaim thou was a nychtbour of this
  toun.'
'I grant I was with thaim agayne my will.
Myn entent is ever to do thaim ill.'    *wish*
1015  Onto the yeitt thir twa pertly furth raid.    *gate; boldly*
The portar come without langar abaid.    *came; long delay*
At Jhone Watsone sone tithandis he couth as.
Opyn he bad, the captayne cummand was.    *Entry he demanded*
The yett but mayr unwysly he up drew.    *without more delay*
1020  Thom Haliday sone be the crag him threw,
And with a knyff he stekit him to dede,    *stabbed*
In a dyrk holl kest him doun in that sted.    *hole*
Jhone Watsone syne has hynt the keyis in    *seized*
  hand.
The power than with Wallace wes
  cummand.
1025  Thai entryt in, befor thaim fand no ma    *more*
Excep wemen, and sympill servandis twa    *harmless*
In the kyching scudleris lang tyme had    *kitchen; scullery boys*
  beyne.
Sone thai war slayne. Quhen the lady had
  thaim seyne,
'Grace,' scho cryit, 'for hym that deit on tre.'    *Mercy*
1030  Than Wallace said, 'Mademe, your noyis    *clamour*
  lat be.
To wemen yeit we do bot litill ill,    *harm*
Na yong childer we lik nocht for to spill.[1]
I wald haiff meit. Haliday quhat sayis thou?    *food*
For fastand folk to dyne gud tym war
  now.'[2]
1035  Gret purviance was ordand thar befor,    *provision; set*
Bath breid and aylle, gud wyne and other stor.
To meyt thai bounyt for thai had fastyt    *eat*
  lang;
Gud men of armes into the clos gert gang.    *courtyard*
Part fleand folk on fute that fra thaim glaid    *Some; went easily*
1040  On the Knokheid quhar gret melle was    *fighting*
  maid.

1 Nor do we like to kill young children
2 For fasting folk now is a good time to dine.

Ay as thai come Jhon Watsone leit thaim in  
And donn to dede withoutyn noyis or dyn,    killed  
Na man left thar that was of Ingland born.  
The castell weyll thai wesyt on the morn.    inspected  
1045 For Jhonstoun send, a man of gud degre:    standing  
Secund dochter forsuth weddyt had he  
Of Halidays, nere nevo to Wallace;    closely related nephew  
Gret captayne thai made him of that place.  
Thai leiffit him thar in till a gud aray,    good order  
1050 Syne wsched furth upon the secund day.    sallied  
Women had leyff in Ingland for to fayr.  
Schyr Jhon the Grayme and gud Wallace  
　　couth cair    go  
To the Corhed and lugyt all that nycht.  
Upon the morn the sone wes at the hycht;  
1055 Efter dyner thai wald no langer byde,  
Thar purpos tuk in Crawfurd mur to ryd,  
Schir Jhon the Grayme with Wallace that  
　　was wycht.  
Thom Haliday agayne retorned rycht  
To the Cor hall and thar remanyt but dred.  
1060 Na Sotheroun wyst prynsuall quha did this    knew; chiefly  
　　dede.  
Kyrkpatrik past in Aisdaill woddis wyd;    Ewesdale  
In saufte thar he thoucht he suld abid.  
Schyr Jhone the Grayme and gud Wallace  
　　in feir,    in company  
With thaim forty of men in armes cleir,  
1065 Throuch Crawfurd mur as that thai tuk the  
　　way,  
On Inglismen thar mynd ramaynit ay.  
Fra Crawfurd Jhon the watter doune thai    Crawfordjohn  
　　ryd;  
Ner hand the nycht thai lychtyt apon Clyd.    Near nightfall  
Thar purpos tuk in till a quiet vaill.    valley  
1070 Than Wallace said, 'I wald we mycht assaill  
Crawfurd castell with sum gud jeperte.    stratagem  
Schir Jhon the Grayme how say yhe best    [what] may be best?  
　　may be?'  
This gud knycht said, 'And the men war    If  
　　without,    outside  
To tak the hous thar is bot litill dout.'    castle  
1075 A squier than rewllyt that lordschip haill,

Of Cummyrland borne, his name was
  Martyndaill.
Than Wallace said, 'My selff will pas in       *go in further*
  feyr
And ane with me of herbre for to speyr.       *shelter; ask*
Folow on dreich giff that we myster ocht.'     *at a distance; need*
1080 Edward Litill with his master furth socht
Till ane oystry and with a woman met.       *inn*
Scho tald to thaim that Sothroune thar was
  set;
'And ye be Scottis, I consaill you pas by,
For and thai may yhe will get evill herbry.    *evil lodging*
1085 At drynk thai ar, so haiff thai bene rycht
  lang.
Gret worde thar is of Wallace thaim
  amang.
Thai trow that he has found his men
  agayne;
At Lowchmaban feyll Inglis men ar slayne.    *many*
That hous is tynt; that gerris thaim be full    *lost; causes*
  wa;                                         *sorrowful*
1090 I trow to God that thai sall sune tyne ma.'    *trust; lose more*
Wallace sperd of Scotland giff scho be.      *for*
Scho said him, 'Ya, and thinkis yet to se
Sorow on thaim throu help of Goddis
  grace.'
He askit hyr quha was into the place.
1095 'Na man of fens is left that hous within.     *guard*
Twenty is her makand gret noyis and dyn.
Allace!' scho said, 'giff I mycht anys se     *once*
The worthy Scottis maist maister in it to    *in charge*
  be.'
With this woman he wald no langar stand.
1100 A bekyn he maid; Schir Jhon come at his    *signal*
  hand.
Wallace went in and bad Bendicite.       *wished 'Bless you'*
The capteyne speryt, 'Quhat bellamy may    *asked; friend*
  thou be
That cummys so grym? Sum tithandis till    *grimly*
  us tell.
Thou art a Scot. The devill thi nacioune
  quell!'                                         *destroy*
1105 Wallace braid out his swerd withoutyn mar;    *drew out*

Into the breyst the bryme captayne he bar,          fierce; struck
Throuch out the cost, and stekit him to          ribs; stabbed
    ded.
Ane other he hyt awkwart upon the hed.          across the head
Quham ever he strak he byrstyt bayne and          shattered
    lyr,          flesh
1110  Feill of thaim dede fell thwortour in the          across
    fyr;
Haisty payment he maid thaim on the flur,          dispatch
And Edward Litill kepyt weill the dur.
Schir Jhon the Graym full fayne wald haiff
    beyne in.
Edward him bad at the castell begyne.
1115  'For of thir folk we haiff bot litill dreid.'          these
Schir Jhon the Grayme fast to the castell
    yeid.
Wallace rudly sic routis to thaim gaiff,          vigorously; blows
Thai twenty men derffly to dede thai draiff.          violently; dashed
Fifteen he straik and fifteen has he slayne.
1120  Edward slew five quhilk was of mekill          great strength
    mayne.
To the castell Wallace had gret desyr,
Be that Schir Jhone had set the yett in fyr;          By then; gate
Nane wes tharin at gret defens couth ma,          make
Bot wemen fast sar wepand in to wa.          weeping copiously in sorrow
1125  Without the place ane ald bulwark was
    maid;
Wallace yeid our without langar abaid.          delay
The wemen sune he sauffyt fra the dede;          death
Waik folk he put and barnys of that stede.          children [out] of
Of purviaunce thai fand litill or nane;          supplies
1130  Befor that tyme thar victaill was all gayne.
Yeit in that place thai lugyt still that nycht,
Fra oystre brocht sic gudis as thai mycht.
Upon the morn the hous thai spoilye fast;          plundered
All thing that doucht out of that place thai          was of use
    cast.
1135  Tre wark thai brynt that was in to tha          Woodwork; burned;
    wanys,          dwellings
Wallis brak doun that stalwart war of
    stanys,          stones
Spylt at thai mycht syne wald no langer          Ruined
    bid;          stay

On till Dundaff that sammyn nycht thai
   ryde
And lugit thar with myrthis and plesance,    *joy*
Thankand gret God that lent thaim sic a    *gave; such*
   chance.

# BOOK SIX

| | | |
|---|---|---|
| | Than passit was utas of Feveryher | octaves |
| | And part of Marche of rycht degestioune; | by; reckoning |
| | Apperyd than the last moneth of wer, | spring [i.e., April] |
| | The syng of somer with his swet sessoun, | sign; sweet season |
| 5 | Be that Wallace of Dundaff maid him boune; | from; ready [to leave] |
| | His leyff he tuk and to Gilbank can fair. | went |
| | The rewmour rais throuch Scotland up and doune, | alarm |
| | With Inglis men, that Wallace leiffand war. | Among; was living |
| | In Aperill quhen cleithit is but weyne | clothed; without doubt |
| 10 | The abill ground be wyrking of natur, | fertile |
| | And woddis has won thar worthy weid of greyne; | woods; got; covering of green |
| | Quhen Nympheus in beldyn of his bour | nymphs; shelter; bower |
| | With oyle and balm fullfillit of swet odour, | sweet |
| | Faunis maceris, as thai war wount to gang,[1] | |
| 15 | Walkyn thar cours in every casuall hour | Follow |
| | To glaid the huntar with thar merye sang. | gladden; song |
| | | |
| | In this samyn tyme to him approchit new | returned |
| | His lusty payne, the quhilk I spak of ayr. | pleasurable pain; earlier |
| | Be luffis cas he thocht for to persew | According to love's chance |
| 20 | In Laynryk toune and thidder he can fayr; | went |
| | At residence a quhill ramaynit thair | Lingered there a while |
| | In hyr presence as I said of befor. | her |
| | Thocht Inglismen was grevyt at his repayr,[2] | |
| | Yeit he desyrd the thing that sat him sor. | troubled him extremely |
| | | |
| 25 | The feyr of wer rewllyt him on sic wis | fire of spring; such a way |
| | He likit weyll with that gudlye to be. | comely one |
| | Quhill wald he think of danger for to rys | At times; on account |
| | And other quhill out of hir presens fle. | times |
| | 'To ces of wer it war the best for me. | war |
| 30 | Thus wyn I nocht bot sadnes on all syde. | I gain nothing except |
| | Sall never man thus cowartys in me se! | cowardice |

1 When nymphs in [the] shelter of his [Faunis's] bower, [which is] sweetly redolent of oil and balm, as officers of Faunus were accustomed to do . . .

2 Even though Englishmen were displeased at his repairing there

To wer I will for chance that may betyd!    *war*

Qwhat is this luff? It is bot gret myschance    *misfortune*
That me wald bryng fra armes utterly.    *would distract me from*
35 I will nocht los my worschip for plesance;    *lose; honour*
In wer I think my tyme till occupy.    *war*
Yeit hyr to luff I will nocht lat forthy;    *to love her; cease*
Mor sall I desyr hyr frendschip to reserve    *keep*
Fra this day furth than ever befor did I,
40 In fer of wer quhether I leiff or sterve.'    *state of war; live; die*

Qwhat suld I say? Wallace was playnly set    *should; determined*
  To luff hyr best in all this warld so wid,    *wide*
Thinkand he suld of his desyr to get;
And so befell be concord in a tid    *agreement; while*
45 That scho maid at his commaund to bid;    *undertook; obey*
And thus began the styntyn of this stryff,    *ending; debate*
Begynnyng band with graith witnes besyd.[1]
Myn auctor sais scho was his rychtwys wyff.    *rightful*

Now leiff in pees, now leiff in gud concord,    *live*
50 Now leyff in blys, now leiff in haill plesance,    *happiness; complete joy*
For scho be chos has bath hyr luff and lord.    *by choice*
He thinkis als luff did him hye avance,    *exalt high*
So evynly held be favour the ballance,    *evenly*
Sen he at will may lap hyr in his armys.    *wrap her [embrace]*
55 Scho thankit God of hir fre happy chance    *great good fortune*
For in his tyme he was the flour of armys.    *flower*

Fortoune him schawit hyr fygowrt doubill face.    *marked*
Feyll sys or than he had beyne set abuff;    *Many times; elevated*
In presoune now, delyverit now throu grace,
60 Now at unes, now in to rest and ruff;    *in distress; quiet*
Now weyll at wyll weyldand his plesand luff,    *well content enjoying*
As thocht him selff out of adversite;    *At this time thought; free*
Desyring ay his manheid for to pruff,    *always; prove*

1 [A] beginning made by agreement before ready witnesses

In curage set apon the stagis hye.                    *placed; high [on Fortune's wheel]*

65   The verray treuth I can nocht graithly tell    *full; readily*
     In to this lyff how lang at thai had beyne;[1]
     Throuch naturall cours of generacioune befell   *it happened*
     A child was chevyt thir twa luffaris betwene,    *conceived; these two lovers*
     Quhilk gudly was, a maydyn brycht and schene.    *comely; fair*
70   So forthyr furth be evyn tyme of hyr age[2]
     A squier Schaw, as that full weyll was seyne,
     This lyflat man hyr gat in mariage.             *wealthy; got her*

     Rycht gudlye men come of this lady ying.        *fine; are descended from*
     Forthyr as now of hyr I spek no mar.
75   Bot Wallace furth in till his wer can ryng;     *went on with his war*
     He mycht nocht ces, gret curage so him bar;     *cease; carried forward*
     Sotheroun to sla for dreid he wald nocht spar,  *spare*
     And thai oft sys feill causis till hym wrocht,  *very often provoked him*
     Fra that tyme furth quhilk movit hym fer mar,   *From; moved*
80   That never in warld out of his mynd was brocht.

     Now leiff thi myrth, now leiff thi haill plesance,   *leave; great pleasure*
     Now leiff thi blis, now leiff thi childis age,       *childhood*
     Now leiff thi youth, now folow thi hard chance,
     Now leyff thi lust, now leiff thi mariage,           *desire*
85   Now leiff thi luff, for thou sall los a gage         *love; lose; pledge*
     Quhilk never in erd sall be redemyt agayne.          *redeemed*
     Folow fortoun and all hir fers outrage.              *violence*
     Go leiff in wer, go leiff in cruell payne.           *live; war; fierce*

     Fy on fortoun, fy on thi frewall quheyll,            *fickle wheel*
90   Fy on thi traist, for her it has no lest;            *good faith; here; lasting*
     Thou transfigowryt Wallace out of his weill          *completely changed; good fortune*

---

1 How long they enjoyed this [married] life
2 So later on when she was the right age

Quhen he traistyt for till haiff lestyt best.   *continued [enjoying] the best*

His plesance her till him was bot a gest;   *happiness here; jest*

Throu thi fers cours that has na hap to ho,   *fierce*

95 Him thou ourthrew out of his likand rest.   *pleasing*

Fra gret plesance in wer, travaill and wo.   *favour in war [to] suffering*


Quhat is fortoune? Quha dryffis the dett
so fast?   *hastens; destiny*

We wait thar is bathe weill and wykit
chance,   *good and evil*

Bot this fals warld with mony doubill cast,   *double dealing [i.e., tricks]*

100 In it is nocht bot verray variance;   *variance*

It is nothing till hevynly governance.   *to*

Than pray we all to the Makar abov,

Quhilk has in hand of justry the ballance,   *justice*

That he us grant of his der lestand love.   *everlasting love*


105 Her of as now forthyr I spek no mar,

Bot to my purpos schortly will I fayr.   *go*

Twelff hundreth yer tharto nynte and sevyn   *1297*

Fra Cryst wes born the rychtwis king of
hevyn,

Wilyham Wallace in to gud liking gais   *happily goes*

110 In Laynrik toun amang his mortaill fais.   *enemies*

The Inglismen that ever fals has beyne,

With Hesilryg quhilk cruell was and keyn   *ruthless*

And Robert Thorn, a felloune sutell
knycht,   *fierce; cunning*

Has founde the way be quhat meyn best
thai mycht,   *[see note]*

115 How that thai suld mak contrar to Wallace

Be argument, as he come upon cace

On fra the kyrk that was without the toune,

Quhill thar power mycht be in harnes   *armour*
boune.   *ready*

Schyr Jhon the Grayme, bathe hardy, wys
and trew,

120 To Laynrik come, gud Wallace to persew

Of his weyllfayr, as he full oft had seyne.[1]

Gud men he had in cumpany fifteen

---

1 Came to Lanark to check on the welfare of good Wallace, as he had often done before

And Wallace nine, thai war na feris ma. — *companions more*

Upon the morn unto the mes thai ga, — *they attended mass*

125 Thai and thar men graithit in gudly greyn, — *dressed in fine green clothing*

For the sesson sic oys full lang has beyne.[1]

Quhen sadly thai had said thar devocioune, — *seriously; their prayers*

Ane argwnde thaim as thai went throuch the toun, — *One [of the English] challenged*

The starkast man that Hesylryg than knew, — *strongest*

130 And als he had of lychly wordis ynew. — *contemptuous; enough*

He salust thaim as it war bot in scorn: — *greeted; only*

'Dewgar, gud day, bone senyhour and gud morn.' — *Greeting!*

'Quhom scornys thou?' quod Wallace, — *Whom do you scorn?*

'Quha lerd thee?' — *taught*

'Quhy, schir,' he said, 'come yhe nocht new our se? — *recently from overseas*

135 Pardoun me than, for I wend ye had beyne — *thought*

Ane inbasset to bryng ane uncouth queyne.' — *ambassador; foreign*

Wallace answerd, 'Sic pardoune as we haiff

In oys to gyff thi part thou sall nocht craiff.'[2]

'Sen ye ar Scottis yeit salust sall ye be: — *yet greeted*

140 Gude deyn, dawch lard, bach lowch, banyoch a de.'

Ma Sotheroune men to thaim assemblit ner. — *More Englishmen; near*

Wallace as than was laith to mak a ster. — *loath; stir*

Ane maid a scrip and tyt at his lang sworde.[3]

'Hald still thi hand,' quod he, 'and spek thi word.'

145 'With thi lang swerd thou makis mekill bost.'

'Tharof,' quod he, 'thi deme maid litill cost.' — *lady; uttered little [on your account]*

'Quhat caus has thou to wer that gudlye greyne?' — *wear; handsome green*

'My maist caus is bot for to mak thee teyne.' — *greatest reason is only; angry*

---

1 Such has long been the custom in this season

2 You shall not be denied such pardon as we are able to give

3 One made gibe/obscene gesture and pulled at his long sword/penis

'Quhat suld a Scot do with so fair a knyff?'          dagger/penis
150   'Sa said the prest that last janglyt thi wyff.          priest; lay with
That woman lang has tillit him so fair               served
Quhill that his child worthit to be thine            Until; grew
      ayr.'                                          heir
'Me think,' quod he, 'thou dryvys me to
      scorn.'
'Thi deme has beyne japyt or thou was                mother; tricked before
      born.'
155   The power than assemblyt thaim about,                armed company
Twa hundreth men that stalwart war and               brave were; bold
      stout.
The Scottis saw thar power was
      cummand,
Schir Robert Thorn and Hesilryg at hand,             close by
The multitude wyth wapynnys burnist                  burnished well
      beyne.
160   The worthi Scottis, quhilk cruell was and            fierce; bold
      keyne,
Amang Sotherone sic dyntis gaiff that tyd            English such blows; time
Quhill blud on breid byrstyt fra woundis             Until; spurted everywhere
      wyd.                                           wide
Wallace in stour wes cruelly fechtand;               combat; fiercely fighting
Fra a Sotheroune he smat off the rycht               severed
      hand,
165   And quhen that carle of fechtyng mycht no            fellow; fighting
      mar,
With the left hand in ire held a buklar;             shield
Than fra the stowmpe the blud out spurgyt            stump; gushed
      fast,
In Wallace face aboundandlye can out                 splattered across
      cast;
Into gret part it merryt of his sicht.               spoiled his sight a great deal
170   Schyr Jhone the Grayme a straik has tayne            blow; delivered
      him rycht
With his gud swerd upon the Sotherone
      syr,
Derffly to ded draiff him in to that ire.            Killed him outright in rage
The perell was rycht awfull, hard and                frightening
      strang,
The stour enduryt mervalusly and lang.               fighting; long
175   The Inglismen gaderit fellone fast;                  extremely
The worthi Scottis the gait left at the last.        street

Quhen thai had slayne and woundyt mony man, — many men

Till Wallace in the gaynest way thai can — To; nearest

Thai passit sune, defendand tham richt weill. — soon

180 He and Schir Jhone with swerdis stiff of steill — swords; steel

Behind thar men, quhill thai the yett had tayne. — [Remained] behind; until; gate, reached

The woman than, quhilk was full will of wayne, — in despair

The perell saw with fellone noyis and dyne, — terrible; din

Gat up the yett and leit thaim enter in. — Raised the gate

185 Throuch till a strenth thai passit of that steid. — stronghold; from; place

Fifty Sotheroun upon the gait wes dede. — street

This fair woman did besines and hir mycht — everything in her power

The Inglismen to tary with a slycht, — delay; stratagem

Quhill that Wallace on to the wood wes past; — While; slipped away to the wood

190 Than Cartlane craggis thai persewit full fast.[1]

Quhen Sotheroun saw that chapyt wes Wallace — escaped

Agayne thai turnyt, the woman tuk on cace, — returned; arrested the woman

Put hir to dede, I can nocht tell you how;

Of sic mater I may nocht tary now. — On such a subject

195 Quhar gret dulle is but rademyng agayne — grief; without remedy

Newyn of it is bot ekyng of payne. — Renewing; increase

A trew woman, had servit hir full lang, — loyal; [who] had served

Out of the toun the gaynest way can gang, — nearest; went

Till Wallace tald how all this deid was done. — To; deed

200 The paynfull wo socht till his hart full sone; — went straight to his heart

War nocht for schayme he had socht to the ground — shame; fallen

For bytter baill that in his breyst was bound. — sorrow; kept fast

Schir Jhone the Grayme, bath wys, gentill and fre, — noble; generous

1 Then made their way quickly to Cartland Crags

Gret murnynge maid that pete was to se,    *mourning*

205 And als the laiff that was assemblit thar    *also the rest*

For pur sorow wepyt with hart full sar.    *pure; sorely*

Quhen Wallace feld thar curage was so small    *sensed*

He fenyeit him for to comfort thaim all.    *concealed his feelings*

'Ces men,' he said, 'this is a butlas payne.    *Cease; unavailing*

210 We can nocht now chewys hyr lyff agayne.'    *bring her back to life*

Unes a word he mycht bryng out for teyne,    *Scarcely; utter; grief*

The bailfull teris bryst braithly fra his eyne.    *woeful; burst suddenly from*

Sichand he said, 'Sall never man me se    *Sighing*

Rest in till eys quhill this deid wrokyn be,    *easy until; be avenged*

215 The saklace slaughter of hir blith and brycht,[1]

That I avow to the Makar of mycht,

That of that nacioune I sall never forber    *spare*

Yhong nor ald that abill is to wer.    *old; fit to fight*

Preystis no wemen I think nocht for to sla    *slay*

220 In my defaut, bot thai me causing ma.[2]

Schir Jhon,' he said, 'lat all this murnyng be,

And for hir saik thar sall ten thousand de.    *die*

Quhar men may weipe thar curage is the les;    *Whenever; less*

It slakis ire of wrang thai suld radres.'[3]

225 Of thar complaynt as now I say no mar.    *lament; more*

Gud Awchinlek of Gilbank, dwelyt thar,    *who dwelt there*

Quhen he hard tell of Wallace vexacioune,    *heard*

To Cartlane wood with ten men maid him boune.    *made his way*

Wallace he fand sum part within the nycht;

230 To Laynryk toun in all haist thai thaim dycht.    *set out*

The wache of thaim as than had litill heid;    *sentries; heed*

Partyt thar men and divers gatis yeid.    *Divided; ways went*

Schir Jhone the Grayme and his gud cumpany

To Schir Robert of Thorn full fast thai hy.    *hasten*

---

1 The slaughter of an innocent creature, blithe and beautiful
2 Wrongfully, unless they give me cause
3 It lessens anger [provoked] by wrongs they should redress

235  Wallace and his to Hesilrige sone past
     In a heich hous quhar he was slepand fast,   *high; sound asleep*
     Straik at the dure with his fute hardely   *Kicked the door*
     Quhill bar and brais in the flair he gart ly.   *Until; floor; made*
     The schirreff criyt, 'Quha makis that gret   *Who*
        deray?'   *din*
240  'Wallace,' he said, 'that thou has socht all
        day.
     The womannis dede, will God, thou sall   *woman's death, God willing,*
        der by.'   *pay for dearly*
     Hesilrige thocht it was na tyme to ly;   *lie [in bed]*
     Out of that hous full fayne he wald haiff   *gladly*
        beyne.
     The nycht was myrk yeit Wallace has him   *dark yet*
        seyne,
245  Freschly him straik as he come in gret ire,   *Vigorously; rage*
     Apon the heid birstit throuch bayne and   *head; broke; bone and flesh*
        lyr.
     The scherand swerd glaid till his coler   *cutting; went smoothly*
        bayne,
     Out our the stayr amang thaim is he gayne.   *over*
     Gude Awchinlek trowit nocht that he was   *didn't believe*
        dede,
250  Thrys with a knyff stekit him in that stede.   *Thrice; stabbed; place*
     The scry about rais rudly on the streyt;   *noise; rose; loudly; street*
     Feyll of the layff war fulyeit under feyt.   *Many; rest; trampled*
     Yong Hesilryg and wicht Wallace is met;   *bold*
     A sekyr strak Wilyham has on him set,   *sure blow*
255  Derffly to dede off the stair dang him
        doune.[1]
     Mony thai slew that nycht in Laynrik
        toune,
     Sum grecis lap and sum stekit within.   *leapt up the flight of stairs*
     A-ferd thai war with hidwis noyis and   *Frightened; were; hideous;*
        dyne.   *din*
     Schir Jhone the Grayme had set the hous
        in fyr
260  Quhar Robert Thorn was brynt up bayne   *burned up bone and flesh*
        and lyr.
     Twelve scor thai slew that wes of Ingland
        born;

1 Violently to [his] death he threw him down the stairs

Wemen thai levit and preistis on the morn
To pas thar way, of blys and gudis bar,[1]
And swor that thai agayne suld cum no
    mar.

265    Quhen Scottis hard thir fyne tithingis of      *heard this excellent news*
    new
     Out of all part to Wallace fast thai drew,      *From all over*
     Plenyst the toun quhilk was thar heretage.      *Settled*
     Thus Wallace straiff agayne that gret      *strove against*
    barnage.
     Sa he begane with strenth and stalwart
    hand

270    To chewys agayne sum rowmys of      *recover; parts*
    Scotland.
     The worthi Scottis that semblit till him      *flocked to*
    thar
     Chesit him for cheyff, thar chyftayne and      *Chose*
    ledar.
     Amer Wallang, a suttell terand knycht,      *cunning tyrant*
     In Bothwell dwelt, King Edwardis man full      *completely*
    rycht.

275    Murray was out, thocht he was rychtwis      *exiled*
    lord
     Of all that land, as trew men will racord;
     In till Aran he was dwelland that tyd,      *dwelling; time*
     And other ma, in this land durst nocht      *many others; dared*
    bide.      *stay*
     Bot this fals knycht in Bothwell wonnand      *i.e., Valence; dwelling*
    was.

280    A man he gert sone to King Edward pas      *made*
     And tald him haill of Wallace ordinance,      *Wallace's actions*
     How he had put his pepill to mischance      *people; misfortune*
     And playnly was ryssyn agayne to ryng.      *had risen; power*
     Grevit thar at rycht gretly wes the king;      *Vexed*
285    Throuch all Ingland he gart his doaris cry      *agents; proclaim*
     Power to get, and said he wald planly      *A call to arms; openly*
     In Scotland pas that rewme to statut new.      *realm; rule anew*
     Feill men of wer till him full fast thai drew.      *Many; war*
     The queyne feld weill how that his purpos      *perceived; what he intended*
    was;

1 In the morning they allowed women and priests to go their way, unhappy
and dispossessed

| | | |
|---|---|---|
| 290 | Till him scho went, on kneis syne can him as | To; then asked |
| | He wald resist and nocht in Scotland gang; | stop; go |
| | He suld haiff dreid to wyrk so felloune wrang. | fear; grievous |
| | 'Crystyne thai ar, yone is thar heretage; | Christians |
| | To reyff that croune that is a gret outrage.' | steal |
| 295 | For hyr consaill at hayme he wald nocht byde; | her counsel; home |
| | His lordis hym set in Scotland for to ryde.[1] | |
| | A Scottis man, than dwellyt with Edward, | |
| | Quhen he hard tell that Wallace tuk sic part, | took such a position [i.e., had rebelled] |
| | He staw fra thaim als prevale as he may. | stole away |
| 300 | In to Scotland he come apon a day, | came |
| | Sekand Wallace he maid him reddy boune. | ready to go |
| | This Scot was born at Kyle in Rycardtoune; | Riccarton |
| | All Ingland cost he knew it wonder weill, | England's coast |
| | Fra Hull about to Brysto everilk deill, | |
| 305 | Fra Carleill throuch Sandwich that ryoll stede, | royal place |
| | Fra Dover our on to Sanct Beis hede. | St Bee's Head |
| | In Pykarte and Flandrys he hade beyne, | |
| | All Normonde and Frans haill he had seyne; | |
| | A pursivant till King Edward in wer, | war |
| 310 | Bot he couth never gar him his armes ber. | make coat of arms |
| | Of gret statur and sum part gray wes he; | size |
| | The Inglis men cald him bot Grymmysbe. | simply called him |
| | To Wallace come and in to Kile him fand; | found |
| | He tald him haill the tithandis of Ingland. | news from |
| 315 | Thai turnyt his name fra tyme thai him knew | changed |
| | And cald him Jop; of ingen he wes trew; | nature; loyal |
| | In all his tyme gud service in him fand; | |
| | Gaiff him to ber the armes of Scotland. | Gave; bear; coat of arms |
| | Wallace agayne in Cliddisdaill sone raid | rode |
| 320 | And his power semblit withoutyn baid. | delay |
| | He gart commaund quha that his pees wald tak, | decreed |

[1] He arranged for his lords to ride to Scotland

A fre remyt he suld ger to thaim mak · *pardon; arrange*
For alkyn deid that thai had doyne beforn. · *every kind; done*
The Perseys pees and Schir Ranaldis wes worn. · *had lapsed*
325 Feill till him drew that bauldly durst abid · *dared to withstand*
Of Wallace kyn fra mony divers sid. · *kinsfolk*
Schir Ranald than send him his power haill; · *entire army*
Him selff durst nocht be knawine in battaill · *known*
Agayne Sotheroun, for he had made a band · *Against the English; bond*
330 Lang tyme befor to hald of thaim his land. · *A long time; hold from*
Adam Wallace past out of Ricardtoun,
And Robert Boid with gud men of renown.
Of Cunyngayme and Kille come men of vaill, · *From Kyle; valuable men*
To Laynrik socht on hors, a thousand haill.[1]
335 Schyr Jhone the Grayme and his gud chevalre,
Schir Jhone of Tynto with men that he mycht be,
Gud Awchinlek, that Wallace uncle was,
Mony trew Scot with that chyftayne couth pas. · *travelled*
Thre thousand haill of likly men in wer · *in all; men fit for war*
340 And feill on fute quhilk wantyt hors and ger. · *many; lacked; weapons*
The tyme be this has cummand apon hand, · *By this time; come*
The awfull ost with Edward of Ingland · *awesome army*
To Beggar come, with sexte thousand men,
In wer wedis that cruell war to ken. · *armour; fierce; see*
345 Thai playntyt thar feild with tentis and pailyonis, · *planted* / *pavilions*
Quhar claryouns blew full mony mychty sonis; · *clarions* / *sounds*
Plenyst that place with gud wittaill and wyne, · *Supplied; food*
In cartis brocht thar purviance devyne. · *God-sent provisions*
The awfull king gert twa harroldis be brocht, · *awesome; made; heralds*
350 Gaiff thaim commaund in all the haist thai mocht · *Ordered* / *might*

---

1 To Lanark made their way on horses, a thousand in all

To charge Wallace, that he sulde cum him
    till                                          command; come to him
Withtout promys and put him in his will:        Unconditionally; submit
'Be caus we wait he is a gentill man,           know; noble
Cum in my grace and I sall saiff him than.      [If] he comes; save
As for his lyff I will apon me tak,             For [the rest] of his life
And effter this gyff he couth service mak,      after; if he serves me
He sall haiff wage that may him weill           payment
    suffice.
That rebald wenys for he has done               rebel is proud; defeated
    supprice
To my pepill oft apon aventur.                  by chance
Aganys me he may nocht lang endur:              Against
To this proffyr gaynstandand giff he be,        If he resists this offer
Her I avow he sall be hyngyt hye.'              Here; vow; hanged high
A yong squier, was brother to Fehew,            Fitzhugh
He thocht he wald dysgysit to persew            disguise himself
Wallace to se that tuk so hie a part;           undertook so much
Born sister sone he was to King Edwart.         He was Edward's nephew
A cot of armes he tuk on him but baid,          without delay
With the harroldis full prevaly he raid
To Tynto hill withoutyn residens,               waiting
Quhar Wallace lay with his folk at
    defence.
A likly ost as of so few thai fand;             impressive army for so few
Till hym thai socht and wald no langer          They made their way directly
    stand.                                          to him [Wallace]
'Gyff ye be he that rewllis all this thing,[1]
Credence we haiff brocht fra our worthi         Credentials
    king.'
Than Wallace gert thre knychtis till him        summoned
    call,
Syne red the wryt in presens of thaim all.      read; writ
To thaim he said, 'Answer ye sall nocht         You won't want for an
    craiff.                                         answer
Be wryt or word, quhilk likis you best till     In writing or verbally which
    haiff?'
'In wryt,' thai said, 'it war the liklyast.'    most fitting
Than Wallace thus began to dyt in hast:         compose a reply hastily
'Thou reyffar king chargis me throu cas         robber-king; because of a
                                                    mere circumstance

355
360
365
370
375
380

1 If you are the leader of all this thing [rebellion]

That I suld cum and put me in thi grace.
Gyff I gaynstand thou hechtis till hyng me.   If I resist; vow; hang
I vow to God and ever I may tak thee   if ever
385 Thou sall be hangyt, ane exempill to geiff   provide
To kingis of reyff als lang as I may leiff.[1]
Thou profferis me thi wage for till haiff.
I thee defy power, and all the laiff   repudiate your power; others
At helpis thee her of thi fals nacioun.   That; here
390 Will God thou sall be put of this regioune,   expelled from
Or de tharfor, contrar thocht thou had   even though you had sworn
    sworne.     the contrary
Thou sall us se or nine houris to morn   see us before nine o'clock
Battaill to gyff magra of all thi kyn,   Ready for battle in spite of
For falsly thou sekis our rewme within.'   to occupy our realm
395 This wryt he gaiff to the harraldis but mar,   at once
And gud reward he gart delyver thaim   had handed to them
    thar.
Bot Jop knew weyll the squier yong Fehew   young
And tald Wallace, for he wes ever trew.   loyal
Than he command that thai suld sone   seize them immediately
    thaim tak.
400 Him selff began a sair cusyng to mak.   severe accusation
'Squier,' he said, 'sen thou has fenyeit   falsely assumed [heraldic]
    armys,     arms
On thee sall fall the fyrst part of thir   these injuries
    harmys,
Sampill to geyff till all thi fals nacioune.'   Example; make
Apon the hill he gert thaim set him downe,
405 Straik off his hed or thai wald forthir go.   Struck; before
To the herrold said syne withoutyn ho,   without pause
'For thou art fals till armys and   perjured
    maynsworn
Throuch thi chokkis thi tong sall be out   cheeks; tongue; cut out
    schorn.'
Quhen that was doyne than to the thrid
    said he,
410 'Armys to juge thou sall never graithly se.'   readily see
He gert a smyth with his turkas rycht thar   made; smith; pair of pincers
Pow out his eyne, syne gaiff thaim leiff to   Pull; eyes; leave
    far.     go
'To your fals king thi falow sall thee leid;   lead

1 To Kings [of the consequences] of robbery as long as I may live

|     | |     |
| --- | --- | --- |
|     | With  my answer turs him his nevois heid. | pack for; nephew's head |
| 415 | Thus sar I drede thi king and all his bost.' | extremely; fear; threatening |
|     | His dum falow led him on to thar ost. | |
|     | Quhen King Edward his herroldis thus has seyne | |
|     | In propyr ire he wox ner wode for teyne, | grew; mad with grief |
|     | That he nocht wyst on quhat wis him to wreke; | way; avenge himself |
| 420 | For sorow almaist a word he mycht nocht spek. | speak |
|     | A lang quhill he stud wrythand in a rage. | |
|     | On loud he said, 'This is a fell outrage. | grievous |
|     | This deid to Scottis full der it sall be bocht; | Scots will pay dearly for this action |
|     | Sa dispitfull in warld was never wrocht. | so malicious [a deed] |
| 425 | Of this regioun I think nocht for to gang | leave |
|     | Quhill tyme that I sall se that rybald hang.'[1] | |
|     | Lat I him thus in till his sorow dwell; | I leave him thus |
|     | Of thai gud Scottis schortly I will you tell. | |
|     | Furth fra his men than Wallace rakit rycht; | Further; went directly |
| 430 | Till him he cald Schir Jhon Tynto the knycht, | |
|     | And leit him witt to wesy himselff wald ga | let him know; reconnoitre; go |
|     | The Inglis ost, and bad him tell na ma, | [To;] ordered; no-one else |
|     | Quhat ever thai speryt, quhill that he come agayne. | asked, until; returned |
|     | Wallace dysgysit thus bounyt out the playne. | set out for the plain |
| 435 | Betwix Culter and Bygar as he past | Culter; Biggar |
|     | He was sone war quhar a werk man come fast, | aware; labourer; approached |
|     | Dryfande a mere and pychars had to sell. | Driving; mare; pitchers |
|     | 'Gud freynd,' he said, 'in treuth will thou me tell | |
|     | With this chaffar quhar passis thou treuly?' | merchandise |
| 440 | 'Till ony, schir, quha likis for to by. | To any; who; buy |
|     | It is my crafft and I wald sell thaim fayne.' | occupation; willingly |

1 Until the day I see that rebel hang

'I will thaim by, sa God me saiff fra payne.   buy
Quhat price lat her. I will tak thaim
ilkayne.'[1]
'Bot half a mark, for sic prys haiff I tayne.'   Only; incurred
445  'Twenty schillingis,' Wallace said, 'thou sall
haiff.
I will haiff mer, pychars and als the laiff.   the mare; also the rest
Thi gowne and hois in haist thou put off   stockings
syne   next
And mak a chang, for I sall geyff thee   change; give
myne,
And thi ald hud becaus it is thred bar.'   old hood; threadbare
450  The man wend weyll that he had scornyt   thought; mocked
him thar.
'Do tary nocht, it is suth I thee say.'   the truth
The man kest off his febill weid of gray,   threw; meagre grey garment
And Wallace his and payit silver in hand.
'Pas on,' he said, 'thou art a proud
merchand.'
455  The gown and hois in clay that claggit   stockings; clogged
was,
The hude heklyt, and maid him for to pas.   fringed
The qwhipe he tuk syne furth the mar can   whip; then summoned the
call.   mare
Atour a bray the omast pot gert fall,   Going over a hill; uppermost
Brak on the ground; the man lewch at his   laughed; way of going
fair,
460  'Bot thou be war thou tynys of thi   Unless; careful; will lose;
chaiffair.'   wares
The sone be than was passit out of sicht;   sun; disappeared
The day our went and cummyn was the   past
nycht.
Amang Sotheroun full besyly he past;   the English
On ather side his eyne he gan to cast   either
465  Quhar lordis lay and had thar lugeyng   camp
maid,
The kingis palyone quhar on the libardis   pavilion; leopards
baid;   stood
Spyand full fast quhar his availl suld be   advantage should
And couth weyll luk and wynk with the   look
ta e.   other eye

1 Let me know [hear] the price. I will take every one of them

Sum scornyt him, sum 'gleid carll' cald him thar; — 'squint-eyed fellow' called

470 Agrevit thai war for thar herroldis mysfayr. — Vexed; mishap

Sum sperd at him how he sald of the best. — what was his best price

'For forty pens,' he said, 'quhill thai may lest.' — pence

Sum brak a pot, sum pyrlit at his e. — poked

Wallace fled out and prevale leit thaim be; — let

475 On till his ost agayne he past full rycht. — host; straight away

His men be than had tayne Tynto the knycht. — by then; seized

Schyr Jhon the Grayme gert bynd him wonder fast, — securely

For he wyst weill he was with Wallace last:

Sum bad byrn him, sum hang him in a cord; — wished to burn; on a rope

480 Thai swor that he had dissavit thar lord. — deceived

Wallace be this was entryt thaim amang; — by this time

Till him he yeid and wald nocht tary lang, — went

Syne he gart lous him of thai bandis new — Then; had him loosed from

And said he was baith suffer, wys and trew. — both trusty

485 To souper sone thai bound but mar abaid. — supper soon

He tald to thaim quhat merket he had maid, — trading

And how at he the Sotheroun saw full weill. — that; English

Schyr Jhon the Grayme displessit was sumdeill

And said till him, 'Nocht chyftaynlik it was — It was not chieftain-like

490 Throu wilfulnes in sic perell to pas.' — headstrong conduct; such

Wallace answerd, 'Or we wyn Scotland fre — achieve Scotland's freedom

Baith ye and I in mar perell mon be, — Both; more; must

And mony other the quhilk full worthi is.

Now of a thing we do sumpart amys, — somewhat amiss

495 A litill slepe I wald fayne that we had, — a little; be glad

With yone men syne luk how we may us glaid.'[1]

The worthi Scottis tuk gud rest quhill ner day. — until near

1 Then consider how we may entertain ourselves [at the expense of] those men

|     | Than rais thai up, till ray sone ordand thai. | to battle order; arranged |
|-----|---|---|
|     | The hill thai left and till a playne is gayne; | went |
| 500 | Wallace him selff the vantgard he has tayne; | vanguard / assumed command |
|     | With him was Boid and Awchinlek but dreid, | without doubt |
|     | With a thousand of worthi men in weid. | men in armour |
|     | Als mony syne in the mydwart put he; | As; middle force |
|     | Schir Jhone the Grayme he gert thar ledar be, | made |
| 505 | With him Adam, young lord of Ricardtoun, |  |
|     | And Somervaill, a squier of renoun. |  |
|     | The thrid thousand in rerward he dycht, | to the rearguard; assigned |
|     | Till Walter gaiff of Newbyggyn the knycht, | gave |
|     | With him Tynto that douchty wes in deid | was bold in deed |
| 510 | And Davi son of Schir Walter, to leid. | lead |
|     | Behynd thaim ner the fute men gert he be | close behind; foot soldiers |
|     | And bade thaim bid quhill thai thar tyme mycht se: | commanded; stay until |
|     | 'Ye want wapynnys and harnes in this tid; | lack; armour; at this time |
|     | The fyrst counter ye may nocht weill abid.' | encounter; withstand |
| 515 | Wallace gert sone the chyftaynis till him call. |  |
|     | This charge he gaiff, for chance that mycht befall, | order; whatever might happen |
|     | Till tak no heid to ger nor of pylage, | pay no heed; pillage |
|     | 'For thai will fle as wod men in a rage. | mad |
|     | Wyne fyrst the men, the gud syne ye may haiff; | Conquer; goods afterwards |
| 520 | Than tak na tent of covatys to craiff. | pay no attention; greed |
|     | Throuch covatys sum losis gud and lyff; | goods and life |
|     | I commaund you forber sic in our stryff. | keep away from such; battle |
|     | Luk that ye saiff na lord, capteyne nor knycht; | spare |
|     | For worschipe wyrk and for our eldris rycht. | ancestors |
| 525 | God blys us that we may in our viage | bless; enterprise |
|     | Put thir fals folk out of our heretage.' | these |
|     | Than thai inclynd all with a gudly will; | bowed |
|     | His playne commaund thai hecht for to fullfill. | promised |
|     | On the gret ost thir partice fast can draw, | these divisions; approached |

530  Cumand to thaim out of the south thai saw        Coming
     Thre hundreth men in till thar armour            bright
       cler,
     The gaynest way to thaim approchit ner.          nearest; close
     Wallace said sone thai war na Inglismen,         soon; not
     'For by this ost the gatis weyll thai ken.'[1]

535  Thom Haliday thai men he gydyt rycht;            those; guided
     Of Anadderdaill he had thaim led that
       nycht,
     His twa gud sonnis, Jhonstoun and
       Rudyrfurd.
     Wallace was blyth fra he had hard thar           pleased when; heard call
       wourd,                                           [lit. voice]
     So was the laiff of his gud chevalry.            rest

540  Jarden thar come in till thar cumpany,           into
     And Kyrkpatrik, befor in Esdaill was,
     A weyng thai war in Wallace ost to pas.          [military] wing
     The Inglis wach, that nycht had beyne on
       steir,                                          astir
     Drew to thar ost rycht as the day can per.      dawned

545  Wallace knew weill, for he befor had
       seyne,
     The kingis palyon quhar it was buskit            pavilion; had been pitched
       beyne.
     Than with rych hors the Scottis befor            fine horses
       thaim raid;                                     rode
     The fyrst counter so gret abaysing maid          encounter; discomfiture
     That all the ost was stunyst of that sicht;      dismayed sight [of the; Scots]

550  Full mony ane derffly to ded was dicht.          Very many were violently
                                                         killed

     Feill of thaim was as than out of aray,          Many; in disarray
     The mair haiste and awfull was the fray.         more; frightening; din
     The noyis rouschit throuch strakis that thai     deafened; blows
       dang;                                          struck
     The rewmour rais so rudly thaim amang            alarm; strongly

555  That all the ost was than in poynt to fle.       at the point of fleeing
     The wys lordis fra thai the perell se,
     The fellone fray all rasyt wes about             terrible din; roused
     And how thar king stud in so mekill dout,        such great danger
     Till his palyone how mony thousand socht

560  Him to reskew be ony way thai mocht.             any; might

     1 For by [the look of it] this army knows the roads well

The Erll of Kent that nycht walkand had          watching
  beyne
With five thousand of men in armour
  cleyne;                                         bright
About the king full sodandly thai gang,          went
And traistis weill the sailye wes rycht          [you may] well believe;
  strang.                                           assault
565  All Wallace folk in wys of wer was gud,      ways of war; experienced
In to the stour syne lychtyt quhar thai stud.    battle; then dismounted
Quham ever thai hyt na harnes mycht
  thaim stynt
Fra thai on fute semblit with swerdis dynt.[1]
Of manheid thai in hartis cruell was,            fierce were
570  Thai thocht to wyn or never thine to pas.    from there
Feill Inglismen befor the king thai slew.        Many
Schir Jhon the Grayme come with his
  power new.
Amang the ost with the mydwart he raid;          middle division
Gret martyrdome on Sotheroun men thai           slaughter; the English
  maid.
575  The rerward than set on sa hardely,          rearguard then; so
With Newbyggyn and all the chevalry.
Palyone rapys thai cuttyt into sounder,          Tent ropes; to pieces
Borne to the ground and mony smoryt             smothered
  ounder.                                        under
The fute men come the quhilk I spak of          spoke; earlier
  ayr,
580  On frayt folk set strakis sad and sayr.      frightened; strokes firm; sore
Thocht thai befor wantyt bath hors and          Although; lacked both;
  ger,                                             weapons
Anewch thai gat quhat thai wald vaill to        Enough; obtained which;
  wer.                                             choose for war
The Scottis power than all togydder war;
The kingis palyon brymly doun thai bar.         fiercely; bore
585  The Erll of Kent with a gud ax in hand
In to the stour full stoutly couth he stand     battle; boldly
Befor the king, makand full gret debait.        offering; resistance
Quha best did than he had the heast stait.      highest place [of honour]
The felloune stour so stalwart was and          terrible fighting
  strang,

1 Whomever they hit with sword blows, no armour could stop them,/ Once
they assembled on foot

| | | |
|---|---|---|
| 590 | Thar to contened mervalusly and lang. | continued |
| | Wallace him self full sadly couth persew | steadfastly conducted himself |
| | And at a straik that cheiff chyftayne he slew. | stroke; prime |
| | The Sotheron folk fled fast and durst nocht byd, | English; dared |
| | Horssit thar king and off the feild couth ride, | Put their king on horseback; rode |
| 595 | Agaynis his will, for he was laith to fle; | loath |
| | In to that tyme he thocht nocht for to de. | did not expect |
| | Of his best men four thousand thar was dede | |
| | Or he couth fynd to fle and leiff that stede. | Before; was persuaded; leave |
| | Twenty thousand with him fled in a staill. | body |
| 600 | The Scottis gat hors and folowit that battaill. | got; battalion |
| | Throuch Culter hope or tyme thai wan the hycht[1] | |
| | Feill Sotheroun folk was merryt in thar mycht, | Many English; injured |
| | Slayne be the gait as thar king fled away. | by the wayside |
| | Bathe fair and brycht and rycht cler was the day, | |
| 605 | The sone ryssyn, schynand our hill and daill. | over; dale |
| | Than Wallace kest quhat was his grettest vaill. | considered; advantage |
| | The fleand folk that of the feild fyrst past | fleeing; battlefield |
| | In to thar king agayne releiffit fast. | Unto; rallied |
| | Fra athir sid so mony semblit thar | From either side; assembled |
| 610 | That Wallace wald lat folow thaim no mar: | not allow [his men] to follow |
| | Befor he raid, gart his folk turn agayne. | In front; rode; made |
| | Of Inglismen seven thousand thar was slayne. | |
| | Than Wallace ost agayne to Beggar raid | Wallace's army; rode |
| | Quhar Inglismen gret purvians had maid. | provision |
| 615 | The jowalre as it was thidder led, | valuables |
| | Palyonnis and all, thai leiffit quhen thai fled. | left behind |

1 Through Culter Valley before they had time to climb the hill

The Scottis gat gold, gud, ger and other wage; — *goods; weapons; reward*

Relevyt thai war at partit that pilage. — *divided; those spoils*

To meit thai went with myrthis and plesance; — *dinner; in good spirits*

620  Thai sparyt nocht King Edwardis purveance. — *They did not skimp with; supplies*

With solace syne a litill sleyp thai ta; — *Refreshed then; took*

A preva wach he gert amang thaim ga. — *secret scout; made; so*

Twa kukis fell, thair lyffis for to saiff, — *fierce rascals; save*

With dede corssys that lay unputt in graiff; — *corpses; unburied*

625  Quhen thai saw weyll the Scottis war at rest,

Out of the feild to steill thaim thocht it best. — *steal away*

Full law thai crap quhill thai war out of sicht, — *low; crept; until*

Efter the ost syne rane in all thar mycht. — *After; English host; ran*

Quhen that the Scottis had slepyt bot a quhill, — *only a short while*

630  Than rais thai up, for Wallace dredyt gyll. — *rose; guile*

He said to thaim, 'The Sotherone may persewe — *English; renew the attack on us*

Agayne to us for thai ar folk enew. — *there are enough of them*

Quhar Inglis men provisioune makis in wer — *provision; war*

It is full hard to do thaim mekill der. — *much harm*

635  On this playne feild we will thaim nocht abid; — *open*

To sum gud strenth my purpos is to ryd.' — *stronghold*

The purveance that left was in that stede — *supplies; place*

To Ropis bog he gert servandis it lede, — *made; lead*

With ordinance at Sothroun brocht it thar. — *the provisions that*

640  He with the ost to Davis schaw can far — *went*

And thar ramaynede a gret space of the day. — *remained; part*

Of Inglismen yeit sum thing will I say.

As King Edwart throuch Culter hoppis socht, — *made his way*

Quhen he persavit the Scottis folowed nocht, — *perceived*

645  In Jhonnys Greyne he gert the ost ly still. — *John's Green*

Feill fleand folk assemblit sone him till. — *Many; soon*

Quhen thai war met the king ner worthit mad     *nearly became*
For his der kyn that he thar lossyt had;     *lost*
His twa emys into the feild was slayne,     *two uncles*
650 His secund sone that mekill was of mayne,     *son; of great strength*
His brother Hew was kelyt thar full cald,     *killed; cold*
The Erll of Kent, that cruell berne and bald,     *fierce baron bold*
With gret worschip tuk ded befor the king.     *died*
For him he murnyt als lang as he mycht ryng.     *mourned; reigned*

655 At this semlay as thai in sorow stand,     *gathering; stood*
The twa kukis come sone in at his hand     *rascals soon approached him*
And tald till him how thai enchapyt war:     *had escaped*
'The Scottis all as swyne lyis dronkyn thar     *like swine lie drunk there*
Of our wicht wyne ye gert us thidder led;     *From; strong wine; lead*
660 Full weill we may be vengit of thar ded.     *avenged; deed*
A payne our lyvis it is suth that we tell:     *On pain of our lives*
Raturne agayne, ye sall fynd thaim your sell.'     *Return / self*
He blamyt thaim and said na witt it was     *reproached; it made no sense*
That he agayne for sic a taill suld pas.     *such a tale*
665 'Thar chyftayne is rycht mervalus in wer;     *war*
Fra sic perell he can full weill thaim ber.     *protect*
To sek him mar as now I will nocht ryd;     *ride*
Our meit is lost tharfor we may nocht byd.'     *food; stay*
The hardy Duk of Longcastell and lord,
670 'Soverane,' he said, 'till our consaill concord.     *counsel / agree*
Gyff this be trew ye haiff the mar availl.     *If; advantage*
We may thaim wyne and mak bot licht travaill.     *defeat / effort*
War yon folk dede quha may agayne us stand?     *Were those; dead*
Than neid we nocht for meit to leiff the land.'[1]
675 The king answerd, 'I will nocht rid agayne,     *ride [back]*
As at this tyme my purpos is in playne.'     *plain*
The duk said, 'Schir, gyff ye contermyt be,     *are firmly set against it*
To mowff you mor it afferis nocht for me.     *move; becomes*
Commaund power agayne with me to wend     *an army; go*
680 And I of this sall se a finaill end.'

1 Then we need not leave the land for food

Ten thousand haill he chargyt for to ryd.          *in all; commanded*
'Her in this strenth all nycht I sall you bid.      *stronghold; await you*
We may get meit of bestiall in this land;          *beasts*
Gud drynk as now we can nocht bryng to
hand.'

685  Of Westmorland the lord had mett him
        thar;
     On with the duk he graithit him to fair.       *prepared to go on*
     At the fyrst straik with thaim he had nocht     *When the first blow was*
        beyne;                                           *struck*
     With him he led a thousand weill beseyne.       *equipped*
     A Pykart lord was with a thousand boune;        *Picard; prepared*
690  Of King Edward he kepyt Calys toun.             *From; held; Calais*
     This twelve thousand on to the feild can        *proceeded*
        fair.
     The two captans sone mett thaim at
        Beggair
     With the haill stuff of Roxburch and            *whole garrison*
        Berweike.
     Schir Rawff Gray saw at thai war Sotheron       *they were like the English*
        leik,
695  Out of the south approchit to thar sicht;       *within sight*
     He knew full weill with thaim it was nocht
        rycht.
     Amer Wallange with his power come als,
     King Edwardis man, a tyrand knycht and
        fals.
     Quhen thai war mett thai fand nocht ellis       *found nothing else there*
        thar
700  Bot dede corsis, and thai war spulyeit bar.     *stripped of belongings*
     Than merveld thai quhar at the Scottis suld     *they wondered where*
        be;
     Of thaim about perance thai couth nocht se.[1]
     Bot spyis thaim tald, that come with Schir
        Amar,
     In Davis schaw thai saw thaim mak repar.        *saw them go*
705  The fers Sotheroun sone passit to that          *fierce English*
        place;
     The wach wes war and tald it to Wallace.        *sentries; aware; told*
     He warnd the ost out of that wood to ryd;       *summoned*
     In Roppis bog he purpost for to byd.            *stay*

---

1 They could see no sign of them

A litill schaw upon the ta syd was    *wood; the one side*

710 That men on fute mycht of the bog out pas.    *from*

Thar hors thai left in to that litill hauld;    *stronghold*

On fute thai thocht the mos that thai suld hauld.    *marsh*

The Inglis ost had weill thar passage seyne    *route*

And folowed fast with cruell men and keyne.    *fierce / bold*

715 Thai trowit that bog mycht mak thaim litill vaill,    *believed / difficulty*

Growyn our with reys and all the sward was haill.[1]    

On thaim to ryd thai ordand in gret ire.    *ordered*

Of the formest a thousand in the myre    *foremost; swamp*

Of hors with men was plungyt in the deipe.    *deeps*

720 The Scottis men tuk of thar cummyng kepe,    *heed*

Apon thaim set with strakis sad and sar;    *firm; severe*

Yeid nane away of all that entrit thar.

Lycht men on fute apon thaim derffly dang;    *Dismounted; violently attacked them*

Feill undyr hors was smoryt in that thrang,    *Many; crushed; throng*

725 Stampyt in mos and with rud hors ourgayne.    *Stamped on; strong / trampled*

The worthy Scottis the dry land than has tayne,    *reached*

Apon the laiff fechtand full wondyr fast,    *rest fighting very vigorously*

And mony groyme thai maid full sar agast.    *men; afraid*

Than Inglismen that besy was in wer    *fighting*

730 Assailyeit sar thaim fra the mos to ber    *Tried hard; carry*

On athir syd, bot than it was no but.    *either side; to no avail*

The strenth thai held rycht awfully on fut    *awesomely; foot*

Till men and hors gaiff mony grevous wound;    *To*

Feyll to the dede thai stekit in that stound.    *Many; stabbed; time*

735 The Pykart lord assailyeit scharply thar    *attacked eagerly*

Upon the Grayme with strakis sad and sar.    *blows*

Schir Jhone the Grayme with a staff swerd of steill    *stabbing sword; steel*

His brycht byrneis he persyt everilkdeill,    *corslet; pierced completely*

[1] Overgrown with brushwood and all the grass was growing vigorously

Throuch all the stuff, and stekit him in that sted; — cloth; place

740  Thus of his dynt the bauld Pykart is ded. — blow; bold

The Inglis ost tuk playne purpos to fle; — clear

In thar turnyng the Scottis gert mony de. — retreat

Wallace wald fayne at the Wallang haiff beyne; — gladly

Of Westmorland the lord was thaim betweyne. — the lord of Westmoreland

745  Wallace on him he set ane awfull dynt, — formidable blow

Throuch basnet stuff that na steill mycht it stynt; — helmet; steel; stop

Derffly to dede he left him in that place. — Violently

The fals knycht thus eschapit throuch this cace. — escaped; chance

And Robert Boid has with a captayne mett

750  Of Berweik, than a sad straik on him set — firm

Awkwart the crag and kervyt the pissane, — Across; neck; severed; gorget

Throuch all his weid in sondyr straik the bane. — armour; and shattered the bone

Feill horssyt men fled fast and durst nocht byd; — Many; remain

Raboytit evill on to thar king thai rid. — Badly repulsed; ride

755  The duk him tald of all thar jornay haill; — feat of arms

His hart for ire bolnyt for bytter baill. — swelled; woe

Haill he hecht he suld nevyr London se — Wholeheartedly; vowed

On Wallace deid quhill he ravengit be,[1]

Or los his men agayne as he did ayr. — lose; before

760  Thus socht he south with gret sorow and cair; — he made his way

At the Byrkhill a litill tary maid, — short halt

Syne throuch the land but rest our Sulway raid. — Then; without stopping; Solway

The Scottis ost a nycht ramanyt still; — remained

Apon the morn thai spulyete with gud will — plundered

765  The dede corssis, syne couth to Braid wood fayr; — Braidwood

At a consaill four dayis sojornyt thar. — stayed there

At Forest kyrk a metyng ordand he. — church

Thai chesd Wallace Scottis wardand to be, — chose; guardian

Traistand he suld thar paynfull sorow ces.

770  He rasavyt all that wald cum till his pes. — received; peace

1 Until he was revenged for Wallace's deed

Schir Wilyham come that lord of Douglas
    was,
Forsuk Edward, at Wallace pes can ass;                    asked
In thar thrillage he wald no langar be.                   subjection to them
Trewbut befor till Ingland payit he.                      Tribute
775  In contrar Scottis with thaim he never raid,          Against; rode
Far better cher Wallace tharfor him maid.
Thus tretyt he and cheryst wonder fair                    treated; dearly
Trew Scottis men that fewte maid him                      fealty
    thar,
And gaiff gretly feill gudis at he wan.                   gave generously many; won
780  He warnd it nocht till na gud Scottis man.            refused
Quha wald rebell and gang contrar the                     go against
    rycht
He punyst sar, war he squier or knycht.                   severely, were
Thus mervalusly gud Wallas tuk on hand;                   undertook
Lykly he was, rycht fair and weill farrand,               Well-made; good-looking
785  Mandly and stout and tharto rycht liberall,           Manly; strong; generous
Plesand and wys in all gud governall.                     Pleasant; leadership
To sla forsuth Sotheroun he sparyt nocht;                 slay in truth Englishmen
To Scottis men full gret profyt he wrocht.
In to the south sone effter passit he;
790  As him best thocht he rewllyt that contre.            governed; region
Schirrais he maid that cruell was to ken                  Sheriffs; fierce; know
And captans als of wis trew Scottis men.                  loyal
Fra Gamlis Peth the land obeyt him haill,                 Gamelspath; entirely
Till Ur watter, bath strenth, forest and                  River Urr; strongholds
    daill.
795  Agaynis him in Galloway hous was nayne                castles
Except Wigtoun byggyt of lyme and stayne.                 built; stone
That captayne hard the reullis of Wallace;                proceedings
Away be sey he staw out of that place,                    sea; stole
Levyt all waist and couth in Ingland wend.                Left; went to England
800  Bot Wallace sone a kepar till it send,
A gud squier and to nayme he was cald
Adam Gordone, as the storie me tald.                      history; told
A strenth thar was on the watter of Cre,                  castle; River Cree
Within a roch, rycht stalwart, wrocht of tre;             rock; made of wood
805  A gait befor mycht no man to it wyn,                  way at the front; find
But the consent of thaim that dwelt within.              Without
On the bak sid a roch and watter was;                     At the rear; river
A strait entre forsuth it was to pas.                     narrow
To wesy it Wallace him selff sone went;                   reconnoitre

810   Fra he it saw he kest in his entent           *considered how*
       To wyn that hauld; he has chosyne a gait      *conquer; way*
       That thai within suld mak litill debait.        *resistance*
       His power haill he gert bid out of sicht,       *whole company; wait*
       Bot three with him, qwhill tyme that it was    *Except; until*
           nycht.
815   Than tuk he twa, quhen that the nycht was
           dym,                                *dim*
       Stevyn of Irland and Kerle that couth
           clyme                          *climb*
       The watter under, and clame the roch so
           strang.                      *climb*
       Thus enter thai the Sothrone men amang.     *English*
       The wach befor tuk na tent to that syd;
820   Thir three in feyr sone to the port thai
           glid.[1]
       Gud Wallace than straik the portar him      *struck*
           sell;                           *self*
       Dede our the roch in to the dik he fell;      *Dead over; ditch*
       Leit doun the brig and blew his horne on     *Let; bridge; loudly*
           hycht.
       The buschement brak and come in all thar    *ambush broke; came*
           mycht,
825   At thar awne will sone enterit in that       *own pleasure soon*
           place;
       Till Inglismen thai did full litill grace.      *To; showed little kindness*
       Sexty thai slew; in that hauld was no ma      *stronghold; more*
       Bot ane ald preist and sympill wemen       *harmless*
           twa.
       Gret purveance was in that roch to spend;     *supplies*
830   Wallace baid still quhill it was at ane end,    *stayed; until; finished*
       Brak doune the strenth, bath bryg and       *bridge*
           bulwark all.
       Out our the roch thai gert the temyr fall,    *timber*
       Undid the gait and wald no langer bid.      *Destroyed; street; stay*
       In Carrik syne thai bounyt thaim to rid,     *prepared; ride*
835   Haistit thaim nocht bot sobyrly couth fair     *steadily travelled*
       Till Towrnbery; that captane was of Ayr     *[castle's] captain went to*
       With lord Persie, to tak his consaill haill.    *sound counsel*
       Wallace purpoisit that place for to assaill.    *planned*

---

1 The watch in front paid no attention to that side; these three together soon moved smoothly to the gate

Ane woman tauld quhen the capitane was gane. — *told [him]; gone*

840 Gude men of fence into the steid was nane. — *defence; place; none*
Thay fillit the dyke with eird and tymmer haill, — *ditch; earth; timber completely*
Syne fyrd the yett na succour mycht availl. — *Then set fire to the gate*
A prest thar was and gentill wemen within — *priest*
Quhilk for the fyr maid hiddewis noyis and dyn. — *hideous*

845 'Mercy,' thai criit, 'for him that deit on tre.' — *died on the cross [i.e., Jesus]*
Wallace gert slaik the fyr and leit thaim be. — *caused the fire to be put out*
To mak defens na ma was levyt thar. — *more were left there*
He thaim commaund out of the land to far, — *go*
Spulyeit the place and spilt all at thai mocht. — *Plundered; destroyed*

850 Apon the morn in Cumno sone thai socht, — *Cumnock; went*
To Laynrik syne and set a tyme of ayr; — *Lanark; for a justice-ayre*
Mysdoaris feill he gert be punyst thar. — *Many wrongdoers*
To gud trew men he gaiff full mekill wage, — *gave; very large rewards*
His brother sone put to his heretage.

855 To the Blak Crag in Cunno past agayne,
His houshauld set with men of mekill mayne. — *appointed; great strength*
Thre monethis thar he dwellyt in gud rest;
Suttell Sotheroune fand weill it was the best — *Cunning Englishmen found*
Trewis to tak for till enchev a chans; — *have a truce; obtain*

860 To furthir this thai send for knycht Wallans.
Bothwell yeit that tratour kepyt still, — *yet; protected*
And Ayr all haill was at the Perseis will. — *completely*
The byschope Beik in Glaskow dwellyt thar,
Throucht gret supple of the captayne of Ayr. — *provision*

865 Erll of Stamffurd, was chanslar of Ingland, — *chancellor*
With Schir Amar this travaill tuk on hand, — *task*
To procur pes be ony maner of cace. — *by any manner possible*
A saiff condyt thai purchest off Wallace. — *safe conduct*
In Ruglen kyrk the tryst than haiff thai set, — *meeting; arranged*

870 A promes maid to meit Wallace but let. — *meet; straight away*

The day of this approchit wondyr fast.
The gret chanslar and Amar thidder past,          Then
Syne Wallace come and his men weill                equipped
    beseyn,
With him fyfty arayt all in greyne.                dressed; green
875  Ilkane of thaim a bow and arrowis bar         Each one; carried
And lang swerdis, the quhilk full scharply         long, very sharp swords
    schar.                                  cut
In to the kyrk he gert a preyst rawes,             put on his vestments
With humyll mind rycht mekly hard a                meekly; heard; mass
    mes.
Syn up he rais and till ane alter went             After he rose
880  And his gud men full cruell of entent.        fierce in purpose
In ir he grew that traitour quhen he sawe;         anger [i.e., Sir Amer]
The Inglismen of his face stud gret aw.
Witt reullyt him that he did no outrage.           Reason
The erlle beheld fast till his hye curage,         took great heed of
885  Forthocht sum part that he come to that       Regretted somewhat
    place,
Gretlye abaysit for the vult of his face.          dismayed; expression on
Schir Amer said, 'This spech ye mon
    begyne.
He will nocht bow to na part of your kyn.
Sufferyt ye ar, I trow yhe may spek weill.         Assured by safe conduct
890  For all Ingland he will nocht brek adeyll     at all
His saiff cundyt, or quhar he makis a              where
    band.'                                  bond
The chanslar than approfferit him his hand.
Wallace stud still and couth na handis ta;         did not take hands
Frendschipe to thaim na liknes wald he             semblance; make
    ma.
895  Schir Amar said, 'Wallace, yhe undyrstand
This is a lord and chanslar of Ingland.
To salus him ye may be propyr skill.'              greet; as is right and proper
With schort avys he maid answer him till:          Without delay
'Sic salusyng I oys till Inglismen                 greeting; use to
900  Sa sall he haiff, quhar ever I may him ken    know
At my power, that God I mak avow,                  I vow to God
Out of soverance gyff that I had him now!          safe conduct if
Bot for thi liff and all his land so braid,        broad
I will nocht brek this promes that is maid.
905  I had lever at myn awn will haiff thee        rather
Without cundyt, that I mycht wrokyne be            safe conduct; revenged

Of thi fals deid thou dois in this regioune,                    does
Than of pur gold a kingis gret ransoune.                        pure; ransom
Bot for my band as now I will lat be.                           Because of my bond
910   Chanslar, schaw furth quhat ye desyr of me.'                expound
The chanslar said, 'The most caus of this                       the main reason for
thing,
To procur pees I am send fra our king                           from
With the gret seill and voice of hys                            seal; support
parliament.
Quhat I bynd her oure barnage sall                              agree to; barons
consent.'
915   Wallace answerd, 'Our litill mendis we haiff                Very little reparation
Syne of oure rycht ye occupy the laiff.                         Since; what is rightfully ours
Quytcleyme our land and we sall nocht                           Relinquish
deny.'
The chanslar said, 'Of na sic charge haiff I.                   I have no such orders
We will gyff gold or oure purpos suld faill.'                   give; before
920   Than Wallace said, 'In waist is that travaill.              That is a useless offer
Be favour gold we ask nayne of your kyn.                        Gold [given as] a favour
In wer of you we tak that we may wyn.'[1]
Abaissid he was to mak answer agayne.                           He was [too] abashed
Wallace said, 'Schir, we jangill nocht in                       bandy words; vain
vayne.
925   My consell gyffis, I will na fabill mak,                    decrees; not lie
As for a yer a finaill pes to tak.                              year; conclusive
Nocht for my selff that I bynd to your seill,                   seal
I can nocht trow that ever yhe will be leill,                   believe; loyal
Bot for pur folk gretlye has beyne                              poor
supprisyt,                                                      oppressed
930   I will tak pees quhill forthir we be avisit.'              until; advised
Than band thai thus, thar suld be no debait,                    agreed formally; strife
Castell and towne suld stand in that ilk                        same state
stait
Fra that day furth quhill a yer war at end,                     until; was
Sellyt this pes and tuk thar leyff to wend.                     Sealed; truce; leave; go
935   Wallace fra thine passit in to the west,                    from there
Maid playne repayr quhar so him likit best.                     went openly where
Yeit sar he dred or thai suld him dissaiff.                     Yet he feared greatly; deceive
This endentour to Schir Ranald he gaiff,                        indenture
His der uncle, quhar it mycht kepit be.                         dear
940   In Cunno syne till his dwellyng went he.                    afterwards


1 We take by conquest what we can from you

|   |   |   |
|---|---|---|
| | In Feveryher befell the sammyn cace | same case |
| | That Inglismen tuk trewis with Wallace. | agreed a truce |
| | This passyt our till Marche till end was socht. | until the end of March |
| | The Inglismen kest all the wayis thai mocht, | considered; might |
| 5 | With suttelte and wykkit illusione, | deceit |
| | The worthi Scottis to put to confusione. | |
| | In Aperill the king of Ingland come | |
| | In Cumerland of Pumfrat fro his home;[1] | |
| | In to Carleill till a consell he yeid, | council; went |
| 10 | Quhar of the Scottis mycht haiff full mekill dreid. | great fear |
| | Mony captane that was of Ingland born | |
| | Thidder thai past and semblit thar king beforn. | assembled / before |
| | Na Scottis man to that consell thai cald | called |
| | Bot Schir Amer that traytour was of ald. | Except; old |
| 15 | At hym thai sperd how thai suld tak on hand | they asked him; undertake |
| | The rychtwys blud to scour out of Scotland. | |
| | Schir Amer said, 'Thar chyftayne can weill do, | Their chieftain is outstanding |
| | Rycht wys in wer and has gret power to, | war; very powerful too |
| | And now this trew gyffis thaim sic hardyment | truce; such / courage |
| 20 | That to your faith thai will nocht all consent. | homage |
| | Bot wald ye do rycht as I wald you ler, | exactly; advise |
| | This pes to thaim it suld be sald full der.' | cost them dearly |
| | Than demyt he the fals Sotheroun amang | he gave his opinion; English |
| | How thai best mycht the Scottis barounis hang. | barons |
| 25 | For gret bernys that tyme stud in till Ayr, | Four large barns |
| | Wrocht for the king quhen his lugyng wes thar, | Made; lodging |
| | Byggyt about that no man enter mycht | Built |
| | Bot ane at anys, nor haiff of other sicht; | Except one at a time; have |

1 In Cumberland from his home in Pontefract

Thar ordand thai thir lordis suld be slayne.    *these*

30 A justice maid quhilk wes of mekill mayne.    *[They] appointed a judge*

To lord Persye of this mater thai laid.[1]

With sad avys agayne to thaim he said:    *stern expression*

'Thai men to me has kepit treuth so lang    *loyalty*

Desaitfully I may nocht se thaim hang.

35 I am thar fa and warn thaim will I nocht;    *foe*

Sa I be quytt I rek nocht quhat yhe wrocht.[2]

Fra thine I will and towart Glaskow draw    *From thence*

With our byschope to her of his new law.'    *hear; administration*

Than chesyt thai a justice fers and fell    *they chose; fierce; cruel*

40 Quhilk Arnulff hecht, as my auctour will tell,    *was called*

Of South Hantoun, that huge hie her and lord;    *very powerful, high magistrate*

He undertuk to pyne thaim with the cord.    *torment*

Ane other ayr in Glaskow ordand thai    *justice-ayre*

For Cliddisdaill men to stand that sammyn day;

45 Syne chargyt thaim in all wayis ernystfully    *Then ordered; earnestly*

Be no kyn meyne Wallace suld nocht chaip by,    *By no kind of means; escape*

For weill thai wyst and thai men war ourthrawin    *knew / overthrown*

Thai mycht at will bruk Scotland as thar awin.    *possess / own*

This band thai clois under thar seillis fast;    *agreement; concluded; seals*

50 Syne south our mur agayn King Edward past.    *Then; moor; again*

The new justice rasavit was in Ayr;    *judge received*

The lord Persye can on to Glaskow fayr.    *went on to Glasgow*

This ayr was set in Jun the auchtand day    *justice-ayre; June the eighth*

And playnly criyt na fre man war away.    *proclaimed; should be*

55 The Scottis merveld, and pes tane in the land,    *since peace [had been] agreed*

Quhy Inglismen sic maistre tuk on hand.    *such a display of might*

Schir Ranald set a day befor this ayr,    *appointed*

At Monktoun kyrk; his freyndis mett him thar.

---

1 They laid this matter before lord Percy
2 So long as I am quit [of responsibility] I care not what you do

Wilyham Wallace on to that tryst couth pas,    *meeting; passed*

60  For he as than wardane of Scotland was.    *guardian*

This maister Jhone, a worthi clerk, was thar;

He chargyt his kyne for to byd fra that ayr.    *kinsfolk; stay away from*

Rycht weyll he wyst, fra Persey fled that land,    *he knew very well, when*

Gret perell was till Scottis apperand.    *imminent*

65  Wallace fra thaim to the kyrk he yeid;    *went*

Pater noster, Ave he said and Creid,    *the Apostles' Creed*

Syne to the grece he lenyt him sobyrly;    *Then; stair; headed resolutely*

Apon a sleip he slaid full sodandly.    *fell into a sleep*

Kneland folowed and saw him fallyn on sleip;

70  He maid na noyis bot wysly couth him kepe.    *protect*

In that slummer cummand him thocht he saw    *slumber; he thought he saw coming*

Ane agit man fast towart him couth draw.

Sone be the hand he hynt him haistele.    *Soon; grabbed*

'I am,' he said, 'in viage chargit with thee.'[1]

75  A swerd him gaiff of burly burnist steill.    *sword strong burnished steel*

'Gud sone,' he said, 'this brand thou sall bruk weill.'    *sword / make good use of*

Of topaston him thocht the plumat was,    *topaz; pommel*

Baith hilt and hand all gliterand lik the glas.    *handle*

'Dere sone,' he said, 'we tary her to lang.    *too long*

80  Thou sall go se quhar wrocht is mekill wrang.'    *much / wrong*

Than him led till a montane on hycht;    *high*

The warld him thocht he mycht se with a sicht.    *at a glance*

He left him thar, syne sone fra him he went.    *then afterwards*

Tharof Wallace studiit in his entent;    *wondered in his mind*

85  Till se him mar he had full gret desyr.    *To; more*

Tharwith he saw begyne a felloune fyr    *fierce*

Quhilk braithly brynt on breid throu all the land,    *vigorously burned extensively*

1 'I am charged with [taking] you on a journey,' he said

Scotland atour fra Ros to Sulway sand.          Over Scotland from

Than sone till him thar descendyt a          soon
    qweyne,

90    Inlumyt lycht schynand full brycht and          Illumined light shining
    scheyne.          clear

In hyr presens apperyt so mekill lycht          much

At all the fyr scho put out of his sicht;          That

Gaiff him a wand of colour reid and          red
    greyne,          green

With a saffyr sanyt his face and eyne.          sapphire blessed; eyes

95    'Welcum,' scho said, 'I cheis thee as my          choose
    luff.          beloved

Thou art grantyt be the gret God abuff          above

Till help pepill that sufferis mekill wrang.

With thee as now I may nocht tary lang.

Thou sall return to thi awne oys agayne;          own way of living

100    Thi derrast kyne ar her in mekill payne.          dearest kin; here; great

This rycht regioun thou mon redeme it all;          must

Thi last reward in erd sall be bot small.

Let nocht tharfor tak redres of this mys,[1]

To thi reward thou sall haiff lestand blys.'          shall have everlasting bliss

105    Of hir rycht hand scho betaucht him a buk.          From; gave to; book

Humylly thus hyr leyff full sone scho tuk,          her leave

On to the cloud ascendyt of his sycht.          from

Wallace brak up the buk in all his mycht.          open

In three partis the buk weill writyn was:

110    The fyrst writtyng was gross letter of bras,          [in] large; brass

The secound gold, the thrid was silver
    scheyne;          shining

Wallace merveld quhat this writyng suld
    meyne.

To rede the buk he besyet him so fast,          busied himself

His spreit agayne to walkand mynd is past,          spirit; waking

115    And up he rays, syne sowdandly furth          then suddenly
    went.

This clerk he fand and tald him his entent          described in detail

Of this visioun at I haiff said befor,          vision

Completly throuch. Quhat nedis wordis          through
    mor?          more

'Der sone,' he said, 'my witt unabill is

120    To runsik sic for dreid I say of mys.          interpret such; fear; amiss

1 Do not fail, therefore, to redress this wrong

Yeit I sall deyme, thocht my cunnyng be small,  *Yet; understanding*

God grant na charge effter my wordis fall.  *God grant that; blame; befall*

Saynct Androw was, gaiff thee that swerd in hand;  *It was St Andrew; sword*

Of sanctis he is vowar of Scotland.  *patron*

125 That montayne is, quhar he thee had on hycht,  *high*

Knawlage to haiff of wrang that thou mon rycht.  *Knowledge; must set right*

The fyr sal be fell tithingis or ye part  *disastrous news before*

Quhilk will be tald in mony syndry art.  *many different directions*

I can nocht witt quhat qweyn at it suld be,  *do not know what queen that*

130 Quhether Fortoun or Our Lady so fre.  *noble*

Lykly it is be the brychtnes scho brocht,  *It is likely by; she*

Modyr of hym that all this warld has wrocht.  *world* *made*

The party wand I trow be myn entent,  *parti-coloured; believe*

Assignes rewlle and cruell jugement.  *fierce*

135 The red colour, quha graithly understud,  *readily*

Betaknes all to gret battaill and blud;  *Betokens; blood*

The greyn, curage that thou art now amang,[1]

In strowbill wer thou sall conteyne full lang.  *painful war; continue*

The saphyr stayne scho blissit thee withall  *stone with which she blessed*

140 Is lestand grace, will God sall to thee fall.  *lasting*

The thrynfald buk is bot this brokyn land  *threefold; simply*

Thou mon rademe be worthines of hand.  *must redeem by*

The bras letteris betakynnys bot to this,  *only*

The gret oppres of wer and mekill mys  *wrong; war; harm*

145 The quhilk thou sall bryng to the rycht agayne;  *which*

Bot thou tharfor mon suffer mekill payne.  *for that; must endure; great*

The gold takynnis honour and worthinas,  *betokens*

Victour in armys that thou sall haiff be  *Victory; through*

The silver schawis cleyne lyff and hevynnys blys,  *signifies pure life; heaven's*

150 To thi reward that myrth thou sall nocht mys.  *joy* *lack*

---

1 The green [signifies] the courageous effort in which you are now engaged

Dreid nocht tharfor, be out of all dispayr. *Fear*
Forther as now her of I can no mair.' *here; can say; more*
He thankit him and thus his leyff has tayne, *leave; taken*
Till Corsbe syne with his uncle raid hayme. *To; then; rode home*
155 With myrthis thus all nycht thai sojornyt thar. *Merrily*
Apon the morn thai graith thaim to the ar *set off; justice-ayre*
And furth thai ryd quhill thai come to Kingace. *rode until*
With dreidfull hart thus sperit wicht Wallace *fearful; asked bold*
At Schir Ranald for the charter of pes. *peace*
160 'Nevo,' he said, 'thir wordis ar nocht les. *these; lies*
It is levyt at Corsbe in the kyst, *left; chest*
Quhar thou it laid; tharof na othir wist.'[1] *
Wallace answerd, 'Had we it her to schaw, *here; show*
And thai be fals we suld nocht enter awe.' *[if] they are; all enter*
165 'Der sone,' he said, 'I pray thee pass agayne. *go back*
Thocht thou wald send, that travaill war in vayne; *Although; send a messenger; trouble; vain*
Bot thou or I can nane it bryng this tid.' *Except; time*
Gret grace it was maid him agayne to ryd. *ride back*
Wallace raturnd and tuk with him bot thre;
170 Nane of thaim knew this endentour bot he. *indenture*
Unhap him led, for bid him couth he nocht; *Ill-luck led [Sir Ranald]; await; could*
Of fals dissayt this gud knycht had na thocht. *deceit; thought*
Schir Ranald raid but restyng to the town, *without*
Wittand na thing of all this fals tresoun. *Knowing nothing; treason*
175 That wykked syng so rewled the planait, *sign; ruled; planet*
Saturn was than in till his heast stait; *in the ascendant*
Aboune Juno in his malancoly, *Above*
Jupiter, Mars, ay cruell of invy *always fierce; malice*
Saturn as than avansyt his natur. *then displayed*
180 Of terandry he power had and cur, *tyranny; responsibility*
Rebell renkis in mony seir regioun, *Rebellious men; different*
Trubbill wedder makis schippis to droune. *Troubled; ships sink*
His drychyn is with Pluto in the se *tarrying*
As of the land full of iniquite.

1 no-one else knows its whereabouts

| | | |
|---|---|---|
| 185 | He waknys wer, waxing of pestilence, | stirs up war |
| | Fallyng of wallis with cruell violence. | |
| | Pusoun is ryff amang thir other thingis, | Poison; rife; these |
| | Sodeyn slauchter of emperouris and kingis. | |
| | Quhen Sampsone powed to grond the gret piller | pulled |
| 190 | Saturn was than in till the heast sper. | sphere |
| | At Thebes als of his power thai tell, | |
| | Quhen Phiorax sank throuch the erd till hell; | earth |
| | Of the Trojans he had full mekill cur | great charge |
| | Quhen Achilles at Troy slew gud Ectur; | |
| 195 | Burdeous schent and mony citeis mo, | Bordeaux ruined; many; more |
| | His power yeit it has na hap to ho.[1] | |
| | In braid Brytane feill vengeance has beyne seyne | Across; great |
| | Of this and mar, ye wait weill quhat I meyn. | more; know / mean |
| | Bot to this hous that stalwart wes and strang | |
| 200 | Schir Ranald come and mycht nocht tary lang. | |
| | A bauk was knyt all full of rapys keyne;[2] | |
| | Sic a towboth sen syne wes never seyne. | Such; tollbooth [i.e., prison] |
| | Stern men was set the entre for to hald; | Strong; guard |
| | Nayne mycht pas in bot ay as thai war cald. | only; called |
| 205 | Schir Ranald fyrst, to mak fewte for his land, | pay homage |
| | The knycht went in and wald na langar stand. | |
| | A rynnand cord thai slewyt our his hed | running cord; swung |
| | Hard to the bauk and hangyt him to ded. | |
| | Schyr Brys the Blayr next with his eyme in past; | |
| 210 | On to the ded thai haistyt him full fast. | death |
| | Be he entrit his hed was in the swar, | As soon as; snare [noose] |
| | Tytt to the bawk hangyt to ded rycht thar. | Pulled; beam |
| | The thrid entrit, that pete was forthy, | therefore |

1 Whose destiny it is not to stop
2 Tightly drawn ropes were fastened all along a beam

A gentill knycht, Schir Neill of Mungumry,
215 And othir feill of landit men about.     *many others; land-owning*
Mony yeid in bot na Scottis com out.     *Many went*
Of Wallace part thai putt to that derff deid;     *party; violent death*
Mony Crawfurd sa endyt in that steid.     *thus; place*
Of Carrik men Kennadys slew thai als,     *also*
220 And kynd Cambellis that never had beyne
fals.
Thir rabellit nocht contrar thar rychtwis     *These did not rebel*
croun,
Sotheroun forthi thaim putt to confusioun.     *therefore; destruction*
Berklais, Boidis and Stuartis of gud kyn,     *kin*
Na Scot chapyt that tyme that entrit in.     *escaped*
225 Upon the bawk thai hangit mony par;     *beam; nobles*
Besid thaim ded in the nuk kest thaim thar.     *corner; cast*
Sen the fyrst tyme that ony wer wes
wrocht,
To sic a dede so mony sic yeid nocht     *such a death; such went*
Upon a day throuch curssit Saxons seid.     *In a single day; accursed*
230 Vengeance of this throuch out that kynrik     *kingdom [i.e., England]*
yeid,     *went*
Grantyt wes fra God in the gret hevyn,     *heaven*
Sa ordand he that law suld be thar stevyn     *So decreed; doom*
To fals Saxons for thar fell jugement;     *cruel judgement*
Thar wykkydnes our all the land is went.
235 Yhe nobill men that ar of Scottis kind,     *descent*
Thar petous dede yhe kepe in to your     *Their wretched deaths*
mynd
And us ravenge quhen we ar set in thrang.     *revenge; placed in danger*
Dolour it is her on to tary lang.[1]
Thus eighteen scor to that derff dede thai     *they killed in that violent*
dycht     *way*
240 Of barronis bald and mony worthi knycht.     *bold*
Quhen thai had slayne the worthiast that
was thar,
For waik peple thai wald na langar spar,     *helpless; would forbear*
In till a garth kest thaim out of that sted     *garden; place*
As thai war born, dispulyeit, bar and ded.     *stripped of belongings, naked*
245 Gud Robert Boid on till a tawern yeid     *tavern went*
With twenty men that douchty war in     *bold*
deid,

1 It is distressing to dwell long on this

| | |
|---|---|
| Of Wallace hous, full cruell of entent; | fiercely enterprising |
| He governyt thaim quhen Wallace was absent. | |
| Kerle turnyt with his master agayne, | turned back |
| 250 Kneland and Byrd that mekill war of mayn. | strength |
| Stevyn of Irland went furth apon the streit; | |
| A trew woman full sone with him couth meit. | loyal; soon met him |
| He sparyt at hir quhat hapnyt in the ayr. | enquired; her; justice-ayre |
| 'Sorow,' scho said, 'is nothing ellis thar.' | else |
| 255 Ferdly scho ast, 'Allace, quhar is Wallace?' | Full of fear; asked |
| 'Fra us agayne he passit at Kingace.' | He left us again |
| 'Go warn his folk and haist thaim of the toun. | hurry; from |
| To kepe him selff I sall be reddy boun.' | protect; all prepared |
| With hir as than no mar tary he maid. | then |
| 260 Till his falowis he went withoutyn baid | delay |
| And to thaim tald of all this gret mysfair. | disaster |
| To Laglane wood thai bounyt withoutyn mar. | headed immediately |
| Be this Wallace was cummand wonder fast; | By this time; came; speedily |
| For his freyndis he was full sar agast. | extremely fearful |
| 265 On to the bern sadly he couth persew | barn resolutely made his way |
| Till enter in, for he na perell knew. | |
| This woman than apon him loud can call: | then |
| 'O fers Wallace, feill tempest is befall! | fierce; great disaster |
| Our men ar slayne that pete is to se, | |
| 270 As bestiall houndis hangit our a tre. | bestial dogs |
| Our trew barrouns be twa and twa past in.' | loyal; in pairs |
| Wallace wepyt for gret los of his kyne, | kin |
| Than with unes apon his hors he baid. | difficulty; stayed |
| Mair for to sper to this woman he raid. | More; ask; rode |
| 275 'Der nece,' he said, 'the treuth giff thou can tell, | kinswoman; if |
| Is my eyme dede, or hou the cace befell?' | how this came about? |
| 'Out of yon bern,' scho said, 'I saw him born, | carried |
| Nakit, laid law on cald erd me beforn. | low; cold earth; before |
| His frosty mouth I kissit in that sted, | place |
| 280 Rycht now manlik, now bar and brocht to ded; | One moment . . . the next; bare; death |
| And with a claith I coverit his licaym, | cloth; dead body |

For in his lyff he did never woman  
  schayme. — *shame*  
His syster sone thou art, worthi and wicht. — *nephew; bold*  
Ravenge thar dede for Goddis saik at thi — *Revenge their deaths*  
  mycht.  
285 Als I sall help as I am woman trew!' — *Also*  
'Der wicht,' he said, 'der God sen at thou — *creature; since that*  
  knew  
Gud Robert Boid, quhar at thou can him  
  se,  
Wilyham Crawfurd als, giff he lyffand be, — *if; is living*  
Adam Wallace, wald help me in this striff!  
290 I pray to God send me thaim all in liff. — *alive*  
For Marys saik bid thaim sone cum to me. — *soon come*  
The justice innys thou spy for cheryte — *love of God*  
And in quhat feir that thai thar lugyne — *company; lodging*  
  mak.  
Son effter that we will our purpos tak — *it's our purpose to go*  
295 In to Laglane, quhilk has my succour  
  beyne.  
Adew merket and welcum woddis greyne!' — *towns; green woods*  
Her of as than till hir he spak no mair, — *Here; then to her; more*  
His brydill turnyt and fra hir can he fair; — *went*  
Sic murnyng maid for his der worthi kyn  
300 Him thocht for baill his breyst ner bryst in — *sorrow; breast; burst*  
  twyn. — *two*  
As he thus raid in gret angyr and teyne, — *rode; grief*  
Of Inglismen thar folowed him fyfteyn  
Wicht wallyt men, at towart him couth — *Specially picked strong; that;*  
  draw — *drew*  
With a maser to tach him to the law.[1]  
305 Wallace raturnd in greiff and matelent, — *turned back; wrath*  
With his swerd drawyn amang thaim sone — *sword; soon*  
  he went.  
The myddyll of ane he mankit ner in twa, — *one [of them]; severed almost*  
Ane other thar apon the hed can ta; — *struck*  
The thrid he straik and throuch the cost — *struck; side of the body*  
  him claiff; — *split*  
310 The ferd to ground rycht derffly ded doun — *fourth; violently cut down*  
  he draiff;  
The fyft he hit with gret ire in that sted; — *place*

---

1 With a law-court servant to bring him before the court

Without reskew dreidles he left thaim ded. — *for sure*
Than his thre men had slayne the tother five,
Fra thaim the laiff eschapit in to lyff, — *rest; with their lives*
315 Fled to thar lord and tald him of this cas.
To Laglane wode than ridis wicht Wallas; — *bold*
The Sotheroun said quhat ane that he hit rycht — *English; whichever one*
Without mercye dredles to ded wes dycht. — *assuredly was killed*
Mervell thai had sic strenth in ane suld be, — *such; one [man] should*
320 Ane of thar men at ilk straik he gert de. — *each blow; caused to die*
Than demyt thai it suld be Wallace wicht. — *thought; bold*
To thar langage maid answer ane ald knycht: — *talk*
'Forsuth,' he said, 'be he chapyt this ayr, — *if he escaped; justice-ayre*
All your new deid is eking of our cair.' — *action; increasing; distress*
325 The justice said, quhen thar sic murmur rais, — *such a complaint* / *rose*
'Yhe wald be ferd and thar come mony fais, — *would; frightened if; foes*
That for a man me think you lik to fle — *one man*
And wait nocht yeit in deid gyff it be he![1]
And thocht it be I count him bot full lycht. — *although it is; lightly*
330 Quha bidis her, ilk gentill man sall be knycht. — *Whoever remains here; each noble*
I think to deill thar landis haill to morn — *deal out all their lands*
To you about that ar of Ingland born.' — *To those of you around*
The Sotheron drew to thar lugyng but mar; — *straight away*
Four thousand haill that nycht was in till Ayr. — *in all*
335 In gret bernys biggyt without the toun — *barns built outside*
The justice lay with mony bald barroun. — *many bold*
Than he gert cry about thai waynys wide — *had proclaimed; camps*
Na Scottis born amang thaim thar suld bid. — *stay*
To the castell he wald nocht pas for eys — *comfort*
340 Bot sojornd thar with thing that mycht him pleys. — *stayed* / *please*
Gret purvians be se to thaim was brocht, — *supplies by sea*
With Irland ayle the mychteast couth be wrocht. — *Irish ale; strongest*

1 And do not know yet if it is indeed he

Na wach wes set becaus thai had na dout          watch; fear
Of Scottis men that leiffand was without.          living; outside

345   Lauberand in mynd thai had beyne all that
      day,[1]
      Of ayle and wyne yneuch chosyne haiff          enough
      thai,
      As bestly folk tuk of thaim selff no keip.          care
      In thar brawnys sone slaid the sleuthfull          limbs; slid; slothful
      sleip,
      Throuch full gluttre in swarff swappyt lik          great gluttony; a stupor;
      swyn;                                               thrown; swine
350   Thar chyftayne than was gret Bachus of
      wyn.
      This wys woman besy amang thaim was;
      Feill men scho warnd and gart to Laglayne          Many; caused
      pas,
      Hyr selff formest quhill thai with Wallace          leading the way until
      met.
      Sum comfort than in till his mynd was set.
355   Quhen he thaim saw he thankit God of
      mycht.
      Tithandis he ast; the woman tald him          News; asked; told
      rycht:
      'Slepand as swyn ar all yone fals menyhe.          company
      Na Scottis man is in that cumpane.'
      Than Wallace said, 'Giff thai all dronkyn
      be
360   I call it best with fyr for thaim to se.'          to provide fire to see them
      Of gud men than thre hundreth till him
      socht.
      The woman had tald three trew burges at          loyal burgesses that brought
      brocht
      Out of the toun with nobill aile and breid,          ale; bread
      And othir stuff als mekill as thai mycht
      leid.[2]
365   Thai eit and drank, the Scottis men at          ate; that might
      mocht.
      The noblis than Jop has to Wallace brocht.          nobles then
      Sadly he said, 'Der freyndis, now ye se          Resolutely
      Our kyn ar slayn, tharof is gret pete,

---

1 They had exerted themselves mentally all that day
2 And as many other supplies as they could carry

Throuch feill murthyr, the gret dispite is
    mor.[1]

370 Now sum rameid I wald we set tharfor.    amends; arrange
Suppos that I was maid wardane to be    Although
Part ar away sic chargis put to me,    Some; placed on
And ye ar her cummyn of als gud blud,    as good blood [birth]
Als rychtwis born be aventur and als gud,    well-born by good fortune; as
375 Als forthwart, fair and als likly of persoun,    As promising; well-built
As ever was I; tharfor, till conclusioun.
Lat us cheys five of this gud cumpanye,    Let us choose
Syne caflis cast quha sall our master be.'    Then cast lots [to decide]
Wallace and Boid and Crawfurd of renoun
380 And Adam als than lord of Ricardtoun—
His fader  than wes wesyed with seknes;    afflicted; sickness
God had him tayne in till his lestand    taken into; lasting
    grace—
The fyft Auchinlek, in wer a nobill man,    war
Caflis to cast about thir five began.    Lots; these
385 It wald on him for ocht thai cuth devys,[2]
Continualy quhill thai had castyn thrys.
Than Wallace rais and out a swerd can    rose; sword
    draw.    drew
He said, 'I vow to the Makar of aw    all
And till Mary his modyr, virgyne cler,    bright
390 My unclis dede now sall be sauld full der,    dearly paid for
With mony ma of our der worthi kyn.[3]
Fyrst or I eit or drynk we sall begyn,    before
For sleuth nor sleip sall nayne remayne in
    me
Of this tempest till I a vengeance se.'[4]
395 Than all inclynd rycht humyll of accord    bowed; humbly in agreement
And him resavit as chyftayne and thar    accepted
    lord.
Wallace a lord he may be clepyt weyll    may well be called a lord
Thocht ruryk folk tharof haff litill feill,    Although rustic;
    understanding

---

1 Cruelly murdered, [making their] contempt seem all the greater
2 It would fall to him [i.e., Wallace]; for anything they could devise
3 Along with [those of] many more of our dear, noble kinsmen
4 For I shall not be idle or sleep [rest?] until I have revenge for this
disaster

Na deyme na lord bot landis be thar part.[1]

400 Had he the warld and be wrachit of hart     *base*
He is no lord as to the worthines.     *worthy of the name*
It can nocht be but fredome, lordlyknes.[2]
At the Roddis thai mak full mony ane     *many a one [knights]*
Quhilk worthy ar, thocht landis haiff thai nane.

405 This disscussyng I leiff herroldis till end;     *discussion; leave*
On my mater now breiffly will I wend.     *On my subject matter*
Wallace commaunde a burges for to get     *ordered*
Fyne cawk eneuch that his der nece mycht set     *chalk enough; mark*
On ilk yeit quhar Sotheroun wer on raw.     *eachgate; together*

410 Than twenty men he gert fast wetheis thraw,     *made quickly twist withies*
Ilk man a pair, and on thar arme thaim threw.     *Two for each man*
Than to the toune full fast thai cuth persew.     *made their way*
The woman past befor thaim suttelly,     *ahead of them stealthily*
Cawkit ilk yett that thai neid nocht gang by.     *Chalked each gate; go*

415 Than festnyt thai with wetheis duris fast     *they fastened; doors*
To stapill and hesp with mony sekyr cast.     *clasp; secure fastenings*
Wallace gert Boid ner hand the castell ga     *on the near side*
With fyfte men a jeperte to ma.     *surprise attack; make*
Gyff ony ischet the fyr quhen that thai saw,     *If; issued; fire*

420 Fast to the yett he ordand thaim to draw.
The laiff with him about the bernys yheid.     *barns went*
This trew woman servit thaim weill in deid     *indeed*
With lynt and fyr that haistely kendill wald.     *flax; kindle*
In everilk nuk thai festnyt blesis bald.     *nook; torches bold*

425 Wallace commaund till all his men about
Na Sotheron man at thai suld lat brek out.
'Quhat ever he be reskewis of that kyn     *Whoever rescues [any] of; kin*
Fra the rede fyr him selff sall pas tharin.'     *red fire*

---

1 Nor consider anyone a lord unless he owns land
2 The character of a lord cannot be without magnanimity

The lemand low sone lanssyt apon hycht.    *gleaming flame; leapt*

430 'Forsuth,' he said, 'this is a plessand sicht;

Till our hartis it suld be sum radres.    *redress*

War thir away thar power war the les.'    *these; less*

On to the justice him selff loud can caw:    *call*

'Lat us to borch our men fra your fals law    *give surety for*

435 At leyffand ar, that chapyt fra your ayr.    *that are living; escaped*

Deyll nocht thar land, the unlaw is our    *Deal; penalty; too*
    sayr.    *severe*

Thou had no rycht, that sall be on thee    *made clear to you*
    seyne.'

The rewmour rais with cairfull cry and    *alarm; painful*
    keyne.    *sharp*

The bryme fyr brynt rycht braithly apon    *fierce; burned; vigorously; on*
    loft;    *high*

440 Till slepand men that walkand was nocht    *To; waking*
    soft.    *gentle*

The sycht without was awfull for to se;    *outside*

In all the warld na grettar payne mycht be

Than thai within insufferit sor to dwell,

That ever was wrocht bot purgatory or
    hell:[1]

445 A payne of hell weill ner it mycht be cauld.    *called*

Mad folk with fyr hampryt in mony hauld:    *trapped in many houses*

Feill byggyns brynt that worthi war and    *Many buildings burned;*
    wicht,    *noble*

Gat nane away, knaiff, captane nor knycht,    *None got away; knave*

Quhen brundis fell off ruftreis thaim    *burning pieces of wood;*
    amang.    *rafters*

450 Sum rudly rais in bytter paynys strang,    *rose violently; strong*

Sum nakyt brynt bot beltles all away,    *undressed*

Sum never rais bot smoryt quhar thai lay,    *were smothered [by smoke]*

Sum ruschit fast tyll Ayr gyff thai mycht
    wyn,

Blyndyt in fyr thar deidis war full dym.[2]

455 The reik mellyt with fylth of carioune    *smoke mingled; foul carrion*

Amang the fyr rycht foull of offensioune.    *Amidst; vile and offensive*

The peple beryt lyk wyld bestis in that tyd,    *were buried; at that time*

---

1 'There might be no greater pain in all the world / than that [of] those
compelled to stay painfully aware within, / except in purgatory or hell'
2 Some rushed quickly to reach Ayr, if they could, / Blinded by fire, they
could not see properly what they were doing

Within the wallis rampand on athir sid, *raging; either side*
Rewmyd in reuth with mony grysly *Lamented ruefully*
  grayne. *groans*
460 Sum grymly gret quhill thar lyff dayis war
  gayne,[1]
Sum durris socht the entre for to get, *doors; reach*
Bot Scottismen so wysly thaim beset,
Gyff ony brak be awnter of that steid
With swerdis sone bertnyt thai war to
  dede,[2]
465 Or ellys agayne beforce drevyn in the fyr. *by force; driven into*
Thar chapyt nayne bot brynt up bayne and *escaped; were burned; bone*
  lyr. *and flesh*
The stynk scalyt of ded bodyis sa wyde *spread; widely*
The Scottis abhord ner hand for to byd, *nearby; remain*
Yeid to the wynd and leit thaim evyn *Went windward; left; alone*
  allayne *indeed*
470 Quhill the rede fyr had that fals blude *Until; red fire; blood*
  ourgayne. *overwhelmed*
A frer Drumlay was priour than of Ayr, *friar; prior*
Sevyn scor with him that nycht tuk herbry *seven; refuge*
  thar
In his innys, for he mycht nocht thaim let. *dwelling-places; stop*
Till ner mydnycht a wach on thaim he set; *guard*
475 Hym selff wouk weyll quhill he the fyr saw *kept good watch until*
  rys;
Sum mendis he thocht to tak of that *amends*
  supprys. *outrage*
Hys brether sevyn till harnes sone thai *seven brothers soon armed*
  yeid, *themselves*
Hym selff chyftayne the ramanand to leid. *rest; lead*
The best thai vaill of armour and gud ger, *chose*
480 Syne wapynnys tuk rycht awfull in affer. *Then; awesome; appearance*
Thir eight freris in four partis thai ga, *These; directions; go*
With swerdis drawyn till ilk hous yeid *swords; each; went*
  twa;
Sone entrit thai quhar Sotheroune slepand
  war,
Apon thaim set with strakis sad and sar. *Set upon them; blows firm*

---

1 Some grimly wept as they departed this life
2 If any happened to escape from that place, / they were soon put to death by
the sword

485 Feill frekis thar thai freris dang to dede; — Many men; slaughtered
Sum nakit fled and gat out of that sted, — got; place
The watter socht, abaissit out of slepe. — startled
In the furd weill that was bath wan and depe — ford well; dark
Feyll of thaim fell that brak out of that place, — Many; broke
490 Dowkit to grounde and deit withoutyn grace. — Plunged to the bottom; died
Drownyt and slayne was all that herbryt thar. — lodged
Men callis it yeit 'the freris blyssyng of Ayr.' — yet; blessing
Few folk of vaill was levyt apon cace — worth; left by chance
In the castell; lord Persye fra that place
495 Befor the ayr fra thine to Glaskow drew, — justice-ayre from there
Of men and stuff it was to purva new. — provisions; furnish anew
Yeit thai within saw the fyr byrnand stout, — Yet; strong
With schort avys ischet and had na dout. — Without delay; hesitation
The buschement than, as weryouris wys and wicht, — ambush; warriors / bold
500 Leit thaim allayne and to the hous past rycht. — Left; alone; castle / directly
Boyd wan the port, entryt and all his men; — reached; gate
Keparis in it was left bot nine or ten. — Defenders
The formast sone hym selff sesyt in hand, — soon; seized
Maid quyt of hym, syne slew all at thai fand. — Dispatched him then; that; found
505 Of purvyaunce in that castell was nayne; — provisions
Schort tyme befor Persye was fra it gayne. — gone
The Erll Arnulff had rasavit that hauld — received; castle
Quhilk in the toune was brynt to powder cauld. — burned; cold ashes
Boyd gert ramayn of his men twenty still; — stationed twenty of his men
510 Hym selff past furth to witt of Wallace will, — learn
Kepand the toune quhill nocht was levyt mar — Guarding; of which no more was left
Bot the wode fyr and beyldis brynt full bar. — Except; houses burned
Of lykly men that born was in Ingland — war-like
Be swerd and fyr that nycht deit five thousand. — By sword; died

515 Quhen Wallace men was weill togydder
        met,
    'Gud freyndis,' he said, 'ye knaw that thar        know
        wes set                                        appointed
    Sic law as this now in to Glaskow toune            Such a law-court
    Be byschope Beik and Persye of renoune.
    Tharfor I will in haist we thidder fair.           go
520 Of our gud kyn sum part ar lossyt thair.'          kin; lost
    He gert full sone the burges till him caw          had; soon; called to him
    And gaiff commaund in generall to thaim
        aw,                                            all
    In kepyng thai suld tak the hous of Ayr,[1]
    'And hald it haill quhill tyme that we her         safeguard it until; hear more
        mayr.
525 To byd our king castellys I wald we had;           await
    Cast we doun all we mycht be demyt our             [If] we cast down; considered
        rad.'                                              too rash
    Thai gart meit cum for thai had fastyt lang;       had food fetched; fasted
    Litill he tuk, syne bounyt thaim to gang.          then they prepared to go
    Horsis thai cheys that Sotheroun had               chose
        brocht thar,
530 A new at will and of the toune can fair.           Newly; went
    Thre hundreth haill was in his cumpany.            in all
    Richt wonder fast raid this gud chevalry
    To Glaskow bryg that byggyt was of tre,            bridge; built; wood
    Weyll passit our or Sotheroun mycht thaim          Passed safely across before
        se.
535 Lorde Persye wyst, that besy wes in wer,           knew; diligent; war
    Semblyt his men fell awfull in affer.              Assembled; very; appearance
    Than demyt thai that it was wicht Wallace;         they believed; stalwart
    He had befor chapyt throu mony cace.               escaped many a lucky; chance
    The byschope Beik and Persye that was
        wicht                                          active
540 A thousand led of men in armys brycht.             Led a thousand men
    Wallace saw weill quhat nowmyr semblit             numbers assembled
        thar;
    He maid his men in twa partis to fair,             divisions to go
    Graithit thaim weill without the townys            Equipped them; outside
        end.
    He callit Awchinlek for he the passage
        kend.                                          knew

___

1 [That] they should defend the castle of Ayr

545 'Uncle,' he said, 'be besy in to wer.                    prepare for battle
    Quhether will yhe the byschoppys taill
    upber,                                                   carry
    Or pas befor and tak his benysone?'                      in front; blessing
    He answerd hym with rycht schort                         little hesitation
    provision,
    'Unbyschoppyt yeit forsuth I trow ye be.[1]
550 Your selff sall fyrst his blyssyng tak for
    me,
    For sekyrly ye servit it best the nycht.                 surely; deserved; tonight
    To ber his taill we sall in all our mycht.'              carry; with all our might
    Wallace answerd, 'Sen we mon sindry                      must go separately
    gang
    Perell thar is and ye bid fra us lang,                   if you stay away from us
555 For yone ar men will nocht sone be agast.                those; afraid
    Fra tyme we meit for Goddis saik haist you               From the time; encounter
    fast.'                                                     [them]
    Our disseveryng I wald na Sotheroune                     separation
    saw;
    Behynd thaim cum and in the northast                     north-east row
    raw.
    Gud men of wer ar all Northummyrland.'                   war
560 Thai partand thus tuk othir be the hand.                 parting; each other by
    Awchinlek said, 'We sall do at we may.                   what
    We wald lik ill to byd oucht lang away;                  not like to stay away long
    A boustous staill betwix us sone mon be,                 strong force; soon must
    Bot to the rycht all mychty God haiff e.'[2]
565 Adam Wallace and Awchinlek was boune,                    were ready
    Sevyn scor with thaim on the baksid the                  Seven; back end of
    toune.
    Rycht fast thai yeid quhill thai war out of              until
    sycht;
    The tother part arrayit thaim full rycht.                division arrayed; directly
    Wallace and Boid the playne streyt up can                open street
    ga;                                                      went
570 Sotheroun merveld becaus thai saw na ma.                 marvelled; no more
    Thar senyhe cryit upon the Persys syde,                  signal
    With byschop Beik that bauldly durst                     boldly dared
    abide.                                                   withstand
    A sayr semlay was at that metyng seyne,                  painful encounter; seen

1 I believe you have not been blessed by a bishop yet, indeed
2 But may almighty God protect the righteous

As fyr on flynt it feyrryt thaim betweyne.                    sparked
575    The hardy Scottis rycht awfully thaim          awesomely
          abaid,                                      withstood
       Brocht feill to grounde throuch weid that      Struck many down; armour
          weill was maid,
       Perssyt plattis with poyntis stiff of steill,   Pierced plate-armour; strong
       Befors of hand gert mony cruell kneill.         By force; fierce men to kneel
       The strang stour rais as reik upon thaim        dense dust rose; smoke
          fast,
580    Or myst throuch sone up to the clowdis          Before sun
          past.
       To help thaim selff ilkayne had mekill neid.    each one; great need
       The worthy Scottis stud in fellone dreid,       stood; terrible danger
       Yeit forthwart ay thai pressit for to be        Yet forward ever
       And thai on thaim gret wonder was to se.
585    The Perseis men in wer was oysit weill,         were experienced in war
       Rycht fersly faucht and sonyeit nocht           fiercely fought; hesitated not
          adeill.
       Adam Wallace and Awchinlek com in
       And partyt Sotheron rycht sodeynly in           parted; two
          twyn,
       Raturnd to thaim as noble men in wer.           Rallied; war
590    The Scottis gat rowme and mony doun thai        mastery; many
          ber.
       The new counter assailyeit thaim sa fast,       encounter attacked
       Throuch Inglismen maid sloppys at the           breaches
          last.
       Than Wallace selff in to that felloune          [threw] himself; terrible
          thrang                                          press
       With his gud swerd that hevy was and
          lang,
595    At Perseis face witht a gud will he bar.         struck vigorously
       Bath bayne and brayne the forgyt steill         bone; brain; forged steel
          throu schair.                                   cut
       Four hundreth men quhen lord Persie was
          dede
       Out of the gait the byschop Beik thai lede,      street; lead
       For than thaim thocht it was no tyme to
          bid,                                            stay
600    By the frer kyrk till a wode fast besyd.         friars' church; close by
       In that forest forsuth thai taryit nocht;        indeed
       On fresch horsis to Bothwell sone thai           soon; made their way
          socht.

Wallace folowed with worthi men and wicht; — strong

Forfouchtyn thai war and travald all the nycht, — Exhausted [from fighting]; toiled

605 Yeit feill thai slew in to the chace that day. — many; in the pursuit

The byschope selff and gud men gat away;

Amar Wallang reskewit him in that place.

That knycht full oft did gret harme to Wallace.

Wallace began of nycht ten houris in Ayr,

610 On day be nine in Glaskow semlyt thair. — by nine o'clock; assembled

Be ane our nowne at Bothwell yeit he was, — By one o'clock; gate

Repreiffit Wallang or he wald forther pas, — Denounced; before

Syne turnd agayne, as weyll witnes the buk, — Then; attests

Till Dundaff raid and thar restyng he tuk, — To; rode; there

615 Tald gud Schir Jhon of thir tithandis in Ayr. — Told; these tidings

Gret mayne he maid he was nocht with him thar. — He greatly lamented that

Wallace sojornd in Dundaff at his will — stayed

Five dayis out, quhill tithandis come him till — altogether; until news

Out of the hycht quhar gud men was forlorn, — Highlands; lost

620 For Bouchane rais, Adell, Menteth and Lorn. — Buchan; Atholl

Apon Argyll a fellone wer thai mak; — grievous war

For Edwardis saik thus can thai undertak. — did they undertake

The knycht Cambell in Argyll than wes still

With his gud men agayne King Edwardis will

625 And kepyt fre Lowchow his heretage, — kept independent Loch Awe

Bot Makfadyan than did him gret outrage. — wrong

This Makfadyan till Inglismen was sworn; — sworn

Edward gaiff him bath Argill and Lorn. — both

Fals Jhon of Lorn to that gyft can concord; — gift; agree

630 In Ingland than he was a new maid lord.

Thus falsly he gaiff our his heretage — handed over

And tuk at London of Edward grettar wage. — payment

Dunkan of Lorn yeit for the landis straiff, — still; contended

Quhill Makfadyan ourset him with the laiff,    *Until; overcame; rest*
635  Put him of force to gud Cambell the
       knycht[1]
       Quhilk in to wer was wys, worthi and     *war*
       wicht.
       Thus Makfadyan was entrit in to Scotland
       And mervalusly that tyrand tuk on hand
       With his power, the quhilk I spak of ayr.    *spoke; earlier*
640  Thai four lordschippis all semlyt till him    *assembled*
       thair,
       Fifteen thousand of curssyt folk in deid    *accursed; indeed*
       Of all gaddryn in ost he had to leid,    *gathering; lead*
       And mony of thaim was out of Irland
       brocht.
       Barnys nor wyff thai peple sparyt nocht,    *Children; wives; spared*
645  Waistyt the land als fer as thai mycht ga,    *Laid waste; as far; go*
       Thai bestly folk couth nocht bot byrn and    *burn*
       sla.    *slay*
       In to Louchow he entryt sodeynly;
       The knycht Cambell maid gud defens forthi.    *therefore*
       Till Crage Unyn with thre hunder he yeid:    *To; went*
650  That strenth he held for all his cruell deid,    *stronghold; despite; action*
       Syne brak the bryg that thai mycht nocht    *Then broke; bridge*
       out pas    *pass over*
       Bot throuch a furd quhar narow passage    *ford*
       was.
       Abandounly Cambell agayne thaim baid,    *Boldly; stood*
       Fast upon Avis that was bathe depe and    *Awe; both*
       braid.    *wide*
655  Makfadyane was apon the tother sid
       And thar on force behuffit him for to byd,    *of necessity beloved; stay*
       For at the furde he durst nocht enter out,
       For gud Cambell mycht set him than in    *place*
       dout.    *at risk*
       Makfadyane socht and a small passage fand;    *found*
660  Had he lasar thai mycht pas off that land    *leisure*
       Betwix a roch and the gret wattersid;    *rock; lochside*
       Bot four in front na ma mycht gang nor    *Only; no more; go*
       rid.    *ride*
       In till Louchow wes bestis gret plente;    *beasts in great plenty*
       A quhill he thocht thar with his ost to be    *while; army*

1 Entrusted himself of necessity to good Campbell the knight

665 And other stuff that thai had with thaim
      brocht,
      Bot all his crafft availyeit him rycht nocht.          skill availed
      Dunkane of Lorn has seyne the sodeyne                   seen; sudden
      cace.                                                   danger
      Fra gud Cambell he went to seik Wallace,               From; seek
      Sum help to get of thar turment and teyne.             anguish; trouble
670 Togydder befor in Dunde thai had beyne,
      Lerand at scule in to thar tendyr age.                 Learning at school
      He thocht to slaik Makfadyanys hie curage.             extinguish; high
      Gylmychell than with Dunkan furth him
      dycht;                                                 prepared
      A gyd he was and fute man wonder wicht.                guide; foot soldier; nimble
675 Sone can thai witt quhar Wallace lugyt was;             Soon; know
      With thar complaynt till his presence thai            grievance
      pas.
      Erll Malcom als the Lennox held at es,                also; in comfort
      With his gud men to Wallace can he pres.              did he press
      Till him thar come gud Rychard of
      Lundy;
680 In till Dundaff he wald no langar ly.                  lie
      Schir Jhon the Graym als bounyt him to               also prepared himself; ride
      ryd.
      Makfadyanis wer so grevit thaim that tid             war; vexed; time
      At Wallace thocht his gret power to se,              That
      In quhat aray he reullyt that cuntre.                state; governed; region
685 The Rukbe than he kepit with gret wrang
      Stirlyng castell that stalwart wes and
      strang.
      Quhen Wallace come be south it in a vaill            by the south of it [the castle]
      Till Erll Malcome he said he wald assaill.           To; attack
      In divers partis he gert sever thar men,             parties; caused to divide
690 Of thar power that Sotheroun suld nocht              should not
      ken.                                                 know
      Erll Malcome baid in buschement out of              waited in ambush
      sicht.
      Wallace with him tuk gud Schir Jhone the
      knycht
      And a hundreth of wys wer men but dout,             warriors; fearless
      Throuch Stirlyng raid gyff ony wald ysche           rode if any; sally out
      out.
695 Towart the bryg the gaynest way thai pas;           bridge; nearest
      Quhen Rukbe saw quhat at thar power was             the size of their army

He tuk sevyn scor of gud archaris was thar.

Upon Wallace thai folowed wondyr sayr.                              extremely hard

At fell bykkyr thai did thaim mekill der.                           fierce encounters; great harm

700  Wallace in hand gryppyt a nobill sper,

Agayne raturnd and has the formast slayne.                          turned back

Schir Jhon the Grayme, that mekill was of                           very powerful
     mayn,

Amang thaim raid with a gud sper in hand.                           rode

The fyrst he slew that he befor him fand;

705  Apon a nother his sper in soundyr yeid;                         shattered

A swerd he drew quhilk helpyt him in
     neid.

Ynglis archaris apon thaim can ranew,                               English; renew the attack

That his gud hors with arrowis sone thai                            soon
     slew.

On fute he was; quhen Wallace has it seyne

710  He lychtyt sone with men of armys keyne,                        dismounted soon; fierce

Amang the rout fechtand full wondyr fast.                           throng fighting

The Inglismen raturnyt at the last.                                 turned back

At the castell thai wald haiff beyne full                           have liked to be
     fayne,

Bot Erll Malcome with men of mekill                                 great strength
     mayne

715  Betwix the Sotheroun and the yettis yeid.                       gates went

Mony thai slew that douchty wes in deid.                            valiant; deeds

In the gret pres Wallace and Rukbe met,

With his gud swerd a straik apon him set;

Derffly to dede the ald Rukbe he draiff.                            Violently to death; dashed

720  His twa sonnys chapyt amang the laiff.                          escaped; rest

In the castell be aventur thai yeid                                 by good luck; went

With twenty men; na ma chapyt that dreid.                           more escaped; peril

The Lennox men with thar gud lord at
     was,

Fra the castell thai said thai wald nocht
     pas,

725  For weill thai wyst it mycht nocht haldyn                       knew; be held [against attack]
     be

On na lang tyme; forthi thus ordand he.                            For a long time; ordered

Erll Malcom tuk the hous and kepyt that                            castle; held it at that time
     tyd.

Wallace wald nocht fra his fyrst purpos bid.                       stray

Instance he maid to this gud lord and wys,

730  Fra thine to pas he suld on nakyn wys

Quhill he had tayne Stirlyng the castell
    strang;[1]

Trew men him tald he mycht nocht hald it    told; hold
    lang.

Than Wallace thocht was maist on     mostly
    Makfadyane;

Of Scottis men he had slayne mony ane.    many a one

735   Wallace avowide that he suld wrokyn be    vowed; avenged

On that rebald or ellis tharfor to de.    rebel; else die in the attempt

Of tyrandry King Edward thocht him gud;    For oppression; good

Law born he was and of law simpill blud.    Low-born; low; blood

Thus Wallace was sar grevyt in his entent;    extremely vexed; mind

740   To this jornay rycht ernystfully he went.    feat of arms; earnestly

At Stirlyng bryg assemlyt till him rycht    bridge; directly

Twa thousand men that worthi war and    were
    wycht.    strong

Towart Argyll he bounyt him to ryd;    prepared; ride

Dunkan of Lorn was thar trew sekyr gid.    reliable guide

745   Of ald Rukbe the quhilk we spak of ayr,    old; earlier

Twa sonnys on lyff in Stirlyng levit thair.    alive; lived there

Quhen thai brether consavit weill the rycht    those brothers understood

This hous to hald that thai na langer    castle; keep
    mycht,

For caus quhi thai wantyt men and meit,    Because; lacked; food

750   With Erll Malcome thai kest thaim for to    prepared
    treit    negotiate

Grace of thar lyff and thai that with thaim    Saving their lives; those;
    was;    were

Gaiff our the hous, syne couth in Ingland    Handed over the castle, then
    pas

On the thrid day that Wallace fra thaim
    raid.    rode

With King Edward full mony yer thai baid,    very many years; remained

755   In Brucis wer agayne come in Scotland.    war

Stirlyng to kepe the toune of thaim tuk on    keep
    hand.

Mencione of Bruce is oft in Wallace buk;

To fend his rycht full mekill payne he tuk.    defend; great trouble

Quhar to suld I her of tary ma?    should; here; more

760   To Wallace furth now schortlye will I ga.    shortly; go

---

1 He entreated this good, wise lord / not to leave there [the castle] on any
account / until he had taken mighty Stirling Castle

Dunkan of Lorne Gilmychall fra thaim send    *sent*

A spy to be for he the contre kend.    *region knew*

Be our party was passit Straith Fulan

The small fute folk began to irk ilkane,[1]

765 And hors of fors behuffyt for to faill.    *horses of necessity behoved*

Than Wallace thocht that cumpany to vaill.    *help*

'Gud men,' he said, 'this is nocht meit for us;    *fitting*

In brokyn ray and we cum on thaim thus    *array if*

We may tak scaith and harme our fayis bot small.    *receive injury; only a little*

770 To thaim in lik we may nocht semble all.    *in the same way; gather*

Tary we lang a playne feild thai will get;    *If we tarry; open battle*

Apon thaim sone sa weill we may nocht set.[2]

Part we mon leiff us folowand for to be;    *Part [of our company]*

With me sall pas our power in to thre.'

775 Five hundyr fyrst till him selff he has tayne    *hundred; taken*

Of westland men, was worthi knawin    *known*

ilkane.    *each one*

To Schir Jhon Grayme als mony ordand he,'    *as many; he decreed*

And five hundreth to Rychard of Lundye.

In that part was Wallace of Ricardtoun;    *division*

780 In all gud deid he was ay redy boun.    *deeds; ready and willing*

Five hundreth left that mycht nocht with thaim ga,

Suppos at thai to byd was wondyr wa.    *Even though; remain behind*

Thus Wallace ost began to tak the hicht,    *army; highlands*

Our a montayne sone passit of thar sicht.    *Over; soon; out of their sight*

785 In Glendowchar thair spy mett thaim agayn,    *Glen Dochart*

With lord Cambell; than was our folk rycht fayn.    *very* / *glad*

At that metyng gret blithnes mycht be seyn;    *joy*

---

1 By the time our party was past Straith Fulan, every one of the small band of auxiliaries began to tire

2 Soon we may not set upon them so well

Thre hundreth he led that cruell was and keyn.    *fierce* / *bold*

He comford thaim and bad thaim haiff no dreid:    *commanded* / *fear*

790 'Yon bestly folk wantis wapynnys and weid.    *Those; lack; armour*

Sune thai will fle, scharply and we persew.'    *and we [will] pursue keenly*

Be Louchdouchyr full sodeynly thaim drew.    *By Loch Dochart; came*

Than Wallace said, 'A lyff all sall we ta,    *take*

For her is nayne will fra his falow ga.'    *here; no-one; fellow go*

795 The spy he send the entre for to se;

Apon the mos a scurrour sone fand he.    *moor; scout soon found*

To scour the land Makfadyane had him send;

Out of Cragmor that day he thocht to wend.    *go*

Gylmychall fast apon him folowed thar;

800 With a gud swerd that weill and scharply schar    *pierced*

Maid quyt of him; at tithandis tald he nayne;    *Made an end of him; so that he told no news*

The out spy thus was lost fra Makfadyhane.    *spy sent out*

Than Wallace ost apon thar fute thai lycht;    *on foot; alighted*

Thar hors thai left thocht thai war never so wicht;    *strong*

805 For mos and crag thai mycht no langar dre.    *bog and rock; endure*

Than Wallace said, 'Quha gangis best lat se.'    *Let's see who makes his way best*

Throuch out the mos delyverly thai yeid,    *nimbly; went*

Syne tuk the hals, quhar of thai had most dreid.    *Then entered the pass* / *fear*

Endlang the schoir ay four in frownt thai past    *Along; shore [of the loch] always; front*

810 Quhill thai within assemblit at the last.    *Until*

Lord Cambell said, 'We haiff chewyst this hauld.    *chosen position*

I trow to God thar wakyning sall be cauld.    *trust*

Her is na gait to fle yone peple can

Bot rochis heich and watter depe and wan.'[1]

---

1 Here there is no way those people can flee / except to the high rocks and the deep dark water

815 Eighteen hundreth of douchty men in deid — *valiant; action*
On the gret ost but mar process thai yeid, — *without further delay; advanced*

Fechtand in frownt and mekill maistry maid. — *Fighting; front; deeds of arms achieved*
On the frayt folk buskyt withoutyn baid. — *scared; set on; hesitation*
Rudly till ray thai ruschit thaim agayne; — *Strongly; array*
820 Gret part of thaim wes men of mekill mayne. — *great strength*
Gud Wallace men sa stoutly can thaim ster — *boldly; bestir themselves*
The battaill on bak five akyr breid thai ber. — *back; wide five acres*
In to the stour feill tyrandis gert thai kneill. — *fighting; many oppress*
Wallace in hand had a gud staff of steyll; — *sword of steel*
825 Quhom ever he hyt to ground brymly thaim bar; — *Whomever; hit; fiercely; dashed*
Romde him about a large rude and mar.[1]
Schir Jhon the Grayme in deid was rycht worthy, — *action*
Gud Cambell als, and Rychard of Lundy, — *also*
Adam Wallace and Robert Boid in feyr — *together*
830 Amang thar fais quhar deidis was sald full der. — *Among; foes; were paid very dearly*
The felloun stour was awfull for to se. — *cruel fighting*
Makfadyane than so gret debait maid he — *resistance*
With Yrage men hardy and curageous; — *Highlanders*
The stalwart stryff rycht hard and peralous, — *struggle*
835 Boundance of blud fra woundis wid and wan, — *Abundance of blood; deep*
Stekit to deid on ground lay mony man. — *Stabbed to death*
The fersast thar ynewch of fechtyn fand; — *fiercest; enough; fighting*
Twa houris large into the stour thai stand, — *long; battle; stood ground*
At Jop him selff weill wyst nocht quha suld wyn.[2]
840 Bot Wallace men wald nocht in soundyr twyn; — *asunder break*
Till help thaim selff thai war of hardy will. — *To*
Of Yrage blud full hardely thai spill,

1 Cleared a space around him, as large as a rood [a measure] or more
2 That Jop himself did not know for sure who would win

With feyll fechtyn maid sloppys throuch the thrang. — *fierce fighting; gaps; throng*

On the fals part our wicht wermen sa dang — *party; strong; struck*

845 That thai to byd mycht haiff no langar mycht. — *stay*

The Irland folk than maid thaim for the flycht, — *Highland; prepared for flight*

In craggis clam and sum in watter flett, — *crags climbed; floated*

Twa thousand thar drownyt withoutyn lett. — *at once*

Born Scottis men baid still in to the feild, — *Native*

850 Kest wapynnys thaim fra and on thar kneis kneild. — *Threw; knees*

With petous voice thai criyt apon Wallace, — *piteous*

For Goddis saik to tak thaim in his grace. — *mercy*

Grevyt he was bot rewth of thaim he had, — *Vexed; pity*

Rasauit thaim fair with contenance full sad. — *Received; stern*

855 'Of our awne blud we suld haiff gret pete. — *own*

Luk yhe sla nane of Scottis will yoldyn be. — *who will surrender*

Of outland men lat nane chaip with the liff.' — *foreign*

Makfadyane fled for all his felloun stryff — *fierce opposition*

On till a cave within a clyfft of stayne, — *stone cliff*

860 Undyr Cragmor with fifteen is he gayne.

Dunkan of Lorn his leyff at Wallace ast; — *permission to leave*

On Makfadyane with worthi men he past; — *followed*

He grantyt him to put thaim all to ded. — *granted [permission]; death*

Thai left nane quyk, syne brocht Wallace his hed, — *none alive; head*

865 Apon a sper throuch out the feild it bar. — *carried*

The lord Cambell syne hynt it by the har; — *then seized; hair*

Heich in Cragmor he maid it for to stand, — *High*

Steild on a stayne for honour of Irland. — *Placed; stone; Highlands*

The blessit men that was of Scotland borne, — *fortunate*

870 Funde at his faith Wallace gert thaim be sworn, — *Found in his allegiance*

Restorit thaim to thar landis but les. — *indeed*

He leit sla nayne that wald cum till his pes. — *let [them] kill no-one*

Effter this deid in Lorn syne couth he fayr; — *After; feat; afterwards; go*

Reullyt the land had beyne in mekill cayr.     Governed; much suffering
875  In Archatan a consell he gert cry,     Ardchattan; had proclaimed
Quhar mony man socht till his senyory.     flocked to; leadership
All Lorn he gaiff till Duncan at was wicht     strong
And bad him: 'Hald in Scotland with the     commanded
  rycht,
And thou sall weill bruk this in heretage.     enjoy possession
880  Thi brother sone at London has grettar wage,     i.e., nephew; reward
Yeit will he cum he sall his landis haiff.[1]
I wald tyne nayne that rychtwisnes mycht     lose none
  saiff.'     protect
Mony trew Scot to Wallace couth persew;     Many; flocked to Wallace
At Archatan fra feill strenthis thai drew.     many strongholds
885  A gud knycht come and with him men
  sexte;
He had beyne oft in mony strang jeperte     dangerous exploits
With Inglismen and sonyeid nocht a deill.     hesitated
Ay fra thar faith he fendyt him full weill,[2]
Kepyt him fre, thocht King Edward had     independent; in despite of
  sworn;     King Edward
890  Schir Jhon Ramsay, that rychtwys ayr was     rightful heir
  born,
Of Ouchterhous and othir landis was lord,
And schirreff als as my buk will record,     also
Of nobill blud and als haill ancrase     sound ancestry
Contenyt weill with worthi chevalre.     Continued
895  In till Straithern that lang tyme he had
  beyne
At gret debait agaynys his enemys keyne;     Offering great resistance
Rycht wichtly wan his leving in to wer.     vigorously; livelihood in war
Till him and his Sotheroun did mekill der;     the English; great injury
Weill he eschevit and sufferyt gret     He accomplished much
  distress.
900  His sone was cald the flour of courtlyness,     son; called; flower
As witnes weill in to the schort tretty     account
Efter the Bruce, quha redis in that story.
He rewllit weill bathe in to wer and pes;     governed; war; peace
Alexander Ramsay to nayme he hecht but     name; called; indeed
  les.

1 If he will come [into Wallace's grace] he shall have his lands
2 He always successfully avoided swearing loyalty to them [the Eng-
lish]

905  Quhen it wes wer till armes he him kest;          war; he devoted himself
     Under the croun he wes ane of the best.
     In tyme of pees till courtlynes he yeid,          courtly pursuits; turned
     Bot to gentrice he tuk nayne other heid.          [noble birth; heed]
     Quhat gentill man had nocht with Ramsay
        beyne
910  Of courtlynes thai count him nocht a              [worth a] pin
        preyne.
     Fredome and treuth he had as men wald
        as;[1]
     Sen he begane na better squier was,               Since
     Roxburch hauld he wan full manfully,              Roxburgh Castle; conquered
     Syne held it lang quhill tratouris                Then; until traitors
        tresonably
915  Causit his dede, I can nocht tell you how;        death
     Of sic thingis I will ga by as now.               such; pass over for now
     I haiff had blayme to say the suthfastnes,        been reproached; truth
     Tharfor I will bot lychtly ryn that cace,         lightly touch on that case
     Bot it be thing that playnly sclanderit is.       Unless; something censured
920  For sic I trow thai suld deyme me no              such; not find fault with me
        mys;
     Of gud Alexander as now I spek no mar.            more
     His fader come as I tald of befor.
     Wallace of hym rycht full gud comford
        hais
     For weill he coud do harmyng till his fais.       certainly; harm; foes
925  In wer he was rycht mekill for to prys,           war; greatly to prize
     Besy and trew, bath sobyr, wicht and wys.         Diligent; both steadfast
     A gud prelat als to Archatan socht;               prelate; made his way
     Of his lordschip as than he brukyt nocht.         possessed
     This worthi clerk cummyn of hie lynage,           high lineage
930  Of Synclar blude, nocht forty yer of age,         Sinclair blood
     Chosyne he was be the papis consent,              by the pope's
     Of Dunkell lord him maid with gud                 Dunkeld bishop; purpose
        entent.
     Bot Inglismen that Scotland gryppit all           seized
     Of benyfice thai leit him bruk bot small.         benefice; allowed; possess
935  Quhen he saw weill tharfor he mycht nocht
        mwte,                                          treat
     To saiff his lyff thre yer he dwelt in But;       save; Bute
     Leifyde as he mycht and kepyt ay gud part         Lived; good faith

     1 Generosity and loyalty he had as much as any one could ask

Under saifte of Jamys than lord Stewart,  protection
Till gud Wallace, quhilk Scotland wan with  Until; won
payne,  difficulty
940  Restord this lord till his leyffing agayne.  land
And mony ma that lang had beyne  many more
ourthrawin,  overthrown
Wallace thaim put rychtwisly to thar awn.  Restored rightfully; own
The small ost als the quhilk I spak of ayr,  also; earlier
In to the hycht that Wallace levyt thar,  In the highlands; left there
945  Come to the feild quhar Makfadyane had  Came
beyne,
Tuk at was left, baithe weid and wapynnys  what; both armour
scheyne;  bright
Throu Lorn syne past als gudly as thai can.  then; well
Of thar nowmer thai had nocht lost a man.  number
On the fyft day thai wan till Archatan  reached
950  Quhar Wallace baid with gud men mony  camped; many a one
ane.
He welcummyt thaim apon a gudly wys  warmly
And said thai war rycht mekill for to prys.  greatly to prize
All trew Scottis he honourit in to wer,  war
Gaiff that he wan, hym selff kepyt no ger.  Gave away what; won; gear
955  Quhen Wallace wald no langar sojorn thar,  stay
Fra Archatan throu out the land thai far  From; travelled
Towart Dunkell, with gud men of renoun.
His maist thocht than was haill on Sanct  His mind was set then wholly
Jhonstoun.
He cald Ramsai, that gud knycht of gret  summoned
vaill,  worth
960  Sadly avysyt besocht him of consaill.  Firmly resolved; sought;
advice

'Of Saynct Jhonstoun now haiff I in
remembrance;
Thar I haiff beyne and lost men apon
chance,  by misfortune
Bot ay for ane we gert ten of thaim de,  always for one [of ours]
And yeit me think that is no mendis to me.  amends
965  I wald assay of this land or we gang  attack; before; go
And lat thaim witt thai occupy her with  let them know; here
wrang.'  wrongly
Than Ramsay said, 'That toune thai may
nocht kep.  keep
The wallis ar laych suppos the dyk be depe.  low; ditch

Ye haiff enewch that sall thaim cummyr sa; — enough; harass
970 Fyll up the dyk that we may playnly ga — Fill; go
In haill battaill, a thousand our at anys; — full battle order; across
Fra this power thai sall nocht hald yon — force; those
wanys.' — buildings
Wallace was glaid that he sic comfort — such
maid;
Furth talkand thus on to Dunkell thai raid. — Forth talking; rode
975 Four dayis thar thai lugyt with plesance, — lodged comfortably
Quhill tyme thai had forseyne thar — Until; made ready their
ordinance. — preparations
Ramsay gert byg strang bestials of tre — had built; siege machines
Be gud wrychtis, the best in that cuntre; — wrights; region
Quhen thai war wrocht betaucht thaim men — made; assigned men to lead
to leid — them
980 The watter doun quhill thai come to that — Down the river until; came;
steid. — place
Schir Jhon Ramsay rycht gudly was thar — was their excellent guide
gid,
Rewillyt thaim weill at his will for to bid. — Directed; to follow his will
The gret ost than about the village past; — army; around
With erd and stayne thai fillit dykis fast. — earth; stones; ditches
985 Flaikis thai laid on temer lang and wicht; — Hurdles; timber; long; strong
A rowme passage to the wallis thaim — clear path; prepared
dycht.
Feill bestials rycht starkly up thai rais; — Many siege engines; raised;
Gud men of armys sone till assailye gais. — soon; attack; went
Schir Jhon the Grayme and Ramsay that
was wicht — powerful
990 The turat bryg segyt with all thar mycht, — besieged
And Wallace selff at mydsid of the toune — middle side
With men of armys that was to bargane — were ready to fight
boun.
The Sotheron men maid gret defence that
tid — time
With artailye that felloune was to bid, — artillery; grievous; endure
995 With awblaster, gaynye and stanys fast — crossbow; bolts; stones
And hand gunnys, rycht brymly out thai — guns; fiercely; shot
cast;
Punyeid with speris men of armys scheyn. — Pierced; bright
The worthi Scottis that cruell war and
keyne,
At hand strakis, fra thai togidder met, — In close combat, from [when]

1000   With Sotheroun blud thar wapynnys sone
      thai wet.
  Yeit Inglismen that worthi war in wer       *Yet; were; war*
  In to the stour rycht bauldly can thaim    *fighting; boldly*
      ber,
  Bot all for nocht availyeid thaim thar deid;   *availed; actions*
  The Scottis throu force apon thaim in thai   *forced their way in*
      yeid.
1005   A thousand men our wallis yeid hastely;   *hurried over walls*
  In to the toun rais hidwis noyis and cry.   *rose hideous noise*
  Ramsay and Graym the turat yet has      *turret; reached*
      woun
  And entrit in quhar gret striff has begoun.   *battle; begun*
  A trew squier quhilk Rwan hecht be     *was called; name*
      nayme
1010   Come to the salt with gud Schir Jhon the   *assault*
      Grayme;
  Thirty with him of men that previt weill   *proved their mettle*
  Amang thar fais with wapynnys stiff of   *Among; foes; strong of*
      steill.                           *steel*
  Quhen at the Scottis semblit on athir sid   *that; assembled; either*
  Na Sotheroun was that mycht thar dynt   *There was no Englishman;*
      abid.                           *blows endure*
1015   Twa thousand sone was fulyeid under feit   *soon; trampled; foot*
  Of Sotheroun blud, lay stekit in the streit.   *Englishmen; stabbed; street*
  Schir Jhon Sewart saw weill the toune was
      tynt,                         *lost*
  Tuk him to flycht and wald no langar   *Fled away; stay*
      stynt;
  In a lycht barge and with him men sexte   *light*
1020   The water doun socht succour at Dunde.   *Down the river; help*
  Wallace baid still quhill the ferd day at   *stayed; till; fourth*
      morn
  And left nane thar that war of Ingland
      born.
  Riches thai gat of gold and othir gud,   *got; goods*
  Plenyst the toun agayne with Scottis blud.   *Settled; Scottish people*
1025   Rwan he left thar capteyn for to be,
  In heretage gaiff him office to fee   *as heritable office*
  Of all Straithern, and schirreiff of the   *[to be] sheriff*
      toun;
  Syne in the north gud Wallace maid him   *Then; set off*
      boune.

| | Verse | Gloss |
|---|---|---|
| | In Abyrdeyn he gert a consaill cry | council proclaim |
| 1030 | Trew Scottis men suld semble hastely. | [To which] loyal Scottish |
| | Till Couper he raid to wesy that abbay; | inspect |
| | The Inglis abbot fra thine was fled away. | from there |
| | Bischop Synclar without langar abaid | delay |
| | Met thaim at Glammys, syne furth with thaim he raid. | then forth |
| 1035 | In till Breichyn thai lugyt all that nycht; | In Brechin; lodged |
| | Syne on the morn Wallace gert graith thaim rycht, | Then; prepare [equip] |
| | Displayed on breid the baner of Scotland | abroad; banner |
| | In gud aray with noble men at hand; | battle order |
| | Gert playnly cry that sawfte suld be nayne[1] | |
| 1040 | Of Sotheroun blud quhar thai mycht be ourtayn. | English; overtaken |
| | In playne battaill throuch out the Mernys thai rid. | open; Mearns; ride |
| | The Inglismen, at durst thaim nocht abid, | that dared |
| | Befor the ost full ferdly furth thai fle | fled in terror |
| | Till Dunotter, a snuk within the se; | Dunnottar castle; promontory |
| 1045 | Na ferrar thai mycht wyn out of the land. | No farther; escape |
| | Thai semblit thar quhill thai war four thousand; | assembled; until |
| | To the kyrk rane, wend gyrth for till haiff tayne. | church ran, thought sanctuary |
| | The laiff ramaynd apon the roch of stayne. | rest; remained; stone rock |
| | The byschope than began tretty to ma, | negotiations; make |
| 1050 | Thar lyffis to get out of the land to ga, | lives; save; go |
| | Bot thai war rad and durst nocht weill affy. | afraid; dared; trust |
| | Wallace in fyr gert set all haistely, | on fire |
| | Brynt up the kyrk and all that was tharin. | Burned; church |
| | Atour the roch the laiff ran with gret dyn: | |
| 1055 | Sum hang on craggis rycht dulfully to de, | hung onto rocks; painfully |
| | Sum lap, sum fell, sum floteryt in the se. | leapt; floundered |
| | Na Sotheroun on lyff was levyt in that hauld | was left alive; stronghold |
| | And thaim within thai brynt in powder cauld. | burned; cold ashes |

1 Had openly proclaimed that there would be no sparing

Quhen this was done feill fell on kneis doun,          many fell
1060  At the byschop askit absolucioun.                       From
      Than Wallace lewch, said, 'I forgiff you all.          laughed
      Ar ye wer men, rapentis for sa small?                  warriors [that] repent; little
      Thai rewid nocht us in to the toun of Ayr,             had no pity on us
      Our trew barrouns quhen that thai hangit               hanged
          thar.'                                             there
1065  Till Abyrdeyn than haistely thai pas,                  To Aberdeen
      Quhar Inglismen besyly flittand was.                   busily were removing
      A hundreth schippys that ruthyr bur and                rudder carried
          ayr,                                               oar
      To turs thair gud, in havyn was lyand                  carry; goods; haven
          thar.
      Bot Wallace ost come on thaim sodeynlye;               Wallace's army
1070  Thar chapyt nane of all that gret menyhe,              None escaped there; company
      Bot feill servandis in thaim levyt nane.               Except many servants; left
      At ane eb se the Scottis is on thaim gayne,            an ebb tide; went on board
      Tuk out the ger, syne set the schippys in              goods, then; on fire
          fyr.
      The men on land thai bertynyt bayne and                battered bone
          lyr;                                               flesh
1075  Yeid nane away bot preistis, wyffis and
          barnys;
      Maid thai debait thai chapyt nocht but
          harmys.[1]
      In to Bowchane Wallace maid him to ryd,                Buchan; went on horseback
      Quhar lord Bewmound was ordand for to                  commanded
          bid.                                               stay
      Erll he was maid bot of schort tyme befor;
1080  He brukit nocht for all his bustous schor.[2]
      Quhen he wyst weill that Wallace cummand               knew
          was,
      He left the land and couth to Slanys pas               travelled to Slains
      And syne be schip in Ingland fled agayne.              then by ship
      Wallace raid throu the northland into                  rode; openly
          playne.
1085  At Crummade feill Inglismen thai slew.                 Cromarty many
      The worthi Scottis till him thus couth
          persew;                                            flocked

1 None went away except priests, women and children; / If they resisted,
they did not escape without harm
2 He did not enjoy possession for all his rude threats

Raturnd agayne and come till Abirdeyn

With his blith ost apon the Lammes evyn; — pleased army

Stablyt the land as him thocht best suld be, — Settled; should

1090 Syne with ane ost he passit to Dunde,

Gert set a sege about the castell strang. — Caused a siege to be laid

I leyff thaim thar and forthir we will gang.

Schir Amar Wallang haistit him full fast, — hurried very quickly

In till Ingland with his haill houshald — entire retinue
past.

1095 Bothwell he left, was Murrays heretage, — [which] was

And tuk him than bot till King Edwardis — only to hire
wage.

Thus his awne land forsuk for evermar;

Of Wallace deid gret tithandis tald he thar. — Wallace's deeds; news told

Als Inglismen sair murnyt in thar mude, — profoundly lamented; minds

1100 Had lossyt her bathe lyff, landis and gud. — [For they] had lost here both

Edward as than couth nocht in Scotland
fair, — go

Bot Kercyingame that was his tresorair,

With him a lord than Erll was of Waran,

He chargyt thaim with nowmeris mony — ordered; large numbers
ane

1105 Rycht weill beseyn in Scotland for to ryd. — well-equipped; ride

At Stirlyng still he ordand thaim to bid — commanded; wait

Quhill he mycht cum with ordinance of — Until; supplied from
Ingland.

Scotland agayne he thocht to tak in hand. — subdue

This ost past furth and had bot litill dreid; — fear

1110 The Erle Patrik rasavit thaim at Tweid. — received; the River Tweed

Malice he had at gud Wallace befor, — Ill-will; towards

Lang tyme by past and than incressit mor,

Bot throuch a cas that hapnyt of his wyff: — circumstance; on account of

Dunbar scho held fra him in to thar striff — struggle

1115 Throuch the supple of Wallace in to — assistance; indeed
playne;

Bot he be meyne gat his castell agayne — means

Lang tyme or than, and yeit he couth nocht — before then
ces. — desist

Agayne Wallace he previt in mony pres, — proved his mettle

With Inglismen suppleit thaim at his — supported
mycht.

1120 Contrar Scotland thai wrocht full gret — Against; wrought
unrycht. — injustice

Thar muster than was awfull for to se,
Of fechtand men thousandis thai war sexte,[1]
To Stirlyng past or thai likit to bid.　　　*before; chose to stop*
To Erll Malcome a sege thai laid that tid　*siege; time*
1125 And thocht to kep the commaund of thar　*keep*
　　　king;
Bot gud Wallace wrocht for ane othir thing.　*planned*
Dunde he left and maid a gud chyftane
With twa thousand to kepe that hous of　*castle*
　　　stayne,　　*stone*
Of Angwis men and dwellaris of Dunde;　*Angus; inhabitants of Dundee*
1130 The sammyn nycht till Sanct Jhonstoun　*same*
　　　went he.
Apon the morn till Schirreff mur he raid　*rode*
And thar a quhill in gud aray thai baid.　*order; stayed*
Schir Jhon the Grayme and Ramsay that
　　　was wicht,
He said to thaim, 'This is my purpos rycht.
1135 Our mekill it is to proffer thaim battaill　*It is too ambitious*
Apon a playne feild bot we haiff sum　*a battlefield; unless;*
　　　availl.'　　　*advantage*
Schir Jhon the Grayme said, 'We haiff
　　　undertayn
With les power sic thing that weill is gayn.'　*has gone well*
Than Wallace said, 'Quhar sic thing
　　　cummys of neid,　*of necessity*
1140 We suld thank God that makis us for to speid.　*succeed*
Bot ner the bryg my purpos is to be　*near; bridge*
And wyrk for thaim sum suttell jeperte.'　*plan; a surprise attack*
Ramsay answerd, 'The brig we may kepe
　　　weill.
Of way about Sotheroun has litill feill.'　*knowledge*
1145 Wallace sent Jop the battaill for to set,　*[time of] the battle; appoint*
The Tuysday next to fecht withoutyn let.　*fight; delay*
On Setterday on to the bryg thai raid,
Of gud playne burd was weill and junctly　*board; firmly*
　　　maid;
Gert wachis wait that nane suld fra thaim　*sentries know; none should*
　　　pas.　　*from*
1150 A wricht he tuk, the suttellast at thar was,　*carpenter; most skilled*
And ordand him to saw the burd in twa,　*ordered; board*

1 Of fighting men there were sixty thousand

Be the myd trest that nayne mycht our it
ga;                                                    Through; middle beam; over
On charnaill bandis nald it full fast and
sone,                                                  hinges nailed
Syne fyld with clay as na thing had beyne
done.                                                  Then filled; as [if] nothing

1155  The tothir end he ordand for to be,
How it suld stand on thre rowaris of tre,              wooden rollers
Quhen ane war out that the laiff doun suld             rest
fall.
Him selff under he ordand thar withall,                underneath; ordered
Bound on the trest in a creddill to sit,               beam; wooden support
1160  To lous the pyne quhen Wallace leit him            loosen; pin
witt;                                                  let know
Bot with a horn quhen it was tyme to be,
In all the ost suld no man blaw bot he.                blow
The day approchit of the gret battaill;
The Inglismen for power wald nocht faill.
1165  Ay sex thai war agayne ane of Wallace;            against one
Fyfty thousand maid thaim to battaill                  went
place.
The ramaynand baid at the castell still;               remainder stayed
Baithe feild and hous thai thocht to tak at            Both; castle; capture
will.
The worthi Scottis apon the tother side                other side
1170  The playne feild tuk, on fute maid thaim to       field of battle entered; foot;
bid.                                                       stand
Hew Kercyngayme the wantgard ledis he                  vanguard led
With twenty thousand of likly men to se.               war-like
Thirty thousand the Erll of Waran had,
Bot he did than as the wysman him bad;                 wise man [see note]
1175  All the fyrst ost befor him our was send.         army; across
Sum Scottis men that weill the maner kend              thought they knew better
Bade Wallace blaw and said thai war enew.              Told; blow [his horn]
He haistyt nocht bot sadly couth persew               did not rush; resolutely
Quhill Warans ost thik on the bryg he saw.
1180  Fra Jop the horn he hyntyt and couth              seized
blaw
Sa asprely and warned gud Jhon wricht.                 sharply; John the carpenter
The rowar out he straik with gret slycht;              roller; knocked; cunning
The laiff yeid doun quhen the pynnys out               rest went down; went out
gais.
A hidwys cry amang the peple rais;

1185    Bathe hors and men in to the watter fell.
        The hardy Scottis that wald na langer
              dwell
        Set on the laiff with strakis sad and sar,                    rest; blows firm; sore
        Of thaim thar our as than souerit thai war.                   over; secured [from attack]
        At the forbreist thai previt hardely,                         van proved themselves
1190    Wallace and Grayme, Boid, Ramsay and
              Lundy,
        All in the stour fast fechtand face to face.                  battle; fighting
        The Sotheron ost bak rerit of that place                     drew back
        As thai fyrst tuk five akyr breid and mar.                    acre more
        Wallace on fute a gret scharp sper he bar;
1195    Amang the thikest of the pres he gais.
        On Kercyngaym a strak chosyn he hais                         stroke delivered; has
        In the byrnes that polyst was full brycht.                   corslet; polished
        The punyeand hed the plattis persyt                          piercing; penetrated
              rycht,
        Throuch the body stekit him but reskew.                      fatally stabbed him
1200    Derffly to dede that chyftane was adew;[1]
        Baithe man and hors at that strak he bar                     dashed
              doun.
        The Inglis ost, quhilk war in battaill boun,
        Comfort thai lost quhen thar chyftayne was                   They lost courage
              slayn,
        And mony ane to fle began in playne.                         many a one; openly
1205    Yeit worthi men baid still into the sted                     Yet; remained; place
        Quhill ten thousand was brocht on to thar                    brought to their
              dede.                                                   deaths
        Than fled the laiff and mycht no langar                      rest; stay
              bid.
        Succour thai socht on mony divers sid,                       Help; many diverse sides
        Sum est, sum west and sum fled to the
              north.
1210    Seven thousand large at anys flottryt in                     in all at once; floundered; the
              Forth,                                                     River Forth
        Plungyt the depe and drownd without                         depths
              mercye,
        Nayne left on lyff of all that feill menyhe.                 left alive; large company
        Of Wallace ost na man was slayne of vaill                    of importance was slain
        Bot Andrew Murray in to that strang                          Except; hard
              battaill.

        1 That chieftain was violently killed

1215 The south part than saw at thar men was
   tynt, — *lost*
  Als fersly fled as fyr dois of the flynt. — *As fiercely*
  The place thai left, castell and Stirlyng toune,
  Towart Dunbar in gret haist maid thaim — *made their way*
   boune.
  Quhen Wallace ost had won that feild
   throuch mycht,
1220 Tuk up the bryg and loussit gud Jhon
   wricht, — *the carpenter*
  On the flearis syne folowed wonder  fast. — *fleers then*
  Erll Malcom als out of the castell past — *also*
  With Lennox men to stuff the chace gud
   speid.
  Ay be the way thai gert feill Sotheroun — *Ever by the way; caused;*
   bleid; — *many; bleed*
1225 In the Torwod thai gert full mony de. — *caused a great many to die*
  The Erll of Waran that can full fersly fle, — *fiercely flee*
  With Corspatrik that graithly was his gyd, — *readily; guide*
  On changit hors throuch out the land thai — *fresh*
   rid
  Strawcht to Dunbar, bot few with thaim — *straight*
   thai led;
1230 Mony was slayne our sleuthfully at fled. — *Many; that fled too slothfully*
  The Scottis hors that had rown wonder — *galloped a very long time*
   lang,
  Mony gaiff our that mycht no forthyr — *Many collapsed; go no*
   gang. — *further*
  Wallace and Grayme ever togidder baid; — *stayed*
  At Hathyntoun full gret slauchter thai maid
1235 Of Inglismen quhen thair hors tyryt had. — *tired*
  Quhen Ramsay come gud Wallace was full
   glad;
  With him was Boid and Richard of Lundy,
  Thre thousand haill was of gud chevalry; — *in all; horsemen*
  And Adam als Wallace of Ricardtoune — *also Adam Wallace*
1240 With Erll Malcome thai fand at — *found*
   Hathyntoune.
  The Scottis men on slauchter taryt was, — *were occupied with slaughter*
  Quhill to Dunbar the twa chyftanys coud
   pas
  Full sitfully for thar gret contrar cas. — *Very sadly; adverse fortune*
  Wallace folowed till thai gat in that place. — *got*

| | |
|---|---|
| 1245 | Of thar best men and Karcyngaym of renoune, |
| | Twenty thousand was dede but redempcioune. |
| | Besyd Beltoun Wallace raturnd agayn; |
| | To folow mar as than was bot in vayn. |
| | In Hathyntoun lugyng thai maid that nycht, |
| 1250 | Apon the morn to Stirling passit rycht. |
| | Assumpcioun day of Marye fell this cas; |
| | Ay lowyt be Our Lady of hir grace. |
| | Convoyar offt scho was to gud Wallace |
| | And helpyt him in mony syndry place. |
| 1255 | Wallace in haist sone effter this battaill |
| | A gret haith tuk of all the barrons haill |
| | That with gud will wald cum till his presens; |
| | He hecht thaim als to bid at thar defens.[1] |
| | Schir Jhon Menteth, was than of Aran lord, |
| 1260 | Till Wallace come and maid a playne record; |
| | With witnes thar be his ayth he him band |
| | Lauta to kep to Wallace and to Scotland. |
| | Quha with fre will till rycht wald nocht apply |
| | Wallace with force punyst rygorusly, |
| 1265 | Part put to dede, part set in prysone strang. |
| | Gret word of him throuch bathe thir regions rang. |
| | Dunde thai gat sone be a schort trete, |
| | Bot for thar lywes and fled away be se. |
| | Inglis capdans that hous had in to hand |
| 1270 | Left castellis fre and fled out of the land. |
| | Within ten dayis effter this tyme was gayne |
| | Inglis captanys in Scotland left was nane, |
| | Except Berweik and Roxburch castell wicht; |
| | Yeit Wallace thocht to bryng thai to the rycht. |

renoune,
*without*
*ransoming*
*Beside*
*any more; then; vain*
*lodging*
*directly*
*this happened*
*Ever praised; her*
*Protector often she*
*many many places*
*soon after*
*oath; every single baron*
*into*
*presence*
*To; plain statement*
*Loyalty*
*agree*
*punished severely*
*Some*
*news; both these*
*negotiation*
*Escaped with their lives*
*castle; occupied*
*past*
*strong*

1 He also gave them an undertaking to work for their defence

1275   That tyme thar was a worthi trew barroun,
       To nayme he hecht gud Cristall of Cetoun.    *name; called*
       In Jedwort wod for saiffgard he had beyne,    *Jedburgh; refuge*
       Agayne Sotheroun full weill he couth
          opteyn.    *win*
       In wtlaw oys he levit thar but let;[1]
1280   Edward couth nocht fra Scottis faith him    *get him [to leave] his*
          get.         *Scottish allegiance*
       Herbottell fled fra Jadwort castell wycht    *strong*
       Towart Ingland, thar Cetoun met him    *where*
          rycht.
       With forty men Cristall in bargane baid    *battle stood*
       Agayne eight scor and mekill mastre maid,    *bold actions*
1285   Slew that captane and mony cruell man.    *many fierce men*
       Full gret ryches in that jornay he wan,    *enterprise [day's work]; won*
       Houshald and gold as thai suld pas away,    *General provisions*
       The quhilk befor thai kepit mony day.    *which; kept many a*
       Jedwort thai tuk; ane Ruwan levit he,    *captured; left*
1290   At Wallace will captane of it to be.    *Wallace's will*
       Bauld Cetoun syne to Lothiane maid repair;    *Bold; then; went*
       In this storye ye ma her of him mair,    *narrative; may hear; more*
       And in to Bruce quha likis for to rede;    *in The Bruce; whoever*
       He was with him in mony cruell deid.    *fierce deeds*
1295   Gud Wallace than full sadly can devys    *firmly arranged*
       To rewill the land with worthi men and wys.    *rule*
       Captans he maid and schirreffis that was gud,
       Part of his kyn and of trew other blud.    *Some; kin; other true blood*
       His der cusyng in Edynburgh ordand he,    *cousin; decreed*
1300   The trew Crawfurd that ay was full worthe,    *always; worthy*
       Kepar of it with noble men at wage;    *Keeper; in his pay*
       In Mannuell than he had gud heretage.
       Scotland was fre that lang in baill had    *free; woe*
          beyn,
       Throu Wallace won fra our fals enemys    *won from*
          keyn.    *fierce*
1305   Gret governour in Scotland he couth ryng,    *ruled*
       Wayttand a tyme to get his rychtwis king    *Awaiting; rightful*
       Fra Inglismen, that held him in bandoune,    *From; subjection*
       Lang wrangwysly fra his awn rychtwis    *wrongfully; own*
          croun.

1 There he lived the life of an outlaw

| | Text | Gloss |
|---|------|-------|
| | Fyve monethis thus Scotland stud in gud rest. | enjoyed peace |
| | A consell cryit, thaim thocht it wes the best | council proclaimed |
| | In Sanct Jhonston at it suld haldyn be. | that; should be held |
| | Assemblit thar clerk, baroun and bowrugie, | clerks, barons; burgesses |
| 5 | Bot Corspatrik wald nocht cum at thar call, | summons |
| | Baid in Dunbar and maid scorn at thaim all. | Stayed |
| | Thai spak of him feill wordis in that parlyment. | many |
| | Than Wallace said, 'Will ye her to consent, | here |
| | Forgyff him fre all thing that is bypast | fully |
| 10 | Sa he will cum and grant he has trespast, | If; admit |
| | Fra this tyme furth kepe lawta till our croune?' | maintain loyalty |
| | Thai grant tharto, clerk, burges and barroune, | granted |
| | With haill consent thar writyng till him send. | full; petition |
| | Richt lawly thus till him thai thaim commend, | humbly |
| 15 | Besocht him fair as a peyr of the land | Beseeched; peer |
| | To cum and tak sum governaill on hand. | government |
| | Lychtly he lowch in scorn as it had beyn, | Contemptuously; laughed |
| | And said he had sic message seyldyn seyne: | such an embassy seldom seen |
| | 'That Wallace now as governour sall ryng | rule |
| 20 | Her is gret faute of a gud prince or kyng. | Here; lack |
| | That king of Kyll I can nocht understand: | |
| | Of him I held never a fur of land. | furrow |
| | That bachiller trowis, for Fortoun schawis hyr quhell, | believes; displays her wheel |
| | Tharwith to lest it sall nocht lang be weill. | last |
| 25 | Bot to you lordis, and ye will understand, | |
| | I mak you wys I aw to mak na band. | let you know; ought |
| | Als fre I am in this regioun to ryng[1] | |
| | Lord of myn awne, as ever was prince or king. | own |
| | In Ingland als gret part of land I haiff; | also, quantity |
| 30 | Manrent tharof thar will no man me craiff. | Homage thereof |
| | Quhat will ye mar? I warne you I am fre. | independent |

[1] As I am free to rule in this region

For your somoundis ye get no mar of me.'    summons; more
Till Saynct Jhonstone this wryt he send    To Perth; writ
    agayne,
Befor the lordis was manifest in playne.    plainly declared
35  Quhen Wallace herd the erll sic answer    such
    mais,    make
A gret hate ire throu curage than he tais;    hot anger
For weyll he wyst thar suld be bot a king    knew; one king
Of this regioun at anys for to ryng;
A 'king of Kyll' for that he callyt Wallace.
40  'Lordis,' he said, 'this is ane uncouth cace.    strange
Be he sufferyt we haiff war than it was.'    If he is allowed; worse
Thus rais he up and maid him for to pas:    rose
'God has us tholyt to do so for the laiff;    permitted; rest
In lyff or dede in faith him sall we haiff,    Alive or dead
45  Or ger him grant quhom he haldis for his    make; admit; regards as
    lord,
Or ellis war schaym in story to racord.    it were a shame; history
I vow to God with eys he sall nocht be    ease
In to this realme bot ane of us sall de,    die
Les than he cum and knaw his rychtwis    Unless; acknowledges;
    king.        rightful
50  In this regioun weill bathe we sall nocht    we both shall not reign
    ryng.
His lychtly scorn he sall rapent full sor,    contemptuous; sorely repent
Bot power faill or I sall end tharfor,[1]
Sen in this erd is ordand me no rest.    Since; earth; decreed
Now God be juge, the rycht he kennys
    best.'
55  At that consaill langar he taryit nocht,    council
With two hundreth fra Sanct Jhonston he    left Perth
    socht.
To the consaill maid instans or he yeid,[2]
Thai suld conteyn and of him haiff no    continue; have no fear for
    dreid.        him
'I am bot ane and for gud caus I ga.'    only one; go
60  Towart Kyngorn the gaynest way thai ta;    Kinghorn; shortest; take
Apon the morn atour Forth south thai    over the Forth [river]
    past;
On his vyage thai haistit wonder fast.    expedition

1 Unless my power fails or I die in the attempt
2 Entreated the council before he left

Robert Lauder at Mussilburgh met
   Wallace,

Fra Inglismen he kepyt weill his place.    *defended*

65  Couth nayne him trete, knycht, squier nor    *None could persuade him*
   lord,

With King Edward to be at ane accord.    *one*

On Erll Patrik to pas he was full glaid;    *advance*

Sum said befor the Bas he wald haiff haid.    *had*

Gude men come als with Crystell of Cetoun;    *also*

70  Than Wallace was four hundreth of renoun.    *Wallace's army*

A squier Lyll, that weill that cuntre knew,    *region*

With twenty men to Wallace couth persew    *rallied*

Besyd Lyntoun, and to thaim tald he than    *told, then*

The Erll Patrik, with mony likly man,    *many war-like men*

75  At Coburns peth he had his gaderyng maid,    *mustered his men*

And to Dunbar wald cum withoutyn baid.    *delay*

Than Lawder said, 'It war the best, think
   me,

Faster to pas, in Dunbar or he be.'    *go; before*

Wallace answerd, 'We may at laysar ryd.    *leisure ride*

80  With yon power he thinkis bargane to bid;    *that force; battle*

And of a thing ye sall weill understand,

A hardyar lord is nocht in to Scotland.

Mycht he be maid trew, stedfast, till a king,    *loyal; to*

Be wit and force he can do mekill thing,    *great things*

85  Bot willfully he likis to tyne him sell.'    *ruin; self*

Thus raid thai furth, and wald na langar    *forth*
   dwell,

Be est Dunbar, quhar men him tald on cas    *men happened to tell him*

How Erll Patrik was warnyt of Wallace,    *warned about*

Ner Enerweik chesyt a feild at vaill[1]

90  With nine hundreth of likly men to vaill.    *warriors at command*

Four hundreth was with Wallace in the    *[on the side of ] right*
   rycht

And sone onon approchit to thar sicht.    *forthwith*

Gret fawte thar was of gud trety betweyn    *want; good negotiation*

To mak concord and that full sone was
   seyne.

95  Without rahers of accioun in that tid

On athir part togydder fast thai rid.    *either*

The stour was strang and wonder peralous,    *fighting*

1 Near Innerwick had chosen a battlefield to [his] advantage

|     | Contenyt lang with dedis chevalrous; | Continued |
| --- | --- | --- |
|     | Mony thar deit of cruell Scottis blud. | Many; died; fierce |
| 100 | Of this trety the mater is nocht gud, | account; subject |
|     | Tharfor I ces to tell the destruccioune. |     |
|     | Pete it was, and all of a nacioun of one. | Pity; of one |
|     | Bot Erll Patrik the feild left at the last, |     |
|     | Rycht few with him to Coburns peth thai past, |     |
| 105 | Agrevit sar that his men thus war tynt. | Grief-stricken; lost |
|     | Wallace raturnd and wald no langar stynt |     |
|     | Towart Dunbar, quhar suthfast men him tald[1] |     |
|     | Na purveance was left in to that hald, | No provisions; castle |
|     | Nor men of fens, all had beyne with thar lord. | defence |
| 110 | Quhen Wallace hard the sekyr trew record, | reliable; report |
|     | Dunbar he tuk all haill at his bandoun, | completely; will |
|     | Gaiff it to kepe to Crystell of Cetoun, | into the keeping of |
|     | Quhilk stuffit it weill with men and gud victall. | furnished; good |
|     | Apon the morn Wallace that wald nocht faill, |     |
| 115 | With three hundreth to Coburns peth he socht; |     |
|     | Erll Patrik uschyt for bid him wald he nocht. | sallied forth; await |
|     | Sone to the park Wallace a range has set; | pursuit |
|     | Till Bonkill wood Corspatrik fled but let | without delay |
|     | And out of it till Noram passit he. |     |
| 120 | Quhen Wallace saw it mycht na better be |     |
|     | Till Caudstreym went and lugit him on Tweid. | Coldstream; lodged |
|     | Erll Patrik than in all haist can him speid. | speed |
|     | And passit by or Wallace power rais, | before; awakened |
|     | Without restyng in Atrik forrest gais. | went |
| 125 | Wallace folowed bot he wald nocht assaill; | attack |
|     | A rang to mak as than it mycht nocht vaill; | chase; avail |
|     | Our few he had, the strenth was thik and strang, | Too; stronghold |
|     | Seven myill on breid and tharto twys so lang. | miles wide; twice as long |

1 Wallace would stop there no longer and turned back / towards Dunbar, where reliable men told him

| | | |
|---|---|---|
| | In till Gorkhelm Erll Patrk leiffit at rest. | lived in peace |
| 130 | For mar power Wallace past in the west. | more forces; went into |
| | Erll Patrik than him graithit hastelye, | prepared |
| | In Ingland past to get him thar supplye; | supplies |
| | Out throuch the land rycht ernystfully couth pas | earnestly<br>passed |
| | To Anton Beik that lord of Durame was. | |
| 135 | Wallace him put out of Glaskow befor, | had put him out |
| | And slew Persye, thar malice was the mor. | [so] their; more |
| | The byschope Beik gert sone gret power rys, | cause; army |
| | Northummyrland apon ane awfull wys.[1] | |
| | Than ordand Bruce in Scotland for to pas | Bruce prepared |
| 140 | To wyn his awne, bot ill dissavit he was; | own; deceived |
| | Thai gert him trow that Wallace was rabell | made him believe; a rebel |
| | And thocht to tak the kynryk to hym sel. | kingdom; himself |
| | Full fals thai war and ever yeit has beyn. | |
| | Lawta and trouth was ay in Wallace seyn; | trustworthiness; always |
| 145 | To fend the rycht all that he tuk on hand, | defend |
| | And thocht to bryng the Bruce fre till his land. | freely |
| | Of this mater as now I tary nocht. | will not linger |
| | With strang power Sotheroun togidder socht, | came together |
| | Fra Owys watter assemblit haill to Tweid. | River Ouse |
| 150 | Thar land ost was thirty thousand in deid; | army; indeed |
| | Of Tynnys mouth send schippis be the se | Tynemouth |
| | To kep Dunbar at nayne suld thaim supple. | guard [entry to] so that |
| | Erll Patrik with twenty thousand but lett | straightaway |
| | Befor Dunbar a stalwart sege he sett. | |
| 155 | The bischope Beik and Robert Bruce baid still | stayed |
| | With ten thousand at Noram at thar will. | |
| | Wallace be this that fast was lauborand, | by this time |
| | In Lothyane com witht gud men five thousand, | Lothian |
| | Rycht weill beseyn, all in to armys brycht, | well-equipped |
| 160 | Thocht to reskew the Cetoun bauld and wicht. | bold<br>valiant |
| | Under Yhester that fyrst nycht lugit he. | Yester Castle; camped |
| | Hay com till him with a gud chevalre: | company of knights |

1 Northumberland [men presenting] an awesome sight

In Duns forest all that tyme he had beyne;
The cummyng thar of Sotheroun he had
   seyne.
165  Fifty he had of besy men in wer;    *active; war*
Thai tald Wallace of Patrikis gret affer.    *array*
Hay said, 'Forsuth and ye mycht him our    *overthrow*
   set
Power agayne rycht sone he mycht nocht    *An army*
   get.
My consaill is that we gyff him battaill.'    *counsel*
170  He thankit him of comfort and consaill    *for his comforting words*
And said, 'Freynd Hay, in this caus that I
   wend,    *take on*
Sa that we wyn I rek nocht for till end.    *So long as; care not; die*
Rycht suth it is that anys we mon de.    *we must die once*
In to the rycht quha suld in terrour be?'    *On the side of right*
175  Erll Patrik than a messynger gert pas,    *sent a messenger*
Tald Anton Beik that Wallace cummand    *[Who] told*
   was.
Of this tithingis the byschope was full    *this news; very*
   glaid,    *pleased*
Amendis of him full fayne he wald haiff    *He was very keen to have*
   haid.    *amends*
Bot mar prolong throuch Lammermur thai    *Without further delay*
   raid,
180  Ner the Spot mur in buschement still he    *ambush quietly*
   baid,    *waited*
As Erll Patrik thaim ordand for to be.    *ordered*
Wallace of Beik unwarnyt than was he.    *was not warned then*
Yeit he befor was nocht haisty in deid;    *Yet; before then*
Bot than he put bathe him and his in    *both; danger*
   dreid.
185  Apon swyft horsis scurrouris past betweyn;    *scouts*
The cummyng than of Erll Patrik was
   seyn.
The hous he left and to the mur is gayn,    *castle [i.e., Dunbar]*
A playne feild thar with his ost he has    *An open*
   tayn.
Gud Cetoun syne uschet with few menyhe;    *issued; a small company*
190  Part of his men in till Dunbar left he;
To Wallace raid, was on the rychtwys sid.    *rode; rightful*
In gud aray to the Spot mur thai ryd.    *array; rode*
Sum Scottis dred the erll sa mony was,    *feared; had so many*

Twenty thousand agayn sa few to pas. *against; advance*

195　Quhen Jop persavit, he bad Wallace suld bid: *saw [this]; begged / wait*

'Tyne nocht thir men, bot to sum strenth ye ryd, *Lose; these; strong position*

And I sall pas to get you power mar. *go; more forces*

Thir ar our gud thus lychtly for to war.' *These are too great; fight*

Than Wallace said, 'In trewth I will nocht fle

200　For four of his ay ane quhill I may be.[1]

We ar our ner sic purpos for to tak; *too close such; take up*

A danger chace thai mycht upon us mak. *dangerous chase*

Her is twenty with this power today

Wald him assay suppos I war away. *[Who] would attack him*

205　Mony thai ar; for Goddis luff be we strang,

Yon Sotheron folk in stour will nocht bid lang.'[2]

The brym battaill braithly on ather sid, *fierce; violently; either*

Gret rerd thar rais all sammyn quhar thai ryd. *Great din; rose there all together*

The sayr semble quhen thai togidder met, *painful encounter*

210　Feyll strakis thar sadly on ather set. *Many blows; firmly*

Punyeand speris throuch plattis persit fast; *Piercing spears; armour*

Mony off hors to the ground doun thai cast;

Saidlys thai teym of hors but maistris thar;[3]

Of the south sid five thousand doun thai bar. *they / overthrew*

215　Gud Wallace ost the formast kumraid sa *foremost overthrew thus*

Quhill the laiff was in will away to ga. *rest wished to go away*

Erll Patrik baid sa cruell of entent *so fiercely determined*

At all his ost tuk of him hardiment. *That; courage*

---

1 Then Wallace said, 'Indeed I will not flee / as long as I have one against four of his [men]'

2 'There are many of them; if we are staunch, for the love of God, / These English folk will not last long in battle'

3 They emptied horse saddles of their masters

Agayne Wallace in mony stour was he.    *Against; battles*

220 Wallace knew weill that his men wald nocht fle

For na power that leiffand was in lyff,    *no power alive*

Quhill thai in heill mycht ay be ane for fyfe.    *strength; one against five*

In that gret stryff mony was handlyt hate;    *were dealt with violently*

The feill dyntis, the cruell hard debait,    *many blows; fierce strife*

225 The fers steking, maid mony grevous wound,    *ferocious stabbing; painful*

Apon the erd the blud did till abound.    *ground; flowed*

All Wallace ost in till a cumpais baid;    *ring formed*

Quhar sa thai turnd full gret slauchter thai maid.    *Wherever*

Wallace and Grayme and Ramsay full worthi,

230 The bauld Cetoun and Richard of Lundy,    *bold*

And Adam als Wallace of Ricardtoun,    *also Adam Wallace*

Bathe Hay and Lyll with gud men of renoun,

Boyde, Bercla, Byrd and Lauder that was wicht,    *valiant*

Feill Inglismen derffly to ded thai dycht.    *Many; violently killed*

235 Bot Erll Patrik full fersly faucht agayn;    *fiercely fought back*

Throuch his awn hand he put mony to payn.    *own / distress*

Our men on him thrang forthwart in to thra,    *pressed forward boldly*

Maide throuch his ost feill sloppis to and fra.    *many breaches*

The Inglismen began playnly to fle;

240 Than byschope Beik full sodeynly thai se,

And Robert Bruce contrar his natiff men.    *against; compatriots*

Wallace was wa fra tyme he couth him ken:    *grieved; recognised*

Of Brucis deid he was agrevit far mar    *distressed; more*

Than all the laiff that day at semblit thar.    *Than all the rest; that*

245 The gret buschement at anys brak on breid,    *ambush; once burst out*

Ten thousand haill that douchty war in deid.    *in all; valiant / deeds*

The flearis than with Erll Patrik relefd    *fleers; rallied*

To fecht agayn, quhar mony war myscheifd.    *many / destroyed*

Quhen Wallace knew the buschement brokyn was,    *ambush / had broken*

250 Out of the feild on hors thai thocht to pas,  *battlefield*
 Bot he saw weill his ost sound in thar weid;  *swoon; armour*
 He thocht to fray the formast or thai yeid.  *scare; before; went*
 The new cummyn ost befor thaim semblit  *newly arrived army;*
  thar             *assembled*
 On ather sid with strakis sad and sar.  *either side; grave and sore*
255 The worthi Scottis sa fersly faucht agayne  *fiercely fought back*
 Of Antonys men rycht mony haiff thai slayne;  *many*
 Bot that terand so usit was in wer  *tyrant; practised; war*
 On Wallace ost thai did full mekill der;  *a great deal of harm*
 And the bauld Bruce sa cruelly wrocht he  *bold; fiercely*
260 Throuch strenth of hand feill Scottis he  *many Scots he*
  gert de.            *caused to die*
 To resist Bruce Wallace him pressit fast,
 Bot Inglismen so thik betwixt thaim past;
 And Erll Patrik in all the haist he moucht  *might*
 Throuch out the stour to Wallace sone he  *battle; soon*
  socht,
265 On the the pes a felloun strak him gaiff,  *thigh-piece; grievous blow*
 Kerwit the plait with his scharp groundyn  *Cleft; armour; sharply*
  glaiff             *ground sword*
 Throuch all the stuff and woundyt him  *cloth*
  sumdeill.           *somewhat*
 Bot Wallace thocht he suld be vengit weill,  *revenged*
 Folowed on him and a straik etlyt fast.  *stroke aimed deftly*
270 Than ane Mawthland rakles betwix thaim  *Maitland; recklessly*
  past:
 Apon the heid gud Wallace has him tane,  *struck*
 Throuch hat and brawn in sondyr bryst the  *helmet; brain shattered;*
  bane,             *bone*
 Dede at that straik doun to the ground him  *stroke*
  drave.            *drove*
 Thus Wallace was disseverit fra the lave  *separated; rest*
275 Of his gud men, amang thaim him allane.  *them [the English] alone*
 About him socht feill enemys mony ane,  *drew; many*
 Stekit his hors; to ground behufid him  *Stabbed; behoved him to*
  lycht             *descend*
 To fend him selff als wysly as he mycht.  *defend; prudently*
 The worthy Scottis that mycht no langar
  bid             *withstand*
280 With sair hartis out of the feild thai ryd.  *heavy; rode*
 With thaim in feyr thai wend Wallace had  *in company; thought*
  beyn;

On fute he was amang his enemys keyn.                    cruel
Gud rowme he maid about him in to breid                  space; all around him
With his gud swerd that helpyt him in neid.
285 Was nayne sa strang that gat of him a strak
Efter agayne maid never a Scot to waik.[1]
Erll Patrik than that had gret crafft in wer            knowledge of war
With speris ordand gud Wallace doun to                   to bear down on Wallace
    ber.
Anew thai tuk was haill in to the feild,                 Enough; unhurt
290 Till him thai yeid thocht he suld haiff no             went
    beild,                                                escape [refuge]
On ather sid fast poyntand at his ger.                   either side; stabbing; armour
He hewid off hedys and wysly coud him wer.               hacked; defend himself
The worthy Scottis of this full litill wyst,            knew very little
Socht to gud Graym quhen thai thar                       Sought out; missed
    chyftane myst.
295 Lauder and Lyle and Hay that was full                  extremely
    wicht                                                 vigorous
And bauld Ramsay quhilk was a worthy                     bold
    knycht,
Lundy and Boid and Crystell of Cetoun
With five hundreth that war in bargan                    ready for fighting
    boun,
Him to reskew full rudly in thai raid,                   vigorously; rode
300 About Wallace a large rowme thai maid.                 space
The byschop Beik was braithly born till                  violently knocked to the
    erd;                                                     ground
At the reskew thar was a glamrous rerd.                  noisy uproar
Or he gat up feill Sotheroun thai slew.                  Before; many
Out of the pres Wallace thai couth                       press of battle; rescued
    raskew,
305 Sone horssit him apon a coursour wicht,                Soon; bold steed
Towart a strenth ridis in all thar mycht,                stronghold rode
Rycht wysly fled, reskewand mony man.                    wisely; rescuing many men
The Erll Patrik to stuff the chace began;                prepare; pursuit
On the flearis litill harm than he wrocht.
310 Gud Wallace folk away togiddyr socht.                  slipped away together
Thir five hundreth the quhilk I spak of                  earlier
    ayr
Sa awfully abaundound thaim and sa sar                   So well defended themselves

---

1 None were so strong that, once injured by Wallace, / ever again troubled a
Scot

Na folowar durst out fra his falow ga, — dared; fellows go
The gud flearis sic raturnyng thai ma. — such counter-attacking; make

315 Four thousand haill had tane the strenth befor — in all; reached the stronghold
Of Wallace ost, his comfort was the mor; — more
Of Glaskadane that forrest thocht till hauld. — hold
Erll Patrik turnd, thocht he was never sa bauld, — returned; bold
Agayne to Beik quhen chapyt was Wallace, — escaped
320 Curssand fortoun of his myschansit cace. — unlucky fortune
The feild he wan and seven thousand thai lost, — won
Dede on that day for all the byschoppis bost. — Died; boast
Of Wallace men five hundreth war slayne I ges, — estimate
Bot na chyftayne his murnyng was the les. — mourning; less
325 Ner evyn it was bot Beik wald nocht abid; — It was nearly evening; remain
In Lammermur thai tranuntyt that tid, — moved camp; time
Thar lugyng tuk quhar him thocht maist availl, — lodging; most; advantage
For weyll he trowit the Scottis wald assaill — believed; attack
Apon the feild quhar thai gaiff battaill last. — gave
330 The contre men to Wallace gaderyt fast. — men of the region
Of Edynburch wyth Crawfurd that was wicht — From; strong
Thre hundreth come in till thar armour brycht, — came
Till Wallace raid be his lugeyng was tayne. — To; rode by the time; chosen
Fra Tawydaill come gud men mony ane — From Teviotdale; many a one
335 Out of Jedwart with Ruwane at that tyd, — Jedburgh; time
Togidder socht fra mony divers sid. — approached; directions
Schir Wilyham lang that lord was of Douglas,
With him four scor that nycht come to Wallace.
Twenty hundreth of new men met that nycht
340 Apon thair fais to veng thaim at thair mycht. — their foes; avenge; with their
At the fyrst feild thire gud men had nocht beyn. — field of battle these; been

Wallace wachis thair adversouris had seyn,  *Wallace's sentries*
In to quhat wis thai had thar lugeyng  *In what manner; camp*
  maid.
Wallace bounyt efter soupper but baid,  *set out; without delay*
345 In Lammermur thai passit hastely.
Sone till aray yheid this gud chevalry.  *Soon; battle order went*
Wallace thaim maid in twa partis to be:  *two divisions*
Schir Jhon the Graym and Cetoun ordand  *commanded*
  he,
Lawder and Hay with thre thousand to ryd;
350 Hym selff the layff tuk wysly for to gid,  *rest; guide*
With him Lundy, bathe Ramsay and
  Douglace,
Berkla and Boid and Adam gud Wallace.
Be this the day approchit wonder neir  *By this time; close*
And brycht Titan in presens can apper.  *i.e., the sun; appeared*
355 The Scottis ostis sone semblit in to sycht  *soon assembled within sight*
Of thar enemys, that was nocht redy dycht;  *ready for them*
Out of aray feill of the Sotheroun was.  *array many*
Rycht awfully Wallace can on thaim pas.  *Relentlessly; advanced*
At this entray the Scottis so weill thaim bar  *onset; conducted*
360 Feill of thar fais to ded was bertnyt thar.  *Many; foes; put to death*
Redles thai rais and mony fled away;  *In confusion; many*
Sum on the ground war smoryt quhar thai  *crushed where*
  lay.
Gret noyis and cry was raissit thaim amang.
Gud Grayme come in, that stalwart was  *powerful*
  and strang.
365 For Wallace men was weill togydder met,  *Because*
On the south part sa awfully thai set  *awesomely*
In contrar thaim the frayt folk mycht nocht  *Against them; frightened*
  stand;
At anys thar fled of Sotheroun five  *once*
  thousand.
The worthi Scottis wrocht apon sic wys  *wrought; such a way*
370 Jop said hym selff thai war mekill to prys.  *greatly to be praised*
Yeit byschope Beik, that felloun tyrand  *Yet; fierce*
  strang,  *powerful*
Baid in the stour rycht awfully and lang.  *Remained; fighting; starkly*
A knycht Skelton that cruell was and keyn  *ferocious, bold*
Befor him stud in till his armour scheyn,  *bright*
375 To fend his lord full worthely he wrocht.  *defend*
Lundy him saw and sadly on him socht,  *resolutely approached him*

With his gud swerd ane awkwart straik him gaiff,    sword; crosswise blow

Throuch pesan stuff his crag in sonder draiff,    Right through the gorget; neck; dashed

Quhar of the layff astunyt in that sted.    Whereof; were dismayed

380 The bauld Skelton of Lundyis hand is dede.    bold

Than fled thai all and mycht no langar bid.    stay

Patrik and Beik away with Bruce thai ryd.

Five thousand held in till a slop away    gap

Till Noram hous in all the haist thai may.    castle

385 Our men folowed, that worthi war and wicht;    valiant

Mony flear derffly to dede thai dycht.    Many; violently they killed

The three lordis on to the castell socht;    went

Full feyll thai left that was of Ingland brocht.    Very many / brought

At this jornay twenty thousand thai tynt,    clash; lost

390 Drownyt and slayn be sper and swerdis dynt.    spear and sword / blows

The Scottis at Tweid hastyt thaim sa fast    to the River Tweed

Feill Sotheroun men into wrang furdis past.    Many; fording places

Wallace raturnd in Noram quhen thai war;

For worthi Bruce his hart was wonder sar:    extremely sad

395 He had lever haiff had him at his large,    would rather have; liberty

Fre till our croun than of fyne gold to carge[1]

Mar than in Troy was fund at Grekis wan.    that; conquered

Wallace than passit with mony awfull man    fearsome men

On Patrikis land and waistit wonder fast,    laid waste

400 Tuk out gudis and placis doun thai cast.

His stedis seven that mete hamys was cauld,    march houses or forts

Wallace gert brek thai burly byggyngis bauld,    strong buildings

Baithe in the Mers and als in Lothiane.

Except Dunbar standand he levit nane.    left

405 Till Edynburgh apon the auchtand day

Apon the morn Wallace without delay

1 Subject [only] to the authority of the crown their fine gold at command

Till Pert he passit quhar the consell was          Perth
    set.
To the barrouns he schawit withoutyn let           revealed without delay
How his gret vow rycht weill eschevyt was.         accomplished
410 Till a maister he gert Erll Patrik pas           superior
Becaus he said of Scotland he held nocht.          held no land
Till King Edward to get supple he socht.           help
The lordis war blyth and welcummyt weill
    Wallas,
Thankand gret God of this fair happy chas.         chase
415 Wallace tuk state to govern all Scotland;        assumed the responsibility
The barnage haill maid him ane oppyn               entire baronage
    band.                          allegiance
Than delt he land till gud men him about           he distributed
For Scotlandis rycht had set thar lyff in          [Who] for; risked their lives
    dout.
Stantoun he gaiff to Lauder in his wage;           as payment
420 The knycht Wallang aucht it in heretage.         possessed
Than Birgeane cruk he gaiff Lyle that was          Birgham lands
    wicht;
Till Scrymgeour als full gud reward he
    dycht,                          assigned
Syne Wallace toun and other landis thar till.      Then; [pertaining] to these
To worthi men he delt with nobill will.            gave
425 Till his awne kyn heretage nayne gaiff he,       own kinspeople
Bot office haill at everilk man mycht se.          Except official positions
For covatice thar couth no wicht him               Of covetice
    blayme.                        accuse
He baid reward quhill the king suld cum            awaited; until
    hayme.
Of all he dyd he thocht to bid the law             abide by
430 Befor his king, master quhen he him saw.
Scotland was blyth, in dolour had beyne
    lang:
In ilka part to gud laubour thai gang.             every
Be this the tyme of October was past;
Ner November approchit wonder fast.
435 Tithandis than come King Edward grevit           News; vexed
    was,
With his power in Scotland thocht to pas,          army
For Erll Patrik had gyffyn him sic consaill.       given; such counsel
Wallace gat wit and semblit power haill,           got to know; assembled his
                whole army

Forty thousand on Roslyn mur thar met. — Roslin

440 'Lordis,' he said, 'thus is King Edward set

In contrar rycht to sek us in our land. — Against the right; seek

I hecht to God and to you be my hand, — vow; by

I sall him meit for all his gret barnage — meet; great baronage

Within Ingland to fend our heretage. — defend

445 His fals desyr sall on him selff be seyn; — be paid back

He sall us fynd in contrar of his eyn.

Sen he with wrang has ryddyn this regioun — ridden over

We sall pas now in contrar of his crown. — in opposition to

I will nocht bid gret lordis with us fayr, — command; to go

450 For myn entent I will playnly declar. — intention

Our purpos is other to wyn or de.

Quha yeildis him sall never ransownd be.' — Whoever surrenders

The barrons than him answerd worthely

And said thai wald pas with thar chevalry. — followers

455 Him selff and Jop providyt that menyhe. — made that company ready

Twenty thousand of vaillit men tuk he; — distinguished

Harnes and hors he gert amang thaim vaill,

Wapynnys enew at mycht thaim weill
    availl,[1]

Grathyt thar men that cruell wes and keyn. — Equipped; fierce; bold

460 Better in wer in warld coud nocht be seyn.

He bad the laiff on laubour for to bid. — commanded; rest

In gud aray fra Roslyn mur thai ryd. — array from

At thar muster gud Wallace couth thaim as, — asked them

Quhat mysteryt ma in a power to pas?[2]

465 'All of a will, as I trow set ar we, — believe determined

In playne battaill can nocht weill scumfit
    be. — defeated

Our rewme is pur, waistit be Sotheroun
    blud. — realm; poor, laid waste

Go wyn on thaim tresour and other gud.' — win from

The ost inclynd all in till humyll will — bowed

470 And said thai suld his commandment fulfill.

The Erll Malcome with thir gud men is
    gayne, — has gone

Bot nayne of rewill on him he wald tak
    nayne. — But he would not assume
        rulership

1 He arranged for them to pick the best armour and horses, / and enough
weapons to serve them well

2 What need was there of a greater force to go [to battle]?

Wallace him knew a lord and full worthi;    knew [him to be]
At his consaill he wrocht full stedfastly.
475  Starkar he was gyff thai suld battaill seyn,    Bolder
For he befor had in gud jornays beyn.    war-like enterprises
A man of strenth that has gud wit withall
A haill regioune may comfort at his call,
As manly Ectour wrocht in till his wer;    Hector
480  Agayn a hundreth countyt was his sper    valued
Bot that was nocht throuch his strenth
    anerly,    only
Sic rewill he led of worthi chevalry.    Such command
Thir ensampyllis war noble for to ken.
Ectour I leiff and spek furth of our men.
485  The knycht Cambell maid hime to that    journey
    wiage,
Of Louchow cheiff than was his heretage.
The gud Ramsay furth to thatjornay went.
Schir Jhone the Grayme forthwart in his    active
    entent,
Wallace cusyng Adam full worthi was,    Wallace's cousin
490  And Robert Boid full blythly furth thai pas;
Baith Awchynlek and Richard of Lundy,
Lawder and Hay and Cetoun full worthy.
This ryall ost but restyng furth thai rid    noble; without resting; rode
Till Browis feild and thar a quhill thai bid.
495  Than Wallace tuk with him forty but les,    indeed
Till Roxburgh yett raid sone or he wald ces.    gate
Sotheroun merveld giff it suld be Wallace
Without soverance come to persew that    safe conduct; attack
    place.
Of Schyr Rawff Gray sone presence couth
    he as    ask
500  And warnd him thus forthwart he wald pas.
'Our purpos is in Ingland for to ryd;
No teyme we haiff of segyng now to bid.    time; besieging; bide
Tak tent and her of our cummyng agayne;    notice
Gyff our the hous, send me the keyis in    Give up; castle; openly
    playn.
505  Thus I commaund befor this witnes large,    these many witnesses
Gyff thou will nocht, ramayne with all the    If
    charge.    responsibility
Bot this be done throuch force and I tak    But if this; capture you
    thee

Out our the wall thou sall be hyngit hye.'  *hanged high*

With that he turnd and till his ost can wend.  *went*

510 This ilk commaund to Berweik sone he
send  *same demand*

With gud Ramsay that was a worthi knycht.

The ost but mar full awfully he dycht,  *without delay; awesomely*

Began at Tweid and spard nocht at thai  *spared none that*
fand,  *found*

Bot brynt befor throuch all  *burned [all] before them*
Northummyrland.

515 All Duram toun thai brynt up in a gleid.  *burned to an ember*

Abbays thai spard and kyrkis quhar thai  *spared; churches*
yeid.  *went*

To York thai went but baid or thai wald  *without delay before*
blyn;  *stop*

To byrn and sla of thaim he had na syne.

Na syn thai thocht the sammyn thai leit us
feill,[1]

520 Bot Wilyam Wallace quyt our quarell  *settled; dispute*
weill.

Fortrace thai wan and small castellis kest  *Fortresses; captured; castles;*
doun,  *down*

With aspre wapynnys payit thar ransoune.  *sharp; ransom [see note]*

Of presonaris thai likit nocht to kep;  *keep*

Quhom thai our tuk thai maid thar freyndis  *overtook*
to wepe.  *weep*

525 Thai sawft na Sotheroun for thar gret  *saved*
riches;

Of sic koffre he callit bot wrechitnes.  *such bargaining*

On to the yettis and faboris of the toun  *gates; suburbs*

Braithly thai brynt and brak thar byggyngis  *Fiercely; burned; broke;*
doun;  *buildings*

At the wallys assayed fifteen dayis,  *Assailed the walls*

530 Till King Edward send to thaim in this  *Until*
wayis

A knycht, a clerk and a squier of pes,  *in peace*

And prayit him fayr of byrnyng to ces,  *courteously to cease burning*

And hecht battaill or forty dayis war past,  *called for; before; were*

Soverance so lang gyff him likit till ast;[2]

1 He did not sin by burning and slaying [the English]. They thought it no sin
when they let us feel the same
2 [And] assurance of safety for as long if he wished to ask it

535 And als he sperd quhy Wallace tuk on hand     *also; enquired*

The felloun stryff in defens of Scotland,     *fierce struggle*

And said he merveld on his wyt forthy     *in his mind therefore*

Agayn Inglande was of so gret party:     *Against; [which] was so huge*

'Sen ye haiff maid mekill of Scotland fre     *Since; much*

540 It war gret tym for to lat malice be.'     *the time was ripe to*

Wallace had herd the message say thar will;     *heard; messengers*

With manly wytt rycht thus he said thaim till:

'Yhe may knaw weill that rycht ynewch we haiff.     *enough*

Of his soverance I kepe nocht for to craiff.     *safe conducts I care not*

545 Be caus I am a natyff Scottis man

It is my dett to do all that I can     *duty*

To fend our kynrik out of dangeryng.     *kingdom from harm*

Till his desyr we will grant to sum thing;

Our ost sall ces, for chans that may betid,     *cease, whatever happens*

550 Thir forty dayis bargane for till bid.     *battle; await*

We sall do nocht les than it mowe in you;     *nothing unless you begin it*

In his respyt my selff couth never trow.'     *reprieve; trust*

King Edwardis wrytt under his seill thai gaiff,     *writ; seal*

Be fourty dayis that thai suld battaill haiff.     *In forty days*

555 Wallace thaim gaiff his credence of this thing.

Thair leyff thai tuk syne passit to the king     *leave; then*

And tauld him haill how Wallace leit thaim feill:     *told; completely; know*

'Of your soverance he rekis nocht adeill.     *safe conduct; cares not at all*

Sic rewllyt men, sa awfull of affer,     *Such well-led; appearance*

560 Ar nocht crystynyt than he ledis in wer.'     *christened [baptised]; leads*

The king answerd and said, 'It suld be kend     *known*

It cummys of witt enemys to commend.     *It is wise; praise*

Thai ar to dreid rycht gretly in certane.     *to be feared; for certain*

Sadly thai think of harmys thai haiff tane.'     *Gravely; suffered*

565 Leyff I thaim thus at consell with thar king

And of the Scottis agayne to spek sum thing.

Wallace tranountyt on the secund day;                   moved camp
Fra York thai passyt rycht in a gud aray.
North west thai past in battaill buskyt boun,           all prepared for battle
570    Thar lugeyng tuk besyd Northallyrtoun
And cryit his pes, thar merket for till stand[1]
Thai fourty dayis for pepill of Ingland,
Quha that likyt ony wyctaill till sell.                 food;  to
Of a thar fer was mekill for to tell.                   all; wares
575    Schyr Rawff Rymunt captane of Maltoun
            was,
With gret power ordand be nycht to pas
On Wallace ost to mak sum jeperte.                      surprise attack
Feyll Scottis men that dwelt in that cuntre            Many
Wyst of this thing and gaderyt to Wallace.             Knew; rallied
580    Thai maid him wys of all that suttell cace.     informed; cunning plan
Gud Lundy than till hym he callit thar
And Hew the Hay, of Louchowort was ayr,                Locharwart; heir
With thre thousand that worthely had                   fought nobly
            wrocht,
Syne prevaly out fra the ost he socht.                 secretly
585    The men he tuk that come till him of new
Gydys to be, for thai the contre knew.                 Guides
The ost he maid in gud quyet to be;
A space fra thaim he buschyt prevale.                  At a distance;  lay in ambush
Schyr Rawff Rymunt with seven thousand
            com in
590    On Wallace ost a jeperte to begyn.              surprise attack
The buschement brak or thai the ost come               ambush; before; army
            ner;
On Sotheroun men the worthi Scottis thai               launched
            ster.                                       themselves
Thre thousand haill was braithly brocht to             violently
            ground.
Jornay thai socht and sekyrly has found.               Combat; certainly
595    Schyr Rawff Rymunt was stekit on a sper;
Thre thousand slayn that worthi war in                 were slain
            wer.
The Sotheroun wyst quhen thar chyftayn                 knew
            wes dede:
To Maltoun fast thai fled and left that sted.
Wallace folowed with  his gud chevalry;

1 And proclaimed his truce allowing normal business [markets]

600  Amang Sotheroun thai entrit sodeynly,        *came in*
Inglis and Scottis in to the toun at anys.        *at the same time*
Sotheroun men schot and braithly kest        *shot; violently*
        doun stanys.        *stones*
Of thar awn rycht feyll thair haiff thai        *their own men many*
        slayn.
The Scottis about that war of mekill mayn        *great strength*
605  On grecis ran and cessyt all the toun.[1]
Derffly to dede the Sotheroun was dongyn        *Violently to death; struck*
        doun.
Gud Wallace thair has found full gud ryches,
Jowellis and gold, bathe wapynnys and
        harnes,        *armour*
Spoulyeid the toun of wyn and of wictaill,        *Plundered; food*
610  Till his ost send with caryagis of gret vaill.        *Sent to the army; value*
Thre dayis still within the toun thai baid,
Syn brak doun werk that worthely was
        maid.
Wyffis and childer thai put out of the toun;
Na man he sawft that was of that nacioun.        *i.e., English-born*
615  Quhen Scottis had tane to turss at thar        *packed up all they desired*
        desyr
Wallis thai brak, syn set the layff in fyr.        *Walls; rest*
The temer werk thai brynt up all in playn;        *timber work; completely*
On the ferd day till his ost raid agayn;        *fourth*
Gert cast a dyk that mycht sum strynthyng        *Had a wall prepared;*
        be,        *strengthening*
620  To kepe the ost for sodeyn jeperte.        *from; surprise attack*
Than Inglismen was rycht gretly agast;
Fra north and south in to thar king thai
        past,
At Pomfray lay and held a parlement.        *[Who] lay at Pontefract*
To gyff battaill the lordis couth nocht
        consent
625  Les Wallace war of Scotland crownyt king.        *Unless*
Thar consaill fand it war a peralous thing,
For thocht thai wan thai wan bot as thai war,        *succeeded; they [only] won*
                                                    *what they already had*
And gyff thai tynt thai lossyt Ingland for        *lost*
        evermar
Apayn war put into the Scottis hand.        *As a penalty were put*

1 Ran up and down stairs and captured all the town

630   And this decret thar wit amang thaim
      fand,[1]
         Gyff Wallace wald apon him tak the croun          If; i.e., crown of Scotland
         To gyff battaill thai suld be redy boun.          all ready
         The sammyn message till him thai send             same messengers to
         agayn
         And thar entent thai tald him in to playn.        intention; told plainly
635   Wallace thaim chargyt his presens till               ordered them to leave his
         absent,                                              presence
         His consaill callyt and schawit thaim his         council; revealed
         entent.
         He and his men desyrit battaill till haiff
         Be ony wayis of Ingland our the laiff.            By any means; above all else
         He said, 'Fyrst it war a our hie thing            were; overly ambitious
640   Agayne the faith to reyff my rychtwis
      king.[2]
         I am his man, born natiff of Scotland;
         To wer the croun I will nocht tak on hand.        wear; undertake
         To fend the rewm it is my dett be skill;          realm; duty; by reason
         Lat God above reward me as he will.'              Let; above
645   Sum bad Wallace apon him tak the croun.              beseeched; to take
         Wys men said, 'Nay, it war bot derysioun          would be only
         To croun him king but voice of the                without approval
         parlyment,'
         For thai wyst nocht gyff Scotland wald            knew not if
         consent.
         Other sum said it was the wrangwis place.         Some others; wrong
650   Thus demyt thai on mony divers cace.                 they offered diverse opinions
         This knycht Cambell, of witt a worthi             distinguished; wisdom
         man,
         As I said ayr was present with thaim than,        earlier; then
         Herd and answerd quhen mony said thar             many expressed their wishes
         will:
         'This war the best, wald Wallace grant thar       were; if Wallace will agree to
         till,                                                it
655   To croun him king solemply for a day,               solemnly
         To get ane end of all our lang delay.'            bring to an end
         The gud Erll Malcome said that Wallace
         mycht
         As for a day, in fens of Scotlandis rycht,        Only for a day; defence

         1 And this they decided amongst themselves
         2 Against good faith to deprive my rightful king

| | | |
|---|---|---|
| | Thocht he refusyt it lestandly to ber, | Although; to bear it lastingly |
| 660 | Resave the croun as in a fer of wer. | Accept; circumstance of war |
| | The pepill all till him gaiff thar consent: | |
| | Malcome of auld was lord of the parlyment. | old |
| | Yeit Wallace tholyt, and leit thaim say thar will. | Yet; was patient; let |
| | Quhen thai had demyt be mony divers skill, | considered; arguments |
| 665 | In his awne mynd he abhorryt with this thing. | own; abhorred |
| | The comouns cryit, 'Mak Wallace crownyt king.' | common people |
| | Than smylyt he and said, 'It suld nocht be. | |
| | At termys schort, ye get no mar for me. | In a few words; more from |
| | Undyr colour we mon our answer mak, | Using pretence; must |
| 670 | Bot sic a thing I will nocht on me tak. | |
| | I suffer you to say that it is sa. | so |
| | It war a scorn the croun on me to ta.' | mockery; take |
| | Thai wald nocht lat the message of Ingland | let; English messengers |
| | Cum thaim amang or thai suld understand.[1] | |
| 675 | Twa knychtis passit to the message agayn, | messengers |
| | Maid thaim to trow Wallace was crownyt in playn, | Made them believe; openly |
| | Gart thaim traist weill that this was suthfast thing. | Gave them to understand |
| | Delyverit thus thai passit to thar king, | Released |
| | To Pomfrait went and tald that thai had seyn | Pontefract |
| 680 | Wallace crownyt, quharof the lordis was teyn, | angry |
| | In barrate wox in parlement quhar thai stud. | contention grew |
| | Than said thai all, 'Thir tithingis ar nocht gud. | |
| | He did so weyll into thir tymys befor, | earlier |
| | And now thar king he will do mekill mor. | [as] their king |
| 685 | A fortonyt man, nothing gois him agayn. | A man favoured by fortune |
| | To geyff battaill we sall it rew apayn.' | offer; regret it possibly/ |
| | And othir said, 'And battaill will he haiff | |
| | Or stroy our land; na tresour may us saiff. | destroy |
| | In his conquest sen fyrst he coud begyn, | since |

1 Come among them before they reached an understanding

690 He sellis nocht bot takis at he may wyn.     *exchanges nothing*
For Inglismen he settis no doym bot ded;     *passes no judgement*
Price of pennys may mak us no ramed.'     *The price paid; remedy*
Ane Wodstok said, 'Yhe wyrk nocht as the     *are not doing this in the*
    wys     *wisest way*
Gyff that ye tak the awnter of supprice.     *If; accept the risk*
695 For thocht we wyn that ar in till Ingland     *overcome [those] that*
The layff ar stark agaynys us for to stand.     *rest; strong*
Be Wallace saiff, othir thai count bot small.     *If; secured*
Forthi me think this war the best of all:     *Therefore*
To kepe our strynth of castell and wall     *defend; strongholds, walled*
    toun;     *towns*
700 Swa sall we fend the fek of this regioun.     *So; defend; main part*
Thocht north be brynt, better of sufferans     *burned; in assured safety be*
    be
Than sett all Ingland on a jeperte.'     *at risk*
Thai grantyt all as Wodstok can thaim say,
And thus thai put the battaill on delay
705 And kest thaim haill for othir governance     *devised; measures*
Agayn Wallace to wyrk sum ordinance.     *Against; plan*
Thus Wallace has in playn discumfyt haill     *completely discomfited*
Agayn King Edward all his strang battaill.     *army*
For throcht falsheid and thar subtilite     *cunning*
710 Thai thocht he suld for gret necessite
And faute of fude to steyll out of the land.     *lack; steal*
And this decret thar wytt amang thaim fand:     *they came to this decision*
Thai gert the king cry all thar merket
    doun[1]
Fra Trent to Tweid of throchtfayr and fre     *thoroughfares and free towns*
    toun,
715 That in thai boundis na men suld wictaill
    leid,     *bring*
Sic stuff nor wyn, on na les payn bot deid.     *Such food; penalty of death*
This ilk decret thai gaiff in thar parlement.     *same decree*
Of Scottis forsuth to spek is myn entent.     *intention*
Wallace lay still quhill forty dayis was gayn
720 And fyve atour, bot perance saw he nayn     *more; he saw no sign*
Battaill till haiff, as thair promys was maid.     *they had promised*
He gert display agayne his baner braid,     *broad banner*
Rapreiffyt Edward rycht gretlye of this     *Condemned*
    thing,

---

1 They had the king proclaim in all the market places

Bawchillyt his seyll, blew out on that fals
king[1]

725 As a tyrand, turnd bak and tuk his gait.     [who] turned back; went away

Than Wallace maid full mony byggyng     buildings
hayt.     hot

Thai rayssyt fyr, brynt up Northallyrtoun,     started fires; burned

Agayn throcht Yorkschyr bauldly maid     set off
thaim boun,

Dystroyed the land als fer as ever thai rid.     rode

730 Sevyn myle about thai brynt on ather sid.

Palyce thai spylt, gret towris can confound,     Palisades; destroyed

Wrocht the Sotheroun mony werkand     Inflicted on; painful injuries
wound.

Wedowis wepyt with sorow in thar sang,     songs

Madennys murnyt with gret menyng     Maidens mourned; lamenting
amang;     among [them]

735 Thai sparyt nocht bot wemen and the     no-one except; church
kyrk.

Thir worthy Scottis of laubour wald nocht
yrk;     weary

Abbayis gaiff thaim rycht largly to thar fud.     supplied them well with food

Till all kyrk man thai did nothing bot gud.

The temperall land thai spoulyeit at thar     plundered
will,

740 Gud gardens gay and orchartis gret thai     destroy
spill.

To York thai went thir wermen of     these warriors
renoun;

A sege thai set rycht sadly to the toun.     siege; resolutely

For gret defens thai garnest thaim within;     those within prepared

A felloun salt without thai can begyn,     terrible assault

745 Gert woid the ost in four partis about,     Divided; army

With wachys feyll that no man suld usche     many watchmen [ensuring]
out.

Aboune the toun apon the southpart sid     Above

Thar Wallace wald and gud Lundy abid.

Erll Malcom syne at the west yett abaid,     gate waited

750 With him the Boid that gud jornays had     expeditions
maid.

The knycht Cambell, that of Louchow was
lord,

1 Held his seal up to disgrace, denounced that false king publicly

At the north yett and Ramsay maid thaim
ford. — a ford

Schyr Jhon the Graym that worthy was in
wer,

Awchinlek, Crawfurd with full manlik affer — appearance

755 At the est part bauldly thai boune to bid. — prepared; stay

A thousand archaris apon the Scottis sid

Disseveryt thaim amang the four party. — Spread themselves

Fyve thousand bowemen in the toun forthi

Within the wallis arayit thaim full rycht; — arranged

760 Twelve thousand and ma that sembly was — gathering
to sycht.

Than said Wallace, 'Thar yond apon a playn — yonder

In feild to fecht me think we suld be bayn.' — ready

Than sailyeit thai rycht fast on ilka sid, — they attacked; every

The worthy Scottis that bauldly durst abid. — withstand

765 With sper and scheild, for gounnys had thai — guns
nayn,

Within the dykys thai gert feill Sotheroun — walls
grayn. — groan

Arowys thai schot als fers as ony fyr — fierce

Atour the wall that flawmyt in gret ire, — Over; flamed

Throuch byrneis brycht, with hedys fyn of — corslets
steyll.

770 The Sotheroun blud thai leyt no frendschip
feyll;

Our schefferand harnes schot the blud so — breaking armour
scheyn. — bright

The Inglismen that cruell was and keyn

Kepyt thar toun and fendyt thaim full fast. — Guarded; defended

Fagaldys of fyr amang the ost thai cast; — Burning faggots

775 Up pyk and ter on feyll sowys thai lent;[1] 

Mony was hurt or thai fra wallys went.

Stanys of spryngaldis thai cast out so fast — from catapults

And gaddys of irne maid mony goym agast, — iron bars; men terrified

Bot nevertheles the Scottis that was without — outside

780 The toun full oft thai set in to gret dout. — risk

Thar bulwerkis brynt rycht brymly of the — fiercely
toun,

Thar barmkyn wan and gret gerrettis kest — rampart breached; turrets
doun.

[1] They got up pitch and tar on many siege engines

Thus sailyeit thai on ilk sid with gret mycht.    *they attacked; each*

The day was gayn and cummyn was the nycht;

785   The wery ost than drew thaim fra the toun,    *weary*

Set out wachis, for restyng maid thaim boun,    *watches* / *ready*

Wysche woundis with wyn of thaim that was unsound,    *Washed; wine* / *injured*

For nayn wes dede in gret myrth thai abound.    *Because none*

Feyll men was hurt bot na murnyng thai maid,

790   Confermyt the sege and stedfastly abaid.    *Reinforced; remained*

Quhen that the son on morow rais up brycht,

Befor the chyftanys semblyt thai full rycht    *gathered*

And mendis thocht of the toun thai suld tak,    *amends*

For all the fens that the Sotheroun mycht mak.    *defence*

795   Arayit agayn as thai began afor,    *They arranged themselves*

About the toun thai sailye wondyr sor,    *attacked extremely hard*

With felloun schot atour the wall so scheyn.    *cruel; over; bright*

Feill Inglismen that cruell was and keyn

With schot was slayn for all thar targis strang.    *strong shields*

800   Byrstyt helmys, mony to erd thai dang,    *Shattered helmets; struck*

Brycht byrnand fyr thai kest till everilk yet.    *every gate*

The entres thus in perall oft thai set.    *entrance*

The defendouris was of so fell defens,    *cruel*

Kepyt thar toun with strenth and excellens.    *Guarded*

805   And thus the day thai dryff on to the nycht;    *force*

To palyounnys bounyt mony wery wycht,    *tents prepared [to go]*

All yrk of wer; the toun was strang to wyn    *weary; overcome*

Of artailye and nobill men with gyn.[1]

Quhen that thai trowyt the Scottis was all at rest,    *believed*

810   For jeperte the Inglismen thaim kest.[2]

---

1 With artillery and noble men with military engines
2 The English turned their minds to finding a stratagem

Schyr Jhon Nowrtoun was knawyn worthy          known [to be]
   and wycht,
Schyr Wilyham of Leis graithit thaim that          furnished
   nycht
With five thousand welle garnest and          equipped
   savage.          eager for battle
Apon the Scottis thai thocht to mak          engage in a skirmish
   scrymmage,
815 And at the yet wschyt out haistely          gate
On Erll Malcom and his gud chevalry.          horsemen
To chak the wache Wallace and ten had          On patrol
   beyn
Rydand about and has thar cummyng seyn.
He gert ane blaw was in his cumpany;          blow the horn
820 The redy men arayit thaim hastely.          arrayed themselves [for
                                         battle]

Feill of the Scottis ilk nycht in harnes baid          each; armour remained
Be ordinance, for thai sic rewll had maid.          order; [a] rule
With schort avys togyddyr ar thai went          Without delay
Apon thair fais, quhar feill Sotheroun was
   schent.          undone
825 Wallace knew weill the erll to haisty was,          too
Forthi he sped him to the pres to pas.          Therefore; press
A swerd of wer in till his hand he bar:
The fyrst he hyt the crag in sondyr schar;          neck in pieces shattered
Ane othir awkwart apon the face tuk he,          crosswise; he hit
830 Wysar and frount bathe in the feild gert          Visor; front
   fle.
The hardy erll befor his men furth past
In to the pres quhar feill war fechtand fast,
A scherand swerd bar drawyn in his hand.          sharp; carried
The fyrst was fey that he befor him fand.          doomed
835 Quhen Wallace and he was togidder set
Thayr lestyt nayn agayn thaim that thai
   met,
Bot othir dede or ellis fled thaim fray.          either died; from
Be this the ost all in gud aray          order
With the gret scry assemblit thaim about.          noise
840 Than stud the Sotheroun in a felloun dout.          terrible danger
Wallace knew weill the Inglismen wald fle,
Forthi he preyst in the thikkest to be,          thickest press
Hewand full fast on quhat sege that he          Hacking; man
   socht;          found

Agaynys hys dynt fyn steyll availyeit nocht. — blow fine; availed

845 Wallace of hand sen Arthour had na mak: — in combat since; match

Quhom he hyt rycht was ay dede of a strak. — always; from one stroke

That was weyll knawin in mony place and thar.

Quhom Wallace hyt he deryt the Scottis no mar. — Whomever; harmed more

Als all his men did cruelly and weyll — Also; boldly

850 At com to strak; that mycht the Sotheroun feill! — That; fight feel

The Inglismen fled and left the feild playnly,

The worthy Scottis wrocht so hardely.

Schyr Jhon of Nourtoun in that place was dede

And twelve hundreth withoutyn ony ramede.

855 Thir mony was left in to the feild and slayn. — Many of these were

The layff raturnyt in to the toun agayn — rest returned

And rwyt full sar that evyr thai furth coud found; — profoundly regretted; forth had gone

Amang thaim was full mony werkand wound. — many painful

The ost agayn ilkane to thar ward raid, — each one; section rode

860 Comaundyt wachis and no mayr noyis maid, — sentries; more noise

Bot restyt still quhill that the brycht day dew, — until dawned

Agayne began the toun to sailye new. — attack anew

All thus thai wrocht with full gud worthines,

Assailyeit sayr with witt and hardines. — Attacked hard; prudence

865 The ostis victaill worth scant and failyeit fast; — army's provisions grew

Thus lay thai thair quhill divers dayis war past. — until; were

The land waistyt and meit was fer for to wyn, — land wasted; too far away; obtain

Bot that wyst nocht the stuff that was within; — knew not; garrison

Thai drede full sar for thar awn
warnysoun.[1]

870 For soverance prayed the power of the     *assurance of safety entreated;*
    toun;     *forces*

To spek with Wallace thai desyryt fast

And he aperyt and speryt quhat thai ast.     *appeared; enquired; asked*

The mayr answerd, said, 'We wald gyff     *mayor; would give ransom*
    ransoun

To pas your way and der no mayr the     *[If you would] go; harm*
    toun.

875 Gret schaym it war that we suld yoldyn be     *were; surrender*

And townys haldyn of les power than we.     *[have] held; less*

Yhe may nocht wyn us, suthlie, thocht ye     *conquer; though*
    bid.     *wait*

We sall gyff gold and yhe will fra us rid.     *give; if you*

We may gyff battaill, durst we for our     *[if] we dared*
    king;

880 Sen he has left, it war ane our hie thing     *too ambitious a thing*

Till us to do without his ordinance.     *For us; orders*

This toun of him we hald in governance.'[2]

Wallace answerd, 'Of your gold rek we     *I don't care about your gold*
    nocht;

It is for battaill that we hydder socht.     *came here*

885 We had lever haiff battaill of Ingland     *rather*

Than all the gold that gud King Arthour
    fand     *found*

On the Mont Mychell, quhar he the gyand     *giant*
    slew.

Gold may be gayn bot worschip is ay new.     *gone; honour; always*

Your king promyst that we suld battaill
    haiff;

890 His wrytt thar to undyr his seyll he gaiff.     *writ; seal*

Letter nor band ye se may nocht availl.     *agreement*

Us for this toun he hecht to gyff battaill.[3]

Me think we suld on his men vengit be;     *be revenged*

Apon our kyn mony gret wrang wrocht he.     *kin; many great wrongs*

895 His devyllyk deid he did in to Scotland.'     *devilish deed*

The mayr said, 'Schir, rycht thus we     *mayor*
    understand;

1 They were extremely fearful about their own provisions
2 This town hold and govern on his behalf
3 He promised to give us battle for this castle

We haiff no charge quhat our king gerris us do,[1]

Bot in this kynd we sall be bundyn you to, — *manner; bound to you*
Sum part of gold to gyff you with gud will

900 And nocht efftyr to wait you with na ill, — *afterwards to lie in wait for*
Be no kyn meyn, the power of this toun, — *manner of means; garrison*
Bot gyff our king mak him to battaill boun.' — *Unless; prepares for battle*
In to the ost was mony worthi man — *Within; many valiant men*
With Wallace, ma than I now rekyn can. — *more; reckon [calculate]*

905 Better it was for at his will thai wrocht, — *performed*
Thocht he wes best no nother lak we nocht.[2]
All servit thank to Scotland ever mar — *deserved; more*
For manheid, wit, the quhilk thai schawit thar. — *prudence; demonstrated; there*
The haill consaill thus demyt thaim amang, — *whole council; considered*

910 The toun to sege thaim thocht it was to lang, — *besiege; would take too long*
And nocht apayn to wyn it be no slycht. — *practicable; by stratagem*
The consaill fand it was the best thai mycht
Sum gold to tak gyff that thai get no mar, — *if they could get; more*
Syne furth thar way in thar viage thai far. — *Then; journey; went*

915 Than Wallace said, 'My selff will nocht consent
Bot gyff this toun mak us this playne content: — *satisfaction*
Tak our baner and set it on the wall
(For thar power our rewme has ridyn all), — *army; realm; ridden all over*
Yoldyn to be quhen we lik thaim to tak, — *Prepared to surrender*

920 In till Ingland residence gyff we mak.' — *If we stay in England*
This answer sone thai send in to the mair. — *mayor*
Than thai consent, the remanent that was thar, — *consented; rest*
The baner up and set it in the toun,
To Scotland was hie honour and renoun. — *high*

925 That baner thar was fra eight houris to none. — *noon*
Thar finance maid, delyverit gold full sone. — *payment; soon*
Ten thousand pund all gud gold of Ingland — *pounds*
The ost rasavit with wictaill haboundand. — *received; abundant food*

1 We have no responsibility for what our king makes us do
2 Although he was the best, we do not find fault with any other

Baith breid and wyne rycht gladly furth
   thai gaiff

930 And other stuff at thai likit to haiff.    *that*
Twenty dais out the ost remaynit thar,    *altogether*
Bot want of victaill gert thaim fra it far;    *lack; provisions; go*
Yeit still of pees the ost lugyt all nicht    *Yet; in time of peace; lodged*
Quhill on the morn the sone was ryssyn on
   hycht.

935 In Aperill amang the schawis scheyn,    *fair woods*
Quhen the paithment was cled in tender    *path; clad*
   greyn,
Plesand war it till ony creatur
In lusty lyff that tym for till endur.    *vigorous life*
Thir gud wermen had fredome largely,    *These; warriors*
940 Bot fude was scant, thai mycht get nayn to    *none;*
   by,    *buy*
Tursyt tentis and in the contre raid.    *Packed up; country rode*
On Inglismen full gret herschipe thai maid,    *destruction*
Brynt and brak doun, byggyngis sparyt thai    *buildings spared*
   nocht;
Rycht worthi wallis full law to ground thai    *sturdy; low*
   brocht.

945 All Mydlam land thai brynt up in a fyr,
Brak parkis doun, distroyit all the schyr.    *shire*
Wyld der thai slew for other bestis was    *deer; none*
   nayn,
Thir wermen tuk of venysoune gud wayn.    *These warriors; quantity*
Towart the south thai turnyt at the last,
950 Maid byggyngis bar als fer as ever thai    *Stripped buildings*
   past.    *everywhere*
The commons all to London ar thai went
Befor the king and tald him thar entent,    *told; intention*
And said thai suld, bot he gert Wallace ces,    *should, unless; made; cease*
Forsaik thair faith and tak thaim till his
   pes.    *peace*
955 Na herrald thar durst than to Wallace pas,    *No; dared*
Quharof the king gretly agrevit was.    *annoyed*
Thus Edward left his pepill in to baill.    *people; woe*
Contrar Wallace he wald nocht giff battaill,    *Against; give*
Nor byd in feild, for nocht at thai mycht    *stay in battlefield*
   say,
960 Gayff our the caus, to London past his    *Gave up*
   way.

At men of wit this questioun her I as,     *knowledge; here; ask*

Amang noblis gyff ever ony that was     *Among nobles if; any*

So lang throu force in Ingland lay on cas     *[Who] so; happened to lie*

Sen Brudus deit, but battaill, bot Wallace?     *since; without*

965  Gret Julius, the empyr had in hand,

Twys of force he was put of Ingland.     *Twice through force; out of*

Wytht Arthour als, of wer quhen that he     *With; also; attempted war*
    previt,

Twys thai fawcht, suppos thai war     *Twice; fought*
    myschewit.     *undone*

Awfull Edward durst nocht Wallace abid     *Formidable; dared*

970  In playn battaill, for all Ingland so wid.     *open; wide*

In London he lay and tuk him till his rest,

And brak his vow. Quhilk hald ye for the     *broke; Which hold*
    best?

Rycht clayr it is to ransik this questioun.     *clear; examine*

Deyme as ye lest, gud men of discrecioun.     *Judge; wish*

975  To my sentence breyffly will I pas.     *subject matter*

Quhen Wallace thus throu Yorkschyr
    jowrnat was,     *had journeyed*

Wictaill as than was nayne left in the land     *Foodstuffs*

Bot in houssis quhar it mycht be warrand.     *Except; protected*

The ost herof abaissit was to bid;[1]

980  Fra fude scantyt na plesance was that tid.     *From the time food grew
    scarce; joy*

Sum bald ryd haym, sum bald ryd     *bold men rode home*
    forthermar.     *further on*

Wallace callit Jop and said till him rycht
    thar:

'Thou knawis the land quhar most
    aboundance is.

Be thou our gyd and than we sall nocht     *guide*
    mys     *fail*

985  Wictaill to fynd, that wait I wonder weill.     *To find food; know*

Thou has, I traist, of Ingland mekill feill.     *knowledge*

The kyng and his to stark strenthis ar gayn.     *strongholds*

Bot jeperte now perell haiff we nayn.'     *Except for surprise attacks*

Than Jop said,' Be ye gydyt be me,

990  The boundandest part of Ingland ye sall se.     *richest*

Of wyn and quheyt thar is in Rychmunt     *wheat; county*
    schyr

---

1 The host on account of this was discouraged from staying

And other stuff of fud that ye desyr,            *food provisions*
Quharof I trow yhe sall be weyll content.'
The ost was glaid and thiddyrwart thai
    went.

995   Mony trew Scot was semblyt in that land,    *gathered*
To Wallace com weill ma than nine             *many more*
    thousand.
Of presone part sum had in lawbour            *Some had laboured in prison*
    wrocht,
Fra athir part full fast till him thai socht.
Wallace was blyth of our awn natiff kyn       *own native kin*

1000  That come till him of baill that thai war in,  *out of suffering*
And all the ost of comforde was the blythar
Fra thar awn folk was multipliand the mar.    *As*
In Richmunt schyr thai fand a gret
    boundans,                                   *abundance*
Breid, ayll and wyn, with other purveans;

1005  Brak parkis doun, slew bestis mony ane,    *woods; many a one*
Of wild and tayme forsuth thai sparyt nane.   *truly; spared none*
Throuchout the land thai past in gud aray.    *order*
A semely place so fand thai in thar way       *handsome; found*
Quhilk Ramswaith hecht, as Jop him selff      *Which was called*
    thaim tald.                                 *Ravensworth*

1010  Fehew was lord and captayne in that hald.  *stronghold*
Five hundreth men was semblit in that         *were assembled*
    place
To save thaim selff and thar gud fra          *goods from*
    Wallace.
A ryoll sted fast by a forest sid,            *royal dwelling*
With turrettis fayr and garrettis of gret prid

1015  Beildyt about, rycht lykly to be wicht,    *Built; strong*
Awfull it was till ony mannis sicht.          *Awesome; any*
Feill men aboun on the wallis buskyt beyn     *Many; above; were prepared*
In gud armour that burnyst was full           *burnished*
    scheyn.                                     *fair*
The ost past by and bot wesyt that place,     *only inspected*

1020  Yeit thai within on lowd defyit Wallace    *Yet; aloud*
And trumpattis blew with mony werlik          *many war-like*
    soun.                                       *sounds*
Than Wallace said, 'Had we yon gallandis      *those gallants*
    doun
On the playn ground thai wald mor sobyr       *temperate*
    be.'

Than Jop said, 'Schir, ye gart his brodyr de    *caused the death of his brother*

1025 In harrold weid, ye wait, on Tynto hill.'    *herald's clothing, you know*

Wallace answerd, 'So wald I with gud will

Had I hym selff; bot we may nocht thaim der.[1]

Gud men mon thoill of harlottis scorn in wer.'    *must endure; scorn of worthless fellows*

Schir Jhon the Graym wald at a bykkyr beyn,[2]

1030 Bot Wallace sone that gret perell has seyn,    *soon*

Commaundit him to lat his service be.    *let*

'We haiff no men to waist in sic degre.    *in such a way*

Wald ye thaim harm I knaw ane other gait    *way*

How we throuch fyr within sall mak thaim hait.    *hot*

1035 Fyr has beyn ay full felloun in to wer:    *ever; harmful in war*

On sic a place it ma do mekill der.    *may; great damage*

Thar auld bulwerk I se of wydderyt ayk;    *old; dried oak*

War it in fyr thai mycht nocht stand a straik.    *on fire; withstand an attack*

Housis and wod is her enewch plente.    *here enough*

1040 Quha hewis best of this forest lat se.[3]

Pow housis doun we sall nocht want adeill;    *Pull; at all*

The auld temyr will ger the greyn byrn weill.'[4]

At his commaund full besyly thai wrocht;    *worked*

Gret wod in haist about the hous thai brocht.    *castle*

1045 The bulwerk wan thir men of armys brycht,[5]

To the barmkyn laid temer apon hycht.    *rampart; piled up timber*

Than bowmen schot to kep thaim fra the cast;    *Then; protect; discharge of missiles*

The wall about had festnyt firis fast.    *they had fastened torches*

Women and barnys on Wallace fast thai cry;

1 'So would I gleefully [deal with] him, / had I the opportunity, but we may not injure them'
2 Sir John Graham was impatient to attack
3 'Let's see who can cut down the forest best'
4 'The old timber will make the new [green] wood burn well'
5 These men in shining armour reached the bulwark

1050  On kneis thai fell and askit him mercy.
      At a quartar quhar fyr had nocht ourtayn,     *place where; overtaken*
      Thai tuk thaim out fra that castell of stayn,  *took; stone*
      Syn bet the fyr with  brundys brym and         *Then beat; brands fierce;*
        bauld.                                        *bold*
      The rude low rais full heych aboun that        *strong flame rose; high*
        hauld.                                        *above; castle*
1055  Barrellis of pyk for the defens was hungyn     *pitch*
        thar,
      All strak in fyr, the myscheiff was the        *burst into flames; damage*
        mar.
      Quhen the brym fyr atour the place was         *flaming; through*
        past
      Than thai within mycht nother schwt no         *neither shoot nor throw*
        cast.                                         *missiles*
      Als bestiall as hors and nowt within           *Also; [such] as; cattle*
1060  Amang the fyr thai maid a hiddvys dyn.         *hideous din*
      The armyt men in harnes was so hait,           *armour; hot*
      Sum doun to ground duschit but mar             *fell without further*
        debait;                                       *resistance*
      Sum lap, sum fell in to the felloun fyr,       *leapt; terrible fire*
      Smoryt to dede and brynt bathe bayn and        *Crushed; burned both bone*
        lyr.                                          *and flesh*
1065  The fyr brak in at all opynnys about;          *openings*
      Nayn baid on loft, so felloun was the          *stayed above; grave; risk*
        dout.
      Fehew him self lap rudly fra the hycht,        *leapt swiftly; top*
      Throuch all the fyr can on the barmkyn         *ramparts*
        lycht.                                        *alight*
      With a gud swerd Wallace strak off his
        hed;
1070  Jop hynt it up and turst it fra that sted.     *grabbed; threw; place*
      Five hundreth men that war in to that
        place,
      Gat nayne away bot dede withoutyn grace.       *None got away; died; mercy*
      Wallace baid still with his power that         *remained quietly*
        nycht;
      Apon the morn the fyr had failyeit mycht.      *diminished in strength*
1075  Beffor the yett quhar it was brynt on breid    *In front of; gate; widely*
      A red thai maid and to the castell yeid,       *clearing; went*
      Strak doun the yett and tuk that thai mycht    *Struck; gate*
        wyn,                                          *pillage*
      Jowellys and gold, gret riches war tharin;

Spulyeit the place and left nocht ellis thar            Plundered
1080 Bot bestis brynt, bodyis and wallis bar.             charred beasts; corpses; bare
Than tuk thai hyr that wyff was to Fehew,               her
Gaiff this commaund, as scho was woman                  she
     trew,
To turs that hed to London to King                      carry that head in a pack
     Edward.
Scho it rasavyt with gret sorow in hart.                She received it; heart
1085 Wallace him selff thir chargis till hyr             these orders gave to her
     gaiff:
'Say to your king, bot gyff I battaill haiff,           unless
At London yettis we sall assailye sayr.                 gates; attack strenuously
In this moneth we think for to be thair.                month; there
Trastis in treuth, will God, we sall nocht              Believe this for the truth
     faill,
1090 Bot I rasyst throu chargis of our consaill.         Unless; stop; orders
The southmaist part of Ingland we sall se
Bot he sek pes or ellis bargan with me.                 Unless; sues for peace; fights
Apon a tym he chargyt me on this wys,                   commanded; manner
Rycht boustously, to mak till him service:              menacingly; subjection
1095 Sic sall he haiff as he us caus has maid.'          Such shall
Than mowit thai without langer abaid.                   moved on; longer delay
Deliverit scho was fra this gud chevalry.               Released; from
Towart London scho socht rycht                          went
     ernystfully,                                       earnestly
On to the tour but mar proces scho went,                Tower without; delay
1100 Quhar Edward lay sayr murnand in his                deeply lamenting
     entent.                                            mind
His nevois hede quhen he saw it was                     nephew's head
     brocht,
So gret sorow sadly apon him socht,                     gravely welled in him
With gret unes apon his feit he stud,                   difficulty
Wepand for wo for his der tendyr blud.                  relation
1105 The consaill rais and prayit him for to
     ces:
'We los Ingland bot gyff ye purches pes.'               will lose; unless; solicit peace
Than Wodstok said, 'This is my best                     counsel
     consaill:
Tak pees in tyme as for our awn availl,                 a truce; own advantage
Or we tyne mar yeit slaik of our curage.                Before; lose; lessen; spirit
1110 Erest ye may get help to your barnage.'             Soonest; baronage
The king grantyt and bad thaim message                  ordered them to send a
     send;                                                  messenger

Na man was thar that durst to Wallace
wend.

The queyn apperyt and saw this gret
distance.

      queen

      reluctance

Weill born scho was, of the rycht blud of
France;

      true

1115 Scho trowit weill tharfor to speid the erar.

Hyr selff purpost in that message to far.

Als scho forthocht at the king tuk on hand

Agayn the rycht so oft to reyff Scotland.[1]

And feill men said the vengeance hapnyt
thar,

1120 Of gret murthyr his men maid in till Ayr.

Thus demyt thai the consaill thaim amang.

To this effect the qweyn bounyt to gang.

Quhen scho has seyn ilk man forsak this
thing

On kneis scho fell and askyt at the king:

1125 'Soverane,' scho said, 'gyff it your willis be,

At I desyr yon chyftayn for to se.

For he is knawin bath hardy, wys and trew,

Perchance he will erar on wemen rew

Than on your men; yhe haiff don him sic
der,

1130 Quhen he thaim seis it mowis him ay to wer.

To help this land I wald mak my travaill;

It ma nocht scaith suppos it do na vaill.'

The lordis all of hir desir was fayn;

On to the king thai maid instans in playn

1135 That scho mycht pas. The king with
awkwart will,

Halff into yr, has giffyn consent thar till.

Sum of thaim said the queyn luffyt
Wallace

For the gret voice of his hie nobilnas.

A hardy man that is lykly with all

1140 Gret favour will of fortoun till him fall

Anent wemen, is seyne in mony place.

Sa hapnyt it in his tyme with Wallace.

In his rysing he was a luffar trew

And chesit ane, quhill Inglismen hir slew.

      trusted; succeed sooner

      proposed; embassy; go

      Also; regretted that

      many; had come

      For; murder

      deliberated

      With this object; prepared

      each; refuse

      knees

      Sovereign

      That; that chieftain

      known as

      Perhaps; sooner; have pity

      done; such

      injury

      moves; always; war

      labour hard

      may do no harm; good [avail]

      were glad

      entreated openly

      Half in anger

      reputation; high

      well-made

      favour

      In respect of women

      true lover

      chose one, until; her

1 Against the right so often take Scotland by force

| | | |
|---|---|---|
| 1145 | Yeit I say nocht the queyn wald on hir tak | take |
| | All for his luff sic travaill for to mak. | such an undertaking |
| | Now luff or leiff, or for help of thar land, | |
| | I mak rahers as I in scriptour fand. | recite; writing found |
| | Scho graithit hir apon a gudlye wis | furnished herself; fashion |
| 1150 | With gold and ger and folk at hir devis; | according to her plan |
| | Ladyis with hir, nane other wald thai send, | no others |
| | And ald preystis that weill the cuntre kend. | old priests; knew |
| | Lat I the queyn to message redy dycht[1] | |
| | And spek furth mar of Wallace travaill rycht. | more; Wallace's right actions |
| 1155 | The worthy Scottis amang thar enemys raid; | rode |
| | Full gret distruccioun amang the Sotheron thai maid; | |
| | Waistit about the land on ather sid. | Laid waste; either |
| | Na wermen than durst in thar way abid. | No warriors; dared |
| | Thai ransoun nane bot to the dede thaim dycht, | ransomed none; death; consigned |
| 1160 | In mony steid maid fyris braid and brycht. | many places; broad |
| | The ost was blith and in a gud estate, | condition |
| | Na power was at wald mak thaim debate; | offer them resistance |
| | Gret ryches wan of gold and gud thaim till, | |
| | Leyffyng enewch to tak at thar awn will. | Provisions enough; own |
| 1165 | In awfull fer thai travaill throuch the land, | awesome state; journeyed |
| | Maid byggynis bar that thai befor thaim fand, | Stripped buildings |
| | Gret barmkynnys brak of stedis stark and strang, | defence walls broke; places; powerful |
| | Thir wicht wermen of travaill thocht nocht lang. | These bold; labour did not weary |
| | South in the land rycht ernystfully thai socht | earnestly; went |
| 1170 | To Sanct Tawbawnys, bot harm thar did thai nocht. | St Albans |
| | The priour send thaim wyne and venesoun, | |
| | Refreshyt the ost with gud in gret fusioun. | good things; plenty |
| | The nycht apperyt quhen thai war at the place: | |
| | Thai herbreyt thaim fra thine a litill space, | sheltered; thence; while |

---

1 I leave the queen preparing for her embassy

| | | |
|---|---|---|
| 1175 | Chesyt a sted quhar thai suld bid all nycht; | Chose a place; stay |
| | Tentis on ground and palyonis proudly pycht | pavilions pitched |
| | In till a vaill be a small ryver fayr, | valley by; fair river |
| | On athir sid quhar wild der maid repayr; | either side where |
| | Set wachis out that wysly couth thaim kepe, | sentries; guard |
| 1180 | To souppar went and tymysly thai slepe. | supper; duly |
| | Of meit and sleip thai ces with suffisiance.[1] | |
| | The nycht was myrk, our drayff the dyrkfull chance; | murky, passed over; dark |
| | The mery day sprang fra the oryent, | merry; rose; east |
| | With bemys brycht enlumynyt the occident. | illuminated the west |
| 1185 | Efter Titan, Phebus up rysyt fayr, | |
| | Heich in the sper the signes maid declayr. | High; sphere; planets decreed |
| | Zepherus began his morow cours, | morning course |
| | The swete vapour thus fra the ground resours, | rose |
| | The humyll breyth doun fra the hevyn availl, | mild breath; heaven descended |
| 1190 | In every meide, bathe fyrth, forrest and daill, | meadow; both stream; dale |
| | The cler rede amang the rochis rang, | clear voice; rocks |
| | Throuch greyn branchis quhar byrdis blythly sang, | |
| | With joyus voice in hevynly armony. | |
| | Than Wallace thocht it was no tyme to ly. | lie in bed |
| 1195 | He croyssit him, syne sodeynli up rais; | made the sign of the cross; arose |
| | To tak the ayr out of his palyon gais. | take; air; tent went |
| | Maister John Blar was redy to rawes, | ready; put on priestly vestments |
| | In gud entent syne bounyt to the mes. | With good intent; prepared for; mass |
| | Quhen it was done Wallace can him aray | dressed himself |
| 1200 | In his armour, quhilk gudly was and gay. | fine; handsome |
| | His schenand schoys that burnyst was full beyn, | shining leg harness; burnished well |
| | His leg harnes he clappyt on so clene; | |
| | Pullane greis he braissit on full fast,[2] | |
| | A clos byrny with mony sekyr cast, | tight corslet; many from clasps |

---

1 From food and sleep they refrained [when they had had] sufficient
2 Knee-armour greaves he clasped on quickly

1205 Breyst plait, brasaris, that worthy was in
    wer. — *Brass pieces of armour for the arms; war*
Besid him furth Jop couth his basnet ber; — *helmet carry*
His glytterand glowis grawin on ather sid, — *gloves engraved; either*
He semyt weill in battaill till abid. — *seemed well; withstand*
His gud gyrdyll and syne his burly brand, — *belt; then; strong sword*
1210 A staff of steyll he gryppyt in his hand. — *steel*
The ost him blyst and prayit God of his
    grace — *blessed*
Him to convoy fra all mystymyt cace. — *preserve; unlucky*
Adam Wallace and Boid furth with him
    yeid — *went*
By a rever throu out a floryst meid. — *river; flowery meadow*
1215 And as thai walk atour the feyldis greyn — *across*
Out of the south thai saw quhar at the
    queyn — *where*
Towart the ost come ridand sobyrly, — *demurely*
And fyfty ladyis was in hyr cumpany,
Vaillyt of wit and demyt of renoun; — *Distinguished; held in*
1220 Sum wedowis war and sum of religioun, — *Some were widows; nuns*
And seven preistis that entrit war in age. — *were advanced in age*
Wallace to sic did never gret outrage — *such; violence*
Bot gyff till him thai maid a gret offens. — *Unless; wrongdoing*
Thus prochyt thai on towart thar presens. — *they approached; presence*
1225 At the palyoun quhar thai the lyoun saw — *pavilion*
To ground thai lycht and syne on kneis can
    faw; — *alight; fell*
Prayand for pece thai cry with petous cher. — *peace; piteous countenance*
Erll Malcom said, 'Our chyftayn is nocht
    her.' — *here*
He bad hyr rys and said it was nocht rycht, — *asked her; rise*
1230 A queyn on kneis till ony lawar wycht. — *any lower person*
Up by the hand the gud erll has hyr tayn, — *taken*
Atour the bent to Wallace ar thai gayn. — *Around the field; gone*
Quhen scho him saw scho wald haiff knelyt
    doune.
In armys sone he caucht this queyn with
    croun — *soon; caught*
1235 And kyssyt hyr withoutyn wordis mor;
So dyd he never to na Sotheron befor.
'Madem,' he said, 'Rycht welcum mot ye
    be. — *You are very welcome*
How plesis you our ostyng for to se?' — *pleases; muster*

'Rycht weyll,' scho said, 'of frendschip haiff
   we neid.            *need*

1240  God grant ye wald of our nesis to speid.    *help us in our hour of need*

Suffer we mon suppos it lik us ill,    *Endure; must*

Bot trastis weyll it is contrar our will.'    *trust; against*

'Ye sall remayn. With this lord I mon
   gang.            *must go*

Fra your presens we sall nocht tary lang.'    *From; tarry*

1245  The erll and he on to the palyon yeid    *pavilion went*

With gud avys to deym mar of this deid.    *consideration, ponder more*

Till consell son Wallace gart call thaim to.    *council soon; summoned*

'Lordys,' he said, 'ye wait quhat is a do.    *know*

Of thar cummyng my selff has na
   plesance;           *pleasure*

1250  Herfor mon we wyrk with ordinance.[1]

Wemen may be contempnyng in to wer    *Women; cause of shame; war*

Amang fullis that can thaim nocht
   forber.[2]

I say nocht this be thir nor yeit the queyn;    *these [women]; yet*

I trow it be bot gud that scho will meyn.    *believe it is only good; mean*

1255  Bot sampyll tak of lang tym passit by.    *example take*

At Rounsyvaill the tresoun was playnly

Be wemen maid, that Ganyelon with him
   brocht,           *By women devised*

And Turke wyn; forber thaim couth thai
   nocht.           *the Turks conquered; resist*

Lang us in wer gert thaim desyr thar will,    *practice; war made*

1260  Quhilk brocht Charlis to fellon los and ill.    *Charlemagne; grievous evil*

The flour of France withoutyn
   redempcioun

Throuch that foull deid was brocht to
   confusioun.           *destruction*

Commaund your men tharfor in prevay
   wys           *secret manner*

Apayn of lyff thai wyrk nocht on sic wys;    *On penalty of [losing their]*

1265  Nane spek with thaim bot wysmen of gret    *No-one*
   vaill,           *importance*

At lordis ar and sworn to this consaill.'    *That*

Thir chargis thai did als wysly as thai    *These commands; carried*
   mocht;           *out; as might*

1 Therefore must we proceed with caution
2 Among fools that cannot keep away from them

This ordynance throu all the ost was
    wrocht.                             *decree*

He and the erll bathe to the queyn thai
    went,                             *conveyed*

1270    Rasavyt hyr fayr and brocht hyr till a tent;    *Greeted her*

To dyner bounyt als gudly as thai can    *made their way as well*

And servit was with mony likly man.    *fitting*

Gud purvyance the queyn had with hyr    *supplies*
    wrocht;                             *carried*

A say scho tuk of all thyng at thai brocht.    *sample*

1275    Wallace persavyt and said, 'We haiff no    *observed*
    dreid.                              *fear*

I can nocht trow ladyis wald do sic deid    *believe; such a deed*

To poysoun men, for all Ingland to wyn.'

The queyn answerd, 'Gyff poysoun be
    tharin

Of ony thyng quhilk is brocht her with
    me,

1280    Apon my selff fyrst sorow sall ye se.'    *grief (ill-effects) shall*

Sone efter meit a marchell gart absent    *the meal; dismissed all*

Bot lordis and thai at suld to consaill went.    *Except; should go to council*

Ladyis apperyt in presens with the queyn.

Wallace askyt quhat hir cummyng mycht    *her coming*
    meyn.                              *mean*

1285    'For pes,' scho said, 'at we haiff to you
    socht.                             *sought*

This byrnand wer in baill has mony brocht.    *burning campaign; sorrow*

Ye grant us pees for him that deit on tre.'[1]

Wallace answerd, 'Madeym that may nocht
    be.

Ingland has doyne sa gret harmys till us    *done so; harms to us*

1290    We may nocht pas and lychtly leiff it thus.'    *go away; leave*

'Yeis,' said the queyne, 'for Crystyn folk we
    ar.

For Goddis saik, sen we desyr no mar,

We awcht haiff pes.' 'Madeym, that I deny.    *ought to have*

The perfyt caus I sall you schaw forquhy;    *show why*

1295    Ye seke na pes bot for your awn availl.    *seek; own advantage*

Quhen your fals king had Scotland gryppyt    *seized*
    haill,                             *entirely*

For nakyn thing that he befor him fand    *no kind of thing; found*

---

1 Grant us peace for him that died on tree [the cross]

He wald nocht thoill the rycht blud in our land,  — permit; blood [lineage]

Bot reft thar rent, syne put thaim selff to ded,  — took by force; property then; death

1300  Ransoun of gold mycht mak us na remed.  — A gold ransom; reparation

His fell fals wer sall on him selff be seyn.'[1]

Than sobyrly till him answerd the queyn,  — gravely

'Of thir wrangis amendis war most fair.'  — For these wrongs; were

'Madeym,' he said, 'of him we ask no mar  — more

1305  Bot at he wald byd us in to battaill,  — that he would stand against

And God be juge, he kennys the maist haill.'  — knows; most righteous

'Sic mendis,' scho said, 'war nocht rycht gud, think me.  — Such amends

Pes now war best and it mycht purchest be.  — Peace; were; obtained

Wald yhe grant pes and trwys with us tak,  — truce; agree

1310  Throuch all Ingland we suld gar prayeris mak  — have prayers offered

For you and thaim at in the wer war lost.'  — war were

Than Wallace said, 'Quhar sic thing cummys throuch bost,  — such; come through menacing

Prayer of fors, quhar so at it be wrocht,  — of necessity where; offered

Till us helpys litill or ellis nocht.'  — To; else not [at all]

1315  Warly scho said, 'Thus wysmen has us kend,  — Carefully; taught

Ay effter wer pees is the finall end,  — Always after war peace

Quharfor ye suld of your gret malice ces;  — cease

The end of wer is cheryte and pes.  — war; charity; peace

Pees is in hevyn with blys and lestandnas.  — bliss; lastingness

1320  We sall beseke the pape of his hie grace  — beseech; pope; high

Till commaund pes sen we may do na mar.'  — To; since; more

'Madeym,' he said, 'or your purches cum thar  — before; soliciting comes there

Mendys we think of Ingland for to haiff.'  — Amends

'Quhat set you thus,' scho said, 'so God you saiff,  — determined / save

1325  Fra violent wer at ye lik nocht to dwell?'  — From; war; stay away

'Madem,' he said, 'the suth I sall you tell.  — truth

Efter the dayt of Alexanderis ryng  — After; time; reign

Our land stud thre yer desolate but king,  — stood three years without a

Kepyt full weyll at concord in gud stait.  — Maintained; in harmony

1 He shall pay dearly for his disastrous false war

| | | |
|---|---|---|
| 1330 | Throuch two clemyt thar hapnyt gret debait, | who claimed [the throne]; happened |
| | So ernystfully, accord thaim nocht thai can. | they could not agree |
| | Your king thai ast for to be thar ourman. | asked; arbiter |
| | Slely he slayd throuch strenthis of Scotland; | Slyly; passed; strongholds |
| | The kynryk syne he tuk in his awn hand. | kingdom then; own |
| 1335 | He maid a king agayn our rychtwys law | contrary to; righteous |
| | For he of him suld hald the regioun aw. | hold in fealty; all |
| | Contrar this band was all the haill barnage | Against; bond; entire |
| | For Scotland was yeit never in to thrillage. | subjection |
| | Gret Julius that tribut gat of aw, | got from everyone |
| 1340 | His wynnyng was in Scotland bot full smaw. | conquest; only very small |
| | Than your fals king, under colour but mar, | Then; pretence forthwith |
| | Throuch band he maid till Bruce that is our ayr, | bond; ancestor |
| | Throuch all Scotland with gret power thai raid, | |
| | Undid that king quhilk he befor had maid. | which |
| 1345 | To Bruce sen syne he kepit na connand. | afterwards; covenant |
| | He said he wald nocht ga and conques land | go and conquer |
| | Till other men, and thus the cas befell. | For other; case |
| | Than Scotland throuch he demayned him sell | throughout; ruled; self |
| | Slew our elderis, gret pete was to se. | ancestors; pity |
| 1350 | In presone syne lang tyme thai pynit me | afterwards; tormented |
| | Quhill I fra thaim was castyn out for ded. | Until; from; dead |
| | Thankit be God he send me sum remed! | remedy |
| | Vengyt to be I prevyt all my mycht; | Avenged; tried with |
| | Feyll of thar kyn to dede syn I haiff dycht. | I have since destroyed |
| 1355 | The rage of youth gert me desyr a wyff; | passion; made; desire |
| | That rewit I sayr and will do all my liff. | sorely regretted; life |
| | A tratour knycht but mercy gert hyr de, | traitor; without; caused her |
| | Ane Hessilryg, bot for dispit of me. | One; only; malice towards |
| | Than rang I furth in cruell wer and payn | prevailed; fierce war |
| 1360 | Quhill we redemyt part of our land agayn. | Until; redeemed |
| | Than your curst king desyryt of us a trew, | accursed; truce |

Quhilk maid Scotland full rathly for to rew.    Which; quickly; repent
In to that pes thai set a suttell ayr,          During; perfidious ayre
Than eighteen scor to dede thai hangyt          death; hanged there
    thair
1365  At noblis war and worthi of renoun,[1]     That were nobles
Of cot armys eldest in that regioun;[1]
Thar dede we think to veng in all our           Their deaths; avenge
    mycht.
The woman als that dulfully was dycht,          painfully was killed
Out of my mind that dede will never bid         stay
1370  Quhill God me tak fra this fals warld so    Until; takes; world; wide
    wid!
Of Sotheroun syn I can no pete haiff.           On Englishmen's sins; pity
Your men in wer I think nevermor to             war; spare
    saiff.'
The breith teris, was gret payn to behald,      vehement tears
Bryst fra his eyn be he his taill had tald.     Burst; when; account; told
1375  The queyn wepyt for pete of Wallace.
'Allace,' scho said, 'wa worth the curssyt       woe betide; accursed case!
    cace!
In waryit tym that Hesilryg was born!           a blighted time
Mony worthi throuch his deid ar forlorn.        worthy men; actions; lost
He suld haiff payn that saikles sic ane
    slewch.[2]
1380  Ingland sen syn has bocht it der enewch,     since; paid dearly enough
Thocht scho had beyn a queyn or a               [As] though
    prynsace.'                                    princess
'Madem,' he said, 'as God giff me gud           so God grant
    grace,
In till hir tym scho was als der to me,         While she lived; as dear . . .
                                                    as
Prynsace or queyn, in quhat stait so thai       estate
    be.'
1385  'Wallace,' scho said, 'of this talk we will ces;
The mendis herof is gud prayer and pes.'        amends hereof
'I grant,' he said, 'of me as now na mayr.
This is rycht nocht bot ekyng of our cayr.'     increasing; distress
The queyn fand weyll langage nothing hyr
    bet.[3]

1 [Bearers] of the oldest coats of arms in that region
2 He should be punished for slaying such an innocent creature
3 The queen discovered words did not help her [case]

| | | |
|---|---|---|
| 1390 | Scho trowit with gold that he mycht be our set. | trusted; won over |
| | Thre thousand pound of fynest gold so red | |
| | Scho gert be brocht to Wallace in that sted. | caused to be brought; place |
| | 'Madeym,' he said, 'na sic tribut we craiff. | no such tribute we crave |
| | A nother mendis we wald of Ingland haiff | Another amends; would |
| 1395 | Or we raturn fra this regioun agayn, | Before; remove |
| | Of your fals blud that has our elderis slayn. | forebears |
| | For all the gold and ryches ye in ryng. | you possess |
| | Ye get no pes but desir of your king.'[1] | |
| | Quhen scho saw weill gold mycht hyr nocht releiff, | help |
| 1400 | Sum part in sport scho thocht him for to preiff. | Some; play test |
| | 'Wallace,' scho said, 'yhe war clepyt my luff; | you were called love |
| | Mor baundounly I maid me for to pruff,[2] | |
| | Traistand tharfor your rancour for to slak. | Trusting; assuage |
| | Me think ye suld do sum thing for my saik.' | sake |
| 1405 | Rycht wysly he maid answer to the queyn: | wisely |
| | 'Madem,' he said, 'and verite war seyn | if it were truly so |
| | That ye me luffyt, I awcht you luff agayn. | ought to love you in return |
| | Thir wordis all ar nothing bot in vayn. | These; vain |
| | Sic luff as that is nothing till avance, | Such love; not praiseworthy |
| 1410 | To tak a lak and syne get no plesance. | suffer censure; then; pleasure |
| | In spech of luff suttell ye Sotheroun ar; | wily |
| | Ye can us mok, suppos ye se no mar.' | mock |
| | 'In London,' scho said, 'for you I sufferyt blaym; | |
| | Our consall als will lauch quhen we cum haym. | council also; laugh; come home |
| 1415 | So may thai say, wemen ar fers of thocht | boldly think |
| | To seke frendschip and syne can get rycht nocht.' | seek; then |
| | 'Madem,' he said, 'we wait how ye ar send. | know; you are sent |
| | Yhe trow we haiff bot litill for to spend. | You believe |
| | Fyrst with your gold, for ye ar rych and wys, | |
| 1420 | Yhe wald us blynd, sen Scottis ar so nys; | You would; since; foolish |

1 You get no peace unless your king desires it
2 This emboldened me to test you

Syn plesand wordis of you and ladyis fair,        *Then pleasing; from*
As quha suld dryff the byrdis till a swar          *drive; to; snare*
With the small pype, for it most fresche           *the whistle; vigorously*
   will call.
Madeym, as yit ye ma nocht tempt us all.           *yet; may*
1425  Gret part of gud is left amang our kyn;      *kinsfolk*
In Ingland als we fynd enewch to wyn.'             *also; enough; capture*
Abayssyt scho was to mak answer him till.          *Afraid; make him an answer*
'Der schir,' scho said, 'sen this is at your       *since*
   will,                                          *pleasure*
Wer or pes, quhat so you likis best,               *whatever*
1430  Lat your hye witt and gud consaill degest.'   *noble mind; counsel settle*
'Madem,' he said, 'now sall ye understand
The resone quhy that I will mak na band.           *no bond*
With you ladyis I can na trewis bynd               *agree no truce*
For your fals king her efter sone wald             *hereafter soon would find*
   fynd,
1435  Quhen he saw tyme, to brek it at his will     *pleasure*
And playnly say he grantyt nocht thartill.         *thereto*
Than had we nayn bot ladyis to repruff.            *none except; reprove*
That sall he nocht, be God that is abuff!          *by; above*
Apon wemen I will no wer begyn;
1440  On you, in faith, no worschip is to wyn.      *honour; win*
All the haill pas apon him selff he sall tak       *the whole responsibility*
Of pees or wer, quhat hapnyt we to mak.'           *whatever we decide*
The qweyn grantyt his answer sufficient;
So dyd the layff in place that was present.[1]
1445  His delyverance thai held of gret availl      *decision; advantage*
And stark enewch to schaw to thar                  *powerful enough; reveal*
   consaill.
Wa was the qweyn hyr travaill helpyt               *Dejected; effort*
   nocht.
The gold scho tuk that thai had with hyr           *she took*
   brocht;
Into the ost rycht frely scho it gayff             *Unto; army; generously*
1450  Till everylk man that likyt for till haiff.   *To every; have it*
Till menstraillis, harroldis, scho delt            *To minstrels, heralds; gave*
   haboundanle,                                    *abundantly*
Besekand thaim hyr frend at thai wald be.          *Beseeching; her friend that*
Quhen Wallace saw the fredom of the                *generosity*
   queyn

1 So did the others that were present in the place

| | Text | Gloss |
|---|---|---|
| | Sadly he said, 'The suth weyll has beyn seyn, | Sternly; truth |
| 1455 | Wemen may tempt the wysest at is wrocht. | wisest creature |
| | Your gret gentrice it sall never be for nocht. | noble conduct |
| | We you assuuer our ost sall muff na thing | assure; not move |
| | Quhyll tym ye may send message fra your king. | Until [such] time as |
| | Gyff it be sa at he accord and we, | If; he and we agree |
| 1460 | Than for your saik it sall the better be. | |
| | Your harroldys als sall saiffly cum and ga; | also shall safely come; go |
| | For your fredom we sall trowbill na ma.'[1] | |
| | Scho thankit him of his grant mony sys | concession; many times |
| | And all the ladyis apon a gudly wys. | goodly manner |
| 1465 | Glaidly thai drank, the queyn and gud Wallace, | |
| | Thir ladyis als and lordis in that place. | These; also |
| | Hyr leyff scho tuk without langar abaid, | Her leave; took; delay |
| | Five myile that nycht south till a nonry raid. | miles; to; nunnery rode |
| | Apon the morn till London passit thai. | |
| 1470 | In Westmenster quhar at the consaill lay | parliament |
| | Wallace answer scho gart schaw to the king. | caused to be shown |
| | It nedis nocht her rahers mar of this thing.[2] | |
| | The gret commend that scho to Wallace gaiff | praise / gave |
| | Befor the king in presens of the laiff, | others |
| 1475 | Till trew Scottis it suld gretly apples, | To; please |
| | Thocht Inglismen tharof had litill es. | comfort |
| | Of worschip, wyt, manheid and governans, | honour, intelligence |
| | Of fredom, trewth, key of remembrans, | noble character; loyalty |
| | Scho callyt him thar in to thar hye presens, | in their august presence |
| 1480 | Thocht contrar thaim he stud at his defens. | Though; in his resistance |
| | 'So chyftaynlik,' scho said, 'as he is seyn, | chieftain-like |
| | In till Inglande I trow has never beyn. | believe |
| | Wald ye of gold gyff him this rewmys rent | realm's revenue |
| | Fra honour he will nocht turn his entent. | From; mind |
| 1485 | Sufferyt we ar quhill ye may message mak. | Assured of safety |

1 Because of your generosity we shall cause no more trouble
2 It is not necessary to repeat here more of this thing

Of wys lordis sumpart I reid you tak                      some; advise; take
To purches pees withoutyn wordis mar;                     solicit peace; more
For all Ingland may rew his raid full sayr.               repent; extremely
Your harroldys als to pas to him has leyff,               also; permission
In all his ost thar sall no man thaim greiff.'            harm
Than thankit thai the queyn for hir                       endeavour
        travaill,
The king and lordis that was of his consaill.
Of hyr answer the king applessit was.                     was pleased
Than thre gret lordys thai ordand for to
        pas.
Thar consaill haill has found it was the
        best
Trewis to tak, or ellis thai get no rest.                 To take a truce; else
A harrold went in all the haist he may
Till Tawbane vaill quhar at the Scottis lay,              St Alban's bulwark where
Condeyt till haiff quhill thai haiff said thar            Safe conduct
        will.
The consaill sone a condeyt gaiff him till.               soon
Agayn he past with soverance till his king.               assurance of safety to
Than chesyt thai thre lordis for this thing.              chose
The keyn Clyffurd was than thar warden                    bold
        haill,                                            wholly
Bewmont, Wodstok, all men of mekill vaill;                great standing
Quhat thir thre wrocht the layff suld stand               these three; others; stand by
        thar till.                                            it
The kingis seyll was gyffyn thaim at thar                 king's seal; given
        will.                                             pleasure
Sone thai war brocht to spekyng to                        Soon; speak with
        Wallace.
Wodstok him schawit mony suttell cace.                    presented; sly arguments
Wallace he herd the sophammis evere deill.                every one of the sophisms
'As yeit,' he said, 'me think ye meyn bot                 mean only
        weill.
In wrang ye hald, and dois us gret outrage,
Of housis part that is our heretage.[1]
Out of this pees in playn I mak thaim                     Out
        knawin,                                           known
Thaim for to wyn, sen that thai ar our                    win back, since
        awin,                                             own

---

1 You wrongfully occupy some of our castles that are our heritage, and commit great outrage against us

| | |
|---|---|
| 1515 | Roxburch, Berweik, at ouris lang tym has beyn, | that ours long time |
| | In to the handis of you fals Sotherone keyn. | fierce |
| | We ask her als be vertu of this band | here also by |
| | Our ayris, our king, be wrang led of Scotland. | justices; wrong led out of |
| | We sall thaim haiff withoutyn wordis mar.' | have back; more |
| 1520 | Till his desyr the lordis grantis thair, | granted there |
| | Rycht at his will thai haiff consentit haill, | according to; all |
| | For nakyn thing the pees thai wald nocht faill. | no kind of thing |
| | The yong Randell at than in London was,[1] | that then |
| | The lord of Lorn, in this band he can as,[1] | |
| 1525 | Erll of Bowchane bot than in tendyr age— | but then; youthful |
| | Efter he grew a man of hycht, wys and large. | tall |
| | | generous |
| | Cumyn and Soullis he gart deliver als, | had freed also |
| | Quhilk efter was till king Robert full fals. | who afterwards; to |
| | Wallang fled our, and durst nocht bid that mute, | overseas; stay in court |
| 1530 | In Pykardte; to ask him was na bute, | futile |
| | Bot Wallace wald erar haff had that fals knycht | would sooner have |
| | Than ten thousand of fynest gold so brycht. | |
| | The Bruce he askit, bot he was had away | asked for; taken |
| | Befor that tym till Calys mony day. | Calais; many a |
| 1535 | King Edward prevyt that thai mycht nocht him get; | proved |
| | Of Glosister his uncle had him set, | placed [there] |
| | At Calys than had haly in kepyng. | That; wholly; keeping |
| | Wallace that tym gat nocht his rychtwys king. | got |
| | The Erll Patrik fra London alsua send | also |
| 1540 | Wyth Wallace to mak, as weill befor was kend, | known |
| | Of his mater a fynaill governance; | affairs; settlement |
| | Till King Edward gaiff up his legeance | gave up; allegiance |
| | And tuk till hald of Scotland evermar. | undertook; remain true to |
| | With full glaid hart Wallace resavit him thar. | received |
| 1545 | Thai honowryt him rycht reverendly as lord; | honoured; respectfully |

---

1 The lord of Lorn's [release] he asked for under this agreement

The Scottis was all rejosyt of that conford.    gladdened; comfort
A hundreth hors with yong lordis of
    renoune
Till Wallace com, fred out of that presoune.    freed
Undyr his seill King Edward thaim gert    seal; had sent
    send
1550 For till gyff our and mak a fynaill end    hand over; final settlement
Roxburch, Berweik, quhilk is of mekill
    vaill,    importance
To Scottis men and all the boundis haill.    bounds entirely
To fyve yer trew thai promyst be thar    a five-year truce; their
    hand.    signatures
Than Wallace said, 'We will pas ner
    Scotland
1555 Or ocht be seld and tharfor mak us boun.    Before anything is sealed
Agayn we will besid Northallyrtoun    We will return
Quhar King Edward fyrst battaill hecht to    promised
    me;
As it began thar sall it endyt be.
Gret weyll your queyn,' he chargyt the    Greet
    message,    messengers
1560 'It is for hyr at we leyff our wiage.'    that; leave off; campaign
A day he set quhen he suld meit him thar
And  seill this pees withoutyn wordis    seal; peace; more
    mar.
Apon the morn the ost but mar avys    without further delay
Tranountyt north apon a gudly wys    Marched; in good order
1565 To the set tryst that Wallace had thaim    appointed meeting
    maid.
The Inglis message com but mar abaid;    messengers; straight away
Thai seyllyt the pes without langar delay.    sealed the peace immediately
The message than apon the secund day    messengers then
Till London went in all the haist thai can.
1570 The worthi Scottis with mony gudly man    many good men
Till Bamburch com with all the power    Bamburgh
    haill,    complete
Sexte thousand, all Scottis of gret vaill.    Sixty; the best
Ten dayis befor All Halow Evyn thai fur;    Hallowe'en; went
On Lammes day thai lycht on Caram mur.    dismounted; Carham Moor
1575 Thar lugyt thai with plesance as thai    lodged; gladly
    mocht,    might
Quhill on the morn at preistis to thaim    that priests sought them
    socht

In Caram kyrk, and sessyt in his hand     *delivered into*
Roxburch keyis as thai had maid connand,     *agreement*
And Berweik als quhilk Sotheroun had so     *held so long*
    lang.
1580 Thai frede the folk in Ingland for to gang,     *freed; go*
For thar lyffis uschet of ather place;     *lives; sallied out; other places*
Thai durst nocht weill bid rekynnyng of     *dared; wait for Wallace's*
    Wallace.     *reckoning*
Capdane he maid in Berweik of renoun
That worthy was, gud Crystell of Cetoun.
1585 Kepar he left till Roxburch castell wicht     *Keeper; strong*
Schir Jhon Ramsay, a wys and worthi
    knycht.
Syn Wallace selff with Erll Patrik in playn     *Then; himself; openly*
To Dunbar raid and restoryt him agayn     *rode; restored*
In his castell and all that heretage,
1590 With the consent of all that haill barnage.     *baronage*
Quhen Wallace was agreit and this lord,     *and this lord were agreed*
To rewll the rewm he maid him gudly ford.     *realm; ready*
Scotlande atour fra Ros till Soloway sand     *across*
He raid it thrys and statut all the land.     *ruled*
1595 In the Leynhous a quhyll he maid repayr;     *Lennox; went frequently*
Schyr Jhon Menteth that tym was captane
    thar.
Twys befor he had his gossep beyn,
Bot na frendschip betwix thaim syn was
    seyn.
Twa monethis still he dwelt in Dunbertane;
1600 A hous he foundyt apon the Roch of     *castle*
    stayne.     *stone*
Men left he thar till byg it to the hycht,     *to build it high*
Syn to the March agayn he rydis rycht.     *Then; directly*
In to Roxburch thai chesyt him a place,
A gud tour thar he gert byg in schort     *tower; had built; short time*
    space.
1605 The kynrik stud in gud worschip and es;     *stood in; prosperity*
Was nayn so gret durst his nychtbour
    disples.
The abill ground gert laubour thryftely,     *fertile*
Wictaill and froyte thar grew aboundandly.
Was never befor syn this was callyt
    Scotland
1610 Sic welth and pes at anys in the land.     *Such; once*

He send Jop twys to Bruce in Huntyntoun,
Besekand him to cum and tak his croun.      Beseeching
Conseill he tuk at fals Saxionis allace!      English
He had never hap in lyff to get Wallace.      the good fortune
Thre yer as thus the rewm stud in gud pes.      realm; peace
Of this sayn my wordis for to ces,[1]
And forthyr furth of Wallace I will tell
In till his lyff quhat aventur yeit fell.

1615

---

1 With these words I cease my account of this

## BOOK NINE

A ryoil king than ryngyt in to France,    *royal; reigned*
Gret worschip herd of Wallace governance:    *repute; leadership*
Of prowis, prys, and of his worthi deid    *prowess; renown*
And forthwart fair, commendede of manheid,    *active conduct, celebrated; courage*
5  Bathe humyll, leyll, and of his prevyt prys,    *loyal; proven prowess*
Of honour, trewth, and void of cowatis.    *fidelity; devoid of cowardice*
The nobill king ryngand in ryolte    *reigning; majesty*
Had gret delyte this Wallace for to se    *desire*
And knew rycht weill, schortly to undyrstand,
10  The gret supprys and ourset of Ingland.    *defeat; overthrow*
Als merveld he of Wallace small power    *Also he marvelled that; army*
That but a king tuk sic a rewm to ster    *without; realm; lead*
Agayn Ingland, and gert thar malice ces
Quhill thai desyryt with gud will to mak pes.
15  And rycht onon a herrold gert he call;    *forthwith; herald*
In schort termys he has rehersit him all    *Briefly; related*
Of his entent completly till ane end,    *intention*
Syn in Scotland he bad him for to wend.    *Then; ordered; go*
And thus he wrait than in till gret honour    *wrote*
20  To Wilyam Wallace as a conquerour:
'O lovit leid, with worschip wys and wicht,    *beloved man; bold*
Thou verray help in haldyn of the rycht;    *true; upholding*
Thou rycht restorer of thi natyff land
With Goddis grace agayn thi fais to stand;
25  In thi defens helpar of rychtwys blud;
O worthy byrth and blessyt be thi fud,    *food*
As it is red in prophecy beforn    *read*
In happy tym for Scotland thou was born!
I thee besek with all humylite    *beseech*
30  My clos letter thou wald consaiff and se.    *sealed; understand*
As your brodyr, I, Crystyn king of France,    *brother*
To the berer ye her and gyff credance.'    *bearer; give a hearing*
The herrold bound him and to the schip is gone;    *prepared to leave*
In Scotland sone he cummyn is onon,    *directly*
35  Bot harrold-lyk he sekis his presens.    *in the manner of a herald*
On land he went and maid no residens    *delays*

In ony steid, quhar he presumyt thar.    *any place*
So on a day he fand him in to Ayr,
In gud affer and manlik cumpany.    *order*
40 The harrold than with honour reverendly    *respectfully*
Has salust him apon a gudly maner,    *greeted*
And he agayn with humyll hamly cher    *humble kindly bearing*
Rasavit him in to rycht gudly wys.    *Received*
The harrold than with worschip to devys    *relate*
45 Betuk till him the kingis wryt of France,
Wallace, on kne with lawly obeysance,[1]
Rycht reverendly for worschip of Scotland.    *respectfully; honour*
Quhen he it red and had it understand    *read*
At this herrold he askyt his credence    *credentials*
50 With aspre spech and manly contenence,    *stern; bearing*
And he him tald as I haiff said befor
The kingis desyr. Quhat nedis wordis mor?
'The hye honour and the gret nobilnas
Of your manheid, weill knawin in mony    *courage; known, many places*
     place,
55 Him likis als weill your worschip till    *as well; honour; praise*
     avance
As yhe war born a liege man of France.
Sen his regioun is flour of rewmys seyn,    *Since; realms*
Als the gret band of kindnes you betweyn,
It war worschip his presens for to se    *honour*
60 Sen at this rewm standis in sic degre.'    *Since; such relationship*
Wallace consavit withoutyn tarying    *immediately understood*
The gret desyr of this gud nobill king,
Syn till him said, 'As God of hevin me    *[the herald]*
     save,
Her efter sone ye sall ane answer have    *Hereafter soon*
65 Of your desyr that ye have schawit me till.    *shown to me*
Welcum ye ar with a fre hartly will.'    *heartfelt*
The harrold baid on to the twentieth day    *stayed*
With Wallace still in gud weillfayr and    *enjoying good hospitality;*
     play,      *entertainment*
Contende the tyme with worschip and    *Passed; honour;*
     plesance;      *pleasure*
70 Be gud avys maid his deliverance,    *After careful consideration;*
         *decision*

[1] Delivered to him the king's letter from France, to Wallace, on [bended] knee with humble deference

With his awn hand he wrait on to the king    *wrote*
All his entent as tuyching to this thing.    *intention; regarding*
Rycht rych reward he gaiff the harrold tho    *rich; gave; then*
And him convoyde quhen he had leyff to    *escorted; leave*
   go
75  Out of the toun with gudly cumpanye.
His leyff he tuk syn went on to the se.    *leave; took; then; sea*
Gud Wallace than has maid his providance:    *arrangements*
His purpos was to se the king of France;
Erest in weyr to Sanct Jhonstoun couth    *At the beginning of spring;*
   fair.    *went*
80  A consaill than he had gert ordand thar.    *council; decreed*
In till his sted he chesyt a governour    *place; chose*
To kep the land, a man of gret valour,    *look after*
Jamys gud lord the Stewart of Scotland,
Quhilk fadyr was, as storys beris on hand,    *histories*
85  Till gud Walter that was of hye parage,    *lineage*
Marjory the Bruce syne gat in mariage.    *afterwards obtained*
Tharof to spek as now I haiff no space;    *speak*
It is weill knawin, thankit be Goddis grace.    *known*
And to the harrold withoutyn residens    *herald [I now return]; delay*
90  How he approchit to the kingis presens.
Fra the Rochell the land sone has he tayn.    *reached*
Atour the landis he graithit him to gayn,    *Across; prepared to go*
Sekand the king als gudly as he may,    *seeking; as well*
So to the court he passit on a day.
95  To Parys went, was peirles of renoun;    *unmatched*
The king that tym held palace in that toun.
Quhen he hym saw, graithly has    *readily*
   understand,
He speryt tithingis and weyllfayr of    *asked news; [about] the*
   Scotland.    *welfare of*
The herrold said in to thir termys schort    *briefly*
100  That all was gud; he had the mar comfort.    *more*
'Saw thou Wallace, the chyftayn of that
   land?'
And he said, 'Ya, that I dar tak on hand    *dare venture to say*
A worthyar this day lyffand is nayn    *more worthy person; living*
In way of wer, als fer as I haiff gayn.    *as far; gone*
105  The hie worschip and the gret nobilnes,    *high honour*
The gud weillfair, plesance and worthines,    *hospitality; dignity*
The rych reward was mychty for to se    *see*
That for your saik he kythyt apon me;    *bestowed*

And his answer in wryt he has you send.'  *writing*
110 The king rasavit it with a lycht attend,  *glad anticipation*
This hie affect and dyt of his writyng.  *strong desire; language*
'O ryoll roy and rychtwys crownyt king,  *rightfully crowned*
Yhe knaw this weill be other ma than me,  *know; through others more*
How that our rewlm standis in perplexite.  *realm*
115 The fals nacioun that we ar nychtbouris to  *neighbours*
Quhen plesis thaim thai mak us ay ado.  *ever*
Thar may no band be maid so sufficians  *bond; complete*
Bot ay in it thai fynd a varians.  *[cause] to vary from it*
To wait a tym, will God at it may be,  *Wait for a while; that*
120 Within a yer I sall your presens se.'  *see*
Of this answer weill plessyt was the king.  *pleased*
Leyff I him thus in ryolte to ryng  *Leave; to reign in majesty*
And glaid comford, rycht as I haiff you
 told.
Of Wallace furth I will my proces hold.  *hold forth my account*
125 In Aperill, the one and twenty day,
The hie calend thus, Cancer as we say,  *high beginning that is*
The lusty tym of Mayus fresche cummyng,  *vigorous*
Celestiall gret blythnes in to bring;
Pryncypaill moneth forsuth it may be seyn,
130 The hevynly hewis apon the tendyr greyn;  *heavenly colours*
Quhen old Saturn his cloudy cours had
 gon
The quhilk had beyn bath best and byrdis  *which; the bane of beast and*
 bon;  *bird*
Zepherus ek with his swet vapour
He comfort has be wyrking of natour
135 All fructuous thing in till the erd adoun  *fruitful; earth below*
At rewllyt is under the hie regioun;  *That is ruled; celestial*
Sobyr Luna in flowyng of the se,  *Moderate*
Quhen brycht Phebus is in his hie  *[astrological] house*
 chemage.
The Bulys cours so takin had his place  *Bull's [i.e., Taurus]*
140 And Jupiter was in the Crabbis face;  *Crab's [i.e., Cancer]*
Quhen Aryet the hot syng coloryk  *Aries; sign*
Into the Ram quhilk had his rowmys ryk,  *rich spaces*
He chosyn had his place and his mansuun  *mansion*
In Capricorn, the sygn of the Lioun;
145 Gentill Jupiter with his myld ordinance  *provision*
Bath erb and tre revertis in plesance,  *plant; restores*
And fresch Flora hir floury mantill spreid

In every vaill, bath hop, hycht, hill and meide;    *valley; glen; mountain; meadow*

This sammyn tym, for thus myn auctor sayis,

150 Wallace to pas of Scotland tuk his wayis;    *depart from*

Be schort avys he schup him to the se    *consideration; made his way*

And fyfty men tuk in his cumpane.

He leit no word than walk of his passage    *let; spread*

Or Inglismen had stoppit him his viage,    *would have stopped; journey*

155 Nor tuk na leiff at the lordis of the parlement:    *leave of*

He wyst full weill thai wald nocht all consent    *knew*

To suffer him out of the land to go.    *permit*

Forthi onon withoutyn wordis mo    *Therefore forthwith; more*

He gart forse and ordand weill his schip;[1]

160 And thir war part past in his falowschip;    *these were some who*

Twa Wallace was his kynnys men full ner,    *close kinsmen*

Crawfurd, Kneland was haldyn till him der.    *were held dear to him*

Of Kyrkcubre he purpost his passage.    *intended*

Semen he feyt and gaiff thaim gudlye wage.    *Sailors; hired*

165 Thai wantyt nocht of wyn, victaill nor ger,    *lacked not; food; equipment*

A fair new barge, rycht worthi wrocht for wer,    *ship; well made for war*

With that thai war a gudly cumpany

Of vaillit men had wrocht full hardely.    *well-chosen; performed*

Bonalais drank rycht glaidly in a morow,    *Farewell drinks*

170 Syn leiff thai tuk and with 'sanct Jhon to borow'[2]

Bottis was schot and fra the roch thaim sent.    *Boats were pushed out; rock*

With glaid hartis at anys in thai went,    *once*

Upon the schip thai rowit hastely.    *Towards*

The seymen than walkand full besyly    *seamen; labouring*

175 Ankyrs wand in wysly on ather syd.    *wound; expertly; either side*

Thair lynys kest and waytyt weyll the tyd,    *sounding lines out; awaited*

Leyt salys fall and has thar cours ynom:    *Let sails; course taken*

A gud gay wynd out of the rycht art com.    *strong; direction*

Frekis in forstame rewllit weill thar ger,    *Men at the ship's prow*

---

1 He had his ship supplied and well prepared

2 Then took their leave and with 'May St John protect you'

180  Ledys on luff burd with a lordlik fer,          Lead on the lee side; bearing
     Lansys laid out to luk thar passage sound,      Lances; to see to the safety of
     With full sayll thus fra Scotland furth thai
          found,                                     went
     Salyt our the day and als the nycht.            throughout; also
     Apon the morn quhen that the son rais
          brycht
185  The schip master on to the top he went.
     Southest he saw that trublyt his entent:        Southeast; troubled his mind
     Saxten salis arayit all on raw,                 sails arranged: in a row
     In colour reid and towart him couth draw.       red; drew
     The gliterand son apon thaim schawit
          brycht,                                    sun; appeared
190  The se about enlumynyt with the lycht.          illuminated
     This mannis spreit was in ane extasy.           spirit; distracted state
     Doun went he sone and said full
          sorowfully,                                soon
     'Allace', quod he, 'the day that I was
          born!
     Without rameid our lywys ar forlorn.            lives; lost
195  In cursyt tym I tuk this cur on hand.           assumed this command
     The best chyftayn and reskew of Scotland,       rescue
     Our raklesly I haiff tayn upon me               Too recklessly; taken
     With waik power to bryng him throu the          weak; over
          se.
     It forsyt nocht wald God I war torment          matters; were tormented
200  So Wallace mycht with worschip chaip            escape
          unschent.'                                 unharmed
     Quhen Wallace saw and hard this mannys
          mon,                                       lament
     To comfort him in gud will is he gon.
     'Maister', he said, 'quhat has amovit thee?'    distressed you
     'Nocht for my selff,' this man said petuisle,   piteously
205  'Bot of a thing I dar weill undertane,          I venture to say
     Thocht all war heyr the schippis of braid
          Bertane,[1]
     Part suld we los, set fortoun had it sworn.     lose; although
     The best wer man in se is us beforn             warrior on the sea; before
     Leffand this day and king is of the se.'        Living
210  Wallace sone sperd, 'Wait thou quhat he         soon asked; know
          may be?'

1 Although all the ships from throughout Britain were here

| | |
|---|---|
| 'The Rede Reffayr thai call him in his still. | *Red Pirate; style* |
| That I him saw evyr waryt worth that quhill! | *Cursed be the time that I ever saw him* |
| For myn awn lyff I wald no murnyng mak. | *own life; lament* |
| Is no man born that yon tyran will tak. | *[There]; that tyrant; take on* |
| 215  He savis nayn for gold nor other gud | *spares none* |
| Bot slayis and drownys all derffly in the flud. | *violently* / *sea* |
| He gettis no grace thocht he war king or knycht. | *receives; [even] though; were* |
| This sixteen yer he has doyn gret unrycht. | *These; wrong* |
| The power is so strang he has to ster | *strong; lead* |
| 220  May non eschaip that cummys in his danger. | *none escape* / *power* |
| Wald we him burd na but is to begyn: | *board; use* |
| The lakest schip that is his flot within | *worst* |
| May sayll us doun on to a dulfull ded.' | *painful death* |
| Than Wallace said, 'Sen thou can no ramed, | *Since you know no remedy* |
| 225  Tell me his feyr and how I sall him knaw, | *about his bearing* |
| Quhat is hys oys, and syn go luge thee law.' | *way of life; lodge below* |
| The schipman sayis, 'Rycht weill ye may him ken | *know* |
| Throu graith takynnys full clerly by his men. | *clear signs* |
| His cot armour is seyn in mony steid | *places* |
| 230  Ay battaill boun and riwell ay of reid.[1] | |
| This formest schip that persewis you so fast, | *foremost* |
| Hym selff is in; he will nocht be agast. | *afraid* |
| He wyll you hayll quhen that he cummys you ner. | *hail* / *near* |
| Without tary than mon yhe stryk on ster. | *delay; must; astern* |
| 235  Hym selff will enter fyrst full hardely. | *valiantly* |
| Thir ar the syngys that ye sall knaw him by; | *These; signs; know* |
| A bar of blew in till his schenand scheild, | *band of blue; shining shield* |
| A bend of greyn desyren ay the feild;[2] | |

[1] Ever ready for battle and with circular decoration always in red
[2] A band of green desiring always

The rede betakynnys blud and hardyment,   *blood; boldness*

240  The greyn curage encressand his entent:   *courage strengthening*

The blew he beris for he is Crystyn man.'   *blue*

Sadly agayn Wallace answerd than,   *Gravely; then*

'Thocht he be crystynyt this war no Godlyk   *God-like*
    deid.   *deed*

Go undyr loft. Sanct Androw mot us   *below deck; help us*
    speid.'

245  Bathe schip maister and the ster man also   *helmsman*

In the holl but baid he gert thaim go.   *ship's hold; made them go*

His fyfty men withoutyn langar rest   *delay*

Wallace gart ray into thar armour prest.   *got them to dress; ready*

Fourty and aucht on luffburd laid thaim   *Forty-eight; the lee side*
    law.   *low*

250  Wylyham Crawfurd than till him gert he
    caw   *summoned*

And said, 'Thou can sumpart of schipman   *know; seafaring ways*
    fair.

Thi oys has beyn oft in the toun of Ayr.   *experience*

I pray thee tak this doctryn weill of me.   *instruction*

Luk at thou stand strekly be this tre.   *firmly by; wooden post*

255  Quhen I bid stryk to service be thou
    bane.[1]

Quhen I thee warn lat draw the saill agane.

Kneland, cusyng cum, tak the ster on   *come cousin; the helm*
    hand.

Her on the vaill ner by thee I sall stand.   *Here; bulwark*

God gyd our schip as now I say na mar.'   *guide; more*

260  The barge began with a full werlik far,   *began [moving again]; show*

Him selff on loft was with a drawyn sword   *deck*

And bad his sterman lay thaim langis the   *helmsmen alongside the ship*
    bourd.

On loude he cryit, 'Stryk, doggis, ye sall   *Aloud*
    de.'   *die*

Crawfurd leit draw the saill a litill we.   *bit*

265  The capdane sone lap in and wald nocht   *leapt*
    stynt.   *stop*

Wallace in haist be the gorget him hynt,   *seized*

On the our loft kest him quhar he stud   *upper deck; threw*

Quhill neys and mouth all ruschit out of   *nose*
    blud.

1 When I command [you to] strike be ready for action

A forgyt knyff but baid he bradis out.   *forged; immediately; draws*

270 The wer schippis was lappyt thaim about.   *were surrounding*

The mekill barge had nocht thaim clyppyt fast;   *great ship had not grappled with them*

Crawfurd drew saill, skewyt by and of thaim past.   *turned obliquely*

The Reiffar criyt with petous voice and cler   *Pirate*

Grace of hys lyff. 'For him that bocht you der.   *Mercy on his life; saved; dearly*

275 Mercy!' he said, 'for him that deit on rud,   *died on the cross*

Layser to mend. I haiff spilt mekill blud.   *Leisure to amend; spilled*

For my trespas I wald mak sum ramed.   *atonement*

Mony saikles I have gart put to ded.'   *innocents caused to be*

Wallace wyst weyll, thocht he to ded war brocht,

280 Fra thaim to chaip on na wyse mycht he nocht,   *From them to escape; no way*

And of his lyff sum reskew mycht he mak.

A better purpos sone he can to tak,   *he soon decided on*

And als he rewyt him for his lyff was ill.   *also; pitied; evil*

In Latyn tong rycht thus he said him till:   *to him*

285 'I tuk never man that enemy was to me.   *took [as prisoner]*

For Goddis saik thi lyff I grant to thee.'

Bathe knyff and swerd he tuk fra him onon,   *immediately*

Up be the hand as presoner has him ton,   *by; taken*

And on his swerd scharply he gert him swer   *swear*

290 Fra that day furth he suld him never der.   *harm*

'Commaund thi men,' quod Wallace, 'till our pes.'   *to accept our peace*

Thar schot of goun that was nocht eith to ces.   *gunfire; easy*   *stop*

The cast it was rycht awfull on athir sid.   *discharge; either*

The Rede Reiffar commaundyt thaim to bid,   *wait*

295 Held out a gluff in takyn of the trew.   *glove; token; truce*

His men beheld and weyll that senye knew,   *signal*

Left off thar schot that sygn quhen that thai saw.   *firing; sign*

His grettast barge towart him he couth draw.   *biggest ship; caused to be drawn*

'Lat be your wer; thir ar our freyndis at ane.     *Let; fighting these; in agreement*

300   I traist to God our werst dayis ar gane.'     *trust; past*

He ast Wallace to do quhat was his will.     *asked*

With schort avys rycht thus he said him till:     *After considering briefly; to*

'To the Rochell I wald ye gert thaim saill.     *made them sail*

For Inglismen I wait nocht quhat may aill.'[1]

305   He thaim commaundit forouttin wordis mair     *without words more*

'Turne saill and wynd, towart the Rochell fair,     *wind*

For thar, God will, is our purpos to be.     *go*

Skour weyll about for scoukaris in the se.'     *Scour; spies*

His commaund thai did in all the haist thai can.     *carried out*

310   Wallace desyryt to talk mor with this man.     *more*

Sadly he sperd, 'Of quhat land was thou born?'     *Seriously; asked*

'Of France,' quod he, 'and my eldris beforn,     *ancestors*

And thar we had sumpart of heretage;

Yet fers fortoun thus brocht me in a rage.'     *cruel; torment*

315   Wallace sperd 'How com thou to this lyff?'

'Forsuth, he said, 'bot throu a sudan stryff.

So hapnyt me in to the kingis presens     *in the king's presence*

Our raklesly to do our gret offens,     *Too recklessly; commit too*

A nobill man of gud fame and renoun

320   That throu my deid was put to confusioun,     *action; ruin*

Dede of a straik. Quhat nedis wordis mor?     *Dead from a stroke*

All helpyt nocht thocht I repentyt full sor.     *sorely repented*

Throu freyndys of the court I chapyt of that place     *escaped form*

And never sen syn couth get the kingis grace.     *afterwards could*

325   For my saik mony of my kyn gert thai de,     *kin were made to die*

And quhen I saw it mycht no better be

Bot leyff the land that me behuffyt o neid,[2]

---

1 Because of Englishmen [there] I know not what trouble there may be
2 But that it was necessary for me to leave the land

Apon a day to Burdeous I yeid.     *Bordeaux; went*
Ane Inglis schip so gat I on a nycht
330 For sey laubour that ernystfully was dycht.     *seafaring; prepared*
To me thar semblyt mysdoaris and weill mo,     *rallied wrongdoers many*
And in schort tym we multiplyit so.
Wes few that micht contrair our power     *against; force*
    gang.     *go*
In tyranry thus haiff we rongyn lang.     *ruled*
335 This sexten yer I haiff beyn on the se
And doyn gret harm, tharfor full wa is me.     *woe*
I savit nayn for gold nor gret ransoun     *saved none*
Bot slew and drownyt in to the se adoun.     *sea below*
Favour I did till folk of syndry land,     *showed to; many lands*
340 Bot Franchmen no frendschip with me fand;
Thai gat no grace als fer as I mycht ryng.     *mercy as far; prevail*
Als on the se I clypyt was a king.     *Also; was called*
Now se I weyll that my fortoun is went,     *has gone*
Vincust with ane; that gerris me sair rapent.     *Vanquished by; sore repent*
345 Quha wald haiff said this sammyn day at     *Who would have; same*
    morn
I suld with ane thus lychtly doun be born![1]
In gret hething my men it wald haiff tane.     *scorn*
My selff trowit till machit mony ane,[2]
Bot I haiff found the verray playn contrar.     *very plainly the opposite*
350 Her I gyff our roubry for evermar.     *Here I give up robbery*
In sic mysrewll I sall never armes ber,     *misrule; bear*
Bot gyff it be in honest oys to wer.     *if; practice of war*
Now haiff I told you part of my blys and     *joy and trouble*
    payn;
For Goddis saik sum kyndnes kyth agayn.     *display in return*
355 My hart will brek bot I wyt quhat thou be     *unless I know*
Thus outrageously that has rabutyt me;     *boldly; overcome*
For weill I wend that leyffand had beyn     *thought; living*
    non
Be fors of strenth mycht me as presoner     *By force*
    ton,     *take*
Except Wallace that has rademyt Scotland,     *freed*
360 The best is callit this day beltyt with brand.     *who carries a sword*
In till his were war worschip for to wak;     *war it would be an honour;*
    *labour*

1 I should by one [man] thus easily be borne down!
2 I believed myself a match for anyone

As now in warld I trow he has no mak.' — *believe; match*
Tharat he smylit and said, 'Frend, weill may be. — *smiled*
Scotland had myster of mony sic as he. — *need; many such*
365 Quhat is thi naym? Tell me, so haiff thou seill.' — *salvation*
'Forsuth,' he said, 'Thomas of Longaweill.'
'Weyll bruk thou it. All thus stentis our stryff. — *You bear it well; ends*
Schaip to pleys God in mendyng of thi lyff. — *Try*
Thi faithfull freynd my selff thinkis to be,
370 And als my nayme I sall sone tell to thee.
For chans of wer thou suld no murnyng mak; — *vagaries of war*
As werd will wyrk thi fortoun mon thou tak. — *fate; work; must*
I am that man that thou avansis so hie; — *praise; highly*
And bot schort tym sen I come to the se. — *[it is] only a short time since*
375 Of Scotland born my rycht name is Wallace.'
On kneis he fell and thankit God of grace.
'I dar avow that yoldyn is my hand — *dare; yielded*
To the best man that beltis him with brand. — *carries a sword*
Forsuth' he said, 'this blythis me mekill mor — *pleases; much more*
380 Than of floryng ye gaiff me sexty scor.' — *florins; score*
Wallace answerd, 'Sen thou art her throu chance, — *since; here*
My purpos is be this viage in France, — *by; expedition to*
And to the king sen I am boun to pas — *since; ready*
To my reward thi pees I think to as.' — *pardon; ask*
385 'Pes I wald fayn haiff of my rychtwis king — *Pardon; gladly*
And no langar in to that realm to ryng, — *realm; hold land*
Thar to tak leyff and cum of it agayn. — *leave; come away*
In thi service I think for to ramayn.' — *remain*
'Service,' he said, 'Thomas that may nocht be,
390 Bot gud frendschip as I desir of thee.'
Gart draw the wyn and ilk man mery maid. — *He caused wine to be poured; each; made merry*

Be this the schippis was in the Rochell raid;   By this time; sailed
The rede blasonys thai had born in to wer.      The red blazons
The toun was sone in till a sudane fer.         soon seized by fear
395  The Rede Reiffar thai saw was at thar       at hand
     hand,
The quhilk throu strenth mycht nayn agayn       might none stand against him
     him stand.
Sum schippis fled and sum the land has          Some fled on ships; taken
     tayn;                                          [to]
Clariounys blew and trumpattis mony ane.        many a one
Quhen Wallace saw the pepill was on ster        in turmoil
400  He gaiff commaund na schip suld ner         approach
     apper;
Bot his awn barge into the havyn gart draw.     own ship; had steered
The folk was fayn quhen thai that senye         pleased; flag [ensign]
     saw;
Rycht weyll thai knew in gold the rede
     lioun.
Leit up the port, rasavit him in the toun       Raised the gate; received
405  And sufferyt thaim for all that he had      gave assurances to them
     brocht.
The rede navyn into the havyn thai socht;       fleet; came
On land thai went quhar thai likit to pas.
Rycht few thar wyst quhat Scottis man           Very few knew
     Wallace was,
Bot weyll thai thocht he was a gudly man        fine
410  And honouryt him in all the craft thai can. in every way they knew
Bot four dayis still at Wallace ramaynyt        Only; that; remained
     thar.
Thir men he callyt quhen he was boun to         These; ready to go
     fair.
He thaim commaundyt apon that cost to           coast to stay
     bid
Quhill he thaim fred for chans at mycht         Until; released them; chance
     betid.
415  'Ber you evyn, quhat gud that ever yhe      Conduct yourselves properly
     spend.
Leiff on your awin quhill tithandis I you       Live; own; until; news
     send.
Ger sell thir schippis and mak you men of       Go sell these ships
     pes;
It war gud tym of wykkitnes to ces.             is a good time; cease
Your captane sall pas to the king with me;

420 Throu help of God I sall his warrand be.'        protection
    He gert graith him in soit with his awin        He had him dressed like;
        men.                                            own
    Was no man thar that mycht weill Thomas         recognise Thomas
        ken.
    Lykly he was, manlik of contenance,             Well-made; manly bearing
    Lyk to the Scottis be mekill governance,        Similar; leadership
425 Saiff of his tong, for Inglis had he nane.      Except for; language
    In Latyn weill he mycht suffice for ane.
    Thus past his court in all the haist thai       went; retinue
        may.
    To Paris toun thai went apon a day;
    Tythingis was brocht of Wallace to the          News
        king.
430 So gret desyr he had of na kyn thing
    As in that tym quhill he had seyn
        Wallace.[1]
    To meyt him selff he waytit apon cace           waited for the chance
    In a gardyng quhar he gert thaim be             garden; had them brought
        brocht.
    Till his presence with manly feyr thai          To; bearing
        socht.
435 Twa and fyfty at anys kneland doun              once kneeling
    And salust him as ryoll of most renoun,         greeted; majesty
    With rewllyt spech in so gudly a wys            polite; manner
    All France couth nocht mair nurtour than        more courtesy; contrive
        devys.
    The queyn had leyff and com in hyr effer,       permission; came; array
440 For mekill scho herd of Wallace deid in         much she had heard; deeds;
        wer.                                            war
    Quhat nedis mor of curtassy to tell?            needs more of courtesy
    Thai kepyt weill that to the Scottis befell.    took good care of
    Of kingis fer I dar mak no rahers;              fare; account
    My febill mynd, my trublyt spreit rewers.       troubled spirit upsets
445 Of rich service quhat nedis wordis mor?
    Mycht non be found bot it was present           except
        thor.                                           there
    Sone efter meit the king to parlour went;       dining; conversation
    With gudly lordis thar Wallace was present.
    Than commound thai of mony syndry               they conversed; many diverse
        thing;

1 He had no greater desire at that time than to see Wallace

450 To spek with him gret desyr had the king.
    At hym he speryt of wer the governance.[1]
    He answerd him with manly contenance      demeanour
    Till every poynt, als fer as he had feill,   On every point; as;
                                                  knowledge

    In Latyn tong rycht naturaly and weill.
455 The king consavit sone throu his hie        understood
      knawlage
    Quhat wermen oysyt be reyff in thar         What warriors practised by
      passage.                                    way of piracy in their
                                                  crossing

    In till his mynd the Rede Reiffar than was;  Red Pirate then came
    Mervell he had how he leit Wallace pas.      He marvelled; allowed
    Till him he said, 'Ye war sum thing to       You were a little to
      blaym.                                      blame
460 Ye mycht haiff send be our harrold fra       sent through
      haym
    Efter power to bring you throu the se.'      For a convoy; across
    'God thank you schir, tharof ynewch had      we had enough [power]
      we.
    Feill men may pas quhar thai fynd na         Many
      perell;                                    danger
    Rycht few may kep quhar nayn is to           defend; [there] is no-one
      assaill.'
465 'Wallace', he said, 'tharof mervell haiff I.
    A tyran ryngis in ire full cruelly           holds sway; fiercely
    Apon the se that gret sorow has wrocht.
    Mycht we him get it suld nocht be for
      nocht.
    Born of this land, a natyff man to me,
470 Tharfor on us the grettar harme dois he.'
    Than Thomas quok and changyt                 trembled; colour
      contenans.
    He hard the king his evill deidis avans.     heard; expose
    Wallace beheld and fenyeit in a part.        dissembled a little
    'Forsuth', he said, 'we fand nane in that    found
      art                                        direction
475 That proffryt us sic unkyndlynes.            proffered; such usage
    Bot with your leiff I spek in haymlynes,     leave; familiarly
    Trow ye be sycht ye couth that squier        Do you believe
      knaw?'

1 He asked him about the conduct of war

'To lang it war sen tym that I him saw.          It is too long since the time
Bot thir wordis of him ar bot in vayn;           these; vain
480   Or he cum her rycht gud men will be           Before; here
        slayn.'
      Than Wallace said, 'Her I haiff brocht with    Here
        me
      Of likly men that was in our countre.        promising
      Quhilk of all thir wald ye call him most     these would
        lik?'                                       like
      Amang thaim blent that ryoll roy most ryk.   looked; king; rich
485   Wesyit thaim weill, bathe statur and curage, Examined
      Maner, makdome, thar fassoun and thar        Appearance; demeanour;
        vesage.                                       faces
      Sadly he said, avysit sobyrly.               Gravely; advised
      'That largest man quhilk standis next you
        by
      Wald I call him be makdome to device.        to judge by appearance
490   Thir ar nothing bot wordis of office.'       These; empty words
      Befor the king on kneis fell gud Wallace.
      'O ryoll roy, of hie honour and grace,
      With waist wordis I will nocht you            vain; trouble
        travaill.
      Now I will spek sum thing for myn availl.    advantage
495   Our barnat land has beyn ourset with wer     stricken; overthrown; war
      With Saxonis blud that dois us mekill der.   Englishmen; great harm
      Slayn our eldris, distroyit our rychtwys     [They have] slain; forebears
        blud,
      Waistyt the realm of gold and othir gud,     Laid waste
      And ye ar her in mycht and ryolte.           are here; royalty
500   Ye suld haiff ey till our adversite,         an eye
      And us support throu kindnes of the band     allegiance
      Quhilk is conservit betwix you and           preserved
        Scotland.
      Als I am her at your charge for plesance.    command and pleasure
      My lyflat is bot honest chevysance.[1]
505   Flour of realmys forsuth is this regioun.    Flower of realms truly
      To my reward I wald haiff gret gardoun.'     For; recompense
      'Wallace', he said, 'Now ask quhat ye wald
        haiff.
      Gud, gold or land, sall nocht be lang to     Goods
        craiff.'                                   crave

      1 My livelihood is but honourable winning

Wallace answerd, 'So ye it grant to me,    *If*
510 Quhat I wald haiff it sall sone chosyn be.'    *soon*
'Quhat ever yhe ask that is in this regioun
Ye sall it haiff, except my wyff and croun.'
He thankit him of his gret kyndlynes.    *kindness*
'My reward all sall be askyng of grace,    *mercy*
515 Pees to this man I brocht with me throu    *Pardon*
    chans.    *chance*
Her I quytcleym all othir gyfftis in Frans.    *Here; relinquish; gifts*
This sammyn is he, gyff ye knaw him weill,    *same; if know*
That we of spak, Thomas of Longaweill.    *we spoke of*
Be rygour ye desyryt he suld be slayn.    *By rigour [of the law]*
520 I him restor into your grace agayn.
Rasaiff him fayr as liege man of your land.'    *Receive; loyal vassal*
The king merveld and couth in study stand,    *marvelled; in thought*
Perfytly knew that it was Longaweill.
He him forgaiff his trespas everilkdeill    *completely*
525 Bot for his saik that had him hydder    *Only; his [i.e., Wallace's*
    brocht;    *sake]; thither*
For gold or land ellis he gat it nocht.    *otherwise*
'Wallace', he said, 'I had levir of gud land    *rather*
Thre hundreth pund haiff sesyt in thi    *put in your possession*
    hand.
That I haiff said sall be grantyt in playn.    *plainly*
530 Her I restor Thomas to pes agayn,
Derer to me than ever he was befor,
All for your sak thocht it war mekill mor.
Bot I wald wyt how that mervell befell.'    *would know; marvel*
Wallace answerd, 'The trewth I sall you
    tell.'
535 Than he rahersyt quhat hapnyt on that day    *related*
As ye befor in my autour hard say.    *according to my authority*
Quhen the gud king had herd this sudan    *about this surprise*
    cas    *adventure*
Apon the se, be forsicht of Wallace,    *sea*
The king him held rycht worthi till avans.    *to praise*
540 He saw in hym manheid and governans;    *leadership*
So did the queyn and all thir lordis.    *these*
Ilk wicht of hym gret honour than recordis.    *Each person*
He purchest pes for all the power haill,    *solicited pardon; armed force*
Fyfteyn hundreth was left in the Rochaill,
545 Gert cry thaim fre, trew servandis to the    *Had them proclaimed*
    king,

And never agayn fautyt in sic thing.    *found fault with such*
Quhen Thomas was restoryt to his rycht    *rightful possession*
Of his awin hand the king has maid him    *With his own hand*
   knycht.
Efter he gaiff stayt to his nerrest ayr    *After; his estate; heir*
550 And maid him selff with Wallace for to fayr.    *go*
Thus he was brocht fra naym of reyff throu    *delivered from; piracy;*
   cace,                           *chance*
Be sudand chans of him and wicht Wallace.    *By a sudden encounter; bold*
Thus leyff I thame in worschip and    *I leave; honour*
   plesance,                          *pleasure*
At liking still with the gud king of France.    *In comfort*
555 Thai thirty dayis he lugyt in to rest;    *at rest*
So to ramayn he thocht it nocht the best.
Still in to pes he couth nocht lang endur;    *Quietly at peace*
Uncorduall it was till his natur.    *Uncordial; nature*
Rycht weyll he wyst that Inglismen    *knew*
   occupyit
560 Gyane that tym, tharfor he has aspyit    *watched out for*
Sum jeperte apon thaim for to mak.    *surprise attack*
A gudly leyff he at the kyng couth tak    *leave; took*
Of Franchmen he wald nayne with him call    *call to arms*
At that fyrst tym for aventur mycht fall,    *chance; happen*
565 Bot Schir Thomas that service couth persew.    *Except; follow*
He wyst nocht weyll gyff all the layff was    *knew; if; rest*
   trew.                           *loyal*
Of Scottis men thai semblyt hastely
Nine hunder sum of worthi chevalry,
In Gyan land full haistely couth ryd,
570 Raissyt feill fyr and waistyt wonnyngis wid.[1]
Fortras thai brak and stalwart byggyngis    *Fortresses; dismantled;*
   wan,                          *buildings conquered*
Derffly to dede brocht mony Sotheron man.    *Violently; death*
A werlik toun so fand thai in that land    *hostile town; found*
Quhilk Schenoun hecht that Inglismen had    *was called*
   in hand.                       *control*
575 Towart that steid full sadly Wallace socht    *place; resolutely*
Be ony wys assailye gyff he mocht,[2]
Bargane till haiff and he mycht get thaim    *Battle*
   out.

1 Started many fires and laid waste dwellings widely
2 If he might by any means attack

Gret strenth of wod that tym was thar          palisade; wood; there
about.

This toun als stud apon a watter sid.          also

580  In till a park that was bath lang and wyd,

Thai buschit thaim quhill past was the          lay in ambush until
nycht.

Quhen the sone rais four hundreth men he          got ready
dycht;

The laiff he gert Crawfurd in buschement          rest; caused; ambush
tak,

Geyff thai mysterit a reskew for to mak.          If; needed

585  Than Longaweill that ay was full savage.          always; eager for battle

With Wallace past as ane to that          together
scrymmage          skirmish

Thir four hundreth rycht wonder weyll          These; wonderfully well
arayit          arrayed

Befor the toun the playn baner displayit,          unfurled banner

Was nocht to thaim weill knawyn in that          known; country
contre

590  The lyoun in gold awfull for to se,          awesome

A forray kest and sessit mekill gud.          foray launched; seized

Wermen within thar playnly understud          Warriors; there

Sone uschit furth the pray for to reskew.          Soon sallied; booty

The worthy Scottis feill Inglismen thai          many
slew;

595  The laiff for dreid fled to the toun agayn.          rest; fear

The forray tuk the pray and past the          foray [party]; spoils; field
playn

Towart the park, bot power of the toun          armed men from

Uschyt agayn in awfull battaill boun,          Sallied forth; battle array

A thousand hayle wyth men of armys          in all
strang.

600  Few baid tharin that mycht to bargane          stayed; fighting
gang.          go

Than Wallace gert the forreouris leyff the          made; foragers; leave
pray,          spoil

Assemblyt sone in till a gud aray.          Assembled; order

A cruell conterans at that metyng was          fierce encounter
seyn

Of wicht wermen in to thar armour cleyn.          bold warriors; bright

605  Feyll lossyt thar lyff apon the Sotheroun          Many
sid

Bot nocht forthi rycht bauldly thai abyd.          nevertheless; withstood

Of the Scottis part worthi men thai slew.     *some*
Wylyham Crawfurd that weyll the perell
  knew
Out of the park he gert the buschement pas    *made; ambush party pass*
610 In to the feild quhar feyll men fechtand    *many; were fighting*
  was.
At thar entre thai gert full mony de.    *caused; many die*
The Inglismen was wonder laith to fle.    *very loath*
Full worthely thai wrocht in to that place,    *performed*
Baid never sa few so lang agayn Wallace,[1]
615 Wyth sic power as he that day was thar;    *such; had there*
On ather syd assailyeit ferly sayr.    *[they] attacked extremely*
                                *hard*

Into the stour so fellonly thai wrocht    *battle; terribly; fought*
Rycht worthy men derffly to dede thai
  brocht,
Wyth poyntis persyt throuch platis burnyst    *[sword] points pierced*
  brycht.                     *armour plate burnished*
620 Wallace hym selff and gud Thomas the
  knycht
Quhom that thai hyt maid never mor    *struck never fought again*
  debait.
The Sotheron part was handlyt thar full    *dealt with; fiercely*
  hayt.
In to that place thai mycht no langar byd;    *stay*
Out of the feyld with sar hartis thai ryd;    *heavy hearts*
625 On to the toun thai fled full haistely.
Wallace folowit and his gud chevalry,
Fechtand so fast in to that thykkest thrang    *press*
Quhill in the toun he enterit thaim amang.
With him Crawfurd and Longaweill of mycht
630 And Rychard als Wallace, his cusyng wicht.    *bold cousin*
Fyfteyn thai war of Scottis cumpany.
Thus hapnyt thai amang the gret party    *they chanced; throng*
A cruell portar gat apon the wall,    *bold porter*
Powit out a pyn, the portculys leit fall.    *Pulled; portcullis let*
635 Inglismen saw that entrit was na ma.    *no more entered*
Apon the Scottis full hardely thai ga,
Bot tyll a wall thai haiff thar bakkis set,    *to; they have set their backs*
Sad strakys and sayr bauldly about thaim    *Firm and heavy strokes;*
  bet.                         *boldly beat down*

1 So few never withstood so long against Wallace

Rychard Wallace the turngreys weill has seyn.    *winding stair*

640  He folowit fast apon the portar keyn,    *fierce*
Atour the wall dede in the dyk him draiff,    *Over; ditch; drove*
Tuk up the port and leit in all the layff.    *Took up; gate; rest*
Quhen Wallace men had thus the entre won    *reached*
Full gret slauchter agane thai haff begon.

645  Thai savit nayn apon the Sotheroun syd
That wapynnys bar or harnes in that tid.    *carried weapons or armour*
Wemen and barnys the gud thai tuk thaim fra,
Syn gaiff thaim leyff into the realm to ga;    *Then gave; leave*
And preystis als that war nocht in the feild,

650  Of agyt men quhilk mycht na wapynnis weild, 
Thai slew nayn sic, so Wallace chargis was,    *such; command*
Bot maid thaim fre at thar largis to pas.    *liberty*
Ryches of gold thai gat in gret plente,
Harnes and hors that mycht thaim weill supple.    *Armour; horses; assist*

655  Wyth Franch folk plenyst the toun agayn.    *filled*
On the tenth day the feyld thai tuk in playn,    *battlefield; openly*
The river doun in to the land thai socht,
On Sotheron men full mekill maistre thai wrocht.    *great deeds of arms; performed*
Quhen to the king trew men had tald this taill,    *tale*

660  Of Franchmen thai semblyt a battaill,    *assembled; battalion*
Twenty thousand of lele legis of Frans.    *loyal vassals*
Hys brothir thaim led was Duk of Orlyans.
Throu Gyan land in rayid battaill thay raid,    *battle order; rode*
To folow Wallace, and maid but litill baid,    *delay*

665  For Frans supple to help thaim in thair rycht.    *From; assistance [they sought]*
Ner Burdeous or thai our tak him mycht[1]
Gud Wallace was and chosin had a playn,
For sum men tald that Burdeous with gret mayn    *told*
   *army*
Within schort tym thocht battaill for to geyff;    *time; offer*

---

1 Near Bordeaux before they could overtake him

670 Bot fra thai wyst that Franch folk couth raleiff — *when; knew* / *relieve*
Wyth gret power for helpyng of Wallace
Uthyr purpos thai tuk into schort space. — *Another; time*
In Pykarte sone message thai couth send, — *Picardy soon; messengers*
Of Wallace com thai tald it till ane end. — *Wallace's coming*

675 Of Glosister captane of Calys was
The hardy erll and maid him for to pas
In Ingland sone, and syne to London went. — *soon; afterwards*
Of Wallace deid he tald in the parlement. — *deeds*
Sum playnly said that Wallace brak the pes. — *broke; truce*

680 Wys men said nay and prayit thaim for to ces. — *no*
Lord Bowmont said, 'He tuk bot for Scotland — *undertook*
And nocht for Frans, that sall ye undyrstand.
Gyff our endentour spekis for ony mair — *If; indenture; claims*
He has doyne wrang the suth ye may declayr.' — *done; truth* / *decide*

685 Wodstok answerd, 'Schir, ye haiff spokyn weill,
Bot contrar resone that taill is everilkdeill. — *against; in every way*
Gyff yone be he that band for him and his — *If that is; signed agreement*
May na man say bot he has wrocht amys, — *amiss*
For pryncipaly he band with us the trew — *agreed; truce*

690 And now agayn begynnys a malice new.
Schyr king,' he said, 'gyff ye think ever to mak
On Scotland wer, on hand now ye sall tak — *undertake*
Quhill he is out, or ellis it helpis nocht.' — *away; else*
As Wodstok said the haill consaill has wrocht. — *whole council; done*

695 Power thai raissyt on Scotland for to ryd — *An army; raised*
Be land and se; thai wald no langar byd. — *wait*
Thar land ost thai rayit weyll in deid. — *host; arranged*
Thar vantgard tuk the hardy erll to leid — *vanguard; lead*
Of Glosister, that of wer had gret feill. — *in war; skill*

700 Of Longcastell the duk demanyt weill — *directed*
The mydillward; on to the se thai send — *middle force*
Schyr Jhon Sewart that weyll the northland kend. — *knew*
The knycht Wallang befor the ost in raid, — *rode*

On sic a way wyth evyll Scottis men he
maid,                                                   *such; evil*

705 Mony castellis he gert sone yoldin be                 *made; surrendered*
Till Inglismen withoutyn mar melle.                     *more fighting*
Or the best wyst that it was wer in playn               *Before; knew; open war*
Entryt he was into Bothwell agane.                      *Entered*
Schyr Jhon Sewart that com in be the se

710 Sanct Jhonstoun sone gat throu a jeperte.             *surprise attack*
Dunde thai tuk and putt Scottismen to
dede.                                                   *death*
In Fyff fra thaim was nocht kepyt a stede,              *from; defended; place*
And all the south fra Chevyot to the se.                *Cheviot*
In to the west thar mycht na succour be.                *assistance*

715 The worthy lord that suld haiff governyt
this,
God had hym tayn we trow in lestand blys.               *taken into everlasting bliss*
Hys son Walter, that bot a child than was,              *youth*
Trew men him tuk and couth in Arrane                    *did; Arran*
pas.
Adam Wallace than wyst of no supple                     *knew; help*

720 Till Rawchle went, and Lindsay of Cragge.            *Rathlin*
Gud Robert Boid in But maid residens.
For haisty desait thai tuk thaim to defens.             *On account of; deceit*
Schyr Jhon the Graym in Dundaff mycht
nocht bid;                                              *stay*
Succour he socht in to the forest of Clid.              *Help*

725 The knycht Sewart a schyrreff maid in
Fyff
Schir Amer brother and gaiff for term of                *of his life*
lyff
The landis haill that Wallang aucht befor.              *possessed*
Rychard Lundy had gret dreid of thar
schoyr;                                                 *shore*
He likyt nocht for to cum to thar pes,                  *peace*

730 Forthi in Fyff thai wald nocht lat him ces.          *Therefore; stop*
To pas our Tay as than it mycht nocht be                *over the Tay river*
For Inglismen so rewllyt that cuntre.                   *ruled*
Out of the land he staw away be nycht,                  *stole; by*
Eighteen with him that worthy war and
wycht,                                                  *were*
                                                        *bold*
735 And als his sone that was of tender eild             *also; son; age*
Bot efter sone he couth weill wapynnys
weild.                                                  *wield*

At Stirlyng bryg or that the wach wes set          bridge before; guard
Thar passyt he away withoutyn let.                 opposition
In Dundaff mur Schir Jhon the Graym he
    socht;
740  A woman tald as than befor was wrocht          told; done
And till a strenth he drew him on the morn.        to a stronghold
Laynrik was tayn with young Thomas of              Lanark; taken by
    Thorn,
So Lundy thair mycht mak no langar                 remain there no longer
    remayn.
Be south Tynto lugis thai maid in playn.           By; camps openly
745  Schyr Jhon the Graym gat wit that he was       got to know
    thar:
Till him he past withoutyn wordis mar.             more
Wallang gart bryng fra Carlele cariage[1]
To stuff Bothwell with wyn and gud                 provision;
    warnage.                                       malmsey wine
Lundy and Graym gat wyt of that victaill;          wind; these food supplies
750  Rycht sudanly thai maid thaim till assaill.    attack
Fyfty thai war of nobill chevalry
Agayn four scor of Inglis cumpany.
Ane Skelton than kepyt the careage;                guarded; baggage
All Brankstewat that was his heretage.
755  Lundy and Graym met with that squier           bold squire
    wicht;
Feill Inglismen to ded derffly thai dycht.         Many; violently killed
Sexte was slayn apon the tothir sid                other side
And five of Scottis, so bauldly thai abid.         boldy; withstood
Gret gud thai wan, bath gold and other ger,
760  Victayll and hors that hapnyt in that wer.
Syn thai haiff seyn weyll lang thai mycht
    nocht lest                                     last
In-to that land tharfor thai thocht it best.
To seik sum place in strenth that thai             a stronghold
    mycht bid,                                     stay
For Sotheron men had plenyst on ilk sid.           English; settled
765  Lundeis luge thai left apon a nycht;           camp
In the Lennox the way thai passyt rycht            directly
Till Erll Malcom, that kepyt that cuntre           To; defended
Fra Inglismen with help of thar supple.            assistance
Cetoun and Lyll into the Bas thai baid,            stayed

1 Valence had baggage brought from Carlisle

770 For Sotheroun folk so gret mastrys had                domination
       maid
    That all the south was tayn into thar hand.          taken
    Gud Hew the Hay was send into Ingland
    And uther ayris to presoune at thar will.            heirs
    The northland lordis saw na help cum
       thaim till.
775 A squier Guthre amang thaim ordand thai              ordered
    To warn Wallace in all the haist he may.
    Out of Arbroth he passit to the se
    And at the Slus land takyn son had be.               soon
    In Flandrys land no residens he maid.                stop
780 In Frans he past, bot Wallace weill abaid            remained true
    On his purpos, in Gyan at the wer.                   To; war
    On Sotheroun men he had doyn mekill der.             done; harm
    Quhill gud Guthre had gottyn his presens             Until; company
    He haistyt hym sone and maid no residens.            soon; stops
785 He has him tald with Scotland how it stud.           told; stood
    Than Wallace said, 'Thai tithingis ar nocht          Those tidings are
       gud.
    I had exampill of tym that is by worn,               past
    Trewys to bynd with thaim that was                   Truce; agree
       maynsworn.                                        man-sworn
    Bot I as than couth nocht think on sic               then; such
       thing
790 Be caus that we tuk this pees witht thar             took; with
       king.
    Be thar chansler the tother pees was bun             By; chancellor; other; agreed
    And that ful sair our for-fadris has fun.            sorely; forefathers; found
    Undyr that trew eighteen scor thai gart de           truce; killed
    At noblis war, the best in our cuntre.               That nobles were
795 To the gret God my vow now her I mak,                here
    Pes with that king I think never for to tak.
    He sall repent that thai this wer began!'
    Thus mowit he with mony ryoll man                    moved
    On to the king and tauld him his entent.
800 Till lat him pas the king wald nocht consent         To let
    Quhill Wallace thar maid promys be his               by
       hand,
    Gyff ever agayn he thocht to leyff Scotland          If; leave
    To cum till him. His gret seyll he him gaiff         [Under] his great seal
    Of quhat lordschip that he likit till haiff.
805 Thus at the king ane haisty leiff tuk he.            from; leave took

Na ma with him he brocht of that cuntre — *more; from*
Bot his awn men and Schir Thomas the — *Except; own*
   knycht.
In Flaundrys land thai past with all thar
   mycht.
Guthreis barg was at the Slus left styll; — *ship*
810 To se thai went wyth ane full egyr wyll. — *eager*
Bath Forth and Tay thai left and passyt by.
On the north cost gud Guthre was thar gy. — *guide*
In Munros havyn thai brocht hym to the — *Montrose harbour*
   land.
Till trew Scottis it was a blyth tithand. — *good tidings*
815 Schyr Jhon Ramsay, that worthi was and
   wycht,
Fra Ochtyrhous the way he chesyt rycht — *From; chose immediately*
To meite Wallace with men of armes — *meet*
   strang.
Of his dwellyng thai had thocht wonder
   lang.[1]
The trew Ruwan come als withoutyn baid; — *delay*
820 In Barnan wod he had his lugyng maid. — *lodging*
Barklay, Besat to Wallace semblyt fast. — *gathered*
With thre hundreth to Ochterhous he past.

---

1 They had thought his staying away [was] very long

## BOOK TEN

The later day of August fell this cace.    *last; case*
For the reskew thus ordanyt wicht Wallace    *prepared*
Of Sanct Jhonstoun that Sothroun
   occupyit.
Fast towart Tay thai passyt and aspyit,    *were on the lookout*
5  Or it was day undyr Kynnowll thaim laid.    *Before; Kinnoull Hill*
Out of the toun as Scottis men till hym    *to*
   said,
That servandys oysyt with cartis hay to    *servants were accustomed*
   feid,
So was it suth and hapnyt in to deid.    *true; indeed*
Saxsum thar com and brocht bot cartis thre,    *Six in all*
10  Quhen thai of hay was ladand most bysse,    *were loading most busily*
Guthre with ten in handys has thaim tayn,    *seized*
Put thaim to dede, of thaim he savyt nayn.    *death; spared none*
Wallace gert tak in haist thar humest weid[1]
And sic lik men thai vaillyt weill gud
   speid.    *by such means; picked*
15  Four was rycht rud; Wallace hym selff tuk    *rough*
   ane,
A russet clok, and with him gud Ruwane,
Guthre, Besat, and als gud yemen twa,    *also; yeomen*
In that ilk soit thai graithit thaim to ga.    *same garb; readied*
Full sutelly thai coveryt thaim with hay,    *cunningly; covered*
20  Syne to the toun thai went the gaynest way.    *Then; nearest*
Fifteen thai tuk of men in armes wicht,    *strong*
In ilk cart five thai ordanyt out of sycht.    *each; ordered*
Thir cartaris, had schort swerdis of gud    *These carters*
   steill
Undyr thar weidis, callyt furth the cartis    *clothes, summoned*
   weill.
25  Schyr Jhon Ramsay baid with a    *waited; an*
   buschement still    *ambush*
Quhen myster war to help thaim with gud    *there was need*
   will.
Thir trew cartaris past withowtyn let    *These loyal; opposition*
Atour the bryg and entryt throu the yet;    *Over; gate*
Quhen thai war in thar clokis kest thaim    *cloaks*
   fra.

---

1 Wallace ordered them to take their uppermost clothing quickly

30  Gud Wallace than the mayster portar can ta  *struck*
      Upon the hed, quhill dede he has him left,  *until*
      Syn other twa the lyff fra thaim has reft.  *Then; taken by force*
      Guthre, Besat did rycht weyll in the toun
      And Ruwan als dang of thar famen doun.  *struck; foes*
35  The armyt men, was in the cartis brocht,
      Rais up and weill thar dawern has wrocht.  *have made their attempt*
      Apon the gait thai gert feill Sothroun de.  *street; made*
      The Ramsais spy, has seyn thaim get entre,
      The buschement brak, bathe bryg and port  *ambush broke; bridge; gate*
          has won;
40  Into the toun gret stryff thar was begon.  *fighting*
      Thai twenty men or Ramsay come in playn  *before; the field*
      Within the toun had saxte Sotheroun slayn.  *sixty*
      The Inglismen on till aray was gayn;  *battle order; gone*
      The Scottis as than layser leit thaim get  *allowed them no leisure*
          nayn.
45  Fra gud Ramsay with his men entryt in  *From when*
      Thai savyt nayn was born of Inglis kyn.  *spared*
      Als Longaweill, the wicht knycht Schir
          Thomas,
      Prevyt weill than and in mony othir place;  *Proved himself; then*
      Agayn his dynt few Inglismen mycht  *stroke*
          stand.
50  Wallace with him gret faith and kyndnes
          fand.  *found*
      The Sotheroun part saw weill the toun was
          tynt,  *lost*
      Freschly thai ferd as fyr dois out of flynt.  *Vigorously; acted*
      Sum fled, sum fell into draw dykis deip,  *deep ditches*
      Sum to the kyrk thar lyvys gyff thai mycht  *lives; if*
          keip;  *preserve*
55  Sum fled to Tay and in small veschell yeid,  *vessels went*
      Sum derffly deit and drownyt in that steid.  *died violently; place*
      Schir Jhon Sewart at the west port out  *gate; went out*
          past;
      Till Meffen wod he sped him wondyr fast.
      A hundreth men the kyrk tuk for succour,  *gave refuge*
60  Bot Wallace wald no grace grant in that  *mercy*
          hour.
      He bad slay all of cruell Sotheroun keyn,  *ordered the slaying of all*
      And said thai had to Sanct Jhonstoun
          enemys beyn.

Four hundreth men in to the toun war ded.

Sevyn scor with lyff chapyt out of that sted.          escaped

65 Wyffis and barnys thai maid thaim fre to
    ga;

With Wallace will he wald sla nayn of tha.          In accordance with; those

Riches thai fand that Inglismen had brocht          recently
    new,

Syn plenyst the toun with worthi Scottis          Then stocked
    trew.

Schyr Jhon Sewart left Meffen forest
    strang,

70 Went to the Gask with feyll Sotheroun          many
    amang

And syn in Fyff quhar Wallang schirreff
    was;

Send currowris sone out throu the land to          Sent couriers soon
    pas

And gaderyt men a stalwart cumpany.

Till Ardargan he drew him prevaly,          secretly

75 Ordand thaim in bargan reddy boun.          for battle get ready

Agayn he thocht to sailye Sanct Jhonstoun          attack

Quhar Wallace lay and wald no langar rest,

Rewllyt the toun as that him likyt best.          Ruled

Schyr Jhon Ramsay gret captane ordand he,

80 Ruwan schirreff at ane accord for to be.          one

This charge he gaif, gyff men thaim          command; if
    warnyng maid

To cum till him withoutyn mor abaid,          delay

And so thai did quhen tithingis was thaim
    brocht.

With a hundreth Wallace furth fra thaim
    socht.

85 To Fyfe he past to wesy that cuntre,          reconnoitre; region

Bot wrangwarnyt of Inglismen was he.          misinformed about

Schyr Jhon Sewart quhen thai war passyt          these were
    by,

Fra the Ochell he sped him haistely,

Upon Wallace folowit in all his mycht,

90 In Abyrnethy tuk lugyng that fyrst nycht.          lodging

Apon the morn with fifteen hundreth men

Till Blak Irnsyde his gydys couth thaim ken.          To; guides directed them

Thar Wallace was and mycht no message
    send

Till Sanct Jhonstoun to mak this jornay          military action
kend,                                            known
95  For Inglismen that full sutell has beyn      cunning
    Gart wachis walk that nayn mycht pas         Made sentries watch; no-one
    betweyn.
    Than Wallace said, 'This mater payis nocht   pleases not
    me.'
    He cald till him the squier gud Guthre,
    And Besat als, that knew full weyll the
    land,
100 And ast at thaim quhat deid was best on      asked; action
    hand,
    'Message to mak our power for to get;        Messengers; bring forces
    'With Sotheroun sone we sall be underset;    the English soon; beset
    And wykked Scottis that knawis this forest   i.e., collaborators
    best,
    Thai ar the caus that we may haiff no rest.
105 I dreid fer mar Wallang that is thar gyd      fear far more; guide
    Than all the layff that cummys on that       others; come
    syd.'
    Than Guthre said, 'Mycht we get ane or       one or two
    tway
    To Saynct Jhonstoun, it war the gaynest      shortest
    way
    And warn Ramsay, we wald get succour         inform; help soon
    sone.
110 Our suth it is it can nocht now be don.       Too true; done
    Rycht weyll I wait veschell is levyt nayn     know no boats are left
    Fra the Wood havyn to the ferry cald
    Aran.'
    Than Wallace said, 'The water cald it is.     cold
    My selff can swym, I trow, and fall na       suffer no
    mys,                                          harm
115 Bot currours oys that gaynis nocht for me;[1]
    And leyff you her yet had I lever de.[2]
    Throu Goddis grace we sall better eschew;     achieve better [than that]
    The strenth is stark, als we haiff men inew.  stronghold; stalwart; enough
    In Elchoch park bot fourty thar war we        only
120 For sevyn hundreth and gert feill Sothron      caused many English
    de,                                           to die

1 'But I am not cut out to be a courier'
2 'And I would rather die than leave you here'

And chapyt weill in mony unlikly place;     *escaped*
So sall we her throu help of Goddis grace.     *here*
Quhill men may fast thir woddis we may     *As long as; these*
    hauld still;     *keep*
Forthi ilk man be of trew hardy will,
125 And at we do so nobill in to deid
Of us be found no lak efter to reid.[1]
The rycht is ouris, we suld mor ardent be.
I think to freith this land or ellis de.'     *liberate*
His vaillyt spech, with wit and hardyment     *well-chosen words*
130 Maid all the layff so cruell of entent     *rest; fierce; purpose*
Sum bad tak feyld and gyff battaill in     *advocated taking the*
    playn.     *battlefield; open battle*
Wallace said, 'Nay, thai wordys ar in vayn.     *vain*
We will nocht leyff that may be our     *leave; advantage*
    vantage.
The wod till us is worth a yeris wage.'     *wood; payment*
135 Of hevyn temer in haist he gert thaim tak,     *hewn timber*
Syllys of ayk and a stark barres mak     *Beams; oak; strong barrier*
At a foyr frount, fast in the forest syd,     *forward position; close to*
A full gret strenth quhar thai purpost to     *place of defence*
    bid;
Stellyt thaim fast till treis that growand was     *Fixed; to trees*
140 That thai mycht weyll in fra the barres pas,     *barrier*
And so weill graithit on ather sid about     *arranged; either*
Syn com agayn quhen thai saw thaim in     *Then*
    dout.     *danger*
Be that the strenth arayit was at rycht,     *By the time; all ready*
The Inglis ost approchyt to thair sycht.
145 Than Sewart com that way for till haiff
    wend     *gone*
As thai war wount, so his gydis thaim kend.     *accustomed; knew*
At that entre thai thocht till haiff passage,     *entrance*
Bot sone thai fand that maid thaim gret     *soon; found*
    stoppage.
A thousand he led of men in armes strang;
150 With five hundreth he gert Jhon Wallang     *ordered*
    gang     *go*
Without the wod that nayn suld pas thaim     *Outside*
    fra.     *from*

1 Therefore each man be of steadfast, hardy will, / And if we do so noble a
deed, / of us hereafter there will be no failing for anyone to read about

Wallace with him had fourty archarys thra;          bold
The layff was speris, full nobill in a neid.          others; spear-carriers
On thar enemys thai bykkyr with gud          attack quickly
     speid.
155  A cruell cuntyr was at the barres seyn.          fierce encounter; barrier
The Scottis defens so sykkyr was and keyn          sure; bold
Sotheroun stud aw to enter thaim amang.          stood in awe
Feill to the ground thai ourthrew in that          Many
     thrang.          press
A rowm was left quhar part in frount          clearing
     mycht fayr;          go
160  Quha entrit in agayn yeid nevermar.          never left again
Fourty thai slew that formast wald haiff
     past.
All dysarayit the ost was and agast,          disarrayed; afraid
And part of hors throu schot to dede was          some horses; shot; death
     brocht,
Brak to a playn, the Sotheroun fra thaim
     socht.[1]
165  The Sewart said, 'Allace, how may this be
And do no harm? Our gret rabut haiff
     we.'[2]
He cald Wallang and askyt his consaill.
'Schyrreff thou art. Quhat may be our
     availl?          advantage
Bot few thai ar that makis this gret debait.'          Only a few; resistance
170  Jhon Wallang said, 'This is the best I          know
     wait:
To ces her of and remayn her besyd,          cease hereof; here
For thai may nocht lang in this forest byd;
For fawt of fud thai mon in the cuntre.          lack; must go into
Than war mar tym to mak on thaim melle.          do battle
175  Or thai be won befors in to this stryff          Before; conquered by force
Feyll at ye leid sall erar los the lyff.'          Many that you lead; sooner
Than Sewart said, 'This reid I will nocht          counsel
     tak;
And Scottis be warnyt reskew sone will thai          If; informed; soon
     mak.
Of this dispyt amendys I think to haiff,          defiance
180  Or de tharfor in nowmer with the laiff.          die; company; rest

1 Fled to a plain, the English sought to escape from them
2 And [yet] we do not injure them? We have too great a repulse

In till a rang myselff on fut will fayr.'            *column foot; go*
Eight hundreth he tuk of liklyest that was
    thair,
Syn bad the layff bid at the barres still           *Then ordered; remain*
With Jhon Wallang to revyll thaim at his            *rule*
    will.
185   'Wallang,' he said, 'be forthwart in this     *active*
    cace.
In sic a swar we couth nocht get Wallace.           *such; snare*
Tak hym or sla, I promes thee be my lyff            *Take him alive or dead*
That King Edwart sall mak thee Erll of
    Fyff.
At yon est part we think to enter in.               *that eastern part*
190   I bid no mar. Mycht ye this barres wyn,        *I stay no longer; capture*
Fra thai be closyt graithly amang us sa,            *quickly*
Bot mervell be, thai sall na ferrer ga.             *Saving a miracle; further go*
Assailye sayr quhen ye wit we cum ner;              *Attack forcefully; know*
On athir sid we sall hald thaim on ster.'           *either; astir*
195   Thus semlyt thai apon ane awfull wys          *assembled; formidable way*
Wallace has seyn quhat was thair haill             *entire plan*
    devys.
'Gud men,' he said, 'understud ye this
    deid?                                            *action*
Forsuth thai ar rycht mekill for to dreid.          *many to fear*
Yon Sewart is a nobill, worthy knycht,              *That*
200   Forthwart in wer, rycht worthy, wys and        *Active; war*
    wicht.
His assailye he ordannys wonder sayr                *attack; marvellously*
Us for to harm, no mannys wyt can do
    mar.                                             *more*
Plesand it is to se a chyftane ga
So chyftanlyk; it suld recomfort ma
205   Till his awn men, and thai of worschip
    be,
Than for to se ten thousand cowartis fle.[1]
Sen we ar stud with enemys on ilk sid               *are placed; each side*
And her on fors mon in this forest bid,             *here of necessity must*
Than fray the fyrst for Goddis saik                 *scare the first [of them]*
    cruellye,
210   That all the layff of us abayssyt be.'         *[So] that; are terrified of us*

---

1  It should encourage / his followers more, if they are honourable, / than to
see ten thousand cowards flee

Crawfurd he left and Longaweill the
   knycht,
Fourty with thaim to kepe the barres wicht.   defend; boldly
With him saxte of worthy men in weid   sixty; armour
To meit Sewart with hardy will thai yeid.   went
215  A maner dyk in to that wod wes maid   A kind of ditch
Of thwortour rys, quhar bauldly thai abaid.   brushwood placed crosswise
A doun with vaill the Sothroun to thaim   downward; advantage
   had.
Son semblyt thai with strakis sar and sad.   Soon they gathered; blows
Scharp sperys fast duschand on ather sid   striking; either
220  Throu byrnys brycht maid woundis deip   corslets
   and wid.
This vantage was, the Scottis thaim dantyt   daunted
   swa,   so
Nayn Inglisman durst fra his feris ga   No; dared; companions
To brek aray or formast enter in.
Of Crystin blud to se it was gret syn
225  For wrangwis caus, and has beyn mony   wrongful
   day.
Feyll Inglismen in the dyk deid thai lay.   Many; ditch dead
Speris full sone all in to splendrys sprang;   splinters broke
With scharp swerdys thai hew on in that   swords; hacked; press of
   thrang.   battle
Blud byrstyt out throu fyn harnes of maill.
230  Jhon Wallang als full scharply can assaill
Apon Crawfurd and the knycht Longaweill,
At thar power kepyt the barres weill,   That; defended
Maid gud defens be wyt, manheid and   manliness
   mycht,
At the entre feyll men to dede thai dycht.   many; killed
235  Thus all at anys assailyeit in that place,   once assailed
Nayn that was thar durst turn fra the   None; dared
   barrace   barrier
To help Wallace, nor none of his durst   dared
   pas
To reskew thaim, so feyll the fechtyng was.   terrible; fighting
At athir ward thai handelyt thaim full   In either group; hotly
   hayt;
240  Bot do or de na succour ellis thai wayt.[1]
Wallace wes stad in to that stalwart stour,   beset; battle

1 But do or die, they sought no other help

Guthre, Besat with men of gret valour,
Rychard Wallace that worthi was of hand.
Sewart merveillyt that contrar thaim mycht stand,    *marvelled*

245 That ever so few mycht byd in battaill place    *withstand*
Agaynys thaim metyng face for face.    *face to face*
He thocht hym selff to end that mater weill,
Fast pressyt in with a gud swerd of steill;    *sword; steel*
In to the dyk a Scottis man gert he de.    *ditch; made; die*

250 Wallace tharof in hart had gret pyte;
Amendis till haiff he folowit on him fast,
Bot Inglismen so thik betwex thaim past
That apon him a strak get mycht he nocht;    *blow*
Wthyr worthy derffly to dede he brocht.    *Other; violently*

255 Sloppys thai maid throu all that chevalry,    *Breaches*
The worthy Scottis thai wrocht so worthely.
Than Sothron saw of thar gud men so drest,    *roughly handled*
Langer to bid thai thocht it nocht the best.
Four scor was slayn or thai wald leyff that steid    *before; leave / place*

260 And fyfty als was at the barrace deid.    *barrier died*
A trumpet blew and fra the wod thai draw;    *from the wood; withdrew*
Wallang left off, that sycht fra that he saw,
To sailye mar thaim thocht it was no speid.    *attack; no use*
Wythout the wod to consaill son thai yeid.    *Outside; soon; went*

265 The worthy Scottis to rest thaim was full fayn;    *content*
Feyll hurtis had bot few of thaim was slayn.    *Many injuries*
Wallace thaim bad of all gud comfort be:    *told to be of good heart*
'Thankit be God, the fayrer part haiff we.
Yon knycht Sewart has at gret jornay beyn;    *exerted himself today*

270 So sair assay I haiff bot seildyn seyn.    *Severe attack; seldom*
I had lever of Wallang wrokyn be    *rather; revenged*
Than ony man that is of yon menyhe.'    *company*
The Scottis all on to the barres yeid,    *barrier went*
Stanchit woundis that couth full braithly bleid.    *Staunched; profusely bled*

275 Part Scottis men had bled full mekill blud.    *Some; a great deal of blood*

For faut of drynk and als wantyng of fud — want; also
Sum feblyt fast that had feill hurtis thar. — weakened; great
Wallace tharfor sichit with hart full sar. — sighed; very heavy heart
A hat he hynt, to get water is gayn; — helmet; seized
280 Other refut as than he wyst of nayn.[1] —
A litill strand he fand that ran hym by; — stream; found
Of cler watter he brocht haboundandly, — plentifully
And drank him selff, syn said with sobyr mud, — then; seriously
'The wyn of Frans me thocht nocht halff so gud.'
285 Than of the day thre quartaris was went.
Schir Jhon Sewart has castyn in his entent: — considered in his mind
To sailye mar as than he couth nocht preiff, — attack again; try
Quhill on the morn that mar men couth raleiff — Until; more relieve
And kep thaim in, quhill thai for hungyr sor — until; acute hunger
290 Cum in his will or ellis de tharfor. — die
'Wallange,' he said, 'I charge thee for to bid — stay
And kep thaim in. I will to Couper rid.
Thou sall remayn with five hundreth at thi will — command
And I the morn sall cum with power thee till.'[2]
295 Jhon Wallange said, 'This charg her I forsaik. — commission here; refuse
Eftir this day all nycht I may nocht waik, — watch
For trastis weill, thai will ische to the playn — sally forth
Thocht ye bid als, or ellis de in the payn.' — Although; wait also; attempt
Sewart bad him byd undyr the blaym: — charged him to stay; reproach
300 'I thee commaund on gud King Edwardis naym, — name
Or thar to God a vow I mak beforn,
And thai brek out, to hyng thee heych tomorn!' — If; escape; hang thee high
Of that commaund Jhon Wallang had gret dreid. — dread

1 He knew of no other [way to] help
2 And in the morning I shall come to you with reinforcements

Sewart went fra thaim with nine scor into
   deid

305 Next hand the wod and his gud men of    *Nearby*
   Fyff,

That with him baid in all term of thar lyff.    *remained for the entire term*

Wallace drew ner, his tym quhen that he
   saw,

To the wod syd and couth on Wallang caw:    *call*

'Yon knycht to morn has hecht to hyng    *promised; hang*
   thee hie.

310 Cum in till us. I sall thi warrand be    *protection*

In contrar him and all King Edwardis
   mycht.

Tak we hym quyk I sall him hyng on    *alive*
   hycht,    *high*

And gud lordschip I sall gyff thee hereft    *hereafter*

In this ilk land, that thi brothir has left.'    *same*

315 Wallange was wys, full sone couth
   understand

Be lyklynes Wallace suld wyn the land,    *likelihood*

And better him war in to the rycht to bid

Than be in wer apon the Sotheroun sid.

Wytht schort wysment to Wallace in thai    *consideration*
   socht.

320 Than Sewart criyt and said, 'That beis for
   nocht,

And fals of kynd thou art in heretage.    *nature*

Edward on thee has waryt evill gret wage.    *wasted his expense*

Her I sall bid my purpos to fullfill,    *Here; stay*

Other to de or haiff thee at my will.'

325 For all his spech to pas he wald nocht spar;    *refrain*

Wyth full glaid hart Wallace resavyt thaim    *received*
   thar.

Be that Ruwan and Ramsay of renown,    *By then*

Be a trew Scot that past to Sanct    *By*
   Jhonstoun,

Thaim warnyng maid that Sewart folowit
   fast

330 Apon Wallace, than war thai sayr agast.    *greatly aghast*

Out of the toun thai uschit with all thar
   mycht,

With thre hundreth that worthi war and
   wicht,

Till Blak Irnsid assemblyt in that place
As Wallang was gayn in to gud Wallace.
335 The knycht Sewart has weill thar cummyng
seyn;
A fayr playn feild he chesyt thaim betweyn.
Eleven hundreth and four scor than had he.
The Scottis men war five hundreth and
saxte;
Thai war bot few a playn feild for to tak.        open battle to undertake
340 Out of the wod gud Wallace can him mak.        went
He wyst nothing of thaim that cummyn
was;
Mar hardement was fra the strenth to pas.[1]
Bot quhen thai hard Ruwan and Ramsay
cry,                                              call [utter war cry]
Of Ouchterhous, blyth was that chevalry.
345 Mycht thai of gold haiff brocht a kingis
rent,                                             ransom
To gud Wallace mycht nocht so weyll
content.                                          please
Than till aray thai yeid on athir sid            order; went; either
In cruell ire in battaill boun to byd.           fierce; ready; withstand
Worthiar men than Sewart semblyt thar           gathered there
350 In all his tym Edward had nevermar.
Bot Sewart saw his nowmer was fer ma;           more
Hys power sone he gart devyd in twa.            army; caused to be divided
To fecht at anys rycht knychtlik he thaim       at once
kend,                                            instructed
In that jornay othir to wyn or end.             combat
355 The worthi Scottis ruschyt on thaim in gret
ire;
The cruell strakis that flawmyt fers as          savage strokes; flamed fierce
fyr.
Wallace and his, als Sotheroun that was
thar,
Few speris had for feyll fechtyng and sar        grievous fighting; fierce
Into the wod at sailye all the day,              [had been] attacking
360 Bot new cummyn men weill vaillyt speris         newly arrived; well-chosen
had thai.
Into the stour thai gart feill Sotheroun de.     In the battle; caused many
Thar cruell deid gret merveill was to se:        fierce action

[1] More courage was [required] from the stonghold to pass

Thai worthi Scottis that fyrst amang thaim
    baid                                    *stood*
Full gret slauchter on Inglismen thai maid;
365  Into the wod befor had prevyt weill,       *proved themselves*
Than on the playn thai sonyeit nocht adeill,   *hesitated not at all*
In curage grew as thai war new begon.     *as [if] they had only begun*
Schort rest thai had fra ryssyng of the son.   *rising; sun*
Be that Ramsay and with him gud Ruwan     *By then*
370  Throu out the thykkest of the pres is gan.    *went*
Sloppis thai maid throu out the Inglismen,    *Breaches*
Deseveryt thaim be twenty and be ten;      *Separated*
Quhen sperys war gang with swerdys of    *had gone; swords*
    metal cler,                           *bright*
Till Inglismen thar cummyng was sauld
    full[1] der.
375  Wallace and his be worthines of hand     *worthy deeds*
Feyll Sotheroun blud gart upon the land.    *Spilled the blood of many*
The twa feildys togidder relyt than.       *armies; rallied*
Schyr Jhon Sewart with mony nobill man
To help thair lord with thre hundreth in
    place
380  About hym stud and did thair besinas,     *utmost*
Defendand him with mony awfull dynt,     *Defending; blows*
Quhill all the outwart of the feild was tynt.   *van; lost*
Of comouns part in to the forest fled     *the common people some*
Succour to sek thar men had thaim so led.
385  The Scottis has seyn so mony in a rout    *[who] have seen; company*
With Sewart stand, na warrand thaim    *protection around them*
    about,
Apon all syd assailyeit wondyr sayr,     *attacked very vigorously*
Throu polyt platis with poyntis persyt    *polished plate armour*
    thair.
The Sotheroun maid defens full cruelly;    *fiercely*
390  All occupyit was this gud chevalry.      *busy*
Schyr Jhon Ramsay wald thai had yoldyn   *had surrendered*
    beyn.
Wallace said, 'Nay, it is all wrang ye meyn.   *intend*
Ranson to mak we can nocht now begyn.
On sic a wys this land we may nocht wyn.   *In such a way*
395  Yon knycht of lang our auld enemy has beyn.  *a long time*
So fell till us of thaim I haiff nocht seyn.    *fierce*

1 The English paid dearly for their invasion

Now he sall de with help of Goddis grace:  
He com to pay his ranson in this place.'    ransom [i.e., his life]  
The Sotheroun wyst all playnly for to de;  
400  Reskew was nayn suppos at thai wald fle.  
Freschlye thai faucht as thai entryt new;    Vigorously; as [if]  
Apon our sid part worthy men thai slew.    some  
Than Sewart said, 'Allace, throu wrangwis    wrongful  
    thing  
Our lyvys we los throu desyr of our king.'    lose  
405  The felloun knycht doutyt his dede rycht    fierce; did not fear death  
    nocht;  
Amang the Scottis full manfully he wrocht.  
Besat he straik to dede withoutyn mar.    Bisset; struck dead; delay  
Wallace prest in with his swerd burnyst bar,  
At Sewart hals he etlyt in gret ire.    Sewart's neck; aimed  
410  Throu pissanis stuff in sonder strak the    gorget metal  
    swyr;    neck  
Dede to the ground he duschit for all his    fell  
    mycht.  
Of Wallace hand thus endyt this gud  
    knycht.  
The ramaynand without mercy thai sla.    Remainder; slew  
For gud Besat the Scottis was wonder wa.    extremely sad  
415  In handis sum thai straik without remed;    fatally  
Na Sotheroun past with lyff out of that    passed alive; place  
    sted.  
Than to the wod, for thaim that left the    Then  
    feild,  
A rang thai set, thus thai may get na beild.    line of men; shelter  
Yeid nayn away was contrar our punyoun.    None escaped; cause  
420  Gud Ruwan past agayn to Sanct  
    Jhonstoun.  
Schyr Jhon Ramsay to Couper castell raid;    rode  
That hous he tuk for defens nayn was    castle; no defence  
    maid.    offered  
Wallace, Crawfurd and with thaim gud  
    Guthre,  
Rychard Wallace had lang beyn in melle,    the fighting  
425  And Longaweill in to Lundoris baid still,    Lindores; remained  
Fastyt thai had to lang agayn thar will.    too long against  
Wallange thai maid thar stwart for to be;    steward  
Of meit and drynk thai fand aboundandle.  
The priour fled and durst na reknyng bid;    dared not await payment

430    He was befor apon the tother syd.       *formerly*

Apon the morn to Sanct Androwis thai
     past,

Out of the toun that byschop turnyt fast.      *evicted*

The kyng of Ingland had him hydder send;      *hither sent*

The rent at will he gaiff hym in commend.      *property; as a charge*

435    His kingis charge as than he durst nocht      *dared not*
     hald.

A wrangwys pape that tyrand mycht be      *false pope*
     cald.

Few fled with  him and gat away be see.      *sea*

For all Scotland he wald nocht Wallace se.

As than of him he maid bot lycht record,      *scornful reference*

440    Gert restor him that thar was rychtwys      *Restored*
     lord.

The worthy knycht that in to Couper lay

Gart spulye it apon the secund day,      *Plundered*

Syn ordand men at the commaund of      *Then*
     Wallace

But mar proces for to cast doun that place.      *Without more ado*

445    Mynouris sone thai gert pers throu the      *Miners; got to bore*
     wall,

Syn pounciouns fyryt and to the ground
     kest all.[1]

Schyr Jhon Ramsay syne to the kyrk can
     fayr.      *went*

Sotheroun was fled and left bot wallis bayr;      *only bare walls*

Eftr Sewart thai durst nocht tary lang.      *tarry long*

450    The Scottis at large throu all Fyff thai rang,      *held sway*

Of Inglismen nayn left in that cuntre;

Bot in Lochlevyn thair lay a cumpane,

Apon that inch in a small hous thai dycht,      *island; mustered*

Castell was nayn, bot wallyt with water      *surrounded*
     wicht.

455    Besyd Carraill thai semblyt Wallace beforn;      *Crail; gathered*

His purpos was for till assay Kyngorn.      *attempt*

A knycht hecht Gray than captane in it      *called*
     was,

Be schort avys purpos he tuk to pas.      *consideration*

Erar he wald bid chalans of his king      *He would rather; have to account to*

---

1 Then set fire to the wooden supports and cast all of them to the ground

460 Than with Wallace to rakyn for sic a thing. — settle the account
That hous thai tuk and litill tary maid. — castle
Apon the morn withoutyn mar abaid — more delay
Atour the mur quhar thai a tryst had set, — Across; meeting
Ner Scotlandis Well thair lugyng tuk but let. — without / hindrance
465 Efter souper Wallace bad thaim ga rest. — After supper
'My selff will walk. Me think it may be best.' — keep watch
As he commaundyt but gruching thai haiff don. — without complaint / done
Into thar slep Wallace him graithit son, — While they slept; got ready
Past to Lochlevyn as it was ner mydnycht,
470 Eighteen with him at he had warnyt rycht. — forewarned
Thir men wend weill he come to wesy it. — These; knew; inspect
'Falows,' he said, 'I do you weill to wyt;
Considyr weill this place and understand — Take good heed of
That it may do full gret scaith to Scotland. — harm
475 Out of the south and power cum thaim till — if an army comes
Thai may tak in and kepyt at thair awn will. — occupy it; defend it
Apon yon inche rycht mony men may be — that island
And syn usche out thar tym quhen at thai se. — then issue; that
To bid lang her we may nocht upon chans. — To wait here for long
480 Yon folk has fud, trast weill, at sufficians. — in plenty
Watter fra thaim forsuth can nocht be set.[1]
Sum uthyr wyill us worthis for to get. — device we need; find
Yhe sall remayn her at this port all still — gate
And I my selff the boit sall bryng you till.' — boat
485 Thairwith in haist his weid of castis he. — Thereupon; off clothes
'Apon yon sid na wachman can I se.' — yonder side
Held on his sark and tuk his swerd so gud, — Kept on; shirt; sword
Band on his nek and syn lap in the flud, — Attached around; leapt; river
And our he swam for lattyng fand he nocht. — obstacle found
490 The boit he tuk and till his men it brocht, — boat
Arayit him weill and wald no langar bid, — Dressed himself quickly; wait
Bot passyt in, rowit to the tothir sid. — rowed
The inch thai tuk with swerdis drawyn in hand — island; captured

1 They cannot be deprived of water

And sparyt nayn that thar befor thaim fand,

495  Strak duris up, stekyt men quhar thai lay.          Broke doors down, stabbed
     Apon the Sothroun thus sadly semblyt thai.          grimly they descended
     Thirty thai slew that was in that samyn             same
       place:
     To mak defens the Inglismen had no space.           opportunity
     Thar women five Wallace send of that                [out] of that place
       sted;

500  Woman nor barn he gart never put to dede.           never had put to death
     The gud thai tuk as it had beyn thar awyn.          goods; own
     Than Wallace said, 'Falowis, I mak you              make known to you
       knawin,
     The purvyance that is within thir wanys.            supplies; these dwellings
     We will nocht tyne. Ger sembyll all at              lose; Have everyone gather
       anys.

505  Gar warn Ramsay and our gud men ilkan.              Alert; every one
     I will remayn quhill this warnstor be gan.'         store of supplies has gone
     Send furth a man, thar hors put to kep,[1]
     Drew up the boit, syne beddys tuk to sleip.
     Wallace power, quhilk Scotland Well ner lay,        Wallace's army

510  Befor the son thai myssyt him away.                 Before sunrise
     Sum menyng maid and merveillyt of that              lamentation; marvelled at
       cace.
     Ramsay bad ces and murn nocht for                   ordered [them to] cease;
       Wallace.                                            mourn
     'It is for gud at he is fra us went.                gone
     It sall ye se, trast weill in verrament,            truly

515  My hed to wed Lochlevyn he past to se.              I pledge my head; see
     Bot that is thar no Inglisman knaw we               there
     In all this land betwix thir watteris left.         These waters
     Tithandis of hym ye sall se son hereft.'            News; see soon hereafter
     As thai about war talkand on this wys               talking

520  A message com and chargyt thaim to rys.            messenger
     'My lord,' he said, 'to dyner has you cald          summoned
     In till Lochlevyn, quhilk is a ryoll hald.          abode
     Ye sall fair weyll tharfor put off all sorow.'      fare well; stop
     Thai graithit thaim rycht ayrly on the             got ready; early
       morow

525  And thidder past of Wallace will to wytt.           of; learn
     Thus semblyt thai in a full blyth                   gathered
       falowschip.

_____

1 A man was sent forth, their horses tethered

Thai lugyt thar till eight dayis was at end,          until eight days had passed
Of meit and drynk thai had inewch to          enough
    spend.          enjoy
Turssyt furth ger that Sothroun had brocht          [They] packed up; gear
    thar,
530    Gert byrn the boit, till Sanct Jhonstoun          Burned
    thai fair.          went
Byschop Synclar, that worthy was and wys,
Till Wallace com and tald him his avys.          told; advice
Thus he desyryt Wallace suld with him ryd
And in Dunkell sojorn that wynter tyd.          Dunkeld; time
535    Bot he said, 'Nay, that hald I nocht the
    best,
And Scotland thus in pes we can nocht          With Scotland
    rest.'
The byschop said, 'Playnly ye may nocht          Openly
    wend.          go
Into the north for men I rede you send.'          advise
'I grant,' quod he, and cheissit a          chose
    messynger;
540    The worthi Jop, was with the byschop ther;
And Maister Blair to Wallace com but baid          came immediately
With that gud lord, that nobill cher thaim          welcome
    maid.
Wallace send Blayr in his preistis weid          priest's habit
To warn the west, quhar freyndys had gret          summon [men from]
    dreid          doubt
545    How thai suld pas or to gud Wallace wyn,          reach
For Inglismen thai held thaim lang in twyn.          kept them long apart
Adam Wallace and Lyndsay that was
    wycht,
Rawchle thai left and went away be nycht;          Rathlin
Throu out the land to the Lennox thai cair          went
550    Till Erll Malcom that welcummyt thaim
    full fair.          warmly
Maister Jhon Blair was blith of that semble.          assembly
Gud Graym was thair and Richard of
    Lunde,
Als Robert Boid that out of But thaim          Bute
    socht.
Had thai Wallace, of nothing ellis thai          [If] they had, they cared
    roucht,          about nothing else
555    Bot Inglismen betwix thaim was so strang          [stationed] between

That thai in playn mycht nocht weyll to    *openly*
  him gang.    *go*
Jop past north, for leiching wald nocht let;    *would stop for nothing*
Gret power thar as than he couth nocht get.    *A large army at that time*
The Lord Cumyn, that Erll of Bouchane
  was,
560 For auld invy he wald lat na man pas
That he mycht let in gud Wallace supple.    *stop from supplying Wallace*
For Erll Patrik a playn feild kepyt he.    *field of battle defended*
Yeit pur men com and prevyt all thair    *poor; proved*
  mycht
To help Wallace in fens of Scotlandis    *defence*
  rycht.
565 The gud Randell, in tendyr age was kend,    *as he was known in his youth*
Part of gud men out of Murray he send.    *sent*
Jop past agayn and com in presens sone    *returned*
Befor Wallace and tauld how he had don.
Bot Maister Blayr so gud tithingis him
  brocht
570 That of Cumyn Wallace full litill rocht.    *cared*
Als Inglismen had than full mekill dreid.    *great fear*
Fra Fyff was tynt the war thai trowyt to    *From [the time]; lost; worse;*
  speid.       *expected to fare*
The duk and erll that in Scotland thaim led
Captanys thai maid, in Ingland syn thaim    *afterwards hurried*
  sped.
575 Wallace hym bounyt qwhen he thocht tym    *prepared*
  suld be
Of Sanct Jhonstoun and with him tuk fyfte.    *For*
Stevin of Irland and Kerle that was wicht,    *bold*
For Inglismen thai had haldyn the hycht    *From; hold; high ground*
In wachman lyff and fayndyt thaim rycht    *On guard duty; proved*
  weill,       *themselves*
580 Till gud Wallace thai war als trew as steill,    *as steel*
To folow hym thai twa thocht never lang;    *never thought twice*
Throuch the Ochell thai maid thaim for to
  gang.
Of mar power he taryt nocht that tyd;    *For a larger force; time*
To keip the land he gert the laiff abid.    *protect; rest stay*
585 To Styrlyng bryg as than he wald nocht pas
For strang power of Inglismen thar was.    *garrison*
Till Erth ferry thai passit prevaly    *Airth; secretly*
And buschit thaim in a dern sted thar by.    *lay in ambush; concealed*

|  | | |
|---|---|---|
| | A cruell captane in till Erth dwelt thar, | *fierce* |
| 590 | In Ingland born and hecht Thomlyn of Wayr. | *called* |
| | A hundreth men was at his ledyng still, | *under his command* |
| | To bruk that land thai did power and will. | *possess; exerted power* |
| | A Scottis fyschar quhilk thai had tayn beforn | *fisherman; taken before* |
| | Contrar his will gert him be to thaim sworn, | *Against; made* |
| 595 | In thar service thai held him day and nycht. | |
| | Befor the son Wallace gart Jop him dycht | *sunrise; made; get ready* |
| | And send him furth the passage for to spy. | *way across* |
| | On that fyschar he hapnyt sodandly | *happened suddenly* |
| | All him allayn bot a boy that was thar. | *except for* |
| 600 | Jop hynt hym son, and for no dreid wald spar, | *seized; soon; fear* |
| | Be the collar and out a knyff hynt he. | *drew* |
| | For Goddis saik this man askit merce. | |
| | Jop sperd sone, 'Of quhat nacioun art thou?' | *asked* |
| | 'A Scot,' he said, 'bot Sothroun gart me vow | *the English made* |
| 605 | In thar service agayn my will full sayr, | *completely against my will* |
| | Bot for my lyff that I remaynit thair. | *Only* |
| | To sek fysch I com on this north sid. | |
| | Be ye a Scot I wald fayn with you bid.' | *be glad* |
| | Than he him brocht in presens to Wallace. | |
| 610 | The Scottis was blyth quhen thai haiff seyn this cace, | |
| | For with his bait thai mycht weill passage have. | *boat; cross* |
| | For fery craft na fraucht he thocht to crave. | *ferry knowledge; fare* |
| | Apon that syd langar thai taryed nocht; | |
| | Till the south land with glaid hartis thai socht, | *bank* |
| 615 | Syn brak the bait quhen thai war landyt thar. | *destroyed; boat* |
| | Service of it Sotheroun mycht haiff no mayr. | *Use* |
| | Than throuch the mos thai passit full gud speid | *moor* |
| | Till the Torwod, this man with thaim thai leid. | |

|     | The wedow thar brocht tithandis to Wallace | news |
|-----|---|---|
| 620 | Of his trew eyme that dwelt at Dunypace. | loyal uncle |
|     | Thomlyn of Wayr in presoun had him set | placed |
|     | For mar tresour na he befor mycht get. | more than |
|     | Wallace said, 'Deym, he sall weill lousyt be | Madam; be released |
|     | Be none to morn, or ma tharfor sall de.' | By noon tomorrow; more |
| 625 | Scho gat thaim meit and in quiet thai baid | got; food; stayed |
|     | Quhill it was nycht, syn redy sone thaim maid | Until; then |
|     | Towart Arth hall rycht sodeynly thaim drew. | |
|     | A strenth thar was that weyll the fyschar knew, | stronghold |
|     | Of draw dykis and full of watter wan. | With ditches; deep water |
| 630 | Wysly tharof has warnyt thaim this man. | |
|     | On the baksid he led thaim prevale, | secretly |
|     | Fra the watter as wont to cum was he. | he was accustomed to come |
|     | Our a small bryg gud Wallace entryt in; | Over; bridge |
|     | In to the hall hym selff thocht to begyn. | |
| 635 | Fra the souper as thai war boun to rys | supper; ready |
|     | He salust thaim apon ane awfull wys. | greeted; awesome way |
|     | His men hym folowit sodanly at anys; | at once |
|     | Haisty sorow was rassyt in thai wanys. | raised; buildings |
|     | With scerand swerdis scharply about thaim dang, | cutting; struck |
| 640 | Feyll on the flur was fellyt thaim amang. | Many; floor; struck down |
|     | With Thomlyn Wayr Wallace hym selff has met; | |
|     | A felloun strak sadly apon him set, | cruel blow |
|     | Throch hede and swyr all throch the cost him claiff. | neck; ribs; cleaved |
|     | The worthy Scottis fast stekit of the layff, | stabbed the rest to death |
| 645 | Kepyt duris and dulfully thaim dycht. | Blocked doors |
|     | To chaip away the Sotheroun had no mycht: | Guarded doors; treated |
|     | Sum wyndowys socht for till haiff brokyn out, | |
|     | Bot all for nocht, full fey was maid that rout. | doomed; crowd |
|     | About the fyr bruschit the blud so red; | gushed |
| 650 | A hundreth men was slayn into that sted. | place |
|     | Than Wallace socht quhar his uncle suld be; | |

In a dyrk cave he was set dulfulle,          dark cave; painfully
Quhar watter stud and he in yrnys strang.    strong fetters
Wallace full sone the brasis up he dang,      bands; broke
655  Of that myrk holl brocht him with strenth    From; dark hole;
     and lyst.                                      cunning
Bot noyis he hard of nothing ellis he wyst.   Except for; heard; knew
So blyth befor in warld he had nocht beyn
As thar with sycht quhen he had Wallace       sight
     seyn.
In dykys out the dede bodyis thai kest,       ditches
660  Graithyt the place as at thaim likyt best,   Prepared
Maid still gud cher and wys wachis gert        quiet; guards; had stationed
     set,
Quhill ner the day thai slepe withoutyn let.  Until; hindrance
Quhen thai had lycht spulyeid the place in    contemptuously plundered;
     hy,                                             haste
Fand gaynand ger, baithe gold and jowelry;    Found suitable; jewellery
665  Our all that day in quiet held thaim still.  Over
Quhat Sothroun come thai rasavyt with gud     welcomed
     will,
In that laubour the Scottis was full bayn.    ready
Inglismen com, bot nayn yeid out agayn;        none went
Women and barnys put in the presonys          [were] put; prison
     cave
670  So thai mycht mak no warnyng to the lave.    others
Stevyn of Irland and Kerle that wes wicht     bold
Kepyt the port apon the secund nycht.         Guarded; gate
Befor the day the worthy Scottis rays,        rose
Turssyt gud ger and to the Torwod gays,       Packed up; went
675  Remaynyt thar quhill nycht was cummyn       Until night; coming
     on hand,
Syn bounyt thaim in quiet throuch the         Then they set off quietly
     land.
The wedowis son fra thai had passit dout      the risk had passed
A servand send and leit the women out,        servant sent; let
To pas fra Arth quhar at thaim likit best.    wherever
680  Now spek of thaim that went in to the        [to] speak
     west.
Wallace hym selff was sekyr gyd that nycht:   a reliable guide
Till Dunbertane the way he chesyt rycht       chose correctly
Or it was day, for than the nycht was lang,   Before
On to the toun full prevaly thai gang.        secretly went
685  Mekill of it Inglismen occupyit.            Much of

Gud Wallace sone throu a dyrk garth hym hyit · *dark garden; hurried*
And till a hous quhar he was wont to ken · *knew well*
A wedow dwelt, was frendfull till our men. · *friendly*
Abone hyr bed on the baksid was maid · *Above her*
690 A dern wyndow, was nother lang nor braid. · *concealed; wide*
Thar Wallace cauld, and sone fra scho him knew · *called*
In haist scho rays and prevaly thaim in drew · *haste; rose; secretly*
Till a clos bern, quhar thai mycht kepyt be. · *nearby barn*
Baith meit and drynk scho brocht in gret plente.
695 A gudly gyft to Wallace als scho gaiff, · *also; gave*
A hundreth pound and mar atour the layff. · *as well*
Nine sonnys scho had was lykly men and wicht; · *well-made*
Ane ayth till him scho gart thaim swer full rycht. · *oath; made them swear*
In pees thai dwelt, in trubyll that had beyn
700 And trewbut payit till Inglis capdanis keyn. · *tribute; cruel*
Schir Jhon Menteth the castell had in hand,
Bot sum men said thar was a preva band · *secret agreement*
Till Sotheroun maid, be menys of that knycht, · *means of*
In thar supple to be in all his mycht. · *To help them with*
705 Tharof as now I will no proces mak. · *account provide*
Wallace that day a schort purpos can tak:
Quhen it was nycht he bad the wedow pas, · *commanded*
Merk all the duris quhar Sotheroun dwelland was; · *Mark; Englishmen were dwelling*
Syn effter this he and his chevalry · *Then after; host*
710 Graithyt thaim weill and wapynnys tuk in hy, · *Equipped themselves; weapons; quickly*
Went on the gayt quhen Sotheroun was on slep. · *into the street*
A gret oystre our Scottis tuk to kep. · *inn; surrounded*
Ane Inglis captane was sittand up so lait, · *late*
Quhill he and his with drynk was maid full mait. · *were overcome*
715 Nyn men was thar now set in hye curage; · *Nine; high spirits*
Sum wald haiff had gud Wallace in that rage,

Sum wald haiff bound Schir Jhon the              captured
   Graym throch strenth,
Sum wald haiff had Boyd at the swerdis           the end of a sword
   lenth,
Sum wyst Lundy that chapyt was of Fyff,          knew; had escaped from
720 Sum wychtar was na Cetoun in to stryff.[1]
Quhen Wallace hard the Sotheroun maid            such a din
   sic dyn
He gart all byd and hym allayn went in.          stay where they were; alone
The layff remaynyt to her of thar tithans.       rest; hear; news
He salust thaim with sturdy contenance.          greeted them boldly
725 'Falowis,' he said, 'sen I com last fra haym  since
In travaill I was our land and uncouth           action; over; foreign seas
   fame.
Fra south Irland I com in this cuntre            From; region
The conquest of Scotland for to se.
Part of your drynk or sum gud I wald             goods
   haiff.'
730 The captane a schrewed answer him gaiff.      wicked
'Thou semys a Scot unlikly us to spy:[2]
Thou may be ane of Wallace cumpany.
Contrar our king he is ryssyn agane,             Against
The land of Fyff he has rademyt in plane.        freed completely
735 Thou sall her byd quhill we wyt how it be.    here; until we learn
Be thou of his thou sall be hyngyt hye.'         one of his; hanged high
Wallace than thocht it was na tym to stand.
His nobill swerd he gryppyt son in hand.         soon
Awkwart the face drew that captane in            Across that captain's face
   teyn,                                         [he] drew it; anger
740 Straik all away that stud aboune his eyn;     Struck; above; eye
Ane other braithly in the breyst he bar,         violently; breast; struck
Baith brawn and bayn the burly blaid             Flesh; bone; strong
   throch schar.                                  cut through
The layff ruschyt up to Wallace in gret ire.     rest of them
The thryd he feld full fersly in the fyr.        struck down; fiercely
745 Stevyn of Irland and Kerle in that thrang     press of people
Kepyt na chargis bot entryt thaim amang,         Disregarded orders
And othir ma that to the dure can pres.          more
Quhill thai him saw thar coud nothing            Until; could nothing stop
   thaim ces.                                     them

1 Some [boasted themselves] stronger than Seton in battle
2 You seem to be a Scot and [so] unlikely to spy on us

The Sotheroun men full sone was brocht to ded.   *soon; death*

750 The blyth hosteler bad thaim gud ayle and breid.   *innkeeper offered them*

Wallace said, 'Nay, till we haiff laysar mar.   *more leisure*

To be our gyd thou sall befor us fayr   *go*

And begyn fyr quhar at the Sotheroun lyis.'   *start a fire*

The hostellar son apon a hasty wys   *manner*

755 Hynt fyr in hand and till a gret hous yeid   *Seized a firebrand; went*

Quhar Inglismen was in full mekill dreid,   *great danger*

For thai wyst nocht quhill that the rud low rais;   *knew nothing until; strong flames leapt*

As wood bestis amang the fyr than gays,   *mad beasts; then [they] ran*

With paynis fell ruschyt full sorowfully.   *terrible pains rushed*

760 The layff without of our gud chevalry   *rest outside*

At ilka hous quhar the hostillar began   *each; started [a fire]*

Kepyt the duris; fra thaim chapyt na man.   *[They] blocked; escaped*

For all thar mycht, thocht King Edward had sworn,   *sworn [the contrary]*

Gat nane away that was of Ingland born,   *Got none*

765 Bot other brynt or but reskew was slayn,   *either burned; without rescue*

And sum throch force dryvyn in the fyr again.   *were driven back into*

Part Scottis folk in service thaim amang   *Some*

Fra ony payn frely thai leit thaim gang.   *From any pain; go*

Thre hundreth men was to Dunbertan send

770 To kep the land as thar lordis thaim kend.   *protect; told*

Skaithles of thaim for ay was this regioun.   *Unharmed because; always*

Wallace or day maid him out of the toun,   *before daylight; left*

On to the coyff of Dunbertane thai yeid   *cove; went*

And all that day sojornd out of dreid.   *stayed; of danger*

775 Baith meit and drynk the hostillar gert be brocht.   *had brought to them*

Quhen nycht was cummyn in all the haist thai mocht   *could*

Towart Rosneth full ernystfully thai gang,   *went*

For Inglismen was in that castell strang.

On the Garlouch thai purpost thaim to bid   *Gareloch; intended; stay*

780 Betwix the kyrk that ner was thar besyd,

And to the castell full prevaly thai draw.   *secretly; drew*

Undyr a bray thai buschyt thaim rycht law,   *brae; lay in ambush; low*

Lang the wattyr quhar comoun oys had
   thai,                                                      Along; use
The castellis stuff, on to the kyrk ilk day.    provision; each
785 A maryage als that day was to begyn.    wedding
All uschyt out and left nayn within    issued
At fens mycht mak bot servandis in that
   place.    That defence; except
Thus to that tryst thai passyt upon cace.    meeting place; chance
Wallace and his drew thaim full prevaly
790 Nerhand the place quhen thai war passyt
   by,
Within the hauld and thocht to kep that
   steid    stronghold; defend; place
Fra Sotheroun men, or ellys tharfor be
   deid.    else / dead
Compleit was maid the mariage in to
   playn[1]
On to Rosneth thai raturnyt agayn.    returned
795 Four scor and ma was in that cumpany    more
Bot nocht arayit as was our chevalry.    dressed [in armour]
To the castell thai weynd to pas but let.    thought; unimpeded
The worthy Scottis so hardy on thaim set,    vigorously
Forty at anys derffly to ground thai bar,    once violently; struck down
800 The ramaynand affrayit was so sayr,    were so extremely afraid
Langar in feild thai had no mycht to bid    power to stay
Bot fersly fled fra thaim on ather sid.    swiftly
The Scottis thar has weyll the entre woun    captured
And slew the layff that in that hous was
   foun,    rest / found
805 Syn on the flearis folowid wondyr fast.    Then; fugitives; very
Na Inglisman thar fra thaim with lyff at
   past.    escaped with his life
The wemen sone thai seysyt into hand,    soon; seized
Kepyt thaim clos for warnyng of the
   land.[2]
The dede bodyes all out of sycht thai kest,    sight; cast
810 Than at gud es thai maid thaim for to rest.    ease
Of purvians seven dayis thai lugyt thar;    [Living on] the provisions
At rud costis to spend thai wald nocht spar.    They were denied nothing

1 When the marriage ceremony was completed fully
2 Kept them locked up [to prevent] them from raising the alarm through the
land

Quhat Sotheroun come thai tuk all glaidly in,  *received gladly*
Bot out agayn thai leit nane of that kyn.  *allowed none*
815  Quha tithandis send to the captane of that  *Whoever sent news*
    steid,  *place*
Thar servitouris the Scottis put to ded;  *messengers; death*
Spulyeid the place and left na gudis thar,  *Plundered; goods*
Brak wallis doun and maid that byggyng  *buildings bare*
    bar.
Quhen thai had spilt of stayne werk at thai  *destroyed; stone; that*
    mocht,  *could*
820  Syn kendillyt fyr and fra Rosneth thai  *Afterwards kindled*
    socht.  *went*
Quhen thai had brynt all tre werk in that  *burnt; woodwork*
    place,
Wallace gert freith the wemen of his grace.  *had the women freed*
To do thaim harm never his purpos was.  *was never his intention*
Than to Faslan the worthy Scottis can pas,  *passed*
825  Quhar Erll Malcom was bidand at defence.  *on guard*
Rycht glaid he was of Wallace gud
    presence.  *company*
Than he fand thar a nobill cumpany:  *found there*
Schir Jhon the Graym and Richard of
    Lundy,
Adam Wallace, that worthy was and wys,
830  Berklay and Boid with men mekill to prys.  *many excellent men*
At Cristinmes thar Wallace sojornyt still.
Of his modyr tithandis was brocht him till  *news; to*
That tym befor scho had left Elrisle;  *[some] time before; Elderslie*
For Inglismen in it scho durst nocht be.  *dared*
835  Fra thine dysgysyt scho past in pilgrame  *From there disguised*
    weid,
Sum gyrth to sek to Dunfermlyn scho  *refuge; Dunfermline; went*
    yeid.
Seknes hyr had so socht in to that sted  *affected her; place*
Decest scho was, God tuk hir spreit to leid.  *Deceased; spirit; lead*
Quhen Wallace hard at that tithandis was  *heard; tidings*
    trew,
840  How sadnes so in ilka sid can persew,
In thank he tuk becaus it was naturaill.  *thanks; took [it]*
He lowyt God with sekyr hart and haill.  *praised; sure; whole*
Better him thocht that it was hapnyt sa;
Na Sotheroun suld hyr put till other wa.  *cause; suffering*
845  He ordand Jop and als the Maister Blayr  *commanded; also*

Thiddyr to pas and for no costis spayr,          Thither; spare no expense
Bot honour do the corp till sepultur.          corpse; burial
At his commaund thai servit ilka hour,
Doand tharto as dede askis till hav.          as befits the dead
850   With worschip was the corp graithit in          placed in the grave
      grave.
      Agayn thai turnyt and schawit him of hir          They returned; made known
      end.                                                      to
      He thankit God quhat grace that ever he
      send;
      He seis the warld so full of fantasie.          illusion
      Confort he tuk and leit all murnyng be.          let; mourning
855   His most desyr was for to freith Scotland.          free
      Now will I tell quhat new cas com on          event
      hand.
      Schyr Wilyam lang, of Douglace daill was
      lord,
      Of his fyrst wyff, as rycht was to record,
      Decest or than out of this warldly cair,          Deceased before then; care
860   Twa sonnys he had with hyr that leyffyt          her; left there
      thair
      Quhilk likly war and abill in curage,          well-made
      To sculle was send in to thar tendre age.          school
      James and Hew, so hecht thir brethyr twa;          were called
      And efter sone thar uncle couth thaim ta,          soon after
865   Gud Robert Keth had thaim fra Glaskow
      toun,
      Atour the se in Frans he maid thaim boun.          Across the sea; go
      At study syn he left thaim in to Parys          then
      With a maister that worthy was and wys.
      The King Edward tuk thar fader that
      knycht
870   And held him thar thocht he was never so
      wicht,
      Till him, he said, assentit till his will.          Until he
      A mariage als thai gert ordand him till          commanded
      The lady Fers, of power and hye blud,
      Bot tharof com till his lyff litill gud.
875   Twa sonnys he gat on this lady but mar.          forthwith
      With Edwardis will he tuk his leiff to far,          approval; go
      In Scotland com and brocht hys wyff on          in
      pes,                                                      peace
      In Douglas dwelt, forsuth this is no les.          these are no lies

Kyng Edward trowyt that he had stedfast beyn,  *believed*

880  Fast to thar faith, bot the contrar was seyn.  *Firmly; opposite*
Ay Scottis blud remaynyt in to Douglace;  *Ever; blood*
Agayn Ingland he prevyt in mony place.  *proved himself*
The Sawchar was a castell fayr and strang;  *Sanquhar Castle*
Ane Inglis capdane that dyd feyll Scottis wrang  *wronged many Scots*

885  In till it dwelt and Bewffurd he was cauld,  *called*
That held all waist fra thine to Douglace hauld.  *a wasteland from thence; castle*
Rycht ner of kyn was Douglace wiff and he,  *near of kin*
Tharfor he trowyt in pes of hym to be.  *believed*
Schyr Wylyham saw at Wallace rais agayn  *that; had risen*

890  And rycht likly to freyth Scotland of payn.  *was very likely to free*
Till help him part in till his mynd he kest,  *in some way; cast*
For in that lyff rycht lang he coud nocht lest.  *life; last*
He thocht na charge to brek apon Ingland;[1]
It was throuch force that evir he maid thaim band.  *homage*

895  A yong man than that hardy was and bauld,  *bold*
Born till him selff and Thom Dycson was cauld,  *Born on his land*
'Der freynd,' he said, 'I wald preyff at my mycht  *attempt what I can*
And mak a fray to fals Bewfurd the knycht,  *make a surprise attack on*
In Sawchar dwellys and dois full gret outrage.'  *violence*

900  Than Dycson said, 'My selff in that viage  *enterprise*
Sall for you pas with Anderson to spek;
Cusyng to me, frendschip he will nocht brek.  *My cousin*
For that ilk man thar wod ledys thaim till,  *same; leads them to*
Throuch help of him purpos ye may fullfill.'

905  Schyr Wilyham than in all the haist he mycht
Thirty trew men in this viage he dycht,  *expedition; readied*
And tauld his wyff till Drumfres he wald fayr.  *told; go*

[1] He thought [there was] no blame in breaking the bond with England

A tryst, he said, of Ingland he had thair. — meeting; with
Thus passyt he quhar that na Sotheroun wyst — knew
910 With thir thirty throu waist land at his lyst. — pleasure
Quhill nycht was cummyn he buschit thaim full law
In tyll a clewch ner the Wattyr of Craw. — ravine; near
To the Sauchar Dykson allayn he send
And he son maid with Anderson this end, — arrangement
915 Dicson suld tak bathe his hors and his weid — both; clothes
Be it was day a drawcht of wod to leid. — By the time; load; lead
Agayn he past and tauld the gud Dowglace, — told
Quhilk drew him sone in till a prevay place. — secret
Anderson tauld quhat stuff that was tharin — garrison
920 Till Thom Dicson, that was ner of his kyn:
'Forty thai ar of men of mekill vaill; — great power
Be thai on fute thai will you sayr assayll. — severely assail
Gyff thou hapnys the entre for to get — If you happen
On thi rycht hand a stalwart ax is set,
925 Thar with thou may defend thee in a thrang.
Be Douglace wys he bydis nocht fra thee lang.' — If Douglas is wise; stays
Anderson yeid to the buschement in hy; — went; haste
Ner the castell he drew thaim prevaly — Near
In till a schaw Sotheroun mystraistyt nocht. — thicket; did not suspect
930 To the next wode wyth Dycson syn he socht, — then; went
Graithyt him a drawcht on a braid slyp and law, — Prepared; load; broad sledge; low
Changyt a hors and to the hous can caw. — call
Arayit he was in Andersonnis weid — Dressed
And bad haiff in. The portar com gud speid. — quickly
935 'This hour,' he said, 'thou mycht haiff beyn away.
Untymys thou art, for it is scantly day.' — Untimely; hardly
The yet yeid up, Dicson gat in but mar. — gate went up; forthwith
A thowrtour bande that all the drawcht upbar, — crosswise band; load
He cuttyt it; to ground the slyp can ga, — sledge went
940 Cumryt the yet, stekyng thai mycht nocht ma. — Blocked; shutting; more

The portar son he hynt in to that stryff, *soon; pulled; fighting*

Twys throuch the hede he stekit him with a *stabbed*
 knyff.

The ax he gat that Anderson of spak,

A bekyn maid, thar with the buschement *signal; ambush*
 brak. *broke*

945 Dowglace him selff was formest in that *foremost*
 pres, *press*

In our the wod enteryt or thai wald ces. *across; before; cease*

Fifty two wachmen sa, of wallis was *guards saw*
 cummyn new,

Within the clos the Scottis son thaim slew. *courtyard; soon*

Or ony scry was raissyt in that stour *Before; cry*

950 Douglace had tane the yet of the gret tour, *gate; tower*

Rane up a grece quhar at the capdane lay, *Ran; flight of stairs*

On fut he gat and wald haiff beyn away. *On his feet he got*

Our lait it was; Dowglace strak up the dur, *Too late; struck down*

Bewfurd he fand in to the chawmer flour, *found on; chamber floor*

955 With a styff swerd to dede he has him *sword; death*
 dycht. *delivered*

His men folowit that worthy was and
 wycht.

The men thai slew that was in to thai *those*
 wanys, *dwellings*

Syn in the clos thai semblit all at anys. *Then; courtyard; assembled*

The hous thai tuk and Sotheroun put to *castle; captured*
 ded, *death*

960 Gat nane bot ane with lyff out of that sted, *Got none but one; place*

For that the yet so lang unstekit was. *Because; gate; unshut*

This spy he fled, till Dursder can pas, *Durisdeer Castle; went*

Tauld that captane that thai had hapnyt sa. *what had happened to them*

Ane other he gert in to the Enoch ga; *Enoch Castle go*

965 In Tybris mur was warnyt of this cas, *Tibbers moor; warned*

And Louchmaban all semblyt to that place. *Lochmaben; gathered*

The cuntre rais quhen thai herd of sic *such a thing*
 thing

To sege Dowglace, and hecht thai suld him *besiege; vowed*
 hyng. *hang*

Quhen Douglace wyst na wayis fra thaim *knew; to*
 chaip, *escape*

970 To sailye him he trowyt thai wald thaim *attack*
 schaip. *proceed*

Dicson he send apon a cursour wycht *strong steed*

To warn Wallace in all the haist he mycht.

Of Levyhous Wallace had tayn in playn · Lennox; taken to the open

Witht thre hundreth gud men of mekill
mayn.

975 Kynsith, a castell, he thocht to wesy it; · inspect

Ane Ravynsdaill held, bot trew men leit · One Ravensworth held [it]
him wyt

That he was out that tym of Cummyrnauld. · Cumbernauld

Lord Cumyn dwelt on tribut in that hauld. · stronghold

Quhen Wallace wyst, he gert Erll Malcom · knew
ly · lie

980 With two hundreth in a buschement ner · an ambush nearby
by,

To kep the hous that nane till it suld fayr. · ground; none; go

He tuk the layff and in the wod ner thar · rest; near there

A scurrour he set, to warn quhen he saw · spy
ocht · anything

Son Ravynsdaill com; of thaim he had na · soon
thocht.

985 Quhen he was cummyn the twa
buschementis betweyn,

The scurrour warnd the cruell men and · spy alerted; fierce
keyn.

Than Wallace brak and folowit on thaim · Wallace's ambush broke
fast;

The Sotheroun fled for thai war sar agast. · English; greatly aghast

Ravynsdaill had than bot fifty men;

990 Amang the Scottis thar deidis was litill to · mentioned
ken.

Quhen Erll Malcom had bard thaim fra the · barred
place,

Na Sotheroun yeid with lyff that thai did · No English went [escaped]
grace.

Part Lennox men thai left the hors to ta; · Some; take

On spulyeyng than thai wald na tary ma. · plundering; make

995 To sege the hous than Wallace coud nocht · besiege; castle
bid; · stay

Throu out the land in awfull feyr thai ryd. · frightening array; rode

Than Lithquow toun thai brynt in to thar · Linlithgow; burned
gayt; · way

Quhar Sotheroun dwelt thai maid thar · set fire to their buildings
byggyngis hayt.

The peyll thai tuk and slew that was tharin; · pele [stockade]

1000  Of Sotheroun blud thai Scottis thocht na syn.    [spilling] of; sin
      Syn on the morn brynt Dawketh in a gleid,    Then; Dalkeith; to an ember
      Than till a strenth in Newbottyll wod thai    stronghold; Newbattle
        yeid.    went
      Be that Lawder and Crystall of Cetoun    By then
      Com fra the Bas and brynt North Berwik    Bass; burned
        toun,
1005  For Inglismen suld thar na succour get;    help
      Quham thai ourtuk thai slew withoutyn    Whoever; overtook
        let.
      To meit Wallace thai past with all thar    meet
        mycht,
      A hundreth with thaim of men in armes
        brycht.
      A blyth metyng that tym was thaim    happy meeting
        betweyn,
1010  Quhen Erll Malcom and Wallace has thaim
        seyn.
      Thom Dycson than was met with gud
        Wallace,
      Quhilk grantyt sone for to reskew    agreed soon; rescue
        Douglace.
      'Dicson,' he said, 'wait thou thar multiple?'    know; number
      'Three thousand men thar power mycht
        nocht be.'
1015  Erll Malcom said, 'Thocht thai war    Although
        thousandys five
      For this accioun me think that we suld
        stryff.'    strive
      Than Hew the Hay, that dwelt undyr
        trewage,    tribute
      Of Inglismen son he gaiff our the wage;    soon; gave up; payment
      Mar for to pay as than he likyt nocht.    More; liked not
1020  With fyfte men with Wallace furth he    forth he went
        socht,
      To Peblis past, bot no Sotheroun thar baid.    Peebles; remained
      Thar at the croice a playn crya thai maid.    [market] cross; proclamation
      Wallace commaund quha wald cum to his
        pes
      And byd tharat reward suld haiff but les.    without a lie
1025  Gud Ruthirfurd that ever trew has beyn,
      In Atryk wode agayn the Sotheroun keyn    Ettrick Forest; cruel
      Bydyn he had and done thaim mekill der;    Waited; great harm

| | |
|---|---|
| Saxte he led of nobill men in wer. | Sixty |
| Wallace welcummyt quha com in his supple | to support him |
| 1030 With lordly feyr, and chyftaynlik was he. | manners |
| Thaim till aray thai yeid without the toun; | went outside |
| Thar nowmer was six hundreth of renoun, | |
| In byrneis brycht, all men of mekill vaill. | corslets; great worth |
| With glaid hartis thai past in Clyddisdaill. | |
| 1035 The sege be than was to the Sauchar set. | siege by then |
| Sic tithingis com quhilk maid tharin a let: | Such tidings; delay |
| Quhen Sotheroun hard that Wallace was so ner, | close |
| Throu haisty fray the ost was all on ster. | confusion; astir |
| Na man was thar wald for ane other byd; | No; there; stay |
| 1040 Purpos thai tuk in Ingland for to ryd. | |
| The chyftane said, sen thar king had befor | since |
| Fra Wallace fled, the causis was the mor. | reasons were all the more |
| Fast south thai went; to bid it was gret waith. | stay; peril |
| Douglace as than was thus quyt of thar scaith. | repaid for the damage they did |
| 1045 In Crawfurd mur be than was gud Wallace. | by then |
| Quhen men him tauld that Sotheron apon cace | told; by chance |
| Was fled away and durst nocht him abid, | dared not wait for him |
| Thre hundreth than he chesyt with him to rid | chose |
| In lycht harnes and hors at thai wald vaill. | light armour; help |
| 1050 The Erll Malcom he bad byd with the staill | ordered to stay; main army |
| To folow thaim, a bakgard for to be. | rearguard |
| To stuff a chace in all haist bounyt he. | provide men for the chase |
| Throu Dursder he tuk the gaynest gayt; | nearest way |
| Rycht fayn he wald with Sotheroun mak debait. | gladly would he fight |
| 1055 The playnest way abone Mortoun thai hald, | most open; above; held |
| Kepand the hycht gyff that the Sotheroun wald | highland [to see] if |
| | would |
| Hous to persew or turn to Lochmaban, | Follow the Ewes [river] |
| Bot tent thar to the Inglismen tuk nan. | But the English took no heed |
| Doune Neth thai held, graith gydys can thaim leyr.[1] | |

1 Down the Nith river they held their way, prepared guides showed them the way

1060  Abon Closbarn Wallace approchyt ner.  *Above Closeburn*
      In ire he grew quhen thai war in his sycht.
      To thaim he sped with wyll and all thar
          mycht.
      On a out part the Scottis set in that tyd;[1]
      Sevyn scor at erd thai had sone a syd.  *on the ground*
1065  The Sotheroun saw that it was hapnyt sa,  *so*
      Turnyt in agayn reskew for to ma.  *Returned; make*
      Quhen thai trowyt best agayn Scotland to  *believed*
          stand,
      Erll Malcom com rycht ner at thar hand.
      The hayll power tuk playn purpos to fle.  *whole army*
1070  Quha was at erd Wallace gert lat thaim be,  *on the ground allowed them*
      Apon the formest folowit in all his mycht.  *foremost*
      The erll and his apon the layff can lycht,  *upon; rest; set*
      Dyd all to ded unhorssyt was that tyd.[2]
      Feyll men was slayn apon the Sotheroun  *Many*
          sid.
1075  Five hundeth larg or thai past  *quite before*
          Dawswyntoun
      On Sotheroun sid to ded was brocht
          adoun.
      The Scottis hors mony began to tyr,  *Many of the Scottish horses*
      Suppos thaim selff was cruell, fers as fyr.  *bold, fierce*
      The flearis left bathe wode and watterys  *fugitives*
          haill:  *completely*
1080  To tak the playn thai thocht it most availl.  *open field*
      In gret battaill away full fast thai raid;  *battalions; rode*
      In to strenthtis thai thocht to mak na baid.  *strongholds; stay*
      Ner Louchmaban and Lochyrmos thai
          went,
      Besyd Chrochtmaid quhar feyll Sotheroun  *many*
          was schent.  *destroyed*
1085  Rycht mony hors at ronnyng had so lang  *that had been running*
      And travalyt sayr thai mycht no forther  *laboured hard*
          gang.
      Schyr Jhon the Graym apon his fut was  *feet*
          set.
      Than Wallace als lychtyt withoutyn let.  *dismounted; delay*
      Thir twa on fute amang thar enemys yeid;  *These two; foot; went*

1 The Scots attacked a party sent out from the main army at that time
2 Killed all those who were unhorsed at that time

| | | |
|---|---|---|
| 1090 | Was nayn but hors mycht fra thaim pas throu speid. | except on horse; quickly |
| | On Inglismen so cruelly thai socht, | fiercely; sought |
| | Quhom thai ourtuk agayn harmyt us nocht.[1] | |
| | To Wallace com a part of power new | some new troops |
| | On restyt hors, that party couth persew. | who could pursue that party |
| 1095 | Adam Corre with gud men of gret vaill, | worth |
| | And Jhonstoun als that dwelt in Housdaill, | Ewesdale |
| | And Kyrkepatrik was in that cumpany, | |
| | And Halyday quhilk semblyt sturdely. | who assembled boldly |
| | Quhar thai entryt the sailye was so sayr, | assault; intense |
| 1100 | Dede to the ground feill frekis doun thai bayr. | many men struck |
| | Seven scor was haill of new cummyn men in deid. | entirely; newly arrived; indeed |
| | The south party of thaim had mekill dreid. | great fear |
| | Wallace was horssyt apon a cursour wicht, | strong courser |
| | At gud Corre had brocht in to thar sycht | That |
| 1105 | To stuff the chas with his new chevalry. | provide pursuit |
| | He commaundyt Graym and all his men forthi | therefore |
| | Togydder byd and folow as thai mycht. | [To] stay together |
| | Thre capdanys thar full son to dede he dycht, | killed |
| | That restyt hors so wondyr weill him bayr. | carried |
| 1110 | Quhom he ourtuk agayn rais never mar. | Whoever; overtook; rose |
| | Raithly he raid and maid full mony wound. | Quickly; rode |
| | Thir thre capdanis he stekit in that stound, | These; at that time |
| | Of Dursdeyr, Enoch and Tybyr mur. | |
| | Lord Clyffurdis eym away to Clyffurd fur, | uncle; went |
| 1115 | The quhilk befor that kepyt Lowchmaban. | kept |
| | Na landyt man chapyt with him bot ane, | land-owning; except one |
| | For Maxwell als out of Carlaverok com | also; came |
| | On to the Sotheroun the gaynest wayis nom. | nearest; took |
| | In to the chas so wysly thai rid | pursuit; rode |
| 1120 | Few gat away that come apon that sid. | |
| | Besyd Cokpull full feyll fechtyng thai fand; | a great deal of fighting |
| | Sum drownyt was, sum slayn upon the sand. | |

1 Whom they overtook never harmed us again

Quha chapyt was in Ingland fled away.   [Those] who escaped

Wallace raturnd. Na presoner tuk thai.

1125 In Carlaverok restyng that nycht thai
   maid.

Apon the morn tyll Drumfres blythly raid.  To; rode

Thar Wallace cryide quha wald cum till his proclaimed
   pes

Agayn Sotheroun thar malice for to ces.[1]

Till trew Scottis he ordand warysoun.   reward

1130 Quha fawtyt had he grantyt remissioun.  had committed a fault

In Drumfres than he wald no langer byd.  stay

The Sotheroun fled of Scotland on ilk sid  every

Be sey and land without langar abaid.  By sea; delay

Of castellys, townys, than Wallace
   chyftanys maid,

1135 Rewlyt the land and put it to the rest

With trew keparys the quhilk he traistyt  keepers; trusted
   best.

The trew Douglace that I you tauld of ayr, told; earlier

Kepar was maid fra Drumlanryk till Ayr,

Becaus he had on Sotheroun sic thing  such deeds
   wrocht.

1140 Hys wyff was wraith, bot it scho schawit angry; showed not
   nocht.

Undyr covart hyr malice hid perfyt,   cove; her malice; completely

As a serpent watis hyr tym to byt.   waits; bite

Till Douglace eft scho wrocht full mekill afterwards; caused;
   cayr;           distress

Of that as now I leyff quhill forthermar.  until later on

1145 Bot Sotheroun men durst her no castell did not dare here
   hald,

Bot left Scotland befor as I you tald,   told

Saiff ane Morton, a capdane fers and fell, Except for; fierce; extreme

That held Dunde. Thar Wallace wald nocht
   dwell.

Thiddyr he past and lappyt it about.   Thither; encircled it

1150 Quhen Morton saw that he was in sic dout such peril

He askyt leyff with thar lyvys to ga.   leave; lives

Wallace denyit and said, 'It beis nocht sa. refused; will not be

The last capdane of Ingland that her was, was here

I gayff him leyff with his men for to pas. permission

1 They would stop their ill-will towards the English

| | | |
|---|---|---|
| 1155 | Thou sall forthink sic maistre for to mak. | regret; such action |
| | All Ingland sall of thee exemple tak. | take an example |
| | Sic men I wend fra thine for to haiff worn. | Such; given protection |
| | Thou sall be hangyt suppos thi king had sworn.' | sworn [the contrary] |
| | He gert commaund na Scottis suld to thaim spek. | |
| 1160 | 'Conferme the sege and so we sall us wrek | Reinforce; wreak [revenge] |
| | On Inglismen has sic will of Dunde.' | [who] take such pleasure in |
| | Scrymjour he maid thar constable for to be. | |
| | A ballingar of Ingland that was thar | small ship from |
| | Past out of Tay and come to Quhytte far. | fair Whitby |
| 1165 | To London send and tauld of all this cace, | told |
| | Till hyng Morton vowyt had Wallace.[1] | |
| | Befor this tym Edward with power yeid | an army went |
| | To wer on Frans, for than he had no dreid. | war; France; fear |
| | Befor he trowyt Scotland suld be his awn. | Before [that]; believed; own |
| 1170 | Quhen thai him warnyt how his men was ourthrawn, | informed overthrown |
| | Agayn he turnyt till Ingland haistely | returned |
| | And left his deid all fykit in to fy.[2] | |
| | Gascone he clemyt as in to heretage, | claimed as his heritage |
| | He left it thus for all his gret barnage, | |
| 1175 | And Flandris als he thocht till tak on hand, | take over |
| | And thir he left and come to reyff Scotland. | these; take by force |
| | Quhen that this king in Ingland was cummyn hame, | had come home |
| | Sowmoundis thai maid and chargyt Bruce be nayme | Summons name |
| | And all uthir that leyffyt undir his croun, | others; lived |
| 1180 | Byschop, barroun to cum at thar sowmoun. | their summons |
| | Quhen Wallace twys throu grace had fred Scotland, | freed |
| | This tyran king tuk playnly upon hand, | tyrant |
| | For sic desyr that he mycht haiff no rest, | such desire |
| | He thocht till him of it to mak conquest, | to himself |
| 1185 | In covatice he had rongyng so lang. | covetice; ruled |
| | Chyftanis he maid; at thai suld nocht pas wrang, | [so] that by the wrong way |

1 [How] Wallace had vowed to hang Morton
2 And left his campaign in a muddle indeed

Gydis thai chessyt fra strenthis thaim to ghy.          Guides; chose; strongholds; lead

Thai thocht no mor to byd at juperty.          await the chance of war

In playn battaill, and thai mycht Wallace wyn,          open          conquer

1190   He trowyt of wer thai wald no mor begyn.          believed; war; more

Lat I this king makand his ordinans;          Leave; arrangements

My purpos is to spek sum thing of Frans.

The Inglis men that Ghyan held at wer,          Guyenne; war

Till Franch folk thai did full mekill der.          great harm

1195   King and consaill sone in thar wyttis kest,          council; minds cast

To get Wallace thai thocht it was the best.

For Gyan land the Inglismen had thai

Thai schup thaim thus in all the haist thai may,          made their way

For thai traistyt and Scotland war weill stad          trusted          settled

1200   Wallace wald cum as he thaim promyst had.

The sammyn harrold befor in Scotland was,          same herald

Thay him commaundyt and ordand he suld pas          summoned; ordered

In to Scotland without langar delay,

Out of the Slus als gudly as he may.          Sluys

1205   Redy he was, in schip he went on cace.          as chance allowed

In Tayis mouth the havyn but baid he has          Taymouth; delay; has [reached]

Quhar Wallace was than at the saylye still,          assault

And he rasavyt the harrold with gud will.          received

Thar wryt he red and said him on this wys,          read

1210   Ane answer sone he couth thaim nocht devys.          devise

Till honest in the harrold than he send          To an honourable inn

On Wallace cost rycht boundandly to spend;          at Wallace's expense; abundantly

Quhyll tym he saw how othir materis yeid.          Until; went

Ane answer he suld have withoutyn dreid.          doubt

1215   The wyt of Frans thocht Wallace to commend.          best minds

In to Scotland with this harrold thai send

Part of his deid, and als the discriptioune          An account of his deeds; also

Of him tane thar be men of discrecioun,          taken there by

Clerkis, knychtis and harroldys that him saw,

| | | |
|---|---|---|
| 1220 | Bot I herof can nocht rehers thaim aw. | *repeat; all* |
| | Wallace statur, of gretnes and of hycht, | *figure; size; height* |
| | Was jugyt thus be dyscrecioun of rycht, | *by right discretion [of those]* |
| | That saw him bath dischevill and in weid. | *both unarmed and in armour* |
| | Nine quartaris large he was in lenth indeid; | *quarters of an ell* |
| 1225 | Thryd part that lenth in schuldrys braid was he, | *A third part of; broad* |
| | Rycht sembly strang and lusty for to se; | *seemly; pleasing* |
| | Hys lymmys gret, with stalwart pais and sound, | *limbs large; step* |
| | Hys browys hard, his armes gret and round; | |
| | His handis maid rycht lik till a pawmer, | *palm tree leaf* |
| 1230 | Of manlik mak, with nales gret and cler; | *make* |
| | Proporcionyt lang and fair was his vesage, | *face* |
| | Rycht sad of spech and abill in curage; | *serious* |
| | Braid breyst and heych with sturdy crag and gret, | *Broad chest; high neck* |
| | His lyppys round, his noys was squar and tret; | *well-shaped* |
| 1235 | Bowand bron haryt on browis and breis lycht, | *Curling brown-haired; eyebrows* |
| | Cler aspre eyn lik dyamondis brycht. | *sharp eyes* |
| | Under the chyn on the left sid was seyn | |
| | Be hurt a wain; his colour was sangweyn. | *Through injury; scar* |
| | Woundis he had in mony divers place, | *many different places* |
| 1240 | Bot fair and weill kepyt was his face. | |
| | Of ryches he kepyt no propyr thing, | *things of his own* |
| | Gaiff as he wan, lik Alexander the king. | *[He] gave; won* |
| | In tym of pes mek as a maid was he; | *peace; meek* |
| | Quhar wer approchyt the rycht Ector was he. | |
| 1245 | To Scottis men a gret credens he gaiff, | *credence; gave* |
| | Bot knawin enemys thai couth him nocht dissayff. | *known; deceive* |
| | Thir properteys was knawin in to Frans | *These attributes* |
| | Of him to be ane gud remembrans. | |
| | Maister Jhon Blayr that patron couth rasaiff, | *description; receive* |
| 1250 | In Wallace buk brevyt it with the layff. | *wrote; rest* |
| | Bot he her of as than tuk litill heid, | *hereof; then took little heed* |
| | His lauborous mynd was all on other deid. | *busy; deeds* |
| | At Dunde sege thus ernystfully thai lay. | |

Tithandis to him Jop brocht on a day,
1255 How Edward king with likly men to vaill, *at command*
A hundyr thousand com for to assaill.
Than Scotland ground thai had tane apon *Scottish territory; taken*
 cace.
In to sum part it grevyt gud Wallace. *grieved*
He maid Scrymjour still at the hous to ly *castle; lie*
1260 With two thousand, and chargyt him forthi
That nayn suld chaip with lyff out of that *escape alive; place*
 sted
At Sotheroun war, bot do thaim all to ded. *That English were*
Scrymgeour grantyt rycht faithfully to bid. *stay*
With eight thousand Wallace couth fra him
 ryd
1265 To Sanct Jhonstoun; four dayis he graithit *prepared*
 him thar,
With sad avys towart the south can fayr; *serious deliberation; went*
For King Edward that tym ordand had
Ten thousand haill to pas at was full glaid,
With yong Wodstok, a lord of mekill *great might*
 mycht.
1270 At Stirlyng bryg he ordand thaim full rycht *Stirling bridge*
And thar to bid the entre for to wer; *wait; signal for war*
Of Wallace than he trowit to haiff no der. *expected; injury*
Thar leyff thai laucht and past but delay, *took their leave; without*
Rycht saraly and in a gud aray, *closely*
1275 To Sterlyng com and wald nocht thar abid; *wait*
To se the north furth than can he ryd, *see*
Sic new curage so fell in his entent, *Such; mind*
Quhilk maid Sotheroun full sar for to *repent full dearly*
 rapent.

This Wodstok raid into the north gud speid;     rode
Of Scottis as than he had bot litill dreid,     fear
For weyll he trowyt for to reskew Dunde.     expected
Thar schippys com to Tay in be the se.     by the sea
5   His gydys said thai suld him gyd in by     lead
Saynct Jhonstoun, quhar passage was playnly.
The hycht thai tuk and lukit thaim about,     hill
So war thai war of Wallace and his rout.     aware; company
In sum part than he remordyt his thocht,     regretted
10   The kingis commaund becaus he kepyt nocht,
Bot quhen he saw thai war fewar than he
He wald thaim byd and other do or de.     wait for them; either
Schyr Jhon Ramsay formest his power saw,     army
He said, 'Yon is, that yhe se hydder draw,     Those are; hither
15   Othir Sotheroun that cummys sa cruellye,     Either; fiercely
Or Erll Malcom to sek you for supple.'     seek help from you
Than Wallace smyld and said, 'Inglis thai ar.     smiled; English
Ye may thaim ken rycht weyll quhar ever thai far.'     know / go
On Schyrreff mur Wallace the feild has tane
20   With eight thousand that worthy was in wane.     extremely
The Sotheroun was rycht douchty in thar deid,     bold
Togydder straik, weyll stuffyt in steyll weid.     struck; equipped / armour
Than speris sone all into splendrys sprent.     spears; splinters shattered
The hardy Scottis throu out the Sotheroun went.
25   In reddy battaill seven thousand doun thai bar,     struck
Dede on the bent that recoveryt never mar.     field; recovered; more
Wyth fell fechtyng of wapynnys groundyn keyn,     cruel fighting / sharp
Blud fra byrneis was bruschyt on the greyn.     corsets; splashed
The felloun stour that awfull was and strang!     fighting

| | | |
|---|---|---|
| 30 | The worthy Scottis so derffly on thaim dang | eagerly / struck |
| | At all was dede within a litill stound; | That; died; while |
| | Nane of that place had power for to found. | go |
| | Yong Wodstok has bathe land and lyff forlorn. | lost |
| | The Scottis spulyeit of gud ger thaim beforn; | plundered; equipment |
| 35 | Quhat thaim thocht best of fyn harnes thai vaill, | armour / choose |
| | Bath gold and gud and hors that mycht thaim vaill. | avail |
| | To Stirlyng bryg without restyng thai raid; | bridge |
| | Or ma suld cum Wallace this ordinans maid. | Before more; order |
| | Past our the bryg Wallace gert wrychtis call, | over; carpenters |
| 40 | Hewyt trastis, undyd the passage all. | Hewed beams; destroyed |
| | Sa tha sam folk he send to the Drip furd, | those |
| | Gert set the ground with scharp spykis of burd. | board |
| | Bot nine or ten he kest a gait befor, | prepared away |
| | Langis the schauld, maid it bath dep and schor. | Along the shallow part / steep |
| 45 | Than Wallace said, 'On a sid we sall be, | one |
| | Yon king and I, bot gyff he southwart fle.' | That; unless |
| | He send Lawder, quhilk had in hand the Bas, | who possessed |
| | Langis the cost quhar ony veschell was, | Along; coast; vessel |
| | And men with him that wysly couth luk | |
| 50 | Of ilka boyt a burd or twa out tuk. | From each boat; board |
| | Schyppys thai brynt of strangearis that was thar. | burned |
| | Cetoun and he to Wallace thus thai fayr, | go |
| | In Stirlying lay apon his purpos still | |
| | For Inglismen to se quhat way thai will. | would go |
| 55 | The Erll Malcom Stirlyng in kepyng had; | |
| | Till hym he com with men of armes sad, | resolute |
| | Thre hundreth haill that sekyr war and trew | in all; sure; loyal |
| | Of Lennox folk, thar power to renew. | reinforce |
| | Schir Jhon the Graym fra Dundaff prevaly | secretly |

| | | |
|---|---|---|
| 60 | Till Wallace com with a gud chevalry, | To |
| | Tithandis him brocht the Sotheroun com at hand. | News |
| | In Torfychan King Edward was lugeand, | Torphichen; lodging |
| | Stroyand the place of purviance that was thar. | Destroying; provisions |
| | Sanct Jhonys gud for thaim thai wald nocht spar. | good [knights] |
| 65 | The gud Stewart of But com to the land; | |
| | With him he ledys weill ma than twelve thousand, | |
| | Till Cumyn past, was than in Cummyrnald. | Comyn |
| | Apon the morn bounyt the Stewart bald | prepared; bold |
| | Sone till aray with men of armes brycht. | Soon to battle order |
| 70 | Twenty thousand than semblyt to thar sycht. | gathered in their sight |
| | The lord Stwart and Cumyn furth thai rid | |
| | To the Fawkyrk and thar hecht to abid. | promised |
| | The Scottis chyftane than out of Stirlyng past; | |
| | To the Fawkyrk he sped his ost full fast. | |
| 75 | Wallace and his than till aray he yeid | |
| | With ten thousand of douchty men in deid. | |
| | Quha couth behald thar awfull lordly vult, | appearance |
| | So weill beseyn, so forthwart, stern and stult, | valiant |
| | So gud chyftanys as with sa few thar beyn, | |
| 80 | Without a king was never in Scotland seyn. | |
| | Wallace him selff and Erll Malcom that lord, | |
| | Schir Jhon the Graym and Ramsay at accord, | |
| | Cetoun, Lawder and Lundy that was wicht, | |
| | Adam Wallace to that jornay him dycht, | undertaking; rallied |
| 85 | And mony gud quhilk prevyt weill in pres. | good men; battle |
| | Thar namys all I may nocht her rehres. | recite |
| | Sotheroun or than out of Torfychan fur, | went |
| | Thar passage maid in to Slamanan mur; | Slamannan moor |
| | In till a playn set tentis and palyon, | |
| 90 | South hald Fawkyrk, a litill abon the ton. | towards; above; town |
| | Gud Jop him selff jugit thaim be his sycht | |
| | In haill nowmer a hundyr thousand rycht. | |
| | Of Wallace com the Scottis sic comfort tuk, | Of Wallace's coming |

Quhen thai him saw all raddour thai forsuk, *fear*

95  For of invy was few thar at it wyst.

Tresonable folk thar mater wyrkis throu lyst, *cunning*

Poyson sen syn 'at the Fawkyrk' is cald, *since then*

Throu treson and corrupcion of ald.

Lord Cumyn had invy at gud Wallace, *malice*

100  For Erll Patrik that hapnyt upon cace;

Cunttas of Merch was Cumyns sister der. *Countess*

Undyr colour he wrocht in this maner, *pretence*

In to the ost had ordand Wallace dede *Wallace's death*

And maid Stewart with him to fall in pled. *argument*

105  He said that lord at Wallace had no rycht

Power to leid and he present in sycht.

He bad him tak the vantgard for to gy; *guide*

So wyst he weyll at thai suld stryff forthi. *argue*

Lord Stewart ast at Wallace his consaill,

110  Said, 'Schir, ye knaw quhat may us maist availl.

Yon felloun king is awfull for to bid.'

Rycht unabasyt Wallace answerd that tyd: *undismayed*

'And I haiff seyn may twys in to Scotland *more than twice*

Wytht yon ilk king, quhen Scottis men tuk on hand

115  Wytht fewar men than now ar hydder socht

This realm agayn to full gud purpos brocht.

Schyr, we will fecht, for we haiff men inew *enough*

As for a day, sa that we be all trew.' *so long as*

The Stewart said he wald the wantgard haiff.

120  Wallace answerd and said, 'Sa God me saiff,

That sall ye nocht als lang as I may ryng, *govern*

Nor no man ellis quhill I se my rycht king. *until; rightful*

Gyff he will cum and tak on him the croun

At his commaund I sall be reddy boun.

125  Throu Goddis grace I reskewed Scotland twys.

I war to mad to leyff it on sic wys, *too*

To tyn for bost that I haiff governd lang.' *lose*

Thus halff in wraith frawart him can he gang. *away from*

Stewart tharwith all bolnyt in to baill. *swelled with anger*

130  'Wallace,' he said, 'be thee I tell a taill.' *by*

'Say furth,' quod he, 'of the fairest ye can.'
Unhappyly his taill thus he began.
'Wallace,' he said, 'thou takis the mekill cur.      responsibility
So feryt it, be wyrkyng of natur,[1]

135  How a howlat complend of his fethrame,      owl complained
Quhill Deym Natur tuk of ilk byrd but      without
  blame      reproach
A fayr fethyr and to the howlat gaiff.
Than he throuch pryd reboytyt all the layff.      repulsed
Quharof suld thou thi senye schaw so he?      ensign; high

140  Thou thinkis nan her at suld thi falow be;      none
This makis it thou art cled with our men.      clad
Had we our awn thin war bot few to ken.'      thine were; indeed
At thir wordis gud Wallace brynt as fyr.
Our haistely he answerd him in ire.      Too

145  'Thou leid,' he said. 'The suth full oft has      lied
  ben,
Thar and I baid quhar thou durst nocht be
  seyn,
Contrar enemys, na mar for Scotlandis
  rycht
Than dar the howlat quhen that the day is
  brycht.
That taill full meit thou has tauld be thi      fittingly; illustrated
  sell;

150  To thi desyr thou sall me nocht compell.
Cumyn it is has gyffyn this conselle;
Will God, ye sall of your fyrst purpos faill.
That fals traytour that I of danger brocht      out of
Is wonderlik till bryng this realm till nocht.      very likely

155  For thi ogart other thou sall de,      pride either
Or in presoun byd, or cowart lik to fle.
Reskew of me thou sall get nane this day.'
Tharwith he turnd and fra thaim raid his
  way.
Ten thousand haill fra thaim with Wallace
  raid.

160  Nan was better in all this warld so braid
As of sic men at leiffand was in lyff.
Allace, gret harm fell Scotland throuch that
  stryff!      strife

1 It happened in the course of nature

Past till a wod fra the Fawkyrk be est.
He wald nocht byd for commaund na
   request,    *command*
165 For charge of nan bot it had ben his king,    *none*
At mycht that tym bryng him fra his
   etlyng.    *intention*
The tother Scottis that saw this discensioun
For dysconford to leiff the feild was boun,    *ready*
Bot at thai men was natyff till Stwart,    *that*
170 Principaill of But, tuk hardement in hart.    *Lord Superior*
Lord Stwart was at Cumyn grevyt thar,
Hecht and he leiffd, he suld repent full sar    *Vowed if he lived*
The gret trespace that he throu raklesnace
Had gert him mak to Wallace in that place.
175 For thair debait it was a gret pete;
For Inglismen than mycht na trete be,
Haistyt sa fast a battaill to the feild,
Xxxti thousand that weill coud wapynnys
   weild.
Erll of Harfurd was chosyn thar chyftane.
180 The gud Stewart than till aray is gane;
The feild he tuk as trew and worthy
   knycht.
The Inglismen come on wytht full gret
   mycht.
Thar fell metyng was awfull for to se;    *terrible*
At that countour thai gert feill Sotheroun de.    *encounter*
185 Quhen speris was spilt hynt out with    *destroyed drew*
   swerdis son;    *soon*
On ather sid full douchty deid was don.
Feill on the ground was fellyt in that place.
Stewart and his can on his enemys race;    *press*
Blud byrstyt out throuch maile and byrneis    *mail armour; corslet*
   brycht.
190 Twenty thousand with dredfull wapynnys
   dycht
Of Sotheroun men derffly to dede thai    *violently*
   dyng;    *strike*
The ramanand agayn fled to thar king.
Ten thousand thar that fra the dede    *death*
   eschevyt    *escaped*
With thar chyftane in to the ost relevyt.    *rallied*
195 Agayn to ray the hardy Stwart yeid.    *battle order*

Quhen Wallace saw this nobill, worthi deid,
Held up his handys with humyll prayer
    prest.                                          pressed together
To God he said, 'Gyff yon lord grace to
    lest
And power haiff his worschip till attend,          honour
To wyn thar folk and tak the haill                 defeat;
    commend.                                        praise
Gret harm it war at he suld be ourset
With new power thai will on him rebet.'             renew the attack
Be that the Bruce ane awfull battaill baid,        battalion commanded
And byschop Beik quhilk oft had beyn
    assayd,                                         attacked
Forty thousand apon the Scottis to fair.           advanced
With fell affer thai raissit up rycht thair        fierce array
The Bruce baner, in gold of gowlis cler.           gules [heraldic red]
Quhen Wallace saw battallis approchyt ner,         battalions
The rycht lyon agayn his awn kynryk,
'Allace,' he said, 'the warld is contrar lik!
This land suld be yon tyrandis heretage,
That cummys thus to stroy his awn
    barnage.
Sa I war fre of it that I said ayr,                earlier
I wald forswer Scotland for evermar.               renounce
Contrar the Bruce I suld reskew thaim
    now,
Or de tharfor, to God I mak a vow.'
The gret debait in Wallace wit can waid           rage
Betwix kyndnes and wyllfull vow he maid.
Kyndnes him bad reskew thaim fra thar fa,
Than Wyll said, 'Nay, quhy, fuyll, wald           fool
    thou do sa?
Thou has na wyt wyth rycht thi selff to leid      mind
Suld thou help thaim that wald put thee to
    deid?'
Kyndnes said, 'Yha, thai ar gud Scottis
    men.'
Than Will said, 'Nay, veryte thou may ken,
Had thai bene gud all anys we had ben;            united
Be reson heyr the contrar now is seyn,            here
For thai me hayt mar na Sotheroun leid.'          people
Kyndnes said, 'Nay, that schaw thai nocht         show
    in deid.

200

205

210

215

220

225

Thocht ane of thaim be fals in till his saw,  *word*

230  For caus of him thou suld nocht los thaim aw.  *Because*

Thai haiff done weill in to yon felloun stour;

Reskew thaim now and tak a hye honour.'

Wyll said, 'Thai wald haiff reft fra me my lyff.  *deprived me of*

I baid for thaim in mony stalwart stryff.'  *stood*

235  Kyndnes said, 'Help, thar power is at nocht;

Syn wreik on him that all the malice wrocht.'  *Then take revenge*

Wyll said, 'This day thai sall nocht helpyt be.

That I haiff said sall ay be said for me.

Thai ar bot dede; God grant thaim of his blys!  *as good as dead*

240  Invy lang syn has done gret harme bot this.'  *Envy long since; apart from*

Wallace tharwith turnyt for ire in teyn,  *from grief*

Braith teris for baill byrst out fra bathe his eyn.  *Profuse tears; sorrow*

Schyr Jhon the Graym and mony worthi wicht  *people*

Wepyt in wo for sorow of that sycht.

245  Quhen Bruce his battaill apon the Scottis straik,  *Bruce's battalion*

Thar cruell com maid cowardis for to quaik:  *coming*

Lord Cumyn fled to Cummyrnauld away.

About the Scottis the Sotheroun lappyt thay.  *drew close*

The men of But befor thar lord thai stud,

250  Defendand him quhen fell stremys of blud  *many streams*

All thaim about in flothis quhar thai yeid.  *floods*

Bathid in blud was Bruce swerd and his weid  *armour*

Throu fell slauchter of trew men of his awn.  *[i.e., own countrymen]*

Son to the dede the Scottis was ourthrawn;  *Soon*

255  Syn slew the lord, for he wald nocht be tayn.  *i.e., Stewart / taken*

Quhen Wallace saw that thir gud men was
gayn,
'Lordis,' he said, 'quhat now is your
consaill?
Twa choys thar is, the best I rede us vaill:   advise us to choose
Yonder the king his ost abandonand,   risking himself for his host
260 Heyr Bruce and Beyk in yon battaill to
stand.   endure
Yon king in wer has wys and felloun beyn;
Thar capdans als full cruell ar and keyn.
Better of hand is nocht leiffand I wys,   certainly
In tyrandry, ye trow me weill of this,   domination, believe me
265 Than Bruce and Beik, to quhat part thai be   whatever they
set.   set [out to do]
We haiff a chois quhilk is full hard but let.   without doubt
And we turn est for strenth in Lowtheane   If
land
Thai stuff a chas rycht scharp, I dar   will mount a chase
warrand.
Tak we the mur, yon king is us befor.
270 Thar is bot this, withoutyn wordis mor,   only this [way out]
To the Tor wod, for our succour is thar.   salvation
Throuch Brucis ost forsuth fyrst mon we far;
Amang us now thar nedis no debayt.
Yon men ar dede. We will nocht stryff for   stand on ceremony
stayt.'
275 Thai consent haill to wyrk rycht as he will;   all consented
Quhat him thocht best thai grantyt to
fullfill.
Gud Wallace than, that stoutly couth thaim
ster,
Befor thaim raid in till his armour cler,
Rewellyt speris all in a nowmer round:   Directed
280 'And we have grace for to pas throu thaim   whole
sound
And few be lost, till our strenth we will
ryd.
Want we mony, in faith we sall all byd.'   If we lose many men; stay
Thai hardnyt hors fast on the gret ost raid.   Those emboldened horsemen
The rerd at rays quhen sperys in sondyr   noise that rose
glaid.   went easily
285 Duschyt in glos, devyt with speris dynt.   Struck with dizziness;
deafened; din

Fra forgyt steyll the fyr flew out but stynt.          sparks; endlessly

The felloun thrang quhen hors and men          cruel press
removyt

Up drayff the dust quhar thai thar pithtis          strength
provyt.          proved

The tother ost mycht no deidis se

290  For stour at rais quhill thai disseverit be.          dust; were separated

The worthy Scottis eight thousand doun
thai bar;          bore

Few war at erd at gud Wallace brocht thar.          Few [i.e., Scots]; to ground

The king criyt hors apon thaim for to ryd,          [his] horsemen

Bot this wys lord gaiff him consaill to bid:          wait

295  The Erll of York said, 'Schir, ye wyrk amys

To brek aray. Yon men quyt throuch thaim          quite
is.

Thai ken the land and will to strenthis
draw;

Tak we the playn we ar in perell aw.'

The king consavyt at his consaill was rycht,          realised

300  Rewllyt his ost and baid still in thar sycht.          Directed

Or Bruce and Beik mycht retorn thar
battaill          rally battalion

The Scottis was throuch and had a gret
availl.          advantage

Wallace commaund the ost suld pas thar way

To the Tor wod in all the haist thai may.

305  Hym selff and Graym and Lawder turnyt          returned
in

Betwex battaillys prys prowys for to wyn;          worthy reputation; obtain

And with thaim baid in that place
hundrethis thre

Of westland men, was oysyt in jeperte,          experienced

Apon wycht hors that wesele coud ryd.          skilfully

310  A slop thai maid quhar thai set on a syd;          breach

Na speris thai had bot swerdys of gud
steyll;

Tharwith in stour thai leit thar enemys feill          the fighting

How thai full oft had prevyt beyn in pres.          proved; battle

Of Inglismen thai maid feill to deces.          many

315  Or Bruce tharof mycht weill persavyng
haiff

Thre hundreth thar was graithit to thar          sent to their graves
graiff.

The hardy Bruce ane ost abandounyt; *allowed to charge*
Twenty thousand he rewllyt be force and
 wit
Upon the Scottis his men for to reskew.
320 Servyt thai war with gud speris enew,
And byschop Beik a stuff till him to be. *support*
Quhen gud Wallace thar ordinans coud se
'Allace,' he said, 'yon man has mekill mycht
And our gud will till undo his awn rycht.' *overly great*
325 He bad his men towart his ost in rid;
Thaim for to sayff he wald behynd thaim
 byd.
Mekill he trowys in God and his awn weid; *armour*
Till sayff his men he did full douchty deid.
Upon him selff mekill travaill he tais; *takes*
330 The gret battaill compleit apon him gais.
In the forbreyst he retornyt full oft; *van of the army*
Quham ever he hyt thar sawchnyng was *'peace-making'*
 unsoft. *rough*
That day in warld knawin was nocht his
 maik; *match*
A Sotheroun man he slew ay at a straik.
335 Bot his a strenth mycht nocht agayn thaim *single*
 be;
Towart his ost behuffyd for to fle.
The Bruce him hurt at the returnyng thair,
Undyr the hals a deip wound and a sayr. *neck*
Blude byrstyt out braithly at speris lenth; *profusely*
340 Fra the gret ost he fled towart his strenth.
Sic a flear befor was nevir seyn! *fugitive*
Nocht at Gadderis of Gawdyfer the keyn
Quhen Alexander reskewed the foryouris, *forayers*
Mycht tyll him be comperd in tha houris,
345 The fell turnyng on folowaris that he maid,
How bandounly befor the ost he raid; *boldly*
Nor how gud Graym wyth cruell
 hardement,
Na how Lawder, amang thar fayis went;
How thaim allayn into that stour thai stud *fighting*
350 Quhill Wallace was in stanchyng of his
 blud.
Be than he had stemmyt full weill his *stemmed [the flow of blood]*
 wound,

With thre hundreth in to the feild can
   found                                *go*
To reskew Graym and Lawder that was
   wicht;
Bot byschop Beik com with sic force and    *cunning*
   slycht
355 The worthy Scottis weryt fer on bak,     *wearied far back*
Sevyn akyrbreid in turnyng of thar bak.
Yeit Wallace has thir twa delyveryt weill
Be his awn strenth and his gud swerd of
   steill.
The awfull Bruce amang thaim with gret    *formidable force*
   mayn
360 At the reskew three Scottis men he has slayn;
Quham he hyt rycht ay at a straik was ded.
Wallace preyst in tharfor to set rameid;    *remedy the situation*
With a gud sper the Bruce was servyt but    *without delay*
   baid.
With gret invy to Wallace fast he raid
365 And he till him assonyeit nocht forthi.    *did not refuse the challenge*
The Bruce him myssyt as Wallace passyt by.
Awkwart he straik with his scharp    *Crosswise sword*
   groundyn glave;
Sper and horscrag in till sondyr he drave.    *horse's neck*
Bruce was at erd or Wallace turned about.    *on the ground before*
370 The gret battaill of thousandis stern and
   stout,
Thai horssyt Bruce with men of gret
   valour.
Wallace allayn was in that stalwart stour.    *severe combat*
Graym pressyt in and straik ane Inglis
   knycht
Befor the Bruce apon the basnet brycht.    *helmet*
375 That servall stuff and all his other weid,    *inferior equipment; armour*
Bathe bayn and brayn, the nobill swerd    *brawn*
   throuch yeid.    *went through*
The knycht was dede; gud Graym retornet
   tyte.    *quickly*
A suttell knycht tharat had gret despyt,    *sly*
Folowyt at wait and has persavyt weill    *Watching his opportunity*
380 Gramys byrny was to narow sumdeill    *Graham's corslet*
Beneth the waist, that clos it mycht nocht    *closed*
   be.

On the fyllat full sternly straik that sle,          loin; rogue
Persyt the bak, in the bowalys him bar
Wyth a scharp sper, that he mycht leiff no
    mar.
385   Graym turnd tharwith and smate that
    knycht in teyn          anger
Towart the vesar, a litill beneth the eyn.          visor
Dede of that dynt to ground he duschyt          blow
    doun.
Schyr Jhon the Graym that swonyt on his
    arsoun          saddle-bow
Or he ourcom till pas till his party,
390   Feill Sotheroun men that was on fute him
    by
Stekit his hors, that he no forther yeid;          stabbed
Graym yauld to God his gud speryt and his          yielded
    deid.
Quhen Wallace saw this knycht to dede was
    wrocht,
The pytuous payn so sor thyrllyt his thocht          pierced
395   All out of kynd it alteryt his curage.          nature
His wyt in wer was than bot a wod rage.          mad
Hys hors him bur in feild quhar so him          carried
    lyst,          wished
For of him selff as than litill he wyst.          knew little
Lik a wyld best that war fra reson rent,
400   As wytlace wy in to the ost he went          Behaving like a madman
Dingand on hard; quhat Sotheroun he          Striking hard
    rycht hyt
Straucht apon hors agayn mycht nevir syt.          Upright
In to that rage full feill folk he dang doun;
All hym about was reddyt a gret rowm.          cleared; space
405   Quhen Bruce persavyt with Wallace it stud
    sa,
He chargyt men lang sperys for to ta
And sla hys hors, sa he suld nocht eschaip.
Feyll Sotheroun than to Wallace fast can          made their way
    schaip,
Persyt hys hors wyth sperys on ather syd;
410   Woundys thai maid that was bathe deip and
    wyd.
Of schafftis part Wallace in sondyr schayr,          shafts [of spears]; pierced
Bot fell hedys in till his hors left thair.          many spearheads

Sum wytt agayn to Wallace can radoun,   *sense; return*
In hys awn mynd so rewllyt him resoun;
415 Sa for to de him thocht it no vaslage.   *To die in such a way; honour*
Than for to fle he tuk no taryage,   *made no delay*
Spuryt the hors, quhilk ran in a gud
    randoun   *swift course*
Till his awn folk was bydand on Carroun.[1]
The sey was in, at thai stoppyt and stud.
420 On loud he criyt and bad thaim tak the flud,   *enter the river*
'Togyddyr byd, ye may nocht los a man.'   *Stay together*
At his commaund the watter thai tuk than;   *took to the water*
Hym returned the entre for to kepe,   *guard*
Quhill all his ost was passyt our the depe;   *across the deep water*
425 Syn passyt our and dred his hors suld faill,
Hym selff hevy, cled in to plait of maill.
Set he couth swom he trowit he mycht   *Although; swim*
    nocht weill.
The cler watter culyt the hors sumdeill.   *cooled*
Atour the flud he bur him to the land,   *Over; he [the horse] carried*
430 Syn fell doun dede and mycht no langar
    stand.
Kerle full son a cursour till him brocht;
Than up he lap, amange the ost he socht.
Graym was away and fifteen other wicht.
On Magdaleyn day thir folk to ded was   *were killed*
    dycht:
435 Thirty thousand of Inglismen for trew
The worthy Scottis apon that day thai slew,
Quhat be Stwart, and syn be wicht Wallace.
For all his prys King Edward rewyt that   *regretted*
    race.   *encounter*
To the Tor wod he bad the ost suld ryd;   *commanded*
440 Kerle and he past upon Caroun syd,
Behaldand our apon the south party.   *Looking across*
Bruce formast com and can on Wallace cry:
'Quhat art thou thar?' 'A man,' Wallace can
    say.
The Bruce answerd, 'That has thou prevyt
    today.
445 Abyd,' he said, 'thou nedis nocht now to
    fle.'

1 To his own people [who] were waiting at the [River] Carron

Wallace answerd, 'I eschew nocht for thee,                    *flee*
Bot that power has thi awn ner fordon.                    *own [countrymen]; destroyed*
Amendis of this, will God, we sall haiff
    son.'
'Langage of thee,' the Bruce said, 'I desyr.'                    *A word with you*
450 'Say furth,' quod he; 'thou may for litill
    hyr.                    *cost*
Ryd fra that ost and gar thaim bid with                    *make them wait*
    Beik.
I wald fayn heir quhat thou likis to speik.'
The ost baid styll, the Bruce passyt thaim
    fra;
He tuk wyth him bot a Scot that hecht Ra.
455 Quhen that the Bruce out of thar heryng
    wer,
He turned in and this question can sper:
'Quhy wyrkis thou thus and mycht in gud
    pes be?'
Than Wallace said, 'Bot in defawt of thee,                    *Only in your absence*
Throuch thi falsheid thin awn wyt has
    myskend.                    *deceived*
460 I cleym no rycht bot wald this land defend,
At thou undoys throu thi fals cruell deid.                    *That*
Thou has tynt twa had beyn worth fer mair
    meid                    *reward*
On this ilk day with a gud king to found,                    *go*
Na five mylyon of fynest gold so round                    *Than*
465 That ever was wrocht in werk or ymage
    brycht!
I trow in warld was nocht a better knycht
Than was the gud Graym of trewth and
    hardement.'
Teris tharwith fra Wallace eyn doun went.
Bruce said, 'Fer ma on this day we haiff
    losyt.'
470 Wallace answerd, 'Allace, thai war evill                    *evilly*
    cosyt                    *exchanged*
Throuch thi tresson, that suld be our rycht
    king,
That willfully dystroyis thin awne
    ofspryng.'
The Bruce askyt, 'Will thou do my devys?'                    *follow my advice*
Wallace said, 'Nay, thou leyffis in sic wys                    *lives*

475 | Thou wald me mak at Edwardis will to be;
Yeit had I lever tomorn be hyngyt hye.'      *I would rather*
'Yeit sall I say as I wald consaill geyff,
Than as a lord thou mycht at liking leiff      *in comfort; live*
At thin awn will in Scotland for to ryng      *liking*
480 | And be in pece and hald of Edward king.'      *hold land*
'Of that fals king I think never wagis to tak      *payment*
Bot contrar him with my power to mak.
I cleym nothing as be titill of rycht,
Thocht I mycht reiff, sen God has lent me      *take by force*
mycht,
485 | Fra thee thi crowne of this regioun to wer,
Bot I will nocht sic a charge on me ber.      *responsibility*
Gret God wait best quhat wer I tak on      *knows*
hand
For till kep fre that thou art gaynstandand.      *standing against*
It mycht beyn said of lang gone her of forn,      *long ago formerly*
490 | In cursyt tym thou was for Scotland born.
Schamys thou nocht that thou nevir yeit      *Are you not ashamed*
did gud,
Thou renygat devorar of thi blud?      *renegade devourer*
I vow to God, ma I thi maister be      *may I overpower you*
In ony feild, thou sall fer werthar de      *more deservedly die*
495 | Than sall a Turk, for thi fals cruell wer.
Pagans till us dois nocht so mekill der.'      *injury*
Than lewch the Bruce at Wallace      *laughed*
ernystfulnas
And said, 'Thou seis at thus standis the cas.
This day thou art with our power ourset,      *overwhelmed*
500 | Agayn yon king warrand thou may nocht      *protection*
get.'
Than Wallace said, 'We ar be mekill thing
Starkar this day in contrar of yon king      *stronger*
Than at Beggar, quhar he left mony of his,
And als the feild; sa sall he do with this
505 | Or de tharfor, for all his mekill mycht.
We haiff nocht losyt in this feild bot a
knycht,
And Scotland now in sic perell is stad      *placed*
To leyff it thus my selff mycht be full
mad.'
'Wallace,' he said, 'it prochys ner the      *approaches*
nycht.

| | | |
|---|---|---|
| 510 | Wald thou to morn quhen at the day is lycht | Would |
| | Or nyn of bell, meit me at this chapel | Before nine o'clock |
| | Be Dunypas? I wald haiff your consell.' | |
| | Wallace said, 'Nay, or that ilk tyme be went, | before |
| | War all the men hyn till the orient | from here to |
| 515 | In till a will with Edward, quha had sworn, | sworn [to the contrary] |
| | We sall bargane be nine houris to morn; | fight by |
| | And for his wrang reyff other he sall think scham, | wrongful plunder |
| | Or de tharfor, or fle in Ingland haym. | home |
| | Bot and thou will, son be the hour of thre | If |
| 520 | At that ilk tryst, will God, thou sall se me. | meeting |
| | Quhill I may lest this realme sall nocht forfar.' | perish |
| | Bruce promest him with twelve Scottis to be thar, | |
| | And Wallace said, 'Stud thou rychtwys to me, | correctly |
| | Counter palys I suld nocht be to thee. | [An] opponent |
| 525 | I sall bryng ten, and for thi nowmer ma, | more |
| | I gyff no force thocht thou be freynd or fa.' | do not care |
| | Thus thai departyt. The Bruce past his way, | |
| | Till Lythqwo raid quhar that King Edward lay, | Linlithgow |
| | The feild had left and lugyt a south the toun, | |
| 530 | To souper set as Bruce at the palyoun | |
| | So entryt in and saw vacand his seit. | vacant |
| | No watter he tuk bot maid him to the meit. | |
| | Fastand he was and had beyn in gret dreid; | danger |
| | Bludyt was all his wapynnys and his weid. | Bloodied |
| 535 | Sotheroun lordys scornyt him in termys rud. | rough |
| | Ane said, 'Behald, yon Scot ettis his awn blud.' | eats |
| | The king thocht ill thai maid sic derisioun. | thought it wrong |
| | He bad haiff watter to Bruce of Huntyntoun. | |
| | Thai bad hym wesche. He said that wald he nocht. | wash |

540 'This blud is myn, that hurtis most my
      thocht.'
      Sadly the Bruce than in his mynd remordyt        regretted
      Thai wordis suth that Wallace had him
      recordyt.                                        said
      Than rewyt he sar, fra resoun had him            repented; deeply when
      knawin                                           he understood
      At blud and land suld all lik beyn his awin.     all alike
545   With thaim he was lang or he couth get away,
      Bot contrar Scottis he faucht nocht fra that
      day.
      Lat I the Bruce sayr movyt in his entent.        I leave; deeply moved; heart
      Gud Wallace sone agane to the ost went,          soon
      In the Torwod quhilk had thar lugyng             camp
      maid.
550   Fyris thai bett that was bath brycht and          beat
      braid.
      Of nolt and scheip thai tuk at sufficiens;       cattle; in plenty
      Tharof full sone thai get thaim sustinens.       got
      Wallace slepyt bot a schort quhill and rais;     only
      To rewll the ost on a gud mak he gais            manner
555   Till Erll Malcom, Ramsay and Lundy
      wicht,
      With five thousand in a battaill thaim           battalion
      dycht.                                           ready
      Wallace, Lawder and Crystell of Cetoun
      Five thousand led, and Wallace of
      Ricardtoun,
      Full weyll arayit in till thar armour clen,      bright
560   Past to the feild quhar that the chas had        chase
      ben,
      Amang the ded men sekand the worthiast
      The cors of Graym for quham he murned            corpse; whom; mourned most
      mast.
      Quhen thai him fand and gud Wallace him          found
      saw
      He lychtyt doun and hynt him fra thaim aw        dismounted; lifted; all
565   In armys up, behaldand his paill face.
      He kyssyt him and criyt full oft: 'Allace!
      My best brother in warld that ever I had,
      My afald freynd quhen I was hardest stad,        true; pressed
      My hop, my heill, thou was in maist              hope; health
      honour,

570    My faith, my help, my strenthiast in stour!    *greatest strength; battle*
        In thee was wyt, fredom, and hardiness.    *wisdom; nobility; courage*
        In thee was treuth, manheid, and nobilnes.    *loyalty*
        In thee was rewll, in thee was governans;    *rule*
        In thee was vertu withoutyn varians.    *virtue*
575    In thee lawte, in thee was gret largnas;    *generosity*
        In thee gentrice, in thee was stedfastnas.    *nobility*
        Thou was gret caus of wynnyng of    *the triumph*
          Scotland,
        Thocht I began and tuk the wer on hand.    *war*
        I vow to God that has the warld in wauld,    *under his government*
580    Thi dede sall be to Sotheroun full der    *dearly paid for*
          sauld.
        Marter thou art for Scotlandis rycht and    *Martyr*
          me.
        I sall thee venge or ellis tharfor to de.'    *else die in the attempt*
        Was na man thar fra wepyng mycht hym
          rafreyn,    *refrain*
        For los of him quhen thai hard Wallace
          pleyn.    *lament*
585    Thai caryit him with worschip and dolour,    *carried; honour; sorrow*
        In the Fawkyrk graithit him in sepultour.    *buried; a tomb*
        Wallace commaundyt his ost tharfor to byd.    *wait*
        Hys ten he tuk, for to meit Bruce thai ryd.
        Southwest he past quhar at the tryst was    *meeting*
          set;
590    The Bruce full sone and gud Wallace is
          met.
        For los of Graym and als for propyr teyn    *pure grief*
        He grew in ire quhen he the Bruce had
          seyn.
        Thar salusyng was bot boustous and    *greeting; rude*
          thrawin.    *angry*
        'Rewis thou,' he said, 'thou art contrar thin    *Repentest; against thine own*
          awin!'
595    'Wallace,' said Bruce, 'rabut me now no    *reproach*
          mar.
        Myn awin dedis has bet me wonder sar.'    *own deeds; beaten; extremely*
        Quhen Wallace hard with Bruce that it stud    *heard*
          swa,    *so*
        On kneis he fell, far contenans can him    *showed a friendly attitude*
          ma.
        In armes son the Bruce has Wallace tane.

| | | |
|---|---|---|
| 600 | Out fra thar men in consalle ar thai gane. | counsel |
| | I can nocht tell perfytly thar langage, | conversation |
| | Bot this was it thar men had of knawlage. | |
| | Wallace him prayt, 'Cum fra yon Sotheroun king.' | beseeched |
| | The Bruce said, 'Nay, thar lattis me a thing. | something prevents me |
| 605 | I am so boundyn with wytnes to be leill, | bound by testimony; loyal |
| | For all Ingland I wald nocht fals my seill. | transgress; seal |
| | Bot of a thing I hecht to God and thee, | vow |
| | That contrar Scottis agayn I sall nocht be. | against |
| | In till a feild with wapynnys that I ber | battlefield; bear |
| 610 | In thi purpos I sall thee never der. | harm |
| | Gyff God grantis of us ourhand till haiff | victory [the upper hand] |
| | I will bot fle myn awin selff for to saiff. | save |
| | And Edward chaip I pas with him agayn, | If; escapes |
| | Bot I throu force be other tane or slayn. | Unless; either taken |
| 615 | Brek he on me quhen that my terme is out, | [If] breaks [his bond] with |
| | I cum to thee. May I chaip fra that dout!' | I will come; escape; peril |
| | Of thar consaill I can tell you no mar. | more |
| | The Bruce tuk leyff and can till Edward fayr, | leave; went to Edward |
| | Rycht sad in mynd for Scottis men that war lost. | heavy |
| 620 | Wallace in haist providyt son his ost. | soon made ready |
| | He maid Crawfurd the Erll Malcom to gid. | guide |
| | The lauch way till Enravyn thai ryd, | low |
| | For thar wachis than suld thaim nocht aspy. | sentries |
| | The tother ost him selff led haistely | |
| 625 | Be south Manwell, quhilk that thai war betweyn. | |
| | Of the out wach thus chapyt thai unseyn. | scouts sent out |
| | The Erll Malcom on Lithquow entris in; | |
| | Our haistely a stryff thai can begyn. | Too; fight |
| | Wallace was nocht all to the battaill boun. | ready for battle |
| 630 | Quhen that thai hard the scry rais in the toun | noise rise |
| | On Edwardis ost thai set full sodandly. | |
| | Wallace and his maid litill noyis or cry | |
| | Bot occupyd with wapynnys in that stour. | busied themselves; fight |

Feill fallen war ded that was without     *Many*
    armour
635   And dysarayit the Inglis ost was than.     *in disarray; then*

Amang palyounis the Scottis, quhar mony     *The Scots slipped among*
    man     *tents*

Cuttyt cordys, gart mony tentis fall.     *made*

Nan sonyeid than, at anys fechtand was
    all,[1]

Gud Wallace ost and Erll Malcom wyth
    mycht.

640   King Edward than with awfull fer on hycht     *awesome company; the hill*

Cryit till aray on Bruce so stern and stout.     *Called to arms*

Twenty thousand in armys him about

In to harnes had biddyn all that nycht,     *In armour; stayed*

Bot frayt folk so dulfully was dycht     *scared; painfully treated*

645   On ilk sid thai fled for ferdnes of other     *each; fear*
    deid.

Wallace and his so rudly throu thaim yeid     *strongly; went*

Towart the king and fellyt feill to grounde.     *struck down many*

Quha baid thaim thar rycht fell fechtyng     *cruel*
    has found.

That awfull kyng rycht manfully abaid:     *withstood*

650   Till all his folk ane gret comford he maid.     *encouragement*

The worthy Scottis agayn him in that stour     *against; battle*

Feill Sotheroun slew in to thar fyn armour,     *Many*

So forthwartlye thai pressyt in the thrang,     *actively; throng*

Befor the king maid sloppis thaim amang.     *breaches*

655   Inglis commounis than fled on ather sid,     *common folk; either side*

Bot noble men nane other durst abid.     *Except for; none; dared*

The Bruce as than to Scottis did no
    grevans.     *injury*

A juge he was with fenyeid contenans:     *feigned*

Sa did he never in na battaill ayr     *before*

660   Nothyr yeit efter, sic deid as he schew thar.     *Nor yet; such; displayed*

The Erll Malcom be than in to the toun     *by that time*

The Erll Herfurd to fle thai had maid     *prepared to flee*
    boun.

The Lennox men set thar lugyng in fyr,     *lodging*

Than ferdly fled full mony Sotheroun syr.     *fled in fear; men*

665   The King Edward that yeit was fechtand     *yet; fighting*
    still

1 None hesitated then, all were fighting at once

Has seyn thaim fle; that likit him full ill.
The worthi Scottis fast towart him thai
    pres,
Hys brydyll ner assayit ar thai wald ces.   *nearly attacked before; stop*
His banerman Wallace slew in that place
670 And sone to ground the baner doun he
    race.                                    *dashed*
The Erll of York consaillyt the king to fle;  *advised*
Than he ratornd, sen na succour thai se.     *turned back since; assistance*
The Inglismen has seyn thar banner fall,
Without comfort, to fle thai purpost all.    *encouragement; all decided*
675 Eleven thousand in toun and feild was
    ded
Of Edwardis folk or his selff left the sted.  *before he himself; place*
Twenty thousand away togidder raid;          *rode*
King and chyftans na langar tary maid.
The Scottis in haist than to thar hors thai
    yeid                                      *went*
680 To stuff the chas with worthi men in weid.  *provide pursuit; armour*
The Lennox folk that wantyt hors and ger      *lacked; equipment*
Tuk thaim at wyll to help thaim in that
    wer.                                      *at their pleasure; war*
At stragyll raid quhat Scot mycht formest
    pas,                                      *In disorder rode*
Of Sotheroun men quhar of gret slauchter
    was.
685 Wallace has seyn the Scottis unordourly      *in disarray*
Folow the chas, he maid chyftanis in hy      *haste*
Thaim for to rewll and all togyddyr ryd,     *rule; together*
Comaundyt thaim ilkane suld other bid.[1]
'In to fleyng the Sotheroun suttaill ar.     *In fleeing; cunning*
690 Se thai the tym, thai wyll set on us sar.    *If they see the opportunity*
Feill scalyt folk to thaim will son ranew,   *Many scattered; soon rally*
For ye se weyll that thai ar men enew.'      *have enough men*
The folowaris was rewllyt weill with skill;  *governed; reason*
In gud aray thai raid all at his will        *as he wished*
695 And slew doun fast; quhat Sotheroun thai     *quickly*
    ourtak                                    *overtook*
Contrar the Scottis com never maistrice to
    mak.[2]

1 Commanded that each one should wait for the other
2 Never again came to fight against the Scots

Into the chais thai haistyt thaim so ner          In pursuit
Na Inglisman out fra the ost durst ster.          stir
The frayit folk at stragill that was fleand          frightened; in disorder
700   Drew to the king, weill ma than ten          more
          thousand.
Thirty thousand in nowmer than war thai,
In till aray togyddyr passyt away.          battle array
Feill Scottis hors was drevyn into travaill,          Many; driven; action
Forrown that day so irkyt can defaill.          Exhausted; tired; [they] failed
705   The Sotheroun was with hors servyt full
          weill;
Of Wallace chais the lordis had gret feill.          Wallace's pursuit; experience
Of hors thai war purvaide in gret wayn.          supplied; quantity
The king changyt on syndry hors of Spayn.          different Spanish horses
Than Wallace said, 'Lordis, ye may weill se
710   Yon folk ar now all at yon king may be.          Those; that
For falt of stuff we lois our mekill thing.[1]
And we wyth hors to pas befor this king          If we had horses
We suld mak end of all this lang debait.          battle
Yeit sum of thaim sall handelyt be full          Yet; hotly
          hayt.
715   Part of our hors ar haldyn fresch and          said to be; strong
          wicht;
Set on thaim sar quhill we ar in this          vigorously; position of power
          mycht.'
Tharwith the Scottis so hard amang thaim
          drew
Of the outward thre thousand thair thai
          slew.
In Crawfurd mur mony man was slayn.
720   Edward gart call the Bruce, mekill of mayn.          strength
Than said he thus, 'Gud Erll of
          Huntyntoun,
Ye se the Scottis puttis feill to confusioun.          many; death
Wald ye wyth men agayn on him raleiff,[2]
And mer thaim anys, I sall quhill I may leiff          destroy; once; live
725   Lov you fer mar than ony other knycht,
And for all this sall put you to your rycht.'          restore; rightful inheritance
Than said the Bruce, 'Schir, los me of my          free
          band;

1 [Because] of lack of provision [specifically horses] we will lose too much
2 [If] you would take men to renew the attack on him

Than I sall turn, I hecht you be my hand.'  promise; by
The king full son consideryt in his mynd  promptly
730  Quhen he hard Bruce answer him in sic  heard; such a way
      kind
Fra Inglismen that Brucis hart set is.  [Away] from
Than kest he thus how he suld mend that  considered; amend
      mys,  wrong
And so he dyd in Ingland at his will.
Na Scottis man he leit with Bruce bid still,  allowed
735  Bot quhar he past held him in subjeccioun
Of Inglismen, held him in gret bandoun.  subordination
He turned nocht, na na mar langage maid;  nor no more words said
In raid battaill the king to Sulway raid  in battle order; rode
With mekill payn fast upon Ingland cost.  much difficulty; coast
740  Fifty thousand in that travaill he lost.  action
Quhen Wallace saw he chapyt was away,  escaped
Upon Annand agayn returnyt thai  Along the Annand River
Till Edynburgh, withoutyn tary mor,  more delay
Put in Crawfurd that captane was befor;  Installed
745  Of heretage he had in Mannuill land.
Wallace commaund ilk man suld hald in
      hand
Thar awin office, as thai befor had had.  own
Thus in gud pece Scotland with rycht he  peace
      stad.  settled
On the tenth day to Sanct Jhonstoun he
      went,
750  Semblyt lordis, syn schawyt thaim his  Assembled; then revealed;
      entent.  intention
Scrymgeour com at than had woun Dunde;  won
Wallace commaund that tym weill kepyt he.  Wallace's command
He sailyeid so quhill strang hunger thaim  attacked so long until; drove
      draiff;  them [the English]
Sa feblyst war, the hous till him thai gaiff.  weakened [they] were; castle
755  Thai wageours sone he put to confusioun,  mercenaries; death
Syn brocht Mortoun to mak a conclusioun
Befor Wallace, and son fra he him saw  as soon as he saw him
He gert hyng him for all King Edwardis  had him hanged
      aw.  menace
Masons, minouris with Scrymgeour furth  miners
      he send,
760  Kest doun Dunde and tharof maid ane  Dismantled
      end.

Wallace sadly, quhen thir dedis war don,   *determinedly; these*
The lordis he cald and his will schawit   *revealed to*
  thaim son.
'Gud men,' he said, 'I was your governour.
My mynd was set to do you ay honour,   *always*

765 And for to bryng this realm to rychtwysnas.
For it I passit in mony paynfull place.
To wyn our awin my selff I never spard.   *own [land]; spared*
At the Fawkyrk thai ordand me reward:   *decreed for*
Of that reward ye her no mor throu me.   *hear*

770 To sic gyftis God will full weill haiff e.   *an eye*
Now ye ar fre throu the Makar of mycht.
He grant you grace weill to defend your
  rycht.
Als I presume gyff harm be ordand me,   *Also; planned for*
Thai ar Scottis men at suld the wyrkaris be.[1]

775 I haiff enewch of our ald enemys stryff.   *enough*
Me think our awin suld nocht invy my lyff.   *[i.e., Scots]*
My office our her playnly I resing;   *give up here*
I think no mar to tak on me sic thing.   *such a thing*
In France I will to wyn my leffyng thar,   *will go; obtain; living there*

780 As now avysd and her to cum no mar.'   *I have resolved; here; more*
Lordis gaynstud, bot all thai helpyt nocht.   *opposed*
For ony thar he did as him best thocht.   *For all that any [said]*
Byschop Synclar was wesyd with seknas   *afflicted with sickness*
In till Dunkell, and syn throu Goddis grace   *Dunkeld; then*

785 He recoveryt quhen Wallace past away;   *went*
Efter the Bruce he lestyt mony day.   *lasted many a*
Gud Wallace thus tuk leiff in Sanct   *leave*
  Jhonstoun;
Eighteen with him till Dunde maid him   *to; his*
  boun.   *way*
Longaweill past that douchty was in deid.

790 The barrounys sone of Brachyn with him   *Brechin*
  yeid.   *went*
Twa brether als with thar uncle thaim   *also; prepared [to go]*
  dycht,
Symon Wallace and Richard that was
  wicht.
Schir Thomas Gray this preist can wyth
  thaim fair,   *went with them*

1 Scottish men will be the ones responsible

Edward Litill, gud Jop and Maister Blayr.
795 *Gude Keirlie past, had bene with Wallace*
       *lang*
*And done full weill in mony felloun thrang.*                    bitter battles
*This Keirlie than that couth with Wallace*                      then
       *fair*
*Will Ker he hecht, myne autor makis declair.*                   go
*Keirl[ie in Iris]ch is bot Ker till cald.*                      was called; states
800 *In Ca[rrik he h]ad heretage of ald.*
*His f[oirbear], quhilk wourthy was of hand,*                    forebears
*Sanc[t David k]ing him brocht out of*
       *Irland.*
*Syne [at Dum]ore, quhar first the Norowais*                     Norwegians
       *come in,*
*This [gude Ke]r maid grete discomfit of thair*                  greatly discomfited their
       *kyn;*                                                    kinsmen
805 *With [sevin hun]dreth he vincust nine*                       vanquished
       *thousand,*
*[Sum drownit i]n Doune, sum sl[ane upon*
       *the land.*
*Thay landis h]ale the gude king gaif him*                       all these lands; gave
       *till.*
*[How Wallace] past now forthir speke we*
       *will.*

Amang merchandis gud Wallace tuk the se.                         went to sea
810 Pray we to God that he thar ledar be!
Thai saylyt furth by part of Ingland schor,                      shore
Till Humbyr Mouth quhen at thai com
       befor
Out of the south a gret rede saile thai se,                      red sail
In to thar top the leopardis standand hye.                       on their topcastle; high
815 The merchandis than that senye quhen thai                     emblem
       saw
Cummand so neir, thai war discumfyt aw,                          all discomfited
For weill thai wyst that it was Jhon of
       Lyn:
Scottis to slay he said it was no syn.
Thir frayit folk yeid son to confessioun,                        These frightened; went soon
820 Than Wallace said, 'Of sic devocioun
Yeit saw I never in no place quhar I past.
For this a schip me think you all agast,                         one
Yon wood cattis sall do us litill der!                           Those wild cats; harm
We saw thaim faill twys in a grettar wer,

825    On a fair field; so sall thai on the se.
       Dyspyt it is to se thaim stand so hye.'          Contempt; so proud
       The ster man said, 'Schir, will ye               steersman
           understand,
       He saiffis nane that is born of Scotland.        spares no-one
       We may nocht fle fra yon barge, wait I weill.    that ship, I know well
830    Weyll stuft thai ar with gun, ganye of           armed; guns, crossbow bolts
           steill.
       Apon the se yon revar lang has beyn;             that pirate
       Till rychtwys men he dois full mekill teyn.      a great deal of harm
       Mycht we be saiff it forst nocht of our gud.     it would not matter for
       This wys he has, in schort for to conclud:       way
835    A flud he beris apon his cot armour,             river; coat of arms
       Ay drownand folk so payntyt in figour.           Always; in an image
       Suppos we murn ye suld haiff no mervaill.'        mourn
       Than Wallace said, 'Her is men of mar            more worthy men
           vaill
       To saill thi schip, tharfor in holl thou ga      the hold; go
840    And thi feris; na mar cummyr us ma.'             companions; do not hinder us
       Wallace and his than sone till harnes yeid.      soon went to [put on] armour
       Quhen thai war graithit into thar worthi         dressed
           weid,
       Himselff and Blayr and the knycht
           Longaweill,
       Thir thre has tane to kepe the myd schip         These; undertaken
           weill.
845    Befor us seven and six be eft was kend,[1]
       Syn twa he chesd the top for to defend;          Then; chose; tophead
       And Gray he maid thar sterman for to be.         steersman
       The merchandis than saw thaim so                 seeing
           manfulle
       To fend thaim selff, be caus thai had no         defend
           weid
850    Out of the holl thai tuk skynnys gud speid,      hold; hides quickly
       Ay betwix two stuft woll as thai mycht           Always between; supplied
           best,
       Agayn the straik at thai suld sumpart lest.      Against; sword blows; endure
       Than Wallace lewch and commendyt thaim           laughed; praised
           aw;
       Of sic harnes befor he never saw.[2]

       1 Seven were directed to the bow, six to the stern
       2 He had never seen such armour before

855 Be than the barge com on thaim wonder    By then
    fast,
    Seven scor in hyr that was nothing agast.[1]
    Quhen Jhon of Lyn saw thaim in armour    them [the Scots]
    brycht
    He lewch and said thir haltyn wordis on    laughed; these haughty;
    hycht:    loudly
    'Yon glakyt Scottis can us nocht    Those foolish; have not
    undyrstand!    understood us
860 Fulys thai ar, is new cummyn of the land.'    Simpletons; newly come from
    He cryit 'Stryk!' bot no answer thai maid.    Strike sail [i.e., surrender]
    Blayr with a bow schot fast withoutyn baid;    hesitation
    Or thai clyppyt he schot bot arowis thre    Before; grappled; only
    And at ilk schot he gert a revar de.    each; made; pirate die
865 The brygandis than thai bykerit wondyr    bandits; attacked very
    fast,
    Amang the Scottis with schot and gounnys    guns
    cast    assailed
    And thai agayn with speris hedyt weill    in return; spears headed
    Feill woundis maid throuch plattis of fyne    Many; plate armour
    steill.
    Ather other festynyt with clippys keyn;[2]
870 A cruell counter thar was on schipburd    fierce encounter
    seyn.
    The derff schot draiff als thik as a haill    deadly shot rained down; hail
    schour,
    Contende tharwith the space ner of ane    Fought; [for] the space of
    hour.    nearly
    Quhen schot was gayn the Scottis gret    gone
    comfort had:    encouragement
    At hand strakys thai war sekyr and sad.    In close combat; resolute
875 The merchandis als with sic thing as thai    also [using] anything they
    mycht    could
    Prevyt full weill in defens of thar rycht.    Acquitted themselves well
    Wallace and his at ner strakis quhen thai be    close quarters
    With scharp swerdys thai gert feill    made many
    brygandis de.    bandits die
    Thai in the top so worthi wrocht with    Those; tophead
    hand,
880 In the south top thar mycht no revar stand.    pirate

1 Carrying seven score intrepid men
2 Each fastened on the other with grappling hooks

All the mydschip of revers was maid waist          pirates; cleared
That to geiff our thai war in poynt almaist.        give up; on the point
Than Jhon of Lyn was rycht gretly agast;            dismayed
He saw hys folk failye about him fast.              fail
885   With egyr will he wald haiff beyn away;        eager
Bad wynd the saill in all the haist thai
      may.[1]
Bot fra the Scottis thai mycht nocht than of
      skey.                                          get clear
The clyp so sar on ather burd thai wey.             grappling hook; cast
Thai saw nothing that mycht be to thaim
      es.                                            comfort
890   Crawfurd on loft thar saill brynt in a bles;   above; burned; blaze
Or Jhon of Lyn schup for to leyff that sted         Before; proceeded; leave
Of his best men saxte was brocht to ded.            killed
Thar schip by owris a burd was mar of               was higher than ours by a
      hycht.                                           board
Wallace lap in amang thai revaris wicht.            bold pirates
895   A man he straik our burd into the se;          dashed overboard; sea
On the our loft he slew son othir thre.             upper deck; three others
Longaweill entryt and als the Maister Blair;
Thai gaiff no gyrth to frek at thai fand thar.      refuge to any man that
Wallas him selff with Jhon of Lyn was met;
900   At his coler a felloun straik he set.          collar; cruel blow; aimed
Bathe helm and hed fra the schuldris he             helmet; shoulders he struck
      draiff.                                          off
Blayr our burd in the se kest the layff             overboard; threw; rest
Of his body, and all the remaynand                  rest of them
Entryt and slew the brygandis at thai fand.         that; found
905   The schip thai tuk, gret gold and other ger,
At thai reiffaris had gaderyt lang in wer.          That these pirates
Bot Maister Blayr spak nothing of himsell,          claimed; for
In deid of armes quhat aventur he fell.             feats
Schir Thomas Gray, than preyst was to
      Wallace,
910   Put in the buk how than hapnyt this cace
At Blayr was in, and mony worthi deid,
Of quhilk him selff had no plesance to              pleasure; read
      reid.
Wallace rewllyt the schip with his awin            commanded; own
      men

---

1 Ordered [his men to] hoist the sail as hastily as they could

And saillys furth the rycht cours for to ken.  *direct*

915 In the Sloice havyn quhill that thai entryt  *Sluys haven until*
be,

The merchandys weill he kepyt in sawfte.  *safety*

Of gold and ger he tuk part at thai fand,  *that*

Gaiff thaim the schip, syn passyt to the
land.

Throuch Flandrys raid upon a gudly wys,

920 Entryt in France and socht up to Parys.  *went*

The glaid tithing at to the king was brocht  *glad news that*

Of Wallace com, it comford all thar  *Wallace's arrival*
thocht.

Thai trowyt be him to get redres of wrang  *expected by*

The Sotheroun had in Gyane wrocht so  *done*
lang.

925 The perys of France was still at thar  *peers*
parlement.

The king commaund wyth trew and haill  *decreed; full*
entent

Thai suld forse a lordschip to Wallace.  *provide*

The lordis all than dempt of this cace,  *considered*

For Gyane was all haill out of thar hand.  *entirely*

930 Thai thocht it best for to geyff him that  *give*
land,

For weill thai trowyt he had so wrocht  *believed*
befor

He suld it wyn, or ellis de tharfor.  *else die*

Alswa of it thai mycht no profyt haiff;  *Also*

This was the caus to Wallace thai it gaiff.  *reason; gave*

935 This decret son thai schawit to the king.  *decision; soon; showed*

Displessyd he was thai maid him sic a  *Displeased; such*
thing.

Of Gyane thus quhen Wallace had a feill,  *knowledge*

No land, he said, likit him halff so weill.  *he liked*

'My chance is thus for to be ay in wer  *fortune; always*

940 And Inglismen has done our realm most
der.  *harm*

It was weill knawin my defens rychtwys  *known; righteous defence*
thar  *there*

Rycht haiff I her, my comfort is the mar.  *encouragement*

I thank your lordis maid sic reward to me:  *such*

Thar purpos is I sall nocht ydill be.'  *idle*

945 The king bad him be Duk of Gyan land.  *decreed*

To that commaund Wallace was
   gaynstandand;                    *opposed*
Be caus that land was haly to conquace,   *entirely to be conquered*
He thocht to wyn erar throu Goddis   *rather to win*
   grace.
Bot nevertheles the king had maid him
   knycht

950  And gaiff him gold for to maynteine his
   mycht,
Syn gaiff playn charge till his wermen of   *Then gave plain orders;*
   France                                 *warriors*
Thai suld be haill at Wallace ordinance:   *wholly in command*
And als of him he bad him armes tak.   *also from; coat of arms*
Wallace forsuk sic changyng for to mak.   *refused such*

955  'Sen I began, I bar the reid lyoun   *Since; bore the red lion*
And thinkis to be ay trew man to that   *always true*
   croun.
I thank you schir of this mychty reward.
Your gyft herfor sall nocht rycht lang be   *therefore*
   spard.
I think to quyt sum part ye kith on me   *repay; bestow*

960  In your service or ellis tharfor to de.'
Gud Wallace thocht his tym he wald nocht
   waist;                                *waste*
On to the wer he graithit him in haist.   *war; set out*
All Scottis men that was into that land
Till him thai socht with thar fewte and   *made their way; fewlty;*
   band.                                *allegiance*

965  Langaweill als a gret power can ras;   *also; raised*
In Wallace help this gud knycht glaidly gais.   *To help Wallace; goes*
Ten thousand haill of nobill men thai war,   *were*
The braid baner of Scotland displayed thar.   *broad*
Thir wermen sone apon Gyane thai fwr,   *There warriors; went*

970  Brak byggyns doun quhilk had bene stark   *Demolished buildings;*
   and stur,                             *strong; sturdy*
Sotheroun thai slew agayn thaim maid debait,   *resistance*
Braithly on breid thai rasyt fyris hait.[1]
Schynnoun thai tuk at Wallace fyrst had
   woun                                 *won*
And slew all men of Sotheroun was thar
   foun.

---

1 They started blazing fires, far and wide

975 In to that toun Wallace his dwellyng maid;
    All thar about he wan the contre braid.    *conquered; wide*
    The worthy Duk of Orliance was lord
    Semblyt his folk in till a gud accord.    *Assembled; order*
    Twelve thousand than he had in armour
       brycht
980 And thocht to help gud Wallace in his
       rycht.
    Leyff I thaim thus, the duk and Wallace    *I leave*
       baithe,
    And spek sum part how Scotland tuk gret
       scaithe.    *harm*
    The fals invy, the wicked fell tresoun,    *envy; disastrous*
    Amang thaim selff brocht feill to    *many*
       confusioun.    *destruction*
985 The knycht Wallang in Scotland maid
       repair,    *repaired*
    The fals Menteth, Schir Jhon, withoutyn
       mair,    *delay*
    Betwix thai twa was maid a preva band.    *secret bond*
    So on a day thai met in till Annand.    *Annandale*
    Of the Leynhous Schir Jhon had gret    *Lennox*
       desyr;
990 Schyr Amer hecht he suld it haiff in hyr,    *promised; as payment*
    Till hald in fe, and othir landis mo,    *hold as a fief; too*
    Of King Edward so he wald pas him to.    *defect*
    Thus cordyt thai and syn to London went.    *they accorded; thus*
    Edward was glaid for to hald that
       poyntment.    *appointment*
995 Menteth was thar bound man to that fals    *sworn*
       king,
    Till forthir him till Scotland in all thing,    *assist*
    Syn passyt haym and Wallang with him    *Then; home; accompanied*
       fur,    *him*
    Quhill he was brocht agayn our Carleill mur.    *Until; over*
    King Edward than in ire and fers outrage    *fierce*
1000 Be thirty dayis raissit his barnage,    *Within*
    In Scotland past and thar na stoppyng    *no obstacle*
       fand.    *found*
    Na chyftane thar that durst agayn him    *dared*
       stand,
    For Menteth tald thai thocht to mak Bruce    *told [them]*
       king.

All trew Scottis wald be plessyd of that thing.

1005 Yeit mony fled and durst nocht bid Edward: *Yet; dared; await*

Sum into Ros, and in the ilis past part. *Some went; isles; some*

The Byschop Synclar agayn fled into But; *Bute*

With that fals king he had no will to mut. *bargain*

Thus wythout straik the castellis of Scotland *without a blow*

1010 King Edward haill has tane in his awin hand, *taken completely under his control*

Devidyt syn to men that he wald lik. *Distributed then*

Strenthis and toun to Ros throuch this kynrik, *Strongholds and castles up to Ross throughout*

Baith hycht and vaill obeyed all till his will. *Both hill and glen*

As he commaund thai purpos to fullfill. *intended*

1015 The byschoprykis inclynyt till his croun, *submitted*

Bathe temperalite and all the religioun. *religious*

The Roman bukis at than was in Scotland

He gert be brocht to scham quhar thai thaim fand, *destroyed*

And but radem thai brynt thaim thar ilkan.[1]

1020 Salysbery oys our clerkis than has tan. *clerics*

The lordis he tuk that wald nocht of him hald, *owe him allegiance*

In Ingland send full nobill blud of ald.

Schyr Wilyam lang Douglace to Londe he send *London*

In strang presoun quhar throuch he maid his end.

1025 The Erll Thomas that lord was of Murray

And Lord Frysaill fra him he send away, *Fraser*

Als Hew the Hay and other ayris ma. *justices more*

He gert Wallang with thaim in Ingland ga; *go*

Na man was left all this mayn land within, *mainland*

1030 Fra Edwardis pees was knawin of ony kyn.[2]

Cetoun, Lawder dwelt still in to the Bas,

With thaim Lundy and men that worthi was.

1 And without exception they burned every one of them
2 From the time that Edward's peace was known to any kinsmen

The Erll Malcom and Cambell past but let          unhindered
In But succour with Synclar for to get.          refuge
1035 Schir Jhon Ramsay and Rowan than fled
       north
To thar cusyng that lord was of Fyllorth,          kinsman; Philorth
Quhilk past with thaim throu Murray
       landis rycht.
Sa fand thai thar a gentill worthi knycht          So found; noble
At Climace hecht, full cruell ay had beyn          That was called Climes; force
1040 And fayndyt weill amang his enemys keyn.          proved himself; fierce
He thocht never at Edwardis faith to be;          in
In till his tym he gert feill Sotheroun dee.          In his lifetime; caused many
He led thir lordis in Ros withoutyn mar;          these; delay
At the Stokfurd a stark strenth byggit thar,          strong fortress built
1045 Kepyt that land rycht worthely be wer;          Protected; from attack
Till thar enemys thai did full mekill der.          great harm
Adam Wallace and Lyndsay of Cragge
Away thai fled be nycht apon the se,
And Robert Boid quhilk was baithe wys          both
       and wicht;
1050 Arane thai tuk to fend thaim at thar mycht.          Arran; defend
The Corspatrik into Dunbar baid still;          remained
Fewte full sone he had maid Edward till.          Fealty; to
Abyrnethe, Lord Soullis and Cummyn als,          also
And Jhon of Lorn that lang had beyn full fals,
1055 The Lord Brechyn and mony other baid          remained
At Edwardis faith for gyftis he thaim maid.          In
Justen of pees for twenty dayis set he          Jousting; for a peace shield
Of Inglismen in Lorn at men mycht be
Playn to declayr, bot for this caus iwys,          reason certainly
1060 That all Scotland be conques than was his.          by conquest
The lordis than and Byschop gud Synclar
Sone out of But thai maid a ballingar[1]
To gud Wallace, tald him thar turmet haill,          entire distress
Than wrait thai thus to get bute of thar          remedy for
       baill:          suffering
1065 'Our help, our heill, our hop, our          health; hope
       governour,
Our gudly gyd, our best chyftane in stour,          battle
Our lord, our luff, our strenth, our          friend
       rychtwysnas,

1 Soon out of Bute made their way on a small ship

For Goddis saik radeym us anys to grace        redeem; once through
And tak the croun. Till us it war kyndar,        To us
1070    To bruk for ay, or fals Edward it war.'        possess [it], rather than [let]
The wryt he gat, bot yeit suffer he wald        letter
For gret falsheid that part him did of ald.
Mekill dolour it did him in his mynd        great sorrow
Of thar mysfayr, for trew he was and kynd.        misfortune
1075    He thocht to tak amendis of that wrang.        revenge for
He answerd nocht, bot in his wer furth        war proceeded
        rang.
Of King Edward yeit mar furth will I        tell
        meill,
In to quhat wys that he couth Scotland
        deill.        divide
In Sanct Jhonstoun the Erll of York he
        maid
1080    Capdane to be of all thai landis braid
Fra Tay to Dee, and undyr him Butlar.
His grantschyr had at Kynclevin endyt        grandfather
        thar,
His fader als; Wallace thaim bathe had
        slayn;
Edward tharfor maid him a man of mayn.        power
1085    The lord Bewmound in to the north he
        send.
Thai lordschippys all thai gaiff him in        assigned to him
        commend.
To Sterlyn syn fra Sanct Jhonstoun he
        went,
Thair to fulfill the layff of his entent.        rest; purpose
The lord Clyffurd he gaiff than Douglace
        daill,
1090    Rewllar to be of the South Marchis haill.
All Galloway than he gaiff Cumyn in hand:
Wyst nayn bot God how lang that stait suld        None knew but
        stand.
The gentill lord, gud byschop Lammyrtoun
Of Sanct Androws, had Douglace of
        renoun.
1095    Befor that tyme Jamys, wicht and wys,
Till him was cummyn fra scullis of Parys.
A preva favour the bischop till him bar;
Bot Inglismen was so gret maisteris thar

He durst nocht weill in playn schaw him kindnes,                                          *openly*
1100  Quhill on a day he tuk sum hardines.              *got up courage*
Douglace he cald and couth to Sterlyng fayr,
Quhar King Edward was deland landis thair.                                            *dividing*
He proferd him in to the kingis service
To bruk his awin; fra he wist in this wys        *possess as; when; knew*
1105  Douglace he was, than he forsuk planle,
Swor, 'Be Sanct George, he brukis na landis of me!                                      *possesses*
His fader was in contrar of my crown,          *opposition to*
Tharfor as now he bidis in our presoun.'             *stays*
To the byschop nane other grant he maid,
1110  Bot as he plesd delt furth thai landis braid.      *wide*
To the lord Soullis all haill the Mers gaiff he
And captane als of Berweik for to be.
Olyfant than, that he in Stirlyng fand,
Quhen he him had he wald nocht kep his band,
1115  The quhilk he maid or he him Stirlyng gaiff.                                             *before*
Desaitfully thus couth he him dissayff:          *Deceitfully*
In till Ingland send him till presoun strang;
In gret distres he levyt thar full lang.
Quhen Edward king had delt all this regioun,
1120  His leyff he tuk, in Ingland maid him boun.
Out of Stirlyng southward as thai couth ryd
Cumyn hapnyt ner hand the Bruce to bid.           *Comyn*
Thus said he, 'Schir, and yhe couth keip consaill
I can schaw her quhilk may be your availl.'        *advantage*
1125  The Bruce answerd, 'Quhat ever yhe say to me
As for my part sall weill conseillyt be.'
Lord Cumyn said, 'Schir, knaw ye nocht this thing,
That of this realm ye suld be rychtwys king?'

Than said the Bruce, 'Suppos I rychtwys      rightful
           be
1130   I se no tym to tak sic thing on me.
       I am haldin in to my enemys hand
       Undyr gret ayth, quhen I com in Scotland
       Nocht part fra him for profyt nor request,   Not to
       Na for na strenth bot gyff ded me arest.     death; stop
1135   He hecht agayn to gyff this land to me.       promised
       Now fynd I weill it is bot sutelte,           deception
       For thus thou seis he delys myn heretage      apportions
       To Sotheroun part, and sum to traytouris
           wage.'
       Than Cumyn said, 'Will ye her to accord,      agree
1140   Of my landys and ye lik to be lord,
       Ye sall thaim have for your rycht of the      in exchange; claim
           croun;
       Or and ye lik, schir, for my warisoun         if; reward
       I sall you help with power at my mycht.'
       The Bruce answerd, 'I will nocht sell my
           rycht.
1145   Bot on this wys, quhat lordschip thou will
           craiff
       For thi supple I hecht thou sall it haiff.'    assistance; vow
       'Cum fra yon king, schir, with sum jeperte.    stratagem
       Now Edward has all Galloway geyffyn to me.
       My nevo Soullis, that kepis Berweik toun,
1150   At your commaund this power sall be boun.
       My nevo als, a man of mekill mycht,
       The lord of Lorn has rowme in to the          space; the highlands
           hycht.
       My thrid nevo, a lord of gret renoun,
       Will rys with us, of Breichin the barroun.'
1155   Than said the Bruce, 'Fell thar sa far a       fain
           chance
       That we micht get agane Wallace of            from
           France;
       Be witt and force he couth this kynryk wyn.
       Allace we haiff our lang beyn haldyn in        too long
           twyn!'
       To that langage Cumyn maid na record,         speech; reply
1160   Of ald deidis in till his mynd remord.         old deals; remorse
       The Bruce and he completyt furth thar
           bande,

Syn that sammyn nycht thai sellyt with thar    sealed
   hande.
This ragment left the Bruce with Cumyn    bond
   thar;
With King Edward haym in Ingland can    went
   far
1165  And thar remaynyt quhill this ragment war    until; indenture
   knawin,
Thre yer and mar or Bruce persewyt his    pursued
   awin.    own [claim]
Sum men demys that Cumyn that ragment    consider
   send;
Sum men tharfor agaynys makis defend.
Nayn may say weill Cumyn was saklasing    guiltless
1170  Becaus his wiff was Edwardis ner cusing.    cousin
He servyt dede be rycht law of his king,    deserved death
So raklesly myskepyt sic a thing.    failed to keep
Had Bruce past by but baid to Sanct    immediately
   Jhonstoun
Be haill assent he had rasavyt the croune.
1175  On Cumyn syn he mycht haiff done the    applied
   law.
He couth nocht thoill fra tym that he him    endure
   saw,
Thus Scotland left in hard perplexite.
Of Wallace mar in sum part spek will we.

## BOOK TWELVE

The sayr travaill, the ernystfull besynas,    hard endeavour; earnest
The feill labour he had in mony place    great
To wyn the land at the gud king him gaiff!
In till his ryng he wald no Sotheroun saiff.    During; government
5  In Gyan land Wallace was still at wer.
Of Scotlandis los it did his hart gret der.    injury
Of trew Scottis in mynd he had pete;    pity
He thocht to help quhen he his tym mycht
    se.
Of set battaillis fyve he dyscumfyt haill,    won completely
10  But jeperte and mony strang assaill.    Excluding surprise attacks
Syn thai forsuk and durst him nocht abid.    withstand
The Sotheroun fled fra him on ather sid.    every side
To Burdeous in gret multiplye    Bordeaux; numbers
Than com thai stufft with victaill be the se.    furnished; sea
15  All Gyan land Wallace brocht till his pees.
To Burdeous yit he past or he wald ces.    before
On out byggyngis full gret maistre thai    buildings; feats of arms
    maid;
Still saxte dayis at sar sailye thai baid.    hard attack; waited
Fortrace and werk that was without the toun    buildings; outside
20  Thai brak and brynt and put to confusioun;    destroyed
Hagis, alais, be laubour that was thar    Hedges; alleys
Fulyeit and spilt, thai wald no froitis spar.    Beat down; demolished
The Inglismen maid gret defens agayn
With schot and cast, for thai war mekill of    missiles; powerful
    mayn.
25  Of gounnys thai war and ganyeis stuffyt
    weill,[1]
All artailye and wapynnys of fyn steill,    artillery
With men and meit within war buskit beyn.    prepared
Thar gret capdane was wys, cruell and keyn,    fierce
Of Glosyster that huge lord and her.    chief
30  This erll had beyn weill usyt in to wer,    experienced in war
Kepyt his men be wit and hardement.    Protected; courage
Without the toun thar durst nane fra him    Out of
    went.
The landis without wer ner waistyt away,    outside
Wermen so lang in to the contre lay.    warriors

---

1 They were well equipped with guns and crossbows

35  In Wallace ost so scantyt the victaill — the food grew so scarce
    Thai mycht nocht bid na langar till assaill. — attack
    Than this wis lord, the Duk of Orlyance, — wise
    To Wallace said, 'Schir, ye suld knaw this
        chance.
    It standis our weill with thir fals Sotheroun — too
        blud,
40  For on no wayis we can nocht stop thar
        fud.
    The havin thai haiff and schippis at thar — haven
        will;
    Of Ingland cummys enewch of victaill
        thaim till.
    This land is purd of fud that suld us beild, — destitute; food; nourish
    And ye se weill als thai forsaik the field.
45  Thai will nocht fecht thocht we all yher — fight; year
        suld bid.
    Ye may of pes plenys thir landis wid. — stock
    My consaill is in playn anent this thing, — completely in respect of
    At ye wald pas with worschip to the king. — honour
    Be his assent ye may at lasar vaill — leisure choose
50  With provisioun agayn for till assaill.' — provisions
    Wallace inclynd and thankit this wys lord. — bowed
    Than thai tranontyt all in a gud concord, — marched
    Past up in France with honour to the king
    And schawit him haill the verite of this thing,
55  And he tharof in hart was wonder glaid. — extremely
    Franch men befor that a hundred yer nocht — a hundred years before
        haid
    Of Gyan halff sa mekill in to thar hand. — in their control
    Wrytting be than was new cumyn of — newly come from
        Scotland,
    Fra part of lordis and byschop gud Synclar, — some of the lords
60  Besocht the king into thar termys fair, — Beseeched
    Of his gentrice and of his gudlye grace, — nobility
    For thar supple to consaill gud Wallace — assistance
    To cum agayne and bryng thaim of — out of subjection
        bandoun,
    And tak to wer the croun of that regioun.
65  This wrytt as than he wald nocht till hym
        schwa. — show
    Rycht laith he war for frendschip, feid or — reluctant; enmity
        aw, — fear

Wallace suld pas sa son fra his presens.                soon
Ane dwelling place he tuk to residens;
In Schynnoun still Wallace his dwelling
   maid
70  And held about rycht likand landis braid.          possessed; pleasant
A keyn capdane than clemyt in heritage              cruel; claimed
Office of it and gret landis in wage,               Feudal service; payment
Tharfor he thocht gud Wallace for to sla.
Undyr colour sic maistre for to ma[1]
75  Lang tym he socht to get a day and place,
Said he desyrd in service to Wallace.
A tryst thai set with sixteen on the sid.           meeting
Fyfty thar by he gert in buschement byd            ambush; lie
Of men in armys. Quhen he with Wallace
   met
80  Rycht awfully he bad thaim on him set.           formidably
Na armour had Wallace men in to that
   place
Bot swerd and knyff thai bur on thaim              carried
   throu grace.
Parteis beyn met ner a fayr forest sid.            The parties
Rycht boustously this capdane said that tyd        menacingly; time
85  At Wallace held of his landis unrycht.           That; wrongfully
Rycht sobyrly he said to that Franch knycht:
'I haiff no land bot quhilk the king gaiff me.
My lyff tharfor has beyne in jeperte.'             jeopardy
The knycht answerd, 'Thi lyff thou sall
   forlorn                                          lose
90  Or ellis that land the contrar quha had          whoever swore the contrary
   sworn.'
On bak he lap and out his swerd he drew;           Back; leapt
The buschement brak quhen he that takyn            ambush; signal gave
   schew.
Gud Wallace thocht that mater stud nocht
   weill.
He gryppyt sone a scherand swerd of steill         trenchant
95  And at a straik the knycht to ded he draiff.     drove
About sixteen sone lappyt all the layff.           encircled; rest
Wallace and his so worthely thai wrocht,
Full feill thai slew that sarest on thaim          many; hardest
   socht.                                           attacked

1 Under pretence to accomplish such a deed

The knychtis brodyr rycht stalwart was and
   strang
100 And thocht he suld be vengyt or thai gang.   *avenged; before; went*
Of Wallace men sum part thai woundyt
   sair.   *severely*
Mawand thar was in till a medow fair   *Mowing*
Nine stout carllis, all servandis to that   *peasants*
   knycht.
Sythis thai hynt and ran in all thar mycht   *Scythes; seized*
105 To the fechtaris. Or thai com ner that place   *fighters; Before*
Of thaim persavyt rycht weill was gud
   Wallace.
Sa awfull thing of sic he nevir saw.
Thaim to rasyst him selff can to thaim   *resist*
   draw,
In to the stour left his men fechtand still   *fighting*
110 To meit thai carllis that com with egyr will.
The fyrst leit draw at Wallace with his sith;   *struck*
Deliver he was and heich our lappyt swyth   *jumped quickly*
And awkwart straik that churl apon the   *crosswise*
   hed.
Derffly on ground he has him left for ded.
115 The tothir he met our lap his syth so keyn,   *leapt over*
On the schulder als straik him in that teyn.   *anger*
Throuch all the cost the noble swerd doun   *ribs*
   schair.   *cut*
The thrid he met with a rycht awfull fayr;   *bearing*
The groundyn syth at Wallace he leit drall.   *sharp scythe; struck*
120 This gud chyftan cleynly our lap thaim all;   *jumped over*
With his gud swerd he maid a hidwys
   wound,
Left thaim for ded syne on the ferd can
   found;   *advanced*
On the wan bayn with gret ire can him ta,   *cheekbone; struck him*
Cleyffyt the cost rycht cruelly in twa.   *Split; rib*
125 Thre formast sythis thus gud Wallace our
   lap
And four he slew; thai saw sic was his hap:   *fortune*
A man he slew ay at a straik.   *ever*
The layff fled fast, thus can the power
   slaik.
Wallace folowed and sone the fyrst our tais,   *overtakes*
130 Straik him to ded that na forthyr he gais,

Syn sped him fast till his awn men again.            .

Be than thai had the knychtis brother slayn.         By then

Sexte and six sixteen to ded has dycht,              killed

Bot saiff seven men at fled out of thar             Except
    sycht.

135   Five malwaris als that Wallace selff with        mowers
        met.

To Franch men syn na sic trystis he set             With; thereafter; such

Be caus at thai him brocht to sic a cace.

The king hard tell weill chapyt was                 heard; escaped safely
    Wallace,

Send for him sone and prayit him for to be

140   Of his houshald, so leyff in gud saufte,          live; safety

For weill he saw thai had him at invye.

Still with him selff he gert him bid forthi.         caused him to stay therefore

Twa yeris thus wytht myrth Wallace abaid             with

Still in to Frans and mony gud jornay               feats of arms
    maid.

145   The king him plessed in all his gudly mayn;       power

Fra him he thocht he suld nocht part agayn.

Lordys and ladiis honoryd him reverently,

Wrechys and schrewis ay had him at invy.

Twa campiouns that tyme dwelt with the              champions
    king

150   Had gret despyt at Wallace in all thing.

Togidder ay yeid thir twa campiouns,                went

Of felloun fors and frawart attenciouns.[1]

Rycht gret despyt thai spak oft of Scotland

Quhill on a day it hapnyt apon hand                 Until

155   Wallace and thai was levit all thaim allayn,       left

Be aventur in till a hous of stayne.                chance; stone

Thai oysyt to ber na wapynnys in that hall,         used

Thai trowyt tharfor a mys thai mycht nocht          believed; wrong
    fall.

Thar commound thai of Scotland scornfully.          talked

160   Than Wallace said, 'Ye wrang us outragely,        outrageously

Sen we ar bound in frendschip to your              Since
    kyng

And he of us is plessed in all thing.

Als Scottis men has helpyth this realm of           out of danger
    dreid.

1 Of terrible strength and perverse intentions

Me think ye suld geyff gud word for gud    *give*
    deid.'
165 'Quhat may ye spek of your enemys bot ill?'
In lychtlynes thai maid answer him till,    *scorn*
And him dispysyt in thar langage als.
'Ye Scottis,' thai said, 'has evir yit beyne
    fals.'
Wallace tuk ane on the face in his teyn    *struck; anger*
170 Wytht his gud hand, quhill nes, mouth and    *With; until*
    eyn,
Throuch the braith blaw all byrstyt out of    *violent blow; gushed with*
    blud.
Butles to ground he smat him quhar he    *Helpless; dashed*
    stud.
The tother hynt to Wallace in that sted,    *drew*
For weill he wend his falow had beyn ded,    *thought*
175 And he agayn in greiff him grippyt sayr    *anger; tight*
Quhill spretis failyeid, ner he mycht do no    *Until; almost*
    mayr.
The fyrst frek rais and smat on Wallace    *man; struck*
    fast.
Bathe to the ded he brocht thaim at the last.
Apon a pillar thair harnys out he dang,    *brains; dashed*
180 Bot with his handis syn out at the dur    *flung*
    thaim flang.
And said, 'Quhat devyll movyt yon churllys    *moved*
    at me?
Lang tyme in France I wald haiff lattyn
    thaim be.'
Traistis for trewth thus war thai ded in    *Believe it truly; indeed*
    deid,
Thocht Franchmen now likis it nocht to reid.    *read*
185 Als I will ces and put it nocht in rym:
Better thar is quha rycht can luk the tym.    *choose*
Mony gret lord was displessyd in Frans
Bot the gud king that knew all haill the chans    *all about the case*
Oft gret dispyt of Scotland spokyn had thai.
190 This passyt our quhill efter a nother day    *over until*
Was nayn of thaim at durst it undertak.    *dared*
He had done wrang nor tharfor battaill
    mak.[1]

1 He was wrong not to insist on battle for this

This ryoll roy a hie worschip him gaiff,                    king; honour
As conquerour him honowryd our the layff          above; rest
195  A fell lyoun the king had gert be brocht                  fierce
Within a barrace, for gret harm that he               Behind barriers
     wrocht,
Terlyst in yrn na mar power him gaiff.                    Caged
Of wodnes he excedyt all the layff,                         wildness
Bot he was fayr and rycht felloun in deid.         cruel
200  In that strang strenth the king gert men               pen
     him feid,                                                                 feed
Kepyt him clos fra folk and bestiall.                      locked away; animals
In the court dwelt twa squieris of gret               importance
     vaill,
At cusyngis war on to thir campiounis twa,    That were cousins of
The quhilk befor Wallace hapnyt to sla.
205  A band thai maid in preva illusioun                       pact; private deception
At thar power to wyrk his confusioun                   bring about his death
Be ony meyn, throu frawd or sutelte.                  means
Efter tharfor thai roucht nocht for to de,         cared not if they died
To ded or schaym sa that thai mycht him         [As long as]; death
     bring.
210  Apon a tym thai went on to the king.
'This man,' thai said, 'at ye sa welthfull              that
     mak,
He seis nocht her bot he wald undertak              sees nothing here
Be his gret fors to put to confusioun.                   By; strength; death
Now he desyris to fecht on your lyoun,             fight
215  And bad us ask at you this battaill strang,
Ye grant him leyff in that barrace to gang.'    enclosure
Sadly agayn to thaim answerd the king:              Gravely
'Sayr me forthinkis at he desiris sic thing,         I sorely regret
Bot I will nothir for greyff nor gret                     anger
     plesance
220  Deny Wallace quhat he desiris of France.'
Than went thai furth and sone met with
     Wallace.
A fygourd taill thai tald hym of this cace.          false tale
'Wallace,' thai said, 'the king desiris that
     ye
Doren battaill sa cruell be to se                               Engage in
225  And chargis you to fecht on his lioun.'
Wallace answerd in haisty conclusioun,
And said, 'I sall quhat be the kingis will           I shall [do]

At my power rycht glaidly to fulfill.'    *Within*
Than passyt he on to the king but mair.    *without delay*
230 A lord of court, quhen he approchyt thar,
Unwisytly sperd withoutyn provisioun,    *Unwisely asked; forethought*
'Wallace, dar ye go fecht on our lioun?'    *with*
And he said, 'Ya, so the king suffer me,
Or on your selff gyff ye ocht better be.'
235 Quhat will ye mar? This thing amittyt was,    *granted*
That Wallace suld on to the lyoun pas.
The king thaim chargyt to bryng him gud harnas,    *armour*
And he said, 'Nay, God scheild me fra sic cas.
I wald tak weid suld I fecht with a man,    *armour; were I fighting*
240 Bot for a dog that nocht of armes can    *knows nothing of arms*
I will haiff nayn bot synglar as I ga.'    *go as I am*
A gret manteill about his hand can ta
And his gud swerd, with him he tuk na mar;
Abandounly in barrace entryt thar.    *Boldly; the cage*
245 Gret chenys was wrocht in the yet with a gyn    *gate / device*
And puld it to quhen Wallace was tharin.
The wod lyoun on Wallace quhar he stud    *wild*
Rampand he braid, for he desyryt blud,    *Rearing he sprang up*
With his rud pollis in the mantill rocht sa.    *paws*
250 Awkwart the bak than Wallace can him ta    *Across; strike*
With his gud swerd that was of burnyst steill;
His body in twa it thruschyt everilk deill.    *cleft*
Syn to the kyng he raykyt in gret ire,    *went*
And said on lowd, 'Was this all your desyr,    *aloud*
255 To wayr a Scot thus lychtly in to wayn?    *waste; scornfully; vain*
Is thar ma doggis at ye wald yeit haiff slayn?
Go bryng thaim furth sen I mon doggis qwell,
To do byddyng quhill that I with you dwell.
It gaynd full weill I graithit me to Scotland;    *It would be very fitting; returned*
260 Fer grettar deidis thair men has apon hand
Than with a dog in battaill to escheiff.    *achieve [victory]*

At you in France for ever I tak my leiff.'  From

The king persavyt Wallace agrevyt was,  resentful

So ernystfully he askyt leiff to pas.

265 Rewid in his mynd at it was hapnyt sa,  Regretted

Sa lewd a deid to lat him undyrta,  base

Knawand the worschip and the gret  honour
  nobilnace

Of him quhilk sprang that tym in mony  was famous
  place.

Humblely he said, 'Ye suld disples you  should not be displeased
  nocht.

270 This ye desyryt; it movyt never in my  never occurred to me
  thocht.

And be the faith I aw the croun of France  owe

I thocht never to charge you with sic  such a venture
  chance,

Bot men of vaill at askyt it for you.'  standing

Wallace answerd, 'That God I mak a vow,  Before God

275 I likyt never sic battaill to be in:

Apon a dog no worschip is to wyn.'

The king consavyt how this falsheid was  understood
  wrocht.

The squiers bath was till his presens
  brocht,

Coud nocht deny quhen thai com him
  befor.

280 All thar trespas thai tald withoutyn mor.  wrongdoing; delay

The king commaundyt thai suld be don to  put to death
  ded,

Smat off thar hedys without ony rameid.  Struck

The campiounis, lo, for invy causlace,  malice

To sodand dede Wallace thaim brocht
  throu cace.

285 The squiers als, fra thar falsheid was kend,  deception; known

Invy thaim brocht bathe till a sodand end.

Lordis behald, Invy the wyle dragoun,  wily

In cruell fyr he byrnys his regioun:

For he is nocht that bonde is in Invy.  nothing

290 To sum myscheiff it bryngis hym haistely.

Forsaik Invy, thou sall the better speid.

Herof as now I will no forther reid,  advise

Bot in my mater as I of for began  before

I sall conteyn als playnly as I can.  continue

295 Quhen Wallace saw thai had him at invy,          malice towards him
    Langar to byd he coud thaim nocht apply.         agree
    Better him thocht in Scotland for to be
    And awnter tak other to leiff or de.             take the chance either
    Till help his awn he had a mar plesance          greater pleasure
300 Than thar to byd with all the welth of
        France.
    Thus his haill mynd, manheid and hye
        curage,
    Was playnly set to wyn out of bondage
    Scotland agayn, fra payn and felloun sor.        cruel suffering
    He woude he suld, or ellis de tharfor.           wished; should
305 The king has seyn how gud Wallace was
        set,                                         determined
    The letter than him gaiff withoutyn let,         delay
    The quhilk of lait fra Scotland was him          lately
        send.
    Wallace it saw and weill thar harmys kend        learned
    Be the fyrst wryt tharto accordiall.             agreeing
310 Thaim to supple he thocht he wald nocht          help
        fall.                                        fail
    Quhar to suld I herof lang proces mak?           account
    Wallace of France a gudly leiff can tak.
    The kyng has seyn it wald nocht ellis be,
    To chawmer went and mycht nocht on him
        se,
315 Gret languor tuk quhen Wallace can
        ramuff.                                      left
    That king till him kepit kyndnes and luff.       showed
    Jowallis and gold his worschip for to saiff      honour
    He bad thaim geyff, als mekill as he wald        give
        haiff.
    Lordys and ladyis wepyt wonder fast
320 Quhen Wallace thar so tuk his leyff and
        past.
    Na men he tuk bot quhilk he hydder               those; thither
        brocht.
    Agayn with him gud Longaweill furth              went forth
        socht;
    For payn nor blys that gud knycht left him       joy
        never,
    For cace befell, quhill ded maid thaim           Whatever happened; until;
        desever.                                         separate

325 Towart the Sluce a gudly fer past he,   *company*
    A veschell gat and maid him to the se;   *ship*
    Eight schipmen feit and gudly wage thaim gaiff,   *hired*
    To Scotland fur, the Fyrth of Tay thai haiff.   *went* / *have docked*
    Apon a nycht Wallace the land has tane
330 At Ernys mouth and is till Elchok gane.
    He gert the schip in covert saill away,   *secret*
    So out of sycht thai war or it was day.   *before*
    At Elchok dwelt ane, Wallace cusyng der,
    At Crawfurd hecht. Quhen thai the hous com ner,   *That was called Crawford*
335 On the baksyd Wallace a window fand
    And in he cald; sone Crawfurd com at hand.   *near*
    Fra tym he wyst that it was gud Wallace   *knew*
    In till his bern he ordand thaim a place.   *barn; prepared*
    A mow of corn he gyhyt thaim about   *heap; arranged around them*
340 And closyt weill, nane mycht persave without,   *shut up* / *outside*
    Bot at a place quhar meit he to thaim brocht,
    And bedyn to, als glaidly as he mocht.   *bedding too*
    A dern holl furth on the north syd thai had   *concealed hole*
    To the watter, quhar of Wallace was glad.   *On the water side*
345 Four dayis or five in rest thai sojornd thar,
    Quhill meit was gayn; than Crawfurd bound for mar   *Until* / *set out*
    Till Sanct Jhonstoun, thar purvyance for to by.   *buy*
    Inglismen thocht he tuk mar boundandly   *plentifully*
    Than he was wount at ony tym befor.   *he usually did*
350 Thai haiff him tane, put him in presone sor.   *seized; harsh*
    Quhat gestis he had, to tell thai mak raquest.   *guests; they asked him to tell*
    He said it was bot till a kyrkyn fest,   *churching feast*
    Yeit thai preiff sone the cumyng of Wallace.   *arrival*
    Knawlage to get thai kest a sutell cace:   *devised a cunning plan*
355 Thai latt him pas with thing that he had bocht,   *bought*

Syn efter sone in all the haist thai mocht     Then soon after
To harnes yeid the power of the toun.     arm went; army
Eight hundreth men with Butler maid
  thaim boun,     ready
Folowid on dreich quhill at this man com
hame.     at a distance
360 Wallace him saw and said he servit blame.     deserved
'In my sleping a fell visioun me tauld     disastrous
Till Inglismen that thou suld me haiff
sauld.'     betrayed
Crawfurd him said he had bene turment sair     tormented severely
With Inglismen that had him in dispair.
365 'Tharfor rys up and for sum succour se.     help
I dreid full sair thai set wachis on me.'     fear; spies
The worthi Scottis thai graithit thaim in
gud weid,     dressed
Thar wapynnys tuk, syn of that hous furth
yeid.     went out
Thus sodandly the fell Sotheroun thai saw;     fierce
370 To few thai war to bid agayn thaim aw     Too; stand
At keynly com with yong Butler the
knycht.     eagerly
Than Wallace said, 'A playn feild is nocht
rycht,     open battlefield
Bot Elchok park is ner hand her besid.
The fyrst sailye we think thar to abyd.     attack; await
375 Nineteen thai war and Crawfurd with gud
will
The twentyd man the nowmer to fulfill.     twentieth; made up
The park thai tuk. Wallace a place has seyn
Of gret holyns that grew bathe heych and
greyn.     holly trees; high
With thwortour treis a maner strenth maid
he;     trees laid crosswise; kind of stronghold
380 Or that war wone thai trowit to gar feill de.     Before; conquered; expected
The wod was thyk bot litill of breid or
lenth;     breadth
Had thai had meit thai thocht to hald that
strenth.
The Inglismen passyt to Crawfurdys place,
Fand in the bern the lugeyng of Wallace.     Found
385 Than Crawfurdis wyff in handys haiff thai
tane     in custody

And ast at hyr quhat way the Scottis war gane.   *asked*

Rycht weill thai trowyt at Wallace suld thar be,

Of France in Tay he was cumyn be the se.   *Out of; by*

Scho wald nocht tell for bost nor yeit reward.   *threat*

390 Than Butler said, 'Our lang thou has beyn spard.'   *Too long*

Tharwith he grew in matelent in ire   *wrath; anger*

And gert thaim byg a bailfull, braid, brym fyr.   *build; woeful; big; fierce*

The Sotheroun swor tharin scho suld brynt be.   *burned*

Than Wallace said, 'Scho sall nocht end for me.   *She*

395 Gret syn it war yon saikles wicht to sla.   *innocent creature; slay*

Or scho suld end in faith thar sall de ma.'   *Before; more*

He left the strenth and the playn feild can ta.   *open* / *entered*

On lowd he criyt and said, 'Lo, her I ga.   *Aloud*

Thinkis thou no schaym for to turment a wyff?

400 Cum fyrst to me and mak end of our stryff.'

Fra Butler had apon gud Wallace seyn   *From when*

Throuch auld malice he wox ner wod for teyn.   *grew; mad with anger*

Apon the Scottis schup thaim all with gret mayn,   *set* / *force*

Bot Wallace son the strenth he tuk again.   *soon*

405 A fell bykkyr the Inglismen began,   *battle*

Assailyeid sayr with mony cruell man,   *Attacked fiercely*

Bot thai within war nobill at defens,

Maid gret debait be force and violens.   *resistance*

At that entra fifteen thai brocht to ded;   *entrance*

410 Than all the lave ramovit fra that sted,   *rest; removed; place*

Yeid till aray agayn to sailye new.   *Rallied again; assail anew*

Wallace beheld quhilk weill in weir him knew.   *knew a lot about war*

'Falowis,' he said, 'agayn all at this place

Thai will nocht saill; bot thus standis the cace:   *attack*

415  Yon knycht thinkis for to devid his men            divide
     In seir parties, the suth ye sall weill ken,        several parties; know
     Agayn on us to preiff how it may be.
     Us worthis now sum wayis for thaim to se,           We must
     Contrar thar mycht a gud defens to mak.             Against
420  Now Longaweill thou sall sex with thee tak.         six
     Wilyam my eym, als mony sall with you ga,
     And five with me, as now we haiff no ma.'           more
     Knycht Butler than partyt his men in thre.          divided
     Wallace wesyd quhar Butler schup to be;             inspected; proceeded
425  Thidder he past that entre for to wer.              defend
     On ilka syd thai sailye with gret fer.             attacked; company
     Wallace leit part in the entre begyn                allowed; come in
     Bot nane yeid out that on the Scottis com           went in
        in.
     Seven formast was quhilk in the forest yeid.        went
430  Wallace five men quhilk douchty was in              brave
        deid,
     Ilkane slew ane and Wallace gert twa de.            Each one
     Butler was vext and said, 'This will nocht          angered
        be.'
     On bak he drew and leit his curage slaik.           drew back; lessen
     The worthi Scottis prevyt weill for
        Scotlandis saik.
435  Gud Longaweill his counter maid sa sar              counter-attack; fierce
     And Crawfurd als, thai sailyeid than no             attacked
        mar.
     Rycht ner be than approchyt to the nycht
     And sternys up peyr began in to thair sycht.        stars; appear
     Sotheroun set wach and to thar souper               appointed sentries; supper
        went.
440  The Butler was sayr grevyt in his entent,           extremely angry
     Yeit fur thai weill of stuff, wyn, aill and         fared well; provisions
        breid.
     Wallace and his thai wyst of no rameid              knew; help
     Bot cauld watter that ran throu out a
        strand.                                          stream
     In that lugeyng nane other fud thai fand.
445  Than Wallace said, 'Gud falowis, think              do not weary
        nocht lang.
     Will God, we sall be sone out of this
        thrang.                                          press
     Suppos we fast a day our and a nycht,               over a day

Tak all in thank this payn for Scotlandis
   rycht.'                                      *suffering*

The Erll of York, was in Sanct Jhonstoun
   still,

450 To Butler send and bad him byd at will;       *await his pleasure*

Till him full sone thar suld cum new power       *reinforcements*

And als himselff thus tald the messynger.        *the messenger reported*

Butler wald fayn Wallace had yoldyn beyn         *have been glad; surrendered*

Or the erll com, for thir causis was seyn,       *Before*

455 His grant schir bathe and his fadyr he slew.

This knycht tharwith towart the park him
   drew.

Quhat cher thai maid, apon the Scottis           *cheer*
   cald.

Than Wallace said, 'Fer better than thou
   wald.'

The Butler said, 'I wald fayn spek with          *gladly*
   thee.'

460 Wallace answerd, 'Thou may for litill fe.'      *payment*

'Wallace,' he said, 'thou has done me gret
   scaith.                                       *harm*

My rycht fadyr and grant schir thou slew
   baith.'

Than Wallace said, 'For stait at thou art in

It war my det for till undo thi kyn.             *duty; destroy*

465 I think als, sa God of hevin me saiff,

At my twa handis sall graith thee to thi         *That; send you*
   graiff.'                                      *grave*

The Butler said, 'That is nocht likly now.

In my credence and thou will fermly trow,        *if; believe*

Of this I ask and thou will mak me grant,

470 Quhat I thee hecht that thing thou sall        *promise; lack*
   nocht want.'

'Sa furth,' quod he, 'be thi desyr reasonable    *Say*

I sall it grant, withoutyn ony fable.'           *lie*

The Butler said, 'Wallace, thou knawis
   rycht,

Thou may nocht chaip for power nor for           *escape; force or cunning*
   slycht;

475 And sen thou seis it may no better be          *since; sees*

For thi gentrice thou will yeild thee to me.'    *honour*

Than Wallace said, 'Thi will unskillfull is.     *unreasonable*

Thou wald I did quhilk is our hie a mys.         *what; great a wrong*

|     | Text | Gloss |
| --- | --- | --- |
|     | Yoldin I am to better, I can pruff, | In submission; prove |
| 480 | To mychty God that makar is abuff; | above |
|     | For everilk day sen I had wit of man | every; been a grown man |
|     | Befor my werk to yeild me I began, | submit myself |
|     | And als at evyn quhen that I failyeid lycht | in the evening; lacked |
|     | I me betuk to the Makar of mycht.' | committed myself |
| 485 | The Butler said, 'Me think thou has done weill; | |
|     | Yeit of a thing I pray thee lat me feill. | tell me |
|     | For thi manheid this forthwart to me fest, | promise; confirm |
|     | Quhen that thou seis thou may no langer lest, | endure |
|     | On this ilk place quhilk I haiff tane to wer | battle |
| 490 | At thou cum furth and all other forber.' | spare |
|     | Than Wallace leuch at his cruell desyr | laughed |
|     | And said, 'I sall, thocht thou war wod as fyr | fierce as fire |
|     | And all Ingland contrar tharof had sworn. | had sworn the contrary |
|     | I sall cum out at that ilk place to morn, | |
| 495 | Or ellys tonycht, traist weill quhat I thee say. | trust; say to you |
|     | I byd nocht her quhill nine houris of the day.' | past nine [in the morning] |
|     | Butler send furth the chak wache on ilka syd. | patrol |
|     | In that ilk place bauldly he bounyt to bid. | prepared; stay |
|     | Thus still thai baid quhill day began to peyr. | waited until / dawn |
| 500 | A thyk myst fell the planet was nocht cleyr. | i.e., the sun; bright |
|     | Wallace assayd at all placis about, | attacked |
|     | Leit as he wald at ony place brek out, | Pretended as if he would |
|     | Quhill Butleris men sum part fra him can ga | |
|     | To helpe the lave. Quhen thai saw it was sa | rest; so |
| 505 | Wallace and his fast sped thaim to that sted. | place |
|     | Quhar Butler baid feill men thai draiff to ded. | stood many; dashed / death |
|     | The worthy Scottis sone past throcht that melle. | |
|     | Crawfurd, thar oyst, was sayr hurt on the kne. | leader |

At erd he was. Gud Wallace turnd again     *On the ground*

510 And at a straik he has the Butler slayn,     *stroke*

Hynt up that man under his arm sa strang,     *Lifted*

Defendand him out of that felloun thrang.     *terrible*

Gud rowm he maid amang thaim quhar he gais.     *gaps*

With his rycht hand he slew five of thair fais,     *foes*

515 Bur furth Crawfurd be force of his persoune     *Carried*

Nine akyrbreid or ever he set him doun.     *Nine acres before*

The Sotheroun fand at thar capdane was ded,     *discovered*

All him about bot than was no rameid.     *remedy*

Thirty with him of the wychtast thai brocht     *strongest*

520 Ded at that place quhar at the Scottis furth socht.     *went out*

Wallace and his be than was of thar sycht;     *out of*

Sotheroun baid still for sor los of that knycht.     *stayed; sad loss*

The myst wes myrk, that Wallace likit weill.

Him selff was gyd and said to Longaweill,     *the guide*

525 'At Meffan wood is my desyr to be,

On bestiall thar for meit that we may se.'     *beasts*

Be than thai war weill cumyn to the hicht.     *By then; high ground*

The myst scalyt, the son schawyt fayr and brycht.     *went away; shone*

Son war thai war a litill space thaim by,     *aware; distance from them*

530 Four and twenty was in a company.

Than Wallace said, 'Be yon men freynd or fa,

We will to thaim, sen at thai ar na ma.'     *[go] to them; since*

Quhen thai com ner a nobill knycht it was,

The quhilk to name hecht Elys of Dundas,     *was called*

535 And Schyr Jhon Scot ek a worthi knycht,     *also*

In to Straithern a man of mekill mycht,

For thar he had gret part of heritage.

Dundas syster he had in marriage.

Passand thai war, and mycht no langar lest,     *last*

540 Till Inglismen thar fewte for to fest.     *allegiance; confirm*

Lord of Breichyn sic connand had thaim maid

Of Edward thai suld hald thar landys braid;     *wide*

Bot fra thai saw that it was wicht Wallace     when
Heyffyt up thar handis and thankit God of     [They] threw up
   grace
545 Of his gret help, quhilk he had sende thaim
   thair.
To Meffen wod with ane assent thai far,     went
Sone gat thaim meit of bestiall at thai fand,     that
Restyt that day; quhen nycht was cumyn on
   hand
To Byrnane wod but restyng ar thai gayne,     without stopping; gone
550 Quhar thai haiff found the squier gud
   Ruwayn;
In utlaw oys he had lang levyt thair     As an outlaw; lived
On bestiall quhill he mycht get no mair.
Thai taryit nocht bot in till Adell yeid     Atholl went
Quhar mete was scant. Than Wallace had     in short supply; anxiety
   gret dreid,
555 Past in till Lorn and rycht litill fand thair.
Of wyld and taym that contre was maid bayr.
Bot in strenthis thar fud was levyt nayn.[1]
The worthi Scottis than maid a petous     lament
   mayn.
Schyr Jhon Scot said he had fer levir de     far rather die
560 In till gud naym and leyff his ayris fre     with his good name intact
Than for till byd as bond in subjeccioun.     bound in subjection
Quhen Wallace saw thir gud men of renoun
With hungyr stad, almast mycht leiff no     stricken; live; longer
   mar,
Wyt ye for thaim he sichit wondyr sar.     Be sure; sighed; deeply
565 'Gud men,' he said, 'I am the caus of this.
At your desyr I sall amend this mys,     wrong
Or leyff you fre sum chevysans for to ma.'     leave; provision
All him allayn he bounyt fra thaim to ga,     All alone; prepared
Prayit thaim to byd quhill he mycht cum     wait until
   agayn.
570 Atour a hill he passit till a playn     Over
Out of thar sycht in till a forest syd.
He sat him doun undyr ane ayk to bid.     oak tree; wait
His bow and swerd he lenyt till a tre.     leaned against
In angwys greiff on grouff so turned he.     anguished; prostrate
575 His petous mynd was for his men so wrocht     wretched; concerned

---

1 Except in strongholds [castles] no food was left there

That of him selff litill as than he rocht.   cared
'O wrech!' he said, 'that never couth be
 content
Of our gret mycht that the gret God thee   With the very great
 lent,   gave
Bot thi fers mynd wylfull and variable   changeable
580 With gret lordschip thou coud nocht so byd   remain
 stable,
And wyllfull witt for to mak Scotland fre.   undertook
God likis nocht that I haiff tane on me.   taken [so much]
Fer worthyar of byrth than I was born
Throuch my desyr wyth hungyr ar forlorn.   lost
585 I ask at God thaim to restor agayn.   pray
I am the caus; I suld haiff all the payn.'
Quhill studeand thus quhill flitand with   finding fault; self
 him sell,
Quhill at the last apon a slepyng he fell.
Thre dayis befor thar had him folowed five
590 The quhilk was bound or ellis to los thar   bound [to do something]
 lyff.
The Erll of York bad thaim so gret gardoun   offered; reward
At thai be thyft hecht to put Wallace doun.   stealth vowed
Three of thaim was all born men of Ingland
And twa was Scottis that tuk this deid on
 hand,
595 And sum men said thar thrid brother
 betraissed   betrayed
Kyldrome eft, quhar gret sorow was raised.   later
A child thai had quhilk helpyt to ber mett   youth; carry
In wildernes amang thai montans grett.   great mountains
Thai had all seyn disseveryng of Wallace   the separation
600 Fra his gud men and quhar he baid on   by
 cace;   chance
Amang thyk wod in covert held thaim law   hiding; low
Quhill thai persavyt he was on sleping faw   Until; perceived; fallen
And than thir five approchit Wallace neir.
Quhat best to do at other can thai speir.   ask
605 A man said thus, 'It war a hie renoun   would earn
And we mycht qwyk leid him to Sanct   lead him alive
 Jhonstoun.
Lo, how he lyis. We may our grippis vaill.   lay hold of him
Of his wapynnys he sall get nane availl.   avail
We sall him bynd in contrar of his will   against

610 And leid him thus on baksyd of yon hill          behind
    So that his men sall nothing of him knaw.'
    The tother four assentyt till his saw,          to what he said
    And than thir five thus maid thaim to           these five
        Wallace
    And thocht throu force to bynd him in that
        place.
615 Quhat! Trowyt thir five for to hald Wallace      Expected
        doun?
    The manlyast man, the starkast of persoun,      strongest person
    Leyffand he was, and als stud in sic rycht       Living
    We traist weill God his dedis had in sycht.
    Thai grippyt him, than out of slepe he
        braid.                                       started
620 'Quhat menys this?' rycht sodandly he said.
    About he turnd and up his armys thrang.          pushed up his arms
    On thai traytours with knychtlik fer he          conduct
        dang.                                        struck
    The starkast man in till his armys hynt he       strongest; seized
    And all his harnys he dang out on a tre.         brains; spattered
625 A sword he gat son efter at he rays.             that; raised
    Campiounlik amang the four he gais.
    Evir a man he gert de at a dynt.                 blow
    Quhen twa was ded the tothir wald nocht
        stynt,                                       stop
    Maid thaim to fle, bot than it was na but;       of no avail
630 Was nane leyffand mycht pas fra him on           living
        fut.
    He folowed fast and sone to ded thaim
        brocht.
    Than to the chyld sadly agayn he socht.          gravely
    'Quhat did thou her?' The child, with a
        paill face,
    On kneis he fell and askyt Wallace grace.        mercy
635 'With thaim I was and knew nothing thar          nothing of their intentions
        thocht.
    In to service as thai me bad I wrocht.'          ordered I did
    'Quhat berys thou her?' 'Bot meit,' the          do you carry here; Only
        child can say.
    'Do turs it up and pas with me away.             pack
    Meit in this tym is fer better than gold.'
640 Wallace and he furth foundyt our the fold.       went across; earth
    Quha brocht Wallace fra his enemys bauld?        Who saved

Quha bot gret God that has the warld in    *in his power*
   wauld.
He was his help in mony felloun thrang.    *terrible dangers*
With glaid cheyr thus on till his men can    *countenance*
   gang.
645  Bathe rostyt flesche thar was, als breid and
   cheis,
To succour thaim that was in poynt to    *at the point of weakening*
   leis.
Than he it delt to four men and fyfte    *shared out*
Quhilk had befor fastyt our dayis thre,    *over*
Syn tuk his part. He had fastyt als lang.    *as long*
650  Quhar herd ye evir ony in sic a thrang,    *of anyone; danger*
In hungry so, slepand and wapynlas,    *without weapons*
So weill recover as Wallace did this cas,    *[in] this case*
Playnly be fors vencust his enemys five?    *force; vanquished*
Yhe men of wit this questioun dyscryve.    *decide*
655  Wythoutyn glois I will tell furth my taill.    *Truly*
'How com this meit?' the falowschip askyt
   haill.
To thar desyr Wallace nane answer yald.    *request; delivered*
Quhar five was ded he led thaim furth, syn    *lay dead; then told [them]*
   tauld.
Gretly displessyd was all that chevalry.
660  Till a chyftane thai held it fantasy    *For; folly*
To walk allayn. Wallace with sobyr mud    *gravely*
Said, 'As herof is nothing cummyn bot    *From this nothing but good*
   gud.'    *has come*
To the law land full fast agayn thai socht,    *low; made their way*
Sperd at this child gyff he couth wys thaim    *Enquired of; direct;*
   ocht    *anywhere*
665  Quhar thai mycht best of purviance for to    *obtain provisions*
   wyn.
Of nane, he said, was that cuntre within,    *There was none; region*
'Nor all about, als fer as I can knaw,    *far*
Quhill that ye cum down to the Ranoucht    *Until; Rannoch Hall*
   hawe.
That lord has stuft breid, aill and gud    *supplies of*
   warnage;    *white wine*
670  Of King Edward he takis full mekill wage.'    *payment*
Than Wallace said, 'My selff sall be your
   gyd.
I knaw that sted about on ather syd.'    *around; either*

Throuch the wyld land he gydyt thaim full
   rycht.
To Ranouch hall thai com apon the nycht.
675  A wach was out and that full sone thai ta;     guard; overpowered
For he was Scottis, that man thai wald      Because
   nocht sla,
Bot gert him tell the maner of that place.     lay-out
Thus entryt thai within a litill space.       while
The yett thai wan, for castell was thar nayn   gate; reached
680  Bot mudwall werk withoutyn lym or stayn.   lime; stone
Wallace in haist straik up the chawmer dur   broke down; door
Bot with his fut, that stalwart was and stur.   Just; strong
Than thai within sa walknyt sodeynly.     inside; awakened
The lord gat up and mercy can him cry.
685  Fra tym he wyst that gud Wallace was thar
He thankyt God, syn said thir wordis mar:   as well
'Trew man I was and woun agayn my will    dwelled against
With Inglismen, suppos I likit ill.
All Scottis we ar that in this place is now.
690  At your commaund all baynly we sall bow.'   readily; yield
Of our nacioun gud Wallace had pete,     i.e., those born Scots
Tuk aythis of thaim, syne meit askyt he.    oaths [of allegiance] from
Gud cheyr thai maid quhill lycht day on   until daylight
   the morn.
This trew man than sone semblit him     assembled
   beforn
695  Thre sonnys he had that stalwart was and
   bauld,                       bold
And twenty men of his kyn in houshauld.    kinsmen
Wallace was blyth thai maid him sic supple,  assistance
Said, 'I thank God that we thus multiple.'
All that day our in gud liking thai rest.    entire day in comfort
700  Wachys thai vaill to kep thaim at coud best.  Sentries; chose; protect
Apon the morn, the lycht day quhen thai   daylight
   saw,
Than Wallace said, 'Our power for to     To know our strength
   knaw,
We will tak feild and up our baner rais    take the battlefield
Of rycht Scotland in contrar of our fais.    Scotland's right against
705  We will no mar now us in covert hid.    concealment hide
Power till us will sembill on ilk syd.     Reinforcements; gather; every
Horsis thai gat the best men at was thar;
Towart Dunkell the gaynest way thai far.   nearest; went

The byschope fled and gat till Sanct
   Jhonstoun.                                     *reached*

710 The Scottis slew all was thar of that           *i.e., the English*
   nacioun,

Baith pur and rych, and servandys at thai
   fand,

Left nane on lyff that born was of Ingland.

The place thai tuk and maid thaim weill to        *captured; good use*
   fayr

Of purviance that byschop had brocht thair.       *Of provisions*

715 Jowellis thai gat, bathe gold and sylver
   brycht,

With gud cheyr thar five dayis thai sojornd        *cheer*
   rycht.

On the sext day Wallace to consaill went,

Gert call the best and schew thaim his            *summoned; revealed;*
   entent.                                          *intention*

'Na men we haiff to sailye Sanct                   *attack*
   Jhonstoun.

720 Into the north tharfor lat mak us boun.         *let us set off*

In Ros, ye knaw, gud men a strenth has            *stronghold*
   maid;

Her thai of us thai cum withoutyn baid.            *delay*

Als into But the byschope gud Synclar             *Bute*

Fra he get wit he cummys withoutin mar.           *gets to know; delay*

725 Gud Westland men of Aran and Rauchle,

Fra thai be warnd thai will all cum to me.'

This purpos tuk and in the north thai rid;

Nan Inglisman durst in thar way abid.             *No*

Quham Wallace tuk thai knew the ald              *Whom; took prisoner*
   ransoun

730 Fra he com haym to fle thai mak thaim          *When*
   boun                                            *ready*

And Scottis men semblyt to Wallace fast.          *flocked*

In awfull feyr throuchout the land thai           *awesome array*
   past;

Strenthis was left, witt ye, all desolate;        *Castles*

Agayn thir folk thai durst mak no debate.         *Against these; resistance*

735 In raid battaill thai raid till Abyrdeyn;       *In battle order; rode to*

The haill nowmyr, seven thousand, than            *entire number*
   was seyn;

Bot Inglismen had left that toun all waist,

On ilka syd away thai can thaim haist,            *every; did; hasten*

In all that land left nother mar nor les.  *neither more*

740 Lord Bewmound tuk the sey at Bowchan  *took to sea*
   nes,

Throu Scotland than was manifest in playn;  *openly*

The lordis that past in hart was wonder  *were very glad*
   fayn.

The knycht Climes of Ross com sodeynly

In Murray land with thar gud chevalry.  *company of knights*

745 The hous of Narn that gud knycht weill has  *castle; taken*
   tane,

Slew the capdane and strang men mony ane.  *many a one*

Out of Murray in Bowchane land com thai

To sek Bewmound be he was past away.  *seek; but; gone*

Than thir gud men to Wallace passyt rycht.  *these*

750 Quhen Wallace saw Schir Jhon Ramsay the
   knycht

And othir gud at had bene fra him lang,  *good men*

Gret curag than was rasyt thaim amang.  *among them*

The land he reullyt as at him likit best,  *ruled; that*

To Sanct Jhonstoun syn raid or thai wald  *then rode before*
   rest.

755 At everilk part a stalwart wach he maid,  *every place; watch*

Fermyt a sege and stedfastly abaid.  *Established; waited*

Byschop Synclar in till all haist him dycht,  *prepared*

Com out of Bute with symly men to sycht;  *good*

Out of the Ilys of Rauchle and Aran  *Isles; Rathlin*

760 Lyndsay and Boid with gud men mony ane.

Adam Wallace, barroun of Ricardtoun,

Full sadly socht till Wallace of renoun,  *resolutely*

At Sanct Jhonstoun baid at the sailye still.  *remained; siege*

For Sotheroun men thai mycht weill pass at
   will,

765 For in thar way thar durst na enemys be  *dared*

Bot fled away be land and als be se.

About that toun thus semblyt thai but mor,  *gathered; immediately*

For thai had beyn with gud Wallace befor.

Cetoun, Lauder and Richard of Lunde,

770 In a gud barge thai past about be se.

Sanct Jhonstoun havyn thar ankyr haiff thai  *anchor*
   set.

Twa Inglys schippys thai tuk withoutyn let:  *hindrance*

The tane thai brynt, syn stuffyt the tother  *one; burned; then supplied*
   weill

With artailye and stalwart men in steyll, *artillery*
775 To kep the port; thar suld cum na victaill *defend; gate*
In to that toun, nor men at mycht thaim
vaill. *help*
Fra south and north mony of Scotland fled, *From; from*
Left castellys waist; feill lost thar lyff to *wasted*
wed. *pledge*
The south byschop, befor at left Dunkell, *English-appointed*
780 Tyll London past and tald Edward him sell *self*
In Scotland thar had fallyn a gret
myschance. *disaster*
Than send he son for Amar the Wallance *soon*
And askyt him than quhat war best to do.
He hecht to pas and tak gret gold tharto, *vowed; go*
785 In to Scotland sic menys for to mak *such means; use*
Agane Wallace, on hand this can he tak. *Against; undertake*
Thai said he wald undo King Edwardis
croun *rule*
Bot gyff thai mycht throu tresoun put him *Unless*
doun.
King Edward hecht quhat thing at Wallang *promised*
band *contracted*
790 He suld it kep, war it bathe gold and land. *keep [honour]*
Wallange tuk leyff and is in Scotland went; *leave*
To Bothwell com, syn kest in his entent *then considered*
Quhat man thar was mycht best Wallace
begyll; *beguile*
And sone he fand within a litill quhill *while*
795 Schyr Jhon Menteth. Wallace his gossop was. *[children's] godfather*
A messynger Schir Amar has gert pas *made*
On to Schir Jhon and sone a tryst has set; *soon; meeting*
At Ruglyn kyrk thir twa togydder met. *Rutherglen church*
Than Wallang said, 'Schir Jhon, thou
knawis this thing. *knows*
800 Wallace agayn rysis contrar the king,
And thou may haiff quhat lordschip thou
will *choose*
And thou wald wyrk as I can gyff consaill. *If; advise*
Yon tyrand haldys the rewmys at trowbill *That; both realms*
bathe;
Till thryfty men it dois full mekill scaith. *To decent; harm*
805 He traistis thee. Rycht weyll thou may him *Trusts*
tak. *take*

Of this mater ane end I think to mak.    matter
War he away, we mycht at liking ryng    Were; pleasure; reign
As lordys all and leiff undyr a king.'    live
Than Menteth said, 'He is our governour.
810 For us he baid in mony felloun stour,    stood; grievous battle
Nocht for him selff bot for our heretage.
To sell him thus, it war a foull outrage.'    betray
Than Wallang said, 'And thou weill
   undyrstud,
Gret neid it war; he spillis so mekill blud    much blood
815 Of Crystin men, puttis saullis in peraill.    souls; peril
I bynd me als he sall be haldyn haill    pledge; kept safe
As for his lyff and kepyt in presoune;
King Edward wald haiff him in
   subjeccioun.'
Than Menteth thocht sa thai wald kepe    so [long as]; the agreement
   connand,
820 He wald full fayn haiff had him of    gladly; [out] of
   Scotland.
Wallange saw him in till a study be,    deep in thought
Thre thousand pundys of fyn gold leit him se
And hecht he suld the Levynhous haiff at    promised; Lennox
   will.
Thus tresonably Menteth grantyt thartill;
825 Obligacioun with his awn hand he maid.    A compact
Syn tuk the gold and Edwardis seill so
   braid    broad
And gaiff thaim his, quhen he his tym
   mycht se
To tak Wallace our Sulway, giff him fre    over; freely
Till Inglismen. Be this tresonabill concord    To; By; agreement
830 Schyr Jhon suld be of all the Lennox lord.
Thus Wallace suld in Ingland kepyt be,
So Edward mycht mak Scotland till him    subject to his sole authority
   fre.
Thar covatys was our gret maister seyn;    covetousness
Nane sampill takis how ane other has beyn    No-one example
835 For covatice put in gret paynys fell,    extreme
For covatice the serpent is of hell.    covetice
Throuch covatice gud Ector tuk the ded,    died
For covatice thar can be no ramed;    remedy
Throuch covatice gud Alexander was lost,
840 And Julius als, for all his reiff and bost;    plundering

Throuch covatice deit Arthour of Bretan,    died
For covatice thar had deit mony ane;
For covatice the traytour Ganyelon
The flour of France he put till confusion;    death
845    For covatice thai poysound gud Godfra    betrayed
In Antioche, as the autor will sa;    author; say
For covatice Menteth apon fals wys    in a false manner
Betraysyt Wallace at was his gossop twys.    Betrayed; that; twice
Wallang in haist with blyth will and glaid
    hart
850    Till London past and schawit till King    To; showed [the agreement]
    Edwart.
Of this contrak he had a mar plesance    contract; more joy
Than of fyn gold had geyffyn in balance.    given
A grettar wecht na his ransoun mycht be.    weight than; ransom
Of Wallace furth yeit sum thing spek will
    we,
855    At Sanct Jhonstoun was at the sogeyng    siege
    still.
In a mornyng Sotheroun with egyr will,    eager
Five hundreth men in harnas rycht juntly,    armour; in close order
Thai uschet furth to mak a jeperty    issued; surprise attack
At the south port apon Scot and Dundas,    gate
860    Quhilk in that tym rycht wys and worthy    who
    was
Agayn thar fayis rycht scharply socht and    Against; foes; fiercely
    sayr.
In that counter seven scor to ded thai    encounter; bore down
    bayr.
Yeit Inglismen at cruell war and keyn    that fierce; bold
Full ferely faucht quhar douchty deid was    actively fought; brave
    seyn.
865    Fra the west yett drew all the Scottis haill    From; gate; completely
To the fechtaris. Quhen Sotheroun saw na    fighters
    vaill    avail
Bot in agayn, full fast thai can thaim sped.    to go in again; speed
The knycht Dundas prevyt so douchty    proved so bold indeed
    deid;
Our neyr the yett full bandounly he baid,    Too near; gate; boldly; stayed
870    Wyth a gud swerd full gret maistre he    sword; deeds of arms
    maid,
Nocht wittandly his falowis was him fra.    Not realising
In at the yett the Sotheroun can him ta;    gate; brought him

On to the erll thai led him haistele.
Quhen he him saw he said he suld nocht de:
875 'To slay this ane it may us litill rameid.'          one; help
He send him furth to Wallace in that steid.          place
On the north syd his bestials had he          siege engines; set up
  wrocht.
Quhill he him saw of this he wyst rycht          Until; knew
  nocht;
Send to the erll and thankit him largelé,          Sent; generously
880 Hecht for to quyt quhen he sic cace mycht          Promised; repay; such as
  se.          opportunity
Bot all her for soverance he wald nocht          here; safe conducts
  grant,
Thocht thai yoldin wald cum as recreant;          surrendered; admitting defeat
For gold na gud he wald no trewbut tak.          nor goods; tribute
A full strang salt than he begouth to mak.          assault; began
885 The Erll of Fyf dwelt under trewage lang          tribute a long time
Of King Edward, and than him thocht it
  wrang
At Wallace sa was segeand Sanct          That; so; laying siege to
  Jhonstoun,
Bot gyff he com in rycht help of the croun.          Unless; properly to help
Till Inglismen he wald nocht kep that          To; keep; bond
  band.
890 Than he come sone with gud men of the
  land,
And Jhon Wallang, was than schirreff of          then
  Fyff,
Till Wallace past, starkyt him in that stryff.          supported; struggle
That erll was cummyn of trew, haill nobill          true, completely
  blud,
Fra the ald thane quhilk in his tym was          old thane
  gud.
895 Than all about to Sanct Jhonstoun thai
  gang          went
With felloun salt, was hydwys, scharp and          fierce attack; hideous
  strang.
Full feill fagaldys in to the dyk thai cast,          many faggots; ditch
Hadyr and hay bond apon flakys fast.          Heather; bound; bundles
Wyth treis and erd a gret passage thai          trees; earth
  maid;
900 Atour the wallis thai yeid with battaill          Across; went
  braid.

The Sotheroun men maid gret defens agayn,
Quhill on the wallys thar was a thousand slayn.
Wallace yeid in and his rayit battaill rycht;                went; ordered battalion
All Sotheroun men derffly to ded thai dycht.                violently killed
905 To sayff the erll Wallace the harrald send,              save; herald sent
Gud Jop him selff, the quhilk befor him kend.               knew
For Dundas saik thai said he suld nocht de;                 sake
Wallace him selff this ordand for to be.                    ordered
A small haknay he gert till him be tak,                     hackney; caused; taken
910 Silver and gold his costis for to mak;                   to meet his expenses
Set on his clok a takyn for to se,                          Placed; cloak; token
The lyoun in wax that suld his condet be;                   safe conduct
Convoyit him furth and na man him with all.                 Escorted
Wemen and barnys Wallace gert freith thaim all,            children; made free
915 And syn gart cry trew Scottis men to thar awn;          then caused to be called; own
Plenyst the land quhilk lang had beyn ourthrawn,            Stocked
Than Wallace past the south land for to se.
Edward the Bruce, in his tym rycht worthe,
That yer befor he had in Irland ben                        year
920 And purchest thar of cruell men and keyn.               obtained; bold; fierce
Fyfty in feyr, was of his moderys kyn,                      company; mother's kin
At Kyrkubre on Galloway entryt in.                          Kirkcudbright in
With thai fyfte he had vencust nine scor.                   vanquished
And syn he past withoutyn tary mor                          more delay
925 Till Wygtoun sone and that castell has tane.            Wigtown; soon; taken
Sotheroun was fled and left it all allane.
Wallace him met with trew men reverently;                   respectfully
To Lowmabane went all that chevalry.                        Lochmaben; army
Thai maid Edward bath lord and ledar thar.                  leader
930 This condicioun Wallace him hecht but mar,              promised immediately
Bot a schort tym to bid Robert the king                     Only; await
Gyff he come nocht in this regioun to ryng,                 reign
At Edward suld resaiff the croun but faill.                 without fail

| | | |
|---|---|---|
| | Thus hecht Wallace and all the barnage haill. | promised / whole |
| 935 | In Louchmabane prynce Edward levyt still | lived |
| | And Wallace past in Cumno with blith will. | Cumnock; happily |
| | At the Blak Rok, quhar he was wont to be, | |
| | Apon that sted a ryall hous held he. | place; royal castle |
| | Inglis wardans till London past but mar | wardens; straight away |
| 940 | And tauld the king of all thar gret mysfar, | told; disaster |
| | How Wallace had Scotland fra thaim reduce | recovered |
| | And how he had rasavyt Edward the Bruce. | welcomed |
| | The commouns swor thai suld cum nevermar | swore / never more |
| | Apon Scotland and Wallace leiffand war. | while; living was |
| 945 | Than Edward wrayt till Menteth prevali, | wrote; privately |
| | Prayit him till haist; the tym was past by | hurry |
| | Of the promes the quhilk at he was bund. | to which he was bound |
| | Schyr Jhon Menteth in till his wit has fund | wisdom; found |
| | How he suld best his purpos to fullfill. | |
| 950 | His syster son in haist he cald him till | called to him |
| | And ordand him in dwellyng with Wallace. | ordered; to dwell |
| | Ane ayth agayn he gert him mak on cace, | An oath; in the event |
| | Quhat tym he wyst Wallace in quiet draw | knew; withdrew |
| | He suld him warnd, for aventur mycht befaw. | alert; whatever might befall |
| 955 | This man grantyt at sic thing suld be done; | that; such |
| | With Wallace thus he was in service sone. | soon |
| | As of tresoun Wallace had litill thocht; | |
| | His lauborous mynd on other materis wrocht. | busy / worked |
| | Thus Wallace thrys has maid all Scotland fre. | thrice |
| 960 | Than he desyryt in lestand pees to be, | lasting |
| | For as of wer he was in sumpart yrk. | war; weary |
| | He purpost than to serve God and the kyrk, | church |
| | And for to leyff undyr hys rychtwys king; | live; rightful |
| | That he desyryt atour all erdly thing. | above; earthly |
| 965 | The harrold Jop in Ingland sone he send | herald; soon; sent |
| | And wrayt to Bruce rycht hartlie this commend, | wrote / commendation |
| | Besekand him to cum and tak his croun; | Beseeching |
| | Nane suld gaynstand, clerk, burges no barroun. | None; oppose |

The harrald past. Quhen Bruce saw his
   credans,                                      *credentials*

970   Tharof he tuk a perfyt gret plesans.      *pleasure*
      With hys awn hand agayn wrayt to Wallace   *own; wrote*
      And thankyt him of lauta and kyndnas,   *loyalty*
      Besekand him this mater to conseill,   *Praying; conceal*
      For he behuffyd out of Ingland to steill;   *needed; steal*

975   For lang befor was kepyt the ragment   *bond*
      Quhilk Cumyn had, to byd the gret
         parlement                                  *Which; await*
      In to London; and gyff thai him accus,   *if; accused*
      To cum fra thaim he suld mak sum excus.   *come away*
      He prayit Wallace in Glaskow mur to walk   *keep watch*

980   The fyrst nycht of Juli, for his salk,   *sake*
      And bad he suld bot in to quiet be,   *ordered*
      For he with him mycht bryng few chevalre.   *companions*
      Wallace was blyth quhen he this writyng
         saw;
      His houshauld sone he gert to Glaskow   *carried*
         draw.

985   That moneth thar he ordand thaim to byd.   *month; ordered; remain*
      Kerle he tuk ilk nycht with him to ryd,   *each*
      And this yong man that Menteth till him
         send –                                     *sent*
      Wyst nane bot thir quhat way at Wallace   *Knew none; these*
         wend –                                   *went*
      The quhilk gart warn his eym the auchtand   *Who; caused; uncle eighth*
         nycht.

990   Sexte full sone schyr Jhone Menteth gert   *caused to be ready*
         dycht
      Of hys awn kyn and of alya born.   *kin; allies*
      To this tresoun he gert thaim all be sworn.   *sworn*
      Fra Dunbertane he sped thaim haistely,
      Ner Glaskow kyrk thai bounyt thaim   *prepared*
         prevaly.                                  *secretly*

995   Wallace past furth quhar at the tryst was   *forth; meeting*
         set;
      A spy thai maid and folowed him but let   *immediately*
      Till Robrastoun, was ner be the way syd   *Robroyston [near Glasgow]*
      And bot a hous quhar Wallace oysyt to   *only one; used; stay*
         byd.
      He wouk on fut quhill passyt was myd   *stood watch until*
         nycht;

1000 Kerle and he than for a sleip thaim dycht.   *got ready*

Thai bad this cuk that he suld wache his part   *traitor; take his turn on watch*

And walkyn Wallace, com men fra ony art.   *waken; any direction*

Quhen thai slepyt this traytour tuk graith heid.   *prompt heed*

He met his eym and bad him haiff no dreid:   *uncle / fear*

1005 'On sleip he is and with him bot a man.   *only one*

Ye may him haiff for ony craft he can;   *skill; knows*

Without the hous thar wapynnys laid thaim fra.'   *Outside; are laid*

For weill thai wyst, gat Wallace ane of tha   *one of them*

And on his feyt, hys ransoun suld be sauld.   *dearly paid for*

1010 Thus semblyt thai about that febill hauld.   *abode*

This traytour wach fra Wallace than he stall   *guard; stole*

Bathe knyff and swerd, his bow and arowis all.   *Both; sword*

Efter mydnycht in handis thai haiff him tane,   *laid hands on him*

Dyschowyll on sleipe, wyth him na man bot ane.   *Unarmed in sleep*

1015 Kerle thai tuk and led him of that place,   *out of*

Dyd him to ded withoutyn langar space.   *Put him to death; time*

Thai thocht to bynd Wallace throu strenthis strang.

On fute he gat the feill traytouris amang,   *foot; many*

Grippyt about, bot na wapyn he fand.   *Felt; weapon; found*

1020 Apon a syll he saw besyd him stand   *beam*

The bak of ane he byrstyt in that thrang   *back; one; broke; crowd*

And of ane other the harnes out he dang.   *brains; dashed*

Than als mony as handis mycht on him lay,   *as many as might hands*

Be force hym hynt for till haiff him away,   *By; seized*

1025 Bot that power mycht nocht a fute him leid   *foot; lead*

Out of that hous quhill thai or he war deid.   *until*

Schir Jhon saw weill be force it coud nocht be,

Or he war tayne he thocht erar to de.   *Before; taken; sooner; die*

Menteth bad ces and thus spak to Wallace,   *ordered [them to] stop*

1030 Syn schawyt him furth a rycht sutell fals cace:   *Then displayed*

'Yhe haiff so lang her oysyt you allane   *here; been accustomed; alone*

Quhill witt tharof is in till Ingland gane.   *While word*

Tharfor her me and sobyr your curage.　　　*listen to me; moderate*
The Inglismen with a full gret barnage
1035　Ar semblyt her and set this hous about　　　*gathered; surround this house*
That ye be force on na wayis may wyn out.　　*by; escape*
Suppos ye had the strenth of gud Ectour
Amang this ost ye may nocht lang endour.
And thai you tak, in haist your ded is　　　*If they take you; death;*
　　dycht.　　　　　　　　　　　　　　　　*certain*
1040　I haiff spokyn with lord Clyffurd that knycht,
Wyth thar chyftanys weill menyt for your　　*well disposed*
　　lyff.
Thai ask no mar bot be quyt of your stryff.　*leave off your struggle*
To Dunbertane ye sall furth pas with me;
At your awn hous ye ma in saifte be.'　　　*own castle; safety*
1045　Sotheroun sic oys with Menteth lang had　　*practice*
　　thai
That Wallace trowyt sum part at he wald　　　*believed; that*
　　say.
Menteth said, 'Schir, lo, wappynnys nane
　　we haiff;
We com in trayst your lyff gyff we mycht　　*good faith; if*
　　saiff.'　　　　　　　　　　　　　　　　*save*
Wallace trowyt weill, and he his gossep
　　twys,
1050　That he wald nocht be no maner of wys
Him to betrays for all Scotland so wyd.
Ane ayth of him he askit in that tid.　　　*oath; at that time*
Thar wantit wit. Quhat suld his aythis
　　mor?[1]
Forsworn till him he was lang tym befor.　　*Perjured*
1055　The ayth he maid. Wallace com in his will;　*oath; submitted to him*
Rycht frawdfully all thus schawyt him till.　*appeared to him*
'Gossep,' he said, 'as presoner thai mon　　*Godfather*
　　you se,
Or thai throu force wyll ellis tak you fra　　*will otherwise take*
　　me.'
A courch with slycht apon his handys thai　　*kerchief; cunning*
　　laid,
1060　And undyr syn with sever cordys thai braid,　*then; strong ropes; bound*
Bath scharp and tewch, and fast togydder　　*tough*
　　drew.

1　[He] lacked wisdom there. What should [he want with] more oaths?

Allace, the Bruce mycht sayr that byndyng *sorely*
rew *rue*
Quhilk maid Scotland sone brokyn apon *soon*
cace,
For Comyns ded and los of gud Wallace! *death*
1065 Thai led him furth in feyr amang thaim *company*
awe.
Kerle he myst; of na Sotheroun he saw. *missed*
Than wyst he weyll that he betraysyt was.
Towart the south with him quhen thai can
pas,
Yeit thai him said in trewth he suld nocht de,
1070 King Edward wald kep him in gud saufte
For hie honour in wer at he had wrocht.
The sayr bandys so strowblyt all his thocht, *troubled*
Credence tharto forsuth he coud nocht
geyff.
He wyst full weyll thai wald nocht lat him
leiff.
1075 A fals foull caus thai Menteth for him
tauld,
Quhen on this wys gud Wallace he had
sauld. *betrayed*
Sum of thaim said it was to saiff thar lord;
Thai leid all out that maid that fals record. *lead*
At the Fawkyrk the gud Stewart was slayn,
1080 Our corniclis rehersis that in playn, *recount; plainly*
On Madelan day, that eighteen yer befor. *i.e., 22 July*
Comyns ded tharof it wytnesis mor. *testified further*
At Robrastoun Wallas was tresonabilly,
Thus falsly, stollyn fra his gud chevalry,
1085 In Glaskow lay and wyst nocht of this
thing.
Thus he was lost in byding of his king. *waiting for*
South thai him led, ay haldand the west *keeping to*
land,
Delyverit him in haist our Sullway sand. *Solway*
The lord Clyffurd and Wallang tuk him
thar;
1090 To Carleyll toun full fast with him thai *Carlisle*
fayr,
In presoun him stad. That was a gret *placed*
dolour.

That hous efter was callyt Wallace tour.                building

Sum men syn said, that knew nocht weill                 afterwards
   the cas,

In Berweik thai to ded put gud Wallace.

1095 Contrar is knawin fyrst be this opinioun;           The contrary

For Scottis men than had haly Berweik                   held wholly
   toun

And Scotland fre, quhill that Soullis it gaiff,         until; gave [up]

For lord Cumyn till Ingland with the layff.             others

Ane other poynt is, the traytouris durst
   nocht pas

1100 At sauld him sa, quhar Scottis men                  That betrayed
   maisteris was.

The thrid poynt is, the commouns of
   Ingland,

Quhat thai desyr, thai will nocht understand

That thing be done, for wytnes at may be,               is done

Na credence geyff forthyr than thai may se.             No; give further

1105 To se him de Edward had mar desyr                   more desire

Than to be lord of all the gret empyr.

For thir causis thai kepyt him sa lang,                 these reasons

Quhill the commouns mycht on to London                  Until
   gang.

Allace, Scotland, to quhom sall thou
   compleyn?

1110 Allace, fra payn quha sall thee now
   restreyn?                                        keep away

Allace, thi help is fastlie brocht to ground:           saviour; quickly

Thi best chyftane in braith bandis is                   strong
   bound.

Allace, thou has now lost thi gyd of lycht.             guiding light

Allace, quha sall defend thee in thi rycht?             who

1115 Allace, thi payn approchis wonder ner,              suffering

With sorow sone thou mon bene set in feyr.              soon; must; fear

Thi gracious gyd, thi grettast governour,               guide

Allace, our neir is cumyn his fatell hour.              too near; destined

Allace, quha sall thee beit now of thi baill?          relieve; woe

1120 Allace, quhen sall of harmys thou be haill?         whole

Quha sall thee defend? Quha sall thee now
   mak fre?

Allace, in wer quha sall thi helpar be?                 war

Quha sall thee help? Quha sall the now
   radem?                                            redeem

Allace, quha sall the Saxons fra thee flem? — expel
1125 I can no mar bot besek God of grace — do no more; beseech
Thee to restor in haist to rychtwysnace, — [your] rightful place
Sen gud Wallace may succour thee no mar. — Since; help; more
The los of him encressit mekill cair. — increased great suffering
Now of his men, in Glaskow still at lay, — who still lay in Glasgow
1130 Quhat sorow rais quhen thai him myst — rose; missed
away.
The cruell payn, the wofull complenyng, — fierce suffering
Tharof to tell it war our hevy thing. — too heavy a
I will lat be and spek of it no mar. — let; more
Litill rehers is our mekill of cair.
1135 And principaly quhar redempcioun is
nayn.[1]
It helpys nocht to tell thar petous mayn; — wretched lament
The deid tharof is yeit in remembrance.
I will lat slaik of sorow the ballance. — allow to lessen
Bot Longawell to Louchmabane coud pas — past
1140 And thar he hecht, quhar gud prince — vowed
Edward was
Out of Scotland he suld pas nevermor.
Los of Wallace socht till his hart so sor — troubled his heart so much
The rewlm of France he vowit he suld — vowed
never se,
Bot veng Wallace or ellis tharfor to de. — avenge; else
1145 Thar he remaynd quhill cummyn of the — until; arrival
king; — i.e., Bruce
With Bruce in wer this gud knycht furth
can ryng. — did rule
Remembrance syn was in the Brucys buk: — afterwards
Secound he was quhen thai Saynct
Jhonstoun tuk,
Folowed the king at wynnyng of the toun.
1150 The Bruce tharfor gaiff him full gret — gave
gardoun; — reward
All Charterys land the gud king till him
gaiff;
Charterys sen syn of his kyn is the laiff. — afterwards; descendant
Quharto suld I fer in that story wend? — go
Bot of my buk to mak a fynaill end:

1 [Even] a little mention [recital] [causes] too much pain, / and chiefly where
there is no / deliverance

| | | |
|---|---|---|
| 1155 | Robert the Bruce com hame on the ferd day | came home; fourth |
| | In Scotland, eft Wallace was had away, | after; taken away |
| | Till Louchmabane, quhar that he fand Edward, | found [his brother] |
| | Quharof he was gretlie rejossyt in hart; | Whereof; rejoiced |
| | Bot fra he wyst Wallace away was led, | when; knew |
| 1160 | So mekill baill within his breyst thar bred | grief; breast |
| | Ner out of wytt he worthit for to weyd. | nearly went mad |
| | Edward full sone than till hys brothir yeid. | went |
| | A sodane chance this was in wo fra weill. | change of fortune |
| | Gud Edward said, 'This helpys nocht adell. | at all |
| 1165 | Lat murnyng be; it may mak na remeid. | Let mourning |
| | Ye haiff him tynt. Ye suld ravenge his deid. | lost; should revenge; death |
| | Bot for your caus he tuk the wer on hand, | Only; war |
| | In your defens, and thrys has fred Scotland, | freed |
| | The quhilk was tynt fra us and all our kyn; | taken from; kin |
| 1170 | War nocht Wallace we had never entryt in. | Were [it] not [for] |
| | Merour he was of lauta and manheid, | Mirror; loyalty |
| | In wer the best that ever sall power leid. | war; army lead |
| | Had he likyt for till haiff tane your croun | taken |
| | Wald nane him let that was in this regioun. | Would; have stopped |
| 1175 | Had nocht beyne he, ye suld had na entres | entrance |
| | In to this rewlm, for tresoun and falsnes. | on account of |
| | That sall ye se. The traytour that him sauld, | betrayed |
| | Fra you he thinkys Dunbertane for till hauld. | possess |
| | Sum comfort tak and lat slaik of this sorow.' | let this sorrow be assuaged |
| 1180 | The king chargyt Edward apon the morou | the next morning |
| | Radres to tak of wrang that wrocht him was. | Redress; had been done to him |
| | Till Dallswyntoun he ordand him to pas, | ordered |
| | And men of armys; gyff thai fand Cumyn thar, | if they found |
| | Put him to ded; for na dreid thai suld spar. | death; danger; spare |
| 1185 | Thai fand him nocht. The king him selff him slew | found |
| | In till Drumfres, quhar witnes was inew. | there were enough witnesses |
| | That hapnys wrang, our gret haist in a king; | too great haste |

Till wyrk by law it may scaith mekill thing. *outside; harm*

Me nedis herof na forthyr for till schaw; *demonstrate*

1190 How that was done is knawin to you aw. *known; all*

Bot yong Douglace fyrst to the king can pas, *went*

In all hys wer bath wicht and worthi was; *i.e., Bruce's war; strong*

Nor how the king has tane on him the croun; *taken*

Of all that her I mak bot schort mencioun; *here*

1195 Nor how lord Soullis gaiff Berweik toun *gave*
away,

How efter syn sone tynt was Galloway; *soon afterwards lost*

How Jhon of Lorn agayn his rycht king *against*
rais; *rose*

On ather sid how Bruce had mony fais; *either side; foes*

How bauld Breichin contrar his king coud *bold; against*
ryd;

1200 Rycht few was than in wer with him to byd; *war; withstand*

Nor how the north was gyffyn fra the gud *given away*
king,

Quhilk maid him lang in paynfull wer to *war*
ryng. *reign*

Ay trew till him was Jamys the gud *Ever true to*
Douglace,

For Brucis rycht baid weill in mony place. *remained*

1205 Undyr the king he was the best chyftayn,

Bot Wallace rais as chyftane him allayn; *rose; alone*

Tharfor till him is no comparisoun

As of a man, sauff reverence of the croun.[1]

Bot sa mony as of Douglace has beyn

1210 Gud of a kyn was never in Scotland seyn. *kind*

Comparisoun that can I nocht weill declar. *state*

Of Brucis buk as now I spek no mar. *more*

Master Barbour, quhilk was a worthi clerk,

He said the Bruce amang his other werk. *composed; work*

1215 In this mater prolixit I am almaist; *prolix; almost*

To my purpos breiffly I will me haist,

How gud Wallace was set amang his fayis. *placed; enemies*

To London with him Clyffurd and Wallang
gais, *went*

Quhar King Edward was rycht fayn of that *glad; capture*
fang.

1 Therefore there is no comparing him [with any other] man, with the
exception, respectfully, of the king

1220　Thai haiff him stad in till a presone strang. *confined; strong*
　　　Of Wallace end my selff wald leiff for dredis *would leave out details / fear*
　　　To say the werst, bot rychtwysnes me ledis. *worst; a sense of right; leads*
　　　We fynd his lyff was all swa verray trew, *so*
　　　His fatell hour I will nocht fenye new. *fated; falsify*
1225　Menteth was fals and that our weill was knawin; *too / known*
　　　Feill of that kyn in Scotland than was sawyn, *Many; were / scattered*
　　　Chargyt to byd under the gret jugement *Commanded; decree*
　　　At King Robert ackyt in his parlement. *enacted*
　　　Tharof I mak no langar contenuans. *continuance*
1230　Bot Wallace end in warld was displesans, *distressing*
　　　Tharfor I ces and puttis it nocht in rym. *rhyme*
　　　Scotland may thank the blyssyt, happy tym *blessed*
　　　At he was born, be prynsuall poyntis two. *That; two principal points*
　　　This is the fyrst, or that we forthyr go, *before*
1235　Scotland he fred and brocht it of thrillage; *freed; out of thralldom*
　　　And now in hevin he has his heretage, *heaven; inheritance*
　　　As it prevyt be gud experians. *proved*
　　　Wys clerkys yeit it kepis in remembrans, *still*
　　　How that a monk of Bery abbay than, *then*
1240　In to that tym a rycht religious man; *At that time*
　　　A yong monk als with him in ordour stud, *also; holy orders*
　　　Quhilk knew his lyff was clene, perfyt and gud.
　　　This fader monk was wesyd with seknace, *afflicted; illness*
　　　Out of the warld as he suld pas on cace. *From this world; in time*
1245　His brother saw the spret lykly to pas. *brother monk; spirit*
　　　A band of him rycht ernystly he coud as, *promise; asked*
　　　To cum agayn and schaw him of the meid *reveal to; reward*
　　　At he suld haiff at God for his gud deid. *That; good deeds*
　　　He grantyt him, at his prayer, to preiff *try*
1250　To cum agayn gyff God wald geiff him leiff. *if; give him / leave*
　　　The spreyt changyt out of this warldly payn, *translated*
　　　In that sammyn hour com to the monk agayn. *same*
　　　Sic thing has beyn and is be voice and sycht. *Such; by*

Quhar he apperyt thar schawyt sa mekill lycht,                                     shone

1255 Lyk till lawntryns it illumynyt so cler                    lanterns
At warldly lycht tharto mycht be no peyr.                     That; equal
A voice said thus, 'God has me grantyt grace
That I sall kep my promes in this place.'
The monk was blyth of this cler fygur fayr;        bright
1260 Bot a fyr brund in his forheid he bayr            brand; forehead; bore
And than him thocht it myslikyt all the lave.                      made all the rest displeasing
'Quhar art thou spreyt? Answer, sa God thee save.'
'In purgatory.' 'How lang sall thou be thair?'
'Bot halff ane hour to cum and litill mair.        more
1265 Purgatory is, I do thee weill to wit,              know
In ony place quhar God will it admyt.
Ane hour of space I was demed thar to be            time; judged
And that passis, suppos I spek with thee.'
'Quhy has thou that and all the layff so haill?'
                                                    sound
1270 'For of science I thocht me maist availl.        knowledge; avail
Quha pridys tharin that laubour is in waist,       Whoever takes pride
For science cummys bot of the haly gaist.'         only; Holy Ghost
'Efter thi hour quhar is thi passage evyn?'         proper
'Quhen tym cummys,' he said, 'to lestand hevin.'   everlasting heaven

1275 'Quhat tym is that, I pray thee now declar?'
'Twa ar on lyff mon be befor me thar.'             alive must
'Quhilk two ar thai? The verite thou me ken.'
                                                    tell
'The fyrst has bene a gret slaar of men.           slayer
Now thai him kep to martyr in London toun
1280 On Wednysday, befor king and commoun.          commons
Is nayn on lyff at has sa mony slayn.'             that
'Brodyr,' he said, 'that taill is bot in vayn,     in vain
For slauchter is to God abhominabill.'
'Than,' said the spreyt, 'forsuth this is no fabill.
                                                    lie
1285 He is Wallace, defendour of Scotland,
For rychtwys wer that he tuk apon hand.            righteous war

Thar rychtwysnes is lowyt our the lave;    *praised above the rest*
Tharfor in hevyn he sall that honour have.
Syn, a pure preist, is mekill to commend.    *Then; poor; greatly*
1290  He tuk in thank quhat thing that God him    *gratefully*
      send.
For dayly mes and heryng of confessioun
Hevin he sall haiff to lestand warysoun.    *Heaven; everlasting reward*
I am the thrid grantyt throu Goddis
      grace.'
'Brother,' he said, 'tell I this in our place,    *[if] I tell*
1295  Thai wyll bot deym I other dreym or    *only believe*
      rave.'
'Than,' said the spreyt, 'this wytnes thou
      sall have.
Your bellys sall ryng, for ocht at ye do    *anything*
      may,
Quhen thai him sla, halff ane hour of that    *for half an hour*
      day.'
And so thai did. The monk wyst quhat    *knew*
      thaim alyt.    *them ailed*
1300  Throuch braid Bretane the voice tharof was    *Throughout; fame*
      scalyt.    *spread*
The spreyt tuk leyff at Goddis will to be.    *spirit; leave*
Of Wallace end to her it is pete,    *hear*
And I wald nocht put men in gret dolour    *sadness*
Bot lychtly pas atour his fatell hour.    *over; fateful*
1305  On Wednysday the fals Sotheroun furth
      brocht
Till martyr him, as thai befor had wrocht.
Rycht suth it is a martyr was Wallace,
As Osuuald, Edmunt, Edward and Thomas.
Of men in armes led him a full gret rout.    *crowd*
1310  Wyth a bauld spreit gud Wallace blent    *bold*
      about.    *looked*
A preyst he askyt, for God at deit on tre.[1]
King Edward than commaundyt his clerge    *clergy*
And said, 'I charge, apayn of los of lyve,    *on pain; life*
Nane be sa bauld yon tyrand for to schryve.[2]
1315  He has rong lang in contrar my hienace.'    *prevailed; against; Highness*
                                                *[royal rule]*

1 He asked for a priest, for [the sake of] God who died on [the] cross
2 None be so bold as to hear the confession of that tyrant

| | | |
|---|---|---|
| | A blyst byschop sone present in that place, | holy |
| | Of Canterbery he than was rychtwys lord, | Bishop of Canterbery |
| | Agayn the king he maid this rycht record | Against; statement |
| | And said, 'My self sall her his confessioun. | hear |
| 320 | Gyff I haiff mycht, in contrar of thi croun. | If; power; opposition |
| | And thou throu force will stop me of this thing, | If you; prevent |
| | I vow to God, quhilk is my rychtwys king, | |
| | That all Ingland I sall her enterdyt | here interdict |
| | And mak it knawin thou art ane herretyk. | known; heretic |
| 325 | The sacrament of kyrk I sall him geiff. | church; give |
| | Syn tak thi chos, to sterve or lat him leiff. | choice; let him live or die |
| | It war mar vaill in worschip of thi croun | more advantage; honour |
| | To kepe sic ane in lyff in thi bandoun, | such a one; subjection to you |
| | Than all the land and gud at thou has refyd, | plundered |
| 330 | Bot covatice thee ay fra honour drefyd. | covetousness; always; drove |
| | Thou has thy lyff rongyn in wrangwis deid: | ruled; wrongful deeds |
| | That sall be seyn on thee or on thi seid.' | offspring |
| | The king gert charge thai suld the byschop ta, | ordered; take |
| | Bot sad lordys consellyt to lat him ga. | grave; counselled; let; go |
| 335 | All Inglismen said at his desyr was rycht. | |
| | To Wallace than he rakyt in thar sicht | went |
| | And sadly hard his confessioun till ane end. | gravely; heard |
| | Humbly to God his spreyt he thar comend, | commended |
| | Lawly him servyt with hartlye devocioun | Meekly; heartfelt |
| 340 | Apon his kneis and said ane orysoun. | prayer |
| | His leyff he tuk and to West monaster raid. | leave; Westminster; rode |
| | The lokmen than thai bur Wallace but baid | executioners; brought |
| | On till a place his martyrdom to tak; | |
| | For till his ded he wald no forthyr mak. | death; go |
| 345 | Fra the fyrst nycht he was tane in Scotland | taken |
| | Thai kepyt him in to that sammyn band. | those same bindings |
| | Na thing he had at suld haiff doyn him gud | done |
| | Bot Inglismen him servit of carnaill fud. | fleshly |
| | Hys warldly lyff desyrd the sustenance, | |
| 350 | Thocht he it gat in contrar of plesance. | against pleasure |
| | Thai thirty dayis his band thai durst nocht slaik, | loosen |
| | Quhill he was bundyn on a skamyll of ayk | fastened; oak bench |

With irn chenyeis that was bath stark and keyn.   *iron chains; strong cruel*

A clerk thai set to her quhat he wald meyn.   *hear*

1355 'Thou Scot,' he said, 'that gret wrangis has don,

Thi fatell hour thou seis approchis son.   *destined; soon*

Thou suld in mynd remembyr thi mysdeid   *wrongdoing*

At clerkys may quhen thai thar psalmis reid   *[So] that priests; read*

For Crystyn saullis that makis thaim to pray,

1360 In thar nowmyr thou may be ane of thai,

For now thou seis on force thou mon deces.'   *of necessity die*

Than Wallace said, 'For all thi roid rahres   *severe recital*

Thou has na charge, suppos at I did mys.   *commission; wrong*

Yon blyst byschop has hecht I sall haiff blis   *That; promised; bliss*

1365 And I trow weill at God sall it admyt.   *believe; grant*

Thi febyll wordis sall nocht my conscience smyt.   *stir*

Conford I haiff of way at I suld gang;   *Comfort; go*

Maist payn I feill at I bid her our lang.'   *[is] that; too long*

Than said this clerk, 'Our king oft send thee till.

1370 Thou mycht haiff had all Scotland at thi will

To hald of him and cessyt of thi stryff,   *struggle*

So as a lord rongyn furth all thi lyff.'   *held sway*

Than Wallace said, 'Thou spekis of mychty thing.

Had I lestyt and gottyn my rychtwys king,

1375 Fra worthi Bruce had rasavit his croun   *received*

I thocht haiff maid Ingland at his bandoun;   *subject to him*

So uttraly it suld beyn at his will,   *entirely*

Quhat plessyt him to sauff thi king or spill.'   *save; destroy*

'Weill,' said this clerk , 'than thou repentis nocht;   *nothing*

1380 Of wykkydnes thou has a felloun thocht.   *grievous*

Is nayn in warld at has sa mony slane,   *that; many slain*

Tharfor till ask, me think thou sald be bane,   *ready*

Grace of our king and syn at his barnage.'   *afterwards of*

Than Wallace smyld a litill at his langage.   *speech*

1385 'I grant,' he said, 'part Inglismen I slew   *some*

In my quarell, me thocht nocht halff enew.      enough
I movyt na wer bot for to wyn our awin;      began no war; what is ours
To God and man the rycht full weill is
    knawin.      known
Thi fruster wordis dois nocht bot taris me.      useless; delay
1390  I thee commaund, on Goddis halff lat me      for God's sake let
    be.'

A schyrray gart this clerk son fra him pas;      sheriff caused; soon
Rycht as thai durst thai grant quhat he      dared
    wald as.      ask
A psalter buk Wallace had on him ever,      psalm
Fra his childeid fra it wald nocht desever.      childhood; be separated
1395  Better he trowit in wiagis for to speid,      believed; expeditions
Bot than he was dispolyeid of his weid.      stripped; clothing
This grace he ast at lord Clyffurd that      asked
    knycht,
To lat him haiff his psalter buk in sycht.      let
He gert a preyst it oppyn befor him hauld      hold
1400  Quhill thai till him had done all at thai
    wauld.
Stedfast he red for ocht thai did him thar.
Feyll Sotheroun said at Wallace feld na      felt no
    sayr.      pain
Gud devocioun so was his begynnyng
Conteynd tharwith, and fair was his      Continued
    endyng,
1405  Quhill spech and spreyt at anys all can      Until; once; did go
    fayr
To lestand blys, we trow for evermayr.      lasting bliss; evermore
I will nocht tell how he devydyt was      divided
In five partis and ordand for to pas;
Bot thus his spreyt be liklynes was weill.      in all likelihood
1410  Of Wallace lyff quha has a forthar feill      greater knowledge
May schaw furth mair with wit and      show forth more
    eloquence;
For I to this has done my diligence,
Efter the pruff geyffyn fra the Latyn buk      evidence given
Quhilk maister Blair in his tym undertuk,      undertook
1415  In fayr Latyn compild it till ane end;      compiled
With thir witnes the mair is to commend.      testimonies; more
Byschop Synclar, than lord was of Dunkell,      Dunkeld
He gat this buk and confermd it him sell      himself
For verray trew; thar of he had no dreid,      very truth; doubt

| | | |
|---|---|---|
| 1420 | Him selff had seyn gret part of Wallace deid. | deeds |
| | His purpos was till have send it to Rom, | |
| | Our fader of kyrk tharon to gyff his dom. | i.e., the pope; judgement |
| | Bot maister Blayr and als Schir Thomas Gray, | |
| | Efter Wallace thai lestit mony day, | survived |
| 1425 | Thir twa knew best of gud Schir Wilyhamys deid | These |
| | Fra sixteen yer quhill twenty-nine yeid. | until; had passed |
| | Forty and five of age Wallace was cauld | called |
| | That tym that he was to the Sotheroun sauld. | betrayed |
| | Thocht this mater be nocht till all plesance, | to all a pleasure |
| 1430 | His suthfast deid was worthi till avance. | true deeds; praise |
| | All worthi men at redys this rurall dyt, | read; unpolished composition |
| | Blaym nocht the buk, set I be unperfyt. | although; imperfect |
| | I suld have thank, sen I nocht travaill spard. | since; labour; spared |
| | For my laubour na man hecht me reward; | work; promised |
| 1435 | Na charge I had of king nor other lord; | command |
| | Gret harm I thocht his gud deid suld be smord. | lost sight of |
| | I haiff said her ner as the proces gais | narrative |
| | And fenyeid nocht for frendschip nor for fais. | not falsified / foes |
| | Costis herfor was no man bond to me. | Payment; bound |
| 1440 | In this sentence I had na will to le; | narrative; lie |
| | Bot in als mekill as I rahersit nocht | related |
| | Sa worthely as nobill Wallace wrocht, | |
| | Bot in a poynt I grant I said amys. | one |
| | Thir twa knychtis suld blamyt be for this, | These |
| 1445 | The knycht Wallas, of Cragge rychtwys lord, | |
| | And Liddaill als, gert me mak wrang record. | wrongful |
| | On Allyrtoun mur the croun he tuk a day | |
| | To get battaill, as myn autour will say. | |
| | Thir twa gert me say that ane other wys; | |
| 1450 | Till mayster Blayr we did sumpart of dispys. | To / disdain |
| | Go nobill buk, fulfillyt of gud sentens, | filled with; subject matter |
| | Suppos thou be baran of eloquens. | barren |

Go worthi buk, fullfillit of suthfast deid,          true deeds

Bot in langage of help thou has gret neid.          need

1455  Quhen gud makaris rang weill in to              poets flourished
        Scotland

Gret harm was it that nane of thaim thee          found you
        fand.

Yeit thar is part that can thee weill avance;          some; recommend you

Now byd thi tym and be a remembrance.          bide your time

I you besek of your banevolence,          pray; benevolence

1460  Quha will nocht low lak nocht my              praise do not find wanting
        eloquence:

It is weill knawin I am a burel man.          rustic

For her is said als gudly as I can;          here; as well

My spreyt felis na termys of Pernase.          knows

Now besek God that gyffar is of grace,          pray; giver

1465  Maide hell and erd and set the hevyn abuff,

That he us grant of his der lestand luff.          lasting love

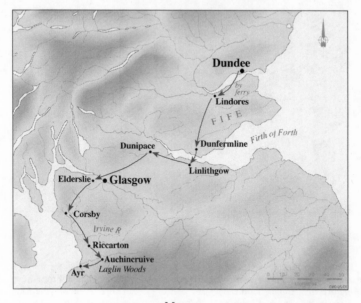

Map 1

Book One, 276–Book 2, 140
Wallace's flight from Dundee with his mother takes him across the Tay to
Lindores by ferry, then on foot (disguised as a pilgrim) across the Ochil hills,
probably along one of the well-trodden pilgrim routes, to Dunfermline. After
a night's rest he crossed the Forth to Linlithgow in the company of other
pilgrims, coming no doubt from the shrine of St Margaret in Dunfermline.
From Linlithgow he proceeded to Dunipace, finding shelter with an uncle
there, then on to Elderslie where he left his mother before going to Corsby
with his mother's brother, Sir Ranald Crawford and then on to Riccarton
into the safe-keeping of his father's brother, Sir Richard Wallace. After a
violent encounter with some of Lord Percy's men while on a fishing trip to
the River Irvine, Wallace flees again, this time to the Auchincruive estate
where another Wallace family member sends food to him as he hides out in
the Laglin woods. From there he makes two forays into Ayr, and is caught on
the second after killing a number of English soldiers, including Percy's
steward.

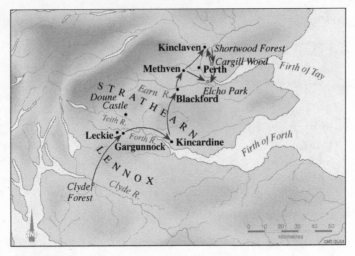

Map 2

Book Four, 100–708
Wallace crosses the River Clyde into Lennox where he camps for a while
before making his way with a small force to a valley above Leckie. From there
he prepares an attack on the nearby peel of Gargunnock. After staying four
days in the captured peel, he leads his men under cover of night to a wood
close by. With the help of Steven of Ireland, Wallace leads his men on foot
across the Forth, over terrain too swampy for horses, camping in forests until
they reach Kincardine. Wallace's party then crosses the Teith River into
Strathearn, attacking Englishmen wherever they encounter them. At Blackford he kills an English squire who is on his way to Doune Castle before
moving north across the Earn to Methven Wood where they camp. Leaving
his men in the forest, he makes his way to St Johnston (Perth), and visits a
paramour before re-joining his men in Methven. From there they move
towards the Tay and in forest there ambush and kill the English keeper of
Kinclaven castle and part of his garrison before going on to take the castle.
After plundering the castle he burns it down and repairs to Shortwood Shaw,
a natural stronghold from which the Scots defend themselves from English
attacks on all sides. After a skirmish Wallace leads his men to Cargill wood
and then to Shortwood again, back to Methven before moving to Elcho Park,
from which Wallace visits St Johnston again.

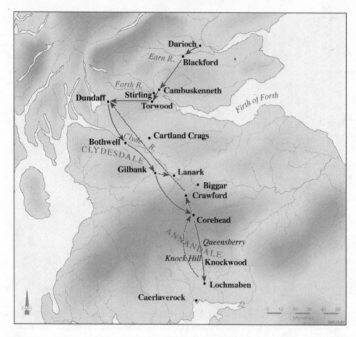

Map 3

Book Five, 279–1140

With the English in hot pursuit, Wallace rides hard from Darioch to Blackford
where he dismounts from his winded horse and proceeds on foot for a good mile
before crippling the horse (originally Butler's) to prevent the English from taking
him. Through moor and heather he makes his way to the Forth and, avoiding the
English watch at Stirling Bridge, goes to Cambuskenneth where at a shallow
place he wades across the river carrying his sword and clothes above his head. He
then crosses the Carse of Stirling to the Torwood where he finds refuge with a
local widow. Once recovered, he heads off with two of her sons to Dundaff where
Sir John Graham joins him as he proceeds to Bothwell Moor. Next morning they
go to Gilbank where they are sheltered by another of his mother's brothers until
Christmas, four months later. From Gilbank he often visits Lanark on account of
Marion Braidfute. He sets off from Gilbank to the Corehead where he meets up
with his kinsmen Thom Haliday and Edward Litill and plans an attack on
Lochmaben castle. Leaving most of the men in the Knockwood, he, Kerle and
the other two go to the town where the keeper's nephew insultingly docks the tails
from their horses. After taking revenge, Wallace returns to the Knockwood,
rallies his men and heads for a hill. Various skirmishes ensue as running battles
take place between Lochmaben and the Corehead. He goes on to attack Crawford
Castle and then returns to Dundaff where he and his men enjoy the hospitality of
Sir John Graham.

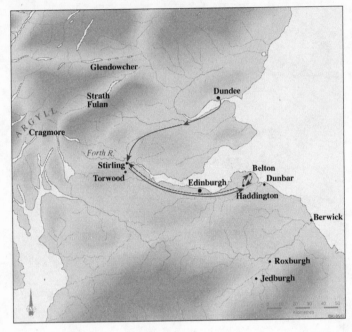

Map 4

Book Seven, 1219–50
After the battle at Stirling Bridge (for which Wallace abandoned his siege of
Dundee), Wallace and his army pursue the English from the field to the
Torwood and after further fighting there and at Haddington on to Dunbar
where Earl Patrick provides refuge for Warenne and the English survivors.
Wallace removes to Belton and then to Haddington for the night, returning
to Stirling next day.

# Notes

**1–19**  These lines provide a short prologue in which Blind Harry highlights the commemorative function of his narrative. Although similar to Barbour's prologue in *The Bruce*, Blind Harry's denigration of the English, the first of many such disparagements in his poem, is not characteristic of Barbour.

**21**  Through the convention of providing his hero's genealogy, Blind Harry traces Wallace's lineage back to the 'gud Wallace' who was a companion of Walter Warayn of Wales (30–32), or Walter Fitz Alan, the first Scottish Stewart. The Stewart dynasty succeeded the Bruces to the throne of Scotland.

**23**  Sir Reginald (Ranald) Crawford, brother of Wallace's mother, became sheriff of Ayr in May 1296.

**28–9**  *Elrisle . . . Auchinbothe.* Elderslie and Auchenbathie, Renfrewshire lands held first by the father, later by the brother of the same name, Sir Malcolm Wallace, as vassals to the Stewart. They were part of the lordship of Paisley and Renfrew and, as Barrow points out, right at the heart of the Stewart fief.

**34**  *the rycht lyne of the fyrst Stewart.* This appears to be a reference to Barbour's long lost genealogy of the Stewarts, a work whose existence is also attested by the fifteenth-century Scottish chronicler, Andrew Wyntoun.

**36**  Sir Malcolm Wallace is the only brother mentioned, although other sources suggest William Wallace had at least one other brother, John, who was executed in 1307 after being captured fighting for Bruce.

**41**  Alexander III (1249–86) whose accidental death when he was thrown from his horse near the royal manor of Kinghorn in Fife left the kingdom without a king. His three children had died before him, his two sons without offspring, so the heir to the throne was his daughter's child, Margaret, the 'Maid of Norway'. On her way to Scotland to ascend her throne in 1290 Margaret died in Orkney. A number of rival claimants to the throne then presented themselves, the strongest two being Robert Bruce, lord of Annandale (grandfather of the future king Robert I) and John Balliol, who did succeed in 1292.

**44**  *a full grevous debate.* Blind Harry provides a very brief and over-simplified account of the succession crisis in the following lines. He identifies the chief competitors as *Bruce* (that is Robert Bruce, lord of Annandale), *Balyoune* (John Balliol) and *Hastyng*

(John Hastings), the descendants of the three daughters of *Our prynce Davy,* David, Earl of Huntingdon, grandson of David I (1124–30). Balliol claimed as the grandson of the eldest daughter, Dervoguilla *(of first gre lynialy)* and Bruce, as the son of the second daughter, Isabel, and the first male descendant *(first male of the secund gre)*; Hastings was the grandson of Ada, the youngest daughter. Edward I (Langshanks) was approached as arbiter and used the opportunity to declare his overlordship of Scotland. Bruce and Balliol emerged as the main claimants, although by the end of 1292, Bruce had resigned his claim in favour of his son and heirs and Edward had decided in favour of Balliol (crowned at Scone on November 30). By the rule of primogeniture, Balliol had the stronger claim but after the succession of Robert Bruce in 1306 history was rewritten to make Bruce appear the divine and popular choice. See Barbour (*Bruce 1*, 37–178) , Wyntoun (*Cronykil*, Book VIII, ccs. i, ii, v, vi, vii, viii, x) and Bower (Book XI, ccs. 1–14) whose accounts clearly influenced Blind Harry.

53–4    These lines may have been influenced by Barbour's passionate reproach:

> A! Blind folk full off all foly,
> Haid ye umbethocht you enkrely
> Quhat perell to you mycht apper
> Ye had nocht wrocht on that maner.
> Haid ye tane keip how at that king
> Alwayis foroutyn sojourning
> Travayllyt for to wyn senyhory
> And throu his mycht till occupy
> Landis that war till him marcheand
> ....
> Ye mycht se he suld occupy
> Throu slycht that he ne mycht throu maistri.
>          (I, 91–112)

56      *Gaskone*. The war with Philip the Fair of France over Gascony did not break out until June, 1294, whereas Blind Harry is clearly referring here to events in 1291–92. Bower's mention of the envoys who journeyed to Gascony in 1286 to seek Edward's arbitration in the succession crisis (Book XI, c. 3) may well account for Blind Harry's mistake, as McDiarmid suggests.

61      *Noram*. Norham on Tweed, Northumberland. It was here in May, 1291 that Edward met the Scots and declared his right to overlordship of Scotland.

65      *Byschope Robert*. Robert Wishart, Bishop of Glasgow (1261–1316), a staunch defender of Scottish independence. Wyntoun and Bower are the sources here.

71      Edward decided in Balliol's favour and the latter was crowned king in November, 1292.

77      *Ane abbot*. Identified as Henry of Arbroath by McDiarmid, who cites Wyntoun and Bower as Blind Harry's sources here.

79      *Werk on Twede*. Up river from Berwick on Tweed.

81      *Corspatryk*. Earl Patrick of Dunbar and March, one of the great magnates of Scotland who supported Edward I. His role in the sack of Berwick is also attested by the English chronicle, *Scalacronica*. He was later appointed keeper of Berwick town (1298). Blind Harry describes him as a traitor, and blames him for the defeat of the Scots at the Battle of Dunbar the following month.

85–6      Several accounts of Edward's sack of Berwick in March, 1296 survive. Medieval Scottish chroniclers represent it as one of the greatest atrocities perpetrated by Edward's forces, because of the slaughter of civilians, including women and children, Wyntoun (Book VIII, c. xi) and Bower (Book XI, c. 20) describe the devastating attack in detail and both reckon the toll at 7500.

98–114      The Battle of Dunbar took place on 27 April, 1296. Blind Harry seems to have used a different source here from Wyntoun and Bower, who mention the presence of only one earl, Ross. The English *Lanercost* chronicle agrees with Blind Harry about the four present. Modern historians tend to agree that three were present, Atholl, Ross and Menteith. (Barrow [1988], 74, Watson, 25)

102      *Mar, Menteith, Adell, Ros*. The high-ranking earls of Mar, Menteith, Atholl and Ross.

115–21      *Scune*. Edward's recorded itinerary after Dunbar places him in the borders during May and early June and then travelling north from 6 June, staying in Perth 21–24 June, Forfar 3 July and arriving in Montrose on 8 July, to which he summoned Balliol. If he included Scone on his route, then he must have been there in the last week of June. Both Bower and Wyntoun state that Balliol was summoned to Montrose and, stripped of the royal regalia, was there forced to resign the kingdom on 8 July, 1296. Whether Edward was ever crowned at Scone is a matter for speculation. He certainly removed the Stone of Destiny to London in 1296.

122      *Gadalos*. Legendary history records that Gaythelos was the husband of Scota, the eponymous mother of the Scottish people and daughter of an Egyptian pharaoh, whose descendants brought to Scotland the Stone of Destiny, which later became the coronation seat of Scottish monarchs and a symbol of Scottish independence. Taken by Edward to London in 1296, it was finally returned to Scotland with the Scottish royal regalia in 1996. See Fordun, *Chronica* I, cc. 8–19 and the expanded version of this origin myth in Bower, *Scotichronicon* I, cc. 9–18.

123      *Iber Scot*. Hiber, the son of Gaythelos who established the Scots in Ireland.

124      *Canmor syne King Fergus*. Malcolm Canmore, king of Scots (1058–93) and the successor of Macbeth. According to legend, Fergus was the first Scottish king.

132      *Margretis ayr*. The descendants of St Margaret, the English wife of Malcom Canmore, became the rulers of England and

Scotland. Blind Harry may be drawing on Bower who inserts an account of their descendants in the midst of his account of the Scottish succession dispute (XI, c. 12).

133    After his triumphant tour through much of central and eastern Scotland, accepting homage as he went, Edward set up an English administration, with headquarters in Berwick. Leading barons and knights, many captured at Dunbar, were taken as prisoners to England.

134    Bruce, i.e., Robert Bruce, the future king.

137    *Blacok mur . . . Huntyntoun.* McDiarmid believes this should be *Blacow mur* as it refers to Blakemore in Yorkshire, where the Bruces held lands. *Huntyntoun* is the vast English Honour of Huntingdon, a third of which had come into the Bruce family through Isabel, one of the three daughters of Earl David.

140    McDiarmid suggests one possible corroboration of this claim that Edward entrusted the government of all Scotland to the earl Patrick of March (*The Wallace Papers, Maitland Club*, 1841, p.5).

144    Blind Harry returns to Wallace and resumes his account of the outbreak of war in early 1296. Later (line 192) Wallace is said to be eighteen years of age when he has his first violent encounter with the English in Dundee. Blind Harry's account of his career doesn't add up. If Wallace is eighteen in 1296 he cannot have been forty-five at the time of his death in 1305, as Blind Harry says he was (Book Twelve, 1427). It may be that Blind Harry thought of eighteen as the age at which a youth could take up arms. In Book Three, Adam, the eldest son of Wallace's uncle Sir Richard Wallace, at the same age is the only one of the three who rides off with William Wallace to pursue a campaign against the English.

147    Malcolm, his father and his eldest brother, also called Malcolm (line 321). The Lennox, in the west of Central Scotland, was one of the oldest earldoms of Scotland. It incorporated Dumbartonshire, much of Stirlingshire, and parts of Renfrewshire and Perthshire.

150    Kilspindie, in the Gowrie district of Perthshire, where a relative on his maternal side offers refuge. Even though he is said to be an 'agyt man' (line 154), it seems unlikely that Blind Harry was referring to the uncle of Wallace's maternal grandfather, as line 152 seems to suggest, but rather to Wallace's uncle.

155    That part of Wallace's education, including going to school in Dundee, ten miles from his uncle's home in Kilspindie, is repeated by Blind Harry in Book Seven, lines 670–71.

159    *Saxons blud.* Blind Harry quite frequently refers to the English occupiers in this racist manner. Another example is the metonym, 'Sothroun' (e.g. line 188). (See Goldstein, 222–3.)

160–70  These sentiments are reminiscent of *The Bruce*, I, 179–204.

165    The English occupation is compared to Herod's slaughter of the innocents.

171–2  Although no other known source claims Glasgow diocese was handed over to the Bishop of Durham, McDiarmid suggests that Blind Harry's conviction about this may be based on a tradition.

175–6 The hanging of Scottish leaders and Wallace's revenge on the English as they slept in barns at Ayr are entirely fictitious events described in Book Seven.

194 Specific examples of the strife Wallace encounters are recounted at lines 205–32 and in Book Two.

201–2 The description of Wallace's appearance and manner is quite conventional. His reticence to speak much is mentioned again at 294.

205 The name of the constable of Dundee castle in 1296 is not known, but the name Selby (207) is that of a Northumberland knight active in the wars of independence.

215 McDiarmid suggests a 'geste' may be Blind Harry's source here.

219 *rough rewlyngis*, that is, roughshod rawhide boots. In his poem on the Battle of Bannockburn, the English poet Laurence Minot used much the same term, 'Rughfute riveling', as a mocking metonym for the Scots. *The Poems of Laurence Minot* ed. Richard Osberg (TEAMS Middle English Text Series, 1996) p. 36.

275 *lawdayis . . . set ane ayr.* Lawdays were the days appointed for holding courts of law and justice ayres were the circuit courts of the Sovereign's justice.

282 St Margaret was Queen Margaret of Scotland (d. 1093), wife of Malcolm Canmore (1057–93). Originally a member of the Saxon royal family, she became renowned for her piety and was canonised in 1249. Her shrine in Dunfermline Abbey (287) was a favourite destination for pilgrims.

285 *Landoris.* Lindores, Fife. This suggests they took the ferry across the Tay at the confluence with the river Earn, rather than the Dundee–Tayport ferry near the firth. Lindores was on a major pilgrim route, and shelter could be obtained at the Grange, the home farm of the nearby abbey.

287 Dunfermline, another early Scottish burgh, was also a major trade and communication centre because of its proximity to the river Forth.

290 *Lithquhow.* Linlithgow, in what is now West Lothian, was one of the earliest royal Scottish burghs.

294 Note the qualities admired in the young Wallace, especially reticence. See lines 200–1.

296–97 One of the main ferry routes for pilgrims and other travellers in medieval Scotland linked Dunfermline and Queensferry (named after Queen Margaret).

299–300 *his eyme . . . persone.* Bower also refers to one of Wallace's uncles as a priest.

304 *sone.* This word is used throughout the poem in addresses by older to younger male relatives generally.

317 *Corsby* (also sometimes anglicised on maps as Crosby) in Ayrshire.

319–21 Blind Harry claims that Wallace's father and his eldest brother

Malcolm were killed at the Battle of Loudoun Hill, but Malcolm Wallace was alive in 1299 and history only testifies to a battle there in 1307. See note to Book Three, line 78.

330     Henry Percy, a Northumberland knight, was appointed Warden of Ayr and Galloway by Edward I in 1296, and played a major part in the Scottish wars. He also appears in *The Bruce* (4, 598–603). Blind Harry describes him as 'captane than of Ayr' at line 379.

355     Another uncle, Sir Richard Wallace of Riccarton in Kyle, Ayrshire, conjecturally one of the Wallace fees (Barrow, *The Kingdom of the Scots, 350*). It was, perhaps, one of his three sons (mentioned first in Book Three, lines 43–4) who married the widow of the earl of Carrick (the father of the future king, Robert Bruce) in 1306.

363–8     Blind Harry becomes specific about the months Wallace spends in Ayrshire, but the year is still unclear.

368–433     The source for this story of Wallace's violent encounter with Percy's men is probably a traditional tale.

383     *Scot martyns fische.* McDiarmid cites an old Scottish proverb which conveys the sense of 'every man for himself'.

399     The Englishman objects to Wallace's use of the familiar 'thou' instead of 'ye' or 'yhe' (385, 391) he adopted earlier in this exchange.

## BOOK TWO

11     *Auchincruff.* Auchincruive castle, Ayrshire, was the fee of Richard Wallace (line 13).

16     *Laglyne wode.* Presumably a nearby forest, later part of the Auchincruive estate. Wallace uses it as a natural stronghold and refuge a number of times in the narrative (2, 66; 3, 421; 7, 262).

27–65     One of three episodes in this book in which Wallace flexes his muscles against the English as he limbers up for organised resistance to the occupation regime Blind Harry has described. Opportunities to display his hero's individual feats of combat are created just as they were for Bruce in Barbour's *romanys*. The motif is repeated at lines 78–136, although this time Wallace does not escape his pursuers, and at lines 384–411.

84     A steward managed a household's domestic affairs, including supervision of his lord's table, hence Blind Harry's joke at line 101.

93     A similarly familiar, so rude, form of address is found at line 391.

124     Ayr castle.

171–359     Note the change of stanza form for Wallace's lament in prison.

234     *Celinus* is another name for Mercury. McDiarmid reads *Celinius* and relates the allusion to Chaucer's *Compleynt of Mars* where Venus flees 'unto Cylenius tour' (113) to avoid exposure by Phebus, who catches her with Mars.

252–5     A.A. MacDonald notes this motif was probably taken from

Valerius Maximus. 'The Sense of Place in Early Scottish Verse: Rhetoric and Reality' in *English Studies* 1991 (Feb.) 72:1, 12–27: 18.

258      *His fyrst norys.* Wallace's former wet nurse (also referred to as his 'foster modyr' at line 270) retrieves his 'body' from the castle walls and arranges for him to be carried across the river to the Newtown on the north bank of the Ayr river. This may suggest that Wallace's birthplace was in Ayrshire. On the other hand, tradition associates Wallace's birth with Elderslie in Renfrewshire, and it may be that the wet nurse came from Ayrshire to nurse the young Wallace. He later sends her, with her daughter and grand-son, to join his own mother in safety there (366–69).

280      To aid the ruse that Wallace is dead the good woman, 'his foster modyr' (270), places a board covered with woollens and surrounded by lights, as if it were a place of honour for mourning the deceased.

288      Thomas of Ercildoune, otherwise known as Thomas the Rimer, is mentioned with other soothsayers in the *Scalacronica*, an Anglo-Norman chronicle begun in 1355 by Sir Thomas Gray. A ballad dating from the fifteenth century recounts some of Thomas's adventures in Elfland. *The Romance and Prophecies of Thomas of Ercildoune* was edited in 1875 by James Murray (EETS o.s. 61). Blind Harry attributes to Thomas the prophecy that Wallace will three times oust the English from Scotland (lines 346–50).

359      Wallace's raids in England are described in Book Eight, 512–620.

387      Longcasteel. A squire who should be distinguished from the Earl of Longcastell, i.e. Lancaster mentioned at Book Six, 669.

416      Sir Richard Wallace of Riccarton. See note to 1, 355. He is said to have three sons (418).

436      Robert Boyd is presented by Blind Harry as one of Wallace's loyal companions, along with Adam Wallace, one Kneland, whose first name is never provided by Blind Harry, and Edward Litill. See Book Three, lines 45–56. Probably he is the Robert Boyd of Noddsdale, Cunningham and coroner of Ayr and Lanark, and possibly the same Sir Robert Boyd that Barbour identifies as one of Bruce's staunchest supporters (*Bruce*, 4, 342, 352–63, 505).

## BOOK THREE

1–14      Compare to the opening lines of Henryson's fable the *Preiching of the Swallow*.

11–20      Historically, the English did not occupy many castles in 1296. Blind Harry establishes another contrast between the suffering and deprivation of the Scots and the well-provisioned English occupying forces. The irony is that harvest time is approaching. Blind Harry is using a literary device, as the opening lines make

|     |     |
| --- | --- |
| 17 | apparent, and creating a motive for Wallace's revenge (40–1). *wyn and gud wernage*. The first suggests *vin ordinaire,* red or white,  while *wernage* is a malmsey or muscadine, a strong, sweet-flavoured white wine. |
| 45–57 | According to Blind Harry, most of Wallace's early companions are his kinsmen: his cousins Adam Wallace and Edward Litill, and another close relative, Kneland ('ner cusyng to Wallace', line 55). Kneland and Edward Litill have not been precisely identified, although families bearing these names are associated with Midlothian and Annandale in the thirteenth century. |
| 48–9 | Adam Wallace, William's cousin, is not mentioned by Barbour. |
| 60 | Mauchline Moor, on the north bank of the River Ayr. Richard Wallace held a fee within the large parish of Mauchline. (Barrow, *The Kingdom of the Scots,* 349). |
| 62 | Fenwicks are known to have been involved in border warfare in the fifteenth century. This Fenwick was probably from Northumberland or Cumberland, given that he is responsible for transporting supplies from England, via Carlisle, to Percy at Ayr, along a major supply route. |
| 67 | Loudoun Hill, just north of the Irvine River, Ayrshire. |
| 72 | Like other medieval writers, Blind Harry uses the authority *topos,* to create the impression of authenticity. |
| 78 | Avondale, not far from Loudoun. McDiarmid suggests that Blind Harry ingeniously created this detour from the usual route from Carlisle to Ayr, via Corsancone, so that he could invent a Battle at Loudoun Hill, drawing details from Barbour's account of Bruce's victory there in 1307 (*Bruce,* 8, 207–358). The use of 'dykes' and the flight of the English are common to both battles. |
| 111–2 | Compare to I. 319–20. Blind Harry has mentioned only one brother, Malcolm. He was alive in 1299. |
| 117–8 | See note to line 62. No specific individual has been identified but McDiarmid points out that a number of persons with this name are mentioned in contemporary records. The expeditions against the Scots may allude to cross-border raids. |
| 129–32 | The polished armour of the English contrasts with the utility of the Scots' armour. The few against the many is a common romance motif, employed by Barbour too. |
| 133–4 | *a maner dyk.* This may well refer to a ditch and wall combination of the kind Barbour describes in *Bruce,* 8, 172–183. See the note on these in A.A.M. Duncan's edition of *The Bruce* (Canongate, 1997), p. 298. |
| 188 | Bewmound. Beaumont is a squire, so is not to be confused with the Bewmound, Earl of Buchan, who appears from Book Seven on. |
| 207 | Kyle and Cunningham were two districts of Ayrshire. Boyd, as noted earlier, held land in Cunningham. |
| 214 | Clyde forest was on the north side of the River Clyde. |
| 261 | Sir Amer de Valence was Edward I's lieutenant in Scotland and was later created earl of Pembroke (1307). He was not a Scot as Blind Harry seems to suggest, although the description 'false |

traytour' may refer to the role he later played in commissioning John Menteith to betray Wallace (Book Twelve). The influence of Barbour is detectable in the reference to Valence immediately after Loudoun Hill, and the connection with Bothwell (similarly in Book Six, 274).

280      The threat of execution in London.

282–306    The dissent of the *lordis* (plural at line 293 probably echoes that at 287) highlights the righteousness of the Scottish struggle as the English king's 'wrang conquest' is juxtaposed with Wallace's 'rycht' (295; 297).

299      *that lord*, i.e., Sir Percy.

316–7     This is more evidence of Blind Harry's sense of humour when he says that the wine was as fine as King Edward's: it is, after all, part of the booty from Loudoun!

342–9     Astrological portents of war are common in medieval literature. McDiarmid cites Chaucer's *Knight's Tale* and *Summoner's Tale,* and Gower's *Confessio Amantis.*

341      *This pees was cryede in August.* In August, 1296, Edward had completed his march around Scotland taking homage wherever he went, and the administration of the occupation regime was set up.

359      *Scrymmage* (same derivation as *skirmish*) was a fencing bout (*OED*).


BOOK FOUR

1–10     Blind Harry's literary pretensions are most evident in rhetorical set pieces of this kind in which the month (September) and the season (autumn) are described.

3       Victuals in this sense include all harvestable foods such as grain, berries, vegetables, and so on.

9       The mutability of worldly things is a commonplace.

15–6     A sheriff was 'the principal royal officer in local districts into which the kingdom was divided for the purposes of royal government'. (Barrow, 1988 p. 8). Sir Ranald inherited the position 'throu rycht' (16), reflecting the tendency for a sheriff's office to become heritable.

18      Another invocation of his written source, or authority. The book cited here is presumably the fictitious one by Blair, which Blind Harry claims as his main authority on Wallace.

22–54    Another instance of aggression between Wallace and Percy's baggage men. See note 2, 379–99.

26      Hazelden, Renfrewshire, south of Glasgow.

104     The Lennox was one of the oldest earldoms in the west of Scotland. Earl Malcolm of Lennox, referred to at line 156, was one of those who swore fealty to Edward I after the Battle of Dunbar (although at line 158 Blind Harry says he had not yet sworn allegiance to Edward), but he was a patriotic supporter of Wallace, just as his son of the same name played an important role in Bruce's reign.

135     *gret ayth.* This was an oath of special solemnity.

147     Annandale in southwest Scotland.

171     The head of the powerful MacDonald clan, whose lordship was
        Kintyre, had sworn allegiance to Edward in 1291 and remained
        a steadfast supporter of the English interest. Alexander Mac-
        Donald of Islay was appointed Admiral of the Western Isles by
        Edward.

173     Like Earl Malcolm, Stephen of Ireland became a staunch
        Wallace supporter. McDiarmid links the latter to the Irelands
        of Murtley castle near Dunkeld, Fife.

175     Men of Argyll come to support Wallace.

185     Fawdoun appears to be Blind Harry's invention since he cannot
        be identified.

190     *the bodelye ayth.* The bodily or corporal oath was 'perhaps an
        oath taken originally on a consecrated host or "body" of Christ,
        but also used of oaths taken with a "bodily touch" of other
        sacred things' (*OED*, which records Blind Harry's usage here as
        the earliest occurrence in English).

194     This is the only mention of Gray in the poem, whereas there are
        frequent references to Kerle, probably William Ker, as lines
        preserved in F and L claim (11, 795–807. Blind Harry identifies
        him as Wallace's steward at line 383 below.

213     *Gargownno.* Gargunnock.

235–9   Wallace's incredible strength is demonstrated when he tears off
        the gate bar with his bare hands.

277     Stephen of Ireland leads them to Kincardine on the east coast,
        and in a forest there Wallace slays a hart.

325–44  Scotland's plenty. Compare with Barbour's account of food
        resources in Aberdeenshire (*Bruce*, 2, 577–84) after his defeat at
        Methven. Methven Park later became a favourite royal hunting
        reserve.

335–40  The device of anaphora (now ... now) is employed to convey the
        range of Scotland's character.

341     Blind Harry points out that Wallace will fight for Scotland for
        six years and seven months, and predicts what is to come, but of
        course the chronology is Blind Harry's own.

343     *left Scotland in playne.* This is presumably a reference to
        Wallace's trip to France (Book Nine).

359     *mar.* The chief magistrate of a town. According to the *Dic-
        tionary of the Older Scottish Tongue* this normally referred to the
        mayor or magistrate of an English town, but is used here of
        Perth, a town occupied by the English. There is also an old
        Scottish Gaelic term, *maor*, meaning steward or bailiff.

395–6   Sir James Butler's son, Sir John, is said to be deputy captain,
        and Sir Garaid (Gerard) Heroun to be the captain of Kinclaven
        Castle (396). A Robert Heron was appointed chamberlain
        comptroller in Scotland in 1305, but no Sir Gerard Heron
        has been identified as active in Scotland during this period.

441     Ninety English soldiers arrive, led by Butler as becomes clear at
        line 457.

583    William Loran, Butler's nephew, arrives to avenge his uncle too. Wallace's fifty men are well and truly outnumbered.

593    Wallace attempts to raise morale in this speech to his men. Compare with Barbour, 2, 340–4.

722    Death by burning was the usual punishment for high treason decreed for women.

723    Wallace is referred to as a *rebell*. He later denies this vociferously.

738–40 Compare to Chaucer, whose narrators in the dream vision poems are often inexperienced in the ways of Venus.

787    *South Ynche*. McDiarmid notes the town had a north and south inch, or lawn.

BOOK FIVE

24–30  The use of a sleuth hound to track Wallace no doubt owes much to a similar episode in *The Bruce* (Book Six, 36–49; 555–674). This sleuth hound is from Gilliesland in Cumberland, not far from the rivers Esk and Liddle (27).

95     Gask wood, like the Gask Hall (179), is on the left bank of the River Earn.

132    Dupplin Castle was west of Perth and Butler stations a large force there (166) when he crosses the river to Dalreach (167) while Wallace and his small company take themselves to the Gask Hˑll (175), where Fawdoun's ghost appears (192–222). This episode appears to have been one of Blind Harry's inventions.

180–213 No specific source for this ghost story is known. Blind Harry refers to Wallace's experience as a *fantase* (212), which McDiarmid notes conforms to what Chaucer calls 'infernals illusions' in medieval dream lore, i.e., fantasies which lured men to their destruction. On possible Celtic sources for the Fawdoun episode, see Balaban, 'Blind Harry and *The Wallace*', *Chaucer Review 8* (1974): 248.

211–24 Blind Harry ponders on the 'fantase' and compares the 'myscheiff' to Lucifer's fall. Note the echo of Barbour (1, 259–60) about leaving discussion of such matters to clerks (223–5).

219–222 McDiarmid refers to Dante's *Inferno*, in which it is disclosed that fiends take over the bodies of traitors once the soul has departed. In his *Daemonologie* (1597), King James VI discussed possession of dead bodies by devils, calling such spectres *umbrae mortuorum* (Chaps. VI, 23–5; VII, 16–18).

246–7  *Schir Jhon Sewart*. The Siwards of Tibbers and Aberdour in Fife were one of the chief Scottish baronial families. Although a Sir John Siward did serve in Edward I's army in Scotland, McDiarmid suggests that Blind Harry has in mind his son, Richard, son-in-law to Sir John Comyn, who had been captured at the Battle of Dunbar, been taken to London, and subsequently became a prominent member of Edward's administration in Scotland. Bower describes how he handed over Dunbar Castle to the English (XI, cap. 24). His son John was later a supporter of Robert Bruce.

298           McDiarmid notes that there are standing stones at several places on Wallace's route here between Blackford and Cambuskenneth.

319           *Kers* is the Carse of Stirling. Wallace travels on foot from south of Blackford along the Forth valley to Cambuskenneth, where he swims across the river.

389–94      Note the appropriate use of the familiar form of address by the parson. When the English adopt the familiar form the intention is to insult Wallace.

412           The Erth ferry ran from Kincardine on the north shore to Airth on the south shore of the Forth.

435–6       Although the pronoun does make this clear, it is Wallace who heads to Dundaff, as becomes evident in lines 449–64. Blind Harry says that the lord of Dundaff was Sir John Graham, and his son, also John, is portrayed by him as one of Wallace's strongest supporters (and kinsman, since related by marriage) until his death at Falkirk (1298). The Grahams became lords of Dundaff in the reign of Alexander II, and their descendants were Balliol supporters, like the historical Wallace, but the name 'John' is more common among the Abercorn branch than the Dundaff branch of the family, so combined family traditions may be Blind Harry's source, as McDiarmid suggests.

456           Blind Harry is partial to such proverbs.

465–6       *In Bothwell . . . With ane Crawfurd*. The Crawford is presumably a kinsman of Wallace. After a night in Bothwell, on the north bank of the Forth, Wallace moves on to Gilbank (467), not far from Lanark, where another uncle, Auchinleck, Sir Reginald Crawford's brother, shelters him (469).

467           Gilbank was identified by Jamieson as a property in Lanarkshire, held in tribute by Auchinleck.

469–74      Presumably family tradition provided Blind Harry with the details of these relationships, for example, that Auchinleck married Sir Reginald's widow, the daughter of the laird of Lesmahagow (474) and fathered three children, one of whom was the son mentioned at line 477. The Crawfords, as noted before, were hereditary sheriffs of Ayr. Percy would have received homage from Sir Reginald when he was installed as part of Edward's administration in 1296.

474           Lesmahagow in Lanarkshire.

479           *he*, i.e. Auchinleck.

481           *Loran*. See note to Book Four, 583.

506           Percy is thinking about the need to appoint a new garrison at Perth and he makes arrangements for this at lines 519–20. No arrangements are made for Kinclaven, which has been reduced to ruins (521).

508           *clerkys*. Another reference to prophecies.

514           *nacione*. One of the earliest uses of this term to refer to an identifiable nation. Wyntoun also uses it in this sense (VII, 408).

519–20      Sir Richard Siward is known to have been sheriff of Fife and

also Dumfries, as well as warden of Nithsdale, but surviving
records do not indicate whether he was ever sheriff of Perth.

533–45 Blind Harry's putative sources, John Blair and Thomas Gray,
are depicted as scholars and eye-witnesses. As Blind Harry had
a friend by the name of Blair, a compliment may be intended.

569–71 William Hesilrig was a Northumberland knight appointed as
sheriff of Lanark in 1296 as part of the new administration. He
is mentioned in the *Scalacronica*, p. 123.

579–710 Blind Harry cites a *buk* as authority for the story of Wallace's
sweetheart. Wallace's courtship of a maiden in Lanark is also
told by Wyntoun, who briefly relates how Wallace's 'lemman'
in Lanark dies at the hands of the town's sheriff for assisting the
hero's escape from the town (VIII, ch. xiii, lines 2075–92).
Unlike the 'lemman' in Perth, this maiden is the daughter of a
late, respectable Lanarkshire landowner. She later declares that
she 'wyll no lemman be' (693). Her noble parentage, beauty,
manners, and virtues are all noticed. Blind Harry names her
father as Hew Braidfute of Lammington (584), which is in
Lanarkshire, but the family has not been identified. He stresses
her vulnerability, as she lacks the protection of parents and her
brother has been killed. Among her qualities is piety: Wallace
falls in love when he first sees her in church. That Blind Harry's
model is Criseyde from Chaucer's *Troilus and Criseyde* is clear
in lines 605–6. The influence of *Troilus and Criseyde* is explored
by Vernon Harward, 'Blind Harry's Wallace and Chaucer's
*Troilus and Criseyde*', *SSL*, 1972, 48–50.

606 *The prent of luff*: Derived from Aristotelian philosophy, this
conception of love as a deep impression made on, and retained
in, the heart is also found in Robert Henryson's *Testament of
Cresseid* (505–11).

609 *hyr kynrent and hyr blud*. These are the credentials that make
her attractive to him.

631–2 Compare Troilus's attitude in Book I of *Troilus and Criseyde*
(lines 191–3).

685 See Chaucer's *Franklin's Tale* (741–50) for a similar *accord*,
especially concerning service in love.

719–61 Wallace moves into Annandale travelling from Corehead, in
Moffatdale, to Lochmaben Castle, where he kills the captain.

720 This familial relationship between Thom Halyday and Wallace
is not otherwise attested. The purported relationship gives
Wallace an extended family and support network. See below
1045 and Book Six, 536–7.

721 *Litill*. Litill from Annandale. See note to 3, 45–6.

737 Sir Robert Clifford, a Westmoreland knight, was active in
Scotland from 1296. He has known associations with Caerlaverock and Carlisle castles, so may well have had a nephew who
was captain of Lochmaben. He was warden of Galloway from
1298 and appointed captain of the south west garrisons, which
were regularly under attack from the Scots. He defended
Lochmaben from Bruce in 1307 and was killed at Bannockburn.

Blind Harry is inclined to make family vengeance a motivating force. Compare his treatment of the Butlers. The uncle of the captain killed here is later killed in Book Ten (1114).

755    A marshall was originally one who tended horses. Later it was the title of a high-ranking officer in a royal court.

757–60    Another instance of Blind Harry's grim humour. As well as shaving, barbers also let blood.

766–970    Wallace and his small company are pursued by soldiers from Lochmaben. Running combat ensues as the English give chase through the Knockwood (777) and Wallace tries to return to Corehead, avoiding open battle. Reinforcements are provided when needed most by Sir John Graham and one Kirkpatrick (see below, 907–15), whereupon the pursuit is reversed.

804–9    This is the 'few against many' motif again.

815–8    Hugh of Morland, another Westmoreland knight, and a veteran according to Blind Harry, was probably involved in border warfare long before the war with Scotland broke out. Although many of the specific persons mentioned by Blind Harry cannot be identified precisely, their names are often authentic in that they can be linked to geographical places.

842    Wallace is presented as an exemplary chieftain.

857    Possibly John Graystok, a Northumberland baron, although McDiarmid thinks Blind Harry may have a later Graystok in mind.

898    Queensberry Hill, near Moffat. Wallace wants the advantage of the high ground.

915    The Kirkpatricks were a knightly family in the feu of the lord of Annandale (Barrow, 21). A Roger Kirkpatrick, justiciary of Galloway (1305–6), aided and abetted at the killing of John Comyn in Dumfries in 1306. This one is said to be the baron of Torthowald, and to be related to Wallace on his mother's side (919–20).

920    Crawford, north of Corehead.

995    *Carlaverok . . . Maxwell.* Caerlaverock Castle, situated between Dumfries and Lochmaben at the mouth of the Nith, and sometimes referred to as Maxwell Castle. It was in Scots hands until 1297, when it was given to Clifford, but not captured by the English until 1300 (Watson, 74). So Blind Harry knows that it was still Scots at this stage. The strategic importance of these castles is recognised, as it was by Bruce.

1040    The English returning from earlier combat with Wallace near Knockwood are killed as they enter Lochmaben.

1045–8    Another of Wallace's kinsmen through marriage, this time to Haliday's second daughter, is made captain of Lochmaben Castle.

1067    Ewesdale and Crawfordjohn.

1071    Crawford Castle, on the Clyde.

1076    McDiarmid confirms that Martindale is a Cumberland name.

1111    Barbour uses a similar phrasing to suggest summary punishment at the point of a sword (*Bruce*, 6, 150).

BOOK SIX

1–104      This preamble links Wallace's fortunes to love, and anticipates
           the loss of his beloved. The metre adopted here is appropriate
           for tragedy, as in Chaucer's *Monk's Tale*, and incorporates
           Wallace's complaint, 29–40. Blind Harry appropriates the
           conventional Spring *topos* for the opening of Book Six, asso-
           ciating April, the last month of Spring (line 3) with Wallace's
           sufferings on account of love. The opening lines are not easy to
           follow though. Blind Harry begins with what seems to be a
           reference to Christian liturgical use, with his allusion to the *utas
           of Feviryher*. *Utas* or 'octave' was the eighth day after a feast,
           reckoning inclusively, so that it always fell on the same day of
           the week as the feast itself. The term was also used of the whole
           period of eight days, so McDiarmid's suggestion that Blind
           Harry may simply mean 'the weeks of February' may be
           correct. The reference to the appearance of April when only
           part of March has passed (line 2), may be explained, as
           McDiarmid suggests, as an allusion to the Roman calends of
           April, which began on March 16.

44–56      *concord.* The influence of the 'accord' between Arveragus and
           Dorigen in Chaucer's *Franklin's Tale* (791–99) is unmistakable,
           especially the echoes in the next stanza. A further debt to
           Chaucer's *Compleynt of Mars*, II, 76–7) is detected by McDiar-
           mid in lines 54–6. An idealised relationship, based on literary
           models, is certainly indicated.

57         The double or duplicitous face of Fortune is frequently used to
           convey the arbitrary nature of her power. See, for example,
           Chaucer's *The Book of the Duchess*, 626–34.

60–1       The rhetorical figures of antithesis and anaphora combine in the
           *now . . . now* construction, and again at lines 81–5.

71         *A squier Schaw.* McDiarmid implies that Blind Harry may have
           been influenced by the fact that around the time he was writing
           his poem, one of James IV's squires was a John Shaw.

88         McDiarmid finds an echo of *Troilus and Criseyde* IV, 296: 'On
           lyve in torment and in cruwel peyne'.

94         *has na hap to ho.* Literally, *no destiny to stop*, i.e., destined not to
           stop.

97–100     The role of fortune and the contrast between this corrupt,
           changeable world and perfect heaven are conventional and
           undoubtedly influenced by Boethean philosophy. An extended
           treatment of the theme can be found in *The Kingis Quair* by
           James I of Scotland (1394–1437).

107–271    The date is very precise and alerts us to his source, Wyntoun's
           chronicle, Book VIII, cc. XIII. Blind Harry lifts the ensuing
           dialogue straight from Wyntoun ( 2038–48), but he elaborates
           on the chronicle in his account of the lead-up to the confronta-
           tion (Wyntoun 2029–37).

113        Robert Thorn, supposedly an English officer too, has not been
           identified.

114–6      'Has found the best way to act against Wallace/by picking a quarrel with him as he happened to come from the church in town, while their company would be unarmed.' Note the assumption that Wallace would be unarmed (i.e., without armour) and so vulnerable. See line 125, where he and his company are dressed in seasonal green.

124–264    Blind Harry may have had another source for his account of the death of Wallace's sweetheart and the revenge killing of Heselrig than Wyntoun's chapter xiii in Book VIII. The killing of the sheriff and the burning of the town are attested in other sources.

132    Wallace replies to the scornful address by contemptuous use of single pronouns in his response.

136    McDiarmid suggests a contemporary reference to Princess Margaret, brought from Denmark to Scotland in 1469.

140    McDiarmid points out that this is a series of sarcastic greetings, initially in dialect, then in Gaelic, meaning: 'Good evening [give me] drink, Lord, furious champion, God's blessing [on you].'

182    *The woman*. This is Wallace's wife, as the following lines make clear.

190    *Cartland Crags*, two miles northwest of Lanark.

193–4    Blind Harry employs the rhetorical strategy of the 'inability' *topos* and as Goldstein observes, 'The episode is no less powerful for its calculated understatement' (*The Matter of Scotland*, 228).

265–6    Wyntoun: 'Fra he thus the Schirrawe slew, / Scottis men fast till hym drew' (VIII, ch. xiii, 2117–18).

268    *that gret barnage*, that is, the English occupying forces.

271–2    The debt to Wyntoun is apparent:

>    And this Willame thai made thare
>    Our thame chefftane and leddare
>        (Book VIII, ch. xiii, 2121–2)

The idea of Wallace as the people's choice is common to both.

275    Murray of Bothwell, said to be the rightful owner of Bothwell Castle, a vital stronghold which commanded the direct route from northern Scotland to the south west (Barrow, 121). This must be a reference to the father of Andrew Murray, later Guardian of Scotland. At this time Bothwell Castle was still the property of the Oliphants. When Andrew Murray inherited it he became known as Murray of Bothwell.

297–318    Jop becomes Wallace's herald. Although Blind Harry gives him a history, he is otherwise unknown. Grimsby is possibly Gilbert de Grimsby who carried the banner of St John of Beverley in Edward's progress through Scotland after Dunbar. McDiarmid notes that a William Grymesby of Grimsby stayed for a while at Linlithgow Palace in 1461 and the poet may well have met him there.

302–12    Compare Chaucer's portraits of the merchant and seaman in the *General Prologue*.

309    A pursuivant was the junior heraldic officer below the rank of herald.

329    His oath of allegiance to Edward must have been made in 1296.

342    This is fabricated, as is the ensuing Battle of Biggar. Edward

did not bring an army to Scotland again until 1298, when the Battle of Falkirk was fought.

363–66 Note the romance motif of disguise in battle. Fehew, or Fitzhugh, is a brother of the Fehew who is later beheaded by Wallace while defending his castle of Ravensworth (Book Eight, 1010–69). McDiarmid notes that a Fitzhugh fought at Bannockburn and refers to another Fitzhugh, who was a prominent contemporary of Blind Harry. The relationship to Edward is a complete fabrication, used to introduce a tale about how a nephew's head was sent to Edward with Wallace's reply to the king's writ.

410 Possibly a reference to the tournaments in which heralds relied on their specialist knowledge of participants' coats of arms.

417–9 Wyntoun memorably likened one of Edward's terrible rages to the writhing effects brought on from eating a spider! (Book VIII, c. xi, 1773–8).

434–73 McDiarmid notes the same story is told of Hereward the Wake.

444 A mark or merk was worth thirteen shillings and four pence.

506 *Somerville*. McDiarmid identifies him as Sir Thomas Somerville. The Somervilles owned lands in Linton, Roxburghshire and Carnwath, Lanarkshire (Barrow, 325).

508–10 Sir Walter and his son David of Newbigging were probably Somerville retainers. Sir John Tynto (509) was another Lanarkshire knight. See earlier mention at line 336.

537 *Jhonstoun* and *Rudyrfurd* are place names, and may refer to Sir John of Johnstone and Sir Nicholas of Rutherford, as McDiarmid suggests. Blind Harry claims they are the sons of Haliday.

540 Members of the Jardine family, associated with Annandale, were active in the wars.

543–765 Battle of Biggar. A fabrication which may very well draw on a variety of sources in which other battles and campaigns are depicted, in particular the accounts by Froissart and Barbour of James Douglas's Weardale campaign, especially the skirmish at Stanhope Park, and details from the Battle of Roslin 1303 found in Wyntoun and Bower. There are many anachronisms therefore in the account of this fictitious battle and its aftermath. Among Blind Harry's most blatant fabrications is his claim that a number of Edward I's relatives were killed at Biggar (649–54).

592 *that cheiff chyftayne he slew*, i.e., the Earl of Kent. The historical earl was actually executed in 1330.

638–41 Supplies are taken to Rob's Bog while Wallace moves his troops to nearby Devenshaw Hill on the right bank of the River Clyde.

645 Johns Green is probably Greenfield near Crawfordjohn.

669 Duke of Longcastle. McDiarmid points out this is an anachronism, like the reference to the lord of Westmoreland (685). The earl of Lancaster at this time was Edmund, brother of Edward I. In 1298 the son Thomas succeeded.

689–91 A Pykart lord as keeper of Calais is another anachronism derived from Edward III's French wars.

694 *Schir Rawff Gray*. Blind Harry makes him warden of Roxburgh Castle (Book Eight, 496–8) but when it was surrendered to

Edward by the Stewart in 1296 the English knight Sir Robert Hastings became keeper (as well as sheriff of Roxburgh) until 1305 when Edward I's nephew, John of Brittany, was appointed the lieutenant of Scotland and keeper of this militarily vital castle (Watson, 216). However, the name of the English warden of Roxburgh Castle 1435–6 according to McDiarmid, was Sir Ralph Gray, so this is another anachronism.

697–8     Because Sir Amer is depicted by Blind Harry as a Scot, there are many such references to his 'fals' conduct and nature.

749     The name of the captain of Berwick in 1297 is not known but, as Watson observes, the majority of appointments do not survive in the official record (p. 33). Both Roxburgh and Berwick were strategically very important, as Blind Harry acknowledges (Book Eight, 1551–2).

761     Birkhall, near Moffat.

765     Braidwood, Lanarkshire.

767     Forestkirk was the old name for Carluke, Clydesdale.

768     The exact date of Wallace's appointment as Guardian of Scotland is unknown, but Barrow believes it must have been before March 1298 (96). Blind Harry's use of Wyntoun here and at lines 784–6 is evident (Wyntoun, VIII, ch. xii, lines 2121–2). See also Bower, XI, c. 28.

771     Sir William Douglas had been the commander of Berwick Castle when Edward sacked it in 1296. He had certainly joined forces with Wallace by May, 1297, when together they attacked William Ormsby, the English justiciary at Scone (of which Blind Harry makes no mention). His son, Sir James Douglas, was Bruce's companion in arms.

802     Adam Gordon, a kinsman of the earls of Dunbar, with Gordon in Berwickshire as his principal estate (Barrow, 189) and a known Balliol adherent. By 1300 he was the Scots warden of the West March. He later became a prominent magnate under Robert Bruce.

836     Turnberry was the chief castle of Carrick. Around the same time Wallace slew the sheriff of Ayr, Robert Bruce led a revolt against Edward, in Carrick.

838–41     These lines from L are missing from the MS, probably, as McDiarmid suggests, because the scribe was misled by the recurrent rhyme *haill*.

851–3     Wallace administers justice, in keeping with his duty as a Guardian. Bruce similarly rewards 'trew' men in Barbour's narrative.

854     McDiarmid takes this as a reference to his elder brother's son. Malcolm would have inherited the patrimony as the eldest son and on his death (which Blind Harry had said took place at Loudoun Hill) his son would have been heir.

855     Blackcraig Castle, in the parish of Cumnock, Ayrshire. 'His houshauld' suggests (like 'his dwellyng', line 940) a reference to Wallace's own castle, and this is confirmed in Book Twelve, 937–8. This has fed the belief retained by some that Wallace was born in Ayrshire.

863     Anthony Bek, Bishop of Durham and Edward's lieutenant in Scotland until Auugust 1296. In Book One (171-2) Blind Harry had said that Glasgow diocese was transferred to the jurisdiction of Durham.

865     Earl of Stanford, Chancellor. John Langton was actually chancellor of England at this time. Blind Harry may be confusing him with Sir Thomas Staunford, a member of Sir Henry Percy's retinue (Watson, 44), especially as he has referred to Percy in the preceding lines (862-4).

869     Rutherglen church near Glasgow.


BOOK SEVEN

1-2     If Blind Harry's chronology were at all consistent, this would refer to February, 1298, since in the previous book he had placed the killing of Heselrig some time after April of 1297; but the Battle of Stirling Bridge (September 11, 1297) will be described later in this book.

7-9     *In Aperill . . . In to Carleill*. According to the records, after he returned from Flanders on April 8 1298, Edward summoned his leading commanders in Scotland to a royal council at York. On the same date he also ordered a muster of Welsh footsoldiers at Carlisle (Watson, 61) as part of his campaign to invade Scotland. Blind Harry may be confusing preparations before the battle of Falkirk with those before Stirling Bridge, the previous year.

16     A very striking image of genocide, as Goldstein notes (*The Matter of Scotland*, 231).

23-9     The plans for the wholly fictitious murder of leading Scots, referred to by Blind Harry as 'the Barnys of Ayr', are hatched. Blind Harry's respect for Percy leads him to dissociate him from the atrocity (31-6).

38     *his new law*. This relates to the justice-ayre that Bek is to hold in Glasgow. McDiarmid finds corroboration in line 517.

40-1     Arnulf of Southampton appears to be fictitious. None of the earls of Southampton had this first name. Later Blind Harry mentions that Arnulf received Ayr Castle, presumably as a reward for the executions (507-8).

56     *maistre*. Barbour also uses it in the sense of display of might. It is clearly seen as a provocative act in time of truce.

58     Monkton Church, near Ayr, in the west of Scotland.

61     *maister Jhone*. Probably another reference to Master John Blair (5, 533). McDiarmid takes it as evidence of Blair's Ayrshire origins, saying Adamton, the seat of the Blair family, was in Monkton parish. He attempts to warn Wallace to stay away from the justice-ayre at Ayr because he knows it is ominous that Lord Percy has left the region (63-4).

68-152     Wallace falls asleep and has a vision in the form of a dream. There are plenty of literary models for this dream-vision, including Chaucer's *Parliament of Fowls* and *House of Fame*. A particular debt to the fourteenth-century alliterative poem *Morte Arthure,* in which King Arthur is visited by Lady Fortune in a dream, has been proposed. In his dream, Wallace is visited first by St Andrew and then by the Virgin Mary. A vision of St Andrew confirming Wallace's divinely ordained role as governor of Scotland is mentioned in the Coupar Angus MS of Bower's *Scotichronicon* (Book XI, c. 28), and probably derived from traditional tales known to both Bower and Blind Harry (Donald Watt, Notes to *Scotichronicon* vol. 6, Book XI and XII, p. 236).

94     The sapphire is interpreted at lines 139–40 as everlasting grace.

123    The 1570 edition by the Protestant printer Robet Lekpreuik substituted 'The stalwart man' for *Saynct Androw,* and 'Goddis saik' replaces *For Marys saik* at 291.

179–89   These lines recall Chaucer's *Knight's Tale* 2454–69, as a number of previous readers have noted. The echoes are particularly striking in lines 183 and 185.

190    *heast sper.* In the earth-centred medieval cosmography, Saturn, like the other planets, moved within its own sphere. The moon moved within the sphere closest to the earth, while Saturn moved in the sphere furthest away, or highest, in the heavens.

191–2    The death of the Argive hero and seer Amphiorax (*Phiorax*), or Amphiaraus, is told at the end of Statius's *Thebaid* 7. McDiarmid cites *Troilus* V, stanza 215 and Lydgate's *Siege of Thebes* as Blind Harry's more immediate sources.

195    *Burdeous.* Bordeaux. McDiarmid reckons Blind Harry is referring to Charles VII's capture of Bordeaux (1453).

197–8   This may be a veiled reference to recent or contemporary history, but it is too vague for more than speculation.

202    Tollbooths were prisons and traditionally execution sites in Scotland.

205–10   Sir Reginald Crawford and Sir Bryce Blair – the latter, like Robert Boyd (2, 436) a Cunningham knight – were actually executed much later: Blair was hanged, possibly in a barn in Ayr in 1306, while Crawford was hanged and beheaded at Carlisle in 1307. Blind Harry's source was *The Bruce* 4, 36–8:

> Off Crauford als Schyr Ranald wes
> And Schyr Bryce als the Blar
> Hangyt intil a berne in Ar.

214    *Schir Neill of Mungumry.* Unknown. McDiarmid suggests Blind Harry may have meant Neil Bruce, Robert Bruce's brother, because his summary execution after a valiant defence of Kildrummy Castle is described by Barbour shortly after the lines quoted above (*Bruce,* 4, 59–61; 314–322).

218    The Crawfords, Kennedys and Campbells came from the south-west (Carrick and Ayrshire), while the Boyds and Stewarts, originally from Renfrewshire, became kinsmen of Robert I through marriage. The Stewarts eventually formed a royal dynasty. McDiarmid may be correct in saying that some are names Blind Harry wished to honour in his own day.

229    *curssit Saxonis seid.* One of Blind Harry's many disparaging

references to the 'enemy'. The English are first referred to as Saxons in Book One, line 7.

237     Blind Harry's partisan view is in evidence and, as in the opening lines of Book One, here he makes an appeal to contemporaries.

280–1     There is a possible echo of Suetonius's account of the covering-up of the assassinated Julius Caesar (to preserve his dignity), which Blind Harry could have known through Fordun (*Chronica* II, cap. XVII).

288     William Crawford, presumably Sir Reginald's son.

331     *deill thar landis*. He refers to the lands of the murdered Scots barons. See lines 436–7 below.

342     McDiarmid says Irish ale is whiskey, but I have been unable to confirm this.

346–9     Note the emotive language used here to condemn the English. Goldstein cites this as an example of Blind Harry's 'racist discourse' (*The Matter of Scotland*, 224–5).

362     A burgess was a citizen of a borough, a freeman.

380     Adam Wallace. See notes to 1, 144 and 3, 45–57. Riccarton, in Kyle, Ayrshire was long associated with the Wallace family as noted earlier (note to 1, 355). See 5, 465 above for a note on Auchinleck (383).

385–6     Wallace's divine mission is thus manifest.

400–1     Compare Chaucer on true nobility in his lyric on *Gentilesse*, and the curtain lecture in his *Wife of Bath's Tale* (1109–64).

403     *the Roddis*. The island of Rhodes. Possibly a contemporary reference by Blind Harry to the Knights of St John, as McDiarmid suggests.

408     *der nece*. This is the 'trew' woman (line 252) who had warned him to stay away from the barns, and advised that the English were drunk.

434–5     The lines are bitterly ironic and allude, of course, to the treachery perpetrated at the barns of Ayr and the revenge about to be taken.

440     A typical example of Blind Harry's grim humour.

450–70     The repetitions and heavy alliterations are particularly effective in conveying the merciless killings described in these lines.

454     *thar deidis war full dym*. McDiarmid interprets this as 'their deaths were in utter darkness', but line 472 makes clear that some did escape.

471     There was a Dominican priory in Ayr, and Drumley was the name of a property not far from Ayr which belonged to the Gilbertine monastery of Dalmulin, according to McDiarmid.

488     *the furd will*. McDiarmid suggests this is St Katherine's Well.

491–2     Compare the irreverent humour here with lines 546–7 below.

559     Throughout *The Wallace* Blind Harry is generous in his praise of warriors from Northumberland. Their mettle would have been tested in border warfare over many years. See line 585 for corroboration.

579–80     *strang stour* is the dust raised by horses and clashing forces. McDiarmid cites James Scott's comment that such vivid imagery is not to be expected from a man born blind.

585     The Percy's men are said to be experienced warriors, just as men of Northumberland are acknowledged as 'gud men of wer' (559).

595–6   Wallace kills Percy. Factually this is untrue since Henry Percy was alive until 1314. Robert Bruce's attack on Percy and his garrison in Turnberry Castle is described by Barbour (*Bruce*, Book 5, 43–116).

607     *that place*, i.e., Bothwell, which is occupied by Valence, as Blind Harry has observed.

609–11  *began of nycht ten houris in Ayr*: 'started from Ayr at ten o'clock at night'. Blind Harry reckons it took Wallace fifteen hours altogether to travel from Ayr via Glasgow to Bothwell. (Ayr to Glasgow 11 hours, Glasgow to Bothwell 4 hours).

613     The impression of verisimilitude is bolstered by another reference to an authoritative source, 'the buk'.

617–954 While disturbances are known to have occurred in the first half of 1297 in the west Highlands, Aberdeenshire and Galloway, Wallace's involvement in any of these is not confirmed by other sources. After he killed the sheriff of Lanark his next recorded strike, with William Douglas, was against the English justice at Scone in May. Blind Harry does not mention this.

620     The recital of names is probably more important than any particular individuals here.

621–3   *Apon Argyll a fellone wer*. John of Lorn is described as 'fals' (629), perhaps because, with his father, Alexander MacDougall, Lord of the Isles, he submitted to Edward in 1296. He was a Balliol supporter, and was related to John Comyn; after the latter's murder, he became Bruce's implacable enemy.

623     Probably Sir Neil Campbell of Lochawe (see Book Eight, lines 485–6) who plays a part as one of Bruce's closest companions in *The Bruce* (2, 494; 3, 392; 570–4)

626–8   *Makfadyan*. Said to have sworn fealty to Edward, but probably not a historical person. As McDiarmid points out, these 'events' are modelled on Barbour's account of the Lorn episodes (*Bruce* 10, 5–134).

633     Duncan of Lorn was Alexander MacDougall's second son.

643     McDiarmid glosses 'Irland' as Hebridean Islands. Harry uses 'Irland' to refer to the Celtic settlements on the mainland and western isles.

647     Louchow. Loch Awe region, near Lorn.

670     This is the second reference to Wallace's schooling in Dundee. Duncan of Lorn is said to have been Wallace's school companion.

673     *Gylmychell*. Possibly a member of the local clan Gillymichael.

679     Sir Richard Lundy is consistently presented as a patriot by Blind Harry, fighting with Wallace at the Battle of Stirling (Book Seven, 1237). The historical Lundy actually went over to the English when the Scots leaders prepared to surrender at Irvine in 1297. He was with the English at Bannockburn (1314). The Lundy family held estates in Angus.

685     *The Rukbe.* Another anachronism, if the allusion is to Thomas Rokeby, mayor of Stirling Castle in 1336–39, as McDiarmid suggests. The sheriff of Stirling, and probably the keeper of Stirling Castle at the time was, Sir Richard Waldergrave.

723     Lennox men were known for their patriotism, and their loyalty to their 'lord', earl Malcolm.

755     *In Brucis wer agayne come in Scotland.* There is no mention of them in *The Bruce.*

757–8    Another reference to the spurious biography by Blair. The claim that Wallace fought for Bruce, *to fend his rycht,* is incorrect, since the historical Wallace fought for Balliol, not Bruce.

764     *small fute folk.* As McDiarmid notes, these were lightly armed auxiliaries.

776     *westland men.* Warriors from the west country, presumably from Argyll.

798     Cragmor. Creag Mhor, facing Loch Awe.

880     John was the heir and Duncan was his younger brother, not his uncle. The MacDougalls were related to the Comyns and were Balliol supporters.

890     Sir John Ramsay is briefly mentioned by Barbour as a member of Edward Bruce's retinue bound for Ireland (*Bruce*, Book 14, 29).

900–2    Although Barbour (14, 29–30) describes Ramsay of Auchterhouse as chivalrous, McDiarmid notes there is no such reference to Sir Alexander Ramsay in *The Bruce.*

913–4    There is no reason to believe that Ramsay held Roxburgh Castle. See note to Book Six, 694.

917     Blind Harry comments on his own inclination to digress and the criticism it attracts, employing a well-known rhetorical *topos.*

927–32   Bishop Sinclair. Another anachronism, as he was not made bishop until 1312. Barbour had celebrated his exemplary leadership against an English invasion of Fife in 1317. Blind Harry's wish to honour the 'Synclar blude', as the Sinclairs were prominent literary patrons in Blind Harry's day, may explain this passage.

938     Lord James Stewart was hereditary lord of Bute (936). He had served as a Guardian during the interregnum and had been given charge of a new sheriffdom of Kintyre by John Balliol during his short reign. He surrendered to Percy and Clifford in July 1297, but had joined Wallace by the Battle of Stirling Bridge.

980     *The watter doun . . . to that steid,* i.e., along the River Tay to Perth, or St John's Town, as it was known.

981     Ramsay is said to be their guide, presumably because he knows the area so well, since he held lands in neighbouring Angus.

983–1027   The assault on Perth. Bruce had mounted an attack on Perth in June, 1306, and as in Blind Harry's account of Wallace's assault, he had approached from the west. The Battle of Methven followed. Perth was not won by Wallace, and the installation of Sir William Ruthven as sheriff in 1297 is another fabrication. See notes 1017, 1025 and 1281 below.

990            The Turret bridge was on the southwest side of Perth (McDiar-
               mid).

1017           Sir John Sewart or Siward. See note to 5, 246. The Siwards
               were a Fife baronial family. The implication is that Siward was
               the keeper of the castle or sheriff of the town who was replaced
               by Rothievan (1027), but this seems unlikely.

1025           *Rwan.* McDiarmid identifies him as Sir William de Rothievan
               (i.e. Ruthven) who swore fealty to Edward in 1291.

1031           Coupar Abbey, in Angus.

1044           Dunnottar Castle, on the east coast of Scotland.

1078           Sir Henry Beaumont, a cousin of Edward II, had married Alice
               Comyn, an heiress to the earldom of Buchan. He fought at
               Bannockburn.

1079           *Erll he was*, but not of Buchan as Harry claims. John Comyn
               was earl of Buchan 1289–1308. He died childless (Barrow, 271).

1082           Slains Castle was on the coast.

1088           *Lammes evyn.* Lammas Day is the first day of August.

1089           *Stablyt*, in the sense of, settled the affairs, of the kingdom, i.e.,
               through the appointment of officers and the distribution of
               lands as rewards.

1090–1127      A number of sources, including Wyntoun (Book Eight, ch. xiii,
               2147–50) and Bower (Book Eleven, c. 27), confirm that Wallace
               was laying siege to Dundee in August, 1297, when he heard
               about the English forces sent by Edward to Stirling.

1102–3         *Kercyingame.* Sir Hugh de Cressingham, Edward's treasurer in
               Scotland. He seems to have become a hated figure in Scotland
               and his corpse was flayed when discovered after the Scottish
               victory at Stirling Bridge.
               *Waran.* Sir John de Warenne, earl of Surrey, appointed keeper
               of the kingdom and land of Scotland, had commanded the
               English army at the siege of Dunbar.

1110–9         These lines refer to the capture of Dunbar which Blind Harry
               has referred to earlier, in Book One. Although earl Patrick was
               an adherent of Edward I, his wife remained a Scottish patriot.
               As the earl of Surrey prepared to take Dunbar Castle in 1296,
               the countess tricked her husband's garrison into admitting the
               Scottish forces to the castle. Some of Blind Harry's details may
               have come from the Guisborough chronicle (977–8). For a full
               account, see Barrow p. 72.

1129           *Angwis men.* Men of Angus.

1144–5         Wallace sends the herald Jop to inform the Scots that the battle
               will take place on the next Tuesday.

1145–1218      Battle of Stirling Bridge. A number of the details given here are
               peculiar to Blind Harry, such as the sawing of the bridge in two
               (1151); the use of wooden rollers at one end of the bridge (1155–
               6); and the use of a carpenter to sit in a cradle under the bridge
               to release pins on command (1158–60). The Scots were prob-
               ably outnumbered by the English, but Blind Harry's figures
               (50,000 English) are fanciful. The number of casualties, in-
               cluding the death of Cressingham at Wallace's hands (1194–9) is

also Blind Harry's invention. Some of Blind Harry's details agree with the account in Guisborough, for example, his figure of 50,000 for the English host (1166), although Guisborough says there were also 1,000 cavalry. Various sources agree that Cressingham led the vanguard across the narrow bridge, while Warenne remained with the other main contingent on the south side of the bridge (1171–5). According to the records, the English made their way to Berwick after the defeat at Stirling, not Dunbar, as Blind Harry says (1218, 1227). See Barrow's account of the battle on pp. 86–8.

1170    *playne field*. Wallace was on the Abbey Crag slope.

1174    An ironic allusion to a popular proverb, as McDiarmid points out, to the effect that the wise man learns by the example of others. Barbour quotes it early in *The Bruce*: 'And wys men sayis he is happy / That be other will him chasty' (1, 121–2).

1214    *Andrew Murray*, father of the regent of the same name. He had been in revolt against Edward in Moray since 1297. See Bower, c. 29, line 19, and Watt's note on p. 237. Although Wyntoun (ch. xiii, 2178) and an inquest of 1300 say that Andrew Murray was killed at Stirling Bridge (*Cal. Docs Scot.*, ii, no. 1178), Barrow and others believe that he did not die until November, probably from wounds received in the battle. Bower's statement that he was wounded and died (XI, 30) bears this construction. Murray and Wallace shared leadership of Scotland during the two months after the Stirling victory.

1222    Dunbar Castle was occupied by Waldergrave at this period, not by the Earl of Lennox.

1234    *Hathyntoun*. Haddington, near Edinburgh.

1251    McDiarmid suggests Blind Harry makes this Assumption Day because of Blind Harry's presentation of Wallace as a special protégé of Mary.

1255–9  Barrow points out that the history of the lordship of Arran is obscure at this time, but the association with Menteith, a member of the Stewart family, dates from this period. It was perhaps conquered by Robert I. Menteith's oath of allegiance to Wallace (1261–2) is richly ironic in view of his later betrayal.

1276    *Cristall of Cetoun*. Sir Christopher Seton, a Yorkshire knight married to Bruce's sister Christian, became one of Bruce's most devoted followers. See also Book Nine, 769. He was captured at Doon Castle and executed in 1306. See *Bruce*, 2, 421–30; 4, 16–24.

1281    *Herbottell*. Herbottle and Jedburgh castles were held against the English until October 1298. Wallace put John Pencaitland in as keeper (Watson, 50). Whether a Ruwan (Rothievan) was installed as captain (lines 1289–90) is unknown.

1293    For the reference to *The Bruce*, see note to 1276 above.

1299–1300  This is historically inaccurate since Edinburgh Castle remained in English hands until 1314.

1302    *Mannuell*. Manuel, in Stirlingshire.

1306–8  Bruce is intended although, as noted earlier, Wallace was a Balliol supporter.

BOOK EIGHT

1 *Fyve monethis thus.* Five months after the Battle of Stirling Bridge would be February 1298, but references to the months of October and November at lines 433–4 only serve to highlight the problems with Blind Harry's chronology. Wallace may well have tried unsuccessfully to win Earl Patrick over at this time.

21 *king of Kyll.* An insulting play on the Wallace lands held in Kyle.

23–4 Corspatrick's dismissal of Wallace as a knight bachelor, i.e., a relative novice, is also meant to be insulting. The earl refers to that well-known image of mutability, the wheel of Fortune, to predict that while Wallace may currently enjoy good fortune, this will soon change.

29 Many Scots lords held land in England at this time, e.g., Robert Bruce.

37 i.e., King Robert Bruce see line 146.

63–6 Robert Lauder became a powerful Scottish magnate under Robert I, richly rewarded by the king for loyalty with grants of lands and the position of Justiciar of Lothian. Blind Harry suggests he is keeper of some castle (line 64), presumably Lauder in Berwickshire.

68 *the Bas.* Bass Rock, off North Berwick.

71 *Lyll.* Unknown, although McDiarmid points out that the Lyles of Renfrewshire obtained property in East Linton in the fifteenth century.

115–121 *Coburns peth . . . Bonkill wood . . . Noram . . . Caudstreym . . . on Tweid.* All of these are in Berwickshire. Norham was on the north bank and Coldstream on the south bank of the river Tweed.

124–9 *Atrik forrest . . . Gorkhelm.* Ettrick forest was in the borders and Gorkhelm has not been identified, although McDiarmid suggests it may have been in the vicinity of the Cockhum stream, by which I assume he means Cockham stream which flows into Gale Water, a tributary of the River Tweed.

137 Bek was sent by Edward I in July, 1298, to capture castles in East Lothian. See note to 179–80 below.

158 *Lothyane* is the shire of Lothian in eastern central Scotland.

161 The Gifford Castle of Yester in East Lothian. Peter Dunwich was the English keeper of this castle in 1296–7.

162 *Hay.* Sir Hugh Hay of Borthwick near Edinburgh, who later fought with Bruce at Methven, where he was captured.

163 Duns forest, in central Berwickshire.

179–180 Bek rides through the Lammermuir Hills and north to the Spottsmuir, south of Dunbar. McDiarmid notes that this was the scene of the Battle of Dunbar in 1296, so the battle described in lines 188–324 may well be fictitious, or a confused rewriting of the earlier battle.

270 *Mawthland.* Robert Maitland was the name of the person who betrayed Dunbar Castle in 1400. According to Hume of Godscroft, *The History of the House of Douglas* ed. David Reid for

the Scottish Text Society (Edinburgh, 1996) vol. I, p. 253, 546.

314     Compare *Bruce*, 3, 45–54, which in turn is influenced by the account of Alexander's defence of his retreating men in the *Roman d'Alexandre*.

317     *Glaskadane* is said to be a forest. McDiarmid places it near Doon Hill in Spott parish near Dunbar.

334     *Tawydaill*, or Teviotdale, in the Borders.

337     *Schir Wilyham lang*, i.e., long or long-legged William Douglas. The Douglas so known was actually the fifth lord of Douglas (c.1240–76). Blind Harry is referring to his son, the seventh lord (1288–1302), whose nickname was *le hardi*. See note to 6, 771.

373     *Skelton*. Probably one of the Cumberland Skeltons active in the borders during the wars. Blind Harry mentions him again in Book Nine, 753.

384     Norham Castle, on the north bank of the River Tweed.

397     An allusion to the pillaging that followed the fall of Troy to the Greeks.

401     *mete hamys*. These seem to be (unnamed) fortified places in the East March, or borderlands, under Patrick's control as Earl of March or Mers (403).

410     Earl Patrick had earlier claimed (line 29) that he held lands in England, presumably directly from Edward, hence the reference to his 'maister' here, to whom he hastens for assistance (line 412). Wallace thinks of his king as 'master' at line 430.

419–20  *Stantoun* is Stenton, near Dunbar. Because Blind Harry considers Valence a Scot, he presents Stenton as forfeited property. Lauders are known to have been in possession from 1337.

421     Birgham, on the Tweed, in Berwickshire. McDiarmid notes that in the 1470s when Blind Harry wrote it was the inheritance of Margaret, Countess of Crawford and wife of the Sir William Wallace of Craigie whom Blind Harry consulted about details of his poem (Book Twelve, 1445).

422     *Scrymgeour* is probably Alexander Scrymgeour, whom Wallace later appointed Constable of Dundee (Book Ten, 1162). Wallacetown may be the one in Dundee.

439     *Roslyn mur*. Roslin, south of Edinburgh, in Midlothian. It was the site of a battle, won by the Scots, in 1303.

479     Hector of Troy was one of the 'Nine Worthies' in medieval tradition, and so authors often commend their heroes through comparisons of this kind. Barbour, for instance, wrote of Sir James Douglas, the second hero of *The Bruce*: 'Till gud Ector of Troy mycht he / In mony thingis liknyt be' (I, 395–6).

494     *Browis feild*. Blind Harry places this near Roxburgh. McDiarmid identifies it as Broxfield.

499     See note to Book Six, 694.

510     Watson attests that Roxburgh and Berwick were besieged in the months after the Stirling Bridge victory, and only saved by the arrival of an English army in February 1298 (p. 50). Both remained in English hands until 1314 and 1318 respectively.

513–9   According to Bower, Newcastle seems to have been the furthest

south Wallace reached in the 1297 raids. In May, 1318, however, Bruce's army raided Yorkshire. Blind Harry's claim that
Wallace's army conducted a burn-and-slash campaign as far as
York which he is supposed to have besieged for fifteen days
(line 529), is not supported by the historical record, but was
probably influenced by Barbour's account of Bruce's raids. On
the extent and impact of the historical Wallace's invasion of
Northern England in 1297, see C. McNamee, 'William Wallace's Invasion of Northern England in 1297', *Northern History*
26 (1990), 540–58.

519    This refers to English conduct during the occupation of Scotland.

522–5    This is the revenge Wallace vowed at line 442. No prisoners are
taken for ransom: all are put to the sword. All these lines re-
iterate this idea. Note the grim humour.

530    Edward was actually in Flanders at this stage, returning in
March, 1298.

570    Northallerton in Yorkshire.

575    Malton is thirty miles southeast of Northallerton (McDiarmid).
Sir Ralph Richmond is not known. McDiarmid suggests that
Blind Harry may have been influenced by Barbour's account of
the ambushing of Sir Thomas Richmond near Linton (*Bruce*,
16, 343).

582    See note 162 above.

623    See note to line 530.

636    *schawit thaim his entent*: revealed to them what Edward intended.

639–72    Blind Harry is at pains to portray Wallace as a loyal vassal with
absolutely no ambitions to usurp his rightful king's place.

651    *Cambell*. Sir Nei Campbell of Lochawe. See note to 7, 623.

662    As a *lord of the parlyment*, Malcolm is a hereditary member of
the Scottish parliament. The other estates of the clergy and
burghesses were also represented

693    *Wodstok*. Blind Harry later describes him as the Earl of Glou-
cester and captain of Calais (9, 675–85), so he seems to have
Thomas of Woodstock in mind. If so, this is another anachron-
ism since Woodstock was the son of Edward III, and the
English did not hold Calais until the latter's reign. See also
Book Eight, lines 1534–7.

714    A free town was one that was allowed to hold its own market.

714–7    The historical record shows that various decrees about provisions were issued in late 1297 and early 1298 as the English tried
to ensure sufficient supplies for expeditions to Scotland as well
as for the garrisons stationed there (Watson, 54).

811–2    McDiarmid notes that these names can be associated with place
names, Norton and Lees, in the vicinity of Malton.

845    Blind Harry several times compares Wallace to King Arthur
(Book Eight, 886, 967; 12, 841).

886–8    Described in *Morte Arthure* (886–7; 1015–6).

945    *Mydlam land* has been identified as Middleham, ten miles

southwest of Richmond (McDiarmid).

953–4      The Commons pressure Edward to accept Wallace's 'pes'.

955      None dare because of what he did to the last ones!

961–72      The posing of a question of this kind to the audience or reader is a typical romance convention. The invited comparison with Brutus, Julius Caesar and Arthur, all well known from the Nine Worthies tradition in the Middle Ages, is intended to favour the hero.

972      *brak his vow*, i.e., to fight a battle within forty days.

1009      *Ramswaith*. McDiarmid reckons this is Ravensworth Castle, northwest of Richmond.

1010      *Fehew*. Fitzhugh, later said to be Edward's nephew, when his head is delivered to the king (1101).

1024–5      This refers to an incident described in Book Six, 363–405.

1031      *lat his service be*. That is, commanded him to refrain.

1047      The bowmen provide the equivalent of covering fire.

1081–3      Wallace's treatment of Fitzhugh's head is deliberately provocative because Edward has reneged on the agreement to offer battle.

1107      *Wodstok*. Woodstock, according to Blind Harry, the earl of Gloucester and captain of Calais (9, 675–85). See note to 8, 693 and below, lines 1534–7.

1113–36      The role of Edward's queen is invented by Blind Harry. As previous editors have noted, Edward's first queen had died, and he did not marry his second, the sister of Philip IV of France, until 1299. McDiarmid suggests a literary model in Lydgate's Jocasta (*The Siege of Thebes*).

1120      An allusion to the hanging of the Scots nobles in Ayr, described in Book Seven, 199–514.

1137      Blind Harry plays briefly with a romance motif when he suggests that the queen may have been motivated by love for Wallace, inspired by his noble reputation. Blind Harry's own comments follow and make conscious use of the authority *topos*.

1147      *luff or leiff*. This does seem to be a tag, as McDiarmid suggests, meaning 'for love or not for love'.

1183–94      Blind Harry normally places such astrological descriptions at the beginning of a new book, for example the opening to Book Four.

1215–21      The queen's retinue, which is all female with the exception of seven elderly priests, is another literary touch.

1225      *lyoun*. The lion rampant of Scotland emblazoned on Wallace's tent is the central emblem of the royal arms of Scotland. The leopard is the corresponding emblem on the English royal arms (Book Six, 466).

1237–1462      Wallace's long dialogue with the queen is a remarkably courteous exchange, evincing the nobility of both parties. Wallace's cautiousness about the queen's motives is expressed to his men, whom he warns to be on guard against the treachery of women. He is nevertheless courteous enough to exclude the queen from his suspicions. The queen in turn

strives to allay suspicions by tasting all the food she has
brought by way of gift. Her mission, she says, is peace.
Wallace resists her overtures by recounting instances of English aggression which have provoked and perpetuated the war,
from the arbitration between the competitors for the throne
through the injustices done to Scotland and the personal
injustice to Wallace, particularly the murder of his wife,
the truce-breaking and the atrocity at Ayr. She hopes to
win him over through offering gold as reparation and tries
to appeal to his chivalry, but he refuses to play the courtly
game. He says he has no faith in a truce which will not
necessarily be binding, or honoured by the English king. In
the end, he is persuaded by her *gentrice* or noble magnanimity
when she generously distributes the gold to his men in any
case.

1256–62    *Rownsywaill*. The epic poem *The Song of Roland* made the
           betrayal and death of Roland at Roncival famous in the Middle
           Ages. Blind Harry may have used the *Historia Karoli Magni*,
           copied at Coupar Angus Abbey in the fifteenth century, for this
           episode as well as for the description of Wallace in Book Ten, as
           McDiarmid suggests.

1281       *marchell*: here a functionary of the kind appropriate in a royal
           court, a stweard.

1286       *byrnand wer*: a reference to Wallace's scorched-earth tactics in
           England.

1320–1     The pope was approached in the late thirteenth century to
           intercede and stop England's suzerainty claims.

1327–8     These lines echo Barbour (*Bruce*, 1, 37–40).

1335       The coronation of John Balliol.

1339       Bower has an account of Julius Caesar's failure to secure tribute
           from the Scots (*Scotichronicon* II, cc. 14–5).

1341–3     These lines refer to the pledge Edward made to Robert Bruce
           the Elder to promote him to the throne of Scotland once Balliol
           was deposed. Bower claims that Edward basically used Bruce to
           ensure the surrender of the Scottish nobles (XI, c. 18).

1344       i.e., Balliol.

1345–7     This derives from Bower XI, c. 25:
           Robert de Bruce the elder approached the king of England
           and begged him to fulfil faithfully what he had previously
           promised him as regards his getting the kingdom. That old
           master of guile with no little indignation answered him thus
           in French: 'N'avons-nous pas autres chose à faire qu'à gagner
           vos royaumes?', that is to say: 'Have we nothing else to do
           than win kingdoms for you?'
           (trans. Wendy Stevenson)

1368       This alludes, of course, to the murder of his wife by Heselrig ( 6,
           124–264).

1391       Red gold was considered the most precious and valuable.

1406–7     A tenet of courtly love was that the loved one should love in
           return or be considered merciless.

1478         Whereas Chaucer made old books 'of remembraunce the keye' (*Legend of Good Women*, Prologue, line 26), Blind Harry represents Wallace himself, through the queen's acknowledgement of his qualities, as the key to remembrance.

1494         *thre gret lordys*: Clifford, Beaumont and Woodstock (1503–4).

1523         Sir Thomas Randolph, later earl of Moray and regent of Scotland. He figures prominently in *The Bruce*.

1525         *Erll of Bowchane*. Sir John Comyn was the earl of Buchan and a Balliol supporter. Blind Harry does not indicate that he is the same person as the John Comyn referred to two lines later.

1527         All the early Scottish chroniclers claim that Sir John Comyn betrayed Bruce to Edward after making a secret covenant with him. See also *Bruce*, I, 483–568. Comyn was killed by Robert Bruce in 1306 (*Bruce* 12, 1185f). Sir William Soules was later executed for conspiracy against Robert I, *Bruce* 19, 1–58.

1536         *Glosister*. The earl of Gloucester, Bruce's uncle through marriage. See note above to 8, 693.

1539–43    As noted earlier, Earl Patrick in fact remained an adherent of Edward I until his death in 1308.

1573–4     Hallowe'en, or the eve of All Saints' Day, October 31 and November 1 respectively, so Blind Harry gives their departure date as October 21, ten days before the feast day, and their arrival at Carham Moor (near Coldstream) as Lammas Day, August 1, the following year, making the raiding campaign in England last over nine months, for which there is no historical confirmation, as noted earlier.

1583–6     The installation of Seton and Ramsay as captains of Berwick and Roxburgh respectively is Blind Harry's invention, as Berwick remained in English hands until 1318 and Roxburgh until 1314.

1597         *gossep*: i.e., Wallace had been godfather to two of Menteith's children.

1602         *March*. The Marches, specifically the border between Scotland and northern England.

1616–8     *Of this sayn my wordis . . . yeit fell*. This should be the last sentence of Book Eight, but the scribe errs and continues for another 124 lines.

**BOOK NINE**

         This book describes the first of two trips to France on which Blind Harry sends his hero, this one before and the other after the Battle of Falkirk (Book Eleven). It is very unlikely that William Wallace visited France between the battles of Stirling Bridge (September, 1297) and Falkirk (July, 1298), but Blind Harry's chronology is so flawed that one has to suspend all belief in the battles, encounters and other events that he assigns to the period between these two major battles involving Wallace. Very little is known of Wallace's movements after Falkirk and before his execution in 1305, but we do know that he went to France around

August, 1299, with five other knights, 'for the good of the
kingdom' (Barrow, 107) and this may have turned into an extended stay, which included visits not only to the French royal
court but to the papal curia. His mission was to persuade Philip
IV (the Fair) to provide military assistance to the Scots and to
help restore Balliol to the throne of Scotland. With Philip's
support, in the form of a letter, he hoped to get the pope to
put pressure on Edward to relinquish claims to Scotland. Blind
Harry may have elaborated on the brief mention of Wallace's
encounters with pirates *en route* and of his warm reception at the
court of Philip the Fair he found in Bower, or known of them
from the same traditional tales and songs Bower himself drew on.

| | |
|---|---|
| 1 | *A ryoll king*. Philip IV (Philip the Fair) of France. |
| 27 | Another reference to the prophecies Blind Harry repeatedly suggests predicted the role Wallace would play in Scotland's struggle for liberation. |
| 56 | This seems to suggest that Wallace is descended from a French family or has inherited land in France for which homage is due to the French king. Bower quotes verses which indicate a tradition existed in the fifteenth century that the French version of Wallace's name was 'Valais' (*Scotichronicon*, XI, c. 30, 54). |
| 58 | A reference to the 'auld alliance' between Scotland and France. |
| 91 | La Rochelle, the main port of Aquitaine, west coast of France. |
| 125–48 | Blind Harry employs the spring *topos* to preface a journey, as Chaucer does in the *General Prologue* to the *Canterbury Tales*. |
| 155–7 | Sir David Graham, the brother of Wallace's ally Sir John, complained in 1299 that Wallace had left Scotland without permission (Barrow, 107). |
| 163 | Kirkcudbright, on the Solway Firth, southwest Scotland. |
| 229–41 | The pirate's coat of arms is described in heraldic terms: *riwell* refers to the narrow band, or *tressure*, near the edge of the coat of arms, here said to be red; *bar of blew* (237) refers to the horizontal stripe on the shield; and *bend of greyn* (238) to a diagonal stripe drawn across the shield from the *dexter chief* to the *sinister base* (*Oxford Guide to Heraldry*, 197). Blind Harry seems to be following the descending order favoured by early heraldic writers: red, blue, green (Gules, Azure, Vert). Differ- ent qualities were attributed to the different tinctures: magna- nimity (red), loyalty (blue) and love or, as here, courage (green). |
| 244 | St Andrew, Scotland's patron saint, has already been intro- duced as Wallace's guide and the interpreter of his inspirational vision at Monkton church (Book Seven, lines 71–152). |
| 252 | Ayr is on the west coast of Scotland. |
| 271 | *The mekill barge had nocht thaim clyppyt fast*. Commonly, sea battles involved grappling vessels together with hooks so that fighting could be engaged on the ship decks. A detailed account of such an operation in given in Book Eleven, 869–88. |
| 284 | Latin is the lingua franca and Wallace, whom Blind Harry has been at pains to describe as a well-educated man, conducts a conversation in it. |

295     A glove was held out or up as a token of a pledge, and cast or
        thrown down as the sign of a challenge to fight.

366     The red pirate identifies himself as Thomas de Longueville, a
        name associated with Normandy. Later Blind Harry says that
        after Wallace's death Longueville fought under Robert Bruce
        and that the king gave him 'All Charterys land' as a reward for
        his service, so the Charteris family can claim descent from him
        (Book Twelve, 1145–52). When Henry Charteris printed his
        edition of *The Wallace* in 1594 he alluded to Longueville as the
        ancestor of his branch of the family, the Kinfauns Charteris.

502     See note to line 58 above.

507–12  Blind Harry's story of how Wallace won a pardon for Longueville
        from the French king resembles the motif of the rash promise
        found in folklore and medieval romances alike. See, for example,
        *Sir Orfeo*.

536     Yet another reference to a spurious authority.

560     Guyenne in southwest France, like Gascony, was an English
        possession in the early thirteenth century but, by the start of the
        Hundred Years' War, French kings had repossessed much of
        this land.

574     *Schenoun*, probably Cenon on the Garonne, twenty kilometres
        from Bordeaux, as Blind Harry says it is in Guyenne (574), on a
        river (579), and after capturing the English-occupied town
        Wallace makes his way along a river towards Bordeaux, where
        he is ovetaken by French reinforcements (665–6). McDiarmid
        may be right in suggesting that Blind Harry might have heard of
        another similar place name, Chinon, where Scots fought under
        Joan of Arc in the mid fifteenth century, but that town was on
        the Vienne river and, though part of the Angevin empire in the
        twelfth century, had become part of the domain of the French
        monarchy before the thirteenth century.

662     *Hys brothir . . . Duk of Orlyans*. Philip's brother was Charles
        Valois, whose son Louis became the first Duke of Orleans later
        in the century.

666     Bordeaux in English-held Gascony.

675     This is the Thomas of Woodstock, earl of Gloucester, first
        mentioned in Book Eight.

681     Sir Henry Beaumont. See note to Book Seven, line 1078.

695–7   The Scottish campaign initiated here does not have a historical
        basis. Blind Harry mentions how the English captured castles in
        the east (Dundee, Perth and in Fife) down to Cheviot; the west
        (Lanark and Bothwell); and in the south of Scotland. The 1298
        expedition, which included the indecisive battle at Falkirk, was
        confined to the area south of the Forth, while the 1300 expedition
        concentrated on the southwest, particularly Galloway (Lochma-
        ben, Caerlaverock, Kirkcudbright), as did the 1301 expedition led
        by Edward, Prince of Wales, although the king led an army from
        Berwick to Selkirk and Peebles, besieging Bothwell in August
        before retiring to Linlithgow, where he was joined by his son.

700     The first duke of Lancaster was created by Edward III. Blind

|     | Harry may, however, be referring to Edmund, earl of Lancaster. |
|-----|---|
| 702 | See note to Book Five, lines 246–7. |
| 716 | This is an error. Sir James Stewart outlived Wallace by four years. |
| 717 | Walter was Sir James Stewart's second son. He succeeded as heir in 1309 because his elder brother had predeceased him. He later married Marjory Bruce. |
| 718 | Arran is an island off the west coast of Scotland. |
| 720–1 | Rathlin, an island off the coast of Northern Ireland, is where Bruce spent several months in hiding in late 1306, after defeat at Methven, according to Barbour (3, 679–88). Blind Harry may be thinking of Lindsay as another of Wallace's kinsmen, since the Lindsays of Craigie were ancestors of the Wallaces of Craigie. Bute was one of the lordships of James Stewart. For Boyd see note to Book Two, 436. |
| 726–7 | Sir John de Valence, said to be Sir Amer's brother. He is referred to as sheriff of Fife in Book Twelve, line 891. Siward, of course, had particular authority in Fife. (See note to 5, 246). |
| 728 | See note to Book Seven, line 679. His fear relates to the possibility of invasion by sea. |
| 742 | *Thomas of Thorn.* Presumably he was related to the Sir Thomas Thorn of Lanark noticed in Book Six, line 113, and killed in the fire set by Sir John Graham (260). McDiarmid suggests he was the son of the former. |
| 744 | Tinto hill, south of Lanark. |
| 747 | Carlisle, in Cumberland, was a major supply base for garrisons and campaigning armies in Scotland. It was well placed to receive provisions by sea, from Ireland as well as England. |
| 754–5 | Presumably the same Skelton mentioned in Book Eight, 373. Branthwaite in Cumberland was a known Skelton property in the fifteenth century. |
| 769 | *Cetoun and Lyll* Sir Christopher Setoun (see note to Book Seven, 1276) and Lyle (Book Eight), 71. Berwick was held by the English, like other garrisons in southern Scotland. |
| 772 | *Hay.* See note to Book Eight, 162. |
| 774 | Most likely a reference to John Comyn, earl of Buchan, and the earls of Atholl, Mar and Ross. |
| 775–7 | *squier Guthre.* Unknown, but perhaps Blind Harry intends a compliment to his contemporaries, the Guthries of Fife who had property not far from Arbroath (777). |
| 778 | Sluys in Flanders was strategically very inportant. It was part of the dominion of Philip IV until given as part of the marriage settlement Edward I negotiated when he married Philip's sister Joan in 1299. |
| 800 | Blind Harry is here suggesting Philip's attachment to Wallace. |
| 803 | The great seal was the monarch's seal used for royal charters. |
| 811 | Guthrie sails north of the firths of Forth and Tay to dock at Montrose further along the east coast because the English are supposed to occupy much of the region. |

| | |
|---|---|
| 816 | See note to Book Seven, 890. |
| 820 | Birnam Wood near Dunkeld, made famous by *Macbeth*. |
| 821 | Barclay and Bisset appear to be the names of local land-owners. Families with these names were later associated with properties near Brechin and Kincardine, not far from Montrose. |

## BOOK TEN

| | |
|---|---|
| 1 | As so often in Blind Harry's poem, the month is declared, but the year is far from clear. |
| 5–46 | Kinnoul hill, east of Perth. McDiarmid was probably correct in suggesting that Blind Harry lifted this whole episode from Barbour's *Bruce* (10, 148–250). |
| 11 | *Guthre*. See note to 9, 775–7. |
| 47 | Longueville is the French knight (and reformed pirate) who accompanied Wallace from France. |
| 57 | Sir John Siward. See notes to 5, 246 and 8, 1017. |
| 59–60 | Wallace does not respect the sanctuary of church, and kills the English who flee there. |
| 71 | Sir John Valence, Sir Amer's brother. See note 9, 726. |
| 74 | Ardagie, near Perth. |
| 80 | *Ruwan*. See note 7, 983–1027. |
| 90 | Abernethy, across from Perth on the south bank of the Tay. |
| 92 | *Blak Irnsyde*. Black Earnside was an ancient Perthshire forest, not far from the Benedictine abbey of Lindores, where various historical battles were fought. Records show that Wallace was here, but in 1304, where he was attacked by the English several times. |
| 98–9 | Indicates that Blind Harry thought of Guthrie and Bisset as local to areas of Perthshire and Fife. See note to 9, 775–7 and 9, 821. |
| 112 | *Wood havyn*. Woodhaven, on the Firth of Tay, opposite Dundee. |
| 119–20 | Wallace is referring to events in Book Five, 19–42. |
| 128 | The sentiment of *pro patria mori*, more or less. |
| 188 | *Erll of Fyff*. Siward is a leading Fife baron. Of course he soon threatens to hang him high if he refuses the order to remain at Earnside forest (10, 300–2). |
| 292 | Coupar, in Fife. |
| 310–9 | Valence going over to Wallace is a fiction, of course. |
| 409–11 | Wallace kills Siward. |
| 421 | Cupar Castle. |
| 426 | A steward's responsibility was to supply households with food and drink. |
| 429–33 | The prior of Lindores and the bishop of St Andrews are said to be English sympathisers or English appointments. After 1296 Edward I is known to have distributed Scottish benefices to English clerics if incumbents did not submit to him. William Lamberton, bishop of St Andrews 1297–1328, was a well-known, unwavering Scottish patriot. He was in France until |

1299, and maintained a close correspondence with Wallace during that time (Barrow, 106). He was appointed as a Guardian with Comyn and Bruce in 1299. Edward II campaigned to have Lamberton evicted from his bishopric in 1319. He was excommunicated by Pope John XXII in 1320.

452   Loch Leven. There are several islands in the loch. The English are not known to have occupied any peel or stockade here in the 1290s. The building is described as a royal dwelling at line 522.

456   Kinghorn, Fife.

457   *Gray*. McDiarmid notes that a Sir Thomas Gray was keeper of Cupar Castle in 1307, so he may have held a similar post at Kinghorn earlier.

464   Scotlandwell, a village on the east side of Loch Leven.

531   *Synclar*. See note to 7, 928–32.

547   Lindsay of Craigie. See note to 9, 720.

565   Thomas Randolph, later earl of Murray. See note 8, 1523.

587   The ferry ran from Kincardine, on the north bank, to Airth, on the south bank of the Forth.

589–90   Thomlyn of Wayr is not known but there was a castle at Airth and action is known to have taken place here in September, 1300 (*Calendar. Documents relating to Scotland*, vol. 2, p. 305). At lines 620–1 Wallace's uncle from Dunipace is said to be imprisoned in the castle, which has a moat and drawbridge (629).

656   Because it is so dark, he can only hear what is happening.

685   Dumbarton is said to be occupied by the English but the Scots controlled this castle from 1297–8. It was Menteith's castle, as Blind Harry notes at line 701. McDiarmid points out that it was in Wallace's hands after Stirling, but recovered by Edward after Falkirk.

773   McDiarmid identifies this as Cove on Loch Long, not far from Rosneath, Wallace's next destination (777). The castle there is occupied by the English (793).

824   *Faslan*, a bay at the Gareloch. The earls of Lennox once had a castle there.

835–6   Compare to 1, 296–7.

857–75   Schyr Wilyam lang of Douglace daill. See earlier note 8, 337. Blind Harry claims he was married twice and had two sons by each wife, Sir James and Sir Hugh by the sister of Sir Robert Keith, and two others by Lady Eleanor Ferrars. In his *History of the House of Douglas* (1633), David Hume of Godscroft also claims this (p. 59), but he is probably following Blind Harry. William Fraser, on the other hand, says the first wife, and the mother of James Douglas, was Elizabeth Stewart, daughter of Alexander, High Steward and that Hugh was one of two sons born to the second wife, whom he calls Elizabeth Ferrars, the other son being Archibald Douglas (*The Douglas Book*, 1885, pp. 73, 104).

865   Sir Robert Keith, Marischel of Scotland, a patriot who supported Wallace until 1300 when he submitted to Edward I.

866–8   Barbour also places James Douglas in Paris during his formative years, *Bruce*, 1, 330–44.

873         *Lady Fers.* Lady Eleanor de Ferrers, or Ferriers, a widow.
883         Sanquhar Castle, Dumfries-shire, possibly built by the English.
            It was not won by Wallace as far is is known.
885         Beaufort is otherwise unknown.
896         Thom Dycson. The Dickson family was associated with San-
            quhar, but the source is probably *The Bruce* 5, 255–462, where a
            Thomas Dickson helps James Douglas capture Douglas Castle.
            Sir William had been Edward's prisoner since 1297 so could not
            be involved in taking Sanquhar at this time.
912         Crawick Water in the parish of Sanquhar.
962         Durisdeer Castle at Castlehill.
964–5       Enoch and Tibbers castles in Durisdeer parish.
976         Ravensdale is said to be the keeper of Kilsyth, near Cumber-
            nauld.
978         Comyn held Cumbernauld Castle.
997         Linlithgow, which Edward held from 1296.
1017        *Hew the Hay.* See Note to Book Eight, 162.
1025        Rutherford. See note to 6, 537.
1055        Morton Castle, in Upper Nithsdale.
1060        Closeburn, a village and castle in Nithsdale.
1075        Dalswinton, Dumfriess-hire.
1083        Lochar Moss, near Lochar Water.
1084        Crochmade Hill.
1095        The Corrie family of Dumfries-shire. McDiarmid notes an
            Adam Corrie was keeper of Lochmaben in 1333.
1096–8      These men were also mentioned in Blind Harry's account of an
            earlier Lochmaben expedition in Book Five.
1114–5      Another of Lord Clifford's relatives is said to be captain of
            Lochmaben.
1117–8      Sir Herbert Maxwell, lord of Caerlaverock Castle. See note to 5,
            995.
1121        Cockpull, near Solway Firth.
1137–8      This is another fiction. Douglas was in prison and so could not
            be appointed warden of the west march.
1147–8      Again, this is unhistorical. This is a repeated episode from the
            earlier account of the siege suspended when Wallace went to
            meet the English at Stirling Bridge. (Book Seven, 1090).
1162        Wallace's charter appointing Scrimgeour as constable of Dun-
            dee survives (*Wallace Papers*, p. 161).
1164        Whitby, Northumberland.
1221–46     Wallace's portrait is drawn from Bower XI, c. 28, who in turn
            derived details and phrases from the Pseudo-Turpin descrip-
            tion of Charlemagne, and from Fordun.
1242–4      Comparisons with the magnanimity of Alexander and the
            audacity of Hector (1244) were conventional. There may also
            be echoes from Chaucer's portrait of the knight in the General
            Prologue to the *Canterbury Tales* (1243).
1259        *Scrymjour.* See note to Book Eight, 422.

**BOOK ELEVEN**

| | |
|---|---|
| 19 | Sheriffmuir. |
| 33 | Siege of Dundee. Woodstock arrives by sea to relieve the siege, but is killed. |
| 37–40 | The tactics used here are reminiscent of those used before the Battle of Stirling Bridge in Book Seven. |
| 42 | Drip ford is near Stirling, where the Teith joins the Forth. |
| 55 | Earl Malcolm is said to hold Stirling still. Wallace expects Edward's invading army to come to recapture it. |
| 62 | Torphichen, south of Falkirk, near Linlithgow. The Knights of St John (64) had a hospital there. |
| 65 | Lord Stewart of Bute, but it should be his brother John. |
| 72–438 | Battle of Falkirk. The historical battle was indecisive (Barrow p. 103) but Scheps notes that in some MSS of the fourteenth-century romance, *Thomas of Ercildoun*, the victory is also given to the Scots, so this outcome is not just Blind Harry's invention. (*Notes & Queries*, April, 1969, p. 126.) |

Blind Harry, like Wyntoun (VIII, xv, 2245–69) and Bower (XI, c. 34), makes the treachery of Comyn a key factor in the failure of Scots to triumph on the first day. The issue of rank is highlighted in Blind Harry's invented exchange between Wallace and Stewart (105–19), in which Stewart articulates the fears of the nobles.

| | |
|---|---|
| 101 | *Cunttas of Merch*. The Countess of Dunbar, wife of Earl Patrick, and sister to Sir John Comyn, whose hostility towards Wallace is attributed by Blind Harry to this alliance. |
| 134–8 | The fable of the owl derives from Richard Holland's *Book of the Howlat* (c.1448), in which the owl is presented as a treacherous upstart. |
| 153 | A reference to the release he negotiated with Woodstock in Book Eight, 1525. |
| 179 | An Earl of Hereford is known to have been an English commander who saw action in Scotland and was in Carlisle in September, 1298 (Watson, 68), but whether he was at Falkirk is not known. |
| 203 | Whether Bruce was present at Falkirk is a much-debated matter. See Barrow, 101. Fordun and Wyntoun say he was; the English chroniclers, including Guisborough, who is the most detailed, do not mention his presence. Blind Harry uses his purported presence to create a confrontation between Bruce and Wallace. |
| 207 | The royal Scottish coat of arms. At line 209: the 'rycht lyon'. |
| 217–40 | Blind Harry moves into allegorical mode to represent Wallace's internal debate or struggle. |
| 279 | *Rewellyt speris all in a nowmer round*. This is the classic *schiltron* formation, in which foot soldiers with long spears were grouped in circular bodies as a first line of defence against advancing cavalry. It has been estimated that some of the *schiltron* formations at Falkirk comprised as many as 1500 men (*Lost Kingdoms*, 122). These *schiltrons* were, however, vulnerable |

to attack by archers, as Falkirk testifies. Protection by cavalry to deflect the archers was lacking.

295    The earl of York. An anachronism, as this title was not created until the reign of Edward III.

342    Comparison with Alexander again, this time against Gadifer. Barbour too uses the analogy to describe Bruce's cover of his men after a skirmish with John of Lorn (*Bruce*, 3, 72–84)

361    This is a tribute paid only to Wallace so far.

378–92    The account of Graham's death owes much to the *Morte Arthure*, as previous readers have noted.

434    *Magdaleyn day.* Wyntoun and Bower also date the Battle of Falkirk on St Mary Magdalene Day, that is July 22, 1298.

440–527    The Bruce-Wallace dialogue across the Carron owes much to Bower's account of a conversation between the two across a narrow ravine. According to Blind Harry, Wallace considers Bruce as the rightful king of Scots, but the historical Wallace was a Balliol supporter. The dialogue focuses on Wallace's rebuke of Bruce for being 'fals' and killing his 'own' people, especially Stewart and Graham. In Bower, Wallace's accusation that Bruce is effeminate and delinquent in not defending his own country persuades Bruce to change sides (XI, c. 34).

454    *Ra.* McDiarmid notes that a Robert Ra of Stirling occurs in the records.

472    *off spryng.* This implies that Bruce is the (unnatural) father of his people.

492    *Thou renygat devorar of thi blud.* The charge conveyed in this startling image is taken to heart when, after Falkirk, Bruce refuses to wash the blood from his clothes and person and endures at supper the scorn of the English: *And said, 'Behald, yon Scot ettis his awn blud.'* (536).

566–82    Wallace's lament for Graham echoes Arthur's for Gawain in the *Morte Arthure.*

620–719    Wallace's pursuit and defeat of Edward's army are fictitious, introduced to make up for the rout at Falkirk.

622    Inveravon, Linlithgowshire.

625    Manuel, near Linlithgow.

721–6    On Edward's false promise to restore Bruce's grandfather to his rightful inheritance, see Bower XI, c, 18.

744–5    Crawford. See earlier note, Book Seven, 1299–1300.

756–8    Morton has been identified by Blind Harry as the English captain of Dundee in Book Ten, line 1147, but he is otherwise unknown.

775    Wallace resigned as Guardian after Falkirk, and Bruce and Comyn became joint Guardians. (Wyntoun, VIII, xv, 2285–92; Bower, XI, 34, 60–7).

790    Sir David Brechin, a Scottish magnate, was active in the war against England until his execution by Robert I for conspiracy in 1320. He certainly did not go to France, as he was one of a raiding party south of the Forth in August 1299.

795–808    These lines are preserved in F and L only, and are introduced here because they preserve some tradition of association with the Kerle family.

809        Wallace sets sail for France again (see headnote to Book Nine), and has another encounter with pirates, this time off the coast of Northumberland.

863        See note to 9, 271.

909–12      Another reference to Gray's book, in which this incident, and Blair's particular contribution, are supposedly recorded.

915        Sluys. See note to Book Nine, 778.

924        See notes 9, 560 and 574 on the English army in Guyenne.

949        Presumably a knight of the realm of France.

977        Duke of Orleans. See note to 9, 662.

989–90      Menteith received the earldom of Lennox in 1306, and seems to have fought for and against Scotland intermittently from 1296 on. He fought for Bruce at Bannockburn.

999–1001   After the Falkirk campaign, Edward did not bring an army through Scotland again until 1300.

1017–20    Rowan and Salisbury refer to liturgical use. The Cistercians are usually credited with introducing the latter to Scotland well before Wallace's time.

1085      Sir Henry Beaumont, later earl of Buchan. See note to 10, 1078.

1089      Clifford received the Douglas lands in 1297 (Barrow, 157). Barbour describes James Douglas's attack on Clifford's garrison there in 1307 (*Bruce*, 8, 437–87).

1094      This reference to James Douglas probably derives from Barbour.

1111      McDiarmid suggests a possible debt to Barbour for the claim that de Soules was given the Merse.

1113      *Olyfant*. Sir William Oliphant, a Perthshire knight, was commander of Stirling Castle when it was heavily attacked by Edward's new siege machines in 1304, despite Oliphant's offer to surrender the castle. In 1299 Gilbert Malherbe was sheriff when John Sampson surrendered. Oliphant was installed by Sir John de Soules.

1122–54    Bruce-Comyn pact. Compare to Barbour, Book One.

## BOOK TWELVE

15        In Blind Harry's account, this is the second time Wallace has subdued Guyenne.

29        Gloucester. See 8, 1536 and 9, 675.

54–5       See headnote to Book Nine.

69        See note to 9, 574.

143       Wallace is in France two years, but Blind Harry's chronology is quite incredible anyway. He ensures that Wallace has some military success after Falkirk and opportunity to display patriotism before his death in 1305.

148–50    Another repetition of a motif already employed, designed to illustrate the envy and malice Wallace had to contend with throughout his career. The motif recurs when the cousins of these two *campiouns* try to humiliate him by getting him to fight a lion (202–80).

287        Like a number of chroniclers, Blind Harry digresses to deliver a short homily on the vice of envy.

333–4      William Crawford, another relative ('cusyng') on Wallace's maternal side, is later identified as his uncle (421). While this uncle dwells at Elcho castle, another uncle resides nearby at Kilspindie (Book 1, 150).

373        (And 525 and 551). Wallace returns to the protection of woods and parks. Historical evidence suggests that Wallace did spend time in forests, especially Ettrick, in his final years. Along with his rebel status, this gave rise to the suggestion he was the original Robin Hood.

402        Blind Harry explains Butler's malice on account of the deaths of his grandfather and father at Wallace's hands (463).

449        Earl of York. See note above, to 11, 295.

534–5      Dundas and Scott. If these names allude to local knights, then McDiarmid's suggestion that a compliment is intended to fifteenth-century knights may be right since only then did these families acquire lands in Perthshire.

595        Possibly influenced by *The Bruce* 4, 109, where a man called Osborne is said to have betrayed Kildrummy Castle.

668        Rannoch Hall. McDiarmid cites a nineteenth-century gazetteer to the effect that this is Ditch Hall in Fortingal.

709        Blind Harry means an English bishop at Dunkeld, reminding his readers that Bishop Sinclair, the rightful incumbent, is in Bute (723). There is further corroboration at line 779.

740        *Bowchan nes*. Literally the nose of Buchan.

743        *Climes of Ross*. Identification is uncertain.

791–5      The role of Menteith in the capture of Wallace is not doubted. He is accused of treachery by Fordun, Wyntoun and Bower. Barrow points out that Menteith was a staunch patriot, but submitted to Edward in 1304 and so was acting in line with this allegiance in handing Wallace over (136).

823        See above, 11, 989–90.

835–48     Another homily, this time on covetousness. The particular allusions to Hector and Alexander suggest a probable debt to Barbour but, of course, such analogies were common. Barbour has a similar descant on treason exemplified in the fates of Alexander the Great, Julius Caesar and King Arthur among others (1, 515–60).

848        See note to Book Eight, 1597.

885–94     Duncan, earl of Fife, was not actually active on the patriot side in Wallace's lifetime. He was later a companion-in-arms when Bishop Sinclair repelled an English attack in Fife. The thane referred to is MacDuff, famous for slaying Macbeth.

918–24     Barbour's mention of Edward Bruce's return to Galloway may be the source here (*Bruce*, 9 477–543).

928        Lochmaben Castle was part of the Bruce lordship of Annandale.

| | |
|---|---|
| 937 | Black Rock. See earlier reference to the Blackcraig (6, 855) and note. |
| 959–82 | Blind Harry has Wallace rescue Scotland three times before he hands over to Bruce. The correspondence between the two is, of course, Blind Harry's invention. |
| 960 | McDiarmid suggests *lestand pees* could mean 'heaven'. |
| 962 | i.e., to enter religious orders. |
| 984 | Glasgow. Bower says it was here that Menteith's men captured Wallace (xii, 8). |
| 1017–20 | Edward I was not responsible for the introduction of the Sarum usage into Scotland, as this had become the regular form of worship in Scotland before Wallace's time. |
| 1023–4 | See earlier note on Douglas at 11, 1137–38. |
| 1025–7 | Randolph did not become earl of Moray until 1312 (Barrow, 196). Lord Frysaill may be Sir Simon Fraser of Oliver Castle in Tweeddale, as McDiarmid suggests. He had been with the English since 1296, but assisted the Scots in 1299 and went over to the patriot side around 1300–1. He was executed in 1306. For Hugh the Hay, see note 8, 162. |
| 1035–6 | *Ruwan.* See note 7, 983–1027. Lord Philorth was the earl of Ross. |
| 1039 | *Climace*, also referred to as Climes of Ross Book Twelve, line 743. McDiarmid hazards two suggestion which associate him with either Fraser estate in Aberdeenshire or Clunes near Nairn, which was held by the Ross family. The latter is consistent with the Philorth connection at line 1136. As McDiarmid notes, Nairn was part of the Murray lands (1137) at the time. |
| 1044 | *Stockford in Ross.* Possibly a reference to Beaufort Castle, a Fraser stronghold. |
| 1053 | Abernethy. See note to Book Ten, 90. |
| 1062–3 | The binding of captured Wallace ironically parallels the break-up of Scotland. |
| 1075 | *thai Menteth.* McDiarmid suggests 'these Menteiths', i.e., kinsmen. |
| 1077 | Blind Harry refers to Sir John Stewart but Sir James was actually chief. Menteith was Sir John Stewart's uncle. |
| 1081 | Falkirk was fought in 1298, so eighteen years makes no sense. Even if eight is meant, this would put Wallace's capture in 1306, which is too late. |
| 1082 | Blind Harry presents Comyn's death as in part a payback for his role in bringing about the death of Stewart at Falkirk. |
| 1089–90 | Clifford. See note to 5, 737. |
| 1093–1108 | The debt is to Barbour, Book One. |
| 1096 | The Scots did not have Berwick at this time. |
| 1109–28 | This is a formal complaint or lament. |
| 1147 | An explicit reference to Barbour's *Bruce*, possibly 9, 396. |
| 1151 | The Charteris family was a prominent one in Blind Harry's day and he pays a compliment by making Thomas of Longueville an ancestor. See earlier note to 9, 366. |
| 1164–76 | Edward Bruce's eulogy on Wallace is an interesting exercise in |

propaganda as once again Blind Harry suggest that Wallace fought to make Robert Bruce's reign possible.

1183-4    The order for Comyn's killing is given because he is seen as responsible for Wallace's death, just as he had earlier been accused by Bruce of a part in the death of Stewart (1079-82).

1195      A reference to Barbour's account in *The Bruce* as line 1212 acknowledges. See also notes above on Berwick as held by the English until 1318 (8, 1583).

1205      A Comparison of James Douglas and Wallace as chieftains.

1226-8    McDiarmid suggests the Black Parliament, held at Scone in 1320 to deal with Soules, Brechin and the other conspirators, described by Barbour (XIX, 46) and Bower (XIII, c. I).

1239-1301 Bower mentions the vision of a holy man in which he saw the ascent of Wallace's soul to heaven. Blind Harry may be expanding on this as he draws on other sources, such as traditional tales about Wallace, to which Bower may also have had access.

1260      *fyr brund*. McDiarmid says this refers to the flame of Purgatory.

1269      The monk asks about the brand on his fellow's forehead.

1280      Erroneous. Wallace was executed on Monday August 23, 1305.

1297      See McDiarmid for other examples of bell-ringing as witness to virtue.

1305-9    Wallace as a martyr is compared to others: Saints. Oswald, Edmond, Edward and Thomas, the great English saints.

1312-37   Edward's prohibition on shriving Wallace and the retort of the bishop of Canterbury who proceeds to hear Wallace's last confession, are entirely fanciful. The intention is to blacken Edward's character further.

1384-6    McDiarmid suggests an echo of Henryson's *Fox and the Wolf* (lines 694-5). Note the contrast Bruce's deathbed words. Wallace is nevertheless presented as devout, in his reading of the psalter to the last.

1400      i.e., torture.

1414      Blair. See notes to 1, 533 and 5, 535-45.

1417      Sinclair. This is Blind Harry's invention.

1427-8    McDiarmid omits these lines which contain a contradiction about Wallace's age at death.

1439      McDiarmid translates as, 'No-one had engaged himself to pay for the writing of this work.'

1445-6    See my Introduction pp. viii-ix for a comment on these two patrons.

1451-66   Note the convention employed in this epilogue. Compare with Chaucer's *Franklin's Tale*.

# Bibliography

PREVIOUS EDITIONS

*Early Printed*
The appendix contains fragments of an edition in the type of
Chepman and Myllar (Edinburgh, 1507/8).
*The Actis and Deidis of the Illuster and Vail-eand Campioun, Schir
William Wallace, Knight of Ellerslie.* Edinburgh: Robert Lek-
preuik, 1570. British Museum. Facsimile edition by William Crai-
gie. Edinburgh, Scottish Text Society, third series, no. 12, 1938.
*The Lyfe And Actis Of the Maist Illvster And Vailyeand Campioun
William Wallace, Knight of Ellerslie.* Edinburgh: Henry Char-
teris, 1594.

*Modern Editions*
Jamieson, John, ed. *Wallace, or, The Life and Acts of Sir William
Wallace of Ellerslie* by Henry the Minstrel Glasgow: Maurice
Ogle, 1869 [1820].
Moir, James, ed. *The Actis and Deidis of the Illustere and Vail-eand
Campioun Schir William Wallace Knicht of Ellerslie* by Henry the
Minstral commonly known as Blind Harry. Edinburgh: Scottish
Text Society 6, 7, 17, 1889.
McDiarmid, Matthew P., ed. *Hary's Wallace*, 2 vols. Edinburgh:
Scottish Text Society fourth ser. 4–5, 1968–9.

SOURCES AND ANALOGUES
Andrew of Wyntoun. *The Orygynale Cronykil of Scotland* ed: David
Laing: 3 vols. The Historians of Scotland 2, 3, 9. Edinburgh:
Edmoston and Douglas, 1872–9.
Barbour, John. *Barbour's Bruce.* Matthew P. McDiarmid and James
A. C. Stevenson. 3 vols. Scottish Text Society fourth series 12–13,
15. Edinburgh, 1980–5.
Bower, Walter. *Scotichronicon* ed. D. E. R. Watt et al. 9 vols.
Aberdeen: Aberdeen University Press, 1987–8.
*Calendar of Documents relating to Scotland* ed. Joseph Bain. 4 vols.
Edinburgh: H. M. General Register House, 1881–8.

438                          THE WALLACE

SELECTED READING

Balaban, John. 'Blind Harry and *The Wallace*' *The Chaucer Review*
    8 (1974), 241–51.

Barrow, G.W.S. *The Kingdom of the Scots*. London: Edward Ar-
    nold, 1973.

Barrow, G.W.S. *Robert Bruce and the Community of the Realm of
    Scotland* 3rd edition. Edinburgh: University Press, 1988.

Brown, J.T.T. *The Wallace and The Bruce Restudied*. Bonn: P.
    Hanstein 1900.

Goldstein, R. James. 'Blind Hary's Myth of Blood: The Ideological
    Closure of *The Wallace*', *Studies in Scottish Literature* 25 (1990),
    70–82.

Goldstein R. James. *The Matter of Scotland: Historical Narratives
    in Medieval Scotland*. Lincoln and London: University of Ne-
    braska Press, 1993.

Harward, Vernon 'Hary's *Wallace* and Chaucer's *Troilus and Cri-
    seyde*', *Studies in Scottish Literature, 10* (1972), 48–50.

McKim, Anne 'Scottish National Heroes and the Limits of Vio-
    lence'. *A Great Effusion of Blood: Interpreting Medieval Violence*
    Ed. Daniel Thiery. Toronto University Press, 2003.

Neilson, George. 'On Blind Harry's *Wallace*', *Essays & Studies 1*
    (1910), 85–112.

Roberts, John. Lost Kingdoms: Celtic Scotland and the Middle
    Ages. Edinburgh: Edinburgh University Press, 1997.

Scheps, Walter. 'Possible Sources for Two Instances of Historical
    Inaccuracy in Blind Harry's *Wallace*', *Notes & Queries* 16 (1969),
    125–6.

Scheps, Walter. 'William Wallace and His "Buke": Some Instances
    of Their Influence on Subsequent Literature', *Studies in Scottish
    Literature* 6 (1969), 220–37.

Scheps, Walter. 'Middle English Poetic Usage and Blind Harry's
    *Wallace*', *The Chaucer Review* (1970), 291–302.

Scheps, Walter. 'Barbour's *Bruce* and Harry's *Wallace*: The Ques-
    tion of Influence', *Tennessee Studies in Literature* 17 (1972), 19–
    24.

Schofield, W.H. *Mythical Bards and the Life of William Wallace*.
    Cambridge, Mass. and London: Harvard University Press,
    1920.

Skeat, W.W. 'Blind Harry and Chaucer', *Modern Language Quar-
    terly 1*(November, 1897), 49–50.

Walker, Ian. 'Barbour, Blind Harry, and Sir William Craigie',
    *Studies in Scottish Literature* 1 (1964), 202–6.

Walsh, Elizabeth. 'Hary's *Wallace*: The Evolution of a Hero',

*Scottish Literary Journal* 11 (May 1984), 5–19.

Watson, Fiona. *Under the Hammer: Edward I and Scotland*, 1286–1306. East Linton: Tuckwell Pess, 1998.

Wilson, Grace. 'Barbour's *Bruce* and Hary's *Wallace*: Complements, Compensations and Conventions', *Studies in Scottish Literature* 25 (1990), 189–201.